THE THORIK DAIN SERIES

Omnibus Volume I

A. G. WEDGEWORTH

Dedication:
For all the years you worked with me as I struggled with severe dyslexia and feelings of inadequacy, your constant encouragement to overcome all the obstacles in my life, and the endless hours you spent editing my manuscript. I love you, Mom.

Acknowledgments:
My lovely wife, Tami, for putting up with my crazy projects and believing in me.

My brother, Rick, for pacifying my wild ideas by creating Runestone cover art and a full 3D rendered map. Thanks for your support.

Everyone who took the time to read my manuscript to help me work out the details and issues. These include Kristina Walker, JoAnn Cegon, Robert Cegon, Michelle Richards, Josh Crawford, Rick Wedgeworth, Alexander Wedgeworth, Tami Wedgeworth, Bob Cegon, Zak Larter, Jonathan O'Brien, Barefoot Editing, Andrew Kelleher, and my business mentor Dennis Shurson.

CONTENTS

FATE OF THORIK

SACRIFICE OF ERICC

ESSENCE OF GLUIC

White Summit
Bay of Sorrows
Kingsfoot
ELDORIC MOUNTAINS
Knic Valley
Haplorhini Range
Farbank
Longfield
Rodent Buttes
Laxwood Forest
Pyrth
Northwall
Shoreview
Waterrun
Spiritwater
WOOLEN
Bridgegate
Coliseum O'Sid
Angry Sisters
Lake Fire
Goodwell
KIRI DUN
Rampart
Volney River
WESTERN WALL
Victory
Portlock
Veil
West Dove
DOVEN
RIVERS' END
Luthralum Tunia
Lu'Tythis
Solani Ridges
Maezoth
Pelonthal City
Mythical Forest
Weir Fortus
PELONTHAL
Rumaldo
Chasque
Shards of Fury
PALM ISLANDS
Breezy Byway

Ambrosius
Darkmere
Gluic
Dare
Thorik & Avanda
Draq
Grewen
Mr. Hempton

FATE OF THORIK
THORIK DAIN SERIES BOOK I

PROLOGUE

Thorik's Log: 1ˢᵗ day of the 9ᵗʰ month of the 649ᵗʰ year.

I am no longer a child. Against my uncle's strict rules and warnings, I plan to wake up early tomorrow and head beyond the safety of my hunting grounds and into the forbidden lands. I can't wait to see what adventures await me.

❧ I ❧

MESSENGER OF DOOM

Grasping the weather-beaten boulder with his blood-covered hands, Ambrosius dragged his torso out of the freezing river water. Fluids oozed out from ruptured burn blisters across his face, neck, and arm. Leaning against the flat side of the cold rock, he rested and reflected on his situation. "Now that the council members are dead, no one else knows of the upcoming attack."

Pressure squeezed his head from all directions, blood tasted coppery upon his lips, and stabbing spikes of pain ran up his legs. Survival was in jeopardy. His first order of business was to get to a safe location and determine the extent of his injuries. Fighting the river's current, he swung his lower limbs out and onto the rocks that lined the rushing waters.

Pulling his body past the top of the boulder, he quickly found himself rolling over the other side onto yet another set of rocks. His spine cracked as he landed flat on his back. Losing whatever breath he had regained since leaving the river, he lay on the newly found surface for a few minutes and stared up at the stars. They were difficult to see as a haze clouded them.

Ambrosius' tall, lean body appeared frail among the resilient stones. Wet, shoulder-length, mahogany-colored hair matted to his face, which was outlined by a properly trimmed beard and mustache. Made of the finest cloths, his clothes were burnt, ripped, torn, and soiled with mud. He was out of his element, but he was a survivor.

Once rested, he dragged himself off the rocky banks and into a grassy area to assess his health in the night's dim light. Starting at his hips, he used his hands to inspect his lower limbs for injuries. Thick, wet fabric made it difficult. Nevertheless, rips in the legs of his pants allowed him to make contact with his skin, and he quickly recognized the problem. His right leg had a long gash with a stone shard wedged deep into one end.

The other leg was broken; he felt one of the bones pushing the skin out an inch from where it should have been. Instinctively reaching for his side bag, he realized it wasn't there, nor was his metal quarterstaff. He would have to get along without them. He had healed his own wounds in the past, and he doubted that this would be his last time.

A sudden overwhelming feeling of sickness washed over him. He felt flushed, nauseous, and lightheaded. Fighting the sensation only increased its intensity. Immediate action was required to prevent him from passing out. His injuries could be worse than he had assumed.

Ambrosius sat quietly for a moment to regain his composure and thoughts before focusing on the stone embedded deep into his thigh. Reaching out with the unique E'rudite powers of his mind, he tugged at the granite shard within his flesh. The stone vibrated and then made a slight lurch forward before being blocked from its escape by threads of his own skin and muscles that had snapped back into place over the entry hole. Pulling harder with his powers, the shard finally ripped out of his leg, tearing the flesh that held it in place. Catching the rock in his left hand, he screamed as blood gushed from the wound.

Tormented by this self-inflicted pain, he tore a piece of his tunic off and wrapped it around his leg to stop the excessive bleeding from the now-larger cut. "One down, one to go."

Reaching out with his powers, he now focused on repairing his broken limb. Normally his abilities were second nature, as walking is for most. Instead, he struggled to use them to do nothing more than lift his lower leg off the ground and begin pushing the bone toward its original position. He was getting weaker with every passing moment.

Excruciating pain shot up his leg, causing him to yell in agony. It was becoming too great to handle. One last quick burst of power from his thoughts gave it the needed shove, popping the bone back into place.

Snap!

Ambrosius screamed, dropping his leg to the ground and collapsing from the pain. His entire body hurt. How much of what he thought to be water was actually blood? How much had he lost?

His self-concern stopped once he heard an animal from behind him, away from the shore. Silence followed. Looking through the haze was difficult and resulted in no answers. Rushing waters raced by on one side, while he could hear trees blowing in the wind on the other. He turned to face the trees, gathering his bearings and options.

Sitting ever so still, he waited to see or hear something. Anything. It finally came as a deep growl from within the trees. Perhaps up in them. It was not the call of a wolf or any large cat species that he knew of. Patiently, he waited for it again. A few moments later, he heard another noise. This time, the sound was from his right as he faced the woods. The growl was slightly higher pitched and had various clicks within it.

"Thrashers."

Ambrosius had seen these savage apes in captivity, but never in the wild. Tribal, thrashers attacked all creatures entering their domain in a crazed frenzy, like a swarm of bees or ants. They were aggressive to anything, regardless of its size.

He dragged himself the short distance back to the rock formations near the river. Intense pain shot through his body with every move he made. Feeling faint once again, he leaned back on a boulder and faced the trees. Taking a needed breath, he looked up at the ever-darkening starlight. He could taste blood dripping down from his face, and his breathing was no longer a subconscious effort as he struggled to keep it under control. He tried to sit still and relax.

A series of barks came from the left, followed by a single howl straight in front of him. If it wasn't the sound of the river drowning out the movement noise of the thrashers, then it was the ringing in his ears that had been nonstop since he woke up on the rocky shore. "Where are you?" Squinting, he tried to see any activity to focus his powers on. "Perhaps a friendly shove will scare you off and send you on your way."

He listened to a few more clicks and howls from the trees at various elevations. By this point, he couldn't see anything. The haze had totally removed all visibility. He focused his thoughts and E'rudite energy on the blackness directly in front of him and waited for a noise to come from it.

Eventually, one bark and set of clicks came from the area of his focus and Ambrosius pushed with his mind, hoping to scare the creature away. Tree limbs snapped and crashed to the ground. A screaming howl shattered a fleeting moment of silence. The trees came alive with noise. Howling and sounds of branches slapping against one another filled the air from every direction along the shoreline woods.

One thrasher jumped out of a tree and landed with a thud. A second one hit the ground, followed by another. Soon, it sounded like an apple tree that had lost its fruit all at once.

Ambrosius' heart sank.

A screaming roar came from directly in front of Ambrosius. A multitude of other growls followed. The first beast charged toward him but was cut short as Ambrosius lifted his hands and used his powers to shove the creature back. Quickly realizing that it did not stop the rest, he spread his arms out to his sides to push them all away. A force emanated from him in a hundred-eighty-degree arc that plowed over everything in its path.

The sounds of surprised creatures resounded from every direction except one: behind him.

It was too late. A slash across his outstretched arm ripped open his forearm. A second assault from the other side caught his neck. Several thrashers on the boulder behind him mauled his upper torso.

The fallen creatures in front of Ambrosius quickly regained their footing and joined the attack. It was only moments before the hairy beasts had grabbed on to his arms and legs to rip them off. They lifted Ambrosius off the ground in a tug-of-war for body parts.

His mind was still fuzzy, and his body had failed him. His mind raced as he started giving up. "No! I can't let it end this way."

In a last-ditch effort, Ambrosius pushed away the pain for one brief moment.

Pulling all of his E'rudite energy into focus in that fraction of a second, he shoved as hard as he could in every direction.

Suddenly, he was airborne, and there was complete silence. Calm encapsulated his body and mind as he floated and recalled the memories of his life. He wondered if he had died.

A wave of wind interrupted his bliss, followed by a thunderous crack of tree limbs. It was the last sound he heard as he crashed back to earth, and he was knocked unconscious.

❧ 2 ❧

FARBANK AND POLENUMS

4th Age, 649th Year, 9th Month, 13th Day

Thorik Dain still had his thin and agile body well into his teens as he pushed his barrow of goods along the forest path with a slight bounce in his step on his way into the village of Farbank. His clothes were clean and neat but without question old and weathered. Like most Polenums, Thorik had soft facial features and hair salted with various colors from nature's palette. His was a mixture of tree-bark brown shades as it feathered back from his face and then down over his shoulders.

Polenums, or "Nums" as they were referred to, had the gift of looking young and spry well into their fifties, making it difficult to tell their real age. That being said, the youthfulness of their exterior was not matched in some attributes. Like most species, the sight and dexterity of the body would fade, and their hair would lose its luster and thickness as it began turning gray. In addition, the minds of Nums tended to regress with age, causing them to regain a sense of childlike play-fulness in their elder years. Fortunately for Thorik he was a young man who would see many years before such things would affect him.

Thorik breathed in the crisp and cool fall morning air as the path turned slightly and skirted the edge of the river. He loved this time of year. The changing colors of the leaves made the entire valley look like a gallery of art. Fall always gave the local villagers a wondrous seasonal sight.

Mountain foothills on both sides of the river were rich in plant life, providing every color imaginable. Areas of exposed rock added their own peculiar scheme of browns, reds, and tans as veins of minerals and uncovered crystal deposits were uncovered by the frequent rains.

Small streams ran down the mountain walls and merged at the bottom with the mighty King's River. Upstream hosted thicker vegetation and narrow valleys, while downstream the river unfurled into softer hills and scattered open ranges. Farbank was nestled in the transition of these two regions.

Living just upstream from the village of Farbank, the young man had taken this windy path as his own. Not because he owned it, but because the only home it led to was his. Seeing that few people came to visit, he had adopted the dirt trail as his responsibility to keep well-trimmed.

A similar path on the far side of Farbank traveled to the Frellican house and not beyond. Farbank was somewhat isolated, and outside trading transpired only a few times a year with their cousins downstream in Longfield.

Working his way from the steep hillside to the boulder-lined King's River, Thorik followed the water flow toward the village. Orange and red leaves, moist with morning dew, clung to his leather boots as he strolled down the path.

His single-wheeled barrow was filled with skins and meat from recent hunting & trapping trips. The skins were cleaned and dried and ready for use while the meat had been smoked and spiced with the Dains' secret family recipe.

Nearing Farbank, he noticed his grandmother, Gluic, on her hands and knees reaching into the bitterly cold water. In her late sixties, she had shown signs of aging for several years now, giving her a more mature and wise look. This was in direct contrast to her actions as she played in the river like a small child.

Swirls of dark skin blossomed from the crest of her nose, up across her forehead, and beyond her dull silver hairline. The same style swirls were on her palms and were known to Nums as soul-markings. These naturally occurring skin paintings were unique for each Polenum and typically formed on their bodies as they became teenagers. Thorik's had not come in yet, which seemed quite odd and was a point of embarrassment for him.

Resting the barrow on its two legs, Thorik stepped over along the shore. "Granna? Have you lost something?"

"Found, my dear boy." Gluic reached deep into the chilled water, soaking her entire sleeve before pulling it back out. "See?" Opening her hand, she showed him a handful of mud and a single black weathered river rock.

Keeping his distance so as not to get mud on his clean clothes, he eyed the river stone. "Very nice. But the water is cold, and the current is moving fast. I don't want my only grandmother to be swept downstream just to be caught by some fishing net in Longfield."

She smiled with a delight that warmed her entire face. Various weeds, grass, and flowers had been used to decorate her hair, clothes, wrists, ankles, and the area around her neck. Stepping forward, she extended her hand out in front of him. "Touch it."

"I'm in a bit of a rush, as you know," he said with a smile. "We don't want our guest to wake up tied up like a prisoner."

"If you tied him up, then he's not going anywhere, is he?"

Thorik knew he wouldn't get out of complying with her request, so he smiled half-heartedly and touched the muddy rock with the tip of one finger in hopes of not getting dirty. "It's a good, smooth rock."

With her other hand, she grabbed his wrist and flipped his hand around to be palm up before she slapped the rock and mud into it.

Gluic's eyes widened as she waited for Thorik to get excited about it as well. "Can you feel its energy? It's very old. Older than me."

He smiled at the obvious ridiculous nature of her comment. "I would assume that to be true."

"I'm older than you think, my dear boy. I remember times before the Mountain King war."

Only partially holding back a laugh, he replied with a smile. "I think you mean you remember stories of the Mountain King. That was thousands of years ago."

"Stories? This stone could tell us many wonderful stories. It even helps you remember what you forgot. It is a good one, isn't it?" She nodded her head to answer her own question.

"It's a fine addition to your collection. You have few that are this..." Thorik stumbled as he tried to come up with the right wording. "...perfectly round and smooth."

She agreed with him. "And as wise. It'll be useful for our journey."

"What journey?"

She slapped the back of his hand, shooting the rock and mud up in the air. Catching the stone in mid-flight, she eyed it like a treasure. Mud had splattered everywhere, coating Thorik's face and shirt with small brown droplets.

Her expression of joy outweighed his feeling of frustration over being dirty, and Thorik grabbed a cloth rag to wipe his face clean. Watching her return to the river to wash the new collectable, he could hear her talking to the stone as she properly cleaned it with no regard to the chilling of her own fingers in the water.

Thorik patted himself down with the rag to soak up any remaining mud on his clothes before putting it away and grabbing the arms of the barrow. "See you later, Granna."

She stopped scrubbing long enough to raise an arm into the air to signal goodbye.

With that, he lifted the barrow's legs off the ground and wheeled it downstream.

It was only a few minutes down the path before he reached the village. The subtle smell of burning logs lofted from the chimneys and mixed with the aroma of meals being cooked.

Out beyond the cattails that lined this part of the river, several children sat on the docks with their fishing poles and lines waiting for some action. Rolled up pant legs exposed their bare feet, which periodically kicked water at one another.

"You won't catch any fish making all that commotion," Thorik yelled over to them.

They laughed and continued to play as they soaked up the last few days of warm fall weather.

The path turned away from the wide river and into the village, consisting predominantly of wooden houses placed on short rock walls. Shared wooden walls separating them and roofs of thatch were the most common, but moss and grass were used as well. A blanket of fall-colored leaves covered everything this time of year.

Each house had a fireplace and smokestack that was often shared with another home. Sometimes, even three or four dwellings would utilize one large chimney in the corner where they all met. They used various barks for sidings, including blackened oak, white birch, and every shade in between. The Nums took pride in their homes and would decorate them with items gathered from nature that best represented their families.

House placement was erratic, and paths often became dead-end streets without warning. As chaotic as the homes and patted down dirt paths were, they kept them quite tidy and clean. Among the odd-shaped alleys were open areas that served as places for entertainment and relaxation. Children would run and swing from tree branches, while adults gathered to talk and play various tile games.

Trees grew in most open areas. Then again, they grew everywhere, including in the streets and in the houses. Many houses used them as part of one wall, while others used the trunk in the center of the home to hang coats and clothes. It was stylish to have a tree as part of the front door frame. Besides its status symbol, it also provided shade from the summer sun.

In the center of the village was a solid stone spiritual building known as the Mori Site. It was a duplicate of the primary spiritual structure on top of Dula Peak. They used this Mori Site for the elders, who could no longer make the trek up the mountainside to teach the writings of the Mountain King.

Thorik wheeled his cart past the Mori Site to the open marketplace in the center of Farbank. Greeted often as he walked down the angled paths, he always returned the sentiment with a smile and a nod.

Small groups of children ran up to him, asking questions about the upcoming Harvest Festival Awards. But Thorik was not willing to give up any of his secrets as he teased them with hints before sending them on their way.

He then stopped and looked across the wide opening for a specific face. This was the only location inside Farbank that was not sheltered by trees. Therefore, several large tents were erected to protect the Nums' fair skin from the sun's rays.

He quickly found the Num he had been searching for and headed straight for her. Emilen had a smile that melted Thorik's heart. Petite in frame, she was far from frail as she bartered with storekeepers for goods. The bright autumn leaf colors of her long, curly, red and gold hair reflected the sunlight peeking between the tents as she stepped out from under one of them.

Thorik couldn't hear or see anything else when he gazed at her face and into her large, greenish blue eyes. Thin lines of darker skin traced over her eyes and extended to her ears. He felt queasy and soft every time he looked at her beauty and soul-markings.

Her demeanor was cheerful as she flirted and sweet-talked several men into giving her what she wanted. She knew how she affected them and used it to her advantage.

Thorik wheeled his cart over and greeted her with excitement. "Good morning, Emilen. How have you been?"

Turning, she smiled. "Fine, thank you. But I haven't changed a lot since yesterday when we talked."

"Oh, right." Pausing, he thought about how to continue. "Speaking of that, remember when I was telling you about the maps I was making of the upstream valley? Well, I brought them to show you."

Taxing her memories from the prior day, she didn't recall the conversation. "We talked about maps?"

"Yes, I told you how I was mapping out the valley to help with my hunting and trapping patterns." He removed a rolled-up map from his pouch and unraveled it for her to see. "So, if this is Farbank and this is the White Summit, then this is what I have mapped out so far. My father knew an ancient path that isn't used any longer."

Glancing over the sketches on the paper, Emilen feigned interest in his interest. "Well done."

"Every peak and valley are labeled. I created names for those that hadn't been given one yet."

"That's very brave of you, Thorik. Taking it upon yourself to name an area that belongs to the Mountain King. He died to free us from slavery. What have you done to earn this right?" she mocked with a giggle. But his excitement was contagious. "This is by far the best map I've ever seen since I left Kingsfoot." A wink of approval comforted him.

Thorik blushed slightly as he rolled up his map to put it away. "Are you going to the festival with anyone yet?"

An expression of surprise crossed her face, but before she could reply, they were interrupted.

"Yes, she is," Wess Frellican announced as he stepped up behind Thorik and put his heavy muscular arm across Thorik's back and onto his far shoulder. "She's going with me, once I ask her." Wess was a few years older than Thorik and more developed. His broad chest and back rested on a lean muscular torso and waist. Sharp soul-markings on his neck and exposed arms resembled long, deep claw marks.

Wess was the youngest of the four Frellican of Farbank brothers who hunted on the downstream open fields. They had always been a successful family with plenty of soft rolling hills to hunt on. The easy hunting grounds provided them with more luxuries than most of the villagers, including nice new clothes and a large hillside house that boasted three trees. Two of them ran along the sides of the front double doors while they used the third tree trunk as a support for the center of the house, much like a tent pole.

Thorik never particularly liked the Frellican family. They had always mocked the Dain family for only having their little cottage, small hunting rewards, and even smaller name. Nums were proud of many things. At the top of the list were their family names and soul-markings. Not only did Thorik not have any soul-markings, but he had the shortest last name of any in the village. The villagers with longer names carried more status in the community and often were viewed as the upper class. Last names like Mullenfrather added credit to your character and respect at gatherings. Trumette Mullenfrather of Farbank was definitely a respected old man.

It was customary for Nums to give their full name at the first meeting with others. This included their first and last name and the place they were born. Some had the slight benefit of having a prefix for spiritual rank that included 'Fir' for the community's spiritual leader and 'Sec' for the Fir's assistants.

"Ah, Dain." Wess always reminded Thorik of his short family name whenever he had the opportunity. "Shouldn't you be in a rush? Fir Brimmelle told me you were all tied up for a while."

Thorik felt the back of his neck heat up while listening to Wess' comments. "No. I'm not in a rush. I can stay and talk," he assured Emilen.

"Are you sure? I thought you had something at your home keeping you preoccupied."

Emilen's interest was growing. "You mean you have something other than maps back at your cottage?"

Glaring at Wess, Thorik obviously didn't want to discuss it. "No. There's nothing at my home. Nothing at all."

Wess nodded with a smile and a wink at Emilen. "You heard the lad. He has nothing. Of course, his family never did." Glancing back down at Thorik and then at his clothing, he continued. "It doesn't even appear that you have anything clean to wear to the festival." He casually tried to dust off the mud droplets on Thorik's shirt with his free hand.

Before Thorik opened his mouth, Emilen stepped in. "I think I will just meet you both there." She smiled, turned, and then walked away to continue her shopping.

The two young men remained standing still as they watched her from a distance.

"She's mine, Dain. You have nothing to offer her."

"Get your arm off me." Thorik pushed out from under Wess' heavy arm and turned to face him head on. "I'm tired of your games, Wess. Just back off!"

Wess looked surprised at the feedback. "Slow down, Fir-pet. What's your problem? Can't you take a little harmless fun?"

Thorik straightened his shirt. "You don't know what it is like to be me. I have duties to perform for the Fir and at the school. I perform all the hunting north of Farbank without any brothers to help," he said, justifying his attitude. "It must be nice to still live at home with your family with no real responsibilities."

Wess smiled at how ruffled Thorik's feathers were. "Yes, it is, no-soul." A sharp nod of his head added extra arrogance to his words. "She's mine," he clarified once again before turning and walking away.

No-soul. The lowest thing that he could be called, especially under the circumstances. Thorik was the only Polenum ever to not have any soul-markings at his age. The embarrassment he could live with, but the thought of disappointing his family with such a deformity was torturesome.

Arms straight and fists clenched, Thorik stood motionless as he tried to regain his composure. Wess' words ate at Thorik, taking bites from his emotional flesh. Ever since he was a child, Wess had always made Thorik feel uncomfortable. He often said that the Mountain King prevented Thorik from having soul-markings because he had caused the death of his own parents. The guilt of being involved in his parent's death was often more than Thorik could handle.

After several minutes of stewing about Wess, Thorik pulled a flat, hexagonal stone from his pocket and held it between his palms while closing his eyes. Taking several deep breaths, his heart rate slowed, and his skin returned from a red to a pale tan.

Putting the stone away, he opened his eyes and started noticing the good things about Farbank again, such as the sound of flutes in the air while people came together and traded and socialized. It was enough to start him on his way again.

He stopped periodically at shops with an armful of skins and meat on his way in and a load of various harvested goods on his way out. Life was grand, and he hoped it always would be.

After a swift day of trading, he returned home to his cottage at the end of his path, in the woods, upstream of the village. In his mind, it was the best place in the world to live. Not a grand house nor colorful, but well built and maintained. Strong and sturdy, it would hold up for many more generations. It was sound and warm, making Thorik thankful for what he had.

He opened the door and exposed the one-room cottage, which included a kitchen, a sitting area, and a table and chairs, as well as a bed. However, the place of rest was occupied by a tall human with mahogany hair who had cuts and burns across most of his body and face. Ambrosius was unconscious in Thorik's bed with several restraints, keeping him from rolling off in his slumber.

"Good evening, friend. I hope you had a fine sleep." Thorik wheeled his barrow right through the doorway. This was much more efficient for putting items away, and he did so in a quick and orderly way. Thorik spun the cart around and then pushed it out of his home, around to the side of the cottage, and up toward the hillside. He stopped at an outcropping of rocks and placed it in a location designed just for his sturdy barrow. A single long rock arched over his tool shed, providing his items with perfect protection from the elements. "Harmony in the home brings harmony to the heart," he said to himself with a smile.

Pleasantly, he walked back to his comfortable single-room home. Once inside, he sat down at his little table and grinned at the human while he had a bite to eat. "I wonder where you've traveled, my friend. What adventures have you taken and what wondrous sights have you seen?" Taking another bite, he could only imagine what existed beyond the limits of his valley.

The fresh fruits and vegetables were better than he had remembered. He loved harvest time. After eating, he cleaned up and boiled a pot of water, to which he added various herbs and pinches of items from many little jars on his open cupboard shelves. All jars were well organized and positioned with their labels facing forward for easy reading.

He let the broth boil for nearly an hour before letting it cool to a simmer. During this time, he spent endless moments looking over maps and drawings at the only table in his home. He had recorded every place he had ever been on various maps with details of unique canyons, bluffs, and rock formations. There were sketches and notes from his travels about various animals he had seen. He removed each valuable sheet from a decorative two-hinged wooden coffer, which he used to store them.

Glancing over at the injured human, he couldn't wait to ask the outsider what lay beyond what he had mapped and perhaps even what was beyond the mountains of the river valley. There were so many questions he had for the unexpected visitor.

Daydreaming of what was beyond the next set of foothills, he drew his own conclusions. This activity was his only escape away from the small village and hunting grounds to the north. If it were up to his Uncle Brimmelle, Thorik wouldn't even go past the first ridge.

Two crisp knocks at the door interrupted Thorik's peaceful pondering of distant valleys. Fir Brimmelle Riddlewood the Seventh of Farbank opened the door and let himself in as Thorik stood from his chair after hiding his maps in his wooden coffer.

Brimmelle was more than twice the age of Thorik and about the same height, but more robust. His dark chestnut and coal-colored hair added width to his already round face, which centered attention on his thick, bushy eyebrows. Broad strokes of dark skin traveled from his left hand up to his neck, stopping abruptly at his jawline.

Fine threads were used in Brimmelle's attire, adding color to an otherwise monotonous man. He was clean and sharp in his mannerisms, yet stale and shallow in his charisma. As the spiritual leader of Farbank, he had respect from the villagers without having to earn it.

"Has he spoken again?" Brimmelle asked, dropping a finely crafted wooden chest hard onto the old table. Carved hexagonal designs coated all sides of the forearm-length box.

Thorik finished cleaning his items off the table while answering. "Yes, this morning I was able to get his name."

"I told you my daily readings would help him." Tugging at his thick eyebrow, he frowned at the human. "He said nothing else?"

"Bits and pieces. He's still saying the same date. The thirteenth day of the twelfth month must be important to him. The rest I can't understand," Thorik answered.

"Have you soaked the wounds yet?"

"The herbs Granna gave me have finished soaking, so I was just about to." Thorik collected several small thick cloths and dunked one into the simmering herbal water he had prepared. Once fully saturated, it was removed and folded tightly to extract most of the water before being placed on the neck of his patient. Humans tended to be a head taller than Nums, with stronger facial features and darker tan skin. This thin human met all those attributes.

Brimmelle looked upon the sleeping man partially covered with a thin blanket. The badly burned side of the man's face and neck was still visible. "And what is it?"

Confused by the question, Thorik continued patting the cloth on the man's burns. "Is what?"

"His name. What are we calling this outsider?"

"Ambrosius."

Fir Brimmelle helped himself to one of Thorik's pears and took a bite. "Well, don't get too attached to him. No good ever comes from dealing with outsiders. The sooner he heals, the sooner he can leave."

Discouraged by the comment, Thorik asked, "Why do you dislike anyone that doesn't live among us?"

"It has nothing to do with disliking them. I don't trust them." Brimmelle's conversations were brief and to the point. He didn't allow pondering on other options. Issues were easier to resolve when they were black and white. "I have had poor luck with the few that have come to our village, including Su'I Sorat. I still blame him for your parents' death. You would have been gone as well if I hadn't saved you." Pear juice sprayed from his mouth as he pointed a stern finger at Thorik. "Remember, outsiders don't do things for others unless there is something in it for themselves. It's that hidden something that costs us in the end."

Thorik lowered his head at the thought of his parents' death and at the debt he owed Brimmelle for saving his life. A moment of guilt strained in his chest as he recalled his responsibility for their deaths.

Moving his wooden chest to the bed, Brimmelle pulled a chair up next to Ambrosius and opened the lid of the box. Selecting one of the many small scrolls that filled it, he unrolled it to expose the writing upon it. He then began reading the spiritual limericks. Each scroll had its own topic that related to a specific rune symbol.

He read the colorful words of inspiration in a dry tone that paled their complexion, much like listening to a beautiful song sung by a tone-deaf singer. It was pointless for Brimmelle to unroll and read each one, for he had a perfect memory and had recited them easily after his first reading. But it was tradition, and he followed the teachings without questioning them.

His monotone scroll reading went on for an hour before he suddenly stopped and stood to leave. Setting the dry pear core on Thorik's table, he walked to the doorway with his chest of scrolls. Pausing for a moment at the open door, he looked into the night and took in a deep breath of cool fall air. "I noticed that you have missed my teachings several times in the past month. It will not happen again. Is this understood?"

Thorik didn't have to speak. He bowed his head, and it was understood. A parishioner missing Brimmelle's reading was unacceptable, but Thorik was Brimmelle's nephew and one of his spiritual assistants. Missing his readings was serious, and Thorik had missed more than one while out on adventurous hunts.

Without turning away from the night sky, Brimmelle made one last comment before stepping out the doorway. "You are too old to be playing with maps and fantasies of distant valleys. I want all of those papers you hid when I arrived to be set aside so you can focus on memorizing the Rune Scrolls. It's time you grow up."

And with that, he left Thorik standing in his one-room cottage with a mysterious man recovering from severe injuries.

Struggling between his mentor's words and investigating this man's journeys would keep Thorik from having a good night's sleep far more than the inconvenience of having to sleep on the floor.

❧ 3 ☙

PAINFUL EXTRACTION

Jolted from his sleep in the middle of the night, Thorik woke to the sound of Ambrosius screaming in pain. The outsider was awake and violent in his attempts to escape the restraints that kept him in bed.

Throwing off his blanket, Thorik quickly stood up to see what the man was yelling about. To his surprise, Gluic was kneeling at Ambrosius' side as she tried to calm him down. Her hooded cloak was still on, and the front door was left wide open. She had just arrived and had left a trail of flowers from her broken necklace through the doorway.

She looked over at Thorik. "Close the door and grab your Runestones," she called out over Ambrosius' screams. "The special stones your parents gave you."

This was not the first time Thorik had witnessed Gluic arrive at just the right moment when someone was in need. In some ways, the locals came to expect it. She had the foresight ability to know when help was needed.

Shutting the front door and grabbing his sack of ancient, flat, hexagonal Runestones, he met Gluic back at the side of the bed. By this point, her cloak was off as she finished checking the straps on Ambrosius' arms and legs to keep him from flailing around and hurting someone.

Ambrosius' entire body exploded with sensations that nearly made him pass out. Instead, he arched his neck, opened his mouth, and let out a murderous cry for help. He grabbed on to the sides of the bed in an involuntary response to his dilemma. His back arched and gasped for breath, as though he had just surfaced from the water after a long dive.

"Shhhh, it will be all right." Gluic spoke in a warm voice as Ambrosius was trying to deal with the pain. "You need to slow down and relax before you pass out again. We thought we had lost you last time."

"Last time?" Ambrosius questioned as he gritted his teeth together. It took a great deal of focus to get out each word. "How many times have I gone through this torture?"

"It's okay, son. Just let the pain flow out of your system. Focus with me." Gluic placed several gems into key positions on his head and body. In addition, she set Thorik's Health Runestone on his forehead. She then placed her hands around the top of his head with her thumbs touching each other between his eyebrows. "Listen to me; we haven't much time. I want you to focus on my hands. We are going to pull the pain out of your body." Her hands moved down his head, past his eyes and nose. "Help me pull it out! I can't do this alone, dear. You have to be here with me." The warmth in her voice was still there, but now much sterner.

The flat, hexagonal Runestone on his forehead had several small gems embedded in it as well as a crystal in the center that was now pulsing with energy, which Ambrosius could feel as heat and could hear as a slow wavelike humming sound.

Listening to her words, he fought the enormous pain and did as she instructed. Impatiently, he waited for the next instruction. Focusing on her voice had reduced his pounding headache and allowed him to hear more clearly. But the overwhelming agony was so strong, and his fingers burned from an internal flame. "What happened to my hands?" Attempting to pull his hand up high enough to see the problem, he found they restricted him from doing so.

Gluic pressed upon him for his attention. "Reach with your mind and push to extract the pain as I pull it out." Her hands worked their way down his neck and then separated as each hand grabbed a separate shoulder. She had noticed that he was slipping again into his own private battle. "Focus! On my hands! Nothing else! There is only one thing important to you right now, and that is my hands."

Her hands stayed firm on his shoulders until she felt he was focused again. "Our thoughts are going to be on your right arm and then down past your fingers. We will not stop at your hand to make sure it is well; otherwise, the rancid energy will stop and fester within it." With both hands on his right shoulder, she pulled the energy down his arm. "Focus on pushing it out of your wrist, across your palm, through your fingertips, and then out past them."

He did as he was told, but then paused for a moment to move his fingers to make sure they were still functional.

"No!" she screamed, tightly squeezing her hands around his wrist; she began moving her grip toward his fingers, which were now turning dark red and becoming increasingly painful to Ambrosius. "Ignore what you feel and focus on me."

It wasn't working; the pain was drawing his attention to it, and his fingers were thinning and turning black. Multiple heat blisters were expanding and bursting on his palms and fingers. Dark blood oozed out of them.

If Ambrosius could imagine what it felt like to have taken all of his pain and condensed it to one spot, it still wouldn't have been this bad. He screamed as though his hand had been dipped in lava. His heart pounded out of control, and his breathing was again erratic. Tossing back and forth, he knocked the gems off his body.

"I can't stop it," she shouted over his screams of pain. "I'm going to have to cut off his arm to prevent the dark energies from going back into his body. I need to get his metal armband out of the way so I can make a clean cut. Give me a saw; I don't care what kind it is," she yelled at Thorik as Ambrosius felt her grab the armband on his forearm. Pulling the band down for the amputation, she quickly removed the leather arm restraint in order to pull the metal band off.

Instinctively, Ambrosius attempted to use his weakened E'rudite powers to keep the armband on to prevent the butchering from happening. He focused on the band with all his might as it continued to slide down. Regardless of his attempts to pull it back up with his mind, she pulled it past his wrist and then palm.

Finally, the metal band flew off the end of his arm and across the room. Several loud noises instantly erupted with a combination of shattering glass and items falling off shelves. The negative energy had followed the armband and shot out of Ambrosius' fingertips, crushing the shelving on the far wall and tipping over a lantern. A small fire broke out, and Thorik ran over to stifle the flames.

"Well done, dear. Now let's get the rest of it out of your body." Her tone had returned to her more usual casual one. His hand was now fine, except for a few remaining blisters. Her deception to get him to focus on her actions, instead of his pain, had worked successfully. She winked at Thorik for helping with the ruse, although he did not know it was one at the time.

Once completed with his other arm, Gluic started in the center of his chest and went down to his stomach before separating at his legs, all along talking him through every step. She finished with the feet in the same manner as the hands, but this time with no issues. It was over, and all his straps were removed. His pain had been washed away, and he could relax.

She brushed his hair off of his face in a warm, motherly way. "Now, Wyrlyn, you lie there and get some rest. You've been through a lot, and I have so much to tell you."

"His name is Ambrosius," Thorik corrected her respectfully. "He told me after your last extraction session."

Smiling, she traced his jaw with a gentle touch. "If that's what he wants to be called, I'll play along." She then collected her gems and cloak before handing Thorik his Runestone of Health. "Keep this handy."

Thorik thanked Gluic for her help and walked her out the doorway and onto the path before watching her head back to Farbank.

She hadn't walked more than a few steps before starting a conversation with one of her many imaginary companions. "Oh, good morning, Rummon. You'll never guess who has arrived…"

Grinning at her typical odd behavior, he soon returned inside to clean up the mess created by the extraction. The fire had been extinguished, but he still needed to clean up the glass and various powders from the jars of herbs that had previously resided on the destroyed shelf.

Ambrosius' throat was raspy even though the pain had subsided. He still didn't understand what had happened or where he was. Regardless, he was relieved not to be in pain anymore. "Thank you."

"You're welcome. I am Sec Thorik Dain of Farbank."

"I am Ambrosius." Finally, having a chance to look at Thorik's face, he recalled fragments of memories, but nothing solid. "You look familiar to me, though I don't recognize your name."

"I would have recalled meeting you." Thorik laughed at the thought. "Very few humans have visited Farbank."

"I never forget a face. We've met before. Have you been to the Dovenar Kingdom or to Kingsfoot?"

"Only in my daydreams. Although I'd love the opportunity to travel upstream to the White Summit." Thorik reapplied the damp cloths to the man's burns. "I found you lying unconscious in the woods during my last hunt, so I brought you here. You've woken several times, and each time you have seen my face before passing out again. It's most likely that which you recall." Returning to the kitchen, he finished picking up the large pieces of debris before grabbing a broom to sweep up.

Twisting his wrists and ankles, Ambrosius stretched them out before reaching for his eye. "Why is my eye covered?"

Thorik glanced over at the leather strap wrapped around his patient's head to hold a paste of root and herbs against his right eye. "It still needs to heal."

"Heal from what? I thought I was healed."

"No. You aren't healed. Granna just removed the pain for a while. She'll return when it starts to get out of control again."

"I'll let you know when I get to that point."

"No need. My grandmother will know before you do." Thorik moved a long stick and some small woodworking tools to his table. "It will take several more sessions. You were badly hurt. As far as I can tell, you were in some sort of fire before you ended up in the river, and then you were nearly torn apart by animals." His tone was observational with a hint of excitement.

"Fire? River?" Ambrosius rolled over to his side before slowly sitting up on the bed. "We were in a council meeting having an argument." He thought for a moment and asked himself, "Then what?" The lapse in memories was frustrating. "The room shook. Everyone was running. The mountain came down on us during the Grand Council meeting." His voice trailed off in dismay.

"You're a member of the Grand Council?" Thorik arranged his tools neatly on his table, from longest to shortest.

"Member?" snorted Ambrosius. "Dear lad, I created the confounded council," Taking a deep breath of pride, he released it while savoring the memories of better times. "I had orchestrated the unthinkable, to hold a Grand Council meeting in the sacred Mountain King Temple to unite ancient enemies against a new common scourge. Together we could cease the hostilities amongst the free people." He paused and then continued in a more humble tone, "But someone attacked us before we could make an agreement. Now the death of the council and the destruction of the temple will be associated with my accomplishments. I have failed our people by bringing all the leaders of our lands into a trap. A single stroke of evil was possible because of my lack of foresight."

Thorik looked on with interest but did not grasp the depth of Ambrosius' words. "I'm sorry to hear about your loss. I've never been that far upstream, but it's my understanding that Kingsfoot and the statue of the king are more inspiring and grander than anything else in the world." He closed his eyes to envision what it could look like. "It seems a shame to deface such a magnificent place."

Gathering his wits about himself, Ambrosius straightened up. "Thorik, this is more than my loss or the devastation to a temple. The tide of Australis will change for the worse without its leaders. I need to return to the Mountain King Temple and find out if there are any survivors. There's still a chance we can save the kingdom and the lands beyond."

Sitting down at the table, Thorik began carving the head of a long, thick wooden staff. "You aren't going anywhere."

"I'm sorry, Thorik, but you cannot stop me," he said in a friendly, authoritative way.

"Nor would I have to try. Your leg will take care of it for me."

Ambrosius recalled the broken leg and cautiously lifted his body to see if his legs could take the pressure of standing. "Not yet. Perhaps with a good walking stick." Disappointed, he sat back down on the bed and noticed that Thorik was creating just that. "How long before I can use my right eye?"

Thorik walked over and sniffed the roots against his eye. "Not long. The root paste is just starting to smell of rot; it will be a few more days before it's finished reducing your swelling. You'll have time to heal and regain your vision before the Harvest Festival, but your leg will take much longer."

Thorik went back to work on the long staff and thought about the destruction at Kingsfoot and the death of various leaders he never knew. Feelings of sadness mixed with the excitement of adventure; he wished he could explore the site to see what had happened. Yet he knew his uncle would never allow that.

Ambrosius returned his head to the bed and stared at the thatched ceiling. He currently depended on the charity of others, which was a feeling that he had come to loathe over the years. On top of that, he knew every day spent recovering reduced the likelihood of him discovering if anyone else survived the Grand Council meeting and who in the meeting was the conspirator that caused the attack. However, he knew he had to wait until he had healed before leaving.

Every morning and evening, Fir Brimmelle came into Thorik's home and read from his Scrolls of Wisdom for an hour.

Ambrosius almost didn't realize he was there. His mind was miles upstream. In fact, he didn't even recall being introduced to Brimmelle. The middle-aged Num arrived, read, and then left the home with no conversation.

Another daily ritual became the cleansing of his pain by Gluic. This odd healing technique seemed to hold off the pain for nearly a day, and each time the effects would last a little longer. She would come in, take control, perform her cleansing, complain about Ambrosius not helping enough, and then leave. This also became a blur to him.

Ambrosius began to slowly walk again with the aid of the staff Thorik had made for him. His life was still in the hands of others. It was a devastating position to be in for such a man who was normally in control.

❧ 4 ❧

HARVEST FESTIVITIES

usic and cheering of crowds could be heard by Thorik and Ambrosius as
they slowly approached the normally open grass field along the river,
downstream from the village. The Farbank Commons had been transformed into a
carnival of celebration and contests. It had been a great year for the villagers, with
bumper crops and an abundance of fish and hunted meats.

Small groups had formed near the tents as the adult men boasted to each other
of their successes throughout the seasons and compared their fortune to past years
when the Mountain King had blessed them with even greater bounties. Each year,
the older stories continued to grow and become more extravagant. Just ten years
prior, melons were said to be twice the size of those of today, but now the stories
told of melons three times that size. The same was true for the tomatoes, deer, and
fish.

Wess, the youngest of the group of men, stretched out his arms while
describing the deer that he had recently hunted. He raised his large muscular arms
on each side of him and spread his fingers apart toward the sky as he conjured up
visions of the size of the deer's antlers. The surrounding men cheered and congratulated him before the next man stepped in to tell his story of triumph.

At the tents near the river, groups of women had gathered to set up tables and
fill them with pies, gourds, melons, and many fragrant dishes. The melons
couldn't compare to how the men had described them, but they were of good size,
nonetheless.

As they worked together, the women chatted and gossiped about who would
win this year's contests and whose husband was going to get hurt in the games.
They also compared how well-behaved and mature their children were to how
childishly their husbands acted.

Using the wooden staff Thorik had made for him, Ambrosius limped his way
past the tents. Gatherings of Nums would quiet down and stare at the intense burns

along the right side of his face and neck. Although he was seen as an oddity to the villagers and a topic of conversation, everyone was respectful, but distant.

Thorik helped Ambrosius past the tents and sat him on a bench facing the temporary stage and the open grass field where the children played.

Ambrosius overheard parts of the women's conversations, but he couldn't keep up with them. They all talked at once about unrelated topics, yet somehow kept up with each other. He resigned his attempts to eavesdrop and relaxed in the cool air and warm sun as Thorik excused himself.

Leaning forward, he rested his staff against his shoulder and watched the children play in the field as they jumped and tumbled into the grass. He smiled for the first time in many a week as he envied the freedom and simple life this village offered.

A short distance away, a group of young and older children stood in a circle chanting a rhyme while tossing pinecones back and forth. One girl stood in the center and watched a dozen cones flying randomly over her head. She was older than most she played with and had a spark in her eye of cleverness and curiosity that stood out from the rest. Her long dark hair was interlaced with various bright shades of spring flowers and swung from side to side while she bobbed her head back and forth to the other children's voices.

When all the jewels are in his crown,
The mighty King will drop it down.
All but one of the gems will break
As it plummets into a nearby lake

At this point in the poem, the young girl glanced over at Ambrosius and grinned before returning to her game. She jumped for the pinecones in the rhythm of the musical poem, missing each and every time. The other children had caught on and tossed their cones on the off-beats to prevent her from being successful.

This treasure will again appear
Striking disbelievers with great fear.
But if the one is cleansed, you see
Rebirth to the kingdom is foreseen

Just before the poem ended, the girl suddenly changed her pacing and jumped up at the right moment to grab several woody cones all at once. Winning that round, she stepped over to be part of the ring, while those standing without a pinecone walked into the center for their turn to catch a cone.

This went on for a few more rounds until the girl left the game and approached Ambrosius. Three thick soul lines twisted into a simple, beautiful pattern around her neck as well as around her wrists. Tilting her head in question, she looked him up and down for answers. "What are you?"

Stunned at first by the brashness of the question, Ambrosius' face softened and warmed up. "Dear child, I am a man, just like those that live here."

"They aren't nearly as tall as you, and you have no soul-markings." Placing her hand on the back of his wrist, she felt its texture. "Your rough skin feels more like an old, dried beaver skin Uncle Wess gave us."

Ambrosius chuckled at the comment. "Sometimes I feel like an old, dried beaver skin."

"Uncle Wess says that you're bad luck and the reason for the dead fish in the river recently," she commented openly, without agreeing or disagreeing with him. "We were having our best fishing year ever until you arrived."

Just then, Thorik returned with drinks and food that he had acquired from the women's tables. "That's enough, Avanda. Go play with your friends," Thorik directed as she removed her hand and quickly smiled before heading back to her group.

"My apologies, Ambrosius." After handing the older man a mug and plate, Thorik sat down to enjoy his meal. "She's only a few years younger than I am, but she doesn't always think about what she says before she opens her mouth. It doesn't help that she's living with Wess while her parents are in Longfield."

Taking a sip of the sweet juice, the drink pleasantly surprised Ambrosius. "She was just curious."

"The last thing she was curious about ended up at the bottom of the river this morning." Thorik noticed Ambrosius' confused look, so he clarified his statement. "Mrs. Grenwicker's nine-time award-winning pie is said to be so fluffy and light it can float on water. Avanda wanted to test that theory by seeing if it could stay afloat between our two main fishing docks." He paused and smiled. "And that pie almost survived the voyage to the second dock before it was pulled sideways in the current, took on water, and sank. Needless to say, Mrs. Grenwicker didn't have a second one to enter into today's contest. So, there are tongues flapping about who will take her place this year."

They both grinned at the thought of the youthful entertainment for a few moments before Ambrosius finally chimed in. "Perhaps if she added a rudder to the bottom, she could avoid the side current next year."

They both went quiet before laughing at the thought.

The day continued with contests for the children first and then the judging of the pies, fruits, vegetables and more. Fir Brimmelle was the head judge for the contests, and by the end of the day his stomach stretched over his trousers, and he wobbled when he walked. Mrs. Grenwicker cried as the winning pie was selected, knowing that it would have been hers if it had not been for Avanda's failed experiment.

Full of food and ale, the men now took their turn to compete in the games as the women and children cheered them on. Contests of strength, speed, and accuracy were usually made to impress the unmarried women of the village. Once in a while, some women would compete just to put the men in their place. Other times, a few married men would enter to show their spouse how young and vigorous they still were.

This was the case of old man Trumette, whose soul-markings circled his mouth and chin and then continued straight down to his chest like a mustache and long goatee. Every year he entered the Dula Peak race. The running contest was from the grassy commons into the woods, through the ancient cliff dwellings, up to the top of Dula Peak and back again. Red flags were made by Trumette's wife, Sorla, and the village's children placed them in the spiritual structure at the top of the peak earlier in the day. The runners would grab them for proof that they made it up to the top.

Many years ago, when Trumette was in his sixties, he took one of the red flags from his wife's bag the night before the festival and hid it deep in the woods. During the race, he fell behind and grabbed his hidden flag halfway up and raced back down to barely win the race. Each year after that, he hid the flag closer to the bottom of the hill, and each year his wife made one extra flag for him to steal from her. It became a tradition to see him take first place as the crowd cheered him on. Sorla always made a big fuss about the event for his benefit, as he would tell her how he was getting younger and faster every year. It was a joy to see him happy, and everyone supported the ruse.

The list of participants in the contests changed for each sporting event, including the Dula Peak Race. This was the only event that Trumette entered; he stood at the starting line with all the young bucks.

Ambrosius glanced at the old man before peering up over the cliff dwellings, which once held their ancestors, to the rocky peak that needed to be hiked to reach the stone spiritual building. He looked forward to seeing how an elderly Num, such as Trumette, could make his way up. "This should be impressive."

Wess stood next to Thorik in line, waiting for the race to begin. He attempted to talk to Thorik to distract him from the race. Thorik did not listen. Wess then pointed at Emilen. Her smile and charm filled Thorik's chest with warmth, and he couldn't help but smile when he saw her. Shaking his head to stop staring at her, he looked back at the track to get his mind focused on the task at hand. Wess blew her a kiss and nudged Thorik to look at her blowing one back at him. Thorik glanced over to see her standing with her arms crossed, just as they gave the signal to start the race. Thorik had fallen for Wess' trick and was now several lengths behind him.

Thirty-four racers ran along the grass field toward the trees, with Thorik at the back as he followed Trumette, who tripped and fell only a few paces out. Thorik stopped and helped the old man up before quickly returning his attention to the race.

The group left the grassy field and ran into the woods with Wess in the lead and Trumette far behind. One at a time, they slowly disappeared into the timber going up the hillside. All except for Trumette, who only made it a few yards into the woods before he slowed down to find the flag he had hidden the night before.

Ambrosius laughed as the crowd cheered Trumette on while they watched him through the trees. Wandering from bush to bush, he searched for where he had placed the hidden flag. Forgetting where he had placed it, he picked up a stick to beat at the shrubs to see if anything would fall out.

The crowd roared with laughter.

Meanwhile, the group of racers had worked its way above the tree line and into the ancient ruins of a Polenum dwelling abandoned long ago. Walls were mere stumps and easily climbable. Each runner was respectful of this spiritual land and dashed between the maze of short borders instead of stepping over them. The time lost was the same for all racers.

They then raced up the rock face toward the peak. Wess was still in the lead, but Thorik was right on his tail and gaining on him. Wess lost his footing when the small rocks gave way, causing him to roll down the steep hill.

Grabbing on to one of the small bushes that grew on the hillside with one hand, Thorik snatched Wess with his other as he slid past. With Thorik's help, Wess stopped and regained his balance. The added weight, however, pulled the small plant out of the ground, and Thorik let go to prepare for his fall. As he slid down, he reached back out for Wess, who retracted his hand, allowing Thorik to tumble down the cliff.

By this point, the crowd was dismayed that Trumette had sat down and given up on his quest. Seeing her husband's frail body exhausted and leaning against a tree, Sorla worked her way over to Avanda. Whispering in the youth's ear, she removed an extra red flag from her apron and handed it to her.

Avanda ran off to the side, into the woods, and then turned sharply toward the old man. She quickly moved in behind him and quietly placed the new flag on the bush just to his right, before sneaking back out the way she came.

Meanwhile, Wess arrived at the top of Dula Peak, ran into the spiritual structure to grab his flag, and began his race down the hill before passing Thorik. As he glanced back and smirked at Thorik, Wess tripped and rolled down the hillside all the way into the cliff dwellings, stopping with a hard crash against the ancient partial wall.

Thorik reached the top and grabbed his own flag. He stopped for only a second, to help a friend up the last rock before he began his chase for Wess. Quick and nimble, Thorik made the loose rock face look very easy to descend.

Shaking off the pain from the impact, Wess pulled himself back to his feet and sprinted over the short walls to ensure his lead over Thorik. Wess knew Thorik would follow tradition and would take the time to weave his way through the ancient site.

Back in the commons, the crowd chanted Trumette's name to get him to search for the flag again. Trumette was still catching his breath, and his poor vision didn't allow him to see the obvious red flag near him. Finally, he stood and turned to his left and began to walk. Everyone screamed, trying to tell him that he was going the wrong way. Looking for a few seconds more, he then followed the crowd's orders by turning around. The villagers went wild with delight. The suspense was killing them as he took a few steps toward the flag while moving the thick fall leaves around with his stick. Just as he started walking past the flag, his stick hit the bush and it fell onto the ground before him.

Trumette stood there staring at the red flag for a moment in disbelief. Picking it up, he started his walk out of the woods into the green grass as everyone chanted his name. Raising the flag over his head, he strolled toward the finish line as quickly as his short steps would take him. His eyes were beaming, and his cheeks were red while he passed the young children on his way to his thirtieth consecutive victory. "Never give up," he told the children as he passed them. "You can make anything happen if you want it bad enough." Trumette huffed as he continued over the last stretch of grass.

But it wasn't over. Wess launched out of the woods and toward the crowd with Thorik in his wake. Dirt and cuts covered their bodies as they rushed in for the finish while Trumette stood in their way. Still several paces from the ribbon, Trumette made a move for it, but he was too late. Wess passed him by in a blur and crossed the finish line first.

Thorik could see Trumette moving the best he could, so he slowed down, allowing the elder man to finish at a respectful second place.

Following in third, Thorik moved to the side and bent over to catch his breath. He looked up to see Wess with his hands over his head, holding the finish-line ribbon as his three brothers ran over to reward him with hugs and pats on the back.

Sorla walked over to Trumette and gave him a big hug, explaining that she was still very proud of him. But it was an end of an era for him. His body language spoke volumes, as though he suddenly felt as old as his ninety-two-year-old body looked.

The crowd was full of mixed emotions. Most of the villagers had never seen anyone but Trumette win the race. Some cheered for Wess, while others stood silent. Most of them still came over to Trumette to congratulate him. Being polite, they also congratulated Wess in a more solemn manner, although Wess ignored them and continued to revel in his victory with his brothers.

Fir Brimmelle stepped in next to Wess with the award and raised his hand in victory. He handed Wess a replica of the Runestone of Success while he read, from memory, a few chapters of the scroll about the meaning of the rune symbol. Smirking at Thorik, Wess stood tall as he listened to Brimmelle's words. Once the reading had finished, the Fir asked Wess for the red flag.

Wess looked down at his hands and realized he didn't have it. Panicking, Wess searched the ground near his feet and then in his pockets while questioning his brothers if they had taken it. But it was nowhere to be found, for he had dropped it during his tumble down the cliff face.

The crowd chanted Trumette's name as the rightful victor of the race.

Tightening his fists, Wess appeared to be ready for a fight. "You all saw me reach the top." Walking over to several spectators, he used his height and broad shoulders to intimidate them. "I still made it there and back first, and you know it."

But they didn't back down and screamed for his elimination from the event.

Brimmelle tried to settle them down by explaining that Wess had made it to the top. However, he was finally pressured to give in to the rule that the contestant must have a flag on their return.

He reached to receive the Runestone from Wess, who clenched his fist around it. "This is your own fault," Brimmelle told him. "I know you've won, but the rules are the rules."

Looking at the group of friends and neighbors getting upset with him, Wess slowly opened his hand and allowed Brimmelle to take the awarded stone. He and his brothers then stomped off to get some ale as Fir Brimmelle awarded Trumette with the Runestone and then read the same passage again for him.

Everyone cheered for Trumette's victory, and Thorik beamed back to life as he looked over at Emilen and winked at her. Caught up in the crowd's enthusiasm, she smiled back at him.

After the group dispersed, Thorik dusted himself off and made his way over to Ambrosius. Allowing himself to fall onto the bench, Thorik wiped the sweat from his face. "That Trumette sure is fast." A long, thin smile grew across his face. "He's like a gust of wind. I didn't even see him pass me."

Ambrosius grinned. "Do you think you'll ever beat him?"

Still smiling, Thorik answered in a thoughtful tone. "I hope not."

"You are very lucky, Thorik. You live in this isolated lush valley, protected from the rest of the world and surrounded by wonderful friends and family." Ambrosius looked upon the bright faces of the young and old. "Yes, you are one fortunate man."

Thorik eyed Wess, who had walked over to Emilen and started a conversation. "Perhaps."

Stretching his back, Ambrosius contemplated his own life. "I don't know if I would say that I have had as much luck over my years."

Thorik continued to watch Wess as he escorted Emilen to the next contest, where he would compete for strength. Wess would win this contest just like he had for the past several years. He was obviously the strongest member of the community. "You're lucky I found you," Thorik said as he returned his attention to his patient.

"Yes, my friend. I was lucky that you found me."

"My mother used to always tell me that things happen for a reason. So, we just need to find out the reason why I found you."

Ambrosius found the comments amusing as he looked about the crowd. "Where is your mother?"

Thorik's lips tightened as he answered. "My parents aren't with us anymore."

Ambrosius realized he hit a sensitive nerve. "I'm sorry to hear that." He let Thorik get some blood back in his face before he continued. "Do you still believe things happen for a reason?"

Thorik nodded his head in a soft motion. "I have to. It's the only thing that keeps me going."

"In that case, I will tell you why you found me."

Thorik's face came back to life with a look of intrigue. "Go on." His brow rose with curiosity as he looked Ambrosius square in the eyes. "Let me hear it."

"I cannot travel up the river valley to Kingsfoot by myself. You will assist my trek and help me determine who destroyed the Mountain King Temple and the Grand Council which held forum within it. Doing so can prevent the next such attack upon the innocent. Why else would you just happen to find me in the middle of the forest?" Ambrosius placed his hand on Thorik's shoulder while finishing his thought. "I've seen you looking over your maps and notes. You want an adventure out of this valley. Finding me gives you that opportunity. It is fate."

Thorik's eyes widened; he had never been that far upstream. "I think not. Even if Brimmelle would allow me to travel such a distance from Farbank, you have not recovered enough to make such a trip. It will take Gluic another few weeks to get you healthy enough."

"I would like you to ask Gluic if she will join us. She can continue healing me during our travels. While at Kingsfoot, you will see a true testament of your faith, and once we have discovered the truth, you can simply ride the river to bring Gluic home to Farbank."

"Do you realize how far downstream we are from Kingsfoot?"

"It couldn't be that far. How else would I have floated down without drowning?"

"You couldn't have without a boat. By walking, I would assume it will take us several weeks," Thorik estimated, not knowing how far Ambrosius could travel in a day.

"All the reason to leave sooner rather than later." Ambrosius twirled the hair of his beard between two fingers, feeling confident that he convinced the young Num to help him.

"You don't understand the dangers of such a trip. You will need to be stronger. The passes will be snow-covered soon, and the river cuts will be overflowing from the after-harvest rains. We should wait until spring."

"Thorik, I cannot wait until spring. Someone has killed the governing body of our world and destroyed a sacred temple of your faith. I need to find out who and how they did this before they strike again." Ambrosius' passion came out stronger than he had intended. "As you said, the after-harvest weather will be moving in soon. We need to leave before it arrives."

"Do you need to be there by the thirteenth day of the twelfth month?" Thorik's scrutinizing look waited for an answer.

Fighting to not display his sudden shock at this question, Ambrosius tempered his voice before replying. "What do you know of this date?"

"I know you repeated it several times in your sleep. Is it important?"

"Extremely, my young friend." Ambrosius made sure no one was standing too near before leaning forward and continuing. "Keep this date to yourself. If we don't stop the murderer of the council by that date, I believe they will unleash a devastating attack on the land which could wipe us all out."

Ambrosius paused until Thorik made eye contact with him again. "So, you see, I will go on my own if I must, but I believe the reason you found me was to help prevent the deaths of hundreds of thousands of innocent people. Children at play, loving wives and husbands, and the elderly all are at risk from this killer. Just because you don't see it here around you doesn't mean it's not coming. It is, and you can help me stop it."

"Why me?"

"You have a firm foundation on which we can build a significant future on. Stronger than most I have met. Plus, there is something about you I still cannot place. Something that tells me you have greatness in your future."

Thorik thought about it for only a few moments before shaking his head as he looked back at Ambrosius. "I'm sorry for what happened to you and about your challenges outside this valley, but there is no way my—"

Brimmelle interrupted Thorik as he walked up to them, "It is time for the Rune

Awards." Towering over them as they sat, he made his presence clear and official, as always. "Come along then. We shall not be late for it." Brimmelle stood firm as an oak tree, waiting for Thorik to jump up and get his items ready for the speech.

After a slight hesitation and a deep breath, Thorik slowly stood and did as he was told by walking over to one of the tents and grabbing various scrolls and bags. He then made his way to the stage and quickly organized his items on a table.

Several children came up to look at what was on display. While performing his spiritual role for the community, they knew him as Sec Thorik to his students, and his students wanted his attention. Showing them various replica Runestones that hung on leather necklaces, Sec Thorik asked them questions as though they were back in school. As they raised their hands, he called on them to give the answers about the rune symbols for each of the stones. Each stone was similar in size, shape, and symbol to the ones used on Ambrosius, but without the radiance or gems embedded within them. Thorik's personal Runestones were ancient and had been given to him by his parents. They were unparalleled in craftsmanship to any seen in the village.

Sec Thorik beamed as the answers came from the children. His weekly teachings of the Runestones and the Rules of Order to the children had obviously paid off. They knew every answer and went on to explain at great length the rune name, its external meaning on the flat side, and its internal meaning on the embedded gem side.

Fir Brimmelle stepped onto the stage and walked to the center before turning toward the crowd. He spied his mother, Gluic, playing with the children as though she were one of them. He had always been uncomfortable with her unorthodox social skills, which had increased during her elder years. Regressing to a childlike mind was common among the older Nums, but she talked to stones and plants, as well as people that didn't exist. She had even informed him that she talked to the Mountain King. In addition, she would change from a playful child to a serious scolding mother in an instant. He never knew who he was going to be approaching. Because of the discomfort he felt with the situation, he never spoke of it, nor did he allow anyone else to. The villagers had learned to ignore her odd behavior if they wished to avoid his punishment.

Sec Thorik quickly waved away the children and grabbed the first of many scrolls on the table before he walked out next to Brimmelle. A crowd formed in front of the stage as Brimmelle reached his hand out to his side, waiting for the placement of the scroll. His Sec removed the string from the scroll before placing it in Fir Brimmelle's hand.

Quieting the crowd, Sec Thorik made an announcement. "It is time now for Fir Brimmelle Riddlewood the Seventh of Farbank to present the Harvest Festival Awards. Can I please have the children come to the front?" Avanda moved to the front with the rest of her young friends and waved at Thorik as he waited for the few stragglers before continuing. "Over the past year, there have been some special accomplishments by our youth. One of which is the saving of Marla Moondy's grazers from a bushdog last spring by Norby Grenwicker."

Everyone cheered as the Sec motioned for Norby to come up on stage. Once there, Thorik placed a leather necklace over the boy's head with a newly carved

Runestone hanging from it. The Sec made sure that the gem face of the stone faced out as he adjusted it to the center of Norby's chubby chest. Thorik then placed his hands on Norby's shoulders and turned him toward the audience as they applauded. Standing directly behind Norby, Thorik asked him to read the rune and describe what it meant to him.

Peering down at the stone now resting in his palm, Norby looked at the symbol in the center of it. "It's the Rune of Symbiosis." He glanced out at his hefty mother and father smiling from the back of the crowd. "It means that I have to help keep Mrs. Moondy's grazers from being eaten, so my mom will have wool to make me clothes and to trade for food." He scrunched up his lips as he worked his brain for more. "So, we all need to help each other to have food?"

"That's pretty close." Sec Thorik smiled as he reached around and flipped the stone over to show the polished stone side. "Go on."

"Well, um." Norby's lips pushed to one side as he thought about it. "It means that each part of my body needs to help the other parts and what I do to one part can affect the others?" He looked up at Sec Thorik in hopes that he had it right.

"Keep going. Give an example that you have experienced."

He thought for a second and then realized he had it. "Last week I ate a whole basket of blueberries that upset my stomach, and I ended up getting sick all over Margi's new dress," he giggled as his belly bounced at the thought. "My mouth loved them, but my stomach didn't. I guess they weren't working together."

Disgusted, Fir Brimmelle glared at Thorik, since he was responsible for educating the children on the Rune Scrolls. Apparently, his Sec had not done his job.

Sec Thorik let it slide. "That's not exactly where I was going. So why don't you listen to Fir Brimmelle as he reads from the Symbiotic Rune Scroll."

With that, Fir Brimmelle uncoiled the scroll and began reading the meaning of the rune, while Norby stood on stage, proudly displaying his award to his friends and waving to his parents. The Fir continued for several minutes in his monotone voice while his parishioners stood quietly and listened.

Once Fir Brimmelle had completed his readings, he coiled up the scroll and handed it back to his Sec, who tied a string around it and set it back with the others. Thorik then handed Brimmelle the next scroll after removing the string from it.

The crowd slowly came back to life with smiles and light chatter as Sec Thorik spoke. "This past winter, someone had stolen a large wall carving from the school. It had been made by last year's graduate Benly Harcaloff in the shape of a huge Runestone of Trust. After several days of questioning, we gave up our search. Not long after, they returned it with an apology. A girl had taken it to be used as a snow sled. And after several successful runs down Turtleback Mound, she lent it to another to ride. But on their way, they crashed into a tree and broke the wood sled in half. The person who returned it blamed herself and took the full punishment without making excuses or accusing others."

The Sec looked down at the children in front. "Avanda, please come up here," he said to the eldest of his students. "This Runestone is for the lesson you learned the hard way, and I hope you are wiser for it." She stepped up on stage, and he placed the necklace over her head. "Now, it's your turn," he whispered into her ear.

Avanda looked down in her open palm at the stone. "It's the Rune of Responsibility. It means that you have to take responsibility for your actions to others and to nature, even if you didn't mean to hurt them." She stopped as she turned the stone over. "Also, I have to be responsible to myself by knowing that I did something wrong, and I did the right thing in the end."

"You're getting there; keep going," Sec Thorik prodded.

Avanda looked behind her and asked, "Would I have still received this Rune-stone if I had told you the truth about Uncle Wess taking it away from me before he broke the sled?"

The crowd overheard and erupted in laughter as Wess' face turned red and his brothers began to laugh and push him around. Humiliated, the youngest Frellican brother left the gathering.

Chuckling at the scene and feeling in his element, Thorik realized the impact he was having on his community. The ability to teach a new generation various lessons for a solid foundation was a wonderful gift that he had the opportunity to be a part of. Gazing out at his students, he thought about how he was instilling in them a higher level of reasoning through his words, but he questioned if that was enough. Fir Brimmelle spoke the words but didn't live them. Thorik was frequently tasking himself to do both.

After everyone settled down, Fir Brimmelle uncoiled the scroll and read the official meaning of the rune.

Several more awards were handed out to the children before a few adults received some. The routine was the same for each, with the Fir reading after each award was given. When they had finished, the crowd dispersed and went back to eating and drinking as the sun set on Farbank Commons.

Lanterns were lit and music played as Ambrosius sat on his bench and watched couples dance. Partners changed frequently, allowing everyone a chance to socialize with each other. The night was still young, but his body was not. Gluic's healing from that morning was wearing off, and he was once again starting to feel the same intense discomfort.

Finally receiving a chance to dance with Emilen, Thorik glanced over at Ambrosius, who was now hunched over. Regretfully, he excused himself and left the dance area to see what was wrong with his patient. "Ambrosius, can you walk?"

"Yes, but the pain is returning with a vengeance," Ambrosius squeezed out.

Thorik helped him to his feet. He then acted as a crutch for Ambrosius as they made their way through the village and to Thorik's cottage, where he laid his tall friend gently on the bed.

Gluic had been waiting there long enough to make herself a pot of tea and sip half a cup down. Her healing stones and gems were laid out and ready to be used as she moved them onto key points of his body.

5

LEAVING FARBANK

Ambrosius opened his eyes the next morning just as the sun warmed the frigid air. He slowly sat up and noticed something different from the other days. Although the room was tidy, like always, there was a pack sitting at the center of the table. Alongside it was a Runestone. He also noticed his wooden staff leaning against the chair. Thorik had fashioned a thumb grip at the top of the staff, ideal for negotiating inclines.

Standing up and moving over to the table, he pulled out a chair and sat down to investigate. He opened the pack to find various items of hiking gear and rations. "He's packed my bags for my trip."

Disappointed that he could not sway Thorik, he took a deep, thoughtful breath and considered his options: wait until he was fully recovered or take his chances now on his own. His frustration at not knowing what exactly happened at the Mountain King's Temple was fueled by the idle time that he had had in the small village. He felt unproductive in not helping any potential survivors of the temple's destruction. He pondered how the council was located and destroyed, and was furious at knowing the assassin was victorious and roaming free. "Where will your next attack be? Who would be there to stop it, if not me?"

Using the wooden staff to lift him from his seat, he threw the pack over his shoulder and grabbed the Runestone to begin his long hike to Kingsfoot. Glancing around the little cottage, he commented to Thorik, who wasn't there, "Thank you for your help, my friend. I understand why you wouldn't want to leave this peaceful place."

He tossed the stone in the air before him and caught it as he turned for the door. Stopping just before opening it, he looked into his palm at the rune in the center of the hexagonal stone. It was the Runestone of Symbiosis. Puzzled for a moment, he suddenly realized what it meant. "I knew you would come through for me." Although Thorik couldn't possibly hear him, ironically the Num approached the door from outside shortly after the words were spoken.

The door swung open and Thorik walked in with a handful of blankets neatly folded after being freshly removed from the clothesline. "Good morning. Do you feel strong enough for a hike upstream today?"

"I've climbed the east face of the Shi'Pel crest; I think I can handle a little tour in the woods," he said with a smile. "I'm glad that I could change your mind about helping me."

Thorik set down the thick blankets and walked to the kitchen area. "You didn't. Looking into my students' faces did." Grabbing several pieces of fruit for them to enjoy on their trip, he tucked some into a sack before tossing one to Ambrosius. "How can I teach the words of the Mountain King if I don't follow them myself?"

"So, it is loyalty that drives you."

"Yes, I guess you could say that. To be honest, what I really want to do is lead others down good paths, but I must lead by example first."

"Being a good leader is more than just that. One must also be willing to make hard decisions that could hurt yourself or others. Either way, leadership or loyalty, you can lead this trek. I appreciate what you're doing for me."

"You're welcome." Thorik went back to his task of collecting items for the excursion. After lining up silverware, plates, oils, and spices on the table, he placed them into his own pack in specific locations around his wooden coffer to keep them protected. Instinctively, he kept the coffer hidden so Brimmelle wouldn't see it and berate him for wasting his time.

Ambrosius stepped out the door into the sun's morning rays peeking between the colored leaves in the trees. Closing the door behind him, he walked out onto the path to test his leg strength as well as Thorik's recent modifications to the staff's handgrip. It felt much better. Not as good as his old metal staff, but an improvement from the prior day. As he walked up toward the hillside behind the cottage to test his leg's capabilities, the outcroppings of rocks acted as ideal sites for stepping up and down. His legs were holding. Weak and wobbly, but holding.

Putting the last few items into their designated locations, Thorik was interrupted by a knock on the door. Upon answering it, he was surprised to find a small party packed for the trip. He had expected Gluic, seeing that she had agreed to help Ambrosius while Thorik led them to Kingsfoot. But he was disappointed to find two others had joined her.

"Brimmelle? What are your plans for this day?" He had hoped that Brimmelle had shown up just to see his mother off on her journey.

The Fir raised his head and chest slightly. "You need a leader for this journey. I'm the obvious choice. And I brought Wess with us to ensure our safety from wild beasts."

This was a direct insult to Thorik by his mentor, the Fir of Farbank. He was just reminded that Brimmelle felt he didn't have what it takes to be a leader or a protector.

Bringing Wess made it even worse. Wess had been malicious and condescending to Thorik, yet he was a loyal follower of Fir Brimmelle and his teachings. The contradiction annoyed Thorik.

Regardless of any feelings Thorik had, he welcomed them both in.

Uncharacteristically, Wess politely thanked him. "You have done well for yourself, Dain." Picking a few jars off the cupboard shelves, he read the detailed labels before setting them back with the labels facing the wall. "Your mother would have been very proud of how clean you kept her little shack." For no apparent reason, Wess pulled a chair out as he rambled on before moving over toward the shelves of books and knickknacks. He observed several items by holding them to the light from the window and then setting them back down in new locations.

Brimmelle, meanwhile, had made himself at home by pulling up his normal reading chair and was entrenched in reviewing the Scrolls of Wisdom as though the journey had been completed and it was time to relax.

By this time Thorik was slowly following Wess around the room, trying not to look obvious as he turned the jars back so the labels faced out, pushed the chair back in, and reorganized the various objects Wess had moved.

Stuffing a bright orange feather into her hair, Gluic looked at the group and shook her head in disbelief. "Are we going to Kingsfoot or rearranging your home? Take the lead," she ordered Thorik, before looking at Brimmelle and Wess. "And I didn't ask either of you two to come, so you walk behind me. I'm not going to spend the next several weeks downwind from you."

Thorik tried not to smile as he grabbed his hunting bow and arrows. She knew just what to say to ruffle Brimmelle's feathers and make Thorik feel better.

Stepping out of the cottage, Gluic turned upstream to head through the woods. Ambrosius was already waiting for the group. Approaching him, she adjusted a shoulder strap. "I see you've found your legs this morning."

He nodded at her statement. "Thank you for your help."

Pulling out a yellowish clear stone from a small sack hanging from her belt, she placed it in his right hand. "Moonstone," she explained. "Releases all the tension and emotions you're hiding inside you." She reached up and pointed at his head. "And you have plenty of that up there."

"Thank you anyway. I'll be fine." Ambrosius politely rejected her help and attempted to give the item back, but was unsuccessful. She had already turned away from him, toward the forest.

"Well, of course you will be, as long as you do as I tell you." Her soft but stern words stopped his efforts to return the gift. "Now hold on to that stone today. I'll need to cleanse it tonight so you can use it again tomorrow." She then walked off into the woods.

Ambrosius chuckled to himself at her odd leadership role and placed the moonstone into one of his pockets before following her through the trees.

Without looking back, Gluic notified Ambrosius, "I'll strap that to your palm if you don't take it back out and hold it on your own."

Stopping in his tracks, he had to give her motherly instincts a nod of praise as he took the stone back out and grasped it in his fist.

Thorik, Brimmelle, and Wess gathered their items and followed as well. Out the door and into the woods they went to catch up to the two in front, who had no idea where they were going.

It wasn't long before they were all together again. Ambrosius was the slowest, but then again, he was the reason they were going. His focus was strictly on pushing his body through any pains that came about. Not overly mindful of the path, he wandered from side to side and required periodic assistance from Thorik. It was a more difficult hike than Ambrosius had anticipated.

Shortly into the walk, Wess and Brimmelle fell a few lengths behind the others to talk privately. Wess watched Ambrosius limp and stumble through the forest like some drunk after a long night of festivities.

"So, this is the one that has put a plague on us? This weak, pathetic man," Wess quietly said to Brimmelle. "Wouldn't it have been easier to just sacrifice him to the Mountain King?"

"We will not taint our village with his blood. He is either the one who will save us or the one who will destroy us, and I will not be the one who orders our savior's death."

Wess slowed their pace a bit more to increase their distance from the rest as they rounded a bend in the old, unused path. "How much more proof do you need that he is evil? The river has been filled with dead fish ever since he arrived. Even with the great harvest we had, we will run out of food if he is not sacrificed and the fish don't return. I know that most of the others agree with me that—"

"Others?" Brimmelle interrupted. "Who else knows that we suspect him of carrying out the words of the Portent Scrolls?" Brimmelle stopped Wess in his tracks and looked him in the eyes. "Listen here, Wesstiford Solen Frellican." He pulled Wess close to him with a handful of his shirt. "I am the Fir, not you. I make this ruling, and I decide who knows what. Is that understood?"

Wess was leaner than Brimmelle, several inches taller, and about half a life younger. Regardless of his physical abilities, Wess was not going to be disrespectful to a Fir. Disagree with him, perhaps, but never disrespect him. Knowing how far he could push the issue, he nodded to Brimmelle, signifying that he would obey.

Keeping his grip tight on Wess' shirt, Brimmelle relaxed his arms to give some distance between them. "Who else knows about this?"

Before he could respond, they both heard a voice in the woods from which they had come. A woman's voice shouted Wess' name. It was Emilen, running through the woods, trying to catch up to them. Her long curly hair bounced with each stride as it was loosely held together with several colorful hair ribbons in a single ponytail. Following behind was the youth, Avanda.

Brimmelle released Wess before they arrived.

Emilen joyfully approached the two while looking past them into the woods. "Where's the rest of the group?"

Brimmelle crossed his arms and pulled his shoulders back. "Young lady, what do you think you're doing?"

Ignoring his question, she walked past both of them and scanned the woods for a direction to travel. "We're going with you. Which way did they go?"

The timber was very thick at this point, but the river could still be heard to her left, so she assumed she was heading the right way.

It seemed very cut and dried to the Fir. "Nonsense. Return home at once. This is no place for the two of you. Return to Farbank and watch Avanda for Wess, like you were instructed."

"My family lives in Kingsfoot, and I want to see if they are safe. As far as Avanda goes, I can watch her while we travel," she replied, before sighting Thorik and Ambrosius. "There they are." Ignoring the Fir, she rushed forward into the woods before Brimmelle could utter a rebuttal.

Brimmelle stood silently and watched her run until she rounded the path's bend. "Is she one that believes he is a savior or a demon?"

Wess finished straightening out the creases in his shirt. "Savior."

"Unfortunate."

"True, but perhaps I could persuade her to think differently." Wess smiled as he watched her leave them.

"You won't get that chance," Brimmelle noted. "It is not safe for Avanda out here."

"She'll be fine. We'll all keep an eye on her."

"Avanda is your responsibility until her parents return to Farbank in the spring. Take this seriously and order Emilen to return with her at once."

Wess was captivated by Emilen's looks. It was difficult for him to stay in Brimmelle's conversation. He eventually added, "It will be good for Avanda to learn how to travel. I'll take care of her, I promise."

"I don't like this," the Fir grumbled as Avanda arrived and then ran past them, following Emilen.

It wasn't long before Emilen had reached the forward group and jumped onto Thorik's back. "Surprise!" she shouted as they both fell to the ground and rolled to a nearby log. Flinching from the stabbing pain inflicted by various objects from within his backpack, Thorik hoped his pack hadn't ripped, spilling out its contents. While on top of him, she laughed at his expression, not knowing why he was making the faces he did.

Hopping off once she saw Ambrosius standing near Gluic, Emilen cautiously approached the older man. "I'm grateful to finally meet you properly. You left the Harvest Festival before I had the opportunity." She searched his eyes to see if he recalled seeing her.

Ambrosius looked down to see Emilen standing next to him. "Do I know you? You look familiar." She wasn't the first Num he thought that about. His head had been scrambled, and his memories were a mess.

"You don't recall seeing me before?"

"Yes… at the festival."

Delighted with the answer, she bowed her head ever so slightly. "I am Emilen. I'm at your service to save our people."

"Save your people? I've tried to save your people. All people in fact, but I'm afraid I have failed. Now I'm struggling just to keep my own vitality."

"But you are the one written about in our Portent Scrolls." She looked into his tired eyes and waited for his reply.

"Emilen, he doesn't know what you're talking about." Thorik inspected his pack and took an inventory of his hunting knives to make sure nothing was lost. "We're just here to return him to Kingsfoot."

Emilen looked in disbelief at Thorik. "Why didn't you tell him?"

Brimmelle responded as he and Wess caught up to them. "We don't even know the truth about the Mountain King statue, the council, and if he is who he claims to be. Contain your excitement until we know what's going on here."

"Why would you think his story is false?" she asked.

Brimmelle answered her loud enough for Ambrosius to overhear. "First of all, how did he end up so far downstream? If he had fallen in the river, he would have surely drowned or froze to death before reaching Farbank."

Thorik attempted to dissolve the friction in the air. "We'll be at Kingsfoot soon enough to determine what happened." Reviewing the items in his pack to ensure nothing was damaged, he noticed Avanda. "What are you doing here?" He was obviously upset that she was subjected to the dangers of the woods.

Avanda frowned. She had hoped Thorik would be excited to see her.

"This is too dangerous for you," Thorik told her before turning his attention to her uncle. "Wess, you need to take responsibility for her and take her back to Farbank."

Wess didn't take kindly to Thorik giving him orders. "Listen, Dain, I gave her to Emilen to watch, so don't be lecturing me. Tell Emilen to take her or, better yet, you can take her back and Emilen and I will lead this group upstream."

Wess saw Emilen's sour look and quickly changed his response. "Personally, if Emilen feels that it is safe out here for Avanda, then I will support her decision." With a quick smile, he added, "Emilen and I will work together to keep her out of trouble."

Thorik couldn't believe his ears and looked at Brimmelle for him to order Wess to take Avanda back.

Brimmelle shook his head at Wess. "Avanda is your responsibility. You better rise to the occasion." It was quickly followed with, "Of course, if anyone asked me, I would tell them that this entire trip should not be taken."

Wess ignored the comments, but he nodded to pacify the elder.

Seeing a quick wink from her uncle Wess, Avanda knew she was in the clear to join the adventure.

6

CURIOUS DISCOVERIES

Once again, the party was on its way through the woods as bushes thickened and boulders became more common. Small hills led the way to steep slopes, which then led to large ravines. The trees in this part of the valley were taller, with trunks the size of three men.

After many more hours of walking into the evening, Wess noticed that moss seemed to grow on almost everything in this area. The exceptions were several logs and a few large rocks scattered about.

Wess, like Thorik, was a proficient woodsman, so when he noticed the unnatural-looking growth, he grew curious and investigated it. Pulling Brimmelle to the side, he pointed to a few odd features. "Take a look at this. There must have been one terrible storm in these parts."

Brimmelle was obviously confused. "Why do you say that?"

"Look at the moss on these logs. It is on the wrong side, so all these trees recently fell."

"Storms knock down trees. What's so odd about that?"

"Normally you would find the base trunk nearby or a small pit from the uprooting. I see neither. This storm tossed these trees away from their growth location."

As the slight breeze changed direction, they noticed a new odor. Brimmelle covered his nose with his hand and looked at Wess.

Squinting, he was starting to get nervous. "I know that smell. It's the smell of death. Rotten flesh." Cautiously, he followed the stench.

Brimmelle didn't want to be left behind, nor did he want to follow. Looking around, he noticed that the rest of the party had left, and he didn't know in which direction. "Let us be on our way."

Wess paid no attention to him as he pinpointed the odor to one of the fallen trees. Noticing a patch of black fur attached to the backside of the log, he took a stick to pry it off to find that it was an arm of some animal. "Thrashers." His eyes darted about before looking over to warn Brimmelle, who was now frozen with fear. Wess had heard the horror stories of those beasts and wanted nothing to do with them. "It's time to go."

Upon reaching Brimmelle, he could see his Fir staring in shock at the sight of a decomposing ape-like beast with both legs missing. Shards of wood pierced through the creature's body. Facial skin had been chewed off half its face, and the insects were running rampant over it.

Brimmelle attempted to clarify the situation. "I've heard that thrashers kill each other for dominance."

"No. This doesn't make sense. A tribe of thrashers ripped apart. What could have done that? And those fallen trees, they don't belong here, and they weren't dragged to this spot either." Looking upwards, he noted a lot of breakage in the canopy. "It's as if they were dropped here. And these large rocks appear water worn from the river. They're out of place as well." He thought for a moment before stating nervously, "I know of no creature that could do this, but I am sure we don't want to run into whatever it is."

Wess had never actually seen a thrasher before, but he had seen hides that had come from the south side of the mountain. He had heard stories. Horrific stories of thrasher raids on villages. Every child had been warned by their parents in an effort to keep them from wandering off into the forest. "Thrashers don't live in the King's Valley." He shook the horrifying children's fable out of his mind. "So why are they here? And why so close to Farbank?"

Though still puzzled, Wess finally decided to focus on getting out of the area to discuss this with the others. In doing so, they caught up to the rest of the group within a few minutes. The party had completely stopped, standing on the edge of a rim, looking across a small valley clearing.

The bowl-shaped clearing in front of them was about half the size of Farbank. Its rim was lined with fallen trees and large boulders that pressed up against the trees still standing along the perimeter.

The small, round valley was free of all life and extended into the river with a dam of earth and rocks, preventing the water from flooding it. It was a strange contrast of rock and dirt surrounded by the lush forest and snowcapped mountains. It was out of place and oddly unnatural. In essence, it was a lifeless crater.

They climbed down the side and then moved toward the middle as the ground grew hard. As they approached the center, the solid rock was stripped clean of all dirt. Deep scars on the bedrock floor pointed away from the center, which is where Thorik led Ambrosius.

Brimmelle stopped next to them as he tried to understand what had happened.

"Do you recall this place?" Thorik asked Ambrosius.

Ambrosius was in great pain by this point. He had pushed too hard throughout the day and was in need of a treatment from Gluic. Regardless, he looked at his surroundings with no memory of them. "No."

"This is where I found you, right here in the center."

Ambrosius slowly looked around. "No, I have no memories of this place." Thinking a bit more, he added, "But I do recall climbing out of a river and onto the rocks near the trees. I remember pain and then being attacked. They came from everywhere. I was certain this was my end. They were clawing and biting and ripping me apart." Ambrosius thought deeply to remember. "Then I pushed them away." He paused as he fought the overpowering urge to collapse from the pain, the day's travel, and the memory of the events. With the help of Thorik, he lowered himself to sit on the ground. "No, not them," he corrected himself. "I pushed everything away. Everything. Then blackness and peace." After a moment, he continued, "I remember nothing else; in fact, I'm uncertain if it's even a memory. It's so unclear, like a faded dream. If I didn't still have the pain in my legs, I surely would have thought it was precisely that."

Thorik noticed Brimmelle's tense expression and face turning deep red. "Brimmelle, I know what you're going to say. However, understand he was going to die, and while his powers to kill the thrashers and create this crater match the powers in the Portent Scrolls about the evil that is coming, they also match the description of the one that will save us."

"You found him out this far?" Brimmelle asked, to Thorik's surprise. "I had forbidden you to exceed the boundaries of Fawn Hollow without others. If you had been hurt out here, we would have never found you. You may play lightly with your life, but I will not."

Thorik's shoulders lowered. "Yes, yes, you are right. But—"

Brimmelle continued over the top of Thorik's words. "Have you forgotten how your parents died? Are you trying to tempt fate?"

"No. You don't understand the entire story."

He grabbed Thorik by his hair with one hand to stifle the young man's words. "No, it's you that doesn't understand the entire ramifications. You knew that thrashers had traveled this close to Farbank, and you never alerted us? You know the stories. You know what they do. And you didn't tell anyone? You endangered all of us so you didn't have to confront me with the extent of your travels?" Angry and disappointed, the Fir looked at Thorik's now sagging shoulders and saddened eyes. "I would not have thought you, of all people, would have put yourself before the village. When are you going to start seeing the greater view of life instead of just your little insignificant piece of it?"

Thorik attempted to get a few words into the conversation. "I was just—"

"I don't want to hear it. When we return to Farbank, you will surrender your family home and your position as our Northern Valley hunter so you can focus on the Rune Scrolls. I will not let you make this mistake again."

Thorik's eyes widened and filled with tears as he began to protest, but he knew that look from Brimmelle. With every word Thorik spoke to argue the point, Brimmelle would make the deal even worse.

�֍ 7 ֍

CAMPSITE

Thorik tried to work off his frustration with himself, the situation, and those he had let down. Rationalizing his decisions, he justified them with the understanding that this trip with Ambrosius was still the right thing to do. He assembled various beds of woven grass, leaves, and sticks for the night to take his mind off his problems.

A campsite had been quickly set up toward the upstream wall to block the wind. Collapsing from the pain and fatigue, Ambrosius rested next to Avanda near the fire as Gluic covered them with blankets.

Fir Brimmelle, Wess, and Emilen argued about what to do with Ambrosius. The options proposed ranged from helping him reach Kingsfoot to leaving him to die where Thorik had found him.

The two men argued that anyone with the power to create this crater was surely a threat. The destruction of so much nature, along with the animals that lived among it, showed a lack of morality.

Brimmelle wasted no time in reading verses from the scrolls which forbade such destruction of nature.

Wess added, "There are dead fish in the river and now thrashers in the valley, near Farbank, no less!" Wess peered into the darkening surrounding woods, partly out of wariness of these predators, and partly to emphasize his point. He continued, "These grave signs shouldn't be ignored. We don't even know what he is. No human can do what was done here. He must be some kind of demon." He enjoyed a heated debate. The outcome meant very little to him. It was the bantering back and forth that excited him.

Emilen held her own against the two. However, emotion played a factor for her. It was very uncommon for anyone to raise their voice to a Fir, let alone publicly disagree with them, but she didn't hold back at all. She pointed out verses in several scrolls that spoke of the coming savior that fell from the Mountain

King's Crown and then helped rebuild their kingdom. "The animals that were killed around the crater were thrashers, who have never come to this valley before. Another day or so and they would have attacked Farbank. Ambrosius prevented the attack and saved our lives. I recall a scroll passage that reads 'where great good comes, great evil tries to destroy it'. It is our responsibility to protect Ambrosius from an evil that will try to kill him."

Fir Brimmelle took offense to being challenged. No one had ever questioned his interpretation of the Runestone Scrolls or the Rules of Order, at least not to his face. He allowed Wess to do most of the arguing and then would interject with phrases from the scrolls when he could.

Wess was quick to return a pointed question back to the sender, and he knew just what to say and how to say it to get under Emilen's mental armor, throwing her off balance. He never lost control of the situation and often flashed that irritating grin of his.

Emilen fought the good fight but became so frustrated with Wess that she finally had to walk away and take a break near the river. "Thanks for your support," she stabbed at Thorik as she walked past him, his shocked look irritating her even more.

Thorik had avoided the debate. His focus was on helping Ambrosius get to the point he could make it on his own, regardless of his intentions. He reached into his sack of Runestones and pulled out one at random for guidance. Mentioning the rune's name, "Respect", he looked at the hexagonal stone's flat side. "Show others the same respect that you would have them show you." Pondering over a few more phrases in his mind helped set him at ease and come to understand his error in judgment.

Brimmelle selected a bed and made himself comfortable with his back turned to the others before he quickly fell asleep. Avanda picked a bed near Emilen, who had distanced herself from Brimmelle. Thorik and Wess took turns as lookouts throughout the night while Emilen slept off her frustration.

After collecting new flora to wear, Gluic ignored everyone and focused on healing Ambrosius before her own slumber. She never got into debates, or the Rules of Order, for that matter. She just did what she felt was right when she felt it needed to be done. Life seemed so much simpler that way.

Ambrosius woke to the sound of a campfire and Brimmelle snoring up a storm. His vision was hazy at first as he looked at the firelight washing against various bodies surrounding the camp. They were all lying on Thorik's thick, neatly constructed beds.

One figure was leaning over the fire and, judging by the smell, making breakfast. As expected, it was Thorik. "You gave us quite a scare again," the Num said. "You passed out when we first arrived and then screamed in pain several times last night." The night's sleep had washed away the arguments from the prior day as Thorik challenged himself to start each day with a fresh outlook.

The Num continued to focus on his cooking. "How are you feeling this morning?"

"I hurt, but I'll survive." Sitting up to face Thorik, Ambrosius squinted as he looked about and realized that he was still in the crater, and still not recalling the place. It meant nothing to him, but something else did. "Do you know the name Ruddlehoth of Kingsfoot?"

"Yes, there's one sleeping right over there. Why? What do you need with Emilen?"

"I'm not sure exactly. I had a dream, recalling someone with that name. What can you tell me about her?" Ambrosius inquired.

Smiling, Thorik glanced over at her sleeping under several blankets. "What do you need to know? She has a splendid gift for teaching the Runestones and helping others. She's strong-willed and can negotiate amazing trades at the market. She's enjoyable to be around. Just don't get on her bad side." Thorik smiled and then noticed that his breakfast hadn't been given attention for a bit.

"Any relationship to Fir Beltrow?"

"Yes, that would be her father. Do you know him?"

"Yes." Now was not the time to inform the young lady of her father's death while he had attended the council meeting. Ambrosius wasn't even absolutely convinced of it himself. It all seemed vague and dreamlike. Instead, he changed the subject. "How is your Order structured? I understand that each community has one Fir of the Order and if I remember correctly, they usually have more than one Sec that is in training who helps with the daily tasks."

Thorik was too busy finishing up the cooking to notice the change in conversation. "We have three; Thea, Shucan, and myself. It is a great honor to be selected. We each have our own ways of supporting Fir Brimmelle. Someday one of us will become the Fir, after Brimmelle has left us."

"So, who does Fir Brimmelle receive guidance from?"

Thorik looked puzzled. "The Order."

Ambrosius also looked confused. "The Order?"

"The Scrolls of Wisdom provide the details of how to live by the Rules of Order."

"Isn't there a higher power than your village Fir to monitor the teachings?"

"No." Brimmelle's unexpected words were abrupt and heavy. "The Rules of Order and the Rune Scrolls tell me what I need to know. Seeing that the Mountain King himself wrote the Scrolls of Wisdom to be self-evident to those who know how to read them, there isn't a need for others to tell me how to interpret his writings."

Thorik looked over. "Good morning, Uncle. Your breakfast is ready." He proceeded to scoop some onto a plate before handing it to him. Thorik continued by making a plate for Ambrosius as well as the rest of the party, as he woke them up, before serving himself.

Brimmelle began shoveling food into his mouth. "Our beliefs are of no concern to you. They have served us well for generations and don't require outsiders poking their noses into our business."

Ambrosius stared at Brimmelle's image, which was slightly clearer now that the sun was starting to rise. "Recently, your Order has acquired representation on the Grand Council, and I haven't had the time to learn much about your beliefs. I was just curious and meant no offense."

Brimmelle continued eating while talking. "I'm not represented by anyone at your council. The Rules of Order and the Rune Scrolls, which the Firs teach to their faction, were written by the Mountain King. The Secs provide support for the Firs and carry out actions to help the faction. The faction provides the needs of the Fir. In return, the Mountain King provides strong crops, abundant fish in the river, and fruitful hunts. It's cut and dried, easy to understand."

Ambrosius questioned Brimmelle again. "Can I safely assume that Gluic is a Channel? I've never met one personally, but she seems to fit the description that I have heard."

Thorik's brow raised and eyes opened large at the question, for he knew how Brimmelle refused to allow anyone to talk about Gluic's odd ways.

Defensively, Brimmelle responded, "She's my mother. Don't you dare try to label her."

Ambrosius took a different angle in his questioning. "Understood. Your mother aside, may I ask how Channels fit into your Order?"

"They don't," Brimmelle replied in a short and irritated tone.

Thorik broke the awkward silence that followed. "Some Nums have been given the gift to channel special powers, which we are thankful for and use from time to time. But they have nothing to do with the Order. There is nothing in our scrolls about them. Historically, Nums have been killed for having such abilities, in the belief that they are evil powers." Glancing at the Fir, he continued. "But Brimmelle has taught us that the powers come from the Mountain King, and we are not to question them, for it would be like questioning the Mountain King himself."

By this point, the rest of the party was eating their breakfast. They all sat on the beddings facing the fire, some with their blankets covering their heads and bodies. The meal was warm and helped them shake off the night's chill.

The camp was oddly silent as they ate, unlike the night before, after Ambrosius had passed out. They quietly finished their breakfast, eyes glaring at each other with obvious tension amongst them. No agreement had been made as to Ambrosius' fate.

Ambrosius noticed his party's disposition with interest, wondering what he had missed. Obviously, he had struck a nerve with his questioning, but the stiffness of the group seemed to be more than just that.

Thorik finally stood, gathered the dishes and his cooking gear, and headed off to the river to clean them. Emilen stood up to help Thorik with the items.

It wasn't far to the water. They had camped near the edge of the crater, toward the river, to reduce the cold winds that came down from the mountaintop and headed down the valley. The crater's northwest edge sloped up to a wall of boulders and dirt that acted as a dam, keeping the water out and encroaching into the river by a fourth of the river's width.

Thorik set his items down on a flat boulder next to the river. "I bet you wish you had brought your fishing supplies." His attempt to lighten the mood received no response, so he continued, "I mean, look at this natural dock. It's perfect for fishing, wouldn't you say?"

Thorik and Emilen started washing the pots as he continued in his pursuit of reducing the uncomfortable silent tension. "I might have to stop here and do some fishing next time I'm in these parts. Yes, some very nice fishing could be done at this location."

"Why didn't you defend my view?" Emilen briskly stated, as her eyes looked up from what she was cleaning to look at him.

Thorik wasn't sure which was worse, the uncomfortable silence or the conversation that was just starting. He looked up from his work and replied. "Hang on a second. I thought you were mad at Wess. Why are you upset with me?"

"Yes, I'm mad that Wess' misguided understanding of the Scrolls of Wisdom could cause an innocent man to die. A man that I believe has been sent here by the Mountain King to strengthen our faith, guide us, and unite us across the land. Of course, it upsets me, and it should upset Brimmelle and you as well. Brimmelle is either too afraid of losing his authority or too bullheaded to see what's going on. On the other hand, you are close to Ambrosius and can surely see that he is not here to harm us. You also know the words of the scrolls and should be helping me in carrying them out. Wess may not agree with me, but I respect the fact that he stands up for what he believes in and is willing to fight for it."

"I just don't see how yelling at each other is going to help any of us."

"So, what would you have me do? Watch as they kill the savior of our people and do nothing? What kind of Sec are you? I thought you were a good person; someone who carries out the Rules of Order and follows the words from the scrolls. At what point do you stand up for what you believe in and fight for it? Or should we just do whatever Fir Brimmelle orders, even though everything inside of us is saying not to?"

Thorik felt this wave of questions crash upon him, and he began to drown in them. He didn't know what question to answer first and was concerned that any answer he gave would unleash another attack. But he had to reply. He wasn't a coward by any means. He just didn't see any reason to make this issue any bigger than it really was. "No, of course not," came out as he kept his eyes on his work. It was a safe answer, simple and not retaliating, which would have caused more conflicts.

"No? No what? No, you don't have the valor to fight for what's right? No, you can't disobey your Fir even when you know he's wrong? Or, no, you don't care about anyone but yourself, and unless it hurts you it isn't worth bothering yourself? Is that why you live outside the village, so you don't have to bother yourself with the problems of others? Ignoring the problems doesn't make them go away."

Thorik was wounded. This wave hit deeper than the prior one, and there appeared to be an endless supply of them ready and waiting. He had worked extremely hard all his life to be the best person that he could and tried to follow the Rules of Order. He thought he performed this better than most others by helping people whenever they asked without looking for anything in return. How dare she suggest otherwise. "You're wrong." He finally looked her square in the eyes. "I'm always helping others. You have no right to question my beliefs and convictions." Pausing to take a breath, he finished with, "I am a good person."

"Yes, you are," she agreed with him. "But it takes more than being a good person to make things better. You have to fight for what's right." Emilen picked up the items she had washed and walked down the hillside and back to camp without saying another word. In her haste, one of her hair ribbons had fallen to the ground near Thorik.

His natural reaction was to return it to her, but instead he picked it up and pulled it tight between his fingers. Tight, just like he felt inside after his confrontation with her. His chest and shoulders were straining, and his stomach churned. Thorik was frustrated and disappointed in himself for not defending himself better. He sat there, near the river, justifying himself to himself before realizing that this wasn't doing him any good.

Looking down at his feet dangling over the boulder, he continued to pull the blue ribbon back and forth between several fingers until he lost control and dropped it. Drifting down, it approached the water's surface and landed on a large frog, that had been warming itself on a rock in the morning sunlight. Thorik gave a slight smile at how it landed on the frog, giving the amphibian a dapper appearance. "Enjoy the scarf, my little green friend. No need to repay me."

The frog leaped into the water and disappeared. Thorik was once again, alone.

❧ 8 ❧

FESH'UNDAY

Thorik's Log: 2nd day of the 10th month of the 649th year.

My journal of our travels begins on a sour note. Our journey up the river has not been as I had hoped. I'm looking forward to reaching Kingsfoot and seeing the Mountain King statue with my own eyes.

Shortly after breakfast, the group had packed and prepared for the day's journey. Most of the group began walking as Thorik doused the campfire ashes before catching up to the rest, following Emilen and Wess, who had been in the back.

Walking next to Emilen, Wess eventually apologized for the confrontation the night before. He explained that he had thought about what she had said, and he would give her ideas a chance. She obviously warmed up to what he was saying and thanked him. Presenting her with one of her many dropped hair ribbons, he explained how beautiful she looked with it in. It happened to be a special ribbon that her mother had made for her. Excited to see it returned, she gave him a quick hug.

Emilen gazed at Wess for a moment. He was actually ruggedly handsome, and he carried himself very well. He had a charm that either had people eating out of his hands or irritated them to no end. But he fought for what he believed in, and that meant a great deal to her. All she needed to do was get him to believe in the right things. "Yes, he could be the one," she thought.

Wess looked down at Emilen and realized he had broken the ice and gotten back into her good graces. The ribbon he had given her was interlaced with variously colored threads that matched her natural flowing locks of hair. She added it to the others already tied up behind her head. Wess watched her shapely figure as they continued. "I bet she joined this trip to spend some more time with me," he told himself.

Thorik had watched the exchange between Wess and Emilen, including the hug.

Avanda stood along the way, waiting for Thorik to arrive. "I'll walk with you," she said once he had caught up to her. Grabbing his hand, she swung it back and forth as she skipped lightly down the way.

It didn't take long for her excitement about the journey to infect Thorik, and they both gained momentum until they were at the front of the party.

The pace was still slow, but faster than the day before. They made several stops for Ambrosius to rest, although Brimmelle and Gluic needed it as well. Thorik and Avanda led the way, followed closely by Gluic and Ambrosius. The rest followed at their own speed.

Ambrosius was still struggling, and the previous day's walking only added sore muscles to his pain. He could not give up, for too much was at stake, so he employed everything he had left to continue. Gluic helped by pulling the pain out of him several times a day, and Thorik was always there to lean on and help him up and down steep hills. In addition, Ambrosius' new staff kept him balanced to make up for his bad leg. It wasn't the highly crafted staff he had traveled the lands with for many an age; it was only a limb stripped of its branches and sanded down, but it served its purpose.

He appreciated his helpers, but Ambrosius missed his old staff. It was a symbol of how things were when he had it. He had seen great battle victories and unions with his staff at his side. Without it, he recalled the defeats and destruction during his youth, and now his current state of helplessness. The staff was symbolic and wasn't the strength of his power, but life felt empty without it, like missing an arm or a leg. He didn't feel whole.

"The grip is bad, it's cutting into my hand," Ambrosius stated as he stopped, handed Thorik the staff, and held out his hand, showing the bloody palm with various cuts in it. He stood silently as Thorik quickly cleaned and wrapped his wounds. Thorik removed the leather from the staff before cutting a few slices out of the wood and then applied new skins to the handgrip.

"Here, this should fit your hand better. I'll work on reducing its weight at our next stop." Thorik firmly placed it back into Ambrosius' freshly wrapped hand.

Ambrosius squeezed his hand around it and moved his fingers a bit to modify his grip. "Better." Nodding, he began limping forward again. The trip was taking its toll on him, physically and mentally. The pain increased progressively throughout the day, even after Gluic's help, and was testing his ability to focus.

Thorik was pleased that the grip was better and proceeded to lead the party along the trail to Kingsfoot. As they reached the narrows where the trail ran through a gorge, they could see that quite a bit of the walls on either side had caved in and blocked the path. The closer they got to the narrows, the more clear it was that they weren't passing through that way. Thorik eyed the bluff's precipitous slope. "This one will take most of the day."

Wess shook his head at the idea. "Why don't we stay by the river? We'll never make it over that cliff face."

Fortunately, Thorik's father had taught him about such things before Brimmelle took over as his guardian. His father had also informed him that the old trail to Kingsfoot lay above the cliff line.

"River cuts," Thorik replied.

"What?" Wess asked, thinking he had heard him incorrectly.

"As we travel farther upstream, the river makes deeper shear cuts into the foothills, carving out gorges straight down into the river. The final gorge doesn't open until Kingsfoot Lake. The river grows more treacherous with less shoreline as we head upstream." He spied what he was looking for and then continued, "Besides, see that large crack a short way up the rock face? That's our passageway through to the other side."

Exhausted, Brimmelle finally arrived. "This is far enough. We cannot climb any further." Breathing heavier than the rest, he sat down on a nearby rock while wiping the sweat from his forehead. Gluic was also showing signs of fatigue as she sat next to him. Wess and Ambrosius followed suit and sat down as well.

Emilen handed around water, starting with Ambrosius, while Thorik pulled some rope out and began tying knots in it. He proceeded to tie the end around himself. Giving several feet of slack, he then tied it to Ambrosius before continuing to Emilen, Brimmelle, Gluic, Avanda, and finally Wess at the far end. While tying everyone on to the rope, he explained that the purpose of the rope was to catch someone should they slip along the way up the steep slopes.

Wess had cited several reasons why he should be tied between Emilen and Ambrosius, but Thorik simply ignored him.

Brimmelle didn't like the idea of continuing. As he ventured farther from his village, he struggled more to hold a leadership role. It also became difficult to obtain passages from his scrolls that would suggest how to handle things differently. Feeling out of place, he attempted several more times to convince Gluic that she should not travel any farther, without any success.

Gluic was too headstrong for him and often would do the opposite of what he asked anyway. Not in an attempt to be cruel, but to teach him. As Fir of Farbank, he had absolute power and in time he had allowed it to corrupt his thinking. He had never traveled to other villages or communities to experience how other Firs taught their students. He had become close-minded and needed to be reminded from time to time of his own mortality and flaws. There was a good man inside him, but only he could bring it out. She felt this trip to Kingsfoot would do him well and hoped he would see it through. However, if he did decide to go back, she still needed to continue on, for her task was not yet completed.

The group was soon up and moving again in an attempt to reach the crack in the mountain before sundown. It took several minutes to get used to the rope's slack between them. If not handled correctly, it was easy to trip on it. Brimmelle learned the hard way more than once.

With the trees slowly starting to give way to more jutting rocks, they worked their way up a long stretch of nearly vertical climbing before opening to a series of rocky shelves which acted as nice rest areas. Thorik climbed up onto the first shelf and turned to help Ambrosius. He could see in the man's eyes that he needed Gluic's touch as he collapsed at the Num's feet and rolled onto his back.

It had taken them longer than Thorik had hoped to reach the upper portions of the cliff. The shadow of the mountain had fallen upon them, and the rising full moon crested over the eastern mountain peaks and bathed them in a blue light.

After adjusting his bow out of the way, Thorik pulled on the rope that linked Ambrosius to Emilen to help her up. While doing so, he was jabbed in the side by Ambrosius' staff. Ambrosius didn't always use the best manners when he needed assistance. Temporarily ignoring him, the Num reached down and lifted Emilen up off the cliff to a standing position in front of him. She was as light as a feather, and for a moment he held her there, looking into her eyes. But the moment ended with another quick jab from Ambrosius' staff.

Thorik broke contact with Emilen and looked at Ambrosius, whose leg bandage was soaked with fresh blood. His injury hadn't healed enough for the trip and appeared to have re-opened. Kneeling next to him, Thorik looked at his wound when he heard Ambrosius whisper, "thrashers."

Thorik didn't believe his ears until he looked at Ambrosius' face to see him eyeing something behind Thorik's back. Thorik turned in a flash, loaded an arrow into his bow, and pointed it to where Ambrosius had been looking.

It was a small outcropping of rocks with a dark cave in the center of it, not far off to the group's right. Stepping out of the cave and into the moonlight, the tribe leader, a large silverhead, eyed Thorik. Three deep blackened scars could be seen on his forehead, one trailing below his left eye. Black hair covered the primate's body, excluding parts of the face and hands. His long muscular arms reached down to the ground as he leaned forward while standing on his shorter back legs. Within one of his large black hairy hands, he held a thick bone that he slowly tapped on the ground. The eyes were the most intriguing; Thorik felt that he could see intelligence within them, even in the modest lighting.

The beast showed his teeth to Thorik before moving back into the darkness.

"Wess!" Thorik yelled. "Watch your back down there. We have thrashers, and they always attack from at least two sides." His father's training raced through his mind.

Brimmelle and Gluic stopped climbing to look around for any attackers while Wess pulled out his own hunting bow. Avanda grabbed several loose rocks to throw.

It was only seconds before the first set of clicks came from a rock shelf above them. A howl followed behind them, in the trees, as a second set of clicks came from the cave where Thorik had his weapon aimed. "Get up here! Now!" Thorik demanded.

Ambrosius rolled back to the edge of the ledge to help Emilen pull the rope that connected her to Brimmelle. The Fir was heavier than Emilen's small-framed body, and he wasn't as sure-footed. His ascent would take longer, especially now that he was panicking.

Wess loaded his bow as he caught a glimpse of several creatures jumping from tree to tree while they moved from the lower trees to the ones above the small band of travelers. It was difficult to prepare a shot at the quick thrashers, even though a Num's vision was reasonably good even in low-light situations. The heavy leaf coverage and the semi-darkness of night added to the challenge. It also didn't help that his footing was nothing more than a few small rocks jutting out of the side of the cliff face.

A series of clicks and a long howl came from the silverhead in the darkness of the cave, causing the trees around the party to shake. Thrashers slapped their hands on the rock shelves above, followed by one loud, high-pitched howl which launched their attack.

Wess began shooting into the trees as the Num-sized apes fell to the ground like rain. He had counted ten that he had shot and twice as many that he had missed.

Thorik stood on the ledge firing his arrows at thrashers emerging from the cave, only to break away periodically to fire at the ones from above. But with no one to watch his back, it wasn't long before he was outnumbered. An attack from the air knocked him to his knees, and he dropped his weapon. Quickly grabbing his knife, he swiveled for a quick stab into the creature's gut. With that one down, two more jumped on him. Thorik caught a glimpse of the silverhead emerging from his security of darkness before barking additional orders to his troops.

Brimmelle pulled himself up onto the ledge, near Emilen, as the first thrasher jumped from above, landing on him. He fell backward and off the ledge, screaming in pain and carrying the beast with him. Avanda shrieked as she saw the thrashers coming from above. Ambrosius let go of the rope as he grabbed his staff and braced it on the ground to stab the next thrasher jumping for Emilen. With the creature landing on the top end of the staff, Ambrosius used the creature's own momentum to propel it down the hillside.

Emilen had continued holding on to the rope that attached her to Brimmelle. This quickly dragged her over the edge, causing her to fall face-first toward Brimmelle and his passenger.

Brimmelle and Emilen clutched on to each other as they slid down the rock with the creature in tow. Without warning, the thrasher was dislodged when the rope abruptly went taut. Ambrosius now held the rope with both hands as he braced his legs against an upright rock to prevent himself from being pulled over along with them. The pain in his weak leg was causing it to tremble, as it felt ready to break again.

Emilen's grip on Brimmelle broke, leaving her hanging in the air from Ambrosius' rope as Brimmelle tumbled several feet before pulling Gluic off her grip. She, in turn, fell into Avanda and Wess, who dropped his weapon to catch her.

Ambrosius leaned forward to grip the rope closer to the edge. He pressed his legs against the upright rock as he leaned back, pulling the rope up. On his second attempt, he heard and felt his leg quiver. Snap! It popped as it gave way. He screamed in pain as he shifted all his weight to his other leg for his next attempt to pull them up. While leaning forward for his new grip on the rope, a mouth full of sharp blackened thrasher teeth sank into the flesh of his left arm.

A few yards away from Ambrosius, Thorik tumbled with the two primates on him as they ripped through his backpack and clothes. His wooden coffer acted as a shield against rear attacks but was a poor excuse for armor. Their speed and upper body strength easily outmatched his. Grabbing the neck of the one on top of him, he began to choke the thrasher while cracking the back of his head against the face of the one underneath him. He squeezed his fingers into the creature's skin and choked him with all his might.

The thrasher's arms and legs went wild as they tore into Thorik's body. Its head tilted as the creature snapped its jaw at Thorik's arms in a chaotic manner. The raised hair on the back of the thrasher's head and the folded-back ears indicated that he was still in an attack posture, in spite of the Num's tight grip on his neck. The creature's eyes showed no fear, only craze, only a desire to kill. Saliva, from its incessant snapping, covered Thorik's face and clouded his vision, as a third beast grabbed at his legs.

Below the ledge, Wess stabilized Gluic and Avanda for the moment. He tried to pull Brimmelle up toward them as the older Num worked his way along the slope. Brimmelle had only taken a few steps before he saw several beasts running up the hill as though it were a flat field. The creatures' strong short bodies seemed to be made for speed in any terrain. Thrashers charged at them from several angles with their drooling mouths biting at the air in front of them, possessed with an uncontrollable rage.

Out of sheer terror, Brimmelle grabbed his chest of scrolls from his belt pouch, closed his eyes, and started reciting the words he had read so often. Before his first verse was completed, he was attacked and pressed against the hillside with his small chest of scrolls between him and the monster, which now had a death grip on the box with its mouth.

Emilen fell from her position, trailed by a severed rope that once connected her to Ambrosius. She tumbled down into Brimmelle, knocking the thrasher off him, along with his wooden chest. The two Nums rolled a few more feet before being stopped by the rope connected to Gluic. Fortunately, Avanda had wedged the ropes under a large rock to keep them from falling.

Wess waved his hunting knife in the air at oncoming attackers as Avanda continued to throw rocks at them. Several dead bodies littered the ground as more continued to attack.

Avanda turned to see a thrasher leap into the air with claws and fangs ready to cut through her skin. Braced for the impact, she watched the body of the creature collapse upon itself from some unseen force. Just prior to landing on her, it shrieked in pain. Blood and vomit rushed out of its mouth as she pushed the dead beast off her.

Two more were at her quickly. The one coming up from below suddenly slammed its head deep into a large rock, literally cracking the skull apart. The other, coming from the side, landed at her feet with an arrow in its throat. She was being protected.

This continued a few more times before she noticed the same was happening for Wess. She peered up to see Ambrosius and Thorik standing on the edge of the rock shelf. Thorik was firing arrows faster than she could count. Ambrosius stood on one leg, propped against a rock, with his left hand holding his staff and the other making various grabbing and slapping gestures in the air.

Thorik yelled down at them. "Climb up! They won't stop attacking while we're still here. Once we move on, they will prey on their own wounded and dead."

Despite their apprehension, the Nums turned their backs to the attacking creatures as they collected their items and started to climb up to the ledge. Bodies collapsed near them as they made the ascent, but they made it without additional confrontations.

Once there, Thorik had the group continue up the hill toward the fissure in the rock that would guide them to safety. Fortunately, it wasn't too steep, and the canyon's exit was only another few minutes away. They quickly proceeded without Thorik and Ambrosius, who continued to hold off any followers.

"I think we're okay now. Start making your way up the hillside," Thorik shouted over the screams of their enemy. But Ambrosius didn't move from his spot and continued to use his powers to crush and knock the creatures back into the forest, even the ones that were no threat. His movements became sharper, with attacks more vicious. The man had exceeded his limits and fallen into an instinctive survival mode.

"Ambrosius, snap out of it!" Thorik ordered, looking up at the focused face of his patient. "Let's go!" Reaching up, he grabbed his arm.

Ambrosius' eyes were glazed over, and his face was rigid, without emotion. He swiftly turned and gestured his hand toward Thorik's chest in a squeezing-type motion.

The semi-darkness of the moonlit night was making it difficult to see details, but Thorik could tell that his own hand was covered in blood from Ambrosius' arm. Thorik's body was now being squeezed, and he reached out to Ambrosius in a plea for mercy as Ambrosius continued to tighten his grip.

Gasping, Thorik fell to his knees before his body went limp. Just before he passed out, Thorik was released. Lying there, he placed his blood-covered hand over his heart and looked over to see Ambrosius lying on the ledge, unconscious.

Fallen and weak, the Num knew there was no way for him to carry Ambrosius out of danger as the thrashers began to regroup. He had to make a decision. He had to grab his weapon and fight the rest of the tribe on his own or he had to run away, leaving the human to be torn apart by the thrashers. Reaching for his dagger, he made his choice.

Wess jumped down off the rock from above and asked Thorik if he could walk. Receiving a nod for a reply, Wess moved over to Ambrosius and maneuvered him onto his shoulders. He slowly carried the man onto the next ledge and then up the hill. Keeping an eye on the injured thrashers, Thorik followed behind Wess, carrying the remains of his backpack and Ambrosius' staff.

They reached the top, where the rest of the group waited for their guides, before Wess lowered Ambrosius. Wess was a muscular individual, but even he had his limits, and today had tested them.

"What happened? How in the king's greatness did we get out of there alive?" Brimmelle asked Thorik when he arrived.

He responded with a hoarse voice, "I don't know. I had just got one of them off me when the other two suddenly died. I looked around and Ambrosius was standing there waving his hand about. Then I grabbed my bow and started firing at them." He stopped to wet his throat as they worked their way through the crack in the mountainside that led to the foothills on the opposite side of the ridge.

Brimmelle didn't like the explanation. "He has more abilities than we know. I told you he is dangerous."

"How will we get past them when heading home?" asked Wess.

"There are boats at Kingsfoot. We'll take the river back downstream," Emilen answered.

"I think there are only a dozen beasts remaining," Thorik told them. "Thrashers don't leave their dens to attack unless they easily outnumber their prey. So, I don't see them as a threat to Farbank until they breed and grow in size. We'll be back long before then." Hearing the distant howl of the thrasher leader, he added, "But for now, we should get some distance between us."

❦ *9* ❦

OV'UNDAY

After traveling a mile or so beyond the cliff face and over the mountain saddle, Thorik's party stopped to make camp and tend to their wounds. A makeshift litter helped transport Ambrosius as he slept off the exhaustion from the day's events.

"Unacceptable!" Brimmelle continued to rant about the battle and losing their rations. "We have but a day's food left, we're badly hurt, we have a child and woman to protect, and on top of it, the guest of honor can't walk, again. This journey has come to an end. Those evil beasts are within two days of Farbank! How are we going to warn everyone? We should have never accompanied this man upstream. I've told you never to trust outsiders."

"He would have died on his own." Emilen cleaned out the deep scratches on Thorik's sides. They were not life-threatening, but were deep enough to give him a lifelong scar. "It is our spiritual duty to help him."

It had become a common disagreement throughout the entire trip, background noise that they carried with them. Nothing ever resolved. No actions ever taken. No give or take. Just a continual disagreement that added a level of discomfort to everything they did.

"But not at the expense of all of our lives." Brimmelle reached for his scrolls to read some comforting words like he usually did, only to find the chest of scrolls gone, taken by the beast that had attacked him. Brimmelle was distraught only for a moment before becoming livid and even more irrational. "That is the last step of the king!" It was a common phrase by the Nums when they had hit their emotional limit. "By the words of the scrolls, we must head home to safety. This outside world is chaotic and unpredictable. We'll float downstream on logs if we must, but it is far too dangerous for us out here."

"Your fears are speaking in place of the king. The scrolls talk at length about accepting nature, for all of its chaos, danger, and beauty, yet you avoid it at all costs." Emilen finished up with Thorik and helped him put his shirt back on.

"I accept nature for what it is, 'A chaotic struggle between life and death with no direction or goal in mind', first line of the third topic in the Nature Rune Scroll," he read from his memories. "We are above that. We do not need to submerge ourselves in this unclean environment to prove anything. We didn't ask him to come to our village; he came on his own. We owe him nothing."

"Actually, he was brought to us." Wess calmly cleaned the thrashers' blood off his hunting knife before continuing. "Dain found him and took him in." He pointed his blade in the direction of Thorik.

The focus was now on Thorik, who was mending his backpack and taking inventory of what had survived the attack. He could feel their eyes gazing at him, waiting for a response. He felt they were pushing him to accept defeat. He was the obvious scapegoat for this disaster of a trip. It had all been his fault from the beginning, and now it was time to come clean.

But it was a lie. He believed in his actions and would do the same again. The pain from the attack was one thing, but the constant bickering was just too much. "Leave!" His statement was strong and crisp to ensure that everyone clearly understood him. "I didn't ask you to come with me. This was my journey, my task. I was doing what I felt was the right thing to do. I talked to Gluic about it, and she informed me when he was able to leave. I never involved you. I didn't ask you to disrupt your life and sacrifice it for him. But all I've heard since we left Farbank is your constant complaining. On top of that, you have blessed yourself with the power of the king's hand to determine if Ambrosius should live or die." He gazed at Brimmelle, Wess, and Emilen as he talked. "This is not your decision. You do not have the authority."

Taking a deep breath, Thorik continued, "Leave; go back home, out of danger. I agree this is no journey for children. Take Avanda with you. Alert the hunting parties to the presence of the thrashers along the gorge rim. You should go. You must go. I will, however, continue to go on my own path despite the hardships it brings upon me, for I know that my heart is in the right place." He turned away from the campfire and walked into the darkness of the trees.

Silence fell over the camp. Brimmelle was appalled at being talked to in such a manner by his own Sec. "How ungrateful, after all I've done for him. There will have to be repercussions."

Wess was without words for the first time on the trek.

Emilen crossed her arms with disappointment. "Look at what you two have done."

Thorik walked a short bit down the hill away from the campfire light and leaned his back up against a large old pine tree. Looking up at the tall, straight trunk, he could see a few stars beyond the top branches as he asked the air above him, "I hope I've made the right choice by helping him. But how do I know if I'm doing the right thing?"

"The best way to predict your future is to create it." A deep voice emanated from around the tree, startling Thorik.

Leaping away, he looked at the tree in disbelief. "What?" He hoped to provide his ears with some validation of the voice.

"There are no guarantees your actions are right. You must trust yourself, make decisions, and let them play out. Take control of your destiny, follow your instincts, and be willing to live with the consequences." The voice had a thunderous effect to it, not loud, but a rumbling that gave off a slight echo.

The Num couldn't quite tell if it was coming from the tree, around the tree, or perhaps above the tree. Could it be the Mountain King himself talking from the sky up above, or was this tree before him actually coming to life?

Nervous, Thorik stared up and down at the tree. "Who are you?"

"Grewen. And who might you be, little man?"

"Sec Thorik Dain of Farbank." Searching for the source of the voice in the low light, he spoke directly to the old tree in order to affix the voice to something.

"A large name for such a small creature."

"Actually, many tell me that it's quite short," he replied with a smirk. "You spoke of consequences. Can you explain?"

"As the great Trewek once said, we've all been altered by the paths we've chosen to take." The voice paused for a moment. "Every decision you make in life changes your future; even the decision not to decide shapes your destiny. You are responsible for your own actions and the fallout from them. If you accept this as truth, you will lead a happier life."

Thorik stepped farther back from the tree before addressing it once again. "What if others take actions that conflict with my own?"

"Blaming others for your misfortunes will only cloud your reality. You cannot control the events that happen around you. However, you have full control over how you react to them. Accept events for what they are and nothing more. To get caught in the web of others will lead you to a path of disillusion and frustration. But this line of questioning most likely requires a longer discussion. Shall we move up to your campsite where it is warmer?"

"You can move?" Thorik questioned.

"Yes. And I must ask, is it customary for you to have your back turned to those you speak to?"

"Back turned?" Thorik looked over his shoulder to see an enormous giant standing a few yards from him, partially obscured by the area's naturally thick underbrush. The gigantic man stood twice that of Ambrosius as he rested his crossed arms in front of him on a thick tree branch. His dark complexion caused him to blend in with the dark surroundings. He looked very relaxed as he stood there with one leg propped up on an exposed root.

Thorik was horrified at the size of him. The dark forest added to his fear as he trembled with shock.

"Now, this is what I'm talking about. You had no way of preventing me from looking the way I do. Your reaction to this situation is in your control, yet you are allowing yourself to be affected by it. Interesting, isn't it?" Grewen mused.

"Interesting isn't the word I would use. Why did you sneak up on me like that?"

"Sneak?" Grewen chuckled at the idea of someone his size sneaking about.

"Again with the blaming of others. I was resting here from my hike up this hillside when you approached us."

"Us? There are more of you?" Thorik questioned, looking wildly around, trying to see through the moonlit forest as he backed up to the old tree and took on a defensive position.

"Slow down, little man. Are you paying attention to how you react to things that don't even exist? You really need to relax."

Thorik heard Emilen scream from up the hill. Looking away from Grewen, he turned from the conversation and ran up the hill as quickly as he could.

Thorik was fast and could easily maneuver within the trees as he quickly returned to camp. Brimmelle, Wess, and Emilen were huddled in the center of the opening, near the fire, as they all looked into the dark woods. Avanda stood on the far side of the fire, curious to investigate what they had seen.

Upon seeing Thorik, Emilen screamed out to him, "There's a winged beast attacking from the woods! Get over here! Now!"

Brimmelle ignored Thorik and continued calling to Avanda. He was terrified for himself as well as for her. "You're in danger; come here at once. Quickly, child."

Ignoring him, she was mesmerized by the image that had flown near the camp and wished to see it again.

"Where's Gluic?" Thorik asked.

Emilen suddenly remembered that Gluic wasn't with them. "She went up the hill before you left."

"She's alone in the forest with a winged beast?" Thorik ran through the camp, out the other side, and then up the hill to find her. He called out Gluic's name several times before finally seeing her sitting in a column of moonlight with a new array of weeds and wildflowers in her hair. Her chin was down, and her eyes were closed as she kneeled on a small boulder with her open hands, palms down, floating over her stones. Spread across the flat top of the rock before her, stones and crystals were set in an artistic flowing pattern.

He had seen her do this before, but he had never disturbed her during a meditation. He approached her from the front, as she faced downhill, and placed his hands on hers to gently wake her.

Her hands grabbed his and began to pull him over the rock toward her. His legs were nearly dangling as he looked up to see her eyes open wide but with a distant look within them. Stretched and tight, her face took on a horrifying appearance.

"Find out his plans and expose the E'rudite," she said in a deep, masculine voice. "Many will die if he is not stopped."

Her grip was tight and was starting to hurt his wrists. "Whose plans? What needs to be stopped?" he asked before she let go of him and blinked her eyes back to normal.

Lowering her shoulders, her body became less tense as she sneered at Thorik. "You've messed up my stones." Her voice had returned to normal, and she lowered herself off the rock after collecting her items, placing each in their correct sacks.

"We have to hurry. There is a—," was all that Thorik got out before a scream was heard behind him. "Let's go!" He then helped her hurry down the hill.

Reaching the camp with Gluic in tow, he saw Brimmelle pointing Ambrosius' staff up at an angle in the air while Wess fired multiple rounds of arrows toward the trees. Emilen now had a firm grasp on Avanda to protect her as they crouched near Ambrosius.

Standing at the edge of the camp was the giant, Grewen, with a shield taller than himself. Arrows being fired shattered as they struck the reflective metal shield. Its shiny metallic surface acted almost as a mirror, causing the campfire behind the group to give off an odd light show while the giant eased his way forward.

No markings or symbols were visible on the shield. There were various waves and creases within it that resembled large wings.

Grewen held the shield out in front of him as he continued to slowly work his way into camp. An arrow could be seen attached to the side of his foot that periodically became exposed from under the lower pointed end of the red-tipped shield.

"Let me see," yelled Avanda as Emilen tried to hide her from the creature entering camp.

"Stop!" Thorik shouted as he raced over to Wess and pushed his bow down toward the ground.

Wess raised it again once Thorik let go, but discontinued the attack.

"Thank you." Grewen's thundering voice caused the Nums to increase their defensive stance. Grewen started lowering his shield and looked over at Wess. "Put that away before someone gets hurt."

Thorik nodded to Wess, who finally lowered the weapon but did not remove the arrow from its position within it.

"See, that wasn't so hard," Grewen said as he let go of the shield, which fell toward the ground. But before landing, it caught itself with a set of back legs. A tail and then a head and neck appeared as the wings folded up and onto its back. The shield had been the back and wings of a silver-scaled creature while its tail, legs, and head had been wrapped around Grewen's massive arm.

Twelve feet of intimidating muscle unfolded before them, reaching from the point of the creature's jagged teeth all the way back to his red-tipped spiked tail. It stretched out to full length as its wings folded up against its body. Reflecting the image of the camp and surrounding woods off of its silver body, it moved through the camp in an awkward and nearly crippled fashion. With wings replacing its arms, long sharp claws protruded from the top of each webbed appendage. This ornery beast was made for flying, not land movement.

Its facial scales were smaller and struggled to cover the redness of his gums and dual rows of teeth that angled in various directions from its mouth. Its eyes stayed squinted, with its scaled eyebrows arching down in a permanent look of anger. Bright red eyelids made it appear that the creature's eyes changed from solid black to red with every blink. The Red-Tipped Silver Dragon ignored the Nums; they were of no interest to it.

Each member reacted differently to the sight. Wess instinctively raised his bow back up. Brimmelle fell backward near the fire while Emilen stood in shock. Thorik stood between the dragon and his group to keep the peace.

"Amazing," Avanda said slowly.

Gluic raised her eyebrows and smiled. "We have guests!"

"Firing that arrow at Draq will only upset him. He isn't as good-tempered as I am," Grewen commented as he plucked the arrow from his foot and then walked further into camp before noticing a figure lying on the opposite side of the fire. "Ambrosius? He's alive! Excellent work, Draq. You led us right to him." In two long strides, he had crossed the camp and reached Ambrosius.

Emilen and Avanda stood in front of the unconscious man as the giant approached. "Leave him alone!" shouted Emilen, while Avanda smiled in awe at his size.

Grewen reached down and gently pushed the two Nums to one side with the back of his enormous hand. "Pardon me, but I need to see if my friend is well."

Draq followed and hissed at the group, preventing them from approaching Ambrosius. Emilen tugged at Avanda, leading her to the safety of Wess.

Grewen and Draq quickly walked around the camp and gathered the items they needed as they assessed Ambrosius' status.

Brimmelle, Avanda, and Emilen stayed near Wess, who still had his arrow in the cocked position, trained on the two enormous creatures as they moved about.

Gluic stood next to Thorik as they watched. Thorik was uncomfortable about them approaching Ambrosius. He had taken such a strong responsibility for the injured man that he didn't like the idea of strangers taking over. Gluic held him back with a slight tug on his arm and assured him that everything would be fine. He trusted her ability to read people, but these were creatures, and he didn't know how well she did with them. Therefore, he watched closely and carefully as the giant and dragon ignored the band of travelers.

As with most mognins, Grewen's dark leathery skin made his face look old, and the back of his bald head looked like the underside of a sack that Thorik had once made out of a banteng skin. His entire body was covered with hairless, tough, brown skin, except for his eyebrows and a patch of dark brown hair on his chin that was neatly woven and tied with leather.

The giant's hands were large in proportion to the rest of his body, with a thumb on each side of three thick square-shaped fingers that had an extra joint in them. His body was enormous in every sense of the word, and he wore a long, light brown robe that was tied above his hips with a thick rope. His feet were bare and nearly as long as Thorik's entire body.

Even with two opposable thumbs on each hand, Grewen couldn't help with Ambrosius' bandages. His fingers were simply too large. Instead, he focused on gathering hot water, soaking rags, and making a comfortable bed for Ambrosius. He also added a few large tree limbs to the fire to increase the light to work by. He didn't move quickly, but was consistent in his efforts before he finally sat down with a rumble that made everyone's footing uneasy for a moment.

Poking his thick finger at several of the packs and bags, he asked, "I'm starving; do you have anything to eat?" Silence filled in for an answer as he continued to investigate their supplies.

The dragon seemed to take the lead role of tending to Ambrosius. Hovering over him with his back to the party, his reflective bat-shaped wings were blocking their view of what he was doing. They could see his head bob up and down and periodically strain upwards as though he was pulling something apart.

It appeared as though the creature was devouring Ambrosius' body, and Thorik couldn't sit quietly any longer. He moved away from Gluic and toward the reflective image of himself on the dragon's back scales.

"It's never a wise move to sneak up on a dragon." Grewen reached over and took a log out of the fire. "Especially one as mean-spirited as Draq."

Thorik was reevaluating many thoughts at this point. Included among them was his approach to the dragon as well as his trust in the giant that now had a flaming log gripped in his hand.

He looked over to see Wess' arrow trained at Grewen while Emilen had now picked up a few hand-sized rocks to help protect the group. Brimmelle held the staff in a defensive manner, as he was still shocked by the entire situation.

Thorik had to think and act quickly to save Ambrosius' life without being crushed by the giant's flaming club. The moment he saw his opening, he took it. The giant was holding the club to his side, which would force him to swing it sideways to hit Thorik. If he could jump a few yards closer to the dragon and then dive out of the way before the log clobbered him, it would crash against the dragon's back instead. It wasn't much of a plan, but it was all he had.

With a few launching steps and a valiant leap of faith, he made it to his intended spot next to the dragon and dove onto the dirt. He rolled slightly from his momentum and landed on his back, looking up at the dragon's face that looked back down at him. Thorik had jumped too far and had rolled under the dragon's wing to his front side, where Ambrosius lay with new bandages and splints.

"Get out, Fesh!" The dragon glared at Thorik.

Thorik complied and rolled back under Draq's wing to find Grewen scratching the bottom of his foot with the end of the flaming log. It was not going to be used as a weapon after all.

"Oh yeah, that feels good." Grewen massaged the arches of his feet with the log. Sparks of hot cinders covered both his feet as he drilled the log into key pressure points with pleasure.

Looking slightly dumbfounded as he moved away from the silver dragon, Thorik looked over at Grewen. "Fesh?"

Grewen shook his head at Draq with disappointment. "Mind your words; we're in mixed company."

Draq ignored Grewen's comments and instead answered Thorik's question. "A Fesh is a lowlife, dimwitted creature so repulsive that one would rather kill it than see it suffer another day eating its own feces."

"It isn't something you want to be," Grewen clarified as he enjoyed the feeling of the fiery log between each of his toes. He then scrubbed the sides and bottom of his feet with it.

"Okay, I understand," Thorik acknowledged. "What kind of creatures are you?"

"They are known as the Altered Creatures," Brimmelle said. "Physical abnormalities of nature created by the Notarians to fight the Mountain King. These filthy beasts are our sworn enemies, designed to kill Polenums. But they were no match for the Mountain King and his army," he ended with a slight smile.

Grewen squinted his eyes and smiled. It wasn't clear if it was the result of the Fir's statement or the digging of the flaming log into his foot. "Legends and folk-lore have distorted the truth," the giant said with a rhythmic grinding of the log. "We are Unday, the descendants of the Altered Creatures. And the tales of the Mountain King War are told differently where I come from. The victors of it are quite mixed."

Brimmelle corrected him instantly. "Mixed by you Altereds. How do you explain the building of the Mountain King statue if he had lost?"

"How do you explain thousands of years of Altered Creature and Unday rule after the war?" Grewen casually tossed back. "Besides, they make statues for martyrs and heroes."

"You grotesque, freakishly large excuse for an overweight hairless bear!" Brimmelle yelled. "How dare you mock the king?"

"Keep it down!" roared Draq, causing even the crickets in the woods to become silent.

Extinguishing the log in the arch of his left foot, Grewen tossed it back into the fire and brushed off the remaining ashes from his skin. "Draq's right. It's late." Lying down, he rested his head on an outstretched arm. "Get some sleep; we have a long walk ahead of us in the morning," he finished before quickly falling asleep.

The dragon finished what he was doing. "You heard him; go to sleep," he ordered as he rested himself next to Ambrosius and covered him with a metallic-looking wing.

The camp went silent. Ambrosius lay unconscious, covered by a Red-Tipped Silver Dragon, a leather-skinned mognin giant stretched out over half the camp, and a group of Nums all stood and watched Thorik sit in the dirt with confusion on his face.

Bewildered by the events that had just unfolded, Thorik looked around the camp to make sense of it all. Thoughts raced through his head. "What just happened to our journey? Is it over? Do I hand Ambrosius over to these creatures who claim to be his friends and return home? Return home to do what? To be what? Brimmelle's Fir-pet, as Wess likes to call it?" The dynamics of the party had changed, and Thorik struggled to understand his place in it. "This was my task, my chance, my opportunity to show that I'm a leader by helping Ambrosius save our people," he thought to himself. "But how will I ever lead these new members? They will easily crush me if I stand up to them."

Feeling desperate, he turned to Gluic for support, but she simply nodded that it would be okay.

There was nothing to do now but keep quiet and out of the way. So, the Nums huddled near each other on the far side of the fire, away from the two uninvited guests, and tried to rest.

RIVER CUT

High overhead, Draq surfed the wind currents as they swept over the mountain's crest. His elegance in the air was accentuated by the nature of his scales. Bursts of sunlight reflected from each of his metallic plates, showering his body with thousands of tiny visual explosions.

Upon flexing his muscles, the scales flattened against his body. A solid reflection replaced the appearance of blinking stars, allowing him to focus the sun's rays intensely onto a nearby bird. Temporarily blinding it, Draq swooped down and captured his prey in midair for a quick meal.

Thorik watched the event above him, nearly forgetting about the dragon's bad temperament. "How wonderful it must be to fly," he said before looking back down at the rock he balanced on.

Jumping onto the next exposed rock, Thorik worked his way across a rushing stream a dozen yards wide. Reaching the far shoreline, he tied his guide rope to the base of an ancient bridge platform. The arch of the bridge had been swept away long ago, but the stone steps leading up to it remained on both banks.

A series of waterfalls were above them as well as below. Fortunately, the old path had led them to an area where a flat rocky ledge allowed them to pass the stream upon the exposed rocks that once held the bridge. The water was perhaps waist high for a Num, and it moved quickly. Even if it was shallow, Thorik knew better than to chance traveling against powerful water currents. The Nums would need to stay up on the rocks.

His viewpoint overlooked the mighty Kingsfoot Valley. He could see the stream run down into the King's River as the sun ignited an amazing inferno of yellows and reds within the tree leaves. Above those colors were strong deep greens of spruce trees that led up to the snow line.

Thorik looked back to the other shore as the rest of the Nums prepared to cross. Grewen moved at a slow pace up the hillside and had fallen behind, just visible through the trees. Ambrosius was still unconscious, but Grewen easily carried him in one of his arms.

Afraid of heights, Brimmelle braced his back against the wall of the mountainside, just prior to the stream. Reciting the words from the Courage Rune Scroll, he continued to visualize himself falling over a waterfall to his death. Never leaving Farbank prevented him from ever being higher than Sammal's old oak tree during his youth. The thought of crossing a stream only a few feet from the edge of the falls caused him to become dizzy.

Ignoring the Fir, Wess double-checked the knot on his end of the guide rope that now spanned the stream. Emilen loosely grabbed it to provide balance while stepping on the moss-covered stones. Even though they were slippery, she skillfully stepped from one to the next with ease. Once Emilen finished her crossing, she motioned for Gluic.

Gluic wasn't as agile, but that did not deter her from slowly working her way across the river, utilizing the rope for balance. As she did, she could hear her son over the slapping water of the falls.

Brimmelle closed his eyes and hugged the rock wall with his back and arms. "Don't look down," he shouted to Gluic as he began visualizing her falling over the cliff. "Get a footing before you move your hands. Only move one hand off the rope at a time."

Fed up with his instructions, she stopped on the next rock and turned halfway back toward him to stop his annoying directions.

Before she could say anything, Gluic noticed Grewen finally catching up to them. It was odd to see him run. His body didn't seem designed for it. Perhaps it was the fact that he was carrying Ambrosius, or was it something else? The trees. The ones from which he had just come. The limbs were moving. Thrashers were in heavy pursuit.

Thorik could see them as well. "Everyone! Get across. Now!" Starting back across the rocks to help them, he quickly reached Gluic and began helping her across.

Wess pulled Brimmelle from his safe location and onto the first rock and led him across the stream. He was halfway across before he turned and realized the Fir was still on the third exposed boulder.

Brimmelle stood solid, frozen with fear. Staring at the edge of the waterfall, his body swayed. He looked over the falls at the long drop beyond and envisioned himself tumbling down it. The rope slipped from his hands and he fell forward, only to be stopped as the rope lodged under his armpits. Light-headed and shaking, he leaned over the water's breaking point in horror. Grabbing the rope at his chest for dear life, his leaning caused an extreme bow in the guide rope that made it difficult for him to balance, and his feet shuffled behind him for grip on the slick rock.

Wess struggled to stay on his own rock. The rope was now out to his side, due to Brimmelle, and no longer helpful. Jumping back across the rocks, Thorik grabbed Wess just as he lost his balance.

Helping Wess to a larger flat rock, the Sec headed back for his Fir, whose feet splashed in the water after he lost his footing.

Grewen pounded his way toward them, breathing hard as he lifted his heavy body with each step toward the group. He realized the error of having Draq fly ahead to look out for assassins. Danger could just as easily come from the local wildlife. The giant could use the dragon's help in these times. There was no way for Grewen to defend himself from these creatures and protect Ambrosius at the same time. The only option he had was to run for safety, Ih was not one of his strongest abilities.

Behind Grewen, the thrashers were catching up quickly. Near the front of the pack, Thorik could see the silverhead at a full gallop. There wasn't time to help Brimmelle step to each stone. Something quick needed to happen. He needed to get Brimmelle across and prevent the thrashers from following them.

Reaching Brimmelle, Thorik pulled him back upright. "Close your eyes." Thorik cut the rope from the thrasher's side of the stream and tied it on to the Fir's belt. A secure knot now linked the Fir to the safe side of the stream. Thrashers didn't like water, so all he needed to do now was have Grewen remove the stepping stones.

The sudden strength Thorik felt by taking charge was quickly suppressed as he looked over the Fir's shoulder. His heart tightened and his throat went dry as he gazed at Avanda. She had been hiding from the group behind the ancient bridge platform. She still needed to cross the river, but Thorik had just cut her guide rope, leaving her stranded on the wrong side of the water.

"Avanda, run this way! You'll have to jump to the third rock before I can help you," Thorik yelled.

"I can't! I'm afraid of the water. I can't swim."

Panicking, Thorik needed to save Avanda's life. "You won't have to be in the water. Just run and jump. I'll catch you!"

She looked behind her to see the tribe of thrashers already attacking Grewen's legs as the giant mognin ran toward her. They would be on top of her within moments. "Promise you'll catch me!"

"I won't let anything happen to you!" he promised.

Grewen and the thrashers were nearly on top of her. Two of the primates had already latched on to his back while a third grabbed his leg. Two raced along each side of him, with several more still chasing. As they approached, a few of them noticed the young Num cowering before the stream. Thirty yards became twenty and then ten as they quickly raced forward.

Trusting Thorik, Avanda stood up and bolted out from behind the stone steps, directly in front of the giant, who nearly stepped on her.

Thorik held on to Brimmelle firmly with one arm as he prepared his footing the best he could. "Get rid of these steppingstones as you cross," he yelled to Grewen as the giant approached the water right behind Avanda.

Avanda jumped to the first one and then the second before closing her eyes and leaping high into the air, trusting that Thorik would catch her.

Still carrying Ambrosius, Grewen reached down with his free arm and started grabbing the exposed rocks and flinging them over the falls as he moved across the water. The surging stream only splashed up to his calves, making it easy for him to cross.

Thorik reached out with his free hand to catch Avanda's outstretched body. He grabbed her, and in return, she grabbed him. Unfortunately, he lost his footing in doing so. Thorik fell backwards into the water, dragging Avanda and Brimmelle with him.

By the time Grewen bent down for the second rock, another thrasher had leaped onto his leg. The giant picked up and tossed the rock before swatting the creatures off of him. Their flailing bodies splashed into the rushing water before its force quickly carried them over the edge and down to the sharp rocks below. Halfway across, the mognin was free of the thrashers and the stream was missing its rocks for passage.

However, Thorik, Avanda, and Brimmelle had been captured by the rushing water and were quickly washed over the edge and out of sight.

A moment later, the rope that Thorik had tied on to the safe side of the stream went tight, knocking Wess off his feet as it shifted directions from the water out to the ledge. Emilen jumped for the rope and attempted to pull it up, but her small body was no match for the weight on the other end. Just as Wess showed up to help, the rope went limp. Their eyes widened with disbelief and concern at the thought of what could have happened. Pulling up the end of the rope, they saw that it was still tied to Brimmelle's broken belt.

LEADERSHIP

Wess moved to the ledge to look for Avanda, Brimmelle, and Thorik. He couldn't see anything from his position, so he jumped to his feet to work his way down from the falls and around a large rock face. Emilen yelled over the edge with no response. The noise from the falls drowned out her voice.

Grewen arrived, splashing out of the water as he kicked his bulky feet onto the dry rocks. He had seen what had happened and gently set Ambrosius down so he could help. Stepping over to the edge, he leaned over Emilen and looked down. He saw three wet Nums holding on to an angled rock. More accurately, Thorik was holding on to the rock with one hand and Brimmelle with the other while Avanda was holding on to Thorik. Brimmelle appeared to have been knocked out; blood was dripping from his head.

Grewen knew that there wasn't enough footing for him to maneuver his large body down the cliff wall. Instead, he gave instructions to Wess, who was currently working his way toward them. "Brimmelle is hurt and unconscious. You need to hurry before Thorik loses his grip," he added to expedite Wess' descent.

Wess yelled back a reply that Grewen's little ears couldn't pick up over the roar of the water.

Emilen went to comfort Gluic. "I'm sure Brimmelle will be fine. They'll make it back up, and we'll all be home safe before you know it."

Gluic untied a bracelet of wildflowers from her arm and wrapped them around Emilen's wrist. "You keep telling yourself that, my dear, if it makes you feel better. But truth be known, we will never see Farbank again."

"Don't give up so easily. We'll reach Kingsfoot in one piece and take a boat swiftly back to the village. We'll survive this journey," Emilen insisted.

The elder woman's face went cold and stiff. "Perhaps you don't understand, my dear. Farbank's future will never see you or me within its boundaries."

Emilen never knew when Gluic was serious or teasing her. She smiled and hoped it was the latter. Channels were known for their strange ways and had no difficulty in reminding others of that.

By the time Wess reached the fallen members, Grewen had dropped one end of the rope to him while the other was wrapped around Grewen's fingers, tightly held by both thumbs of his right hand.

Wess reached out as he told Thorik to swing Brimmelle over. Within a few slight swings, Wess was able to grab his leg and pull him off to a safer place where he laid him down. Helping Avanda and Thorik off the outstretched rock, he then returned to Brimmelle to check his injuries. The elder Num was bleeding from a nasty cut to his forehead as well as his hands, which he apparently sustained in an attempt to catch himself.

Wess tied the rope securely around Brimmelle and Avanda. Once he gave a tug on the rope, Grewen quickly pulled them up and had Emilen and Gluic remove the rope before he lowered it again for Thorik and Wess. They both tied themselves on and grabbed hold of the rope over their heads.

"Thanks for helping me up there. Another second and I would have lost my balance on that rock," Wess said to Thorik.

"I'm sure you would have done the same for me," he replied.

"Let's not test that theory." He then gave that arrogant smile of his. But this time it didn't bother Thorik as much. Wess looked up, and with a tug on the rope, they launched up into the air and landed in Grewen's grasp.

Howling and clicking from the far side of the water continued, but the apes made no attempt to enter the rushing waters.

After the group moved out of view, Emilen began cleaning Brimmelle's cuts and scrapes as he slowly started to wake. He moaned about the pain and mumbled various passages from the Scrolls of Wisdom to calm his headache.

They rested and recovered as berries, roots, and mushrooms were picked and eaten. The autumnal palette of the hillside was a feast for the eyes as well as the stomach.

Grewen ripped entire shrubs out of the ground. After a quick slap against the side of his foot to dislodge most of the dirt, he placed them in his mouth, dirt and all. His constant hunger was easily quenched with nearly every plant he walked past.

Gluic returned to Brimmelle with a few dark green leaves with reddish veins as he complained about his head pounding with pain. She rubbed the leaves together between two small rocks to squeeze out the liquids from within them. After removing the solid remains of the plant from the rocks, she softly rubbed the moist rocks on his temples.

"Pepper's mint will remove your pain," she informed him as Brimmelle blinked his eyes from the strong vapors the liquid gave off. Moments later, his headache reduced, and his thoughts cleared.

Thorik sat near Ambrosius with a handful of berries. "You're looking a little thin; what do you say about some ciderberries? Ambrosius?" With concern, he placed his pale hand on Ambrosius' chest to make sure he was still with them. He was. "You've overslept and missed the high adventure. Come on now; let's see a bit of life in you."

"He'll be fine," Grewen stepped in, "but I'd suggest keeping your distance from him if you know what's good for you."

Surprised at the comment, Thorik asked, "Are you threatening me?" He took two firm steps toward the giant who had him shaking with fear just the previous night.

"No. Just stating the facts. You put your life in danger each time you get close to him," Grewen said as he watched Draq swooping in out of the sky toward them.

"And how is that?" Thorik asked as he turned back to Ambrosius just in time to be knocked down by the landing dragon.

"Get away from him, Fesh," Draq demanded.

Thorik slid on his back halfway to Grewen before rolling back to his feet and dusting himself off. "Now you wait just a minute. We've saved this man's life more than once, and we deserve the right to continue to…" He stopped as the dragon moved up and over him, leaning his head down to press his forehead against Thorik's tilted head. Draq's black eyes stared at Thorik while he started pressing Thorik down.

"Until we know who you are, you have no right to anything." Draq defined the new rules of their journey. "You will provide food, water, and shelter for us, and we will provide it to him. You will not touch him or be near him without our permission." He had pressed Thorik down to his knees. "Do you understand?"

"No, I do not," Thorik pushed back. "You don't know us, but we don't know you either. Ambrosius has never told us about you, let alone that he is safe with you. Yet we are expected to trust you when you aren't willing to do the same for us." His short little body pressed his head up a few inches against the dragon, who was now starting to breathe hard.

"I don't have to trust you. You, on the other hand, have no choice." Draq reached out with his leg and kicked Thorik onto his back again before leaning over him and pressing one of his claws on Thorik's chest. "One or more of you may be a traitor, and I cannot take the chance of him being harmed."

By this point, Avanda and Emilen were furious at the situation. "Leave him alone," shouted Avanda.

"Thorik, get out of there," Emilen called, fearing for his life.

Thorik thought about how unfair this was. He had jeopardized everything to bring Ambrosius this far, and now these strangers were going to take over. In addition, he had lost his leadership role again. Every time he felt that he had control of his life, it was taken away from him. "Not this time," he said to himself as he continued to be pressed into submission from the weight of the dragon leaning on his chest with one leg.

Thorik glanced over at Grewen, who was relaxing against a tree, watching for Thorik's reaction to Draq's demands.

"You're right," Thorik squeezed out.

Emilen was relieved that there would be no more bloodshed today. Wess, on the other hand, was disappointed that he had given up so quickly. He was just starting to respect the Num and felt this character flaw had resurfaced.

Draq's narrow eyes never left Thorik as he backed away and let him stand.

"You're correct. I have no choice but to trust you." Thorik brushed himself off again before glancing over at Grewen and then back at the reflective scaled face of the dragon. "You will take care of Ambrosius while I lead us to Kingsfoot."

Grewen's left eyebrow rose as he looked over to see Draq's response.

"I follow no one," Draq replied, standing his ground.

"Fine. Then leave us," Thorik continued. "Ambrosius asked me personally to lead him to Kingsfoot to find the truth of what happened. And unless you wish to defy his wishes, I will lead us."

"I could kill you all in but a moment's time," Draq replied.

"Yes, you could," Thorik said honestly. "And then you would need to explain to Ambrosius how you killed us for trying to protect him. I'm sure he would be grateful."

"What faith do you have that I won't kill you now and tell him that you were ripped apart by thrashers?" He cocked his head slightly as he edged it forward. "Why should I trust that you have had such words with him?"

"The way I see it, you can kill us at any point you wish. Believing that you will or won't take such actions will not help my mission to bring Ambrosius to Kingsfoot. Although killing us prior to talking to Ambrosius could cause you significant issues. I don't think Grewen would lie about such things to him. So I don't have to trust you. You, on the other hand, have no choice." He stared Draq in the eyes while his stomach fluttered from the stress of his bluff.

The eyes of the other Nums darted back and forth between Thorik and the dragon, waiting to see the next move.

Draq reached out, grabbing the Num and lifting him off his feet as the dragon's wings wrapped around, surrounding them from all outside influences. Cramped and encased inside the creature's wings, Thorik was pressed up against the silver-scaled body. Draq breathed out hot, dry air and flared his nostrils down at Thorik. His large teeth began to show as the right side of his lip rose to expose the black of his gum line.

Thorik was now a prisoner, as his feet dangled off the ground and his arms were locked at his sides from the pressure of the surrounding wings. He pushed his head back to look up at the dragon's face that hovered above him. Perhaps he had taken too big of a risk. Stepped too far. Pushed too hard. He sweat from the hot air, which was hard to breathe.

Draq finally broke the stressful silence of staring Thorik down. "Don't play your games with me, Fesh. If I feel at any time that you pose a threat to Ambrosius, I will strike you down without warning."

Thorik gasped for breath in the tight environment and replied, "Same goes for me."

Draq squinted, trying to see more than what was on the surface. "You have courage, little Num, and a fierce loyalty to Ambrosius. I can respect that. Just remember that you will be no good to him dead." Draq eyed him again as Thorik mustered up the strength to raise his head and eyed him back. Draq continued, "He was lucky to have found you. You may lead the group to Kingsfoot while I scout ahead for trouble."

"More thrashers?" Thorik squeezed out.

"No, Fesh." He pulled him in even closer. "Thrashers are the least of your concerns. We need to avoid hunters."

"What are they hunting?"

"Ambrosius."

From the outside of the glossy winged cocoon, the group watched as it finally opened up and Thorik was set down on his feet. He was paler than normal and weak in the knees, but he stood up as strongly as he could manage.

"We have come to an understanding," Draq stated to the other Nums. "Thorik will be leading you to Kingsfoot, and Grewen will care for Ambrosius while I scout ahead."

"Thorik?" Brimmelle spoke up as he lay on the ground with a bandage around his head. "I lead this trip. I am in control here. I'm the Fir!"

"This is not a debate!" Draq ordered. "Thorik is in charge, or you will answer to me."

Oddly enough, no one argued with the dragon.

12

REUNION OF OLD FRIENDS

Avanda's playful laugh could be heard as she told Grewen of her misadventures. "And then Uncle Wess crashed into a big willow tree. It broke our wooden Runestone sled in half and nearly did the same to him. He walked funny for weeks." Finishing her story, she laughed at Wess' painful experience.

Ambrosius woke to find himself near a warm campfire in the mountainous forest. He couldn't believe his eyes when he saw Grewen sitting near him, chatting with young Avanda on his lap. "Grewen! How did you? Where did you?" Ambrosius didn't know where to begin as he struggled to sit up straight.

"You have the name right. After that, I lost you," Grewen replied with a smile. "It's good to see you as well. It has been a long time. Fortunately for me, I ran into an old friend of ours who told me that you were in trouble." He pointed in the sky toward the reflective creature flying above.

Ambrosius glanced up for a few moments to watch Draq scouting for any potential threats. "You did it, my friend. You brought help. I knew you wouldn't abandon me in the temple's rubble."

"So, you trust him?" Avanda's question was blunt and to the point.

"Oh yes. I trust no one more than Draq. We fought through decades of battles together. Although Grewen is a close second. I couldn't have made it through the Civil War without him."

She nodded. "I'm going to tell Gluic she was right." Hopping off Grewen's leg, she left the two alone.

"It is good to see you, my mognin friend. I never expected to see you after the Battle of Maegoth."

Grewen plucked a handful of grass from the ground and began chewing on it. "I drifted on my own afterward in an attempt to come to terms with what I had witnessed. The horrors of the Dovenar Civil War's final battle should have never happened."

"I agree. I was attempting to prevent another such catastrophe from happening when we were attacked, and I ended up clinging to life in a small village.

Grewen glanced across the camp at Thorik, who was diligently working on Ambrosius' staff. "Luckily, you acquired a new friend in your time of need, who has protected you."

Ambrosius also noticed Emilen sitting next to Thorik, making suggestions for designs that could be etched into the sides of the staff. Their body language spoke volumes of their current feelings for one another as she placed her hand on his leg while they talked. His self-confidence had grown after the run-ins with the thrashers, Brimmelle, Wess, and Draq. Emilen found it very appealing.

Brimmelle and Wess sat on the ground playing a heated game of Runeage. Wess was losing and complaining about Brimmelle's strategies. Brimmelle's exceptional memory had allowed him to recall every strategy Wess had ever played against him. He was going to easily defeat the young man.

Gluic had settled herself in a clearing to meditate. After she had weeded out the limp vegetation she was wearing on her own body, she placed various sticks and leaves around her. She softly touched them in what appeared to be a random sequence while sitting cross-legged on the ground.

Watching closely, Avanda had walked over and sat near the elder Num, and then tried to perform the same meditation as Gluic. It was difficult to do while talking at the same time, but the young Num would do her best.

Ambrosius sat up a little straighter. "I don't know if I would call myself lucky. I am of ill health." He rubbed his forehead and lowered his voice. "My body and mind are weak. My powers are questionable at best. And if it was not for a gullible young Num's belief in fate and a story contrived, I would still be downstream."

"This Num takes great pride in helping you. You have deceived him?" Grewen asked.

"No, it's not like that. I told him it was fate that we met. Just because I don't believe in it doesn't mean it's not true for him," Ambrosius reasoned. "But I can't help feeling that there is something about him that makes him stand out."

"You are fortunate to be alive, fate or no fate. Draq said no one else survived. What happened?"

Ambrosius looked up at Grewen. "Darkmere has once again waged war upon us, and this is only the first wave from his hand. He will destroy anyone and anything that does not serve him. His minions are now everywhere, and we can trust few. They reach beyond his sight with the help of small groups that carry out his orders. War is here. I must gather the armies to stop him."

Grewen looked uncomfortable about what he had to tell Ambrosius, but he was not going to keep secrets from him. "I don't think you will be able to."

Ambrosius was slightly surprised by the comment, especially from Grewen. "And why is that?"

"I believe you are wanted for the death of the Grand Council members. Word is out that you called the council meeting to destroy them, giving you absolute power. This would allow you to go head-to-head with Darkmere without their approval."

"How could the council members' deaths be known by others so quickly?" Ambrosius questioned.

"Better yet, I came across travelers with this information before the Grand Council was even murdered."

"I was led into a trap, but did they mean for me to survive? If so, why?" Thinking out loud, he continued. "Someone invited to the meeting worked for Darkmere." He began playing the chain of events over in his mind. For months he'd worked to rouse the people out of their slumber. Ambrosius had single-handedly brought all of the principals of the clans and nations to their ultimate demise. "How foolish I've been. I've trusted too many and grew myopic upon my quest." He paused as he came back to the conversation with his old friend. "The attack on the Grand Council surely will spur people to action." Ambrosius caught Grewen's smirk, indicating Ambrosius was missing the point. "Regardless, few would believe that I would do such a thing," he said proudly, coming back to Grewen's topic.

"But they have seen you do such acts in your past," Grewen noted factually, without criticizing Ambrosius. "They've seen you fight for the rights to your dead father's kingdom. They fought in your wars, and their families have died in your battles. And they watched as their coastline cities sank under the water of the great flood." Grewen shook his head at the memories of the horrific battles that still lingered in his mind. "These people have watched you destroy the mightiest kingdom Australis has ever had." Relaxing his shoulders, he continued, "Changing your ways may help the future, my friend, but it does not erase your past. So yes, I can see how they could accuse you of doing such things."

"Grewen, you know the reasons behind that war, yet you question my motives and make me sound like a criminal?"

"No, I'm just telling you the facts. However, many others are questioning them. Once they realize that the council has in fact been killed, they will question why you are the only survivor. Their thoughts will develop to the same end. Ambrosius, you will be killed once you are discovered to be alive."

Ambrosius didn't know how to respond. He had worked so diligently to accomplish so much, but having it stripped away wasn't enough for Darkmere; he had to make sure that no one would ever listen to Ambrosius again. And it appeared he had succeeded. There might not be anyone or anyway to stop him at this point. Ambrosius stroked his beard with a few fingers. "Was it luck that I lived, or was it Darkmere's way of making sure that I suffered?"

"We may never know," Grewen replied.

"I wish I could just remember what had happened. It's foggy, and parts are missing."

He looked up and was surprised to see Gluic quietly standing next to them, holding a sack of items. It was an unsettling encounter as the two realized they hadn't observed her approaching. Ambrosius looked back over to where she had been meditating, only to find Avanda was still there, lying on her side, taking a nap.

Gluic had overheard the conversation and pulled out a small sack from her cloak. She emptied the contents, several smooth black stones, into her hand to show them.

Ambrosius looked over at them and smiled. "Yes, they are very nice stones." His dismissive way was gentle, but made it obvious that he wished to return to his conversation with Grewen.

"Is that volcanic glass?" Grewen asked as he reached over to touch one.

She quickly slapped his large forefinger before he could reach it. "They have been cleansed by the moon. Your touch will weaken them."

Grewen retracted his hand and looked at the end of his finger to see how it yielded such powers.

"Thank you for showing them to us, Gluic," Ambrosius responded politely, hoping she would take the hint and leave.

She picked one of the stones up by its sides and held it toward Ambrosius' forehead. "They can help you remember what you are missing."

"I don't think your pebbles can help, but I value the offer."

She continued to hold them out in front of him as she smiled and nodded her head up and down to convince him to let her try.

Grewen grinned. "Go ahead, Ambrosius. It's worth a go."

Ambrosius didn't appreciate Grewen aiding her fantasies, but now he felt locked into attempting it. "You need to know that I'm not going to swallow those." A bitter look crossed his face.

"No, no. You will lie down on the ground, and I will build a net of the stone's energy around you." She glanced behind her at one of her unseen friends. "No, it won't cause seizures like last time. I have better stones this time."

Ambrosius shot Grewen a disgruntled look for getting him into this.

"What's the worst that could happen?" Grewen asked. "You lie down and take a nap for a few minutes?"

Gluic looked up to correct Grewen's statement. "Few days."

"Excuse me?" Ambrosius asked.

"It will take several days of sleep to recover from the memory reading, but you will be very refreshed upon wakening, hopefully with all your memories intact," she reassured him.

Once again, he looked at Grewen with concern.

Grewen smiled and mocked his situation. "Did you hear that, Ambrosius? You'll awaken refreshed."

Gluic started by laying Ambrosius down on his back with his arms down along his sides. She placed one of the rocks on the ground near the top of his head. After adding one over each shoulder, she placed one on the outside of each ankle. Prior to setting each stone, she whispered instructions to them.

Thorik looked over from across the camp to see his grandmother performing some sort of ritual around Ambrosius. Just then, Gluic looked up directly at Thorik and waved him over.

As he approached, Gluic began giving instructions. "Thorik, give me the Runestones for trust and enlightenment." Reaching down, she adjusted the stone near his right shoulder.

Curious, Thorik dutifully pulled out a dozen before he found the two that she had requested. He quickly handed them to her.

She placed one over each of Ambrosius' eyes while kneeling next to him. Keeping his elbow on the ground, she raised his left hand. A thin, yellowish crystal was set in his palm, and she placed his fist firmly between both of her hands. Speaking softly, she closed her eyes and began to see his thoughts while he drifted into a dream state.

It was only a moment before he had immersed himself into his memories of the past. So vivid and real, they played out as though he was living them for his first time.

13

HIDDEN MEMORIES

A two-thousand-foot high vertical slice out of the White Summit Mountain gave way to a stone statue just over half the height of the cliff face. This statue of the Mountain King stood with its back flat against the cliff wall as its feet rested in a half-circle lake, surrounded by stone and crystal statues of various animals. The king looked down toward his crown, held in his hands, with warmth and kindness on his face.

The accuracy was amazing. At a great distance, a traveler would see a king in his flowing robes and a few scars from his war with the Notarians. If they had swum across the lake to touch the statue, they would feel each individual fiber that made up the threads of his grand clothes.

Built next to the lake, against the same carved wall as the king's statue, was the city. Ambrosius had walked onto the third terrace of the main garden in front of the city, overlooking the lake, to find Beltrow along with many other Nums. They were all preparing the plants for the winter. The morning sun had worked its way down the Mountain King's body, on to the city of Kingsfoot, and then across the terrace they stood upon.

"Bless the king's travels," Fir Beltrow Ruddlehoth announced. "How many years has it been?" Short and stocky, even by Polenum standards, Beltrow had a solidness to his stature and an honest tone to his voice. Curly light red hair covered his head as well as his chin. Small, thoughtful eyes looked out from under graying eyebrows as he smiled from behind his overgrown mustache.

"Too long, Fir Beltrow, too long. I apologize for not visiting you sooner; there is so much to be done, and my youth has been lost in the wake. You, however, look as if you haven't aged at all," Ambrosius said.

"Maybe not on the outside, but I can feel it in my bones. For the first time in decades, my legs weren't able to make the journey to Shoreview for the annual trade visit. My daughter traveled with the group in my stead." Beltrow motioned

Ambrosius to come over and help him lift and flip a clay pot over the plant he was working on.

"I want to thank you for agreeing to host the Grand Council at your temple. It is important that no one feels at a disadvantage. It was also of great help for you to send out escorts, helping us find our way. I now understand why this valley is unknown to the rest of us in the south. Has anyone else arrived yet?" Ambrosius continued helping Num with his chores.

Only a handful of spiritual leaders and a small group of residents knew the location, for they lived among it as the temple's caretakers. Typically keeping to themselves, this was a unique situation that required a secluded location out of evil's view. They had extended the offer to hold the meeting after hearing of Ambrosius' desire to revive the Grand Council and restore peace.

"A few arrived last night, but they asked not to be disturbed." He continued to work on his plants as he said goodbye to them for the winter. "It looks like we have a group that will arrive in the next few hours," he noted, while motioning his head toward the lake.

Ambrosius looked to the far side of the lake and up on the valley's southern mountainside. "Your eyesight is as keen as any Num I've ever met. I don't think you're as old as you claim."

Scoffing at the comment, Beltrow peered up at the Grand Mountain King statue standing in the center of the half-circle lake. "It will be a long, cold climb up those steps in the morning. I hope I'm up for it."

"If you're not, I'll have Draq fly you to the crown. His tongue may be sharp, but the ride will be as smooth as yakka cream."

"Draquol is here? How are he and his family?"

"He's scouting for uninvited guests at the moment. His family is of good health and wellbeing."

"Last I heard, he was going to be a father. Did the hatchling survive the escape from his egg?"

"Yes, he and Melendrol are parents of a little hell-raiser named Fraquendol who broke open that thick shell like it was parchment. He needs a lot of taming before meeting you."

"Ah, yes. I recall the first time I met Draquol." Beltrow placed a hand on his thigh and patted it a few times. "I can't say that he had a lot of restraint himself."

They both laughed at the fond memories.

Reaching out with a strong two-handed handshake, he properly welcomed Ambrosius. "Welcome to Kingsfoot, my friend. My people will tend to your needs inside. I will join you later."

"I shall look forward to it," Ambrosius responded before leaving to stroll around the city.

Although the city's architecture was not from the Polenum culture, the courtyard floor had been built with large interlocking hexagonal Runestones. Carved vertical stones, resembling open scrolls, lined the courtyard's perimeter as they unraveled from eight feet in the air down to the ground.

Approaching the city, Ambrosius marveled at the exterior wall filled with a collage of animal and plant carvings in various scenes. Beltrow had neglected to tell him about the beauty of Kingsfoot and its valley. They had met during the Fir's annual summer trade visit to Shoreview, many ages ago, and the Fir had only mentioned that they lived in a small spiritual community.

Ambrosius wandered inside and found it was filled with oddly shaped rooms and walkways to give way for artistic structures. One room was carved out to look like the inside of a whale, while another had carved insects across the walls. Every surface was designed to look like some part of nature.

The floors depicted sand, leaves, water, and rocks. Ambrosius thought this was amusing, seeing that it was all rock. The designs on the floor were visually bold but subtle to the touch and could only be felt with bare feet or the touch of one's fingers. He was again amazed by the detail and bent down to feel a pebble; he couldn't quite tell if it was real or carved into the floor.

"Did you drop something?" a soft voice said.

Ambrosius looked up to see a lean and voluptuous woman in a long gown of red and black as he realized he was grabbing at an etching in the floor. "No." He stood back up. "Just admiring the workmanship. Isn't it amazing?"

"Yes, of course it is. Irluk built it," she said to educate him.

"The Death Witch?" he replied with amusement.

"Long before being murdered by Wyrlyn, and prior to the Alchemist and E'rudite War. When she ruled Australis as the most powerful Alchemist ever. She was practically a god."

Before opening his mouth, he remembered why he asked the council to attend this meeting and decided to let it go, for now. "I see." He controlled his tone the best he could. "I am Ambrosius, founder of the Grand Council. And you are?"

"Megyn." She eyed him up and down with distaste. "I am the new Prominent of EverSpring. I have heard your name before, and you are not welcome in our lands."

Ambrosius had a history of conflicts with the Alchemists and had hoped that his actions over the past several years had improved relations between them. Apparently, they had not.

"All the more reason we convene in a neutral location such as this. Where is your predecessor, Bryus Grum? Has he retired at an early age?"

"He no longer leads us. I am authorized to speak for the guild now, but you will not like what I have to say."

"I'm sure that Bryus passed down his knowledge of our intent to you. We wish to mend old ills and build an alliance against the coming threat of war. Surely, we can agree to that."

"Perhaps the approaching threat is only coming after you and your power. It might be the change that the rest of us need. Is it your fear of losing what you have that would drive us to battle and sacrifice our lives?" She sneered at him out of disgust. "The changes before us are confrontational only because you and the other leaders have made them such. Accepting Darkmere's rule would stop all conflicts."

Ambrosius raised his voice. "I know Darkmere's treachery and tyranny all too well. He will only give you what you want until he needs you no more. The opportunity that you seek with him is a spell of your own illusions. Do not be fooled by your own desires."

"You're too closed-minded to see what opportunities lie ahead," she said as her servant approached and whispered in her ear. When she was finished, Megyn returned her attention to Ambrosius. "I must be leaving now. We can continue this debate at the council meeting tomorrow. I think you will find that I do not stand alone."

"Megyn!" He paused to relax his voice before continuing. "Please think about my words."

"Likewise." She began to leave, but suddenly stopped and swiveled on the toes of her feet back toward him. "I nearly forgot something. Oddly enough, Darkmere gave me a message to give to the mighty Ambrosius, just in case I should ever run into you. He has a thirtieth-anniversary gift for you."

Ambrosius' face became motionless as the blood appeared to leave his face. A message from Darkmere was unexpected and was more of a threat than a gift. It had been thirty years since the end of the Civil War, a time and battle he'd rather forget. Many thoughts raced through his mind. Bryus Grum, who had been one of Ambrosius' most difficult but critical converts, now was suspiciously absent from the equation. This new Prominent now seemed more entangled with the enemy than he had first assumed. Was she a spy? Not a very subtle one, if so. But what if there were a spy in the valley and Megyn was there to keep Ambrosius off-balance enough not to uncover the truth? Sounded like Darkmere, devious but not too creative. Vigilance was required.

She watched his tension with pleasure for a moment before she turned and walked around the bend of the corridor with her servant.

Ambrosius woke up early the next morning to walk with Beltrow up to the temple, situated inside the Mountain King statue's crown, which was held in front of the main statue, within the king's open palms. The trek required climbing hundreds of steps up to the sacred room.

As they made the pilgrimage up the long stairway inside the mountain, they rested in each of the small sitting areas along the way. Every platform had a bench from which to view the glorious valley through its windows. The rising sun warmed the stairwell as light refracted off the small etched glass, shining prisms of color up and down the angled hallway.

Ambrosius sat with Beltrow in the window seat and listened to the Fir's lyrics of the Rune Scrolls come alive. It had been a shame that he had never spent any time learning about this culture.

Periodically, a few other council members would pass them by as they sat. Often a nod would suffice as they climbed the steps, trying not to interrupt Beltrow's readings. Others never even gave them a glance.

Climbing the stairs became less of a task and more of a spiritual journey through poignant thoughts being read out loud. Time was given to quietly contemplate each verse prior to ascending to the next window seat. The journey took most of the day, and Ambrosius felt he had gained years of insight from it and was thankful for the enlightenment.

They rested one last time at the final complex of rooms just below the temple.

Food and drink were set out as servants calmly and quietly organized the area for the long meeting ahead.

Beltrow and Ambrosius continued to ascend the last few steps up to the opening of a large glass-domed room, which overlooked the entire valley. The view was even more breathtaking than Ambrosius was expecting as he walked over to the far side of the temple. He could see the valley open up to a gorge where the winding river ran from the lake below him toward the distant Lake Luthralum.

After gazing like a child out into the valley, Ambrosius looked up and out of the glass ceiling to see the pronounced chin and face of the Mountain King several hundred feet above them. The cold autumn air had left a strong beard of white from the night's mild storm. As odd as it might seem to Ambrosius, the ice below the king's eyes made him look disheartened.

He felt a slight chill from the sight of the cold outside. Lowering his eyes, he watched one of the servants light eight large oil vats near the walls of the temple. A second servant lifted a long rod above her head to open a hinged glass tile in the ceiling in order to allow the smoke to escape.

The pillars around the temple's exterior were carved to look like open scrolls hanging from the glass ceiling. They unraveled fluidly down onto the temple floor, sometimes extending into the room a foot or two. Facing inward toward the center of the room, the scrolls listed out each of the Rules of Order. The details of the stone carvings were remarkable; the rips and folds of the paper where they had hit the floor and bounced into the room suggested they had been released from above and frozen in time during a fluid motion.

Making up the walls of the temple, the pillars also were the sides of the crown. The king held the crown slightly out in front of him as though he was giving it to those who wished to have it.

By the time all the council members had eaten and rested from their trek up the long staircase, the evening light was starting to fade. Opening proceedings would take place for a few hours on the first night to voice all of the concerns that needed to be discussed over the next week.

Beltrow called the meeting to order. The council members were a variety of several Del'Unday and Ov'Unday species as well as humans and a single Polenum. Ambrosius sat across from Beltrow in hopes of not implying his allegiance with him. The rest began to sit as he had expected. Those with similar beliefs tended to sit together.

The Grand Council convened at the large, round granite table. Carved into its surface, twelve oil vats formed a circle, providing each member with equal lighting. The flames shone evenly upon the faces of the various creatures sitting around the massive stone. Many had sent their servants to their quarters after bowls of fruit and decorative crystals had been placed on the table for the debates.

Beltrow started the meeting off. "Welcome. I am your host, Fir Beltrow Ruddlehoth of Kingsfoot." The group nodded respectfully. "Before we begin these talks, I need to impress upon this council the fact that our temple is a neutral center where everyone should feel equal. I hope this will reduce the apprehension that has been troublesome in prior council meetings. I commend each one of you for having the courage to attend today. This single gathering is going to be a historical event that will shape the future of Terra Australis."

The conference had begun. Beltrow sat down, motioning for Ambrosius to take over.

Ambrosius rose from his chair with the help of his black metal staff. His mahogany hair fell down to his royal blue cloak, flowing under its own magical capacity. His mannerisms were refined from years of public speaking, and his words were clear and precise.

"It is of these times that I speak, when alliances and a man's word have been blurred by the dishonesty and treachery of those who would see us all suffer," Ambrosius stated. "Members of the Grand Council, Province and City Leaders of Terra Australis, I implore you to heed my warnings. Darkmere is prepared to strike, and this time it is not merely to conquer, but to destroy."

It was the first council meeting since they had disbanded the Grand Council years prior due to frustration and distrust infecting its members. Servants of Darkmere had contaminated the once powerful alliance of leaders with historical prejudices. This was their last chance at unification.

Ambrosius continued with a poignant and factual oration. He then paused long enough to take a sip of his drink. "This is our last stand. I have presented the evidence before you." He pointed to the marked-up maps spread out on the table. "These demonstrate the same movements of forces that my messengers sent you earlier. Darkmere has tightened his claws around your lands and pitted us against one another to do his bidding. Further debate only acts to delay action while he continues his sedition. We must unite against Darkmere, the scourge upon our world, before it is too late." His eyes thinned as he watched his audience for a reaction.

"Why should we follow you?" Megyn asked. "We don't need another one of your bloodbaths."

"True, many have died under my command on the battlefield, both in victory and defeat. I have a full understanding of the horrific nature of war, but I still believe that a battle for freedom is a justified cause. Peaceful slavery is no way to live."

The Del'Unday representative, Volnic, spit on the map in front of him before standing. Rich, dark red skin covered his giant seven-foot-tall muscular frame supported by two thick hairy wolf-like legs. His exposed upper body was lined with various bladed spikes that jutted out from his shoulder blades, spine, and elbows. Self-inflicted scars across his chest were worn as badges of honor for successful battles and conquests. Light from the oil vats reflected off his solid red eyes set inside a dragon-like head. Volnic was a blothrud, creatures which were known for their bad tempers and warrior mentalities. He embraced both of these attributes as critical qualities of Del'Unday leadership.

Making a point, Volnic raised his head up and looked down over his long bony face at Ambrosius. Thin layers of skin stretched out over the ridged bone structure of his hairless wolf-like snout. "I have been offered expansion to my lands with full authority over them. You have offered me nothing, and yet you would put the

Del'Undays on your front lines to fight for your safety." His voice was powerful and successfully filled the others with unease.

Ambrosius replied calmly. "We offer to aid you in keeping your freedom. Darkmere only offers you false promises."

Gregory Marl of the Eastland Province shook his head. "You Altereds make my stomach turn. You would allow the destruction of peaceful societies for your own greed." Eastland was a human province that had seen more battles with the Del'Unday than any other. The resentment in Gregory ran deep into the roots of his family tree.

Volnic erupted with fury over the comment and quickly knocked over a servant and a few council members before grabbing Gregory's body and lifting it into the air. "Peaceful? I should rip out your tongue for such lies!" Volnic screamed in the man's face while veins in his neck and along the bony structure of his face pulsed with heated blood. "You humans have enslaved my people for centuries, and now you have the audacity to say peaceful?"

Gregory's pain went deep into his ribs from Volnic's grasp, but his hatred of the Altereds was too great to show it. "Only after your species enslaved us for thousands of years. You and all your filthy and vile type are an abomination of nature. You don't deserve any better."

The thought of a Del'Unday being subservient to a lesser creature was repulsive to Volnic, who threw Gregory across the room toward one of the large windows that overlooked the valley. Ambrosius reacted and used his E'rudite powers to stop the man from crashing through the glass and falling to his death. Instead, he fell to the stone floor with only a slight bounce.

"Volnic, this is not a place for you to wage war!" Ambrosius shouted.

"But it is for you. That's why you've brought us all together. To wage war against a growing power that threatens your own, not mine. I will not be a part of your next Maegoth massacre!"

The comment hit Ambrosius hard, for his history with Darkmere would provide Volnic with the evidence that the blothrud could use to convict Ambrosius of such crimes. The city of Maegoth had been in the center of the Civil War, which destroyed the Dovenar Kingdom. The battle left many tens of thousands dead and felled the once great civilization. Blood from these deaths still stained Ambrosius' hands and dreams, even after thirty years.

Ambrosius was not willing to give up, knowing all too well what was at stake. He began to walk around the table as he spoke to the entire committee. "Say what you will about my dealings with Darkmere, but I can tell you that his only interest in you is to carry out his own wishes."

Megyn watched Gregory being escorted out of the chamber while his arms protected his ribs, broken by Volnic's grasp. "Darkmere has approached many of us, and it is true that his words come at a cost. But so do yours." Her hooded cloak showed only her beautiful face and soft hands as they extended beyond its black emptiness. Light literally did not reflect from her cloak, appearing as though there was a hole in space.

Ambrosius conceded. "Agreed; my price is high." He ran a finger along his short beard that shaped his face without hiding it. "The alternative price of forever living under his rule is higher. He is not what you think he is."

"Are you?" she tossed back at him.

He stopped walking and placed his hands on the back of the chair previously used by Gregory Marl. "I will not debate with you about my history." Glancing down, he noticed a decorative round metal object on the floor and knew instantly what it was. Looking back up at the faces in the council, he continued, "We are here to make a choice for our world. Do we leave here as a united front to end the attacks that have caused our people to suffer and live in fear, or do we act like cowards, give into his threats, and kneel at his feet?"

"Cowards?" Volnic roared at the accusation.

Ambrosius was not going to let go of his control over this discussion. He leaned down and picked up the metal disk and leather necklace before making his way back to his chair. "Volnic, I have received information that one among us is working directly for Darkmere with the sole purpose of stopping us from uniting. You seem to be an advocate for him. Where does your allegiance lie? Have you become one of his minions here to spy on us?"

The council erupted with protest while a few members were stunned at the allegation.

"How dare you accuse me of being a servant of a human?" Volnic yelled as he pounded both of his massive fists on the thick granite table, causing it to crack in many directions.

Ambrosius turned to look at the Guild Prominent of EverSpring. "Or perhaps you, Megyn. You speak kindly of Darkmere's barbaric ways."

Megyn's emotions exploded. "We all know your feelings about Alchemists and the Del'Unday, and it is not surprising that you selected us to accuse of these baseless crimes against the council. You have no proof of such an act, and you're using this premise to scare us all into agreeing with you."

"But I have such evidence. There is a traitor here, among us," Ambrosius held up the round brass disk he had found on the floor. It held a spherical gem in the center that was foggy and peppered with red glowing dots. The disk that held the gem was fashioned with Darkmere's symbols. His was the ancient E'rudite power of alteration that was used by the Notarians, which is a forbidden power in Terra Australis.

Ambrosius tossed the item out into the center of the table for all to see. "Someone at this meeting has been spreading Darkmere's poison into our thoughts. We now have the opportunity to capture his servant as well as turn the tide on his quest for power."

"Outrageous!" Fir Beltrow shouted from the opposite side of the table. "You have compromised our location and used our sacred temple as a trap for Darkmere's servant? Blasphemy, I tell you! Blasphemy!" Beltrow slammed his fists on the table, causing it to rumble from his attack. Then the floor began to shake and tremble. And it continued to the walls, ceiling, and beyond.

Everyone stepped back from the table as the vibrations increased.

Across the room, Ambrosius caught a glimpse of a shadowy figure of mist and ashes. Bloodstained eyes were covered by a veil of long black hair. No flesh, only bones and veins could be seen. Burnt debris mingled in the smoke that comprised a female body. The Death Witch, Irluk, had arrived, and Ambrosius knew too well what this meant. She was here to collect the souls of those lost in violent deaths.

A loud crack of thunder erupted from above the glass ceiling. Looking up, the members could see the glass cracking under the quake's stress as well as from rocks falling from above. Beyond the glass, something wasn't right. A fissure opened above them in the Mountain King's neckline. It spanned from his left shoulder, across the front, to the right side of the neck. The width of the crack increased and decreased as the shaking continued.

And then it stopped. The room went silent. The world seemed to stand still, and everyone struggled to absorb what was happening. Thousands of images and thoughts rushed through their minds in that fraction of a second before the crack under the king's neck burst open with flaming red magma erupting from it.

The explosive power lifted the statue's head up and then out. The stone face tilted forward as it fell off the cliff and rushed down toward the council members. Red, glowing molten rock trailed behind the head as it roared down the cliff face.

The members looked up at the ominous sight, only for a moment, before the statue's head crashed into and through the temple's dome.

❁ 14 ❁

KINGSFOOT LAKE

Thorik's Log: 16th day of the 10th month of the 649th year.

We have reached Kingsfoot Lake. I now understand why this is our spiritual center, for no other place on earth could look this beautiful and feel this refreshing.

Ambrosius woke up mentally relaxed and refreshed, but the visions he had seen were unsettling. His memories of the council meeting were clear, yet the traitor's identity had been missed or blocked from his thoughts. For the first time in many weeks, he was feeling more like himself and ready to find out the truth.

During Ambrosius' sleep, Thorik had successfully led the party up the ancient trail atop the rim and then the rest of the way to Kingsfoot Lake without any issues. Friendship had quickly united Grewen and Thorik along the way, and the Num had also continued to slowly earn Draq's trust and respect, which was more than Ambrosius had hoped for.

Waiting for the group to get moving again, Avanda tested her climbing skills on one of many stone statues in the area. Twice the height of Grewen, it was in the form of a giant cat on its hind legs.

Gluic had kept to herself, like always, but seemed to be spending more and more time talking to unseen members of their party. "Yes, Rummon, we're on our way. Be patient." Turning around, she shook her head. "No, Zixi, I'm not chasing you down the tower's stairwell again." She continued her discussion while gathering grass and wildflowers to make herself a new necklace.

Brimmelle and Wess sat by the shore looking across the half-circle lake. Against the flat mountainside, the Mountain King statue's head and hands were in rubble at his feet. Cold morning air swirled with the mist rising from the lake water, covering the Mountain King's toes.

They were all relieved to have arrived at Kingsfoot but disappointed to find the statue destroyed. They had hoped Ambrosius was wrong. It was a sad sight, as they stared at the cooled dark lava rock that ran down the Mountain King's headless body. It was now clear that the molten rock and ash had poisoned the waters downstream. The mystery of the dead fish in Farbank may have been solved, but the destruction of the Mountain King Temple and Grand Council still raised many questions.

The perimeter of the lake was lined with large statues of various animals, all on large cube stone bases. Most bases rested on the shoreline, while some sat nearly submerged in the lake's water. All of the statues faced the Mountain King. A bear stood up on its back feet, and a deer looked to be leaping off its base. Each statue had an astonishing level of realism that reminded Ambrosius of what he had seen inside the city.

Above and beyond the Mountain King statue rose a mighty snow-covered volcanic peak that was seen from Farbank. Glaciers hugged the White Summit's sides as mist rose from its natural chimneys. Its clouds of steam had grown over the years. Recently, the pillars of vapor had been thick and dark.

Along the sides of the valley, green spruce trees ran up the half-bowl-shaped foothills toward the steep barren peaks that lined them. No roads, paths, or buildings could be viewed, other than the stone city of Kingsfoot on the far side of the lake.

Opposite the cliff face, the lake's water ran through a thin canal under a bridge and into a large river. This was the official source of the King's River, which wound back and forth around various foothills as it made its way past Farbank and Longfield and then to the distant Lake Luthralum.

Contrary to the obvious devastation of the Mountain King's statue, the valley continued to emanate feelings of wellbeing.

Splash!

Brimmelle jumped up to his feet and ran over toward his mother, who was several steps into Kingsfoot Lake. She was searching for new stones, and her dress was soaking from the knees down. "Mother, get out of the sacred water," Brimmelle ordered with no results.

She spied something under the water that interested her greatly. She bent her knees to lower her entire body under water for several seconds as she retrieved what she was looking for. It was a long clear crystal the length of her palm. Cylindrical in shape and as thin as her finger, it was smooth along the sides and sharp on the ends. Holding up her treasure, she turned with her dripping hair and clothes to show it off to her son. "I wondered where this one was."

"Please get out of there before you freeze to death," her son shouted to her.

She ignored him and hid the crystal away before she cupped her hands and scooped up water to wash her face. "I miss this water. Warm and cleansing. Good for healing the body and soul."

Brimmelle had taken his boots off and began to wade into the water to escort her to shore. As he stepped into the water, he was amazed at how warm and soothing it was. Natural springs of mineral water had kept the lake at a comfortable temperature.

~

AFTER STANDING UP, Thorik reached down to help Emilen up from where they had been sitting. He gathered his updated maps and notes of their journey and carefully placed them into his wooden coffer, which was then tucked away into his mended backpack.

"Em, could you please hand me my carving knives?" Thorik requested as he gestured toward the ground where he had worked on Ambrosius' staff.

Emilen quickly gathered the neatly placed tools and handed them to him before grabbing the staff. "We should get over to the city before nightfall to avoid the cool night air," she announced as she handed the staff to Ambrosius. "I had Thorik add a few extra runes on your staff to help you during your travels." She gave a pleasant smile and eyed the newly added Portent Scroll Rune.

Afterward, she worked her way down to the waterfront, where Wess waded with his sore feet in the warm water. Placing one hand on his shoulder to get his attention, she announced that the break was over. It was time for the last hike of the day, to the city of Kingsfoot.

The touch rejuvenated Wess. She had not made any physical contact with him for days, and her unexpected gesture caused him to realize how much he missed it. Wess' sense of comfort ended when she removed her hand. He wasn't used to losing, especially to Thorik.

"Avanda?" Thorik called up to the top of the huge statue of a wild cat roaring with its face tilted upward toward the Mountain King. She had been climbing and playing on it for some time now.

From within its open mouth, she peered over the edge at him. Tossing one leg over the side to start her descent, she was suddenly jerked back up and out of view from the rest of the party.

"Help!" Avanda reached her arms up in the air from inside the cat's mouth before they were once again ripped away.

Racing to the statue, the Nums could hear her shrieks of pain. Sweat collected upon Brimmelle's forehead at the thought of her danger as Wess loaded his bow and aimed it at the statue before realizing his misguided logic.

"It's eating me alive!" she yelled by the time Thorik had climbed up to the knee of the petrified animal. "Where is my handsome hero to save me?" She giggled and then broke out laughing at everyone's emotional response. "Am I doomed to be devoured by a cat?" she called down to the group as she dramatically flung her upper body over the edge of the open mouth.

Brimmelle patted his brow dry with a cloth. "Not funny, young one. Get down here right now."

Chuckling at the ruse, Thorik stopped climbing. "Grewen, can you help her down, please?"

"At your service, little man." Stepping up on the square base, he reached up for her.

She continued to laugh as she hopped into Grewen's enormous hand before he gently set her down in front of the group.

Pretending to be ashamed, she apologized with a smirk. "Sorry about that, Fir Brimmelle. I was just playing."

Brimmelle dismissed her weak attempt at an apology. "Help my mother out of the lake and get her items together. It's time to go."

Gluic smiled and reached out for the girl to approach. "Come out into the water and help me back to shore, dear. And don't mind him. He doesn't like it when I play either."

Ambrosius slowly stood up with the assistance of his newly modified wooden staff. "My mind is clear, but my body feels like I've been in a fight with a chuttle-beast," he said to Grewen.

"Looks like the beast won." Chuckling, he then watched his friend to ensure he could stand without assistance. His hand was ready to catch him, should he fall.

Ambrosius was impressed to find that he was able to walk better than he had in a long time. The E'rudite quietly thanked Gluic for her help under his breath as he and Grewen began to lead the group toward the city.

"You're welcome," Gluic casually replied from a distance, as she walked out of the lake with several new stones for her collection.

Avanda quickly helped Gluic gather her items while Brimmelle and Wess waited for her. Once she was ready, she led them across the lush grassland around the lake.

It wasn't long before the four Nums had caught up to the mognin and human. By that point, Avanda was bored and asked Grewen if he would carry her. Traveling with her in one arm was effortless for the giant, and it gave her the chance to ride high enough to see the distant city's unique features.

Shortly after heading out, Emilen stopped Thorik to point out several unique landmarks in the valley, causing the two Nums to fall behind the others.

Draq scouted from high above, watching the party break up into three groups. Three Nums had moved up front. Grewen's slow heavy steps now set the pace for Ambrosius and the giant's passenger, Avanda. However, Thorik and Emilen had stopped at the lake's shoreline. The dragon's only concern was for Ambrosius, and he stayed within a few air maneuvers of reaching him.

Calmness made Draq uneasy. He would much rather be engaged in battle and know where his enemy was than sit idle and wait for them to come out of hiding.

Ambrosius and his escorts continued working their way to Kingsfoot, walking in the wide field of shallow grass that covered the land between the water and the woods. Steam continued to rise from the lake and poured out under the bridge at the halfway point around the lake. The stone overpass spanned the lake's only outlet, which fed the King's River.

The bridge was carved with the same devotion as the local statues. It was in the shape of an enormous scroll that had unraveled across the river's width. It appeared frozen in time, as though a breeze pushed the center of the paper bridge up off the water. Railings were made from the sides of the scrolled paper as it reacted to the artistic wind and folded upwards. The bridge was flawless, except for one section of the railing. It had been broken, and the rough stone was exposed from the top of the handrail.

Gluic, Brimmelle, and Wess crossed the bridge and continued to work their way around the lake toward the city.

Leaping out of the mognin's arms without warning, Avanda raced up to the crossing. Hopping up onto the railing, she made her way across with skill and grace. Her descent was a quick cartwheel on the railing with a tumble in the air before landing in the grass on the far side. She loved being playful and hoped to never grow up.

Not long after, Ambrosius and Grewen reached the bridge but stopped abruptly when they came upon the damaged railing. Ambrosius felt the rock with the tips of his fingers. It stirred up painful memories within him, but the flashes of his past were too vague to understand why. The broken stone was sharp to the touch, and shards of the railing lay scattered about on the bridge and on the ground below. Curious, he slowly worked his way off the bridge and around the railing. Following the outside of the bridge, he found his way back underneath it, where the river met the lake.

Grewen watched Ambrosius set his wooden staff down to reach under the bridge and grab a long, black, metal rod. It was his old quarterstaff. The one he had used to defeat the Sathoids of Lutin. The staff he used when he held Wilken Pres at bay during the Trial of the Humorics. It had survived, apparently better than he had. The crystal top piece sat neatly in the thin black iron rod, flaring out just above and below his hand. The grip was of the finest leather, and its sister handhold was down the staff farther, for use when two-handed gripping was needed for battle. A decorative counterbalance was placed toward the bottom that could also be used as a long-handled mace-like weapon. It was a glorious piece of art and weaponry he had commissioned for himself long before the Battle of Maegoth.

Grinning with satisfaction, Ambrosius clutched it with both hands. It revived him and gave him a sense of strength and security that everything would be back to normal. Back to how he had made it. He felt that everything in his life would soon be heading in the right direction.

"Darkmere." Grasping his metal staff tight in his fists, Ambrosius peered up across the lake at the headless King. "You made a mistake by not killing me when you had the chance." With his newly found staff in hand, he used it to walk back up to Grewen, who was standing at the end of the bridge waiting for him.

"It is good to see you holding your quarterstaff again," Grewen commented as they began to distance themselves from the bridge. It was part of the E'rudite's identity and charisma. As he walked with Ambrosius, the mognin couldn't help but notice his human friend was standing up straighter and with more confidence. "You look more like your old self now." Allowing his hand to drag near his feet, the giant ripped a handful of grass out of the field and tossed it into his mouth while continuing the conversation. "Is that a good thing?" he half-joked, spilling some of the grass from his lips.

15

HOT SPRING MINERAL WATERS

Emilen and Thorik had stopped short of the bridge while the rest of the group moved on. Emilen continued telling him about how the Mountain King once stood proud with his hands out in front of him and how they would decorate the animal statues around the lake during festivals, even the ones on bases that required swimming out to.

She reminisced about growing up near the lake. "On cool days like this, my friends and I would swim over to that statue of the dolphin and play for hours. We had a rope tied to the end of its nose that allowed us to swing way out and drop into the lake. Afterward, we would all sit on its tail to relax." She finished and smiled at the statue and her memories.

He glanced out at the dolphin statue as it arched forward toward the Mountain King. Its tail was half submerged, as though it was pushing itself out of the water. The statue's square base sat a foot above the water's surface like a large mat ready to catch the dolphin should it fall backwards. It was the same base that all the statues had. Some animals stood on them, some were stepping off of them, while this one had the tail hanging off one side and dipping into the water.

Emilen's face brightened as she spied a rope that had been left tied around the dolphin's open mouth. "Come on; we're going for a swim," she insisted as she started removing her gear.

"What? Now? We're already behind the rest of the party." Nervous, he darted his head around to see if anyone was looking their way. Ambrosius and Grewen could be seen beyond the bridge, walking toward the city, while the rest were much closer to the city's perimeter. "I'm not sure that this is the right time. We need to get to the city." Watching her out of the corner of his eye, he tried not to stare as she removed her clothes and reached back to tie her hair up tight.

She turned toward him with her hands still fiddling behind her hair knot and looked at him in a questioning way. "I would suggest you undress before getting into the water." Laughing, she left her scattered clothes on the shore, walked into the warm, inviting water, and submerged her entire body before resurfacing. Sighing, she relaxed a moment before turning around.

Thorik was extremely uncomfortable about the situation and tortured himself with guilt as he slowly undid his shirt. As much as he wanted to just rip off his clothes and jump right in, he was conflicted whether or not he should.

"It's not against the Rules of Order to swim." She watched him slowly undress. "Also, the Scrolls of Wisdom talk at length about the beauty of our bodies and not being ashamed of them."

"I'm not ashamed of my body." His hands shook nervously. "Aren't you concerned about being caught?"

She looked around at the open valley. The only other people were out of sight due to the light veil of mist rising from the lake. "No, I'm not. And even if they did, we aren't doing anything wrong. We're just swimming." She smiled. "Perhaps they'll join us."

The thought of the entire party frolicking in the buff did not appeal to Thorik at all, yet he removed his shirt and folded it properly before setting it square on his backpack. Still conflicted, he started with his pants until he noticed Emilen watching him. He hesitated and looked around the lake one last time for a reason not to continue. "Perhaps the party is returning to see if we're okay."

No such luck.

His heart raced, his chest tightened, and his emotions upset his stomach. Terrified to follow her lead, he had the same level of desire to let go of his self-inflicted inhibitions and be free. As he watched her swim away, he swallowed hard and chose the latter. He removed the rest of his clothes and neatly folded them before setting them between his shirt and backpack. He then made a mad dash for the water, diving head-first and returning to the surface with a sigh of relief. It felt like nothing he had ever experienced before. Freedom, openness, and total relaxation. He couldn't describe to himself how great it felt to conquer his anxieties and be free of his fears.

After floating in the warm water for a bit, he wondered if he had ever truly relaxed before that moment. It was a new feeling for him, and he soaked it up. The lake was more than warm water; there was something special about it. Something spiritually uplifting. He also took notice of the pleasant tingling sensations around the souvenirs left on his sides by the thrashers.

"Enjoying yourself?" Emilen asked with a chuckle as he floated on his back with his arms straight out to his sides. Seeing him smile without opening his eyes for his response, she laughed at his reaction to the warm water. "These waters will prevent your wounds from souring and will even heal our bodies if we stay long enough. We'll revive ourselves for a bit before we enter the city."

Grabbing his hand, she led him toward the statue. They parted from each other halfway there and swam the remaining distance due to the depth of the water. Emilen quickly out-swam Thorik and headed to the far side of the dolphin's statue, out of sight.

Not nearly as strong of a swimmer, he slowly approached the dolphin and worked his way around, holding on to the base to help him move along. As he rounded the second corner, he saw her lying on the statue's giant, half-submerged tail that had a slight cupping on both sides. This gave her some privacy without preventing her from seeing the Mountain King side of the valley. She folded her hands behind her head as she leaned back in the tail fin, far enough down so that her body was still mostly in the water, as a thin layer of steam coated the water's surface. She was a vision of beauty with skin that looked like silk. Her soul-markings fell from her neck and down the center of her chest. The misty sunlight glistened on the clear water as it warmed her exposed neck and arms with each passing wave. Her calm and natural state put Thorik at ease as well.

Working his way over, he lifted himself onto the giant tail next to her. He also put his hands behind his head as they both looked up at the headless Mountain King statue, across the lake, towering over the valley. It was sad, actually, to look upon it in its current condition. The king looked so helpless and betrayed, yet it couldn't break the overwhelming harmony of the valley and the warm mineral lake.

Emilen sighed loudly as she gazed up at the statue. "You know, if it weren't for a few thousand years, I'd say he looked like he could have been your father." Rolling over, she snuggled up to Thorik. "You know what's unfortunate about this?" she asked, resting her head on his shoulder.

He couldn't think of anything at the moment. He had never felt so peaceful and relaxed in his entire life. So, he stayed mute to listen to her answer.

"I never really appreciated seeing the Mountain King while I lived here. He had always been watching over us, and I guess I assumed he always would be. But now it's gone, and I realize that I never really treasured it." Her heartfelt tone helped set the mood.

Thorik listened, while running his finger along her arm that rested on his chest. "How could you not see the magnificence in it? Even now it's overwhelming and by far the most impressive monument to our faith that has ever existed. I don't understand."

She lowered her head onto his chest as the warm water and mist covered most of their bodies. "It's like seeing a cloud out your window every day of your life. Never a day without it. It becomes lost in the background, and you just assume that it is always going to be there." She paused to look up into his eyes. "Haven't you ever had that happen?"

He gave it some thought. "The only thing I can compare it to is my parents. I suppose I had assumed that they would always be there for me. So, I never truly cherished what I had while they were alive." He inhaled deeply and pulled her in tight as he recalled their faces.

"I'm sorry to hear about your parents. You've never told me what happened to them." She then rested her head on his chest again.

Thorik swallowed at the thought. "It was an accident that nearly killed all three of us. We had befriended a traveler. A man named Su'I Sorat, who told of great treasures in the mountain's valleys. He had ancient maps of the valleys and canyons, but no references on how to get there."

He continued after a few moments of thinking about his past. "My father was a skilled hunter, far better than I am. Mum had a keen eye for tracking. When I was little, I would often join them on hunts, learning the trade. By the time I was of age, I was able to hold my own. Yet my parents wouldn't allow me to travel with them when Sorat was there. Instead, I had to be watched like a hatchling by my Uncle Brimmelle in Granna Gluic's house."

"It was during one of their travels that we had a big storm in Farbank. Biggest one I had known. Thunder woke me from a nightmare of my parents in trouble. Somehow it seemed more than a dream, though. I don't know why, but it was so real to me. However, Brimmelle refused to believe me, and he escorted me back to bed. I couldn't help believing that my parents really were in danger. So, it wasn't long before I quietly snuck out of the house. I had spent so much time looking at Sorat's maps, I knew them by heart. I also knew that my father was planning to check out a valley across the King's River past Spirit Peak. So off I went in the middle of the night to find them. Fortunately, there were some breaks in the storm, but it was a long difficult walk as I navigated the best I could with the light I had and the memory of the maps I had seen. Eventually, I reached the valley I believed they had traveled to." Thorik paused and looked into the missing face of the Mountain King.

Waiting for a resolution, Emilen asked, "Did you find them?"

"Yes." He took a long, deep breath. "But I was too late. The storm had caused a rock and mudslide that flooded the valley and littered it with mud, boulders, and tree limbs."

Continuing his story, he added, "Eventually, I was able to find my mother. But during my attempt to free her, she was swept away in a river of debris. Grabbing a still rooted tree, I clung to it as I reached for safety. It was still too far for my weakened body to reach the mud-free canyon walls. I couldn't pull myself out. I just didn't have the strength. My parents had been killed and washed away, and I feared that it would be the end of me as well."

Thorik straightened up and finished his thoughts. "That's when Brimmelle reached in and saved my life. He had figured out where I was going, followed me up the mountainside, and had just caught up with me. He was so angry; I'm not sure he will ever fully trust me again. He didn't talk to me for days as we recovered my parents' bodies and buried them nearby. He didn't even say goodbye to them as I erected stone markers. I think he was as angry with them as he was with me."

Thorik sighed and remembered his parents' laughter and hugs. "I sure miss them. What I wouldn't give to have one more day with them. Just one more." Tears of sadness and happiness due to his thoughts ran down his cheeks.

"Sorry; I didn't mean to upset you." She started to pull away to give him some space.

He didn't allow her to go far; his arm behind her stopped her from leaving. "No, Em, it's fine. I'm okay. It's just that this is the first time I've talked about it." His other hand started to gently touch her face as he stared into her green-blue eyes. They were the same color as the lake and gave him the same calm feeling as the water. He continued to look deep into her eyes as he softly traced the lobe of one ear.

"We don't have to talk about it anymore if it upsets you." She knew that, after all they had been through lately, he was emotionally tired, so she changed the subject. "I think you will like my parents. My father is a Fir, but he is nothing like Brimmelle. And my mother is a lot like me." She smiled, hoping to move on to a more pleasant conversation.

"Your parents?" Thorik squeaked out, wondering how they would feel about him swimming naked with their daughter. If it wasn't for the mist, they would be within eyesight of the city.

She could see that he was anxious again and realized that it was time to leave. "It's okay, Thorik. We can go. Thank you for talking with me. We don't seem to get the opportunity to be alone much."

Thorik realized how important it was for her and softly nudged her back to him. "Em, we can talk a little longer before we have to go." Not even his anxieties could shake him from this dream; he held her tight in the water, resting on the tail of the dolphin, looking out at the Mountain King statue.

She talked about all the things she and her friends used to do around the lake while growing up. They continued for another half an hour before making the short swim back to land. After they dried off, they got dressed and headed out.

Once at the bridge, Thorik noticed an area on the right-side railing that was damaged and went to investigate. He looked at the debris and tried to determine what could have caused the destruction of the railing. Peering over the edge, he looked down and saw Ambrosius' wooden staff with the antler trim, the one that Thorik had worked so hard on making sure it supported all of his needs. But obviously it didn't and was not needed anymore as it lay tossed against the rocks like any other branch that had been washed up on shore.

Emilen looked to see what was so intriguing and quickly realized what it was. She placed a hand on his shoulder and comforted him. They left the stick and moved on toward the city. It didn't matter anymore, for this journey was coming to an end anyway. "We should keep moving. Now that our group has reached the city, my family will be out looking for me." Trying to distract him from the thoughts of the staff, she held his hand and led him off the bridge.

Neither her words, nor the walk, relieved his disappointment.

⌒

HIGH OVERHEAD, Draq arched his long, scaled neck as he made a quick turn to the left while flying over the forest beyond the lake. He had been scouting for several hours in search of signs of danger but found the valley to be peaceful. His trained eyes worked their way back and forth to ensure he had not missed anything before he turned to head back.

Once he made this decision, he straightened out his body and leaned his head slightly down, increasing his speed. His wings flapped hard before he tucked them in back to stabilize his flight as he shot like an arrow across the valley. The angle of his descent had him heading near the bridge at the mouth of the river. He was uncannily fast.

From the air, it would have looked as though Draq was about to crash into the river just before the bridge as he rapidly approached it. With ever-increasing speed, he pulled up just far enough to rocket his way under the bridge and out over the lake, where he glided mere inches from the calm water, twirling the layer of mist above it.

Craning his neck to improve his streamlined shape, he lowered himself into the water. The massive speed and his aerodynamic features allowed a smooth entry into the water with nothing more than a ripple.

Flying underwater was slower than in the air, but Draq was just as graceful. Turning and gliding like a giant manta, his only limitation was how long he could hold his breath while searching for food. Fortunately, he didn't have to test his endurance since he spotted a three-foot-long toothfish. It darted quickly to the side, causing Draq to fly by it on his first pass. The chase was on.

Diving down after the fish, Draq performed an underwater ballet of twists and turns, racing around ancient columns and arches. Frightening away schools of smaller fish during his pursuit, he turned quickly to avoid parts of the Mountain King statue's face, as it rested on the lake's bottom. It was at that point where he captured his prey and bolted to the surface for air.

Thrusting his body out of the lake with his meal in his strong jaws, his wings quickly shed their water. Spreading his wings back out to full length, he flew up toward the headless Mountain King, finally landing and eating his dinner on the empty neck of the statue. He was able to view the entire valley from that vantage point as he watched Ambrosius pass the boat docks near the city.

Gluic was up front by this point, along with her son and Wess, as they approached the city's outer barrier. Brimmelle stopped at the series of perimeter statues in amazement as he saw his beloved Runestone Scrolls spelled out in massive stones. Every passage and every verse were exactly as he remembered seeing them every morning and evening during his readings to his village. His blood raced with excitement as he slowly approached and touched them, tracing the etched letters with his finger.

The scrolls had been carved in granite to appear to be unraveling from an invisible holder eight feet in the air. Each scroll cascaded down to the ground and rested on a large hexagonal granite slab with a rune symbol in its center. These stone carvings had a detail that became more obvious as Brimmelle inspected them closer. Imperfections in the parchments had been added, as well as eloquent waves in their journey to the ground. Each scroll was carved in a unique way, and they rested back-to-back, one facing out to the party as they approached, and another scroll facing in toward the city. Between each set of scrolls was an opening to allow entrance onto the city's property.

Wess moved between the scroll pages and emerged inside the perimeter where scattered animal statues stood on a grid of hexagonal granite slabs, as if protecting the city. Past them lay a wide stairway leading up to three garden area levels. Several chunks of dried magma had landed in the open gardens from the destruction of the Mountain King statue. These black rocks were jagged and smelled of sulfur, causing the entire area to smell of rotten eggs. "Is this place safe?"

Gluic walked past Wess and noted, "Don't worry. There's nothing to fear until nightfall. Build a campfire near the entrance of the city." She pointed to the top tier.

Wess agreed before thinking about what she had said in such a dry tone. "What is there to fear after nightfall? And where is everyone?" he responded with more of a nervous touch in his voice than he had planned.

She did not answer as she walked away, up the stairway.

∼

AMBROSIUS FINALLY ARRIVED at the outer row of scrolls with Grewen as they met Brimmelle reading his favorite verses from the courtyard's carvings. The Fir's glee at the monuments to his faith came through his loud reading of the words to his bored student, Avanda.

It wasn't long before she slipped away to see everything she could with the remaining light of the day.

Following Ambrosius, Grewen turned sideways to work his way between the large stone scrolls, into the courtyard, and then up to the roaring fire at the top of the stairs near the entrance of the city.

The city looked so empty compared to the last time Ambrosius had visited. "The survivors must have abandoned the city after the attack." He didn't see any traces of them. Everything looked as though they had left without any provisions. "Although there doesn't seem to be enough damage to warrant an evacuation."

Wess passed Ambrosius and Grewen on his way down the stairway as he went for more firewood. "Where is everyone?" he asked in passing. He only received a shaking of the head from Grewen, implying he didn't know.

Upon reaching the top tier, Ambrosius and Grewen rested on a stone bench as they watched the last two Nums work their way around the lake toward them. "Keep your eyes open, my friend; we may not all be what we appear to be," Ambrosius quietly commented to Grewen.

"It would seem unlikely these little ones are anything but what they seem. Are you sure you aren't just becoming paranoid after this last incident?" Grewen calmly replied as he reached over to grab a flaming stick out of the fire and began using it to scratch between his toes.

"I'm not sure who I can trust anymore."

"You must trust those that have earned it." The giant wrinkled his dark leathery face with pleasure from the toe cleaning.

"I'm not sure I can do that."

"What's your other option? Live on your own, always fearing that everyone will back-stab you? That's no life. That's self-inflicted torture." Changing hands, Grewen started on his other foot.

They quieted down as Wess returned.

Wess tossed an armful of sticks near the fire. "Where's Gluic?"

Grewen and Ambrosius looked at each other in question before looking about the open gardens. They soon surmised that she must have entered the city. With the evening light fading and darkness soon to set in, Grewen removed the flaming stick from between his toes. "Grab a torch; it looks like we're heading in."

Wess still had a lot of distrust for the two, but he knew Brimmelle would take it out on him if his mother was lost, so he followed the other two into the city in an effort to find Gluic.

16

ABANDONED CITY OF KINGSFOOT

Astonished by the city's design, Thorik and Emilen walked toward the perimeter scrolls. Brimmelle was now resting on one knee, reading the runes in the center of one of the many granite tiles, tracing the letters with his fingertips as the light diminished.

Avanda came running up to them and grabbed Thorik's hand, pulling him from Emilen. "You have to see this place! It is so different from Farbank." She dragged him past the scrolls and into the courtyard. "Look at all of these animal statues. I counted over thirty that I could identify. I bet you know them all."

Thorik brushed his hands along the stone animal statues as he accompanied Avanda and Emilen into the courtyard. "This is amazing, Em. What a wonderful place to grow up." Looking around and seeing almost everything in perfect shape, he added, "Why was it ever abandoned?"

She had been looking about for signs of life, and his words finalized her thoughts. Leaving him, she ran across the stone courtyard and up the stairs.

Thorik and Avanda only watched for a moment before they followed her as she ran past the campfire and into the city, yelling various people's names.

Thorik yelled up to her while in pursuit, "I'm sure your family is fine. They must have just left because of the damage or simply gone someplace safer."

It was all he and Avanda could do to keep up with Em as she darted from one winding corridor to another in the limited light still emanating from the windows. She rushed into several rooms, only to find them empty of life. By the time Thorik and his student had entered behind her, she was already pushing past them on the way back out. This continued until Thorik decided to wait outside in the hall for her to return from each room. This approach worked much better until she didn't return from one of the rooms.

With very little light left in the hall, Thorik and Avanda peered into the room expecting to see her resting with exhaustion, but instead they found a storage room with an open door on the far side. He sprinted over to it and looked both ways down the now pitch-black hallway without seeing or hearing any sign of her. "Em?" He called down one way and then the other without receiving any response. "Now what?" he asked, knowing they were. The last bit of light had diminished from the storage room and left Thorik and Avanda lost in the dark.

Feeling her way about the room, Avanda opened a cabinet engraved with decorative designs. Inside she felt cloths, a chalice, ornamental objects, and other ceremonial items. She stopped at a familiar object. "Thorik, I think I found a full oil flask."

"Excellent," he replied. He had found a lantern.

After locating his flint in his backpack, he filled the lantern with oil before lighting it. Their eyes adjusted and started to focus on the room. It had turned yellowish green from the oil's flame.

Humming could be heard, soft at first, then growing in strength. It was familiar and vibrated from every direction. Not from behind the walls, but from the walls themselves.

The walls and ceiling quickly pulsed to life as they saw bees covering every inch of the stone surfaces.

Avanda stood still, watching in amazement.

Chills ran down Thorik's spine. He grabbed Avanda's hand and pulled her out the nearest door, into the corridor where Emilen had exited. He slammed the door behind them and rested his back against it while catching his breath. Struggling to understand why they hadn't seen or heard any bees until that moment, he fought off Avanda's pleas of curiosity to investigate it.

Instead, he selected a direction and started down its path with the lantern out in front to show the way, with its sickly green light with hues of yellow and brown fading in and out against the walls and floor.

Avanda ran her fingers along the carvings of plant life on the walls as they moved forward. She could almost see the plants move from her touch. They seemed so lifelike.

After a sharp turn in the corridor, the plant life became covered with carved cobwebs. Thorik strived to walk quickly in an attempt to catch up to Em, although in reality he was slowing down from an uncomfortable feeling about the place. As they progressed, the cobwebs had turned to stone spider webs that covered all surfaces.

Out of the corner of his eye he saw the webs shake and stir, causing him to become tense and nervous. "Avanda, stop touching the wall."

"I'm not. It's moving on its own," she replied with renewed interest in it.

"Just stand on the other side of me, so you're not accidentally brushing up against it."

"Why? Isn't it amazing? The stone is actually moving!"

"Yes, amazing. I'm sure it's just a trick of our eyes. We are tired and not used to the lantern's light yet." He spotted several large spiders carved into the webs. "Now please walk on the other side of me."

"I'm not tired," she said. "It's really moving. They're alive; watch." Stopping next to the wall, she plucked a few spider webs with her fingers. They vibrated for a moment before subsiding.

"It's stone, Avanda. Stone carvings don't sway or move. It's our eyes or something. Just because you can't explain it, doesn't mean that the stone has come alive."

Disappointed in the response, she challenged him. "If it's just stone, then you wouldn't be scared to touch one of the carved spiders, would you?"

"Avanda, we don't have time for this."

She smiled in the greenish light, giving her an eerie look. "Hold your finger up against a stone spider and prove me wrong. Then I'll drop it forever."

Thorik sighed. "Avanda, please. We need to find Emilen."

"The Runestone of Bravery says…"

"All right, that's enough. You win. I get plenty of those reminders from Brimmelle, and I don't need to start getting them from you, too." To free up his hands, he handed her the light source. "Pick a spider so we can get this over with."

Her lantern was lifted toward the stone wall that displayed layers of webs and periodic palm-sized spiders. After finding the largest one available, she pointed at it.

He moved closer to the one she selected. It was about eye level, and he slowly reached out to touch it. But before he did, he retracted his hand and lowered it to the web below. He wanted to prove to himself that this was still a carving before touching the spider itself. Thumping the web caused it to move. "It must be some kind of twine made to look like stone." He plucked the web a few times with his fingers, each instance getting a bit closer to the center of that specific web, near the spider. "This is a waste of time," he muttered, stepping back from the wall.

He looked over at Avanda, who was smiling at his inability to prove her wrong.

"Fine, here is your answer." He took the lantern back from her so he could get better lighting on the wall image. He stepped in closer to the wall and placed his first two fingers squarely on the spider carving. He could make out the tiny hairs on the spider's back. The details were amazing.

Turning and smiling at Avanda, he stood there relieved, still pressing his fingers against the stone wall for a few more moments. He had conquered his fears and was now ready to move on. It felt good. It felt fulfilling. It felt like the spider had just moved out from under his fingers and was now climbing on his hand. Peering down, his eyes agreed.

Avanda screamed as the spider ran up onto the back of his wrist.

Thorik's left arm was occupied with the lantern, preventing him from swiping at it. Instead, he tried to quickly shake it off. But it was too late. The arachnid was already crawling up his sleeve. Startled, he tossed the lantern to Avanda and began removing his backpack and shirt. He felt a bite on his upper arm and screamed from the pain. Ripping off the rest of his shirt, he felt the spider run onto his back where it couldn't be reached. Thorik panicked and slammed his back against the wall to squish it. He felt the creature crack behind him and looked down to see it fall to the floor.

Avanda quickly stomped on it. She then attempted to kick it off to the side, only to find that its squashed body was only a carving in the floor.

Success was short-lived as Thorik realized that his bare back was now stuck to the wall carvings of webs.

Looking around for support to peel himself off, he noticed several more fist-sized spiders moving toward him from all directions on the wall. He pulled his chest forward, causing the granite webs to stretch as they held on to his shoulder blades.

Avanda began to pull his arms to free his body. Small pieces of his skin ripped off and dangled from the wall carvings. Excruciating pain from the ripping of flesh increased as two more spiders jumped onto the back of his neck while another leaped onto his head. Fear increased and adrenaline rushed through his body, giving him the willpower to rip himself free of the granite illustration. Portions of stone web clung to his back, while the wall had claimed segments of his skin. It was an even swap that Thorik had no interest in checking at this time as he stumbled away from the webs.

Avanda could see more spiders on him and grabbed the only weapon available: Thorik's backpack. She swung the pack as hard as she could to crush or at least knock off the spiders. She failed, however, to warn Thorik of the upcoming attack.

Thorik screamed as she knocked him down to his knees.

"It's okay," Avanda notified him. "I got one off. Just a few more to go!"

Thorik rolled out of the way of Avanda's overhead crushing blow with the pack. It smashed against the floor with the sounds of breaking items within the pack.

"Avanda, stop! Trust me; I've got this," he told her as she prepared for another strike.

Reaching up, he grabbed the spider that was now biting the back of his neck and threw it off into the distance. The other burrowing in his hair was more difficult. It clung to the Num's hair, and he was only able to lift it an inch from his head. The lantern's light gave Thorik the view of several more spiders making their way toward him, so he knew that his time was limited.

Using his free hand, he pulled his hunting knife out of his belt holder as he continued to lift the spider from his head. With one quick swipe, he cut just below the spider, removing its legs and a large section of his hair. The spider was extracted and then tossed down the hall.

More spiders fell from the wall next to them and prepared to attack.

Thorik grabbed Avanda's hand and their gear before the two of them ran down the open corridor as quickly as they could, but they couldn't outrun the army of attacking spiders.

Noticing a set of closed doors, he threw them open, ran through them, and quickly turned to shut them once Avanda was inside the room. Closing the doors tightly, he looked at the edges of the door and the floor beneath it to see if any were coming through. It looked as though they had escaped them.

He breathed deeply as he rested his hands on his knees. His back was bloody from the webs as well as the spider bites on his arm and neck. The scratches and bruises from his backpack didn't help either. He could feel drips of blood running down his skin and grabbed a cloth out of his worn backpack to clean some of it off before putting his shirt back on.

The pack was ripped and stained from liquids and powders from broken canisters. His coffer was intact, but it had crushed many of the other items. Disappointed, he looked over at Avanda's innocent face.

She brushed herself off and softly smiled. "I told you they were alive."

Putting on his torn shirt, he noticed movement from within the new room. Stone murals of a tropical forest bordered the grand chamber, and granite trees created a canopy of limbs and leaves overhead. Although the light from the lantern wasn't particularly bright, its beam carried for quite a distance, allowing Thorik to see a door on the far side of the room.

Turning to the nearest wall and raising his light higher, he looked out past the wall's foreground bushes for some sign of life. He placed a hand on a carving of a bush in front of him in an attempt to look past it. Remarkably, it worked, and he could see the leaves move when he pushed it to the side. Thorik wondered if he was hallucinating or whether the stone was behaving in this very unstone-like manner.

A slight movement under the next shrub caused Thorik to go on the defensive. "Back up. Something is out there."

"Out where?" she replied, confused at what was happening. "You mean inside the wall?"

He nodded, eyeing the carvings that were only an inch or two in depth.

Backing away, she noticed a sound and then an object moving toward her. She stumbled and fell onto her backside, away from the wall, as a creature jumped from its coverage and entered the room at her feet. A clear, crystal, long-eared hare hopped past Avanda quickly before disappearing into the adjacent wall.

"I'll take a few crystal hares over granite spiders any day," Thorik chuckled before hearing a large catlike growl from the wall he had just investigated. They froze. His heart missed a beat. "Not again. What is this place?" He gently helped Avanda to her feet.

Keeping an eye on the wall illustration, he could hear the breathing of a large animal following their slow movement into the room. His experience with large cats in the wild had been enough to know to keep his distance and also not to act like prey by running. It didn't help that he had fresh blood on his back, assuming stone predators could smell.

Curious as to what they were up against, he grabbed one of the broken jars from his pack and threw it in the direction of the sound, attempting to scare it off. The glass jar traveled deep into the flat carving of the forest and shattered against a tree near the hidden creature. It had no effect. Thorik's depth perception struggled as he tried to focus on various distances within a carving that was no more than a finger's length deep.

Placing his pack on his back, he grabbed a dagger. Taking Avanda's hand, he continued working his way out into the center of the room, toward the far door. The unseen cat moved along the wall with him, hidden from their sight.

The hunt lasted until the cat had an opportunity. It leaped out of the wall at Thorik, pushing the Num to the ground and knocking the dagger from his grip.

Landing past Thorik's fallen body, the black marble panther circled quickly before jumping onto the Num.

Fleeing was unlikely, since the cat easily outweighed Thorik. Stretching and grasping a sharp piece of glass, which had fallen out of his pack, he stabbed the sharp edge toward the cat's stone leg, hoping it could feel pain. Unfortunately, the cat grabbed the Num's arm in his mouth, preventing the strike.

Unwilling to sit by and do nothing, Avanda attacked from behind, swinging the lantern at the panther's head with all of her might. It hit her target, breaking the side of the lantern and snuffing out all the light from the room. Everything went quiet. There was only one way to know if she had succeeded in frightening the cat away. She reached her hand out into the darkness to see if anything was still on top of Thorik. The silence added to her hesitation as she stretched her arm closer to where she thought they had been.

Her hand landed upon Thorik's arm and then chest before she felt the stone claw of the panther still resting on him. She knew there was no escape. Avanda screamed.

❧ 17 ❧

SPEAK OF THE DEAD

A large rib cage arched upward over Grewen's head and connected at a vertebrae which ran the length of the hall. Each rib bone acted as a column in the corridor, as though Ambrosius, Grewen, and Wess were walking inside the body of a giant snake. Several doorways exited the corridor along both sides, blending in to keep the carved atmosphere.

A muscular structure could be seen on the walls between the bones along the way. Grewen stood up straight and ran his fingers on the textured ceiling overhead before holding up his torch to see all of the imperfections that had been purposely carved in great detail. "Amazing. The last time I've seen this level of craftsmanship was on the Tower of Lu'Tythis," Grewen commented as he noticed a small symbol carved into the end of one of the ribs. It was a glyph of some type that he didn't recognize, perhaps an artistic signature. It featured a series of connecting circles and lines. It reminded him of the symbol of the E'rudites.

Ambrosius had walked ahead while Grewen conducted his investigation and Wess cautiously peered into several rooms on the sides of the hallway.

"Grrrrrrrr." The sound echoed in the long corridor.

Wess felt an overwhelming desire to hide near the giant. Trust or not, the Ov'Unday was more comforting than the beast making the odd growling and rumbling. Bow and arrow ready, he had backed up against Grewen and tossed his torch before him, hoping that this new unknown would leave once it gazed upon Grewen's massive size.

"Grrrrrrr," the gurgling of the growl was more apparent this time.

"Show yourself." Wess spoke out into the darkness.

Grewen reached down with his free hand and patted his belly. "Oh, sorry about that," the giant commented about his stomach's rumblings. "I'm so hungry I'd consider eating meat." Glancing down at Wess, he compounded the Num's uneasiness. Grewen chuckled at Wess' reaction to his joke until he heard Ambrosius asking for him.

Ambrosius was standing at the end of the hall in a large doorway that held two thick wooden doors which opened into the corridor. Beyond the entrance was a room, round in shape with a domed ceiling. In the center, it hosted a large granite table with many chairs around it.

"It's the temple within the crown," Ambrosius said.

Leaning down to get through the doorway, Grewen stood back up to observe what Ambrosius was describing. "It appears to be in better shape than you let on," he jested.

Wess, who was much more nervous than the others, walked in behind them. "I don't think we should be in here. It smells of death." He still didn't fully trust either one of them, but at this point, he was more concerned about the odd feelings he was getting from the carved-out rooms in the city.

Ambrosius walked farther into the room and looked about. "Gluic?" He spotted her sitting on the floor beyond the table, placing stones in various patterns within a larger circle of stones that surrounded her.

She looked up only for a moment as she continued her work. "Oh good. You're here. We're almost ready."

Smiling, Ambrosius shook his head at her odd ways before returning his attention to the room. Walking around the table, he softly touched the back of the chair that he remembered standing at when the Mountain King's head came crashing down through the glass ceiling. "It is nearly identical, with a few modifications. These statues of Polenum warriors now stand where the windows were, and the ceiling is stone instead of glass."

Grewen reached up to touch the carved ceiling and knocked his knuckles on it several times. "Sounds like stone." He then walked over to sit on the large granite table to rest. "So, why the duplication of rooms?"

"It must be their Mori Site." Wess immediately noticed their gazes at him with questioning expressions. "A Mori Site is built for the elders that can no longer make it up to the spiritual sites on top of the valley walls. It allows them a chance to conduct business as well as to atone for disrespecting the Rules of Order. We have one in the center of Farbank. I assumed everyone had them."

Wess realized that he had captured both of their attentions. He was not going to lose this opportunity to be in control for a while. Rolling up his sleeves and placing his hands behind his head, he sat down in a chair and kicked his feet up onto the table. It was at this point that he began to enlighten them about his culture and his own stories of success in the community.

This continued for a short time before two short figures approached the doorway.

Thorik limped into the room and saw Wess sitting at the table telling Grewen a clever little tale about his past, while Gluic was busy giving a stern lecture to one of the many statues in the room. Ambrosius had his back to the group as he investigated one of the stone warriors.

Avanda followed Thorik, carrying the unlit lantern along with some of the items that had fallen out of his ripped backpack. Wonder still filled her eyes with every new experience and room she entered. She was ready for anything.

Thorik, on the other hand, appeared to have already been through everything the city had to offer. His clothes were bloodstained, and his backpack was torn and dragging behind him. With slumped shoulders and a dazed expression, he fell into a chair near Wess.

"Nice hair, Dain," Wess said of Thorik's self-inflicted haircut. The last time Wess had seen Thorik, he was talking to Emilen prior to crossing the bridge. Since then, the rest of the party hadn't had any conflicts, so this appearance of a disheveled and bleeding Thorik was unexpected. He grinned and assumed that Emilen had rebuffed Thorik's advances with hostility. "Where's Emilen?"

"I don't know. But I'm fine. Thanks for asking." Thorik's comments were meant for the group, but none paid any attention. "We followed her into the city, but then she lost us. I was hoping she was with you. She knows her way around the city, but we should still go look for her. I don't like the idea of her being alone."

Grewen's eyebrows crunched in the middle of his face. "What did you run into, or should I ask what ran into you?"

Wess was suddenly reminded of Gluic's warning that they had nothing to fear until after dark. It was definitely after dark, and Thorik's wounds instantly alerted his senses. His face gave a nervous twitch as he waited for Thorik's response. It most likely would be something hideous. "We should stay here. Safety in numbers."

Thorik motioned his head to Avanda as he replied to Wess, "Not likely; we brought the danger with us."

She walked over and set their damaged lantern on the table.

Thorik pointed to the bent object. "This is the cause of my pain."

Wess chuckled. "Dain, you may want to practice fighting flint boxes before you move up to lanterns."

Grewen's eyebrows relaxed at his answer. "The lantern attacked you?"

"In a way, it did. Would you like me to demonstrate?"

Grewen looked over at Wess, who was confused at Thorik's answer and still nervous about what really could be out there in the dark. "Wess, you better stand behind me before he releases that lamp; it looks of foul temper."

Wess began to move out of his chair before realizing that Grewen was playing with him. Irritated that he was on the wrong side of the joke, he sat back down and folded his arms across his chest. "Okay, Dain, release your lantern of terror."

Gluic interrupted, as normal, on a completely different subject. "Ambrosius, we're finished. They are here now and prepared to talk to you."

"Who wants to speak to me?" Ambrosius waited for someone to enter the room.

"Those who died in the temple. They are here among us." She reached out into the air as though to hush a voice that only she could hear. "They are speaking about the killing of the council."

The rest of the party looked about for something to happen, but nothing presented itself.

Ambrosius gave her a strong gaze. "Thank you, Gluic; this is what I came for. Ask them who destroyed the temple and killed the council members."

"They don't wish to talk to me. Ask them yourself." Gluic was apparently having a conversation with someone else and didn't appreciate being interrupted. "He'll find it and bring it to you. Be patient. You'll be out of your slumber soon enough." She continued her conversation with her unseen friend as she walked out the doorway into the large ribbed corridor.

Ambrosius looked around for something to speak to. He finally walked up to the statue that Gluic had spent time with and asked, "Who did this to you? I need to know to prevent others from your same fate."

There was no response.

Frustrated, Ambrosius called out to the other statues, "If you wish to speak, now is your time." No response. "Who did this to you? Come alive and talk, or we shall leave here with no idea of how to achieve justice for your murder."

"Are you sure you want them to come alive?" Thorik asked.

All attention turned to Thorik as he opened a small glass door on Avanda's lantern.

Ambrosius stepped over to the table and braced himself against it. "Thorik, I need to know who did this. If you have some way to help, you need to do so."

Thorik lit the oil wick in the semi-functional lantern, and sickly green dancing light painted the room, overpowering the yellow light of the groups' torches. The lantern's illumination kissed the decorative walls and statues, providing them with a burst of life and freedom to move about, just as it had to the spiders in the hallway and the panther in the room after.

One of the statues began to move. First its eyes and then its fingers and mouth. Wess gasped and jumped up from his seat. Intrigued, Grewen scanned the room to see all the activity, while Ambrosius stepped back from the animated statue.

Eventually, all of the statues came to life and began moving toward the group. Wess took a defensive stance with his back to the center of the room. Thorik ushered Avanda under the table for safety.

"Why has the slayer of the council returned?" asked the statue in front of Ambrosius.

Ambrosius corrected their statement. "He has not. However, I have returned to discover who your assassin is, so I may vindicate your deaths."

Another statue repeated the question. "Why has the killer of the council returned to Kingsfoot?"

All of the statues now had their weapons and shields forward and were ready to start fighting. They independently moved inward from the outside walls, each restating the phrase at random times with slight variations.

"No, you have it wrong," Ambrosius announced. "I didn't kill you; I'm a victim of this as well," he firmly stated to the statue in front of him, whose speed was increasing as his spear rose toward Ambrosius' head.

Eight armed statues surrounded the group, all just a few steps away from attacking the travelers. All were chanting the same accusation over and over again.

Ambrosius stood firm and shouted, "Stop! You have made a mistake." Each of his words came out strong and clear. Controlling his temper was becoming strenuous as the side of his face became rigid and menacing. "I command you to stop!"

It was too late. Wess picked up a thick wooden chair and crashed it into the statue closest to him. Wooden splinters and debris showered the area, while the force of the impact knocked the statue over. It landed hard and shattered into pieces across the floor.

One of the statues swung at Thorik. The Num ducked and rolled to the far wall to escape the blow. By the time he got back up, he could see Wess on the back of one of the statues while Grewen calmly held two of them at bay with his huge hands.

Oblivious to Wess and Thorik's challenges, Ambrosius easily held off several statues with his own powers as he tried to understand what was happening.

A statue grabbed Wess off the back of another stone warrior. Tossing him to the ground, it prepared to stomp its granite foot on the Num's head.

Having seen enough, Avanda jumped out from under the table, reached for the lantern, and then blew out the flame, returning the yellow light from the torches. All unnatural life had ceased once the wick had been extinguished and the green light had faded, much like when the large cat attacked Thorik.

Wess squeezed his face out from under the statue's boot. He had been just a second away from being crushed. Rolling away, he pushed himself up onto one knee to catch his breath as he pointed at Ambrosius. "I knew it!" Wess claimed as he worked both legs under him and stretched his back. "You killed all those people. You destroyed the Mountain King statue. You are behind this."

Ambrosius sat down in disbelief. "Why would they blame me?"

"Because it was you," Wess answered.

Thorik stepped in. "He's not the kind of person who would kill others for power. He's just not like that."

"Oh, you would be surprised. He's clever, but Brimmelle and I were right about him all along."

"Wess, why would he ask us to help him come all the way here if he had killed them?"

Wess thought quickly and replied, "Because he came back for something. Something he didn't have an opportunity to grab last time, but now, with everyone out of the way, he can find it."

"Like what? What have you seen him take? You've been with him the entire time."

Wess was a little puzzled by the questions, but that didn't stop him. "Perhaps he hasn't found it yet." He gave a slight pause before he smiled and continued. "Or maybe he has already acquired what he came back for."

Stepping over, he grabbed Ambrosius' metal staff that had been leaning against the table. "Thorik, where's the walking stick you made for him? I don't recall him having this quarterstaff while he was in Farbank."

It was a sensitive subject for Thorik, but he didn't let that change his mind. "Finding his staff doesn't make him a murderer. You have to trust me; he didn't do this."

"How do you know for sure? Tell me, what should we believe? His words or the words of those he has killed? The ghosts of his victims have pointed to him," Wess added.

Ignoring Wess, Ambrosius sat and scratched his beard while trying to figure out why the spirits of the Grand Council were accusing him of such crimes. "Frustrating," he acknowledged. "This hasn't helped us discover any clues as to who is working with Darkmere. Without this lead, we will have to go directly after Darkmere himself."

Thorik responded to Wess' comments, "We don't even know where those voices came from. Were they indeed spirits? Or were they controlled by someone else? There are a lot of questions to be answered before accusations can be made. Besides, don't you think Ambrosius would know if he did this or not?"

Wess, dismissing Thorik's logic, was quick on the offensive again. "Let's say for a moment that he's not lying to us. Maybe he's still missing some of his memory from when he got hurt and ended up in that crater. He could be telling us the truth that he doesn't remember, and yet still have killed them." He turned and looked directly at Thorik. "Remember when Trumette fell and knocked his head against the village well? He lost two days of memory and swore he hadn't been in Sammal's tree house, didn't he?"

Thorik argued the point, "Trumette loses two days of memory every time his wife makes him take a bath. Ambrosius' memories were restored by Gluic. He recalls exactly what happened."

"Maybe Wess is correct." Ambrosius spoke up. "Perhaps I am missing some facts. I keep having dreams of the destruction and what happened afterward, but I lose the specifics by the time I wake. Gluic helped regain most of my memories, but not all of them."

"There, I knew it," Wess proudly acclaimed as he pointed the black iron staff in judgment toward Ambrosius.

Thorik thought for a moment before responding to Ambrosius. "There is a way to find out and end this discussion. Gluic, can you restore the rest of his thoughts?"

The lack of response reminded them all that she had wandered off again.

Thorik quickly put his items together in what remained of his backpack, grabbed a torch, and headed out the doorway to find Gluic. "Come on, Avanda, we still need to find Em as well."

She grabbed her lantern and its flask of oil before following him out of the room.

Wess slowly positioned himself between Ambrosius and the doorway with the quarterstaff gripped for combat. He bent his knees slightly and hunched forward in case Ambrosius made a leap for him.

Instead, Ambrosius leaned farther back into his chair and continued stroking the path of his mustache that led to his beard. He tilted his head and looked at the ever-so-quiet giant. "Grewen, what do you suppose they meant? If these statues were indeed speaking for the spirits here, do they blame me for bringing them here in the first place?"

Oddly enough, Wess was startled since he had forgotten about Grewen. He was so large and still that he almost blended into the room. Wess moved his way behind Ambrosius, pulled out a hunting knife, and held it up in a threatening manner. "Grewen, keep your distance, or Ambrosius' blood will be on your hands. This murderer is in my custody until we can get him to a higher authority."

Grewen ignored Wess and answered Ambrosius. "The spirits' questions are vague. But if it is true that you don't recall what happened, how can you honestly say that you didn't kill them?"

Wess nodded his head in agreement with Grewen.

It was difficult to accept Grewen's words, but Ambrosius acknowledged the possibility. "I suppose that I, at least indirectly, am responsible for their death."

With some confidence that Grewen was on his side, Wess stepped forward and placed the sharp blade of his hunting knife against the side of Ambrosius' neck. "We've had enough of your lies and games. Tell us why you have destroyed this Temple, killed these people, and then returned here." Wess stood as though he was going to sever the older man's head from his shoulders if he didn't get the answer he wanted to hear.

Grewen lowered his head into one of his large palms in disbelief. The giant could only hope that Ambrosius wouldn't get angry at the Num's actions.

Wess only had a moment to look up and see Grewen's response before he was knocked off his feet by an invisible force that lifted him high in the air. The impact of the Num's body against the stone surface knocked the wind out of him and caused him to drop his blade. Pinned to the ceiling, facing down, a mixture of fear and confusion crossed his face. He was unsure what to do.

Ambrosius had moved only one eyebrow. Lifting Wess up like this was like brushing away a fly. Ignoring the annoying Num, he continued his conversation with Grewen as though Wess had never been in the room. "Though the implication was that I had planned it. Why would I create a council to unite Australis only to destroy it? I'm trying to rebuild our world, not overthrow it."

"The Del'Unday would disagree with you. So would the servants of Darkmere." Grewen also ignored the body above them. "It is well known that you have been displeased with the council's progress over the past many years and have been pushing for a more aggressive response to Darkmere. Because of this, you were seen as a threat to the council's power, and likewise, the council was a threat to you."

"Disagreements that have been blown out of proportion." Ambrosius dismissed them with a wave of his hand. "The council did not understand Darkmere like I do. He extends branches of friendship that are laced with poison thorns."

Grewen continued his analysis of the situation. "The fact that your conflicts are publicly well known will make it difficult to persuade others to believe that you are not behind this disaster. In addition, your history of conflicts with Alchemists, Del'Unday, and during the Dovenar Civil War has crippled your persona in many ways."

"And you, Grewen? Where do you stand on my character?"

"I believe you are a man of many challenges and responsibilities. I fought alongside you during the Civil War and have killed for your cause. I have watched as you have taken justice into your own hands when others would not. You are a man who has had everything, yet has nothing to show for it. You are my friend and an honorary Ki-Ov'Unday family pod member. I see no reason you would lie to me about being innocent. So, I will continue to trust you until you are proven untrustworthy."

"Thank you, my friend."

"But be aware that the evidence is starting to stack up against you," Grewen continued. "You have nothing but your character to stand on at this point. And there is still the issue of your memory. Truth be known, you haven't even proven to yourself that you didn't destroy the temple in a fit of rage."

Ambrosius took a deep breath and slowly let it out as he thought about the comment, before looking over to see Thorik and Brimmelle stepping into the doorway.

"Brimmelle," Wess managed to get out as he gasped for air.

Brimmelle stumbled back a step and grabbed the doorframe with one hand. "By the Rune of Reason, what is the meaning of this?" Brimmelle shouted up to Wess, who was lying on the ceiling.

Ambrosius looked up and casually lowered Wess to the stone floor. Floating down, Wess tried to look in control by holding Ambrosius' staff before him. Once on his own feet, he backed up toward Thorik and Brimmelle.

Wess explained to the other two Nums what he had heard. "He's made many enemies and killed before. This isn't his first time. He confessed to these crimes."

"Perhaps you'd like to spend some more time on the ceiling." Ambrosius eyed the spot where Wess had been. He was already in a bad mood about being accused of the murders, and his patience was getting thin with Wess' incessant accusations.

Wess backed up into the doorway, next to Thorik and Brimmelle. "We're getting out of here before he kills the rest of us." Glancing over at Grewen, his hands were shaking. "Or we get eaten by that one."

"Nah, I don't really care for Nums. Too stringy." Grewen smirked, picking at his teeth as though something was between them. His subtle humor didn't always come across well to some.

"Give me that." Thorik snatched the iron staff out of Wess' hands before he hurt himself.

Without a weapon for defense, Wess turned and bolted down the hallway, followed quickly by Brimmelle.

As the Fir's footsteps faded off, Thorik walked over to Ambrosius and leaned the dark metal staff against the table. "This is yours." He then turned to leave the room. Stopping on his way out, Thorik stared into the empty corridor before him while addressing Ambrosius. "I hope you found what you came for." Standing up straight, he pulled his shoulders back, clasped his hands together behind his back, and gave a deep sigh. "We found Emilen in her old living quarters, if you happen to be curious as to her fate. She and Gluic are now preparing our beds for the night in the main hall. We will be heading home to Farbank at sunrise." And with that, he left the Mori room.

Ambrosius glared at Grewen over the giant's last comment. "This is not a good time for you to be joking around."

"Maybe you're right. Nums take things so seriously. Are you sure they aren't related somehow to the Del'Unday? We never did come to an agreement on the origins of those family trees."

"This is not the time to continue our debate over the lineage of species." The pressure from the day was getting to him, and he rubbed both eyes with the thumb and forefinger of his right hand. "I need to get the word out about how the council was destroyed. I'll call a meeting of the remaining leaders to explain my findings. We must address this threat from Darkmere before he attacks again."

"Perhaps you don't understand. The first sighting of you will probably create a mob that will hunt you down. You may very well be an outlaw. A wanted criminal. Already convicted and sentenced by all the northern provinces."

Ambrosius shook his head in disbelief. "It can't be that bad. I have been a head of state or council member my entire life. They wouldn't dare accuse me so quickly without any proof. I think you underestimate the following I have."

"And I think you underestimate Darkmere's ability to influence others. Perhaps you should know that he is scheduled to speak in Woodlen."

"Denrick Copperman won't let it happen. His loyalties are with me."

"Denrick invited him."

Ambrosius was disheartened. His face went cold, and his eyes searched for an answer. "We need to go there and confront him."

"You're going to confront Darkmere during his visit? How do you intend to find out where he will be? Woodlen is a large province with several cities. You can't just show your face around there to ask questions. And last time I checked, Undays were only allowed as slaves or gladiators." Grewen's fist hit the stone table a few times to add emphasis to his last few words. The pounding echoed out the doorway and down the hallway.

Ambrosius stood up and grabbed his staff, which he raised and pointed up toward Grewen's large face. "I don't know how I will find out where he is, but I must," he argued. "I have nothing to lose at this point, do I? Darkmere has destroyed everything in my life up to this point. I will not sit back and let him win."

"Win? Is this about you winning? Is this just a continuation of the Civil War to you? Or worse, some out-of-control rivalry?"

"No, that's not what I meant." Ambrosius lowered his voice and weapon. "I mean win, as in him taking over Australis in a cruel dictatorship. If he succeeds, everyone will give up their own independence and beliefs in order to follow his. You know this." Ambrosius sat back down. "I can understand how people hate me for the things I've done. I also have had great friction with many cultures. But I have never forced them to change their ways to follow me. I've only asked them to understand and accept other beliefs." Leaning forward onto the table, he looked at the giant's leathery face. "I need to confront Darkmere head-on."

The giant frowned at the idea. "Again, I will ask, how will you walk freely inside the Dovenar Wall of Woodlen to find out where he will be? You are too well known, and you will be captured immediately. I'd help, but Ov'Undays can't freely enter the land. Only humans and Polenums are allowed to go beyond the wall."

A moment passed before a grin grew upon the E'rudite's face. "We have allies."

Grewen leaned forward and softened his deep, powerful voice the best he could. "They just left here with ill feelings and are heading downstream in the morning. How do you plan to turn that around?"

"I don't know. But I must. Too many lives are depending on me." He stroked his beard as he considered the options. "We need their help… Actually, we only need one of them."

18

TURNING POINT

Draq nested on the headless neck of the Mountain King statue for the night. A small cave had been created when the head had fallen off, and steam was continually rising out of it. It was a warm spot to sleep for the night with a perfect view to see any intruders arriving.

He looked down to his right to see the campfire light outside the main entrance of the city. Memories of past crusades with friends tempted him to go down, but he no longer was one to socialize, nor did he enjoy being inside. He felt confined and helpless when he entered buildings or tunnels. He had comparatively little in the way of defending himself against those who would threaten him or his friends. He needed space to fly, to glide, to swoop, to strike.

The Red-Tipped Silver Dragon missed the days of battles and then returning home after the victories. It had been a long time since he and Ambrosius had a victory to celebrate. It had also been a long time since he had been home with his family, and he didn't see that changing any time soon.

Coiling up near the steam vent, Draq rested his head over the edge of the statue's neck so he could view the valley at all times. After the long road Ambrosius and he had traveled, the dragon no longer could look out and see such a valley as beautiful. Instead, all he saw were hiding places that others could be using before they attacked. The world was now a large, continuous battlefield.

~

The Num's campfire sat in the center of the first huge hall of the city, while the original fire could be seen flickering in the cold breeze just outside the main doorway. Snow was starting to accumulate in small drifts just inside the doorway.

It looked frigid and dismal to the group as they kept warm near the second fire.

It was not the cold of the winter storm that caused them to stay silent; it was the chill of emotional conflicts.

Emilen was cuddled up against Thorik under a shared blanket, her eyes sad and wet from weeping. "I miss them."

"I'm sure they're safe." He leaned his head against hers to comfort her in her time of need. "Perhaps they went downstream to Farbank or Longfield. I'll help you find them."

"Thorik." She gazed into his eyes. "You're very sweet, but they could have traveled across the mountains to Shoreview for all we know." She placed her finger up to his mouth as he began to respond with some heroic comment. "Just hold me. If the Mountain King wishes for me to see my parents again, then it will happen. I will not waste your efforts if it is not what he wishes for us to do." Smiling at him, she brushed her fingers against his cheek and softly nodded her head, telling him that it would be all right.

Thorik felt a surge of love toward her, which he hadn't anticipated. He didn't know if it was from the soft strength in her voice or from the warmth of her hand against his skin. Pushing back the hood of his cloak, he held her hand against his neck, closed his eyes, and leaned toward her.

Wess sat with Avanda, jealous of Thorik's relationship with the curly redhead. He had sat on the opposite side of the fire from Ambrosius on purpose and kept his eyes focused on the elder human while sharpening his hunting knife. The rhythm of the grinding metal was nearly hypnotic as it echoed off the walls.

Grewen sat with his feet up against the lapping flames of the fire and wiggled his toes to get the flames between them. He sighed and groaned several times as the heat touched just the right spots.

Meanwhile, Brimmelle tried to get Gluic to sit down and warm herself under their blanket, but she was busy placing various stones near the fire. "Mother, please sit down before you catch yourself on fire."

Ignoring him, she pulled another small river-rock out of her pouch and held it near her lips, speaking quietly to it for a short time. She traced it with her finger as she nodded, listening to what it had to say. Afterward, she gently placed the stone in a specific place up near the fire with the many others that were already warming. This ritual continued until she had nearly thirty stones and crystals laid out in various groups and distances. It wasn't a particularly uniform placement, but somehow it was organized in a naturally pleasing sort of way.

Grewen looked over at the stones as Gluic returned to Brimmelle and got under her son's blanket. "Why the grouping? Wouldn't they warm faster if they were evenly dispersed?" the mognin asked.

She looked at the stones with a puzzled look on her face. "I'm not sure. I would guess they work better in groups than individually spread out." The patterns made by the rocks pleased her. "Or perhaps some of them just don't get along with others. I just put them where they tell me to."

Grewen's right eyebrow rose as he turned toward her with his smile. "Well, that's very nice of them to take the pressure off of you in having to decide their resting spots." There was a hint of sarcasm.

"Yes, it is," she concluded in a serious tone. "It's a lot like us." She nodded in agreement with her own statement. "We all make our own choices as to where we sit and who we like and dislike. I wonder if we're as smart as the stones."

Silence fell back on the group as they listened to the crackling of the fire and the wind blowing through the distant front doorway.

Ambrosius finally broke the silence with a question. "Thorik, do you believe in your heart that I killed these people?"

Thorik answered in a slow, thoughtful manner. "I believe that it is in your nature to do whatever it takes to succeed, regardless of who gets hurt. Your focus is so strong that you might forget about the cost of your victory. You are much like Wess in that manner."

Offended, Wess straightened up, but Thorik continued before the larger Num could speak.

"I also believe you are doing your best to help our world become a better place. And sometimes it takes fighting for what you believe is right and fighting those who would hurt you more in the long run. So, do I believe that you killed the Grand Council and destroyed the Mountain King statue? I don't know anymore. I want to believe you, but it's difficult. It also shouldn't matter to you if I believe you or not. After daybreak, you will never see me again."

"But it does matter, Thorik. It matters to me because you are what I'm trying to save. You, your family, your village, and your way of life. There are people like you all across this land that will no longer be free to enjoy life if I don't help them by stopping Darkmere from conquering the free lands." Ambrosius sighed at the thought of the terrible consequences. "I am not fighting for my personal gain. I am fighting for the freedom of others."

Thorik absorbed his comments and then noted, "Good; I'm glad we could be of service to your cause, and I hope we helped. May the king's vision help you foresee trouble and his sword give you the strength to win your battles."

"I can't do this alone," Ambrosius added. "I need your help to stop Darkmere."

"My help? Why my help?" He glanced at Grewen's massive size. "Surely you have more powerful friends at your call. You don't need us. Gluic has healed you enough that you can travel without her. We are tired and want to return home. It's over. What more could we possibly give you?" Thorik concluded.

"Your friendship," Ambrosius stated. "It is more powerful and reliable than the mighty Spear of Rummon. It's not about power or strength; it's about attitude and desire. Real power comes to those with the drive to accomplish a goal. Real power is within you, my friend."

"Where is this headed?" questioned Thorik.

"I need your help in leading my people."

"Into war? I'm not the person you think I am."

"No, not to war, to freedom." Ambrosius continued, "It is quite simple. I need your help in finding out where Darkmere is so I can stop him from his oppressive takeover. He has many that follow him because they have had no one else to trust, until now. Thorik, you have a gift. They will trust you. They will listen to you. And you can help them understand what he's really trying to do."

"I don't think I can live up to those expectations."

"Do you remember when I told you that you looked familiar?"

Thorik nodded.

"I've recalled where I've seen your face before. It was here, up on that mountain. Your face is the same as the Mountain King's." Ambrosius paused to let it sink in. "Thorik, I believe you are a descendant of the Mountain King."

Brimmelle choked on the water he was drinking. Spraying a mist toward the fire.

Thorik smiled. "And seeing that the head is gone, I am supposed to just believe it to be true."

Ambrosius thought about his lack of evidence as Brimmelle continued his coughing spell. "True, I have no proof. Although Emilen could most likely tell you better than I."

Emilen looked into his eyes. "You do look a lot like him."

The words made Thorik feel good, but again, there was no proof. "It is very nice that I have facial features similar to the Mountain King's, but that does not prove that I am related in any way. Ambrosius, perhaps you weren't aware that our scrolls say he died in the Great Emancipation before he had any children. Therefore, there are no descendants."

Brimmelle nodded his head as he began to gain control over the water he had been choking on.

Ambrosius played his last game piece on the table. "Understood. But you did promise me that you would see this through. Surely, you're not going back on your word."

"I am doing nothing of the kind. You asked for help getting to Kingsfoot. I have fulfilled that."

Ambrosius answered back in a softer tone to defuse Thorik's new edge. "Actually, I told you that I was heading upstream to Kingsfoot. I asked you if you would help me find the ones responsible and prevent their next attack."

"You played your words on me," Thorik protested, realizing Ambrosius was correct.

Brimmelle laughed at Thorik. "I warned you about this. Outsiders cannot be trusted. You would be a fool to follow him now that you know that he has the tongue of a serpent."

Emilen voiced her opinion. "I think we should go. We can do this. If we can help in some way to save lives, then we should. You could be a great leader, Thorik. I can feel it."

Her comments were quickly followed by Brimmelle's rebuttal. "He's no leader. A leader must take charge and make decisions that may not be popular. He doesn't have it within him. His heart is too soft. He cares too much about how his orders will make others feel. He is now, and will always be, a follower."

Brimmelle glared at Ambrosius. "I've had enough of you and your stories. It's time we set our sights on Farbank before winter fully arrives. You've filled the boy's head with ideas that will get us all killed. Leave him alone and go about your business. And for the record, the rest of us made no commitment to you nor your quest to save the world."

Feeling powerful, the Fir looked back over at Thorik. "You're no descendant of a king, you're not a leader, and you're not capable of turning the tide of some war. Most of all, you know I'm right. Don't let this man entice you into believing that you're more than you really are. You're a Sec, and you used to be a hunter; a questionable one, I might add. And the only reason you hold the position of Sec is because of me." Lying down, he got comfortable for his night of rest. "You're lost without my guidance. You always have been."

Thorik stared at his uncle and thought about his words before looking back at Ambrosius. "I'll go with you."

Ambrosius was relieved at his answer and was thankful that Thorik still trusted him.

Brimmelle, on the other hand, was outraged. "How dare you disobey me! After all I have sacrificed for you. You miserable ingrate! You will never become a Fir now." Suddenly aware of his surroundings, and his lack of control within them, he stopped his rant and gave Thorik a disappointed fatherly look before rolling over and turning his back on him. "I won't be there to save you this time," he mumbled loud enough for his nephew to hear.

Emilen smiled at Thorik. "I will be there for you."

Her words put any criticism from Brimmelle out of Thorik's head. For the first time in his life, he felt liberated.

Wess had been watching Thorik and Emilen. Their relationship had been getting steadily stronger since the river-cut crossing, and if it wasn't broken up soon, he knew that he may never have a chance with her. All he needed was to wait for an opening. And if he knew the Dain well enough, Thorik would create an opening, hopefully prior to the party splitting in two and going their separate ways.

Thorik's Log: 17th day of the 10th month of the 649th year.

Emilen and I have joined Ambrosius, Draq, and Grewen to travel to the Woodlen Province in an effort to prevent the destruction of the kingdom by Darkmere. I hope I won't regret this decision.

MORNING CAME, and a light fog had covered the valley. The freezing mist attached itself to the city's external walls and the statues in the courtyard, coating them with a thin layer of ice.

Draq continued to watch from the Mountain King's neck. He knew peaceful times could change to dreadful encounters in a few heartbeats.

Thorik and Emilen had said goodbye to the other Nums during breakfast and were leaving the city and following Ambrosius and Grewen by a few stones' throws. The two Nums held hands while listening to the cracking of frozen grass under their feet as they headed around the lake.

Emilen turned around and waved at Avanda, Brimmelle, and Wess as the three loaded their gear into one of the several rowboats that rested at the slippery docks just outside of the city.

"Uncle Wess, I don't want to go back without Thorik and Emilen." Avanda struggled with the idea of splitting up the party.

"I know. Nor do I. But it looks like we missed our chance."

"Our chance for what?"

"Nothing." He realized he had been caught in an emotional moment while gawking at Emilen. Wess waved back to her, disappointed that his chance with Emilen had just ended. He turned and prepared the boat for the downstream voyage, following orders from his Fir, whose voice was loud enough to carry across the lake.

Finished loading the boat, Brimmelle realized that Gluic wasn't around. She had run off ahead to show Ambrosius and Grewen her new stones and nuggets of gold.

Brimmelle yelled for his mother several times before he raced his stocky body from the docks toward her, slipping on the ice and falling twice along the way. At his pace, it took several minutes to pass Thorik and Emilen and reach his mother. He was out of breath. "Mother, we're leaving."

"Yes, we are. I didn't think you were coming," Gluic said to her son before she continued to explain what each of her stones was used for. "These red rubies help energize and motivate you, and this pink crystal removes emotional debris from your heart," she informed Grewen.

Brimmelle caught his breath enough to speak again. "We're not going to Woodlen; we're leaving to go back home to Farbank."

Gluic stopped and kissed his cheek. "You have a safe trip and button up that shirt. I don't want my son to catch a cold while I'm not around to help." She buttoned up his shirt for him while talking.

"No, Mother, you're coming with us to Farbank."

"I can't right now, dear, but I'll meet you when we get done." She turned and walked toward Grewen, leaving Brimmelle confused and frustrated.

"Wess!" Brimmelle yelled back toward the docks. "Unload my things. I'm going to Woodlen." Slumping his shoulders, the Fir began his walk back to the docks, passing Thorik and Emilen again.

"Yes! Here we come," Avanda sang out from the dock's edge.

Not overly surprised with the change, Wess unloaded the supplies while the group moved around the lake. He once again would have a chance with Emilen. All he needed was the right opening.

As Wess and Avanda approached the Fir with all the gear, Brimmelle said, "I told you to unload my things. You two are still going back to Farbank."

Avanda looked down, disappointed.

Wess took the Fir aside, "If Ambrosius is the man we think he is, you're going to need my help. Thorik will be of no value."

Brimmelle thought for a moment. "True. But we still have to warn Farbank of the thrashers, and traveling beyond the valley is not for children."

"We can send a boat downriver with a message. The current should get it caught in the pond, like everything else that floats down the river." The 'pond' was actually an eddy in the river near Farbank that had widened the banks so much that debris riding the river often would get caught and circle there for days before continuing downstream. "If it should make it past the pond, it will get caught in the Longfield fishing nets, and they will send someone upstream to warn Farbank. And as far as Avanda goes, she's in no more danger with us than trying to get past thrashers along the river's banks."

Brimmelle sighed as he saw Wess' reasoning and welcomed the thought of an ally on their journey. "Fine. Send the note, and let's hope it finds its mark. We're going to Woodlen," he commanded, as though it was his idea.

Avanda's face lit up as she raced ahead to tell the rest of the party.

Brimmelle followed her while Wess returned to the dock and prepared the boat for its own journey downstream.

As the five leading members approached the stone bridge, Ambrosius stopped, while the other four continued over it. Grewen, Gluic, Avanda, and Brimmelle stopped halfway across to wait for the E'rudite, who had disappeared from their sight for a minute, only to return again from alongside the bridge's entrance.

Just before Thorik and Emilen had arrived at the bridge, Ambrosius rounded the corner to make his way up onto the deck of the crossing. Thorik immediately realized that Ambrosius had gone underneath and swapped out his original metal staff with the antler-crowned hazelwood one that Thorik had carved out for him.

Ambrosius glanced over at Thorik and then at his staff. "New beginnings." With a soft grin, he turned back toward Grewen to move forward, to their destination.

❦ 19 ❦

FROZEN SLOPES

The group rounded the lake and walked up the mountain's foothills, which were covered in sheets of ice that increased in thickness the higher they climbed. Several layers of clothing were donned to fight the chilling wind that raced down the mountainside toward them as a winter storm rolled into the valley.

Bundled and cold, the members slipped several times on the icy slopes. They had been walking the better part of the day and were only a little over halfway up to the pass. Frost built up on faces and exposed skin while backpacks and supplies stiffened like bricks. Their fingers began to burn from the freezing temperatures to the point that they were of little use anymore.

All of Gluic's decorative feathers and plants had frozen or blown off. Survival was their only concern as the storm intensified.

Ambrosius ordered Draq to fly above the storm and wait for them on the far side of the mountain's ridge. It was not without an argument from the silver dragon, but the E'rudite's orders were clear and were followed.

Although he had not been to this part of the King's Valley, the general terrain was familiar to Thorik. He was able to keep them on the buried trail.

Ambrosius had been using his powers to create a shield of energy. It held off most of the wind, but hours of sustaining this level of focus exhausted him, and the shield was shrinking in size and strength. It had been too long to continue such a task, and Ambrosius began slowing and stumbling. Thorik moved to his side for support.

Reaching the pass before nightfall was not going to happen. Everyone was tiring out with each painful step; feet began to feel more like blocks of ice, and toes lost total feeling and movement.

Brimmelle, who had been complaining most of the day, finally yelled out, "We're going to die on this mountain unless we turn around and go back to the city of Kingsfoot. It's our only hope!"

Grewen disagreed. "It's too far." He looked at Gluic and Emilen struggling to keep their legs moving. His eyes lowered to Avanda, who was already curled in a ball between Grewen's massive hands and arms. "We'll never make it back down, and I don't think we can reach the pass."

Ambrosius intensified his powers to block the mighty winds. "Pushing forward is our only option."

"No!" Thorik yelled over the wind. "We will have to find shelter here, right now, if we wish to survive. This entire mountain range is filled with small caves. We just need to find one for the night."

The group continued to walk for another painful half-hour as they looked for such an opening in the rocks.

"Over there!" shouted Thorik as he pointed to an angled crack in the mountainside. "I'll bet there's a cave in there. We should stay the night in it, if there is." Walking toward it, he stopped at a tree near the entrance in order to remove a few layers of bark before entering the opening.

Nobody argued or commented. Physically and mentally drained, they followed Thorik's instructions to the temporary shelter.

Ambrosius, Gluic, and Brimmelle were exhausted and immediately dropped onto the rock floor inside the crack in the mountain. The cave was not large, but it provided substantial shelter from the wind. It had a moderate sized opening to the outside and just enough room for Grewen to crowd into.

With everyone in, Thorik began directing their survival. "Grewen, break off a few limbs and then move that boulder in front of the cave so it blocks most of the wind, but leave a gap at the top."

On a normal day, it would have been an easy task for Grewen, but with hands trembling uncontrollably from the cold, it would be difficult. "I'll see what I can do." He set Avanda inside the cave prior to trying.

"Do your best." Thorik turned to see his shivering party sitting along the walls of a small triangular cave. With shaking fingers of his own, he removed a flask of oil and some flint from his backpack.

"Wess, pull the weeds and dead brush out of the ground and stack them over there." Thorik pointed at the wall near the entrance. His upbringing prevented him from telling Brimmelle and Gluic to help, so he continued without them, "Emilen, grab a few of your hair ribbons and start fraying the ends."

Wess looked around at the brush near the entrance and began his duties while Emilen worked with Gluic to unravel the cloth.

Ambrosius used his weakened powers to help Grewen move the boulder in front of the cave. Afterward, Grewen began breaking down the limbs for firewood as Ambrosius used his depleted energy to hold off the cold winds from blowing into the cave.

Thorik made a clean area to work and prepared the piece of bark that he had stolen from the tree. He placed the unraveled cloth into the now curved bark holder. He sprinkled some oil on the wood to help it get started.

With his hands still shaking from the frost, he struck the flint to create a spark over the oil-stained cloth, but instead, he caught his finger in the process. The numbing pain shot through his hand, and he wrenched away in agony. His nearly frostbitten fingers were already sensitive, and this process was becoming too much for him to handle. Clutching the flint in his unsteady hand, he tried again in vain to get a spark.

After Thorik's break from Brimmelle's years of domination, a newfound determination had welled within him. By the time they had reached the cave, he was fully in charge of the party. He was also fully responsible for their lives. Thorik had to succeed. He had to save everyone. He had to prove that he could be a leader when a leader was needed the most.

Again and again, he tried to start the fire, but his inability to control his exposed fingers made it impossible. He refused to give up as he continued his effort, even though his fingers and knuckles took a serious beating. The burning sensation of the frostbite had already started.

Wess reached over and grabbed his wrist. "It's okay, Thorik. Let me have a go."

It was the first time Wess had called him by his first name, and Thorik hoped Wess was actually sincere. As a Sec, he knew from the Runestone Scrolls that leading was as much about giving directions as it was about knowing when to ask for help.

Reaching out with stiff clawed hands, Thorik dropped the tools into Wess' hands.

Wess had been warming them inside his clothes for the past several minutes, and they were much more flexible. After a few quick strikes, the shower of sparks lit the fire. Wess blew on it. Small at first, cupped in the bark tray, they slowly added more fuel until they had a controlled fire with the smoke leaving by way of the gap left at the entrance. Smiling at his accomplishment, Wess winked at Emilen.

She nodded in appreciation.

Ambrosius released the wind shield once he was comfortable that the fire was strong enough to fight the gusts on its own.

After warming up a little, Grewen broke the branches into pieces small enough to be usable as firewood. As he snapped them down to size, Wess stacked them along a wall.

Thorik located a dozen fist-sized rocks and placed them near the fire, along with all of his Runestones.

"Not you too?" Brimmelle commented. "Does mother now have you cleansing stones?" Glancing at Gluic, he shook his head.

Thorik finished his work, ignoring Brimmelle's words, and allowed the rocks to absorb the heat of the fire. Reaching over with a mink skin, he grabbed the first rocks that he had placed near the fire and handed them to Avanda, Gluic, and Emilen. "Place these between your layers of clothes and in your boots to warm you up. Then place your hands near the area as well."

After taking care of them, he handed warmed stones out to the rest of the party before enjoying a few for himself.

As the stones lost their heat, they were set back near the fire and replaced with hot ones. The rotation of rocks went on all night as they slept for an hour at a time.

❧ 20 ☙

DEL'UNDAY

Ascending the remaining mountainside consumed most of the following day. That afternoon, they exited the crevasse that linked the Mountain King Valley to southern Lakewood Valley. It was a welcoming sight. The wintry storm had not passed over the crest of the mountain range, and the snow and wind were captured within the northern valley. To the south, the sun was shining among the scattered rain clouds onto green slopes and the land beyond.

The entire southern lands could be seen for hundreds of miles in a panoramic view that took the Nums' breaths away. Never had they assumed the world was so vast.

Thick, rich forests and distant mountains covered the east, while scattered lakes and hilly woodlands covered the land just southeast of the mountain pass. The southwest had more mountains as well, but with less vegetation at the upper heights, which abruptly sprung up from the low flat lands. Soft wisps of smoke rose from two distant twin mountain peaks.

To the south and southwest was a great lake that had no end in sight. In the far distance, perhaps on an island, stood a tall, slender line. Its height was even with their own.

"What is that?" Thorik asked.

Ambrosius looked over at the vertical black line in the landscape. "Lu'Tythis."

"What is it?"

"It is a tower."

"It can't be. The top is as tall as a mountain." He was spellbound at the possibility.

Ambrosius agreed. "That's a fair estimate. The large crystal in its pointed top sits several thousand feet high. You will see the crystal's rhythmic light display at night, high in the sky. It's very soothing."

Turning his attention away, Ambrosius focused on the southern valley. "Before us lies the Lakewood Forest. That thin wavy line running from east to west is the Cucurrian River." He glanced over at Thorik, who was fixated on the tower. "Thorik, keep focused." Ambrosius raised his voice. "The river," he repeated and pointed back at its location.

Thorik shook it off and searched for a moment before seeing the thin line that weaved between lakes. "Yes, I see it."

"Good. Along that river is the Dovenar Wall, which borders the entire Dovenar Kingdom. This section protects the province of Woodlen. We will travel down to the entrance of the city of Pyrth. You will go into Pyrth to determine if it is safe for my arrival. You'll have to start conversations and overhear others. Perhaps you can find out something from the local pub or marketplace."

Grewen added, "Also, keep your ears open for someone who goes by the name of the Terra King. I would very much like to know where and when he will be speaking to the people."

"Exactly what kind of conversations are we listening for?" Thorik found himself staring again at the black vertical line of Lu'Tythis Tower in the background.

"You're looking for information about the murder of the Grand Council. Grewen has heard that I may be a suspect, so we need to know how prevalent that rumor is in order to determine our next step. Your best source of information will be the Gentry, but I do not think they will talk to you, so you will need to talk to the Plebeians for information."

"Gentry? Plebeian?" Thorik was confused.

"Simply put, Gentry have the power, and Plebeians do not," Ambrosius summarized.

"How will I tell them apart?"

"If not by the attitude, look at the clothing and jewelry," Ambrosius mused. "You also need to stay clear of the Alchemists. They have great powers and will read you like an open scroll."

"Alchemists?" Thorik asked.

"Yes; you know, wizards, mages, witches, sorcerers, and the like. They wield powers that are magic in nature."

"Is that what you are?" Thorik asked.

Filling his mouth with a handful of local weeds, Grewen smirked and raised his eyebrows, waiting for Ambrosius' response.

Ambrosius was slightly shocked at the question, but attempted to downplay it. "No, I am an E'rudite," he said proudly and humbly.

"What's the difference?"

"We are students of true nature, not just of what you see, hear, and feel, but of the fundamental fabric of everything around us. Over time, this allows us to be closer to the very structure and makeup of all life. One result is that we can, if needed, manipulate many of the threads of this fabric, such as energy, gravity, time, space, and the elements. It is a studied art that requires many years of discipline and guidance to be responsible for such great knowledge. It can take a lifetime to master just a single natural art. To be an E'rudite, one must understand the forces of nature to such a great degree that those forces become an extension of oneself."

Ambrosius continued. "Alchemists, on the other hand, have a spiritual belief that guides them to natural energies, which they harness. They use and mix these energies together to create various reactions, much like a recipe to make a cake. They do not understand why it rises and tastes the way it does, only that it will when ingredients are mixed in the correct manner. This, they call 'magic'."

"Often these 'magic' recipes are complex and sensitive to variation. They struggle to control these reactions, so the Alchemists often enchant objects for later use. Enchanted objects can then be activated in a number of different ways, depending on the substance and enchanter. They have verbal or physical commands, such as breaking objects or getting them wet. This allows others who have even less understanding of these forces to be able to use them." Ambrosius sighed. "Ignorance and power are dangerous bedfellows."

Thorik scratched behind his ear in thought. "So, they're kind of the same but just have different ways to get there?"

"Close enough."

"I'm still confused. Why don't you like the Alchemists?" Thorik asked.

"It's not that I don't like them. I simply find their ways to be very hazardous. They do not understand what they are dealing with, for they focus on the results regardless of the energy they are tapping into. In addition, they don't have the discipline to use it correctly and responsibly, causing them to be reckless."

"They're all like that?" Thorik questioned.

"Most of them. Magic is dangerous; you would be well advised to stay clear of it."

"So are E'rudites more powerful than Alchemists?"

"Not always. It isn't that simple." Ambrosius was tired of the line of questions and ready to move down the mountainside once Draq gave the signal from the air.

"Did the E'rudites create Lu'Tythis?"

"Enough questions for now, my curious friend." Ambrosius could see Thorik was again staring at the tower. "Thorik! There are a lot of things in this world that will be new to you. If you stop to dwell on them all, we will never get anywhere. You must learn to focus on your mission."

Thorik apologized, "Sorry, you're right. We will pass the Woodlen gates and inquire around in the city of Pyrth. If your name is still in good standing, we will find out. We'll return with our findings, make our plans, and then determine who destroyed the Mountain King statue."

"Excellent." Ambrosius looked up into the sky. A solid glare of reflected sun interrupted the shimmering from Draq's scales. "Draq has given us the all clear. It's time to travel down into Lakewood Forest."

"Then let's be on our way," Gluic said, standing next to him, ready to head down into the valley. She had already donned a headdress of local weeds, and she began stuffing a feather in one of the holes in Ambrosius' leather vest.

The day's travel down the mountain was much easier than any other during the trip. A fire-free camp was established that evening to prevent any potential assassins from locating them. It was a cool night for sleeping without a campfire, but they would enjoy it much more than sleeping in the frozen cave on the other side of the mountain.

"Thorik." Emilen gazed up into the southern night sky.

He turned from his camp duties to follow her line of sight. Above the trees, semitransparent ribbons of green, blue, and red waved in the sky like flags in the wind. These misty banners flapped in the windless breeze as they decorated the night's black pallet.

Thorik walked up behind Emilen and wrapped his arms around her waist, pulling her in tight. "Beautiful. This must be the light display from Lu'Tythis Tower." He recalled his conversation with Ambrosius.

They stood, holding each other, watching the event for what seemed like hours before retiring for the night. Upon waking, the colored waves had been banished by the rays of the morning sun.

There wasn't much of a trail as they traveled down the foothills into heavier woodlands. A week or more had passed before they reached the scattered lakes. By doing so, they lost sight of Draq and assumed all was well until he came swooping in to alert them of a small army of enemy warriors.

"How many?" Ambrosius asked the dragon.

"A few hundred, armed with various launchers."

"What kind of close-range weapons are they traveling with?"

"Nothing special; just standard hand-to-hand combat items."

"No rams or bores?" Ambrosius questioned.

"No."

"Odd. Why would they attack the wall without any weapons to get inside it?" Ambrosius considered the options. "There must be another target for their attack. Where are they located?"

"They are camped in a river basin downstream, out of your current path. You should be able to pass through without having any confrontation with them," the dragon said.

"That doesn't sound like the Draq I know." Ambrosius grinned at the thought. "Lead the way. I want to see what they're up to. It may be a small clue to a larger plan."

The party continued in the direction led by Draq while Brimmelle complained that he thought this was a bad idea. With his protest falling on deaf ears, they eventually reached a rim looking down into a river basin filled with creatures.

The Nums gasped at the many Del'Unday species that existed and how fierce most of them looked. When asked, Grewen was indulgent enough to answer the Nums' questions about the various species.

A few tall, red-skinned and red-eyed blothruds barked out orders at the rest of them. Hairless skin stretched over their long snouts, exposing lower and upper teeth. Armed with spikes that naturally grew out of knuckles and elbows, many didn't feel the need to carry additional weapons. Jagged, angled blades grew out of their back spines, undoubtedly for rear attacks. Two large, hairy, wolf-like legs supported razor-sharp claws and thick, pointy spikes. Standing tall with their shoulders back, they were clearly in charge of this battle campaign.

Hunched over, the two-legged Krupes appeared to be the common military guard and soldier. They wore sharply cut dark metal armor and were equipped with various weapons. Since they were completely covered with metal, it was impossible to see the color of their skin or the shape of their face. Only glimpses of eyes could be seen from within the slots of the helmets. Krupes carried out the orders of the blothruds without question and kept the site in order. In fact, they never spoke. They were silent as they went about their chores. The unknown nature of these beasts spooked the Nums.

Several brandercats wandered the camp on all fours in search of their next meal. When standing on their back legs, these lizard-skinned cats were as tall as the Krupes. Crouching down and sitting quietly, they waited for opportunities to eat. While idle, their scales would quickly change colors to match their surroundings, causing them to vanish from sight.

During a delivery of raw Fesh'Unday meat, a brandercat leaped from its hiding place and snatched a hundred pounds of the uncooked food with its multiple layers of teeth. In the few seconds that it took for a Krupe to catch up to the brandercat, over half of the meal was consumed. The cat laughed in a human tone about the event. Running for cover after being poked sharply with the Krupe's spear, it swore bitterly back at it.

It took the Nums by surprise to see all of these new species.

Avanda pointed at a dragon, less than half the size of Draq, with dark coal-colored scales. "That one looks like Draq, but I can't find any that look like you," she said to Grewen.

It was Ambrosius' turn to widen his eyes and raise his eyebrows as he waited for Grewen to respond to Avanda's comment.

"That's because I am an Ov'Unday, not a Del'Unday."

"What's the difference?" she replied.

"Delz are bred for war and conquest. We, on the other hand, are at peace with nature and accept what we have," Grewen taught his class of one.

Brimmelle entered the conversation, saying, "So, Ov'Unday are good and Del'Unday are evil?"

"No, life is not that black and white," Grewen explained. "They justify their actions with their beliefs, teachings, and traditions. What seems evil to us is not an act of evil in their minds. Also remember, history is written by those who are victorious. When the Delz conquer lands, they record themselves as good and the destroyed civilization as evil. Most aggressors do the same."

Brimmelle voiced his thoughts. "I don't trust any of them. Filthy Altereds are all alike."

Grewen flinched at the term. "We prefer to be called Unday. Altered Creatures are things of the past. Slaves of a race long gone."

Thorik added his thoughts with his limited knowledge. "Draq is a Del'Unday, but you get along with him."

"Rare as it is, sometimes Del'Unday and Ov'Unday can coexist. The Delz also have been known to take Fesh'Unday as pets and laborers, something we Ov'Un-days typically do not do."

Seeing Avanda's questioning face, Grewen decided to answer it before it was spoken. "Fesh'Unday are the wild creatures such as wolves, grazers, thrashers, bushdogs, and faralopes."

"Quiet," Ambrosius ordered. Several of the Del'Unday infantry marched toward their position, but fortunately, they marched by without issue. After veering off, they were soon out of sight.

Looking at the camp, Ambrosius thought it seemed odd that they weren't preparing for battle. He then focused on the water system being built along the river. "They plan to stay for a while. They're spending a lot of time making shelters instead of sharpening their blades."

"Perhaps they are training," Grewen suggested.

"Or they are waiting for more reinforcements to arrive." It just didn't look right to Ambrosius.

"Why attack now?" Grewen asked.

"Maybe they have received word that the council has been destroyed. They lost some of their key commanders as well and could be seeking retribution. Also, they know there is no longer any power to hold them responsible for such an attack on Woodlen."

Ambrosius' lips tightened as he thought about his prior statement. "But how would news get all the way to Ergrauth or Corrock in time to prepare an army and have it travel this far within a cycle? I think whomever was feeding the information you intercepted has also been informing Ergrauth. Who else received this information before the incident even occurred? This net of deception is far wider than I had imagined. We must proceed even more cautiously."

"I say we leave before we get caught." Brimmelle's visions of the creatures were making him uncomfortable.

Ambrosius nodded. "I agree; we must depart before dark. There is no more to learn here without putting ourselves at risk."

With that, they cautiously left the Del'Unday area and were back on their way to Woodlen.

Their travels continued without issue for days. Nearing the Dovenar Wall, they camped in a small clearing encircled by thick trees and brush to hide their location. A small stream ran through the camp, providing fresh water and a pleasant sound for sleeping. The plan was set for the Nums to head south to Woodlen after breakfast.

21

WOODLEN PROVINCE

Leaving their companions at camp, the Nums followed the stream down through the woods for a few miles until it spilled over into the side of a deep, fast-paced river.

It was just prior to that junction where an old wooden bridge spanned the stream they had been following, allowing a dirt road to follow the large river along their side of the newly found waterway. The far side of the river hosted an old stone and mortar wall which reached up to the top of the forest's canopy.

Thorik was in awe of the structure's size. "Why would anyone need a wall of such magnitude?"

Brimmelle glared at the unnatural sight in the middle of the lush forest. "Most likely to keep their people locked up inside."

Glancing up and down the raging river, Thorik couldn't see any gateway beyond the wall. With map in hand, he added a quick sketch of their location. "I suggest we go upstream." They had been going upstream most of the trip; going downstream somehow felt like they were heading backward.

"No, the entrance is downstream," Emilen corrected him.

He scanned for any obvious reason why she would contradict him but saw nothing. "Why do you say that?"

"When my father was ill, I took the summer trade visit for him. I'm pretty sure I traveled across this bridge."

Once again, Thorik searched up and down the long road that followed the river and the wall. "It all looks about the same in both directions. It could have been any bridge that you recalled."

"No, it was this bridge."

He made a few more notes on his map. "There could be hundreds of crossings in these parts; how can you tell them apart?"

"Thorik, you have never been outside of the King's Valley. It could be the only bridge in the entire kingdom, as far as you know."

Holding his map before him, he tried to envision the idea. "I find that hard to believe with all the streams around here. Are you suggesting it is?"

"No! I'm not suggesting anything like that."

"Okay. Okay. I just wanted to make sure we head the correct way."

"Next time, I would appreciate it if you would just listen to me, like you do Ambrosius," Emilen said with a verbal stab.

Wess followed Emilen onto the bridge. He hoped that this was the chance that he was looking for to start getting close to her again. "I don't see how you put up with someone that doesn't trust your judgment."

He received no reply from Emilen.

Unsure why she was upset, Thorik tucked his map back into his coffer.

Brimmelle looked over at Thorik in another disappointed moment. "You won't listen to anyone but Ambrosius, will you? The world is filled with good and evil people, and you need to learn who you can and cannot trust." Brimmelle lowered his thick, wild eyebrows and looked straight at Thorik. "You can't rely on anyone but your own kind. You can only trust Nums," he said, thumping his finger against Thorik's chest. Brimmelle turned and headed out to catch up with his mother, who was already on the far side of the stream.

After putting his pack on, Thorik slowly started behind the others. "I don't believe that, Uncle." His voice was far too soft for Brimmelle to hear, which was intentional.

Avanda had waited on the small wooden bridge for him and then walked alongside Thorik for a few moments before taking his hand in hers. "I believe there are good and bad in every type of people." Remembering Grewen and Draq, she added, "Or creature."

Thorik didn't reply as they continued to walk along the road, avoiding the mud puddles from recent showers that accumulated in the wagon wheel grooves. The warmth of Avanda's hand in his made the travel less depressing.

It wasn't long before they reached an old, thick, stone bridge crossing the robust river. With missing stones, it was poorly maintained and was built strictly for function with no artistic designs. Across the river was an area of the Dovenar Wall that jutted out slightly on both sides of a gated entrance. The walls turned at sharp angles and continued into Woodlen for approximately forty feet and stopped at a second similar gate entrance. Both gates had been lifted straight up several yards and could quickly be dropped back down if needed. The catwalk above the wall continued between both gates, with several guards posted upon it.

A large solid metal door hovered horizontally overhead, hinged near the first gate. The removal of a single pin would allow the door to swing down against the wooden seal, preventing any enemy ingress in a moment's notice. The idea of being in the way of it when it swung down made Thorik very uncomfortable.

Wess led them over the bridge and under the first gate before falling in line behind several locals entering and waiting their turn to pass the second gate and then enter the city.

At the front of the line was a faralope-pulled wagon of goods. It had traveled a quarter of the way between the two vertically lifted gates before stopping to be inspected. The wagon was followed by three fishermen carrying the day's catch, and then the Nums. While waiting for the guard to finish talking to the wagon owner, Thorik moved up in front of Wess to lead them into the province. Brimmelle and Wess pulled him back behind them to make sure he didn't say anything they all would regret.

"Where's your permit for this Fesh?" the sergeant on duty asked about the creature harnessed to the front of the wagon. "No Unday is allowed in Woodlen without proper papers unless they are dead and will be used for skins and meat, especially here in the city of Pyrth."

An elderly man sat on the front of his wagon, holding the creature's reins. "I have recently captured this Fesh'Unday and have not had a chance to register it."

Stepping up to the creature, the sergeant inspected the beast. Large hairy hooves braced the two thick legs under its heavy center while the long tail acted as a counterweight to its wide and stubby neck and head. Covered in thin, coarse, white hair over black skin, the Fesh'Unday snarled at the military official who was now standing next to it.

"Wild faralopes are untamable creatures that are dangerous and outlawed." The sergeant raised his gauntlet and slapped it against the creature's back. "You will not receive a permit for this type of a Fesh unless it is for the Melee Matches." He grabbed the creature's mouth with both hands to hold it closed as he used his thumbs to check its teeth and gums. "Looks like we've got a nice one here. She might be entertaining to watch in a fight at the Coliseum."

"She's not for sale nor for fighting," the wagon owner noted. "I need her to haul my goods. The law states that I have one day to register her. Now leave her alone."

Releasing the Fesh'Unday, the sergeant walked over to the man. "Listen up, Plebeian, don't you tell me what to do. I'm Sergeant Borador. Here in Pyrth, I am the law. I could kill this beast right now, throw you in prison for talking back to me, and still sleep well tonight." Grabbing the reins from him, the sergeant began to whip the weak man with them. "You need to think twice before disrespecting Gentry."

The old man fell to his side from the lashings, causing the sergeant to reach farther with the reins. The tugging caused the faralope to rear backwards, losing control and slamming her way free of the wagon's arms. Spooked, it ran wildly.

"Gates down!" commanded a guard from above. The metal rods of the gates were as thick as Thorik's thumb, and were separated at a hand's width apart. Hanging by chains that coiled around large spools on the far side of the wall, the gates were held vertically up in the air by a locking lever, which the guards released.

Both mighty gates came crashing straight down, one just missing Thorik. The first set separated the male Nums from Emilen and Avanda.

The Sec looked at the downed gate and realized he was fortunate not to have been crushed under its tremendous weight. His thankfulness for a lucky break came to an end once he realized he and several others were trapped between the two gates with a crazed rampaging creature.

Avoiding the strong legs of the faralope, the three Nums ran behind and then under the wagon for safety.

Chaos ensued as the Fesh'Unday made its way behind the wagon and lapped the caged area.

Arrows and spears flew from above as everyone except the sergeant ran for cover. An arrow shot into one of the fishermen's legs, making him fall, only to be trampled by the beast on its next loop. Several spears broke through the wagon's deck, nearly catching the three Nums that hid under it.

Sergeant Borador calmly watched the mayhem as he grabbed one of the thrown spears out of the ground. Waiting for the creature's next lap around the temporary pen, he positioned his weapon over his shoulder and behind him, ready to release it with all of his might.

Racing with fear in her eyes, the panicked Fesh'Unday moved out from behind the wagon, only to receive the blade of the sergeant's spear in her chest. She fell to the ground in a cloud of dust as additional arrows shot from above to ensure the sergeant's safety.

As the chains coiled up, the gates lifted, allowing several guards to enter the area.

The sergeant admired his handiwork. "Take the beast in for butchering and push that wagon out of here." He gave his men their orders before addressing the old man again. "If I ever see you trying to enter my gate again, I'll be sending you in for butchering."

The elderly man and his wagon were taken out across the stone bridge and dumped onto the dirt road.

With their day's catch flattened into the ground, the two remaining fishermen carried their injured friend into Woodlen to find him some medical treatment.

Emilen, Avanda, and Gluic caught up to their party as they passed the sergeant's watchful eye. He seemed to like the quiet and obedient Nums with their heads down and eyes lowered, and he let them pass without issue.

Beyond the extremely thick province wall was a large common area for military personnel, including blacksmith shops, armories, a mess hall, sleeping barracks, and stables. Several Unday were chained up along stable walls, only to be released when needed. Beyond this area was a smaller defensive wall that led into a commerce area just beyond two large wooden doors, standing ajar.

Concerned, Thorik didn't like the idea of seeing any creature in chains. "Do you suppose they are Ov'Unday? They look more docile than the Del'Unday we've seen."

Brimmelle grumbled with disgust. "It doesn't matter. They're all the same. Wild, dirty, and dangerous, like the one that just about killed us at the gate."

"I don't think they are all like that. How about Grewen and Draq?" Thorik asked.

"Draq is without a doubt dangerous. I think Grewen can be as well, if provoked. And he's definitely dirty. Either way, none of these creatures should be trusted." Brimmelle ended the conversation by turning away from the stables and toward the marketplace.

Despondent faces were common upon the enslaved creatures chained to walls as well as to the fronts of various military carts and wagons. One creature was seen tied to a post as it was being whipped in punishment for some wrongdoing.

Thorik felt terrible about how they were being treated and extremely guilty about not doing anything to help them. "This is wrong. We can't just leave without trying to help."

Brimmelle fired back over his shoulder, "Leave it alone, Thorik. Every issue in this world is not our responsibility to fix. We're over our heads as it is, so unless you plan on taking on the entire military single-handedly, I suggest you pay attention to what we came here for."

Feeling uncomfortable at the Fir's agitated tone, Avanda moved up toward Gluic and the rest of the Nums that had continued walking.

As he slowly followed Brimmelle, the sight of slavery hit Thorik hard; he wouldn't give the issue up. "Ambrosius wouldn't stand by and allow such things to continue. He would take action and make a difference. He would change things."

Brimmelle turned around and stopped Thorik in his tracks at his disobedient tone. "Change? Ambrosius has corrupted your mind. Change does not lead us to the positive outcome you believe. What good has it done for us?" His voice rose as he lectured his nephew. "We were nearly killed by thrashers, living statues, a freezing winter storm, and a racing Fesh'Unday. For what, I ask you, for what?" He ended with a huff and a glare that weakened Thorik's legs. The Fir was at his limit.

Thorik heard the words and struggled to answer. "To help others. To prevent another attack."

"Another attack? As far as we know, there may have never been a first one. Ambrosius could have simply killed the council. And even if there might be an attack, who are we here to save? These people?" He looked at the military and their enslaved Unday. "Why is it our responsibility to take care of their problems? Shouldn't they deal with it themselves? When have we ever asked for outside help?" It was a rhetorical question, but he waited for Thorik to absorb the obvious answer. "I don't trust outsiders."

Thorik countered his claim. "That's not true. How about Emilen? She didn't grow up in Farbank, so technically she's an outsider."

"She is a Num, born in our spiritual city of Kingsfoot. She's completely different."

"That's the reality of this, isn't it? This is about other species more than about outsiders. What is it about them that you fear?"

Brimmelle rebelled against the questioning with a roar that put Thorik back into his place. "Don't you take that tone with me, Sec Dain. You owe me your life for more than one occasion. The least you could do is show me some respect." Silence fell as Brimmelle straightened his clothes and puffed out his chest while looking at Thorik's disheartened expression. Softening his voice to a stern fatherly level, he added, "There is nothing wrong with keeping things the same. Don't you like our life in Farbank?"

Thorik cast his eyes down to the ground. "Yes, very much so."

"So why would we risk changing it by deluding our minds with their thoughts?

The Mountain King has provided us with rules to live by, and, as long as we do, he keeps the crops strong and the fish plenty." Brimmelle looked at Thorik's lowered head and knew he had captured the obedient boy he once knew. "Let us stop this march across lands that are not ours. We need to take everyone home. This is not our fight, nor is it our responsibility. Our obligation is to Farbank. We should be making sure that our people are safe." Brimmelle was finally comfortable that he had won his case and they would soon be home with things back to normal.

Thorik looked over at Avanda and Emilen and realized the danger he had put them in. Nodding his head a few times, he admitted Brimmelle was right. "Yes, we need to bring them home to safety... once we finish this last request for Ambrosius." Brimmelle was not pleased about Thorik's last comment, but before he could say anything, Thorik continued. "I made a commitment to Ambrosius to find out if it was safe for him to enter the province, and I intend to live up to it. The Mountain King's words in the Responsibility Rune Scroll state—"

"I know what the scroll states," Brimmelle interrupted. He wasn't going to fight the words of his own teaching. Besides, he had won. They were going home very soon.

Thorik and Brimmelle quickly caught up to the others as they reached the open gates leading out of the military area.

Entering Pyrth's market area, Thorik noticed that all the vendor stands were on raised tiled areas, a few fingers above the vine-infested street of worn and broken flat stones. Unlike the tents of Farbank, these were solid structures with overhangs that routed rain away from their patrons.

The other obvious difference was how they conducted business. Bickering and loud haggling back and forth took the place of pleasant conversations and updates on family members. They also did not exchange or trade goods. Instead, customers provided metal pieces much smaller than Thorik's Runestones to pay for their items.

Respectfully leery of humans in this city, they found a Num selling her fruits and vegetables. Produce seemed so much larger and vibrant back at the Harvest Festival, but they were famished and wished to eat.

Greeting the fellow Num with a cheerful attitude, Thorik hoped to start up a pleasant conversation. Periodically, he would stop in hopes that she would join into his dialog. Perplexed, she stared at him, waiting for his selection of items.

He finally realized that she was not going to add to the discussion, so he chose the items they required. Once completed, she requested payment.

"I have no metal pieces. Will you accept a mink skin?" Thorik asked. He received his answer in her impatient facial expression.

Gluic stepped forward with her open bag of gems and gold nuggets. "Maybe I have something she would like?"

"Mother, she doesn't want your river rocks." Assuming they had no value, Brimmelle helped her put the pouch of stones away.

Thorik had to come up with some form of payment. They hadn't eaten in days, except for a few berries and roots. Thinking of options, he pulled out his sack of Runestones. Pausing, he questioned his possibilities one more time before emptying a few into his palm. He knew they had to eat, and the Runestones were the only thing he had of value. As much as his heart told him not to, the looks of his starving family and friends pressured him into making the trade.

The vendor's eyes lit up. "They look authentic. Where did you get those?"

"From the Mountain King," Thorik replied as she took one from his hand. "Would you accept one as payment?" he asked, yet he hoped in a way she would say no.

She inspected it closely. "These are the real thing? How did you come by these?"

Thorik nodded. "My parents gave them to me."

She looked the group over and then returned her attention to Thorik. "So, you must be a Fir. I apologize for my rudeness. I know that the Terra King has several groups of spiritual leaders that journey for him. I just didn't realize that you were one of them."

Brimmelle nearly fell backwards from the shock of Thorik being called a Fir. "Wait! I am Fir Brimmelle Riddlewood the Seventh of Farbank," he corrected her. "These are my followers." He had established their significance with his words as well as with a change of his voice. Suddenly feeling important again, and in charge, he knew things would soon be getting better. It had been a long time coming.

"Joyous," the vendor said. "And I am Mira Shovell of Pyrth. I have so enjoyed your master's resurgence. It has been inspirational to us as of late, seeing that we are under constant threat of being attacked by the Altered Creatures." She continued her conversation as she loaded up several items into a sack for them. "Ever since the Prominent of Pyrth left for the Grand Council, the Terra King has been here to help keep our hopes up."

Excited by her comments, Thorik couldn't believe his luck. "He's here?"

She looked a little confused. "Of course. Aren't you among his core spiritual leaders?"

Emilen thought quickly. "Yes. However, we have just returned from a lengthy special mission for the Terra King and haven't seen him yet. Could you tell us where he is?" Emilen smiled and used her natural charm in hopes that the lady would accept the story.

Mira handed Emilen the sack of fruits and vegetables. "At the theater. Today's resurgence will start soon." She looked back at Thorik and held up the Runestone that she had taken from him. "I'll take this one as payment."

Reluctantly, Thorik parted with the object and tucked the rest back in his sack before tying it off and storing it away. "Where is the theater?"

Mira pointed down the main street and explained some simple directions as she watched Thorik get out a blank parchment to draw a map of the area. He was quick and accurate, but left out many details for now that he would fill in once he had time to sit down.

Brimmelle took another bite of his meal before nudging Thorik. "Put that away and eat something. We all need our strength." As ordered, Thorik returned his notes to his scuffed-up wooden box and grabbed a handful of berries to eat as they walked down the main road.

The road was filled with large two-story houses and shops that peddled everything from jewelry and clothing to house goods and foreign wares. A bright glazing of color and fascia boards covered ancient buildings in the hope of looking fresh and new. But once Thorik looked past the exterior glamor, he saw foundations cracked and walls struggling to support ceilings, while watermarks on the walls exposed prior rain leaks in the roofs.

Avanda did not see any of those things; instead, she ingested the energy of the city with all of the hustle and bustle of its busy streets. The colors of signs and clothes exploded in a vibrant collage everywhere she looked. "This is amazing. I never knew there was so much life and excitement outside of Farbank."

"It's not real; these people are living a fabrication of their own making," Thorik responded as he saw many people wearing old and dirty clothes under their crisp and clean robes and coverings.

Emilen looked over at him. "You sound more like Brimmelle every day. Why are you picking it apart? Just enjoy it."

Wess couldn't resist adding to Emilen's sting. "She's right, Fir-pet, you need to be less critical. Start enjoying life, like these people do." He used the opportunity to once again get between Thorik and Emilen by stepping in front of him, causing Thorik to slow down.

Thorik fired back, "We have a specific task to get done here. We aren't on a holiday."

Wess turned around and walked backwards, keeping pace with Emilen. "You have a task, not us. We didn't make any commitments. Besides, who said you can't enjoy yourself while performing it?" Once completed, he spun around on the ball of his foot to walk along with Em.

Thorik let the conversation end. For years he had heard Wess' speeches about letting go of rules and responsibilities to enjoy life. Right now, the Sec was more interested in finding out more about the Terra King and overhearing any comments about Ambrosius. In doing so, he isolated himself from his group, like he usually did when in deep thought. He fell behind the other Nums as they continued toward their destination.

Stopping periodically to look in the large picture windows of the shops, Wess and Emilen enjoyed seeing the foreign items for sale. They pointed and laughed as they moved from shop to shop, guessing what the use was for many of the unknown objects. Feeling right at home in the city, they greeted oncoming traffic with waves and smiles as though they were locals themselves.

Thorik was jealous of Wess and Em's easy rapport with the locals as well as each other. He felt threatened and inept as he walked down the road behind them, pondering his dilemma. He quietly talked down his emotions. "Now is not the time to take issue with it. Now is the time to get information and get back to camp. I will deal with this later."

He felt several taps on his hand before looking over to see Avanda trying to wake him from his own world. "What is it, Avanda?"

She grabbed his hand before replying. "Did you see that lady back there with the three large feathers for a dress? How about the man walking on sticks as tall as Grewen? Or the kids with blindfolds trying to run across the street without getting hurt? These people are crazy. Isn't it great?" She was beaming from ear to ear.

Avanda had several reasons to be pleased. First of all, they were in a fun place with a lot of new things to see. Second of all, she was happy to see Wess and Emilen spending time together again. She didn't want Thorik's feelings hurt, but she had wanted her uncle to meet someone soon so he would be happy and Avanda could have cousins to play with.

Thorik smiled at her unusual appetite for the insane as they followed the rest of the Nums down the crowded road.

Brimmelle and Gluic led the group around a corner toward the gathering. Stopping for a moment, she searched the ground. "There are no good stones here."

"I'm sure they are the same here as they are in the King's River Valley."

She kneeled down a few times as they walked and picked up a few small rocks. "No, the stones here are dead. They don't speak."

"Well then, it's a good thing you brought your own stones to talk to."

They turned again to see hundreds of people lined up to enter a large open amphitheater. The crowd flooded in and swept Brimmelle and Gluic quickly in its tide; they were washed to the far side of the theater before they could sit down. They were isolated from their party with no way to change seats.

Despite the cramped conditions, additional audience members continued to push their way in on the sides until there was no room left on the long arched stone benches that surrounded the lower stage. Room to stand along the sides filled in quickly, and Brimmelle started to feel claustrophobic.

The remaining four members of Thorik's party only made it as far as the seating near the entrance before they were blocked by others. Split into two groups on opposite sides and one row behind, Brimmelle and Gluic were too far away to hear them over the crowd. Thorik was just happy that they didn't get separated even more before sitting down.

Several red-cloaked guards kept the front seats open for the Gentry. These people were the upper class and apparently had better privileges than everyone else. They wore nicer garments and jewelry and seemed to walk more stiffly and slowly than the rest. The Gentry were humans, whereas the Plebeians were a mixture of human and Polenum races.

"I heard that the Terra King will be granting healings today," a member of the crowd behind Thorik commented.

Another added, "He is also supposed to select his new core spiritual leaders."

Thorik was confused and asked the two men behind him about their statements. "What happened to his last core leaders?"

"They were sent off on a quest. Now he needs a new group for another important task," one answered back.

Large wooden hexagons with rune symbols had been moved onto the stage, followed by large signs painted to look like scrolls with large text for the audience to read. The stagehands finished placing the props on stage as Brimmelle read the scrolls from afar. He was instantly upset as he noticed missing words and passages.

Thorik also noticed these right away and made comments to Emilen and Wess.

"They couldn't write down everything on the scroll and still expect us to read it." Emilen tried to calm Thorik. She was still energized from the excitement of the city and the current crowd.

Thorik looked across the way to see Brimmelle upset and having many words with other audience members near him. The dispute went on for a short time before Gluic ordered him to sit down and be quiet. He was obviously not pleased with the situation.

22

TERRA KING

With a striking of a hammer to the enormous hexagonal gong, everyone in the audience cheered as a tall, thin man walked out into the center of the stage in white flowing robes that covered his feet and dragged behind him. His hands were together in front of him, hidden by the robe's long sleeves. The hood of the robe also covered most of his face, allowing only his long white beard to be seen.

Without saying a word, he raised his right hand with his palm out to the audience to silence the applause. His wrist and arm were thin, pale, and bony with several age spots. Everyone went quiet as the white-robed man waited for all attention to be on him.

"Before the Age of Man, and the prior Age of Altered Creatures, there was the Age of the Notarians. These rulers used their powers to breed the Altered Creatures to enslave our ancestors." The man had a strong commanding voice for all to hear. "During this dark age for humans and Nums, our ancestors created the Rules of Order and the words of the Runestones in an effort to free themselves of the Notarians' torturous rule and stop the devastation of Australis. This is not Num folklore. It was the beginning of the strongest unification of our people in history."

Motioning at himself, he continued, "I know this to be true, for I was there. I was the Mountain King." He paused, and the audience gasped. "My body has been reborn, but my soul and spirit are the same. I recall the paradise we had lived in prior to the destruction brought on by the Notarians."

"Threatened by the movement for freedom from myself and my allies, the Notarians ordered the Altered Creatures to destroy all human and Polenum life. Thousands of additional creatures were created from the depths of evil to wage war upon us and hunt us down. But in doing so, they not only destroyed our civilization, but their creatures went wild and turned on the Notarians in order to take over the world for themselves. I was killed during the final battle, and my thoughts and energy were set adrift."

Brimmelle was shocked at the concept. Sitting motionless, his anger grew over the misrepresentation of his faith. "This is obviously a hoax," Brimmelle said to his mother. "The blood of a Polenum runs through the Mountain King's body. A warrior, a leader, born of grace and honor. Not a human who hides his face and blurs the words of the ancient stones."

The Terra King signaled to one of his red-cloaked guards, who then swung a hammer and hit the gong again. Two Unday were released onto the stage as the crowd gasped and screamed at the sight of these oddities of nature. One resembled a large wolf with long muscular tentacles out of its back that thrashed about as small lightning bolts emanated from the ends. The second creature was about the height of the Terra King's knee as it slithered onto the stage with its slug-like features. It spat acid from extendible spouts, which covered the boneless body.

Ignoring the deadly creatures sneaking up on him from behind, the Terra King calmed everyone down. "After my death, the Altered Creatures ruled Australis for thousands of years, while our people lived as nomadic tribes or as their slaves."

Gurgling and twitching its body, the giant slug turned from a dull brown to a bright red before shooting a stream of acid onto the man's back. His cloak instantly began to dissolve, followed by layers of flesh from his leg. Bleeding on the stage, he was fortunate enough to have most of his muscle still intact. In great pain, he withheld his scream and stumbled a few steps to the side, pointing at the creature. "They tortured us and entertained themselves by having us fight to the death. When we could do no more, they ate us raw while we were still alive."

The crowd shuddered in horror while listening to the tale and watching the creatures surround him for the kill. It somehow justified the current reverse scenario that took place, where all three types of Unday were forced to kill each other for the sport of men.

The Terra King removed his hood. His bald head and thin face were plain, causing onlookers to focus on his large solid white eyes, recessed in pools of shallow gray skin.

Limping away from the two beasts, he had become cornered against the back of the stage. "And although the Age of Man has arrived, it still has not fulfilled itself. Instead of removing the Altered Creatures from our lands, we cower behind walls like rabbits hiding in their holes. This must stop." Stepping forward, he slapped his palm on the slug's body, causing it to change. Starting at the place of contact, the soft mass of the creature turned into water and splashed onto the stage. "We cannot continue to live in fear from them any longer. Why would we hand a coward's legacy down to our children? It is an outrage to procrastinate on such an issue."

The mutated white wolf curtailed his advancement after seeing the watery demise of the other. Growling, he stood his ground and looked at his options to attack.

Turning, the Terra King walked toward the Del'Unday wolf and pointed at it. "We have made attempts to work with these beasts, these deformities, these aberrations with no honor. But we continue to pay the price. Three hundred years ago, the last Dovenar Wall was built, stopping the expansion of men and Nums. Peace was achieved, until we were attacked in Eastland time and time again. And here in Woodlen as well. Unprovoked! Unwarranted! Inexcusable! We gave them no threats." He touched his own leg, and the flesh grew back into place, to everyone's amazement, including the wolf-like creature. "Our only crime was not torching them and returning their ashes to the soil from which they were created." Retreating, the Del'Unday backed off and lowered its head to admit defeat.

The crowd jumped to their feet, yelling death threats to the Altered Creatures. Raised fists and daggers showed signs of anger and a desire for revenge. It took several minutes for the Terra King to regain control. While doing so, he waved the creature away, and his guards escorted it behind the stage curtains.

"Caution, my friends. The winds are changing, and the creatures are gaining ground. We could easily lose everything we have and return to the Age of Altered Creatures. It is at your doorstep right now, as we speak. You must make a choice to help our cause or die under the ruling of beasts."

He paused to get a sense of the crowd, who were violently agitated at the creatures as well as themselves, for not taking action. Yelling protests against the creatures, the crowd was nearly out of control. Those without anger in their eyes pleaded to the king for help against these beasts. Their body language showed him that he was getting the response he wanted.

The Terra King continued, "But all is not lost, for there is still hope. Actions can be taken to help us against them. With the guidance of the Rules of Order and the words of Runestone Scrolls we shall take back this land which is rightfully ours. And those who help will live forever as the Grand-Firs that saved Australis."

He paused again, allowing the audience to cheer and scream in support. Soaking it in, the king allowed the crowd's energy to become contagious to those still unconvinced. Even Emilen and Wess had been swept up in the shouting as the king continued. "Some of you have the strength to be the new heroes of this age. Legends will be written about you, and lyrics will be sung about your courage. You know who you are, down deep in your heart. You know you can make a difference if given the chance. But I cannot take you all, so be sure you will commit to carrying out your forefathers' dreams before standing and joining my core of spiritual leaders," he ended on a very passionate note.

The crowd cheered and applauded enthusiastically.

Em stood up on her seat and raised her arms. "I will join you!"

Thorik was shocked that she had been caught up in the excitement of the speech and forgotten what they had come to do. "What are you doing? Get down before someone sees you." Red-cloaked guards were moving toward various people that stood up. Thorik spotted one guard making his way up the crowded stairs toward her.

Emilen spoke to Thorik as she gazed at the Terra King. "Don't you see, Thorik? This is our way of helping revive our beliefs. We finally have the help we've been looking for to spread our words of wisdom." She looked down at him and reached out her hand for him to take. "Come with me. We will spread the glory of our faith across the land. We will be heroes, and we will be honored. You've been looking for a way to be respected. Here it is. Take it."

"No. This is wrong," he replied as the guard moved closer to them. "This is not how we learned our faith."

"Maybe we weren't told everything we needed to know." She stepped down off the seat, grabbed both of his hands, and looked deeply into his eyes. "Please Thorik, for me. I want you to come with."

He clutched her hands tight, and tears swelled up in his eyes. "I can't. Please don't leave."

"I must," she said as the guard reached them.

"Just you?" the guard asked her.

"No. I'm joining also," announced Wess, quickly stepping forward and placing an arm around Emilen to ensure they wouldn't be separated.

"Wess!" Thorik and Avanda choked out at the same time.

Wess glanced over his shoulder as the guard escorted them down toward the stage. "Sorry, Dain, but I'm taking my opportunities when I can find them. Take care of Avanda for me," he said to Thorik before looking over at his niece. "Enjoy every moment in your life, little girl. Thorik will bring you back home to your parents. Tell them about my heroic contribution to save the world."

Laughing, he walked down the steps holding on to Emilen before yelling back to Thorik, "And good luck with your quest."

Avanda tried to follow her uncle, but Thorik wouldn't allow her to go. He held on to her tightly as she cried for Wess to return.

The crowd showed their support with overwhelming approval as the new core of leaders stood before them. The Terra King asked each one to announce their name so that all could hear who the saviors of destiny were. As each one did so, the Terra King placed a leather necklace over their head. Hanging from the leather was a decorative brass disk with a small crystal sphere in its center.

Thorik's heart broke as Em announced her name and then churned when Wess called out his.

Avanda clung tightly on to Thorik. "Don't leave me, Thorik. Promise that you won't."

"I won't leave you, Avanda. I promise," Thorik said softly as his anger at Wess' irresponsible action grew. He looked over at Brimmelle, who was just as furious at their actions.

After the new group of leaders had announced their names, they were all led off the stage to begin the teachings that were needed to reach new levels of wisdom. It was announced that isolation from all others would be required for an extended amount of time to prepare the new recruits for these tasks.

Thorik now sat with Avanda, wondering to himself as to what he could do. "What were they thinking? We have a promise to keep for Ambrosius. They have a responsibility to Avanda."

He finally turned back to the people behind him that seemed to know a bit more about this process. "Where are they taking them?"

"Don't know. No one knows. Many people have tried to stop their husbands, fathers, and other family members from joining, but have never found them. You would think that they would just be proud of them for their contribution."

It wasn't the answer that Thorik wanted to hear.

Time felt as though it was running fast and standing still all at the same time for Thorik. His mind was spinning with questions about what to do next. He couldn't leave Brimmelle and Gluic at the resurgence, and the crowd was too tight to make his way over to them, so he sat idle as it continued.

The Terra King walked over to one of the large wooden Runestone mockups. It was the Health Rune. "As the reborn Mountain King, I have the responsibility and burden to provide all of the Firs with proper instructions as to how to interpret the Words of Wisdom."

Brimmelle couldn't believe his ears. "Firs are not told how to interpret them. The words are sound and solid, and they speak for themselves."

The people around Brimmelle tried to get him to quiet down.

The king continued, "With this burden, I also have my original abilities to carry out the true powers of the Runestones. This Health Rune, for example, means more than internal and external health. It holds the secret to physical repairs of the body. A broken limb or burns can be healed with it. Come to me if you have ailments and I will demonstrate."

Several people stood up. The guards directed them to Brimmelle's side of the seating area before heading down to the stage.

Brimmelle stood up and shouted, "This is an outrage! The Runestones are not to be used as some spectacle in a theatrical show. They are a belief system of words and the meanings of them. You don't learn the true nature of what these rules and scrolls were created for by being entertained." He looked sharply over at Thorik, who was watching him with more interest than ever before. "You have to read them with your own eyes and come to your own understanding." He had finished with a passion in his voice that he himself did not know he had.

Brimmelle turned to Gluic to see her reaction, only to find her gone. In her place were two red guards who grabbed him and dragged him out of the event. While doing so, he looked toward the stage to see Gluic standing in line to be healed by the Terra King.

He panicked. Never in his adult life had anyone ever physically restrained him. The thought of it wasn't even in his mind until after it was being done. He suddenly realized that he could be in danger from authorities with a higher power than himself. It was a terrifying concept that he had only just begun to understand.

What would become of him? More importantly, who would take care of his mother? The situation became even graver as he realized that his mother was in danger, and he would not be able to help. Not now, perhaps not ever again. "What have I done?"

"Where will he be taken?" Thorik asked the people behind him.

"The Southwind Mines are where most protesters are sent." He was uninterested in Brimmelle's fate.

Thorik's world was quickly falling apart, and, to add to that, Gluic was now walking onto the stage as the man in front of her reached the king.

Gluic smiled and waited patiently in line as others were being healed by the touch of the Terra King. As usual, Gluic had her own agenda that occasionally crossed paths with everyone's goals. It was always a question of how her actions would help later, more than if they would.

"My leg was crushed while logging and had to be removed." The man displayed the wooden replacement below his knee.

"I can see that," the Terra King said. "Do you believe in the Rune of Health's healing powers?"

"Yes sir, I do."

"Do you believe in my power as the Mountain King?" Placing his hands on the man's wooden appendage, he used his powers to alter the makeup of the material into flesh and bone, veins and arteries, and fat and muscle.

"Yes, I believe," the man shouted.

"Again." The Terra King continued the manipulation of matter from wood and air to living tissues. Everyone sat in silence as they watched in awe.

"I believe in your powers and in the words of the Runestones."

Lowering the old man's leg to the ground, the Terra King removed the man's cane. "Walk."

The man stood on both legs and took a step forward, followed by another.

The crowd went wild.

Gluic was next in line, and she smiled at the white-cloaked man while walking over to center stage. She grasped a thin crystal tightly in her left hand. Its powers would be needed.

"I have stones," Gluic told the Terra King in a serious manner.

"And how long have you had them, dear lady?"

"For many years now, long before you were born."

"Show me where you hurt, and I will lay my hands upon you so you will be healed."

Gluic smiled and reached out for his hands. "I will guide your hands to the spot."

He allowed her to take his hands, and upon touching them a sudden shock ran through his body. His chin wrenched down into his chest, and his legs buckled, knocking him to his knees. Spasms shook his body as she held his hands tight within hers. Continuing to shake, he collapsed to the floor.

Lowering onto one knee, she peered into his white eyes as she tightened her grip. "Do you hear me?" she asked in her thoughts to him.

Shaking uncontrollably, he stared into her eyes and responded. "Yes," his mind replied back to hers.

"Good. Now, what's behind this deception? What are your plans?"

A flood of thoughts poured into her head. The images of violent deaths and suffering were overwhelming. Battles of creatures and humans were seen in her mind, as well as a flood wiping out a city and people drowning in horror. She saw his past and his plans for the future: slavery of humans and a Del'Unday kingdom of great power. Trying to wade through all of his hatred, she focused on his thoughts of his current plans. And she saw them. She then saw his silhouette standing above her as she lay dead.

Her mind link had been broken. She looked down to see new life in his eyes, and he smiled from the visions he had just given her. She quickly placed the crystal in her side pouch as she stood.

But it was now Gluic's turn to suffer as he clutched on to her hand. She froze in her tracks for a few moments before she fell to her knees. Her floral decorations quickly began dying and tumbling off her. She reached over with her free hand, grabbed his wrist, and channeled her pain back into his hand, which had a hold on her. Squeezing his wrist, she prevented the pain from diluting itself up his arm. His hand turned dark as heat blisters formed, and his fingers thinned.

Everyone was speechless as they watched the two struggle back and forth on stage.

The Terra King shouted in pain as his hand burned from the acid that oozed out of the blisters on his hand. He released her, and she did the same.

She stood and stumbled a few feet away while regaining her balance. Turning toward the audience, she pointed at the king and announced, "This is…" Nothing else came out.

The Terra King stood up slowly as he watched her. He had used his powers of alteration to change all the air around Gluic into a poisonous gas. She could not breathe.

Gasping for air, she tried to make it off the side of the stage. She needed to get away from him before it was too late. A guard stepped in her path, blocking her escape. A second guard stepped in between her and the Terra King to prevent her from returning. Both guards choked from the poisonous gas, which extended from the Terra King's hands and surrounded her body. She fell back to her knees, then to her side. Then, calmly and quietly, Gluic died.

Silence came over Pyrth's amphitheater while the Terra King worked his way back to the center of the stage. As he regained his strength, one of his servants ran over to show him a document and whisper in his ear.

Thorik was physically and mentally numb. He didn't know how to react to the sight of his grandmother lying dead on stage. He couldn't even feel Avanda holding on to him and burrowing her face into his chest, crying. He couldn't hear or feel anything.

"We are under attack, my friends, my patrons." The Terra King broke the odd air about them. Pointing down to Gluic's body, he said, "This was a servant of Ambrosius, sent here to kill me."

"And it continues to get worse. Our Grand Council has been destroyed, and our final attempt to bridge this species gap has ended. Ambrosius, a longtime supporter of the Altered Creatures and their Unday descendants, has destroyed the Grand Council. Desire for corruption and his personal agenda has removed our only remaining chance for peace." The Terra King knew how to play the crowd with a dramatic pause. "He has been spotted north of Woodlen traveling with several of these perversions of nature. He has come for you and your children. He plans to destroy everything you have in order to return the Altered Creatures to power. For he, my followers, is a Notarian E'rudite, a servant of the original Notarians who enslaved our forefathers."

Over half of the crowd stood up to flee the theater as Thorik debated his options with lightning speed. Grabbing Avanda's hand, he guided her toward the exit along with many others in the audience, who wished to save their families. Thorik's goal was to alert Ambrosius of the Terra King so that the E'rudite would save his family and friends.

"Be seated, my children. You are safe for now. The guard duty at the gates is being tripled, and we have dispatched several of my best enforcers to bring him to justice."

A few of those on the ends of the rows had already left, including Thorik and Avanda, as the red guards regained control and ordered the audience to sit back down to continue with the long ceremony.

23

VENGEANCE

"I loathe hiding!" Ambrosius' current situation was getting the better of him. "I struggle to believe that I cannot show my face inside the Dovenar Walls. The land that I fought my entire life to protect and save." He frequently spiked the end of his staff into the ground in anger while stomping around the temporary campsite.

The camp was far enough from the Dovenar Wall to hopefully evade detection. The open area was hidden with thick brush and had a few logs to sit on next to the small passing stream. They had selected this location to wait for the Nums to return with information because it was off of the main roads and the Nums could simply follow the water back upstream from Woodlen.

"Relax, Ambrosius." Grewen rested on his back with his head propped up on a large, flat rock. Taking a bite from one of the fire logs, he chewed on it while watching the large white clouds pass behind the thick green covering of leaves. With a full inhale of the fresh air, he closed his eyes to take his own words to heart before letting the air out with a slight whistle of his pursed lips. "If the Nums come back and say it is clear, you'll walk right in. This is just a precautionary measure. Think of it as a temporary exile before your triumphant return." Grewen smirked and opened one eye to see his friend's response.

Ambrosius did not react to his words.

Perched on one of the larger logs, Draq watched his companion pace back and forth. "I could fly over to see where the Nums are. Perhaps they have the information you need. I can fly back with it to save time."

"If there are truly assassins looking for me, your recent flying may have already placed us in jeopardy. And if it is not true, Del'Undays are still captured for just being near the Dovenar Wall. You'll end up fighting a chuttlebeast or some other Unday at the next Coliseum event," Ambrosius replied.

"I'd like to see them try. I have no fear of them," Draq replied in a challenging manner.

"I don't want you to take that risk. I need you to care for Ericc if something should happen to me."

Draq lowered his posture a bit. "Your son is safe with my family."

"Son?" Grewen's little ear stubs perked up. "Why, congratulations, my brother. Why didn't you tell me you had spawned new life?" Grewen leaned onto his left elbow and reached over to pat Ambrosius on the back with his other hand. "How old is the little guy?"

Ambrosius nodded a thank you to Grewen with sadness in his eyes. "He's fourteen," he said slowly. "But I haven't seen him since he was six."

Grewen was shocked at this news and stood up. "For the love of Trewek, why not?"

Draq realized that Ambrosius would struggle with this line of conversation, so he intruded in it. "Stay out of his affairs, Grewen. You don't understand what it takes to be in his position."

"What I don't understand is how you could not see your son for eight years," Grewen replied.

"It's for his own safety." Draq worked his way between the two.

Grewen could no longer see Ambrosius behind Draq. "Draq, please move to the side so we can have a conversation." Waiting for a response from the dragon, he eventually reached forward and calmly grabbed the dragon around the neck with one hand and moved him to his side so he could see Ambrosius. He held the dragon out of view with the same level of emotion he would have had with moving a rock. It was just an annoyance; nothing to get upset about.

Draq despised his emotionless removal from the scene, and he thrashed about. Grewen's grasp was too tight to break free from, but wasn't enough to cut off the airflow. To escape, the dragon's tail violently slapped the ground, his wings flapped, and his claws scratched in an effort to break free of the mognin's hand.

"Ambrosius, what's going on?" Grewen asked as Draq swung his spiked tail and lower claws up onto Grewen's outstretched arm. Grewen's skin was thick, but Draq's razor-sharp points impaled him and drew blood. Draq tightened his claws with all of his strength.

"Ouch!" Grewen yelped. Releasing his grip, he tried to shake the dragon off his arm.

"It's okay, Draq. No need for secrets," Ambrosius said.

After one final squeeze on the giant arm, Draq let go. "I will kill you if you ever touch me again," he snarled. Lifting off the ground with his powerful wings, he flicked the mognin blood off his claws down at Grewen before he flew off into the woods, out of view.

Draq was one of the meanest Del'Unday the giant had ever met; he was short-tempered and violent in a fight. Grewen knew the only reason the dragon didn't attack him with full force was because of Ambrosius. Draq was many things, but most of all, he was loyal. He would never abandon Ambrosius in his time of need.

"He'll be fine once he has some time to himself," Ambrosius advised the mognin.

"Tell me about your son," Grewen requested again as he started to bandage the claw marks on his arm.

"After the Dovenar Civil War and the Battle of Maegoth, you left to find inner peace. I had a similar journey of my own. I went to seek guidance from the Third Oracle in the Northern Wastelands. He helped me understand my role as a leader and the need for a council of peers from every part of Australis. Returning to the six remaining provinces, I created the Grand Council and became its facilitator instead of a member, to ensure I didn't influence it."

"I know about the council. But what does this have to do with your son?" Grewen asked as he finished tending to his bleeding wounds.

Ambrosius ignored the question and continued with his story. "During the third year of the council I met Asha at the Greensbrook conferences, and we quickly fell in love. The Grand Council had begun to unite and take important steps forward. Life was good."

"My success must have struck a bad vein with Darkmere since he stirred the hatred within the city of Corrock toward those who followed the council. His legions of Del'Unday would try to stop everything we put in place. But it was me he wanted, not the council. So I resigned my position and began a family hidden away from the public's eyes. My son, Ericc, was born in secrecy and was never told of his heritage. The less he knew about my past, the less likely it was that he would be pulled into my affairs."

"Darkmere must have redirected his forces to search for us, for all was quiet during my absence. Asha and I were able to evade them, often moving just before they arrived to kill us. It was aggravating to always be hiding and living in the shadows, never knowing who our enemies were."

"Our luck ran out while we lived in a small shack on Ki'Volney Lake, just east of your birthplace, near Lagona Falls. I returned home after a day of fishing to find that Asha and Ericc had been taken." Ambrosius fought off the vivid memory as he talked his way through it.

"I followed the tracks of the Del'Unday captors northwest to Corrock, where I found my wife strung up on the city's locked gates. Her arms and feet were tied secure and her dress was ripped and bloody from their torturing of her. They had let her hang there, starving. She hung from the barred door for days, mocked by locals, staring out across the landscape, waiting for me to save her. She was dead before I arrived. The Death Witch, Irluk, had taken her soul and left an empty shell of a body. I had failed her."

Ambrosius stopped only a moment to take a sip of water before he continued, "After lowering her from the gate and saying goodbye, I turned my attention to finding my son. I was furious as I tore the gates apart and entered the city looking for him. I tortured and murdered many Del'Unday before I was told that my son was to be ceremoniously killed by Alchemists in an attempt to prevent Darkmere's premonition of my son killing his own child. I left the devastated south entrance of Corrock with Asha's lifeless body to bury her properly and begin the hunt for my son."

"I searched for months until I got wind of the location where my son was to be sacrificed for Darkmere. During the Eve of Light, in the Alchemist's Temple of

Surod, I found him, and I would have never gotten out of there with him if it weren't for the help of Draq, Chella, and Bovel. Unfortunately, Chella and Bovel did not make it out alive."

"Darkmere and his people have been hunting for my son ever since. Being constantly recognized from my past, I had two options: hide away from civilization with my son or hide him until I could stop Darkmere. It was then that I asked Draq to take Ericc to his home and raise him with his own son and wife. He agreed and has done so ever since. I don't know where he is, for I do not want my own thoughts to betray me. I only know that Draq will keep him safe until he is of mind and strength to protect himself."

Ambrosius looked at the sad face of Grewen before concluding his story, "And now here I am again, hiding. I'm too old for this game, and I refuse to live my life in fear."

"Fear will do you no good, old man," said an unexpected voice from the woods behind him.

The E'rudite used his staff to quickly get on his feet before swiveling to see a man walk out into the small clearing. Middle-aged with short, straight black hair, he wore a red and gold cloak, colored with magical symbols that lined the bottom as well as around the neckline. He held a mere stick of a wand before him in one hand and several strings of beads in the other.

Ambrosius quickly recognized several Del'Unday species moving in the woods as they surrounded the two. He motioned for Grewen to watch his back as he placed his attention on the Alchemist who was approaching him.

Grewen stood up to his full height of over twelve feet, hoping that it would intimidate them and prevent an attack. In addition, he smiled as though he was looking forward to a good fight. His huge leathery hands slapped together with a crash that made everyone stop in their tracks before he rubbed them together to loosen up his wrists and fingers.

Grewen had no intention of hurting anyone; he had vowed not to attack anyone after the massacre at Maegoth. Regardless, he understood that the majority of warfare was mental strategies more than brute strength. He was willing to play this deception of potential violence.

Ambrosius was not one to be intimidated. He took charge of the situation and demanded information from the uninvited guests. "Speak of your business quickly, for I am in no mood for games."

"Your game has ended today." The unknown man nodded his head at one of his Del'Unday.

Without taking his eyes off the intruder, Ambrosius could see a hairy hunchedback Del'Unday move into the clearing. The creature limped from old battle wounds as it dragged something forward. It stopped, leaned down to grab the item, and threw it into the camp.

Thorik was tossed to the ground. He rolled to a stop near Ambrosius, only to quickly jump back to his feet in defiance. He had several scratches and bruises but quickly regained his composure and dusted himself off. "His name is Sharcodi," he told Ambrosius. "They ambushed us halfway here."

Ambrosius glanced over at Thorik in disappointment before returning his gaze back at Sharcodi.

"Don't blame the Num; he actually was of little use to us." Sharcodi had an arrogance that came across in his tone and body language. "When I found them, they wouldn't have seen me even if they were standing next to me," he said with a cocky display of his thorn bush wand.

"Them?" Ambrosius questioned himself. Not knowing if Sharcodi had all the Nums or just a few more, he kept his question silent. "Invisibility spells to sneak up on a Num are not impressive. A wizard worth his weight would have easily found a mognin in a forest from the pounding of his enormous heart. Yet you prefer to capture and interrogate defenseless Polenums."

"I told them nothing," Thorik defended himself. "I promise."

It made no difference to Ambrosius. He had given no information to the Nums that could leak out and harm him. He was much too wise for that. Ambrosius was more interested in knowing where the rest of the Nums were, but he knew better than to ask in front of their company. Perhaps one or more were hiding safely.

"He's quite correct, you know." Sharcodi's smug attitude was thicker than tar. "He wouldn't even give up his own name. Really, it was quite improper, especially for a Num. But the fact is, I found you easily enough without his assistance."

Sharcodi nodded to his strongmen again, who this time brought out Avanda. She was kicking and biting as the Unday attempted to keep hold of her.

"I thank you for the safe return of our companions. But we really must be on our way," Ambrosius stated to Sharcodi.

"I'm afraid I did not come here to reunite you with old friends. I came here for you. Your young one here will stay with us until I am comfortable that you have been properly detained."

The Del'Unday pulled out a long deformed blade and held it to Avanda's throat. The blade appeared to have been bent and hammered back out many times in the past, but the edge was still sharp. Battle-beaten points across the blade pressed against her skin.

Thorik screamed, "No! Don't hurt her!" If it were not for Ambrosius holding on to the back of his cloak, Thorik would have made a run for her. As it was, his actions made the Del'Unday pull the knife up, creasing Avanda's skin.

"What is it that you seek of me?" Ambrosius said without emotion.

"I seek many things from you. First of all, I want to hear you apologize for the Civil War destruction of the Dovenar Kingdom as well as for the attack on the Temple of Surod." Sharcodi looked at a few of the Del'Unday that had surrounded the camp and continued, "Then apologize to these fine Del'Unday for crushing the buildings and innocent families in the fourth district of Corrock. Some of them had families that died in that attack of yours."

Sharcodi stepped toward Ambrosius and Thorik feeling pretty confident about his situation as he continued his speech. "You also owe your Num an apology for destroying his spiritual temple, the Mountain King statue." He patted Thorik on the shoulder and gave him a wink to imply that he was helping him out.

Thorik listened to the speech and was again questioning what other secrets of Ambrosius's past may still be hidden from him.

"But before I forget, I want to thank you for the destruction of the Grand Council. It has allowed us to take back that which is rightfully ours. Now that the council is out of the way and martial law has taken over each city, we can quickly fix those things that aren't up to our standards." Sharcodi smiled as he finished.

Ambrosius stood calmly as his senses monitored Sharcodi's movements walking about the camp. His concern was more for Thorik and Avanda at this point. As dangerous as Sharcodi was, he was no match for Ambrosius. At least he wasn't the last time he saw him eight years ago in Surod as an apprentice. It had taken a while, but Ambrosius finally recognized the name, the voice, and the egotistical Alchemist wannabe that fought alongside his master, the High Wizard Noreldi.

"Typical," Ambrosius said. "You want me to grovel to make you look superior to your small army of misfits."

"Oh, dear, no," Sharcodi replied with a cavalier wave of his hand. "I already know I'm superior to you in many ways. While you were out trying to run Australis with your council, I was working on my craft and perfecting it over the years for just this meeting. You see, you are a relic of what was, and now I am the vision of what will be."

"You're delusional, just like your old master, Noreldi," Ambrosius remarked with a lack of fear. The calmness was bothering Sharcodi, but the use of his prior master's name pushed him to the edge of anger.

It was obvious that he wanted to make Ambrosius squirm and ask for forgiveness, but he would not get any of that on this day. Ambrosius had been broken and struggling for many weeks now and had little patience for this man's futile threats.

"Delusional, am I?" Sharcodi turned his back on them and walked toward the woods. Facing Avanda, he smiled at her as he began to speak quietly. Raising a string of red beads, he moved one bead at a time over his finger to the other side.

Thorik looked to Ambrosius for direction, only to see him tilt his head slightly and squint as though he was trying to listen for something. Moments later, Thorik could see the tops of the trees blowing in the wind and a large dark cloud approaching overhead.

"If you leave now, I will let this intrusion pass," Ambrosius announced. "But I warn you, if you provoke me, my retaliation will be swift."

The wind immediately picked up, causing Thorik to separate his feet for traction against it. He struggled to keep his balance as the wind shifted directions and pulled him back and forth.

Grewen didn't react to the wind as branches and sand blew against him. However, even he had to shield his eyes a few times as the blowing dirt was getting so thick, he could hardly see the surrounding trees anymore.

Ambrosius stood firm as his cloak and tunic flailed in the gusts while he stared at Sharcodi, who was turning toward Ambrosius with his magical components at chest height. His fingers were fumbling with the beads as he softly chanted to them. He then opened his hand enough to drop the string of red beads to the ground.

"Look out!" Thorik shouted as he pushed Ambrosius to his side just as a falling fiery rock missed Ambrosius' back. A shower of flame had begun to strike the group of three with flaming liquefied rocks the size of a Num's fist.

Ambrosius had fallen to his knees. He was smacked several times on the back, preventing him from standing. The fiery rocks had also lit his clothes on fire. Regardless, he continued to make his way to his feet until he was struck in the head, knocking him back down to the ground.

Thorik had his arms over his head as he tried to protect himself and make it over to Grewen. The sand continued to get into the Num's eyes while the wind knocked him over twice more. A falling flame smacked him in the right shoulder just as he reached Grewen's leg.

The rocks pounded on Grewen's back and head as he started on his way to find his friends through the cloud of swirling dirt. He picked up Thorik and shielded him from the falling balls of fire before making his way over to Ambrosius. The back of Grewen's robe had started on fire, and the flames spread across his back.

Ambrosius could feel the burning of his hair and skin as the fire quickly overtook him. The magically invoked wind fanned the flames in every direction as he yelled in pain.

Grewen heard Ambrosius scream and quickly plucked him from the ground only to toss him into the small stream that ran through the camp. Following him to the water, he knelt down over Ambrosius to protect him from the onslaught of burning hail.

Ambrosius raised himself slightly out of the stream and spit out the water that had rushed into his mouth. Taking only a moment to shake off the chill of the water, he sat up next to Thorik, who was also being protected under Grewen's large body.

Sharcodi's sinister laugh could be heard over the howling winds that continued to blow at their faces and the firerocks slapping against Grewen's back as he arched over his friends. "This is the reason I have been looking for you. I have come to slay the mighty Ambrosius. I came to pay you back for the destruction you unleashed on this land and for all the lives you have taken." Sharcodi walked closer to the threesome and smiled as the chaotic weather avoided his own body and those of his companions.

Thorik looked about, seeing several Del'Unday creatures coming out of hiding and into the camp. Thorik and his friends were surrounded by dozens of vile-looking beasts, most with horns, fangs, or claws ready to strike the small group of three.

Grewen's robe had burst into flames across his back as he continued to protect his two friends. In all reality, the attack didn't bother him. In fact, he enjoyed the pounding heat. He could have stood there for hours if it weren't for the other issues at hand.

"You will suffer greatly, but I will not kill you. Darkmere wishes you to be alive to watch your son's death." Sharcodi slightly lowered his wand, which reduced the wind noise. He wanted Ambrosius to hear him loudly and clearly. "Perhaps you are not aware that your son has been spotted by Darkmere's followers. They will soon have him captured."

Ambrosius' blood boiled as he heard the words, and he rose out of the water with a single purpose in mind. Standing up and away from Grewen, he walked to Sharcodi and held his staff out to his side as he lowered his eyebrows and focused on the wizard. "Where is Darkmere?"

A slight flick of Sharcodi's wrist caused the storm to intensify, and Grewen pulled Thorik farther under him to protect him from the increased frequency of the raining fire. The wind was becoming so severe that even Grewen had to brace himself with one arm.

Ambrosius was furious and stood firm while the sand and fiery rain continued to increase directly around him. Even at this great intensity, it never reached his body since it was deflected a short distance before hitting him. "Where is he?" he demanded again of the Alchemist.

Sharcodi appeared concerned that Ambrosius was not affected by his magic and lifted his arm and wand directly at Ambrosius as he chanted a few unrecognizable words.

Ambrosius glared at Sharcodi's outstretched arm and reached out with his mind powers to snap the middle of the wizard's forearm backwards. A loud crack was heard over the howling wind as the end of Sharcodi's forearm was flung up into the air for a moment before falling.

Sharcodi looked on in horror as his useless forearm and hand hung from the rest of his arm like a possum from a tree limb.

Ambrosius used his powers to quickly break the bones every few inches up the same outstretched arm, working from the initial break toward his shoulder.

Before Sharcodi could react, his upper arm snapped in half with a loud crack and fell downward, hanging from the flesh on the remaining stub of his arm past his shoulder.

As quickly as it had started, the wind and fire ended with no traces of ever having existed. Thorik watched his damaged clothes and burns disappear. "What happened?"

Grewen had seen the same events unfold. "It appears to be a masterful illusion."

"I asked you a question," Ambrosius said through gritted teeth. He approached Sharcodi to look at him eye to eye.

Upon seeing this, the Del'Unday launched their attack on the small group. Several ran at Ambrosius and were quickly knocked back into the trees by his E'rudite powers. With a glance at the creature holding Avanda, he used his mind to crush the Del'Unday's hand, forcing the knife out of his grip. His attention to that specific Del'Unday was only momentary as he returned his anger toward Sharcodi.

Grewen grabbed two of the Del'Unday and held them out to shield himself from the oncoming attacks. His enormous hands fit around the back of their waists with an unbreakable grasp. Oncoming Del'Unday swung weapons at Grewen's hands to release them, only to hit their own clan members time and time again. The Del'Unday that were held in Grewen's grasp fought back and blocked the oncoming attacks of swords and spears.

Concerned about Thorik's well-being in the face of an oncoming brandercat attacker, Ambrosius utilized his powers to lift Thorik up out of the way and onto a large tree branch.

Thorik was startled by the aerial flight but quickly stabilized himself on the branch and loaded his bow. He pointed the arrow down at the scaled cat, only to find that it had disappeared. Thorik searched everywhere near the base of the tree and found the same results. The cat was gone.

More Del'Unday left their hiding places to join the attack.

The E'rudite controlled his powers to rotate Sharcodi's feet backward, snapping the man's ankles. This act prevented the spellcaster from running away while Ambrosius addressed the wave of new attackers.

Unable to stand, Sharcodi fell backwards and scattered his magical items across the ground at the edge of the campsite. They were now out of his reach, and he was temporarily without power.

Ambrosius turned around to see eight more Del'Unday attacking. Spears and arrows as well as one of the Krupes who had leaped at the E'rudite were in flight toward him.

He raised his staff in front of him to shield himself from the multitude of attacks from every direction. Just as the invisible shield began to form, the earth below his feet fell inward, causing him to land on his back after a ten-foot drop. A giant Del'Unday terragrub had dug the hole and moved toward Ambrosius, showing its five-foot round mouth of spiraling teeth. Preparing to fight off the carnivorous earthworm, he was struck by the Del'Unday jumping down onto him.

Thorik peered back and forth, looking for the brandercat along the ground, his weapon cocked and ready to fire. His focus was only interrupted when he saw the earth swallow Ambrosius, followed by many Del'Unday, who jumped in after him. It was at this moment that the brandercat leaped from an upper branch onto Thorik, knocking him to the ground.

Thorik quickly rolled to his feet and ran into the woods, away from the cat.

The feline purred with pleasure as it ran to catch him. "Good. Run. The chase adds to the taste of the meal. Your raised heartbeat fills your flesh with hot blood, sweet and juicy."

Thorik darted in and out of the thick woods faster than ever before in his life. He knew of no one that could keep up with him until now. The creature was not only keeping up with Thorik, but he was also gaining on him.

The Num checked over his shoulder to see the creature closing in on him and then fading off. It had blended into the colors of the terrain. Still visible, it blurred and became unfocused. Unable to stop and look, he only had a fraction of a second to peer back, and the creature was no longer visible to him.

Not knowing what to do, Thorik heard the crunching of leaves and sticks under the brandercat's heavy paws. The sounds approached closer and closer until there was a sudden quiet. Thorik darted to the right, assuming the creature was airborne and couldn't make the turn.

He was correct; the brandercat skidded to a halt and turned to run after him back toward camp.

Nearing the campsite, Thorik was exhausted. Splashing his way across the stream, he turned around and fell to one knee. Aiming his bow at the empty forest on the far side of the water for several minutes, he waited for some sign of the creature.

The brandercat slowly moved across the water just downstream of the Num. It moved one foot at a time, slowly in and out of the water, trying not to disrupt the water flow. Success would have been his if it were not for the exceptional eyes of Polenums.

Thorik noticed the small changes in the water downstream and didn't think twice before shooting.

The arrow flew toward the creature as the Del'Unday attempted to jump out of the way, but it wasn't fast enough. The head of the arrow lodged deep into its right shoulder, piercing its chest, causing it to fall with a splash and reveal its location.

The creature's natural brownish-green scales came back to life as it stood up and limped to shore before falling again.

Thorik armed his bow with another arrow from his quiver and walked toward the wounded cat. "Don't move!"

The fallen creature coughed and laughed back at the short hunter. "You Fesh don't have what it takes."

The adrenaline from being chased was still hot within Thorik. He raised his bow up to put the creature out of its misery. Staring down at it, he realized that his goal was not to kill it. Instead, it was to preserve the lives of his friends and himself. "I've done my part with you. The local Fesh'Unday can finish you off." He then turned away.

Blood poured out of the wound of the brandercat as it gasped for breath. "You coward. Kill me now, or the next time we meet, I shall eat you alive!" it shouted as Thorik ran back to the battle.

As Thorik approached the campsite, the ground began to rumble. The hole where Ambrosius had fallen was emitting shockwaves of tremors. In addition to the E'rudite's challenges, more Del'Unday had arrived to surround Grewen. Even so, Thorik had to leave Grewen and Ambrosius to defend themselves. He needed to find Avanda.

With a screech that nearly pierced Thorik's ears, Draq rocketed out of the woods, through the open area, and back into the woods on the far side, picking up one of the Del'Unday in his passing. He was so fast that nobody even saw him. They wouldn't have even noticed him if it hadn't been for the sound and the breeze that followed.

His time away from Grewen had cooled him off, but his return to camp to find them fighting filled him with excitement and the thrill of taking out his victims.

Draq did not slow down as he released the Del'Unday, slapping the creature hard against a large tree, killing him instantly. Turning around for another run, he blasted his way between the trees, back to the opening. Once there, he corrected his course and grabbed his second victim with his claws, launching it off its feet without warning. This time Draq arched his back, bolting his way above the trees and beyond before releasing the creature in midair. He raced the falling creature back to earth with great pleasure. Draq enjoyed the attacks far too much and made this into a game as he passed by his falling victim on his way to the next.

Thorik rushed out of camp towards where he had last seen Avanda. Upon entering the woods, he found the jagged dagger that had been held against her neck. It lay in the dirt, covered with blood. His heart raced at the thought of her being hurt, or worse.

A path of blood trailed its chaotic way amongst the ground, bushes, and tree trunks. Thorik frantically followed the fresh blood droplets to a tree. He stopped and looked for the next clue to their direction.

A high-pitched scream was heard from beyond the next grouping of red-thorn bushes. Racing around them, he found her sitting with her back to him, legs crossed, hunched forward.

He stopped to look for the Del'Unday that had captured her. Not seeing it, he slowly stepped closer to her, only to notice blood on Avanda's clothes. She wasn't moving.

Looking back into the woods for her attacker, he quietly asked, "Avanda? Are you okay?"

She sat up and turned her head toward him. Blood had been splattered, covering her face and shirt, and tears ran down past her cheeks. "I'm fine." After placing a few oddly shaped items into a red and gold pouch, she sniffed and wiped her face with her sleeve. She had found Sharcodi's purse of magic and was intrigued by its contents, but she knew better than to show an adult who may take them from her.

Still very leery, Thorik kept his eyes on the woods while helping her up. "You're covered with blood; are you sure you aren't hurt?"

"It's not my blood," she stammered, and sniffed. "That creature's hand exploded like squished grapes." Twitching at the memory replaying in her mind, she continued, "After dropping the knife, he chased me into the woods."

"So, you lost him. Well done. But he may return." Thorik cautiously led her back to camp.

"Oh, I don't think he'll bother us any longer," she commented. During her fight with the creature, she had thrown several objects at him from within the magical pack she had found. To her surprise, his body shrunk to a mere tenth of his original size and was last seen being chased by a hawk.

She knew her tale of adventure would surely have the purse of magical items taken away, so she placed it under her cloak to keep it in hiding until she returned to Farbank and showed her friends.

Back at camp, an enormous ground quake lifted Grewen and the Del'Unday off their feet before they fell to the quivering earth. A moment of absolute silence blanketed the woods.

Just as everyone started getting back up, a second ground blast occurred. This time several Del'Unday were thrown from the terragrub hole, landing in nearby trees and in the stream.

Ambrosius climbed the walls of the hole. Cut and bleeding, he had survived the many attacks, but his business was not yet completed. The ground was littered with Del'Unday. Some were dead; some were unconscious; others groaned in pain. However, Sharcodi was still alive, and he held valuable information.

Thorik and Avanda had just entered the camp and ran over to help their E'rudite friend out of the hole.

Ambrosius glared at the remaining Del'Unday. Not a word was spoken as the creatures gained their footing and rushed out of the camp, into the deep woods, and away from the E'rudite.

He returned his gaze to Sharcodi, who by this point had dragged himself into the woods. Ambrosius walked over to the spellcaster as Sharcodi got on his knees to beg for his life.

"For the last time, where is my son?" Ambrosius demanded.

Sharcodi groaned as his ribs cracked from Ambrosius' power. "I will not betray the Terra King's orders." He hadn't given up yet. With one last effort of strength, he used his remaining arm to reach for powder within a small side pouch and threw it at Ambrosius' face.

The E'rudite quickly used his powers to redirect the unknown red dust back at him. The powder hit Sharcodi's face and launched a series of horrifying events that ended with his head slowly dissolving away in a gruesome fashion.

Ambrosius took the end of his staff and pushed the headless kneeling body over before checking out the rest of the camp. By this time Draq had the trees littered with creatures and Grewen still held a few battered, but alive, creatures out in front of him.

"Terra King?" Thorik asked as he moved toward the middle of camp. "He's the one that killed Gluic, and his men have taken Brimmelle to a mine in Southwind."

Grewen turned his attention to Thorik. "Gluic's dead? By the hands of Darkmere? Where?"

"No, not Darkmere, the Terra King. And it happened in Pyrth's amphitheater."

Grewen dropped the unconscious Del'Undays that had been used as his shields. "Darkmere and the Terra King are one and the same," he informed Thorik.

Ambrosius declared, "We are going to Pyrth!" He stormed past them as he marched to the Dovenar Wall.

Before following him, Thorik and Avanda quickly moved around the camp, picking up arrows and placing them in his quiver for future battles.

Grewen's face saddened before continuing, "I'm sorry to hear about your grandmother's death, and your uncle's capture. We should be able to cut through River's Edge to get ahead of them and free him in Pelonthal. Where are Wess and Emilen? Are they safe?"

"I don't think so. It's a long story. I'll tell you on the way," answered Thorik as they rushed downstream to catch up with the angry E'rudite.

❦ 24 ❦

FRONTAL ASSAULT

By the time the small group neared the Dovenar Wall, Ambrosius was more furious than ever. He had played back every one of Darkmere's attacks on him and his family's lives over and over again. Visions of his wife and her death flashed through his mind, as well as the battle to save his son. He recalled various arguments of their youth and how they escalated into a Civil War that ended with the horrors of the Battle of Maegoth. Memories of the day when Darkmere killed the king caused Ambrosius to tighten his fists. An endless line of death and pain existed every time he thought about his nemesis.

He had instructed Draq to fly home to see if Sharcodi's claim about Ambrosius' son was true, but Draq would not leave Ambrosius on the eve of battle. The protection of Ambrosius was his primary reason for living; besides, he never turned down an opportunity to enjoy a good fight.

"It's conceivable that Ericc has been seen," Draq admitted.

Already furious, Ambrosius snapped back at Draq, "How is that possible? You have him protected away from civilization."

"He has run off twice before, but we have located him with my son's help and brought him back. No harm was done," Draq responded.

Ambrosius' voice deepened as he addressed his winged friend. "No harm? If he has been seen and identified by any of Darkmere's vultures, his life is in danger, along with your family." Fuming over this new information, he asked, "How could you let this happen?"

"Ericc loathes being confined and refuses to follow anyone's rules but his own. He's much like his father in that regard," Draq spit back with a chilled tone as he distanced himself from the E'rudite and flew over the treetops.

The dragon's words only added fuel to the E'rudite's anger as he stomped through the forest.

The walk toward the Dovenar Wall had given Thorik and Grewen time to think clearly. Walking into the city of Pyrth was not a good decision for any of them. Their attempts to convince Ambrosius of this were wasted as he had already made up his mind.

Draq flew high overhead to warn them of traps, but apparently no one had planned for a frontal assault by an E'rudite, a dragon, a mognin, and two young Polenums. Draq had not led them down the winding stream that Thorik had taken. Instead, he gave them a more direct route to the front gate.

Ambrosius approached the Dovenar Wall gates as the locals moved out of the way and the guards approached. It was an odd sight to observe as a well-known dignitary, now outlaw, walked up defiantly with a huge Ov'Unday and two little Nums in tow.

Emotions were high as the guards along the upper catwalk of the wall loaded their arrows in their bows. A small group of military personnel broke up a quick huddle as the leader motioned for a squad of men to stand on each side of the gate's entrance.

Avanda held on to Thorik's hand and couldn't believe the level of focus everyone was giving them. She had been the center of attention before, but never by such a tense group.

Thorik looked at Grewen for reassurance that they wouldn't be sent to death for this. Grewen responded with a shrug that informed him that he didn't know what would happen.

They both continued in their attempts to talk Ambrosius out of this approach all the way to the gate, which was now lined across the top with guards and a few dozen more on the ground in his way. In the center, Sergeant Borador stood with his hand raised to stop Ambrosius. Thorik recognized him from his first crossing into Pyrth and was not looking forward to meeting him again.

"By the local authorities of Pyrth and the province of Woodlen, you are hereby ordered to surrender yourself for crimes against the Dovenar Kingdom," the sergeant ordered.

"Then it is crimes against myself, for I am the Dovenar Kingdom authority," Ambrosius commanded without changing his stride. "Now get out of my way!"

The sergeant asked again for Ambrosius to stop with no results. "Prepare to fire on my command!" he shouted at the rows of archers on the wall in hopes of making his point clear to Ambrosius. It did not, and the sergeant was not going to allow the most notable criminal ever known to just stroll through his gates. "Fire!" he finally shouted. The bowstrings twanged as they released their arrows.

Grewen quickly leaned over the Nums to protect them from any arrows coming their way. However, it wasn't needed, for halfway through their flight, the arrows took a sudden turn away from Ambrosius and went instead toward the guards in front of him. The military group panicked and tried to get out of the way as the arrows shot into their legs and arms during their escape. The E'rudite powers of Ambrosius were stronger than they had been in some time and were charged with energy from his anger at Darkmere.

Sergeant Borador stood firm in the center of the two gates, waiting for Ambrosius. He had easily evaded the oncoming arrows with a few quick turns of his body. Sliding the broadsword out of its sheath, he grasped it firmly with both hands. "I will enjoy this." He pointed the end of the sword directly at the approaching man.

The rest of the guards ran or crawled to safety behind the second open gate as Borador gave his next order to them. "Lower both gates," he said once Ambrosius was past the first one.

Both gates came crashing straight down, locking Sergeant Borador and Ambrosius in a cage.

Grewen saw the falling gate but could not reach it before it had hit the ground. The gate was quickly locked into place with many metal beams, preventing Grewen from lifting it back up. Once he realized this, he grabbed the gate's thick iron rods and tried to pull them apart. Welded horizontal rods provided extra strength to the gate, making his attempts very difficult. The giant mognin pulled with all of his might, and the bars slowly bent; the snapping of weld joints could be heard over the creaking of metal as he slowly increased the size of the opening.

Thorik yelled through the gate, "Ambrosius, there's too many of them above you on the wall. Get out of there!"

Ambrosius walked toward Sergeant Borador and glanced at the outstretched shining metal blade in front of him. He finally stopped as he heard the rumbling of guards, preparing for their own assault on him from the catwalk above.

Sergeant Borador had him within his snare of fifteen-foot-thick walls topped with heavy armaments and thick wrought-iron gates on each side. At his call, a hailstorm of spears, arrows, and boiling oils would flood down on top of Ambrosius. His captive was trapped. The E'rudite was his.

"I was told to take you alive, but I can live with the consequences of your death." Borador raised his masterful sword over his head to attack the silent prisoner.

Ambrosius abruptly raised his arms out to his sides. His fingers fanned out in his right hand while he grasped his wooden staff in his left.

Fractions of time felt like long frozen moments as everyone felt the enormous power building within the E'rudite.

"Fire!" Borador shouted, causing a launch of a hundred projectiles toward Ambrosius from above.

It was at that moment the walls on both sides of the E'rudite's outstretched arms exploded with fury, shattering the individual blocks into small shards of flying debris. The gate and catwalk behind the sergeant also erupted away from them, sending sharp broken metal rods into the distance.

The guards that once stood on the wall had been catapulted a great distance along with the wall fragments; some landed on roofs of buildings while others were crushed by tumbling blocks. Limbs and clothes were ripped from guards at the time of the detonation, as they flew through the air and struck other military personnel that happened to be in the area.

The devastation to the walls and the surrounding area was immense. Dust from the eruption of power started to settle in on the traumatized environment. Every structure in the vicinity had taken some level of damage from the E'rudite's blast, and the survivors began to slowly move about in confusion.

Sergeant Borador stood paralyzed with fear as he realized the unbelievable force that had just been wielded. He no longer stood in a cage of strength, but instead he was encircled with waist-high rubble. The firm hold he had on his sword, still over his head, weakened under his own trembling.

Reflexively, Borador moved to the side as Ambrosius started his walk forward again, but the military leader had a last moment burst of courage and took a large swipe with his weapon at the passing man.

The sword struck at Ambrosius' back, only to be stopped by an invisible shield just a few hairs' widths prior to hitting him.

Ambrosius glanced over at a large piece of wall that had fallen only twenty yards from them. He enlisted his powers to pull it toward them at a great speed, as though it had been kicked by an invisible giant tenfold the height of Grewen. Just missing Ambrosius' back, the stone slab grabbed Borador in its flight and struck a building on the opposite side.

Ambrosius never looked back to see Grewen bending the gate apart. Nor did he see Thorik and Avanda screaming at him to stop before it was too late. He only focused on what was before him.

He had been in Pyrth enough times to know exactly where the amphitheater was located. The most direct route would be through the marketplace and then a line of government buildings.

Draq screeched into the dysfunctional military courtyard with air acrobatics and assaults on armed soldiers and guards along the walls and rooftops. Attempting not to steal Ambrosius' thunder, the dragon had waited intently for the first explosion before starting his attack. As he flew just feet over the wall's catwalk, guards jumped off both sides to find safety. Those that didn't jump were grabbed during the dragon's passing and tossed over into the river.

The archers fired rounds of arrows and watched in vain, as they could not penetrate the silver dragon's scales. However, if any of the large ballista arrows had hit Draq, he would have been knocked out of the air. Fortunately for Draq, his speed and agility prevented their ability to properly aim such weapons.

A good battle rejuvenated Draq. It was natural and instinctive in every way, as if he was born to do. He teased the rooftop soldiers with false injuries as he plummeted toward the ground, only to pull up at the last second, causing them to jump from their perches. He enjoyed seeing the fear in their eyes.

Ambrosius firmly walked forward, forgetting about his friends, as Grewen continued to bend the bars on the remaining outside gate. His thoughts were primarily on his son as well as the destruction and death he had seen over the years, all caused by Darkmere. "This madness must stop, and it must happen today."

Storming forward, he reached the closed wooden doors that led to the commercial market area. The few guards that tried to defend the city were quickly disposed of with a flick of the E'rudite's fingers as he advanced toward the heavy, wide oak doors. With a clap of his hands, the doors exploded away from him, sending missiles of splinters in every direction but his own.

All went silent as the dust settled and the victims of the attack began to shake off their shock.

Bent door hinges clung to the block wall as the E'rudite entered the next area, which was covered in wood chips, splinters, and dust. Local residents screamed and ran from the destroyed doors as well as the powerful man who emerged from them.

Merchants and patrons rushed out of Ambrosius' path while he marched his way across the large market area toward the steps of the old and decrepit Taxation building. Never veering from his course, he removed shacks and toppled wagons that lay before him. Nothing which might have diverted from his route stood long. Approaching the series of government buildings, he vaguely recognized some of the scattering officials from the area. He only saw one last obstacle in his path between Darkmere and himself. Reaching his arms out and squeezing his fists, a high-pitched wave of energy shot forward, striking and imploding the ancient vine-covered building. It crumbled before him, and a dust cloud rolled high into the air, while rats scurried for new hiding places.

Ambrosius stepped up to the top of the rubble as the dust cleared and the ringing in his ears subsided. Once it did, he heard the screaming of men, women, and children. Thorik and Grewen could also finally be heard from the market. They had broken through the gate and were running up to him while Avanda stopped to help a small child out from under a collapsed wooden roof.

In a nightmarish sensation, he looked behind him to see his friends as they approached, begging him to stop. Past them, he saw a marketplace in ruin as injured people made their way to safety. Children cried while blood dripped down their bodies from cuts and deep gashes caused by flying wooden splinters.

It was a terrible sight of innocent people, bloody and broken. A tornado of anger had caused pain to everyone in its path. Nearly a third of the market buildings had been severely damaged, and distressed residents reached out from under rubble in a plea for help.

"What have you done?" Thorik screamed at Ambrosius.

Ambrosius came out of his rage-filled trance and noticed his trail of destruction all the way from the front gate. It was horrific, and he was distressed in his realization that he had done this to the people he was trying to help.

As the dust finally settled, he turned back around to see the amphitheater filled with injured people from the devastation he had caused. Beyond the crowd was the stage where Darkmere stood, posing as the Terra King.

"I told you he would come for you! Rise, my family, and take him down!" The Terra King pointed at Ambrosius.

The audience members quickly turned into a mob as they stood up on their benches, blocking Ambrosius' view of Darkmere. Picking up stones from the destroyed building, they began throwing them at him as they crowded around.

Stones were easily deflected, but Ambrosius had to choose how many more lives he was willing to put in danger to capture or kill his enemy. At the same time, he had come this far; to stop just feet away from this barbaric killer would be a waste. How many lives would he save by killing him on this day?

He continued to hear Thorik and Grewen yelling for him to stop. But the damage was done, and he pushed toward the stage as the mob was pushed back against his invisible powers. All he needed was a clear view of Darkmere to incapacitate him, so he continued to press forward as best he could without causing any more injuries. He was tempted to simply swipe the crowd off to the side in order to have a clear view of the Terra King in order to stop him. Instead, he elected to avoid causing any more injuries or deaths with such an aggressive move.

The mob continued to grow in size as they screamed and smashed rocks against the E'rudite's invisible protective shield. It had no effect on Ambrosius or his shield. His mind was still focused on the man on stage.

Additional people arrived from the direction of the marketplace, surrounding Grewen. These locals turned into a second mob as they approached with weapons and ropes. Military forces had shown up with large nets and shackles to capture the uninvited Ov'Unday. Grewen turned his back to Ambrosius in order to deal with his own immediate threat.

Draq landed behind Grewen in an attempt to scare off the gathering of humans and Nums. "Ambrosius will take out that other group before he goes after Dark-mere. You and I can take out this one." Draq was clearly enjoying the chaos and battle. His Del'Unday roots were showing through his impenetrable scales.

Grewen's choice to fight would not only cause the death to the frail humans and Polenums, but it would go against his vow not to strike out against others. His opportunity to escape had been closed off with lines of archers along the wall that separated the marketplace from the military courtyard. He realized he was trapped, and that surrendering was the only way to survive without killing someone. "This fight will have to take place at another time. I will not harm these people."

Thorik looked at him in despair. "No, Grewen. Don't give up. Run for it. Get out while you can."

Grewen looked over at Draq as the crowd moved toward them. "Take Ambrosius to safety and then go to Pelonthal to save Brimmelle. They will have to use the River-Green Road to get to Southwind. If I can escape, I will meet you there."

"I will not let these Fesh take you into slavery." Draq moved toward the crowd to attack. His eyebrows lowered and his teeth began to show in a successful attempt to intimidate the locals.

"No more death today, my friend. No more." Grewen extended his arm to his side, preventing Draq from charging them. "I will be okay. Save Ambrosius." He nodded to Draq, indicating that it would be fine, and to do as he asked.

"See you in Pelonthal." Draq lifted off to fly over to Ambrosius.

Grewen looked down at Thorik. "Disappear and blend in. You will be difficult to find in this city. Men think all Nums look alike." He gave a halfhearted grin as he nudged him back into the crowd.

The mob attacked. Grewen stood still as locals applied shackles and chains to him, removing his freedom of movement. He looked up from his newly applied metal neck braces and watched as Thorik found Avanda in the back of the crowd that cheered the capture of this twelve-foot beast.

Meanwhile, Ambrosius carefully pushed his way forward and opened up a gap to see the stage again. This time it was empty, with no signs of Darkmere's exit. There were too many options to check as Ambrosius searched around for a clue. But it was too late, for Darkmere had escaped.

The Terra King's followers continued to tighten around him as the ones in front were being pressed against the invisible barrier. He watched as several of them gasped for air from the pressure of the crowd. Finally, one passed out and fell, only to be replaced by another body being pushed to the front.

Ambrosius realized that even by standing still, he was hurting these people. Civilians that were doing nothing more than protecting their families from the obvious threat: himself. "Attempting to explain to them that the Terra King is the real threat would be wasted energy after what I have done," he muttered to himself. "What have I done? I allowed the end to justify the means, just as Thorik had said I would."

Draq flew overhead. "Bust out of this, Ambrosius. Where to next?"

Ambrosius was feeling sick with regret and disappointment. "Can you lift me?"

"For a short distance." Draq looked up at the row of stores behind the back of the stage. "I can easily get you over the buildings for you to continue your pursuit."

"No," he replied and looked back toward the front gate. "Back to the woods."

"I don't understand. We haven't caught Darkmere yet." Draq looked at the mob around his friend. "And I know you can get out of this situation. Why leave now?"

"Can you or not?" he asked again.

"I can," the reflective dragon responded, frustrated that the attack was over without a victory.

"Then do so." Raising his staff horizontally above him, he held it tightly with both hands.

Draq reached down and grabbed the staff, lifting Ambrosius off the ground. The vacuum of the E'rudite's absence caused a wave of people to flood into the center.

As they lifted over the marketplace, they could see Grewen chained up by the second gathering with the support of many brightly colored military uniformed men. Thorik and Avanda, on the other hand, were nowhere to be found.

"What have I done?" Ambrosius asked Draq as he looked at the destruction that he had caused.

"You were trying to save them from Darkmere's impending wrath," replied Draq, who was working hard to keep them in flight.

"At what cost? At the cost of those I'm trying to save?"

Arrows shot from the ground and tops of walls as they escaped the city limits. Those that hit Draq's scales bounced off with no effect. The same could be said about those hitting Ambrosius' energy shield.

Although they were not fast, they were able to fly into the woods far enough to find a location to land that provided temporary safety. It would take some time for the men to cross the rivers and streams to catch up to them.

Ambrosius commanded Draq to fly home and find out if his son was missing. He needed to know if he was chasing a ghost in another one of Darkmere's games. While he did that, Ambrosius would work his way to Shoreview and then down to Pelonthal before Brimmelle was lost forever in the Southwind Mines.

"Meet me in Pelonthal with good news of my son." Ambrosius raised his hand to signal farewell to his companion, who was flying away.

Lowering his hand back to his side, he sighed and reflected on his mognin friend. "Grewen, what harm have I put you into?" He walked toward Lake Luthralum as he continued his conversation with the giant, who was now many miles away. Grieving would have to come later, for Ambrosius needed to sustain his hope. It was still up to him to prevent the next major attack, which would happen in just five weeks. Everything rested on his shoulders to find out where it would happen and prevent it.

"Now it will be up to Thorik to show his valor and wit to save you, Grewen. The Num is special; you will see. He will rise to the occasion. Yes, it is his time to shine," he told his friend silently, speaking into the breeze, hoping the giant would be safe.

❧ 25 ❧

COLISEUM

―――――

Thorik's Log: 13th day of the 11th month of the 649th year.

Returning to the amphitheater, we were unable to find Granna's body. In fact, the Terra King, his servants, and the new Grand-Firs had all left without a trace. I still can't understand why Em and Wess would leave us so easily. Uncle Brimmelle has been sent to the mines far to the south, which we will travel to after freeing Grewen. We had been told that all unauthorized Altereds must fight to the death in the games at the arena. We met a local named Tilli, who gave us directions to find the Coliseum. We hope to get there in time to save our giant friend.

―――――

Bouncing back and forth from the crowd on all sides, Thorik and Avanda tried to keep up with them in the darkness of the night. Streaming around corners and up steps with the flow of the other patrons, they finally made their way to the inside of the Coliseum and to some open seats.

Flames from large stone oil-filled vats provided light throughout the entire complex. In the center of each vat rose a statue of various small animals, which were displayed brightly by the burning oil that surrounded them.

It had been a difficult weeklong journey to arrive at this event on time, and the two Nums were exhausted, dirty, and hungry. Fortunately, they blended in with the crowd.

The Coliseum was enormous and sat tens of thousands of people in multi-tiered circles that surrounded a sand-filled base. Four significant areas could be seen from Thorik's vantage point. At the bottom was the sandy arena filled with various white marble statues and large bowls of burning oil. The walls around this level were decorated with additional statues depicting scenes of battles and celebrations. Thick wrought-iron gates blocked doorways.

The next level up was for the Gentry and other nobility, decorated with flags and banners of many color combinations. Situated along one side of the Coliseum, it was comprised of several rows at twice the height of everyone else's seating. It also supported its own entrance from one side.

The Plebeian section was dull in comparison, being crowded and poorly cleaned. It was the largest area of the complex and provided multiple entrances for dozens of levels. Filled with various races of humans and Nums, seating was tight, and viewing was not always the best.

Caged sections of the Coliseum filled in as the fourth unique part of the Coliseum. Thorik could see two such sections from where he sat, but assumed that more could be hiding from his view. They branched off from the sandy arena floor level and had iron bars that covered the walls and ceilings of corridors and rooms. They seemed out of place with the white marble backdrop of the rest of the architecture which was coated with lush green plant growth.

Thorik opened his battered coffer and grabbed a few of his drawing supplies as he recorded the Coliseum's layout while they waited for the Melee Matches to begin. Bumped several times by excited viewers, Thorik protected his work from their spills of drinks and food. He sketched out each of the areas to the best of his knowledge with the view that he was given. Adding more detail later, such as the floor statues, caged rooms, overrun ivy walls, and flaming vats for light, he was nearly finished by the time the event started.

Avanda craned her neck to see everything going on. "It's been a while since we've seen Grewen. I hope he isn't injured."

Thorik looked at her concerned face. "I'm sure he's fine. They wouldn't allow him to fight in the games tonight if he wasn't well."

"Are you sure he's going to be fighting tonight?" she asked.

"We just have to hope the information we gathered is correct."

"And if it isn't?"

Thorik didn't like the line of questioning. He knew that the information could be wrong, and Grewen could be on the far side of Australis by this point. "If Grewen were here with us right now, he would say, 'Worrying about it doesn't do any good. It is what it is'. Therefore, we will have to just wait and see."

Avanda crunched her face at Thorik. "You don't do a very good imitation of Grewen."

Thorik chuckled. "Sorry."

She added, "And if he was here to say that, we wouldn't be worrying because we would know where he was."

Thorik opened his mouth to explain what he meant and then decided not to bother.

Spectators roared as several high-level officials walked out to their seats in the Gentry section, signaling the onset of entertainment. Thorik and Avanda watched the best they could as people frequently stood up in front of them to cheer.

A large man walked out into the base level and kicked the sand around a bit as he practiced a few jabs of his sword with one of the statues. He was taller than any human Thorik had ever seen, with arm muscles the size of tree trunks. Blue-colored cloths were waved above many audience members' heads as they chanted his name. "Asentar, Asentar," they continued as the man's muscles rippled with each practice maneuver.

"For the first match tonight, we have Doven's champion of champions, the supreme knight of the Dovenar Kingdom, Asentar, who will single-handedly fight off a tribe of thrashers," a man in bright green and yellow robes announced using a large horn.

The crowd cheered again when they heard his name and clapped, randomly at first. After a short time, everyone fell into sync. Clap, clap, clap, pause, clap, clap, clap, pause. The beat from the audience was strong and intoxicating as each clap was accompanied by part of his name. "As-en-tar, As-en-tar." It was hard not to get caught up in it.

Asentar worked his way past several statues to the center of the sandy stage. Once there, he bent his knees in a wide-leg stance with nothing more than a short sword in his left hand and a thin long sword in his right. Slightly hunched over, ready for the attack, he looked over at the announcer and nodded his head.

All of the thrashers were released from one entrance into the arena and made their way toward the muscular man. Some jumped from statue to statue as they made their approach from the air while others galloped straight for him.

The sight brought back frightening memories for the two Nums and they wondered how this single man was going to fight off over two dozen of these beasts.

A few of the thrashers turned and started to climb the walls to attack the audience. The first of these climbed up a few rows in front of Thorik and pounced on the man in front of him. Clawing at the man's arms, which protected his face, the creature jumped to the man next to him. It continued to leap and attack until a few guards were able to catch it in a net and carry it off.

Though the men were still bleeding from their injuries, the crowd seemed to dismiss the assault as nothing more than a minor accident, and they quickly returned their attention to the battle with Asentar.

A second off-course thrasher climbed up the wall below the Gentry seating area. This one was quickly shot by several nearby guards prior to the beast harming anyone.

Thorik watched as Asentar spun his swords around and sliced at the attackers with an unexpected grace. Using both swords, he moved his body in complete rotations as he fought them off. He stopped momentarily and repositioned himself when time allowed, but never looked overly challenged in his continuing battle.

Over twenty creatures lay at his feet as he spun the swords in the palms of his hands while walking over to the remaining ones, devouring their own dead tribe members. Not missing a beat in his steps, he slashed the last few creatures without an issue.

Asentar walked over to the Gentry and bowed as they politely applauded for him. The mighty warrior turned to the Plebeians and waved his sword in the air as they cheered and praised the Dovenar knight's name.

"I heard that he once killed a chuttlebeast with his bare hands," a member of the audience said enthusiastically.

His neighbor replied, "I heard it was two chuttles at once!"

Eavesdropping on their discussion, Thorik didn't know if they were speaking the truth or if it was the ale talking. Then again, he didn't know what a chuttlebeast was, so it really didn't matter.

Wagering on each fight increased the excitement for the audience, and men in bright yellow clothes walked up and down aisles, taking bets before each battle. Coins were exchanged and sides were selected as they prepared for the coming event.

Some matches included several humans against various Unday, although most of them were strictly creature against creature. Avanda quickly picked sides for each match as she cheered them on. Somehow it didn't seem real to her as she sat in the stands, becoming caught up in the excitement.

Cataloging all the names he could, Thorik struggled to watch the matches themselves because of the bloody content. He even had difficulty watching thrashers being slaughtered.

Sometimes it was difficult to tell the Del'Unday from the Ov'Unday, but the Fesh'Unday were pretty easy to recognize. They acted on pure instinct and had limited communication. A pack of wolves barked and growled together as they fought a family of tigrons. Both appeared to be Fesh'Unday with minimal intelligence.

Melee after melee continued late into the night until the final event. The tired spectators regained their excitement and anticipation as this ultimate rumble was about to start. The yellow-clothed men were surrounded by betting patrons hoping to cash in big.

Thorik watched the insanity of people being entertained by watching creatures fight to the death. If he could have left the event, he would have done so long ago. But he couldn't abandon the possibility that Grewen was still going to show up.

"And now, what you've all been waiting for, the Tri-Unday Midnight War," the announcer said before he attempted to subdue the cheering and yelling of the Plebeians so he could continue. "As you know, before Victor Dovenar built the first wall and safe haven for men, the Altered Creatures ruled Australis." The crowd hissed at the remarks. "As the expansion of the Dovenar Wall continued, men and Nums were no longer threatened by them. The remaining unwanted lands were shared between the three clans of Altered Creatures until a war began. A fight for dominance."

"Tonight, we will reenact their final battle for you. You will see the reason why men cannot trust these evil creatures and why your taxes go to protect our great walls." The announcer paused for the applause and looked over at one of the lead Gentry who nodded back at him.

"Place your bets on which Unday clan will win the Midnight War," he shouted as the crowd scrambled for their last chance to bet.

Thorik and Avanda watched the chaos; they were elbowed and jabbed several times as people made their way toward the sides to bet on the winning clan.

Once that was completed, Thorik could finally see the arena again. White, black, and gray flags hung behind the announcer on a wooden tree stand for all to see. It was a score-tracking system of some type.

The arena's iron-gated entrances also had these same colors hanging over them, although Thorik could only see the white-flagged and gray-flagged entrances. The black-flagged one faced toward the Gentry, not viewable from Thorik's location.

Thorik watched as audience members waved various colored cloths over their heads, as they had done at many of the previous matches. The only difference this time was that more flags were waved and that three colors were in play. It was almost even between the number of gray and black flags, and only a small scattering of white.

Trumpets sounded as the gates opened, and the audience sat on the edge of their seats, waiting for the match to start.

A rumbling could be heard as creatures trampled the hard dirt below their feet on the way out to the arena. One by one, creatures appeared from each gate, many at a full run as they headed toward the center.

Under the gray flag came out the wild creatures, the Fesh'Unday. They were disorientated, angry, and looking for a kill.

"I hope they weren't fed anything for a few days. I want them hungry!" a man waving a gray cloth yelled to his buddy over the crowd's cheering.

His friend waved a black flag as he watched the creatures enter from below their seats in a much more calm and ready-for-battle manner. "Yes! I have a blothrud!" Turning and pointing at his friend, he laughed. "You don't have a chance now."

The blothrud stepped out several yards into the arena before stopping and eyeing the Gentry leaders. Within the Gentry seating area, several Alchemists stood up to make their presence known to the beast. The on-looking Del'Unday stood up like a man with dark red skin and long, powerful, hairy, wolf-life legs. Bladed spikes extended from his shoulder blades and down his massive spine. A large scar on his back could be seen from a distance, running from his upper left shoulder blade down to below his belt on the opposite side. Whatever had caused it had also broken several of the angled spikes on his back. A symbol had been branded by a hot iron on his right shoulder blade.

Turning his head to watch the Fesh enter the arena, the blothrud's long bony face resembled a mix of dragon and wolf features. Sharper and less fleshy than both, his lips struggled to cover his full set of glazed teeth. His eyes were solid red and shimmered in the flickering light of the fiery vats. Wearing no more than a few ripped cloths around his waist, he stood up straight and defiant.

The other Del'Undays kept their distance from the blothrud, and instinctively so did most of the Fesh'Unday as the towering creature stood his ground, surveying the new landscape. He was not nearly as tall as Thorik's friend Grewen, but he looked a lot more intimidating.

Thorik listened to the two men next to him as they named off the creatures fighting on their sides. Every once in a while, they would make a comment about the white team of Ov'Unday but never with much interest.

"Oh, no!" shouted the second man. "You have a chuttlebeast!" He shook his head in disappointment while his friend stood up on the seat and cheered.

The chuttlebeast charged out from under the hanging gray flag with its large cube-like head. Long clumped and matted wool covered this four-footed thick-legged creature. It was nearly as wide as it was tall, and it stood eight feet to the top of its shoulders. This clumsy looking animal apparently only had one strength; to charge and bulldoze anything in its path. It ran straight for the center, crushing every Fesh'Unday and marble statue in its way. If the initial striking of its flat face didn't kill its victims, then the trampling of its massive hooves.

The chuttle raced around the arena, hitting anything in sight, and clobbering several creatures while they stepped into the arena from the entrances. Recessed eyes were covered by the thick wool and could have been part of its misguided head-on attacks. As it continued to charge and run into the side walls, Avanda real-ized it had less to do with the wool and more to do with lack of intelligence.

The beast ran past her location, flooding the area with a pungent, vile, acid-like smell. The crowd had been prepared and held their breath while it passed. However, Avanda and Thorik breathed in the vapors, not knowing any better. They instantly felt the fumes burn the inside of their nasal cavities and spike a quick and powerful headache and lightheaded feeling that lasted only a few seconds. The creature and smell were gone as quickly as they had come.

Thorik listened to the two men continue as creature after creature was released.

"Shane, look over there," said one of the men. "The white team has a mognin."

Grewen stepped out from under the white flag and looked around at the chaos in the arena. Fresh cuts and whip marks were visible on his body, and his ripped robe hung down from his waist. He had been beaten severely and not cleaned up afterward. A large branded symbol could be seen on his right shoulder blade. Despite the injuries, he stood up straight with dignity. It easily made him the tallest creature in the arena.

"He's huge," said the other. "I've never seen a Mog that big before. Is it too late to change my bet?"

Grewen stood on the sand, examining his new surroundings and the audience cheering him on. Spectators waved white flags harder as they realized what they had.

Avanda screamed with excitement. "Thorik, he's here! You were right!"

Thorik was torn between being glad at being correct that Grewen would be here and mortified that his friend was now a slave and gladiator. "Now all we need to do is free him," he said softly as he looked at everything he was up against. Thousands of onlookers wanted to see him battle to the death. There would be no simple way to sneak their main attraction out of sight.

Grewen stood motionless as he watched creatures of all types wage war. thrashers were jumping about while bears stood on their back legs trying to scare off creatures approaching them. It was pandemonium. Over a hundred Unday were now packed into the walled sandy pit.

A tigron leaped at the blothrud with full force, nearly knocking him over. Holding back the tigron's head with his hands, the blothrud reached down with his own mouth and made a large bite into its neck, killing the smaller creature instantly. Releasing the tigron from his bloody jaws, he tossed the dead carcass up into the stands.

The announcer removed one of the gray flags from his three-branched score tree. Several flags had already been removed, and the white team was not doing well.

The Plebeians screamed and yelled as creatures were killed and flags were removed. The fierce thrashers spent most of their time eating from the ever-increasing dead bodies. One by one, the numbers dwindled down until only a few creatures were left.

Grewen had survived mostly because of his size. Most creatures wanted nothing to do with him, fearing his strength. The same could be true about the chuttlebeast and the blothrud.

The chuttlebeast continued to run amuck, destroying everything in its path. During its last tour around the outer wall, it wiped out two Del'Unday, one Fesh'Unday, and four Ov'Unday before seeing Grewen.

The chuttlebeast charged with full force at Grewen, who was still on Thorik's right side. The crowd had been waiting to see this for a long time, and they stood up with excitement. Thorik couldn't see and grabbed his pack to move up to the front.

Thorik nudged Avanda. "It's time."

She grabbed her belongings and followed him.

People were standing everywhere as they waved their cloths for victory, allowing the two small Nums easy maneuvering between them.

"Do we have to use it all?" Avanda asked as they continued down toward the arena.

"Yes, we can't take a chance. We don't know how much will be required."

Thorik reached the front stone railing to see the chuttlebeast collide with Grewen, who had his hands out, ready to catch the beast's cube-shaped head before it slammed into him. His braced feet slid in the dirt as the creature pushed him backwards. He held on to the chuttle with one hand on its flat-boned nose and the other at the ridge over its ear, while he held his breath from the vapors it gave off.

The mognin grappled with the creature and pushed with his mighty legs to slow it down. But the weight and momentum of the chuttle continued to push him back toward the blothrud, who was now seeing an opportunity to attack Grewen from the back as he skidded toward him.

The black and gray team supporters yelled and cheered in delight as they saw the last Ov'Unday prepare to die.

Thorik could tell that Grewen did not know he was about to be attacked from behind. In addition, Grewen's head was nodding forward as the beast's vapors were knocking him out. It was time for them to act.

"Hand it over," Thorik said.

Avanda reached into her sack and removed the flask of Kingsfoot oil. "Not all of it. I want to save some. It may come in handy."

Grewen's backward slide was nearing the two Nums.

"Avanda, there's no time." Thorik's voice was more stern than normal.

Seeing Grewen's dilemma, she quickly handed the glass flask to Thorik.

Thorik wasted no time in throwing it as hard as he could. The central decorative statue within the flaming oil-filled vat was the target, and the Num's aim was right on target. The flask crashed against the stone art of a squirrel and sprayed its contents into the vat, which immediately changed the flame to an ill-green color. The flaming squirrel immediately came to life and leaped off the vat and into the crowd, causing them to scream with fright.

The light from the magical-colored flame quickly coated the inside of the Coliseum. Within seconds, the statues within the arena and along the walls suddenly came to life, just as they had done in Kingsfoot. As the mystical oil continued to work in the arena area, the wall sculptures behind the audience of the Plebeians and the Gentry emerged from their hibernated state. Slowly at first, each newly living being emerged from the hanging vines and from behind tall ferns.

The crowd panicked as the threat of this magic became all too real. The creatures were stone, but they acted like the wild animals they resembled.

Confusion ran everywhere as the stone structures had a life of their own while interacting with the crowd. Gigantic prehistoric creatures moved from their resting places and stepped on those in their way, while stone spiders, snakes, and bugs were released among the crowd.

The Gentry were trapped. The only exit from their seating area was now blocked by several moving statues. In an attempt to escape, they started lowering themselves over the wall near the Ov'Unday entrance.

The blothrud noticed the escaping Gentry and then looked back at Grewen, still sliding backwards. He jumped at Grewen, knocking him off his feet. Both of them rolled to the side, out of the chuttlebeast's path.

"Get on your feet and run this way," the blothrud shouted at Grewen while he got back on his own wolf-like legs and began to run.

Grewen obliged out of sheer confusion at the scene he was now viewing. He didn't understand why the blothrud had saved his life, but this was no time to ask. Standing up, he followed the blothrud at his own lumbering fast pace.

They ran past several animated statues, and the blothrud knocked a few over with his swinging forearm. Grewen looked back to see that the chuttlebeast had turned around and was charging behind them.

"Get ready to jump when I give the word," the blothrud instructed. He watched as the Gentry leaders made their way down the fabric of the white flag to the sandy arena and gated entrance. One of the Alchemists said a few words and pointed his wand toward the locked gate. It unlocked and opened for the Gentry as Grewen and the blothrud stormed toward them, followed by the chuttle.

The Gentry and the two spellcasters raced inside, closing and locking the iron gates behind them just as the giant Undays arrived. The blothrud slowed down to allow Grewen to catch up to him, with the chuttle just steps behind them both.

The Gentry and one Alchemist raced down the caged corridor. The second spellcaster was a witch who held her ground while watching the two tall creatures run at her, side by side. She knew the gate would hold, but didn't want anything thrown through the wrought-iron gates that could hurt her companions. The witch pulled out a small object from her cloak and said a few magical words. In the blink of an eye, she transformed her body into a rock wall just behind the gate.

At the last second the blothrud yelled, "Jump!" and pushed Grewen to the right as he jumped to the left, allowing the chuttlebeast to race between them into the locked iron gates. The bulky beast crashed through the entrance at full force. The gate snapped off its hinges as the massive face of the chuttle charged forward. A momentary scream could be heard as the Fesh'Unday hit the rock wall, exploding debris in every direction, trailed by droplets of red blood. The beast continued to race down through the corridor after the remaining Alchemist and Gentry.

The blothrud stood back up and looked over at Grewen, who had fallen face-first into the sand. Pointing at the mognin, he said, "You owe me one, Mog." He turned and headed down after the chuttle to finish his attack on the Gentry who had imprisoned him. He would now take out his revenge for the torture that they had inflicted upon him.

Grewen finally stood and looked around to find Thorik lowering Avanda and himself down the black fabric over the Del'Unday entrance. Grewen hurried over to them, avoiding the still animated statues.

Avanda greeted him with a hug to his leg. "Grewen, I was so afraid I'd never see you again."

Looking down at the little Num on his calf, he replied, "You worry too much, little one. That never solves anything."

Thorik smiled at Avanda over Grewen's comment. Perhaps he had rendered a better impression of Grewen than she had given him credit for.

Respectfully, Thorik looked at the blood and dirt that covered his large friend, who was giving advice on not getting stressed about life. Grewen was always a source of calm for Thorik, regardless of the situation.

Looking around at all the chaos in the Coliseum, Thorik commented, "Let's get out of here and save Brimmelle in Pelonthal, if it's not too late."

Grewen agreed. "From what I've heard, the Terra King's enemies are being shipped to the Southwind Mines. Their wagons will have to go across the bridges at Eastland. We should be able to get in front of him by crossing the river at River's Edge."

The three entered the Del'Unday tunnel to make a quick escape from the Coliseum and the Woodlen Province.

❧ 26 ❧

SHOREVIEW

Tall thick grass arched from the breeze rolling in off Lake Luthralum. The grasslands ended abruptly at the edge of the bluffs. Dramatic breaks from the rolling fields and mountain foothills were common along the northern shores of the lake.

The grass had turned brown and had gone to seed as the autumn's temperatures fell. On the top of each enormous blade of grass was a feathery bright white plume containing hundreds of grass seeds. Wind blowing off the lake scattered the seeds in the air, giving the appearance of a wintry blizzard.

Ambrosius softly parted the tall stalks of grass in his path to see where he was going. The floating seeds clumped onto his clothes as he headed against the wind toward the lake.

He saw the edge of a bluff and a large oak tree after the grass finally parted. The tree was one of the few that dotted the hills. The grasslands had become so thick that it was uncommon for anything else to grow. This tree must have come of age before the grass had taken over the landscape.

Ambrosius stopped at the tree. Its roots gripped the edge of the bluff as though it was hanging on for its life. Long, thick roots worked their way down the rock walls and into cracks. Nearly a third of the tree's base was hanging over the edge.

Reaching over, the E'rudite touched the old tree with great respect. He understood the tree's daily struggle to fight the strong winds that wished to push it over while the ground underneath it slowly eroded away with each rain.

The long walk from Pyrth had given Ambrosius time to think about what had happened over the past few months. His life had been turned upside down. His mistakes had amplified as his anger got the best of him, perpetuating the issue. Again, a vicious circle of his own making.

"Ambrosius, you fool. How did you let yourself get to this point?" he asked himself.

He could feel the energy flow from the tree into his hand. It was massively strong and rejuvenated his own strength to carry on and to make things right. Patting the tree like one would pat the back of an old friend, he looked down over the edge of the bluff at the city of Shoreview.

The city was in a shallow beach area surrounded by the bluffs on three sides. A large system of buoyant platforms supported streets, homes, and stores. Nearly half the city was floating on the water, while the other half kept it anchored to the land. The thriving city was landlocked and grew in the only direction it could; out into the lake. Thin, long flags flapped in the wind above every home with the colors and crests of the families who lived within them.

Ambrosius stood near a trail leading down to the city. The windy path snaked its way past cliff dwellings randomly carved into the bluff walls. Wooden ladders and walkways connected the dwellings vertically and horizontally in a chaotic maze, working their way down to the dock-like city below. People flooded the wooden walkways as they went about their daily chores, while children played on the interlocking system of bridges, stairs, ladders, ramps, and poles as though it were a giant play area.

Ambrosius worked his way down the trail; it led to a wooden walkway and then to a ladder and then to another walkway before going down one more very long ladder and down several flights of stairs. Stepping out onto the street, he knew there was a less physically challenging way down. He just couldn't recall it. Every time he had visited Shoreview, the path had changed. The city was dynamic and seemed to redesign itself every few years.

The humans and Nums of the city politely greeted him as he passed. A few Ov'Unday could be seen on a distant street, while three children followed him in a game of curious discovery about the outsider. The city, for the most part, felt as he had remembered it to be.

With his feet firmly on the ground, so to speak, he walked across the raised street and out onto the floating section of the city. Pausing several times to gain his bearings from his last recollection of the town, he finally stopped at a shop. The sign out front read, 'Dare to Trade.'

As he attempted to enter, he found the door to be locked. Pulling his staff before him to knock on the door, he heard a snort from behind the door. A second snort and a cough followed.

Ambrosius stepped to the side of the store to discover an open window hanging over the water, several lengths from the storefront. Two boots extended out the window, one resting on the other, toes up to the sky. A fishing pole also extended from the opening, and a line had been cast into the water below.

The snort was heard again as the owner of the boots shifted his feet slightly. A pause of silence was broken with light snoring.

Ambrosius grinned at the opportunity.

Using his E'rudite powers, he slowly unbuckled and then lifted one of the boots off the owner's foot and then lowered it to the water. Raising the end of the fishing line, he attached the boot to the fishhook and placed it back into the lake. A firm pull of the line with his E'rudite powers startled the person in the window.

The remaining boot and the tattered sock disappeared from the windowsill as an unshaved chunky man leaned out of the shop to grab his fishing pole, which had slipped from his grip. Upon grabbing the tool, he reached his thick hand out to pull the line out of the water. His hopes were high as he licked his lips and gazed down into the lake for some sign of his catch.

Unfortunately, his desire was quickly dashed as he saw a boot instead of an enjoyable meal. Leaning out of the window, he pulled the boot up to him, unhooked it, and tossed it back into the water with a grumble. Just as he let go of the item, he recognized the clasp on the side of the boot. Pulling himself back into the store, he looked down and realized he was missing one of his boots.

Back at the window, the hairy-backed shirtless man rested his weight on the sill. Bewildered, he looked out to where he had tossed his boot.

"Looking for this?" Ambrosius said from the other direction.

Swiveling his head and heavy body, he saw the lean man standing on the dock platform, pouring the water out of his boot. "Ambrosius! You son-of-a-Krupe!" he jested. "Best respects. When did ya get in town?"

"Only now."

The man disappeared from sight, and heavy footsteps pounded their way to the front of the store. The lock was quickly released, and the door swung open, exposing the filthy inside of the shop and letting out a foul odor.

The man in the doorway was about a half a head shorter than Ambrosius but weighed twice that of the E'rudite. Shirtless, his large hairy stomach hung over his pants and was coated with leftovers from several meals. Less than a beard and more than stubble, Dare's face was dirty and unkempt. He had limped into the doorway due to an old wound to his hip, which he offset by using a large Fesh'Unday leg bone as a cane. The thick and dirty bone had battle scars and engravings. Fresh blood coated an area toward the bottom of the cane where gray rat fur still clung.

"Dare, it is good to see you." Ambrosius held his breath a few seconds afterward while the smell dissipated in the breeze.

"And I you," he replied, before noticing the burn marks down Ambrosius' face and neck. "What happened to yer face?"

Ambrosius had completely forgotten about his physical scars. It took him a second to realize what Dare was asking about. Touching his tender skin he said, "The Grand Council has been destroyed, and nearly took me down with it."

"You be at Kingsfoot during the purification?"

Stunned, Ambrosius asked, "How do you know what happened at the council meeting, let alone where Kingsfoot is?"

Scratching his chest before removing a few unwanted items from the hair on it, he replied, "Know of Kingsfoot, but not where it is. Beltrow was one of my best customers. Came down from the mountains every summer ta trade. Good man, he was. I knew somethin' was amiss when no one from Kingsfoot came down for the annual trade this year."

"You said 'he was'. How do you know of his death?"

"A flock of them faith-followers came through 'ere after the destruction. They stated their scrolls called it a 'purification' to start over. Said their valley's air went sour and they had ta leave. Talked General Stickwell into trading one of his boats for some gems. As quick as they arrived, they set sail for a place called Elysian."

Ambrosius absorbed the new information. "These have been some troubling times, my friend."

"Better days ahead with you back, I think." Dare rubbed his thumb and finger together over an imaginary coin.

"My last purchase from you filled your pockets full," Ambrosius commented. "Times should have been good to you with such wealth."

"Aye." Dare's eyes shifted as he thought about his reply. "Sweet Nectar of Irr, she is a troubling wench. Her vile grasp drained me within inches of me life and left me dry."

Ambrosius looked at him shamefully. "You traded your full purse for a taste of spirits? Nectar of Irr, no less? You've never been able to stop once you start drinking. You know better."

"I does now. Have no more taste for her. The thought sours me mouth as we speak."

"I hope so." Ambrosius looked around the busy street before he added, "May we talk in private?"

"At your service. Come aboard." Dare allowed Ambrosius to enter his store of odds and ends.

Before shutting the door, Dare noticed two young Nums spying on his affairs and pointed the bloody end of his cane at them. With a loud stomp of his foot onto the street deck, he yelled, "Be gone, ya snooping tadpoles!"

The curious children ran off as Dare limped back into the shop and slammed the door behind him. "Shouldn't 'av used the foot without my boot," he grumbled to himself while shaking off the pain under his torn sock.

Piles of abnormally shaped objects were along every wall. Mostly junk left over from when his shop was filled with exquisite items from all over the land. These items were what didn't sell and had been collecting dust and insects for a long time.

It took Ambrosius a few minutes to get used to the thick air from the decaying musk of dead rats in the corner as well as Dare's own sweaty clothes that lay about. "I am in need of your services."

"What 'tis ya wanting?" Dare rummaged through the junk piles and lifted his remaining valuable items up to show his customer. "A rack of a three-horned estoo?" he asked, but quickly read Ambrosius' facial expression. Kicking a large fanged sandrat out of his way, he collected several other objects. "Cloth fashioned from the webs of Kiri Desert Spiders? Moon Lake gribson peddles? Map of the fabled Pwellus Dementa' city? Seeing orb of the ancient dwellers? Mask of a knight slayer? Ergrauthian spices?" All were answered by Ambrosius' deadpan expression.

"Information," the thinner man explained.

"Ah." Dropping the items on the floor where he stood, he used his cane to walk across the room and right up to him. Leaning his hairy arms against Ambrosius' chest, he moved his face close and looked up at his patron. With over-exaggerated mouthing of his words he said, "Me specialty."

The stench coming off the man's body was nothing compared to the death vapors released from his mouth. Ambrosius turned and walked to the window where Dare had earlier been fishing in his sleep. Clutching the sill, he leaned his body on his straightened arms and took a deep breath of the air from outside. "No games this time. I have to know some critical facts. Do not appease me with half-truths to support your purse."

"Misinformation, I swear. I didn't know it had been tainted." The fat man scratched his backside as he thought. "Never on purpose. Never to my favorite customer." He gave an uncomfortable trustworthy smile to persuade Ambrosius to trust him.

Collecting one last breath of fresh air from outside the window, Ambrosius turned around and leaned lightly on the windowsill before addressing the pathetic-looking man in front of him. "Where is Darkmere going to strike next?"

"Darkmere?" His voice gave away his surprise. "Ain't been 'ere for ages. Last I 'eard, he vanished into the east."

"He is often disguised and goes by the alias of the Terra King."

"Terra King, you say? Name plucks my cobwebs. Again, not through these parts, but within the Dovenar Walls he makes his mark." Dare taxed his brain. "I know of the ill magot and his sickly followers."

"Good. Tell me what you know."

"Not so fast, friend." Dare ran his dirty fingers through his thinning hair to act more businesslike. His hair ended up sticking out at an awkward slant while a fresh coat of thick natural grease covered his hand. "What we be talking in payment?"

"Your life."

"Not like ya to threaten me. What's come over ya?"

"No threat. The information I am looking for will allow me to stop Darkmere from his next attack. If I am unsuccessful, he will probably take over these lands. He eventually will catch up to you."

"There ain't never been a prison I can't escape," Dare boasted. "Proved that to Darkmere himself."

"Who said anything about him sending you to prison? After what you've done in your past, I don't see him keeping you around long."

Swallowing hard, Dare agreed. "Truth it be. But my purse runs dry. Surely it is worth something for my efforts."

"I will make good on my account. But the price will depend on the information given."

"Heave ahead." Dare rested his bone cane at his hip and extended his oily hand out to Ambrosius to lock the deal.

"Agreed." He reached out to shake the man's hand.

Dare slapped his hand into Ambrosius', causing a squishy popping sound from within the grip. Dare placed his other hand on Ambrosius' forearm and held it firm as he tightened his hold on the taller man's hand and shook hard. "Like times of old it is." Releasing his grip, he turned away.

Stepping up to a table, Dare cleared off all objects with one swipe of his cane, crashing the collection to the floor. Grabbing a map from a wall rack, he unscrolled it onto the now empty table. "Terra King been racing up'n down the outer wall like a feline after a sandrat." He pointed to various cities on the map of the Dovenar Kingdom. "Avoids the lake like the plague. Fear of water after the Civil War, I venture." Chuckling at his own joke, his raspy voice caused it to almost sound like a cackle.

"Has there been any pattern to his movements? Any location that he visits more often?"

Dare tried to put the sightings he had heard about into some type of order. Scratching under the roll of his stomach with both hands, he said, "Paces like a caged tigron, it seems. Back and forth, north and south. Never still for long. Only in one place long enough to shout his anger at them Altereds. Flighty as a bird, he is. Lands, squawks, and leaves, he does."

"Is there anyone he has befriended along the way? Any leads we can follow?"

"Friends? Nay. Fear keeps them closer than stink on chuttles." Looking intensely up from the map, he scratched his backside once more. "Promises immortality fer joining his cause. Collecting corpses is more like it. Never seen again are they who join him in crusade. Taken in by the words of the Mountain King to do his bidding."

Looking back to the map, Dare continued, "No battlefield I see for his next attack."

Ambrosius was disappointed. "Keep working on it. Perhaps you will recall more with time."

"Doubt that, I know what I know. That's all there is," Dare admitted. "What else ya be needing?"

"Transport to Pelonthal."

"A ship and a crew, ya say?" Dare stood up straight. "Costly request. Coins needed up front for provisions."

"I have friends here from whom I can obtain the funds. How soon can we sail?"

"Ship I have, captain I be, but a crew and supplies will take a few days to rustle up."

"That will be fine. We sail in two days."

27

DEAD WATERS

Thorik's Log: 18th day of the 11th month of the 649th year.

Thanks to the chaos in the Coliseum that caused local hysteria throughout the surrounding city, Avanda and I were able to escape with Grewen past the outer Dovenar Wall and into the O'Sid Fields. Now that we are free, we wish to give Brimmelle this same gift.

"How did you meet Ambrosius?" Thorik asked his giant companion as they walked along the edge of a shallow gorge. The summer had dried up most of the water at its base, leaving only a small stream until the spring rains could refill it.

The open, dry landscape was colored with patches of short golden grass. Splashes of purple from hard little seeds that clung to the stems of the local govi-weed added color to the O'Sid Fields. The land was dreadfully hard and flat, except for the dry waterbeds and the tall termite mounds.

They had been walking for days outside the Dovenar Wall without the fear of being attacked by humans. Of course, walking in the open Fesh'Unday land was not the safest way to travel.

"It was before the Civil War." Grewen moved Avanda's sleeping body from his left arm to his right to prevent his muscles from stiffening up. His long robe had been patched up as best as possible after being ripped up prior to, and during, the Coliseum games. "Ambrosius had come to Pelonthal after it had been invaded by the Ov'Unday."

"I thought Ov'Unday were pacifists. Why would they invade a human province?"

"It's complicated, Thorik." Grewen walked over to one of the tall, thin mud mounds.

"Everything about Ambrosius seems to be complicated. The facts that I continue to learn seem straightforward and, so far, support Darkmere more than Ambrosius."

"Like I said, it is complicated." Grewen made a fist with his free hand and slammed it deep into the mud mound before stirring it around inside.

"It appears simple enough to me. The Unday continue to attack men and Nums. Darkmere is fighting for the men while Ambrosius is fighting for the Altered Creatures."

The mognin pulled his hand free of the mound. Giant biting termites coated his fist as they attacked his thick skin. "Don't always believe what you hear." Sucking the insects off his hand, one finger at a time, he pushed a few trying to escape back into his mouth.

"I don't have to. I've seen it with my own eyes. We both heard the ghosts in Kingsfoot accuse Ambrosius of murdering the Grand Council. We watched the E'rudite destroy the buildings of Pyrth and kill many of its residents. His allies are Altered Creatures. What more proof do I need?"

Licking the remaining termites from his palm, Grewen looked down at the little Num. It appeared that Thorik was struggling with his own argument. "So why is it even you don't believe it to be true?"

"I don't know; maybe that's what bothers me the most. My heart does not agree with my eyes."

They continued walking in silence for a short time.

"Thorik... did you fight alongside Ambrosius and me against the Del'Unday and the human Alchemist, north of Woodlen?" Grewen asked.

"Of course, I did. You were there."

"Do you consider me your friend?"

"I tracked you down and saved you in the Coliseum Melee Matches, didn't I?"

"So, are you against Del'Unday and humans working together for peace?" Grewen asked.

"No. What kind of question is that?"

"The evidence would imply it. You befriended an Ov'Unday and then fought Del'Unday and a human. Even though these facts are true, they are obviously not complete. You are accusing Ambrosius of the same thing. Seeing his battles and my friendship has given you facts but not the entire story, yet you are using them against him," Grewen stated with no response, so he continued, "Do you consider Draq your friend?"

Thorik gave off a half smile. "I don't know yet."

Grewen nodded his head in agreement. "Me either."

They both lightened the serious mood with a long-overdue laugh.

Thorik's smile lessened a bit. "I wish I knew where I fit into all of this."

"What do you mean?"

"What's my purpose here? I feel I can make a difference in this world, but how? And who am I to become?" Thorik took a deep breath while reflecting on his own questions. "Following Brimmelle's words of wholesome tradition fills me with comfort, but Ambrosius' conviction to change things for the better feeds a fire within me that I feel destined to follow. I struggle between the security of Farbank and the adventure over the next hill." Looking up at the gentle giant, he said, "I want both, but neither of the extremes. How do I find out who I am and what I should believe?"

Grewen warmly grinned and tilted his head toward the Num. "My dear little friend, life isn't about finding yourself, it's about creating yourself."

Thorik pondered the words and returned his gaze to the path before them. It would take some time to fully digest Grewen's comments.

The friends headed south over the O'Sid grasslands that slowly turned to sparse vegetation and Kiri Drylands, always keeping the Dovenar Wall just within sight to their west. Bands of Del'Unday and Fesh'Unday were occasionally seen. Hiding from them often slowed down the trip to a snail's pace. Grewen taught Thorik and Avanda what plants and roots were edible as they stopped frequently to fill Grewen's rumbling stomach.

Avanda made several attempts to catch a horned toad before she was successful. "I'll call you Ralph," she told the critter who rested in between her hands. Its confinement was short-lived as she dropped it and wiped her hands off. "Yuck! It peed on me." She then started the chase again.

Thorik had finished eating and began working on his maps and notes again while Grewen continued to search for enough food to fill his large body.

Chewing on various plant roots, Grewen asked Thorik, "What made you decide to become a Sec?"

"I really didn't have a lot of choice."

Grewen's face shifted and appeared confused. "What do you mean?"

"After my parents died, I was too young to live on my own, so my Granna Gluic took me in to live with her and Brimmelle. He didn't appreciate my moving in, feeling I was too unstructured and childish. I lived with them until this past spring."

"Surely he could remember what it was like to be a youth."

"No, I don't think so. His father had trained him to be a Sec since he was seven. Then he passed away when Brimmelle was only eleven, handing over the Fir status to him. He quickly became the leader of our village with no time to be a child. I think he has always held that against me; the fact that I still choose to enjoy life instead of giving in to be an adult."

"Becoming an adult doesn't mean giving up your ability to have fun and enjoy life," Grewen replied.

"To him it does. And I have failed in doing so. During my long three years living with them, he trained me endlessly to become a Sec. He still insists on it, but I frequently let him down."

"Why do you let him get to you? He's your uncle, not your father."

"He's the closest thing I have to a father. He has saved me from myself on more than one occasion."

"According to him or to you?"

Thorik looked confused. "What do you mean?"

"He has convinced you that you need him. From what I have seen, you do not."

Thorik became defensive. "He's done a lot for me and has looked after me when I needed it."

"Don't get emotional, little man. I was just saying that you have proven on this journey that you can handle yourself. His words should be used more for guidance rather than as orders to be taken."

Thorik sighed. It was easy to say, but he couldn't ever see himself standing up against Brimmelle. Just the thought made him uncomfortable.

Avanda returned to them, displaying her newly caught common brown-back snake. The two-foot-long snake coiled around her wrist and hung its head down, looking for insects as Avanda tried to feed it grass. "Thorik, would you like to meet Ralph?"

"Ralph?" Thorik questioned. "I thought the horned toad had that name."

"Yes. It's easier to remember their names if they are all the same," she added. "Here, you can hold him."

Thorik instinctively stepped back. "No thanks. We need to get going soon. You should put your friend back with his family."

"All right. I think I saw about twenty of his brothers and sisters near here earlier. I'll see if I can find them again," she responded.

Thorik took a quick survey of the ground near him to make sure none of Ralph's family had dropped by to visit.

Grewen smirked. "It's only a snake."

"I know. I was just checking to make sure we aren't forgetting anything."

"You're a terrible liar, Thorik." Grewen chuckled to himself as they prepared to leave the site.

Slightly embarrassed, Thorik looked up to see the endless horizon of the desert. "How much farther do we have to travel?"

"Well, we passed the Woodlen Province, so we probably have a day before we finish passing the province of Doven and arrive at River's Edge."

"Is River's Edge a nice place? I would assume that they allow Ov'Unday if they are going to allow you to cross," Thorik surmised.

Grewen looked a little setback at the question. "It wasn't Para'Mathyus, but it was very nice. Like all provinces, the Dovenar Wall surrounds it to prevent Unday from entering. In River's Edge, the wall lined the province along the crest of the shallow river valley bluffs. The entire province is less than a mile wide in spots, but follows the river for probably eighty miles upstream from Lake Luthralum."

"You said it 'was' very nice. Does that mean it was destroyed by the Del'Unday?"

"It means that it was once a rich valley of growth and prosperity from both a natural and economical standpoint. It was caught up in the middle of the Dovenar Civil War and became the final battle point between the North and the South."

Avanda released the reptile, returned, and started gathering her things so they could start heading south again.

"Who won the Civil War?" Thorik asked.

Grewen shook his head at such a black-and-white thought. "No one. During the last battle, a great wave from Lake Luthralum came ashore and destroyed all lakeside cities. River's Edge was hit the hardest since the wave rolled up through that low river valley all the way to the end of the province. It was eventually stopped by the Dovenar Wall, near Ki'Volney Lake."

"Did they rebuild once the water receded?" Thorik asked.

"Interestingly enough, the waters didn't recede. They stayed at the higher levels, and the coastline cities as well as most of River's Edge remain submerged. The majority of all humans and Polenums at that time lived on Lake Luthralum's shores and were killed by the wave. What you have seen outside your valley is the starting over of a new civilization. You were one of the few totally isolated from these major events of our time. Consider yourself lucky."

As predicted, the landscape became barren and opened up to sand dunes just before they reached River's Edge's exterior province wall. They constructed it with better quality than the Woodlen Province Wall, although it was not as tall.

Unable to climb up the wall, Grewen took a brief break and enjoyed his time basking in the warmth of the hot desert sun as he sank his exposed feet into the hot loose sand of a Kiri sand dune. He missed this kind of weather that reminded him of his days as a youth collecting sand crabs along Ki'Volney Lake.

He sat on the top of a tall dune and leaned back on the Dovenar Wall. Daydreaming of past and future events, he was struck on the head with a metal chain. Looking up, he found Thorik leaning over the edge of the wall.

"Sorry about that." Thorik stood on the massive abandoned wall as he struggled to maneuver the chains he found to make four loops hanging off the side down to Grewen.

Grewen stepped back to ensure he wouldn't get clobbered again. The tall sand dune had already taken care of half the wall's height, so the chains would only have to support him climbing the second half. "Are these going to hold me?"

"Yes. As long as the links are still strong… and these old metal brackets hold tight."

"Thanks for the vote of confidence." Grewen held the four loops of chain links in his hands. Using the different height loops for footholds and pulling hand over hand, he scaled the wall within a few minutes. The hard part was still to come when he tried to pull his body up onto the ledge.

Thorik and Avanda attempted to help the giant, who was at least twenty times their own weight. Grewen barely seemed to move, and their pulling was having little impact on his ascent. But pull they did, and they finally rolled his exhausted body onto the top of the wall.

"That was easy enough," Grewen said between breaths.

"Our next path appears easy as long as you can swim." Thorik peered out across the mile to the far wall of River's Edge. "You can swim, can't you?"

"Not one of my strengths, little man."

"Well, I forgot to bring my boat on this trip. So, unless you have one hidden under your robes, I think you need to learn quickly."

Grewen smiled at the candor and wit of the remark. "It's good to see you found your sense of humor."

"Oh, and by the way, Avanda will ride on your back. She doesn't know how to swim either."

Avanda's ears perked up. "I'm not riding on him. He'll sink."

"I'm inclined to agree with Avanda on this one. mognins sink like a rock," Grewen said.

Thorik replied to the giant, "Is crossing these waters our only chance to catch up with Brimmelle before he goes to the mines?"

"Yes, as far as I know," the mognin answered reluctantly. "They will take the prisoners all the way upstream to the Eastland bridge in order to cross the river. Crossing here is our only chance of getting in front of them."

Thorik nodded. "Avanda, do you want Fir Brimmelle to be lost forever in some mine? Never to see Farbank again? Is that the fate you wish upon him?"

"No," she replied.

"Then we need to get past our fears and cross River's Edge province to save him." Thorik was fully in charge.

All in agreement, they worked their way down the steps on the inside of the Dovenar Wall to the flooded province valley. Grewen slowly stepped into the cloudy water and found that it only came up to his thighs. "Perhaps I'll just walk across. Want a ride?"

After Grewen backed up to the wall's staircase, Thorik climbed onto his back and straddled the mognin's neck while holding on to his large head for support. Avanda stepped onto Grewen's large palm before sitting down for the ride. They were ready for their casual stroll to the far wall.

Making their way toward the center, the water continued to work its way up Grewen's body until Thorik's feet were getting wet. It didn't bother him until he thought he saw movement within the murky water.

"What's the matter, Thorik? I thought you knew how to swim." Grewen chucked as he kept lifting his hand higher to prevent Avanda from getting wet.

"I do, but I thought I saw something."

"In the water?" Grewen glanced down, but the muddy brown water gave little to view.

Avanda had no luck either, although she was excited to see anything to bring some life into the boring river crossing.

"Yes…" Thorik's head spun back and forth, searching the water until he saw a bony figure rise near the surface for a brief moment. "In the water! I saw it again!"

"Where?" Avanda nearly fell off Grewen while jumping around with excitement at the opportunity.

Grewen chuckled at the skittish nature of Nums. "Did you see a ghost or something?"

"Grewen, how did you know?" Thorik kept a sharp eye out for more signs in the river flowing through River's Edge.

"I was just poking fun, Thorik. Legends of this river being haunted by Irluk's drowned Civil War souls are just folklore."

"Your folklore just surfaced and looked me in the face," Thorik rebutted.

Grewen chuckled as the water reached a new level that came up to his chin. "The only haunting of River's Edge is down by Lake Luthralum, where Maegoth used to stand. The rest of the river is safe, as far as I know," Grewen added and winked at Avanda.

She played along. "You're not scared, are you Thorik?"

"No, Grewen's words have given me great comfort," Thorik said with dry sarcasm. He then lifted his feet out of the rising water and grabbed his backpack to set it on Grewen's head. "I hope this is the deepest part of the valley."

Grewen's step fell a little deeper. "I don't think we have even hit the original river yet, so you two will need to swim for it soon. I'll do my best to hold my breath and run along the bottom until I reach the safe levels."

Nervous about what he had seen, Thorik got his gear ready for the swim. "I hope your knowledge of folklore is better than my vision."

Avanda eyed several old metal poles sticking out of the water. She was very nervous about swimming and willing to try anything before having to do so. "Grewen, do you see that row of lamp poles? Perhaps that is a bridge over the old river base." A sparkle of hope was in her voice.

"It's worth a try," Grewen agreed while moving over to it. "Your eyes have done it again, little one; we have found an old stone bridge. I hope it's intact all the way across."

They were now moving slowly as Grewen walked on his toes and paddled with his free hand. This continued for nearly an hour as he tried to maintain his balance so he wouldn't spill his passengers or their supplies into the water. They eventually crossed the bridge and made their way toward the far wall without any issues.

Finally, the water level began to recede down Grewen's neck to his chest.

Relieved, Thorik sighed. "I have to admit that you were correct, Grewen. My eyes must have been playing tricks on me. It should be smooth sailing from here. I'm glad that's behind us."

"See, worrying only adds stress to your life, and it usually has no validity in the first place," Grewen added.

Avanda laughed at both of them. "Come on, Grewen, you both were scared. I saw your face when you thought you had to run along the bottom holding your breath."

"Don't confuse being concerned with worrying," Grewen said calmly just before he shouted out in pain. "Ouch! Something just bit my leg."

Thorik laughed. "I'm not falling for it, Grewen."

"I'm serious. That really hurt."

"Fine, I'll have a look at it when we get to the wall."

"Ouch!" Grewen jerked forward to pull his foot free, nearly knocking Avanda out of his hand. It didn't help. "Something has a hold of me."

Grewen was slowly being pulled backward by one leg while attempting to stop himself with the other leg pressing against the muddy lake bottom.

"What's happening?" Thorik asked.

"I told you; something has a hold of my leg. It's dragging us back into deeper waters." Grewen clenched his large jaw as he made another attempt to pull free with no success. "You two need to jump off and swim the rest of the way while I try to free myself."

Thorik pulled out his hunting knife. "I'm not leaving you again." He then tied Avanda's and his items together and tossed one sack on each side of Grewen's neck for safety. "Stay still, and I'll swim down and cut you free from the plants you most likely got caught in."

Second-guessing himself only for a moment, Thorik jumped into the water and swam down in the thick, murky waters. Even with no cloud cover, it was difficult to see anything as he followed Grewen's body down to his captured leg.

Expecting to see some aquatic vine wrapped around Grewen's foot, Thorik was terrified to find an army of skeletons pulling on him. Remnants of flesh and mud covered the animated bones as they worked together to pull Grewen into darker waters.

Blood could be seen spilling out of Grewen's leg from what appeared to be bite marks. Thorik didn't take time to think as he reacted to the situation. He reached down and grabbed Grewen's thick leg for balance and used his own feet to kick off as many of the skeletons as he could.

Three of the partially flesh-covered dead floated forward and grabbed Grewen's other leg, causing the giant to lose his balance. Avanda splashed into the lake as he was forced to use both hands to stabilize himself.

As his mighty hand reached over to grab her, she was pulled under the murky water, out of his sight.

"Avanda!" he yelled and plunged both arms under the surface to find her. His huge limbs swung back and forth in his attempt to grab her body.

After a few quick passes, he clutched on to her and raised his hand above the water to investigate. To his surprise, he found an animated corpse in his hand instead of the little Num. He tossed its bones into the distance before submerging his massive hands for another attempt.

Thorik held on to Grewen's leg as the large limb thrashed about. He continued to kick the skeletons off Grewen's body one by one. However, it wasn't long before a few of them began attacking Thorik's grasp with a series of bites and by clawing at his own arms and hands.

Feeling another hand on his leg, Thorik reached down to remove it. But upon touching it, he felt more flesh than bone. He grabbed the wrist and pulled it off his leg before raising it toward him. It was Avanda, and she was in a state of horror.

She screamed in fear as her remaining breath escaped from her mouth and floated upward.

Thorik pulled her toward him just as a fleshless face looked over her shoulder at him. This latest skeleton was armed with a rusty sword, and he prepared to shove it through Avanda's back and into Thorik's chest.

Thorik let go of the security of Grewen's body. Kicking hard at the bony arm that held on to Avanda's leg, he pushed Avanda up toward the surface with all his might as the skeleton's weapon made its way toward them.

The water erupted with bubbles in front of Thorik as he waited to feel the rusty blade penetrate his chest. Instead, a large hand reached out and grabbed Thorik around his chest and shoulders. He was instantly raised above the surface to see Avanda in Grewen's other hand.

Grewen was violently kicking at the attacks on his legs. He laid the two Nums over his shoulders and began to swipe at the skeletons crawling up his sides out of the water.

Thorik and Avanda held on to Grewen with their remaining strength as they both gasped for air.

Grewen removed the clinging skeletons from Thorik and Avanda's bodies as he headed for the wall. Once there, he set the Nums down on the wall's lower dry platform and sat down to remove the stragglers hanging on to his own legs.

Thorik choked his way back to life. "Folklore?"

"So I've heard," Grewen replied as he tended to his own wounds.

❦ 28 ❧

MYTH'UNDAY

The three friends had climbed out of River's Edge by passing over the southern Dovenar Wall. They walked toward Pelonthal on a dirt path that followed the province's wall to the west. It wasn't long before they were again dry from the day's sun and heat.

After several long, hot days, they had made it past Solann Ridge. The temperatures had begun to fall, and the foliage was much more pleasing to the Nums. Lightly wooded areas along soft grassy hills and meadows greeted the travelers.

Grewen could tell the Nums enjoyed this climate much more than the dry heat of the desert. "Welcome to the edge of the Mythical Forest," he announced. "Home of the Myth'Unday."

"There's another Altered Creature clan?" Thorik asked.

"Not exactly. Myth'Undays were created by the Great Oracle to bring a playfulness to our land, as well as to entertain her. Instead of being an alteration of other animals and creatures, they were created from the energy that exists in the forest."

Avanda's curiosity kicked in, and she questioned the giant before Thorik had the chance. "What do they look like?"

"I'm sorry to say that you most likely will never find out."

"Why not?" she asked.

"Because they may not wish to be seen," Grewen continued. "They would rather play with you."

"How can they play with me if I can't see them?"

Grewen smiled. "Have you ever walked through the woods and heard noises like someone else is there, but they are not? Or have you seen movement out of the corner of your eye, but it stops before you can focus on the area?"

Avanda nodded her head. "Yes."

"That would be them. They live in most forests, but this region is their home.

The Floral Faeries, Brush Brownies, Leaf Pixies, and the rest of the inquisitive Myth'Unday species all originated from this forest.

Thorik listened to the tale. "Sounds much better than living corpses." He smiled at his young student. "Avanda, if we are lucky, maybe you'll get to see one."

Grewen cleared his throat and shook his head at Thorik. "I don't think you want to meet any Myth'Unday."

Thorik was confused. "Why not?"

"Many have gone into the timberland to see or catch a Myth'Unday, and most never returned. The few that have were changed for life: always looking over their shoulders and afraid of their own shadows." Grewen searched for a moment in the trees. "No, I wish not to see any Myth'Unday during our travels."

As darkness approached, they stopped just off to the side of the road by a small spring to stay the night. A canopy of light green leaves overhead acted as a blanket to keep the warmth in the campsite.

"Grewen, are we going to be safe here from the Myth'Unday?" asked Avanda in a timid voice.

Grewen waved her over to him as he lay on his side. "Come over here, little one. I won't let anyone harm you."

Avanda came over to him and cuddled up against his chest. He covered her with a blanket before placing his hand just above her to keep her warmth in and any night dew out.

Thorik lay down and relaxed near the spring. "How much farther until Pelonthal?"

"We have less than a day's walk to get there. Once we enter, the River-Green Road follows the inside of Pelonthal's Dovenar Wall from River's Edge all the way to Greensbrook."

"Shouldn't we be walking all night to make sure they don't get ahead of us?" Thorik asked.

"No. Remember, they will have to go all the way around River's Edge, through Eastland, before traveling all the way back to Pelonthal. They will have to pass us on this road to pass us at all."

"Why wouldn't they take a boat or ferry across?"

"Apparently, some legendary folklore seems to scare them away from crossing over River's Edge." Grewen winked at Avanda.

She smiled and closed her tired eyes.

Thorik rested his head in his palms as he visualized the map of the landscape. "Aren't we going the wrong way? Shouldn't we be heading toward Eastland to free Brimmelle when they leave the Dovenar Wall's gates?"

"Eastland has been the center-point of conflict between men and Unday for many centuries," Grewen answered. "I'm not getting any closer to that province than I have to."

Grewen stretched his neck and looked down to make sure Avanda was comfortable. "Trust me, Thorik. We're headed the right way. Now get some sleep."

Thorik looked up at the stars between the trees for a bit, thinking of the events along his travels. Thoughts of Emilen crept back into his head, and he began missing her. How he wished she was with him snuggling up under the blanket. For a moment, he thought he could smell her scent and feel her touch. Holding on to these feelings, he soon drifted into a deep sleep as he dreamed about his memories of her.

~

THORIK WOKE up from a dream about Emilen arguing with him back at the crater along the King's River. Blinking himself awake, he could see that Grewen was wrapped up with glowing threads that danced in various colors. Glistening sparkles appeared, floating in every direction.

Thorik adjusted his eyes to see hundreds of little shiny dots flying around them. He lay on his back and looked about at several small beings playing and frolicking around the campsite. Singing songs and dancing to their own light and airy music, they tried to wake Grewen by tickling his feet and face as he lay in his constraints. Neither seemed to faze him.

Bending his knees, Thorik pushed his body up with his arms, only to find a miniature girl with two red oak leaves for wings sitting on his left knee. She was no bigger than his finger, and her reddish glowing body shone brightly like a flame.

"What kind of game is this?" Thorik asked, still half asleep.

"A game? What a brilliant idea. Let's play a game!" a male voice responded from the natural spring behind Thorik. "What kind of game do you like to play?"

Thorik rotated his body toward the small pond, scaring the winged girl away. The water had a slight blue glow about it that brightened the underside of the tree coverings. It also illuminated the grass and rocks that lined its shores.

A large frog was sitting upright on one of the rocks, holding a fishing pole whose line sank deep under the water. An acorn shell fit firmly on his head as a hat, and around his neck he wore a blue ribbon fashioned like a scarf. He looked very dapper and strangely familiar.

Thorik leaned forward and squinted to see if his eyes and ears would work better at less of a distance. Surely, he was seeing things.

One of the frog's legs dangled over the rock's edge while the other was bent, allowing for his foot to be flat against the top of the rock. "It's a wonderful natural dock. I bet you wish you had brought your fishing gear."

Thorik was confused. He wasn't sure what bothered him more, the idea of a knee-high frog talking to him or what he had to say. Everything was oddly familiar and yet barely understandable. Blinking his eyes to wake himself up did no good.

"Mr. Theodore J. Hempton, at your service." The frog tipped his hat with his free hand. "And who might you be, my lad?"

Thorik leaned back to a normal sitting position while watching the talking frog in amazement. It seemed awkward not to reply, even if he didn't fully believe his own eyes.

"Sec Thorik Dain of Farbank," he responded, still confused at the possibility of the conversation.

"Well, of course you are. That sounds like a right good name for such a lad as yourself." The end of Mr. Hempton's fishing pole tugged down a few times. Gripping the rod with both hands, he backed up on the rock to pull his catch out of the water. "So, do you like a taste of the unknown in your games?"

"What?" Thorik replied.

"Your games," he continued. The fishing line pulled hard, causing Mr. Hempton to fly forward and land very close to the end of the rock before stopping himself. He didn't allow his fishing to interrupt the conversation. "Do you like livin' a little on the edge? Peeking in the neighbor's windows, if you know what I mean?"

"No, of course not," Thorik replied quickly.

Mr. Hempton pulled back on his foot-long fishing rod, and it bowed in a strained arch. "No, no, obviously not. Right you are. Who would?" The line in the water thrashed about before heading out toward the center of the natural spring pond. "But don't you ever wonder what it would be like to lose your restrictions and inhibitions and just do what feels right?"

"Sure, I suppose."

"Good, now we're getting somewhere." He continued to struggle with his footing as the line kept pulling. "What would you say to a little game?"

Thorik looked over at Grewen, who continued to have movement confinements placed across his body and even over his mouth. Avanda was secure under his arm, but for how long? "Tell them to let my friends go first."

"Heavens, no. That would spoil the game. They are the prize, you know."

"What?"

"Well, you must have a prize at the end of a game; otherwise, it's not worth playing, I always say." Mr. Hempton pulled back on the line with all his might but struggled to make any headway. "Be a good lad and hold on to the pole for me while I grab a net."

"I'm not helping you."

"Come on, be a sport. Grab the line, we'll play a game, and then you'll be off on your way. Simple as that; no harm done." Mr. Hempton suddenly fell forward from the pull on the line and grabbed hold of the sides of the rock with his back feet as his body hung over the edge.

Instinctively, Thorik grabbed the rod to help out. "What kind of game is this?"

"It's called Hang On."

"Hang On? Never heard of it. How do you play?"

"You hang on." Mr. Hempton's smile made Thorik's heart sink.

Thorik was instantly pulled from the grassy shore into the shallow pond, only to find himself deep underwater, still holding on to the short fishing pole. Looking around, he felt the current taking him away deeper into the water. He was no longer in the natural spring near Mr. Hempton. Instead, he was in a moving river.

Afraid to let go of the rod, he held on for dear life as he descended into the water's depths. Holding his breath and attempting not to panic, he saw a flesh-deprived body move out of the darker water and into view. Chunks of flesh clung to its bones as it swam toward the Num. To Thorik's horror, not only was it getting closer, but several more were emerging from the dark to block his route. Memories of the undead within River's Edge flashed through his mind as the fishing rod line pulled Thorik toward the center of a crowd of partially skinned skeletons, who had suddenly realized that he was drawing near.

Thorik knew that if he let go now, they would easily overtake him. His only other option was to hope the moving catch at the other end of the fishing line continued its pace or sped up. Perhaps he could just race his way past them before they got a hold of him.

Several bony fingers grabbed at his arms and legs while he advanced past the first group, only to find his hooked fish had stopped running from him. The fishing line went limp. Groups of full and partial corpses surrounded him as he looked about for his options. Above him, he spotted the light of the sun and a way to escape. Without any hesitation, he began his swim to the surface in an attempt to reach it before the dead caught up with him.

The half-flesh bodies effortlessly moved toward him as he closed in on the surface. The water cleared, and the sun's warmth could be felt through the top of the water.

Just as his left hand breached the surface, his other hand was tugged down by the fishing rod. His air wouldn't last much longer. The only chance available to get away from the swimming dead was to let go of the rod and swim to shore. It was the only logical decision, but it didn't feel right. It wasn't within the rules of the game. It had been called 'Hang On' for a purpose, and he wasn't going to jeopardize Grewen's and Avanda's life by messing this up.

It was only moments before the bony fingers grabbed his ankles and then his legs. He held on to the little rod with all of his might as one of the skeletons bit into the back of his right hand.

Thorik's underwater scream came out as a large bubble of valuable air, and he watched it float up and burst onto the surface as the dead pulled him down. He continued to fight them off, but there were too many of them, and it was difficult to do as he held on to the fishing pole whose line was now tangled around and through his attackers.

As he was about to give up from lack of oxygen, the fishing line went tight, snapping several skeletal bodies into pieces and launching Thorik in a new direction. He reached over with his left hand to hold on to the rod just as it started to slip out from his right.

The water drove hard against his face as he fought off the feeling of passing out, and then he stopped. The line went limp again, and he looked up to see a green light from above. With a few minor strokes of one arm, he reached the surface and gasped for air.

He panted for a few minutes, trying to regain control of himself. Thorik eventually realized he was in a large granite room with one door on the far side. In the center of the wall on his side of the room was a fountain that sprayed water into a small shallow stone pool. Numerous vats of burning oil displayed a green flame as the wall and floor carvings began to come to life. Spiders, bees, panthers, and other creatures pulled away from their stagnant hibernation and started moving toward the pool where Thorik sat.

Holding the tiny fishing pole in one hand, he made a dash for the far door as heavy water-soaked clothes weighed him down, making it difficult to run. Rays of soft blue light peeked out from underneath the closed door.

Halfway across, his path was blocked by a white crystal brandercat. "I only have one chance at this. I can't stop," he told himself. Leaping up and rolling over the back of the cat, he landed on his feet and continued running toward the door, which opened for him under its own power. A column of blue moonlight beamed into the room, washing out a section of the room's green light.

Black marble bees swarmed around him, stinging him violently. He slowed as he tried to protect himself from them. Swatting at the ones near his face, he looked about to see what else in the room was coming his way. While he was doing so, the door began to close again.

Larger creatures broke free of the walls, slowly making their way toward Thorik, while the smaller ones quickly attacked. Spiders of ruby crystals lowered themselves from the ceiling, while granite beetles ran up under his pant legs.

"NO!" Thorik shouted in defiance. Turning sharply back toward the doorway, he focused on his destination and ignored the pain that the animated attackers were inflicting upon him. Charging for the door, he accepted every bite and sting along the way. It was the price of freedom, and he was willing to pay it.

The door began to open again as he approached its archway with new strength and attitude in his shoulders. The room exited a few yards above the center of a small pond within a forest. Mr. Hempton waited patiently for Thorik to arrive.

Numb to the ongoing attack, Thorik reached the doorway and entered the moonlight. The stone animals that entered the light with him began to petrify and harden. The rest of the creatures stopped their approach at the edge of the blue moonlight. At last, he was free.

The fishing line went tight.

Thorik grabbed the pole with both hands and looked back at the line as it led to the fountain at the far end of the room. It began to pull him out from the archway, back into the green light. He turned to see Mr. Hempton, who was waiting for Thorik's reaction.

"Not this time." Thorik made an aggressive posture, leaned toward the pond, and pulled on the string. It was a struggle, but this time he was in control; he lost his footing only once. Pulling hand over hand, the fishing line coiled near his feet.

"What are you?" he asked as the line stopped. It was stuck. "Oh, no you don't. I've come too far to not finally catch you."

He pulled with all his might, and the line finally gave way, knocking Thorik onto his back, landing on the ledge of the doorway before it dropped off to the small pond below. Quickly reeling up the loose line, he stood back up.

He squinted to see what type of fish he was dragging across the floor, past the idle stone creatures. But the string was no longer tight as he coiled. Either he had lost his catch, or it was moving toward him.

Jumping out from over the top of the animated statues, a thrasher roared as it attacked the Num with its snapping jaw and clawed hands. The fishing line was wrapped around the primate's hand as it landed on Thorik, knocking him backward, through the doorway and into the natural spring below.

Grewen snored away as various colored flickering pixies and faeries entertained themselves on top of his huge sprawled-out body. They bounced on his stomach, put flames to his feet, played hide-and-seek in his robes, and even opened his eyelids in an attempt to wake him up, all with the goal of teasing him more. Remarkably, none of this woke the giant up from his slumber, and the Myth'Unday lost interest in their games.

Thorik emerged from the pond with a splash, still holding on to the frog's little fishing pole. Quickly realizing that the thrasher was gone, he stood up to walk out of the shallow spring toward land. His legs shook under his body with each step he took. Walking to the edge, he fell onto the green grass where he had been sleeping before all this had started.

Mr. Hempton sat on the edge of his rock with his thin legs crossed and his hands folded politely in front of him on his lap. "Good show, dear boy. Well done."

Thorik reached over and handed the twig of a pole back to him.

Mr. Hempton looked it over to ensure it was in good shape. "That was entertaining. I do so love a spirited game. You're quite good yourself. Would you like to play another?"

"No." Thorik rolled over onto his back to rest. "For what purpose would you put me through such a thing?"

"Purpose? It's just a game, lad. Not everything has to happen for a purpose."

The statement irritated Thorik, for it went against his mother's favorite saying. "That's not true. Everything happens for a purpose."

"You'd like that to be true, but even you have doubts about it. That's why it bothered you so much when I said that. Just like you have been questioning the purpose of your adventure with your friends."

Thorik shook it off and went back to the original questioning. "How do you know these things? Why did you put me through such a horrible, torturous game?"

Mr. Hempton looked at Thorik with intrigue and smiled. "Dear boy, it was your game."

Still breathing hard from the underwater experience, he asked, "What? I don't understand."

"You made up the game, the rules, and the challenges out of your own fears and desires."

"You read my thoughts and used my fears against me?"

"Goodness, no. You used them against yourself. Just like you do in real life. The only difference is when you are with Myth'Undays, your thoughts become more real to the senses. Take me, for example. What am I?"

Thorik was still trying to digest this new information as he answered. "A frog, of course."

"Am I now? The last person who saw me thought I was a Tree Nymph." Mr. Hempton adjusted his hat and winked before continuing. "You see, everyone sees things differently. That does not make you right and them wrong."

"Does it make me wrong and them right?"

"No, neither has to be false to make the other true. Lad, they both can be correct, yet see two different things. Truths and reality are unique to the individual. Everything exists differently for each of us."

"Are you saying there's nothing to believe in? Nothing to fight for? Is everyone right from different perspectives?"

Mr. Hempton laughed. "Don't fool yourself. There is plenty of wrongdoing in this world, and you usually know when you are a part of it. The challenge comes when you are so focused on what you know is right that you refuse to even listen to other perspectives. This can be just as dangerous."

Thorik sat for a short time, thinking about the conversation and the pain he had caused himself in the game. "So… What's my prize?"

"Pardon me?" Mr. Hempton replied, slightly surprised at the question.

"My prize for holding on to your fishing pole while I was attacked by all of my fears. What is it?"

Mr. Hempton appeared perplexed. "I'm not sure. It's been a long time since anyone has won one of my games. Well played, by the way. Bravo," he said with a polite clapping of his hands.

"Your prize was to have Grewen and Avanda if I lost." Thorik turned and looked over to see the little flying Myth'Unday untie the giant as he continued to sleep. "What's my prize for winning?"

Mr. Hempton gave the question some serious thought before responding. "Where are you traveling?"

"What does that have to do with it?" Thorik was slightly annoyed by all the games.

"Entertain me for a bit more, won't you?"

"We are en route to meet with others on a journey."

"To do what, may I ask?" the frog questioned.

"My uncle has been captured and is being sent to the Southwind Mines. We've come to save him while they transport him along this road. After that—"

Mr. Hempton interrupted Thorik in mid-sentence. "There's your prize, you silly Num. And a grand reward it will be for you. Of course, it's not much of one for me, or most people, for that matter."

"What are you talking about?" Thorik asked.

"I will free your uncle," he said with a smile and a wink.

Thorik thought about his offer and gave a wide grin. "Perhaps things do happen for a reason."

～

"A FINE GAME this is but, although it has strategic qualities, it lacks the excitement of survival," Mr. Hempton commented to Thorik as they played another game of Runeage. "Perhaps if a player were to lose a toe or finger with each tile surrendered."

They continued playing as the other Myth'Unday creatures sprinkled sleeping dust over Grewen and Avanda.

"Is that absolutely necessary?" Thorik asked again. "Grewen could really come in handy with stopping the guards to free Brimmelle."

"If they wake and see me, I insist they play a game. And I can't guarantee that they will win." Mr. Hempton took a moment and set down his next Runestone tile.

"Are you saying that no one can see Myth'Unday without playing a game?" Thorik asked.

"Not true in the slightest. How did you ever win our game in the pond?" Mr. Hempton said to himself before continuing. "Young children can see through our illusions, but who will believe the words of a child? In addition, I ask for payment to see me in the form of a game. Some Myth'Unday do nothing, but many others require a great deal more. You're quite lucky you ran into me. My sister would have ripped out your eyes for gazing upon her. She's extremely vain, you know. The arrogant twit will never let me live down the day I broke her mirror. 'Get over it already,' I says to Raython. 'Look in a mud puddle. It reflects your face better,' I added." The frog laughed at his own memories.

Thorik had an odd expression on his face as their conversation led to Mr. Hempton's personal memories. "Based on that, Avanda should be able to see you without playing a game."

"Don't be so sure about that. Kids grow up fast nowadays, and innocence is quickly lost. As much as I'm up for another game, I think we'll have our hands full in a very short time."

The sun rose and turned the sky light shades of blue before a leaf-winged Myth'Unday flew down from a tree to notify Thorik of an approaching wagon.

Thorik climbed up into the tree and watched the wagon work its way to the apex of a hill before going back down into the next shallow valley. He called down to Mr. Hempton. "I see a wagon and several riders approaching. It looks like the Terra King's guards." He climbed out of the tree and hid behind some bushes.

Mr. Hempton nodded at a Tree Faerie wearing a walnut shell for a hat and a hollowed-out pinecone for a dress.

The Faerie nodded back to Mr. Hempton and went right to work. It ran out into the middle of the road and stopped before it began spinning around like a top. It gathered more speed as it spun and eventually drilled itself into the ground.

All was quiet for a few seconds, then the ground rumbled. Earth pushed up from the center of the dirt road and a tree sprouted out of it. Limbs formed, and the tree's height and width increased at an incredible rate.

Once its branches were long enough to span the road, it stopped. A slight pause was taken before a series of eruptions near the tree exploded dirt into the air. Thick roots pushed their way out of the ground in every direction. They pulsed and grew until they were easily over a foot thick.

The oncoming wagon would not be able to pass this obstacle.

Thorik was pulled down into hiding by the Myth'Unday as the wagon approached. He was still in awe of seeing a tree grow in a matter of minutes.

The wagon arrived over the hill and came to a stop before the tree. Two soldiers sat on the front of the wagon, which was being pulled by a four-legged Fesh'Unday that was long and thin with tan hair. Six guards rode on the backs of faralopes and other similar two-legged species. Two of the riders took the lead, followed by the wagon and then the other four riders.

The wagon itself was a cage on wheels and contained a dozen human and Polenum captives. Thorik immediately saw Brimmelle sitting in the back corner, hot and depleted of energy from the trek across the desert. He did not look well.

Once they stopped, the first two guards got off their beasts and started discussing how they could cut out the roots for the wheels of the wagon. One grabbed his battle-axe from his mount and walked over to chop at the roots blocking the path. He swung the axe with full force, and it cut deeply into the root. Pulling it out for another swing, he stopped when he noticed blood on his blade.

The guard next to him noticed it as well. They both looked down at the root to see blood pouring out of the wound.

As they looked upon the root with disbelief, the tree limbs from above attacked. The tree grabbed both guards and lifted them up, stripping them of their weapons.

It was at this time that the Myth'Undays attacked like a swarm of multicolored fireflies. Large blankets were flown over from the woods and placed over the prisoners' cage. It was held down to prevent those inside from seeing the Myth'Unday.

Glowing threads wrapped around the guards as sleeping dust was sprinkled in their faces.

The guards fought back and shielded themselves the best they could. One guard near the back grabbed one of the faeries out of the air and held her tight in his fist. The glowing Myth'Unday brightened her intensity as the guard gazed upon streams of light shining out between his fingers before feeling the flesh in his palm burning. He opened his hand quickly and blew on his palm to cool it down as the faerie escaped and then crammed faerie dust up his nose.

Other guards made futile attempts to swing swords and maces at the tiny creatures, often resulting in their own injuries. This continued as the Myth'Unday teased and tied up the guards, who were now falling off their rides.

Chaos around the wagon quickly subsided as each of the guards fell into the Myth'Undays bindings. All but the wagon driver had been tied up and moved into the woods, out of view.

Mr. Hempton hopped up onto the front of the wagon and then onto the captive driver, stopping on his shoulder. He showed the man his fishing rod. "I hope you're up for a game."

It was impossible for Thorik to know what the guard saw when he looked at Mr. Hempton, but it was obviously something that struck fear in him, for he screamed in horror at the sight.

The driver was quickly bound and removed from the visibility of the prisoners.

Thorik ran out to the road and grabbed the fallen battle-axe near the tree. Looking down at the bleeding wound in the exposed root, he asked, "Are you going to heal?"

Hundreds of little tree seeds emerged from the limbs and floated to the ground in helicopter casings. Upon landing, they sprouted legs, arms, and heads. They all quickly scurried into the woods as the tree itself decayed before Thorik's eyes.

Tree limbs drooped, then fell, before the entire plant turned to dust and swirled softly away in the breeze.

"Thank you," Thorik said to the Tree Faerie. "Farewell," he said to an empty road, for they had all vanished.

Moving to the back of the wagon, Thorik pulled off the blanket and busted the lock apart with his new double-bladed weapon. He swung the door open, freeing the captives. They all looked drained and thin from lack of food and water as well as burned from the desert's hot rays.

Reaching into the cage, Thorik began helping people out of the wagon and down to the road. In his haste to help, he almost didn't notice his grandmother. "Granna Gluic? Is that you? I thought you were dead."

"It wouldn't be the first time, dear." She then held up her sack of stones and winked. "I had a bit of help."

Thorik hugged her tighter than he had ever done before. He had missed her greatly and suddenly realized how much he enjoyed her company. He never wanted to let her go again.

"She was unconscious for a few days." Brimmelle followed her out. "But I nursed her back to health with my readings of the scrolls."

Still hugging Thorik, Gluic commented softly into his ear, "It was the stones."

The prisoners stretched their legs and bodies as they made their way to the natural spring. To their surprise, a bountiful feast of fruit was next to the water's edge. They quickly enjoyed the gift of food and thanked Thorik for it time and time again.

"You're welcome, but it wasn't me. The Myth'Undays must have gathered it for you." No one listened to Thorik's explanation as they took in the hospitality.

It was at this time that Grewen and Avanda woke to the sight of the group enjoying their feast. There was more than they could eat, but perhaps less than Grewen could.

"Hello?" Grewen sat up behind bushes that hadn't existed when he had fallen asleep.

The sight of the giant mognin caused immediate fear throughout the crowd.

"It's okay," Thorik announced to the recently freed people. "He's our friend."

Taking some time to calm everyone down, Thorik gathered some food for Grewen and Avanda.

Thorik loaded his new battle-axe onto his back as several people asked how he had saved them.

"I had help from some Myth'Undays that I befriended," Thorik said. "I won a game with Mr. Hempton. He's a big frog…" He smiled as he used his hands to show everyone how tall Mr. Hempton was. "…with an acorn hat…and a blue scarf…and a fishing pole…" Seeing the awkward glares, he hoped to continue without sounding any crazier. "He helped me free you as the reward for winning the game."

"How did these well-dressed frogs help you?" one of the older men asked.

"No, there was only one frog. The rest were little forest people with mystical abilities. Some had wings, some could glow, others dressed themselves with leaves and nuts," Thorik explained.

The group laughed at his far-fetched story of magical little people and dismissed it as they thanked Thorik again for the rescue and food.

Keeping the celebration short, they wished to start their return trip to see family and friends. The group boarded the wagon and mounts to head back toward Eastland in a state of jubilation.

Brimmelle and Gluic said goodbye to the group as they rode away before turning back to Grewen and Avanda. Avanda and Brimmelle quickly began telling their own adventures as the two stories bounced back and forth on top of each other.

It was only a matter of minutes before old habits returned as Avanda started telling Gluic of her exciting adventures while Brimmelle explained his own hardships with the journey to Grewen.

Enjoying the sight of them back together again, Thorik leaned against a nearby tree. Chuckling at the scene, he noticed something move out of the corner of his eye. "Thank you," he said without veering his focus.

Mr. Hempton stood on a branch, leaning on the trunk. "No, no. Thank you, my lad. You have a good head on your shoulders and play a fine game. Just remember, you always control the game until you stop believing that you do."

"I'll remember that next time I meet another Myth'Unday."

"Lad, I was talking about your games outside the Mythical Forest."

Thorik understood and nodded.

Theodore J. Hempton gave Thorik a slight bow and a tip of his hat before jumping off the tree. He then hopped across the forest floor and behind the brush, where the bound guards hung upside down from the trees. Finding the first contestant for his personal entertainment, he gave an evil smile.

Seeing Grewen pack up all the supplies and the remaining food, Thorik knew it was time to leave.

29

PELONTHAL

Thorik and his party made their way along the River's Edge southern perimeter wall toward Pelonthal. The farther west they traveled, the more hospitable the climate became, with lower temperatures and comfortable humidity levels. Grass turned greener and pockets of timber continued to increase in size as they continued to skirt the northern edge of the Mythical Forest.

At the top of one of the many rolling hills, the Pelonthal Dovenar Wall could be seen running south from the River's Edge Province. With each hill they walked over, the wall became more defined, and details of the gate's opening came into view.

Getting sidetracked again, Thorik questioned the wall acting as a dike. "Grewen, what holds the water inside River's Edge? Wouldn't it run out through the gates into the land beyond?"

Chuckling at Thorik's ever-inquisitive mind, he replied, "Only if they were open. The solid protective metal doors can be dropped, closing them tight from the inside to prevent any kind of attack. The pressure from the water continues to force them into a tight seal."

"Let's focus on this gate right now," Brimmelle suggested as he pointed forward. He was very nervous as they approached the entrance with an Unday as part of their party. Flashbacks of the faralope incident at the Woodlen Gate kept popping into his head. "I don't like this."

Grewen noted, "It's fine. The only purpose of the guards at Pelonthal's gate is to keep out warmongering Del'Unday or Fesh'Unday that may eat the local crops or livestock. Ov'Unday have been living in Pelonthal for decades."

Few words were spoken as they approached the beautifully designed wall. Decorating the outer wall, patterns of trees and hills could be seen at first glance, while plants and animals were visible with more effort. The wall was not carved out like the objects in Kingsfoot or the Woodlen Coliseum. Instead, it was artistically placed colored rocks that created various scenes of nature across its entire length.

The road led to the gate. From this vantage point, Thorik could see both north and south walls of River's Edge with the lake in between them, as well as the tops of several buildings above the surface near the center. Many more buildings existed in this location than where Thorik had crossed. He assumed it most likely meant more dead souls rummaging around as well.

Thorik commented to Grewen, "The River's Edge Lake looks wider here, and there doesn't seem to be a straight path across without going through a building. I can see why no one passes here."

"Looks pleasant enough." Brimmelle was unsure what all the fuss was about as they stepped up to the open gates.

Thorik smirked at Brimmelle's words as he politely waved at one of the guards on the wall. Cupping his hands on either side of his mouth, he called up to the guards. "Gentlemen, how are you on this fine day?"

A guard walked over and peered down at the group. "All quiet, as usual. How are the roads toward Eastland? We heard of a devastating storm that blew out many bridges and towers in Southwind, and the winds were heading northeast along the Southern Mountains. Did you get any of it?"

"No sir; perhaps we left before it hit," Thorik replied.

"Praise your timing. She sounds like a mean witch."

The guard uniforms were of blue and white, uncomplicated and functional with no frills or lace. Their simplistic look gave more of a clean and genuine look than the uniforms of Woodlen.

"What be your business on this day?" the guard asked.

"We come to visit friends."

"What part of Greensbrook?"

"No, in Pelonthal."

The guard looked perplexed. "River-Green Road runs through the heart of the forest, straight to Greensbrook and then on to Southwind. There are no side roads to the lakeside cities in Pelonthal. Never been a need."

Grewen realized the potential confusion of the Nums and entered the conversation. "I used to live here and still have family in the capital. I know the way." Looking at the sun as it lowered in the west, he knew they wouldn't be able to make the trek through the forest before nightfall. "Do you have lodging for the night?"

"Stables are large enough to hold you, as long as you get along with faralopes and uderipes," he answered as Brimmelle flinched at the idea. "That should keep you dry and safe until morning. But even with daylight, you don't want to get lost in the forest or the Myth'Unday will have at you."

A second guard came out from below, at the gate entrance. "There'll be a fee for the lodging, and you'll still have to pay the same toll even if you're not following the entire length of the road."

"Accepted. Thank you." Grewen had to bend down as they walked under the hanging gate.

Gluic walked over to the tollman and emptied a few gold nuggets into his open hand.

He shook himself out of his boredom as he gazed at the precious tender provided.

"That should be enough," Grewen said as he stopped her from adding more to the already high price she had paid.

Once inside, the road turned sharply to the left and followed along the inside of the wall for as far as they could see. The path was made of flat stones wedged together in a skillful manner. Over the years, the odd-shaped stones had lost their luster, and grass formed in the seams, but instead of looking old and unmanaged, this gave the road character and a charisma of its own. It felt as comfortable and relaxing as Thorik's path from his cottage to Farbank.

They stayed the night without issue and began following the River-Green road first thing in the morning. They traveled south for several miles with the wall on their left and the thick forest to their right. The wall and road cut straight through the middle of the Mythical Forest with a forty-foot-wide opening.

"Here it is. This is the way." Grewen had turned abruptly from the road and started walking toward the trees.

The Nums looked around for some kind of sign.

"How do you know?" Thorik asked.

"It's the seventh double-root tree we've seen since we entered the province."

Skeptical, Brimmelle looked into the dark forest and at the double-root tree, which was actually two trees that grew together in various twisting fashions. "Are you sure?"

"I think so."

"And if you're wrong?" Brimmelle asked in the commanding Fir voice that he used often on Thorik.

"Then I'm wrong, and we'll miss the city and have to sleep in the forest. Hopefully, I got it right." He entered the forest.

Brimmelle did not like the response or the fact that Grewen walked away without providing the Fir with an opportunity to argue the point. Standing his ground for a moment, he knew he had no choice but to follow the giant to continue the discussion.

Thorik entered the dark woods, followed by Avanda, Gluic, and then Brimmelle.

The forest was thick with ferns and trees with exposed roots on land that never seemed to flatten out. Small creeks and streams sporadically appeared from ground springs and ended under rocks and vegetation. The ground was covered with a soft red mud and clay that clumped onto everyone's boots as well as Grewen's feet. It made the constant up and down hike slippery and dangerous.

The wind rustled the upper leaves of the trees and gave off a soft whistling sound, much like music. It was followed by soft voices in the background that could not be understood. Motions in the forest were seen out of the corners of their eyes but never where they were directly looking. The group had an uncomfortable feeling that they were being watched.

Grewen kept his senses on alert. "I have the feeling the Myth'Unday are toying with us."

Brimmelle looked up at the enormous man. "You mean the little forest folk that Thorik was telling us about earlier? I'll keep my eyes open for any flying frogs," he sarcastically replied. His uncomfortable laugh was an attempt to block the noises in the woods.

"Thorik never said the frog could fly." Avanda glanced over at the other Num. "You didn't, did you, Thorik?"

Thorik smiled at Avanda's attempt to defend him. "No, he didn't fly. But I don't think these Myth'Unday know of my good relations with Mr. Hempton. They may not take so kindly to our trespassing."

Thorik's apprehension about the odd noises and soft voices that he heard was stiffening his stride. Mr. Hempton's game had taught him that his fears were his worst enemy. It wasn't easy, but he needed to control his emotions and relax.

Grewen's small ears didn't catch all the sounds that the Nums' did. Unlike the rest, Gluic chatted away with the unseen guests. Then again, she had been doing that for years. Thorik wondered if she had been talking to the Myth'Unday all that time.

After his taunting of Thorik was over, Brimmelle became edgy with each new sound from the forest. "Did you hear that? I heard footsteps following us." He turned and walked backward as he scanned the terrain. It wasn't more than a few steps before he fell from his haste and clumsiness. He crashed through a fern, down a small slope, and into a muddy puddle with a loud splash.

"Perhaps you're right. I think I just heard something myself," Grewen teased.

Brimmelle's backward fall had coated the Fir's backside with thick clumps of wet red clay. But instead of lashing out in anger, he became alarmed by growls and snorts from every direction, interlaced with whispers and distant conversations. "We aren't alone. There must be Del'Unday out here with us." His heart quickened as the soft voices became louder while the sounds of snapping branches and heavy footsteps increased in frequency and volume.

"It's not Del'Unday, Brimmelle. It's the forest folk," Avanda replied. "Oh, Thorik, do you think I'll be lucky enough to see a Myth'Unday?"

"Keep your eyes open," Thorik said kindly, hoping that they wouldn't run into any. He had no desire for another Myth game.

Brimmelle continued to panic. He was seeing movement in every direction, but couldn't focus on any of it. The snapping of sticks and slushy footfalls in the mud continued to get closer to him. "We need to get out of here!"

Of course, they had not seen or heard nearly what he had.

Avanda smiled back at the Fir. "I thought you didn't believe in them."

Thorik shook his head, cautioning her not to tease. Brimmelle was having a hard time in this forest, and they needed everyone to keep their wits about them.

With fresh flora crammed in her hair, Gluic walked back to Brimmelle. "Take these, dear." She placed two black spherical smooth rocks in her son's hand. "Hold them tight, and they will calm you down."

"Your river rocks will not save us from the creatures in these woods." Brimmelle quickly placed the stones in his side pouch.

"Yes, they will," Thorik said in support of his grandmother's advice. "The Myth'Unday have obviously chosen you to entertain them. They play on your thoughts and your fears. What you believe is real, is real… at least to you."

Grewen stopped and looked back at Thorik. "Nicely spoken, little man." Turning back, he led his friends farther west, hoping they would see the city soon, for the evening was not far off.

Brimmelle followed behind as he continued to gawk at the trees that began to bend from their own power instead of the wind. He stopped in his tracks as the large double-root tree in front of him looked to be waiting for him, though the other party members passed it by. It stared him down from unseen eyes.

The outstretched arms of the massive tree twisted their end branches toward him, and a knot in front opened as a mouth. Brimmelle was frozen with fear for several seconds before he realized he was sinking in the thick mud. Attempting to lift his feet was useless as he sank even deeper.

"Help!" Brimmelle screamed. "Come back!" he shouted. But the rest of the group was long gone, out of sight.

Mud soon covered his knees as he struggled to free himself until he saw the large double-root tree step forward, dragging its root system out of the ground. Earth around it popped up in the air in small clumps as the roots lifted from beneath it.

Watching the tree make its slow way toward him, Brimmelle spotted a brown squirrel running at him. It made tracks across the mud and onto the Fir's shirt, leaving a trail of tiny footprints. The squirrel jumped up onto his shoulder and looked him square in the eyes before squeaking out a barrage of chattering sounds.

"Go away! Leave me alone!" Brimmelle demanded of the rodent.

It replied back to him with an open mouth of large dangerous teeth and a violent scream, chilling Brimmelle to the bone. Only inches from his face, the squirrel continued to bare its teeth at him. Brimmelle attempted to slap it away, only to find his hands were stuck at his sides.

Looking down, he saw several roots from the oncoming tree had already wrapped themselves around him. Moving ever so closely, the tree purposely broke off one of its own limbs. The Fir was certain that the sharp end of the limb was to be used for thrusting into his chest.

The squirrel ran down his arm and bit his wrist, causing his reflexes to move his arm forward within the restrictions of the roots. Moving to his front, the critter opened one of Brimmelle's side sacks, which was no longer covered by his arm. It pulled something out and raced back up to his shoulder.

Screeching at Brimmelle with its high-pitched terrifying sound, it almost bit the Num's nose off before it ran back down his arm. It then placed the two round black stones, which it had stolen from the sack, into the Fir's hand.

He grasped the items tightly as the tree reached down and picked him up out of the mud and into the air. Dangling like a lifeless sack of rice in its two largest limbs, the Fir was moved toward the tree's open mouth. He was to be taken in with a single bite.

"Are you with us?" the tree's thunderous voice asked.

Brimmelle's entire body shook with fear. "What?"

The squirrel ran along the ground next to him and asked, "Brimmelle, do you feel any better?"

"That sounds like Thorik's voice." He searched the woods for the boy.

"He's coming out of it," the tree said in Grewen's voice.

Brimmelle's eyes widened as he beheld a hideous Del'Unday Krupe walking toward him. Its sharply cut black armor covered everything but the glowing eyes that stared at Brimmelle. It spoke. "You just couldn't keep the stones in your hand like I asked, could you?" His mother's voice echoed out of the metal armor.

Brimmelle tried to understand but couldn't. Sounds and sights blurred and faded in and out. He held his mother's precious stones, which the squirrel had given to him, tightly. Closing his eyes, he hoped it would all go away.

Thorik's voice hit Brimmelle's ears clearly this time. "It's just a hallucination caused by the Myth'Unday. Your own fears are betraying you. Pull yourself out of it."

"We've lost a lot of time. We need to hurry if we plan to make it out of here before nightfall," Grewen said. "It's not wise to stay the night in the depths of the Mythical Forest, especially if you have a chance not to."

Brimmelle slowly opened one eye to see Gluic, Thorik, and Grewen standing over him. "How did they do this to me?"

Grewen set him on his feet. "It's their forest. They can do what they want. Entertaining themselves by making your emotional thoughts come alive is what they enjoy, especially at night. So, let's hurry so we don't have to sleep here."

"Look, everyone," Avanda yelled, standing a few yards from Grewen. "I caught one of them. I have my own Myth'Unday."

Thorik and Grewen's eyes widened and hearts sank at the thought of the potential issues to follow.

"You what?" Thorik hoped he had heard her wrong.

She smiled as she stepped up to the group with her hands cupped, top and bottom, around her prisoner. "I jumped around a tree and surprised her. She had just started to fly away when I caught her."

Grewen glanced around the forest for an attack from her Myth friends.

"Wonderful!" Gluic moved closer to Avanda. "Let us see her. Show us her beauty and her magic."

"I don't want her to fly away," Avanda said. "Can we put her in a sack to keep safe?"

Thorik stepped behind her and placed his hands on her shoulders. This was just like he used to do in class in Farbank, when he wanted the students to think deeply about something before speaking to the class. "Avanda, I want you to concentrate on the Runestone that you are wearing around your neck. How does it apply to this situation?"

Avanda thought about it and nodded in agreement. "We have a responsibility to all life. Only take what we need and give back what we can," she recalled from his teachings and took a deep breath. "Goodbye, little winged lady." She opened her hands to reveal a colorful butterfly. It flapped its wings a few times before it left Avanda's palm and began circling around Gluic's head.

"Beautiful!" Gluic was obviously delighted. "I so miss them."

"But that's not what I caught," Avanda explained, as the winged insect flew once around the entire group before disappearing into the forest. "Honest, it wasn't."

"We believe you." Thorik was happy with the way things turned out.

The group hurried off in a race against the daylight. Up and down the small folds of land and through periodically dark areas, shaded by heavy tree growth, until it opened into an airy slope leading to a distant city near the lake. The last bit of sun was falling as they made their way across an open grassy knoll.

Night had fallen before they reached the city. Lanterns lined the streets and buildings with a glow of energy about them. Music and merrymaking could be heard while passing the first row of odd-shaped homes. No exterior boundaries or walls protected the city, and the gradual increase of houses led them toward the inner city that was situated along the water's edge.

Thorik heard horns and flutes playing exciting new tunes, while drums and string instruments supported them. Each instrument played its own melody, which complimented all the others. This organized chaos was relaxing and uplifting at the same time.

They rounded the corner to see a cobblestoned open area along the lake, filled with artists of all kinds. Painters and pot makers crafted their wares as sculptors and ironworkers showed off their latest creations. The well-lit lakeside festivities included musicians, chefs, acrobats, and more. Jewelers developed custom designs for waiting customers who were already wearing a ridiculous number of accessories. Flaming foods were served to patrons as they watched glassblowers create wonderfully colored glassware.

Grewen sighed with relief. "Pelonthal City, the last safe haven for mixed cultures."

The area teemed with life and vitality as all races and species coexisted together, enjoying each other's company. A young mognin played tag in the streets with a gathler and Num while a large bird-like man used his own feathers to paint on a canvas of flattened bark.

Clothing styles varied as well as the fabric used, but for the most part the theme was loose fitting and relaxed. No guards were seen, and no walls loomed over them as the people enjoyed life along the docks. It was hard to believe this was in the same kingdom as the other cities they had passed through.

Thorik walked along the boardwalk looking out at the boats swaying back and forth from the shallow waves. A light breeze blew off the lake into town, cooling the sun-baked brick streets and buildings. It was a perfect evening to unwind from the grueling experiences of the past few weeks. The air had the smell of the beginning of fall when the first rush of mountain air cooled Farbank after a warm, sticky day.

Walking past artwork of wood, clay, and metal, they stopped frequently to admire the ingenuity and creativeness that was required to make the objects. Shiny brass and metal sculptures of abstract ideas were on display, as well as statues of known and unknown animals.

Thorik sat down on the side of a large fountain decorated with metal sculptures, some in the water while others were mounted along the outer short half-wall. Turning his back to the fountain, he watched his friends and family enjoy what the city offered. He only wished that Emilen was there to enjoy it with him.

"Don't turn your back on me, Fesh," said a growling voice from behind Thorik.

Thorik whipped around to realize that he had mistaken an old companion for one of the metal sculptures. "Draq? Is that you?" he said softly to the unmoving silver dragon perched on the fountain's edge.

"Yes. Why are you whispering?"

Thorik was surprised and relieved that he wasn't hearing things again. The Mythical Forest had him questioning everything.

"Draq!" Grewen strolled across the open area toward them.

"Grewen." He nodded respectfully. "Good to see that you broke free. I knew they couldn't keep a hold of you."

"Actually, Thorik freed me." He looked down at the young man. "I'm in his debt."

Politely, Thorik added, "Avanda helped. We make a good team."

Skeptical, Draq looked at the little Num and began to make his compliment to Thorik. "So, you saved… Gluic?" He had interrupted his own sentence with the sight of the elderly Num.

"What?" Thorik questioned.

Draq continued in a controlled voice, "Gluic, you're alive?" Lowering his eyebrows, the dragon looked back over at Thorik. "You said she was dead."

"Oh, I was, dear. But I never let that hold me back before," she replied.

Draq paused before he shook off his perplexed expression. "I suppose Thorik saved you as well," he remarked with dry sarcasm.

Gluic shook her head. "No, there were too many guards. Thorik's friend, the frog, and his butterfly companions saved us." She was absolutely sincere in her statement.

Draq looked up to Grewen for a proper answer.

While mouthing the word 'frog', Grewen used his hands to show the small size of the frog that had helped them.

"I don't want to know." Draq hoped to end the confusing conversation.

Brimmelle stepped up to the group, holding Avanda's hand. "We are here also," he announced, alerting Draq of his freedom.

"Good," Draq replied with little interest. "Ambrosius' son, Ericc, is no longer at my lair, but we have no evidence that he has been captured by Darkmere. If he has been, Darkmere will want to be present before the Alchemists attempt his assassination. Therefore, we need to find Darkmere. To do that, we need to determine where his next target will be. Unfortunately, we haven't found any leads yet."

"We know where he is going." Gluic started digging for something within her many pockets as feathers and dried weeds tumbled out.

"How is that possible?" Draq's interest was piqued, yet he was skeptical that these Nums could accomplish a task which an E'rudite and dragon could not.

She pulled out a large cylindrical crystal, the one she had found in Kingsfoot Lake. Smiling and nodding, she held it out in front of them. "In here."

Draq's head drooped as he realized she didn't have the information he needed, and they were no closer to finding Ambrosius' son today than a week prior. "I don't think Darkmere is in your crystal."

"No, but his thoughts are trapped in here," she told him.

Draq lowered his head toward Gluic's open hand and eyed the crystal. "How is that possible?"

"Darkmere gave them to me when we held hands." She gave a quick wink. "Go ahead, touch it and see."

Draq backed off. "I don't touch anything having to do with Darkmere unless it involves his death."

Grewen reached out his hand only to retract it at the last second. "Last time I tried this you slapped my finger and told me I would suck the energy out of it," he jested before he opened his palm for her to place it.

"That's true," she reminded herself. "They still haven't forgiven your species. Amazingly vast memories. They never do forget." Turning to Thorik, she left Grewen slightly stunned by the comments.

She set the crystal in the center of Thorik's palm and closed his fingers around it. Gluic placed one of her hands on top of his fist and the other below. "Close your eyes. What do you see?"

Immediately, visions of horrible acts flashed through his mind. Torture, pain, beheadings, mutilations, and more. Visions of Darkmere and Ambrosius in battle, crushing waves from the lake, sacrificing a child at an altar. He was obviously disturbed by the images and tried to turn his head away. "So much evil. So much hatred. I can see so much pain in his life."

"Where is he headed?" Draq barked.

Thorik focused for a few seconds as he mentally asked the same question to the crystal. A room came into view. A man, Darkmere, stood at a table looking at a map. Pointing to the western coastline of Luthralum, where a mountain range came into view. A break in the range exposed an arched line and words describing the location. "Australis Weirfortus," Thorik responded as his eyes opened wide, breaking the trance-like state which held him. "What's a Weirfortus?"

Grewen and Draq looked shocked as they turned their heads out to the lake, looking into the moonlit horizon.

"He wouldn't dare," Draq growled.

"To what end?" Grewen questioned. "What possible purpose could he have?"

Draq clenched his jaw. "If this vision is correct, this will be the end of Australis."

"As we know it?" Thorik questioned, hoping for clarification of changes they may see.

Grewen shook his head. "It could mean the end of our land and the end of all life that lives on it."

30

FRIEND OR FOE

As instructed by Grewen, Thorik led the Nums along the shoreline street toward the Crab Pot Inn. Glistening ribbons of color danced high in the atmosphere extending from the Lu'Tythis Tower. They had seen the distant flowing lights every cloudless night since they had left Kingsfoot. The locals thought nothing of it, but Thorik and Avanda were always captivated by the beautiful light show. He recalled the first time he had seen the tower after exiting the pass. Memories of Em revealed images of them cuddling together as they watched the tower's lights. It seemed so long ago. Only a month or so had passed, yet he felt he had experienced a lifetime of adventures. "She would have loved to have seen them this close to the tower," he mumbled to himself.

Reaching the inn, Thorik opened the front door, which led them into a grand room supporting dining and drinks. Thick wooden beams arched up the walls to the peak in the center of the ceiling. A large open fireplace was the primary light, with scattered lanterns attempting to back it up. Wet fishing nets dried on large rusty hooks, and crab baskets hung from the walls along with several trophy-sized crab skeletons. Some were larger than Thorik and had pincers the length of his arm.

The room smelled of seafood and ale. Pungent, but not to the point of being unbearable. The dozen or so diners didn't seem to complain as they broke open crab legs ripe with meat.

Ambrosius sat at one of the tables along the far wall from the fireplace. It was poorly lit and isolated from the patrons who sat among the other tables. He was quiet and reserved, bringing no attention to himself as he kept his face in the shadows.

Thorik walked over to him but wasn't sure how to start the conversation. The last time they had seen each other Ambrosius was destroying the northern Woodlen city of Pyrth and its residents along with it.

Ambrosius looked up and noticed the group approach him. He smiled and rose to his feet. "Welcome to Pelonthal City, my friends. I am glad to see you are all well. Especially you, Gluic. I had heard that you had passed away."

She smiled at the sentiment. "Who's to say I hadn't?"

Ambrosius wasn't sure how to take her comment, so he redirected the conversation to Thorik. "Your travels have been long and far. It is good to see you have saved Gluic and Brimmelle. What came of Grewen's fate?"

"Avanda and I broke him out of the Coliseum Melee Matches. He is here with Draq, currently visiting family to arrange for transportation."

"So, the stories are true. I heard word that the Coliseum magically awoke and attacked its attending audience with a life of its own. I could only hope that it was your doing in saving Grewen. You have done well, my friend."

The words bothered Thorik. He turned to his grandmother. "Granna, can you and Uncle Brimmelle please secure rooms for us and put Avanda to bed? I need to talk to Ambrosius."

Afraid she would miss some excitement, Avanda protested slightly as Gluic pulled her from the table and to the innkeeper before heading up to their rooms.

Brimmelle stayed at the table for a moment, shaking his head at Ambrosius. "I have nothing to say to him, anyway. He's the cause of all our problems," he said to Thorik in a fatherly way. The Fir was exhausted from the day's travel and didn't have it in him to argue any further. Wishing to clean the dried mud and clay from his clothes, he turned and went up to the rooms with his mother.

Thorik snapped back toward Ambrosius. "Get this straight." He leaned forward onto the edge of the table. "I have not 'done well'. I have done nothing but what I had to because of your attack on Pyrth and on helpless innocent people. We wouldn't be here right now if it weren't for your uncontrolled anger and reckless disregard for others in your pursuit to take revenge on Darkmere."

Ambrosius was solemn in his response as he relaxed in his chair. "You don't understand, Thorik. It is very complicated."

Thorik's fists flexed. "I am tired of being told it's complicated. It's an easy way out for you to defend your actions. In your mind, the end justifies those who get hurt. But you don't want to be held responsible for those details. You want the recognition of the eventual result, hoping that everyone in the end will forgive and forget what it took to accomplish it, as well as those who died in your wake."

Ambrosius kept his voice low, hoping to encourage Thorik to do the same. "That is not true."

"Oh no? Then what are you doing here?" Thorik's voice had raised instead of lowered. "Brimmelle's captors would have rolled right past this province toward Southwind while you sat here in this inn. You made no attempt to save him!"

"It wouldn't have done any good to save him if he and tens of thousands of others would die just a few weeks later from Darkmere's attack. Now lower your voice," Ambrosius said sternly while keeping his own intensity at bay. He didn't like the attention they were gathering from the nearby diners.

"I will not! Not until you provide me with an answer of substance." He stood up straight and continued, "I trusted you. I fought for you. I believed in you!"

Ambrosius glanced back and forth at the other tables, concerned about what might be overheard. He then returned his gaze to Thorik's eyes. They looked stronger than before: more assured and less apprehensive. "You have grown during your travels, my friend. I was correct, you know. You will make an outstanding leader someday." He pulled out the chair next to him and motioned to it. "Please sit. I have put you through great dangers. I owe you an explanation."

Hesitating at first, the Num sat down at the table while Ambrosius waved the barkeeper over to order drinks. After the drinks had been served, Ambrosius began his story.

"I was born a prince to the Dovenar Kingdom. My twin brother Tarosius obviously had the same fate. It was our responsibility to keep the kingdom strong and prosperous. I was educated in the fundamentals of finance and legislation. My brother was educated in military tactics with the aim being for him to protect the Dovenar Walls from invasions."

"Ru'Mere, the king's advisor, taught us in the ways of the E'rudites. A skill that has been forbidden in Australis for thousands of years. He had been born an E'rudite and had concealed it throughout his years."

"Tarosius embraced his powers of matter alteration and eventually traveled out of the kingdom for more advanced training by an Oracle named Deleth. I stayed behind and continued my training of gravitational control by Ru'Mere, who taught me massive powers and the responsibilities that accompany them. He was a great mentor, leader, and friend."

"Tarosius returned years later from his distant training to regain his position and become the next King of our land. He had changed his name to Darkmere, a name Deleth had crowned him with. It wasn't long before he and King Gorren began their same old disputes. Ultimately, Darkmere killed the king, followed by many of the king's faithful supporters."

Thorik tried to absorb this information as quickly as it came at him. "The Terra King, which is Darkmere and your brother, killed your father?"

Ambrosius raised a finger to stop the interruption. He knew that this line of questioning would derail him from saying what he needed to. "Darkmere quickly took strength in the military and began a campaign to rule the kingdom. Ru'Mere advised our mother, the queen, to crown me as the new king, providing me with the power to stop Darkmere. When she did, my brother was furious and attacked city after city that supported my throne. Eventually cities followed him out of fear, and a separation was created between the northern and southern provinces."

"The capital city of the Dovenar Kingdom at that time was Maegoth. It sat in the middle of this conflict and was constantly being fought for. A battle of horror rampaged the earth at Maegoth as the final battle of the Civil War. Prominent Alchemists joined Darkmere's forces, and they cast spells of eternal life and mind control on their warriors but failed to grant them freedom from pain."

"Darkmere's strategic moves were well played, and his army was strong, but we surpassed their efforts with sheer heart and desire to win. My army of men and Ov'Unday quickly took control of the battle. However, we realized that the enemy was not defeated when we killed the same warriors time after time, as they screamed in horror. They began begging for death as they were forced to continue their battle against us. Out of mercy, we dismembered their bodies and decapitated their heads to remove them from this life, but they would not die. Those incapable of fighting anymore stared at us in desperation to end their life, crying in horrific sounds that still haunt us in our nightmares. It was the most unsettling massacre that has ever taken place."

"Even some of the Alchemists had a change of heart and began granting death. Darkmere quickly found out about the spell reversals and swiftly killed those Alchemists for such treason."

"It took the Great Wave from the lake to rise up and wash the blood from the earth to end the battle. The battlefield, along with the city, now resides underwater in the mouth of River's Edge."

Thorik thought out loud, "Those were the living dead we saw in the river."

"Yes. The battle ended thirty years ago on the thirteenth day of the twelfth month. We are less than three weeks from this anniversary."

"He's going to finish the war on the date he left off," Thorik surmised.

Ambrosius nodded to confirm Thorik's words while taking another sip of his ale.

Thorik's face still looked puzzled. "But what caused the Great Wave?"

"We did. Darkmere and I are at fault. I used to blame my brother, but with age, I have come to realize that both of us caused it. Our stubbornness drove Ru'Mere to do whatever it took to stop us from killing everyone. Ru'Mere released a wave of water on our battle and was willing to sacrifice both of us and the coastal cities in an effort to save the rest of Australis."

Ambrosius continued, "Darkmere was defeated and retreated to the city of Corrock. There he fought for leadership and slowly gained his army of Del'Unday warriors and assassins.

"While he trained his military machine, I sought out guidance from the Oracle of the North, Feshlan. He instructed me to establish a great council of all creatures. One that would unify the land and bring peace back to Terra Australis after four thousand years. I traveled the land in search of all races, beliefs, species, and clans. Excluding Corrock and Ergrauth, most were willing to at least listen to the idea. The Alchemist Guild joined, as well as several families of the Ov'Unday clan. A few Del'Unday clan cities also joined to keep abreast of our talks. One member from each of the six remaining Dovenar Provinces also attended.

"Great strides were taken over the years to bring peace to the land. A decade later, the societies of our people had blended and meshed. Borders seemed vague, and fears dropped.

"Darkmere resisted the movement and sent his vile serpents to uproot our work. However, years of attacks only led to unification and strengthening of the council as they worked together to fight him. He quickly realized his errors and focused on coming after me, knowing that I was the catalyst in organizing his defeat.

"I went into hiding, and Darkmere faded from the people's view in his pursuit of my family. He eventually murdered my wife and is still in pursuit of my son. He intends to stop the prophecy, which states that my son will cause the death of his son.

"Time passed before he returned to his primary mission of total dominance.

But this time it would be different. Darkmere discovered a new way to fight the council. Instead of head on, he would poison them from within. He changed his physical appearance and took on the persona of the Terra King, evading those looking for Darkmere. Through the use of the ancient Mountain King spiritual beliefs, he acquired small bands of locals to infiltrate their own lands and cause pain. He deluded them into believing his interpretation of the scrolls and appointed himself as their new king with the power to carry out the Mountain King's words.

"With this newfound power, he used his followers to remind their citizens of the terrors and fears of the past. Mistrust led to prejudice and intolerance. Small-scale attacks provoked retaliation of larger ones, only to be returned again. Humans and Altereds parted ways as anger and fear erupted across the land.

"The Terra King preached to humans and Nums with words of courage and safety while his alter ego, Darkmere, quietly deceived the Del'Unday about their banishment from the Dovenar Kingdom as he prepared them for war.

"Allegations of bigotry climbed all the way up to the Grand Council. Key members that spoke openly against each other began to mysteriously die. This validated that members of the council couldn't be trusted. No longer was there a safe haven to hold meetings, and so it was disbanded.

"Authority over individual cities was splintered, and martial law took hold. Chaos ruled in areas of weak military powers. Humanity was quickly being lost, and kinship among species seemed doomed. The Unday were expelled or enslaved in every province except here in Pelonthal and parts of Southwind and Greens-brook. Humans and Nums were treated no differently in the Del'Unday cities. Our civilization had stepped backward several centuries.

"Once I heard of the abandoned council, it took me nearly a year to find a safe location and hold a new meeting. I was able to get a message to Beltrow's annual trading party while visiting Shoreview. They, in turn, responded to my contact with a date and location to be escorted to the temple. It was our last chance to right Darkmere's wrongs. But again, he circumvented our goals and put an end to peace by destroying the entire council."

Ambrosius changed his tone as he stepped away from the story to talk directly to Thorik. "What I did to those people in Pyrth was unfortunate, and I will never forgive myself. They were going about their lives in peace, free to live how they wished. But understand, my friend: either Darkmere or freedom must die. They cannot coexist."

"Unfortunate?" Thorik's face tightened at Ambrosius' attempt to not fully apologize for his actions. "How do you justify your actions as unfortunate?"

Ambrosius relaxed into his chair again and looked straight into the Num's eyes. "There will come a day when you must make choices and take actions that may seem wrong to your closest friends, and even yourself, but you must do them anyway for the betterment of all humanity. If I had stopped my brother on that day, I could have saved hundreds of thousands of lives. Now they are all still in jeopardy."

"But you hurt others in your failed attempt. I don't believe that I would have made the same choices," Thorik replied.

"And that may be your weakness. You try too hard to please everyone. In doing so, you may be putting them all at risk."

Thorik didn't know how this conversation changed to his own flaws. He took a quick sip of his drink and moved back to Ambrosius' challenges. "If you are the true Dovenar King, take charge of your land. Reunite your people to fight Darkmere. Performing this by yourself only pits them against you. It is not the way for a king to rule."

Ambrosius took a moment to wet his own dry throat. He also took the opportunity to look for others listening to the conversation. All was clear. He leaned forward and talked softly.

"I am not the rightful king. I am an E'rudite. You see, just before the Battle of Maegoth, I discovered that for us to have E'rudite powers our parents must have them as well. My mother didn't, nor did the king. It was Ru'Mere who claimed this ability and therefore was our true father. Our mother, Rubecca, and Ru'Mere had fallen in love prior to her being forced to marry Gorren. She was pregnant at their wedding, but early enough along to assume we were Gorren's children. To give up this information would have caused the deaths of Ru'Mere, Tarosius, myself, and our mother. Knowing this, everyone remained silent."

"So there is no rightful King?" Thorik asked.

Ambrosius stroked his beard. "There is another Dovenar family line that gave birth to a royal child. But that young man is not ready for the throne."

Thorik questioned his thinking. "Your mother was still the queen. Why can't you rule? Why does your E'rudite blood scar over this option?"

Ambrosius realized Thorik's misunderstanding and looked for a way to put it into perspective for him. "Fir Brimmelle has absolute power in your village of Farbank, and look at how it has affected his relationships with others." He raised his hand to prevent any protest from Thorik. "Hear me out on this."

"Imagine if he also had the power of an E'rudite. Fear and resentment would begin to brew among those he ordered. Eventually, his powers would have to be used to stop those that would see him overthrown. Use of his powers would only perpetuate the issue. He would eventually have to rule as a god or be killed. He would have no choice. There is no middle ground to stand on."

"My brother and I should have never been given the kingdom in the first place. It has disrupted the entire land. The time of the E'rudites is over. We should not exist anymore." He took a moment of thought before continuing. "The Alchemists have lost strength every generation since the master book of spells, *Vesik*, was lost in the Govi Glade. They too will soon be a thing of the past."

"I am the only one that can stop Darkmere from taking over Australis. I must do this to allow the land to evolve naturally. It will soon be time for the rightful King to take the throne and for men, Nums, Ov'Unday and Del'Unday to live together."

Thorik cocked his head slightly. "Who is the rightful King?"

"I cannot say without putting his life in danger. He is out among the people and gaining allies as we speak. He will be ready once Darkmere and I are gone. All that is left for me to do is to find Darkmere before the thirteenth day of the twelfth month."

Thorik folded his napkin into a perfect triangle and set it up against the corner of the table as he watched Ambrosius quench his parched mouth after all his talking. Adjusting the napkin to line it up with the table's edge, Thorik asked, "Did you believe it was fate that I found you on the King's River shoreline, or was that just a lie to get me to help you?"

Ambrosius' face saddened as he set his mug down. The smell of ale filled the table as he exhaled deeply. "Obviously it was a lie, my friend." He lowered his eyes. "Otherwise, we would have found Darkmere in time. But with no leads and only a few weeks to go, I don't see how this can be accomplished." Raising his eyes back up to meet Thorik's, Ambrosius said with all sincerity, "I am sorry."

Thorik nodded. "Thank you for being honest with me. But you are wrong; it was fate. For I know where Darkmere is."

Ambrosius wasn't sure what to make of the response. "Don't toy with me."

"He is traveling to Australis Weirfortus," Thorik noted.

Ambrosius' face sank in disbelief. "Then he has found out how to get in."

31

LUTHRALUM TUNIA

Thorik helped Grewen load the boat just as the first light of day crested over the distant mountains. The cool, moist air felt good as it drifted off the lake into Thorik's face. "I'm glad your nephew was willing to lend us his boat."

"He doesn't use it anymore."

The long rowboat was wide enough for Grewen to sit in. Toward the back on both sides, long thin floating stabilizers were connected by angled beams to make sure that they were not in the way of rowing. It was seaworthy and functional, but not fancy. No markings or trim to add any class; however, the design was smooth and pleasing to the eye.

Thorik turned to see Brimmelle running after Gluic as she raced down the street wearing nothing but her undergarments. She was free, like always, enjoying life wherever it took her. She reminded Thorik of his mother and how she never seemed to let things get her down. She could roll with whatever came at her as she enjoyed the ride. Somehow, he felt he was losing that part of himself.

"Thorik?" Grewen asked. "You with me?"

Thorik snapped out of his daydream and answered, "Yes, what do you need?"

"Round everyone up so we can leave."

Thorik did just that. He walked off the dock and back onto the cobblestone way, informing Brimmelle and Gluic that it was time to leave before heading toward the inn to inform Ambrosius and Avanda. He met the two halfway to the inn. The E'rudite's face was hidden by the hood of his cloak as he walked with the Num youth.

"And then I caught a Myth'Unday in my hands," Avanda told Ambrosius as they walked along. She had been explaining all of her high adventures to him ever since they left the inn. "You should have seen it. She was so adorable with her little wings. And then she changed into a butterfly and flew away."

"Why hide?" Thorik asked Ambrosius once Avanda finally took a breath. "These people aren't looking for you. You're safe here."

"You are mistaken. I am currently not safe anywhere. Safer, perhaps, but not safe."

They walked to the boat where they met Brimmelle and Gluic climbing aboard. Circling overhead, Draq waited impatiently for the group to leave.

Grewen was the last to get on. Sitting in the center to help balance out the boat, the mognin pushed off from the dock. Grabbing the paddles, which were attached to the boat with metal pivot joints, he turned the boat around to head away from the shore.

The giant slowly rowed the boat between the many obstacles in their path. Sunken chimneys and roof peaks covered the watery landscape, looking like tombstones floating on the misty lake. Branches of forgotten trees scraped the bottom of the boat like fingers of those who had been lost in the great flood. The old city of Pelonthal rested under the water. It was a constant reminder of the Civil War.

SNACKING ON SEAGULLS IN MIDAIR, Draq flew overhead and helped guide his comrades toward a small island chain filled with palm trees. It was a welcome rest on their journey across the water, but it was only temporary, and the boat soon cast off again to reach Australis Weirfortus before Darkmere did.

While Grewen rowed, Brimmelle took a nap after rigging up a blanket and equipment to provide a small area of shade for his fair-skinned face. Thorik used the free time to update his maps and notes, while Avanda attempted to understand Gluic's unique stone designs.

Thorik's Log: 5th day of the 12th month of the 649th year.

We have set sail and are in a race against time. We have but a week left to cross the lake of Luthralum Tunia and stop Darkmere, assuming he is there at all.

"WHERE DID you get that wooden box?" Ambrosius asked.

"I've had it for years."

"How come I've never noticed it before?"

"Brimmelle doesn't like me wasting time writing in my journals, so I keep it tucked away. Why?"

"It appears very similar to one I once owned." Ambrosius realized he was growing impatient with the slow pace of the boat. He knew Darkmere was about to destroy the kingdom, while he sat there doing nothing more than watching Grewen row. Little things were agitating him. "Don't be hiding things."

"I'm sorry. I didn't realize you hadn't seen it before."

Ambrosius stopped himself and placed a soft hand on the boy's shoulder. "No, I'm sorry. You did nothing wrong."

While weeding the limp plants from her clothes, Gluic had watched the discussion and turned her attention to Ambrosius. "What's on your mind?"

"It's what's not in it." Ambrosius sighed. "I still don't understand how Darkmere found and destroyed the Grand Council. Each member had to be shown the way. I don't believe he knew how to get there. And yet I'm certain he was behind its destruction."

Gluic removed one of her small sacks of stones from her belt. "We never finished regaining your memories, and now is as good a time as any."

"I would appreciate that. In fact, I truly need to know what happened, if for no other reason than for myself."

There was just enough room in the boat for Ambrosius to lie down and receive Gluic's help. She began the same as before with the placing of the stones and then her hands. It wasn't long before his mind drifted off to a faraway place and a memory of the Mountain King statue, the temple room, and the Grand Council.

AMBROSIUS TOSSED Darkmere's disk to the center of the granite table for all to see. It was still attached to the broken necklace that had fallen from its owner's neck. "Someone at this meeting has been spreading Darkmere's poison into our thoughts."

The Grand Council erupted with anger and accusations against one another.

Beltrow put a stop to all conversation as he hammered his fist on the table. "Blasphemy!"

Ambrosius felt the floor below him shake as he saw Beltrow still standing with his hands on the table, frozen with frustration.

Across the room, the E'rudite caught a glimpse of Irluk, the Death Witch, waiting for her new arrivals. Her swirling appearance of ash and coal-colored debris floated a few feet above the temple's floor. Her presence was a sure sign that death would soon be at hand.

A thunderous crack from above caused him to look up and see the neck of the statue crack and the head fall. Irluk faded from Ambrosius' view as he raised his staff in the air. Using his E'rudite powers, he pushed with all his might against the oncoming mountainside. He pushed up into the air against the falling face as it rocked back and forth between nature's gravity and his powers. What felt like minutes to Ambrosius was only seconds to those in the temple as they panicked.

Streams of glowing fiery red lava shot from the now-larger crack below the king's neck. It was too much for even Ambrosius to hold up any longer. The giant face lurched forward and came screaming down at him with the light of the flaming magma surrounding it. There was no time to run or escape.

Time slowed as Ambrosius watched his colleagues run for cover into the chest of the Mountain King statue, but time was not their friend. He stood alone on the far side of the entrance to the temple while the rest pushed their way out.

He braced for the impact in the fraction of the second that was given by holding his staff in both hands above him and creating a shield of energy around himself. But time wasn't on his side either as molten rock crashed through the ceiling and struck the side of his face and chest, knocking him to the floor just as the face of the Mountain King breached the glass ceiling.

All went silent for Ambrosius as he felt himself being crushed by the rock face. His energy shield pushed against his body and then shot him out of the temple. He tumbled through the air and wind, fanning the flames of his burning flesh as he was hurled across to the far side of the lake.

He landed with a crash onto the side of the bridge that spanned the lake's outlet into the river. Sending stone fragments of the railing in every direction, he bounced like a limp doll down to the ground underneath the bridge. Ambrosius had lost control of his powers long enough during the impact to feel his legs slap against the stone before he landed and rolled on the ground toward the lake.

Lying on the shoreline of where the lake met the river, he was in extreme pain. It was overpowering, unlike anything he had ever felt before. Lungs crushed from the crash, he gasped for air. The side of his face and chest was burned, and he couldn't move one of his legs.

Ambrosius rolled over to gaze back across the lake. It was a horrific sight as the glowing red lava poured out of the Mountain King statue's neck and down the front of his body. The staircase windows exuded magma as it worked its way down to the city.

The E'rudite watched for quite some time, grieving the deaths and contemplating the ramifications of what had just occurred. Incapable of getting up, he then pondered his own fate until a cloaked figure in a small rowboat pulled up to shore. The person helped him into the boat and covered him with a blanket. They headed under the damaged bridge and then downstream. Ambrosius fell in and out of consciousness as the river ran down the center of the river-cut gorge before opening up to periodic wide shorelines and occasional rapids.

As they continued, the rapids picked up again and tossed the little boat around in circles until it finally capsized, ejecting both of them into the fast-moving water. Still in deep pain, Ambrosius worked to stay afloat as he watched the other person swim toward the boat that was quickly moving out of Ambrosius' reach downstream.

With the cloak now off the other person's head, the E'rudite could see the face of the one who saved him. It was a servant of the Mountain King's Temple, the one who had been knocked over during Volnic's outburst. Her eyes reached out to him as she grabbed hold of the boat and watched Ambrosius sink under the water.

He struggled to make his way back to the surface as he fought with everything he could against the undertow. He lost his bearings until he cracked his head against a large object. Finding the rocky shoreline, he climbed his way out of the water and onto a large, smooth boulder. He looked back to find that the cloaked figure and the boat were gone.

~

Ambrosius woke with a jolt, soaked in his own sweat. Shaking off the dream-like state, he realized he was back in the mognin rowboat. They had run aground on a small island to take a break from rowing on Lake Luthralum. Thin, tall columns of rocks pierced the sky from the tiny island, which only had a few safe sandy beaches to land on. Draq could be seen perched on top of the rock pillars surveying the ocean landscape.

Everyone stared down at the E'rudite, quietly waiting for him to speak.

Ambrosius organized his thoughts and realized that his pushing of the Mountain King statue's face caused the rocking of the giant stone head and the final tumbling onto the council. "It was I," he exclaimed. "I was the one who destroyed the temple and killed the council.

32

AUSTRALIS WEIRFORTUS

Thorik walked through the story with Ambrosius. "Are you saying that you pushed the head of the Mountain King up, causing it to crack at the neck in the first place?"

"Yes, that is now my belief."

"Why would you do that?" Thorik questioned.

"I thought it was falling down toward us. I was trying to save everyone."

"What made you think it was falling? Didn't you say the quake started before you looked up?"

Ambrosius thought again about his memories. "It was Darkmere's disk. The gem in the center must have been enchanted with a spell of grand illusions," he realized. "It was on the table for all to see. All that needed to be said was the proper word for its spell to be cast on everyone present."

"What word?"

"Blasphemy."

Thorik looked shocked. "Fir Beltrow?"

Ambrosius nodded. "That is when the illusion started."

Brimmelle was not going to listen to them talk badly about a Fir such as Beltrow. "Impossible! No Fir would plan to kill others, let alone destroy his own temple and people. I don't believe it," he protested.

"Nor do I, my friend. Nor do I." Ambrosius' words surprised Brimmelle as the E'rudite stroked his beard. "But that was the word that activated the enchantment. So, if he didn't know, then someone else knew him well enough to gamble on him saying it."

The group thought about his comments as they launched off the sandy beach and continued across the lake. Grewen's rowing provided a respectful speed across the often-choppy waters. It was a long eventless trip that caused the discomfort and edginess that boredom often brings. However, they eventually saw an ominous wall on the horizon.

The Dovenar Wall paled in comparison to the structure rising out of the water before them. This new wall stood taller than the Mountain King statue and bridged a distance of such great length that Thorik could only speculate on its size. It was as if the earth had been turned up on its end, protecting them from falling off the edge.

Closing in on the great wall, they could see slight seams between the massive blocks stacked from deep below the water, and all the way up to the clouds. The sun worked its way into the clear water, showing the seemingly unending depth of the wall.

"What is it?" Thorik was in utter amazement.

"This?" Ambrosius gazed at the overwhelming size of the structure with great respect. "This, my dear friend, is what allows us to exist. It gave birth to our land and allows life to spring forth. This is Australis Weirfortus."

Confused, Thorik asked the obvious question, "How does this wall do all of that?"

"It protects us. If this were not here, we would have never been born, for there would not have been any land to be born to."

Thorik pushed for more clarification. "I don't understand."

"This is not just a wall. It is a barrier that holds back the ocean from regaining this inlet that we call home. If this dam should break, a mountainous wave, thousands of feet high, would rush in and consume everything you have ever seen during your lifetime." Ambrosius glimpsed at Thorik's worried face. "And yes, that means Farbank as well."

"Who could build a mountain of stone blocks?" Thorik asked.

"Notarians, along with the help of E'rudites, the Unday, Humans, and Nums. At one time, they all worked together to create a paradise called Terra Australis, a few thousand feet below sea level. Weirfortus was built, and they removed the ocean waters from the sea inlet to make way for fresh water and new life. But something in paradise went wrong, and a battle ensued, killing most of the humans and Nums while leaving only a few E'rudites and Notarians."

Ambrosius stretched his back and continued. "The remaining Notarians are known today as the three Oracles: Ovlan the Great, Deleth the Dark, and Feshlan the Lost. But even they stayed at odds with each other, which is how the Altered Creatures took over Australis for thousands of years. Finally, humans came into power, allowing for great strides in advancement. But they also fought amongst themselves as well as against the Del'Unday and Ov'Unday. It was at this time that the discovery of the Weirfortus water reservoirs was made. Shortly after that, one of the reservoirs was opened, causing a great flood that wiped out all coastal living."

Thorik opened his coffer to take notes. "The Civil War Flood?"

"That is correct, Thorik. And that was only one reservoir. There are many more, and they continuously fill themselves back up while pulling the salt out of the ocean's water."

"How do you know this?"

"Because after the flood, I was the one who found and then closed the Weir-fortus reservoir doors."

"But why would Darkmere wish to flood the valley?"

Ambrosius thought about the answer before giving it. "I have been asking myself that same question ever since we left port, and I don't think he would. I see no reason for him to destroy everything when he has already removed the council and myself from challenging his authority. But I do believe he will open at least one reservoir to raise the waters higher."

"How high?" Thorik asked.

"Only to the top of the Dovenar walls," Ambrosius answered. "Walls have two potential uses. To keep things out or keep them in." The E'rudite stroked his beard as he spoke. "Disguised as the Terra King, he has scared men into believing that the Del'Unday are on the move. They have all returned home to take refuge behind their tall, sturdy walls that surround Lake Luthralum. The water he releases from Weirfortus will fill in the human provinces, just like it did in River's Edge at the end of the Civil War."

Thorik looked at Ambrosius in disbelief. "He means to kill all humans and Nums in one wave of water."

"I believe so," Ambrosius confessed.

"But won't the water flow through the gates and flood the land beyond?"

"Do you recall the armies of Del'Unday we saw north of Woodlen? They were preparing for an attack that they could not win. In hindsight, it is now obvious they had no intention of breaking through the Dovenar Wall. Only to launch an attack against it."

"Why?"

"So, the Woodlenders would close their solid doors to defend themselves. If Darkmere has set up a minor attack at every gate, then I would assume that every one of them will be closed up tight at the time the wave strikes."

Thorik finished the thought. "Trapping in all the water and the people from escaping as the wave blankets the land."

Not a word was spoken for some time as everyone thought about how it would affect their families, their friends, and the world they knew.

They continued traveling north along the Weirfortus' gigantic structure, passing several half-moon-shaped platforms that extended into the water. Hexagon stone tiles with engraved rune symbols covered the constructed landings, which supported two closed doorways. Each docking plateau looked the same, and the group continued to pass them by until Gluic told them to stop once she felt a change in the wall's energy. The group landed the boat along its thick tiles and got out to stretch their legs and backs after the long day.

"I don't think I will ever get onto another boat again." Brimmelle complained as he groaned from his aches. He placed his hands at his hips and stretched as he reviewed the various rune symbols below his feet.

Grewen glanced over at him and thought about how Brimmelle was fortunate enough to be able to stand and stretch while in the boat. "It's a long swim home, little man."

Draq had already landed and rested, roosting on a long stone slab that spanned over both entrances into the Weirfortus Dam.

Thorik started removing gear from the boat as Gluic and Avanda wandered off to explore the docking platform. He gazed up at the constructed stone cliff as it reached high into the sky and then back down toward the two closed stone doors. "Which one?"

"I thought you were the one with all the answers," Draq sarcastically stabbed from above.

"Well, just because…" Thorik began to defend himself while watching Ambrosius walk past him and approach the left doorway. Puffing up his chest, Thorik replied to the dragon's comment with a grin. "This one," he ordered, pointing toward the left door. Internally, he was hoping Ambrosius wouldn't change his mind.

Grewen turned to Draq. "He's our leader." He held a straight face before cracking a smirk.

The Red-Tipped Silver Dragon wasn't impressed. Frustrated, he yelled at Brimmelle to get his mother before she fell into the lake as she reached out into the water to pet a passing fish.

Thorik and Grewen had followed Ambrosius to the large smooth stone door. The doorway was covered with a row of hexagon tiles, each with a separate rune. The tile placement arched along the inside of the frame, and several of them were missing.

Thorik was confused as he watched Ambrosius search for a way to open the stone door. "I thought you had been here before."

Frustration filled Ambrosius' expression. "Yes. It was a different reservoir, and the door was open at the time I arrived."

Grewen stepped over to investigate the second door. "If Gluic is accurate in saying this is the correct platform, then either Darkmere hasn't arrived yet, or he figured out how to get in and then closed the entrance afterward."

"It's about time we got the upper hand on him," Thorik gladly commented.

Ambrosius was not ready to join Thorik in his enthusiasm. "We don't have anything on him yet. He managed to send a spy into the secret and hidden council meeting. He successfully baited me into attacking Pyrth to strike fear into the populace against me. And he knows my son is out of hiding. I can only hope this is not another trap. No, my friend, we do not have the upper hand yet."

Ambrosius continued searching. "It would appear that these tiles are about the same size as the ones you carry. Hand me one from your collection."

Thorik took out his sack of Runestones and looked inside it.

Ambrosius answered Thorik's question before he could utter it. "Any of them will do fine."

Thorik reached in, pulled one out, and looked at it briefly as he handed it to him. It was the Unity Runestone. Finding it appropriate for the situation, Thorik smiled at the irony. "Who would have ever thought they would see Del'Unday, Ov'Unday, Nums, and an E'rudite all working together?"

Ambrosius began to place the stone in one of the missing tile locations. It looked like it was going to fit. He retracted his hand. "Yes, I think these will work.

Now, we need to determine the correct order to place them in. Hopefully, once all are in place, the door will open."

"We have a problem," Grewen announced. "This door already has all of its Runestones in place. So, if our presumption is correct, they have entered here and closed the door behind them."

Ambrosius realized they may already be too late, and the water could be entering the spillway at any moment. "Thorik, see if the Runestones are in the same sequence on that door frame," he ordered with urgency in his voice.

Thorik ran over and quickly had his answer. "They are completely different." On his way back to Ambrosius, he looked into his full sack of flat Runestones. "We could just start trying them until it opens, although it may take some time."

Scratching his beard, the E'rudite's eyes darted back and forth while contemplating the situation. "No, the wrong combination could cause this door to open with a wave of water behind it, or this entire platform may drop into the lake. I know not what traps lie within this. The same could be true if I force it open. I tread lightly on Notarian artifacts." He raked his fingers through his hair as he tried to contain his emotions.

Grewen returned to the first door, and they all continued to search for a pattern within the symbols. Every second that passed could be the one that they needed to stop Darkmere's plan. "Death is among us on this day," the giant said to Ambrosius.

"It is not like you to give up so easily, my old friend," the E'rudite commented before he noticed Grewen gazing out on the water. Following his line of sight, the rest of the group saw Grewen's concern.

A partially transparent woman stood just above the surface of the water. Her clothes were made of shadows and mist, which evaporated as they drifted away from her. Dark smoky ashes gave depth to her body and face as she scowled at the group from behind her flowing dark gray hair made up entirely of burnt debris.

"Irluk," Ambrosius told them. "To see the Death Witch before a battle is a bad omen." Looking at Thorik with concern, he added, "I saw her in the fog before the battle of Maegoth and again before the destruction of the council. There will be a battle here today, and death is certain."

Gluic eyed the apparition. "You were once so beautiful. It's such a shame what you became."

Thorik watched the ghostly shadow of a woman fade away in the breeze, but her absence didn't calm his nerves. A shiver ran down his spine, and the hairs on his body stood on end. "Who will die today?"

Ambrosius struggled with her image as well. Few had seen Irluk and lived to talk about it. He knew she was closing in on him, for he had seen her far too often. However, he needed to evade her just one more time.

"Thorik, back to the doorway and the runes. This is your area of expertise. Tell us what to do!" Ambrosius snapped as he ran his fingers through his hair again, nearly pulling handfuls out by the roots.

Thorik racked his brain over the puzzle with no obvious answer. He had inspected the runes in the tiles on the platform they stood on, finding no common series. "I don't know!"

"Quickly, Thorik. We have no time for this!"

Guilt set in as the Num tried to determine the answer that Ambrosius demanded. "I'm sorry!"

By this point, Brimmelle strolled up to them after settling his mother's needs and glanced at the missing tiles. "Looks like you're missing the Justice, Courage, Compassion, and Harmony Runestones," he said very matter-of-factly.

The group turned in disbelief and looked at the hefty Num for an awkward moment.

Abruptly, Ambrosius questioned his comment. "And what makes you say this?"

As always, Brimmelle didn't appreciate being questioned, especially on Runestones. "The rest of them are in the same sequence as the ones outside the city of Kingsfoot." Periodically, his natural ability to memorize everything he saw came in handy. He had never been wrong about such things and did not like being questioned.

For the first time, Ambrosius looked at the Fir with respect. "Thank you. I'm glad you came on this journey. Quickly, Thorik, put them in place."

He reached into his bag and began pulling out the needed stones. It wasn't long before he had all but one of them. And then it hit him. He had given the merchant in the Pyrth market one of his Runestones, but which one? She had selected one from his hand, and the rest were quickly set back into the bag.

Frantically, he dug in his bag to find it. "Could I have traded the key to unlocking this door and saving the valley for a mere sack of fruit? What have I done?"

"Hurry, Thorik!" Ambrosius ordered.

Thorik dumped the bag on the ground, got down on all fours, and separated them. "Please, Mountain King," he prayed out loud. "I'll never give out another of your sacred Runestones again. I'll cherish them and protect them." As the last word crossed his lips, he recovered the Runestone he needed. With a sigh of relief, he solemnly thanked the king as he placed the stones where Brimmelle pointed.

A low rumbling could be heard and felt under their feet. The group backed away from the doorway, nervous of the unknowns on the other side. Grinding rock moaned as the door slab slowly slid to the side. Ambrosius leaned forward to see the darkness from behind it. He held Thorik back from doing the same.

A long granite corridor was exposed. Its once-polished floors and walls were now covered with dust and cobwebs. Carved symbols and unknown writing decorated the walls, which stood several shoulder lengths apart.

The E'rudite stepped forward and peered deeper into the passage. Putting one foot inside, he waited for any potential trap or reaction. None emerged, so he stepped fully through the archway.

A ground-shaking thud followed his entrance. Brimmelle jumped for cover. Thorik leaped in after Ambrosius to save him, startling the man from behind.

Grewen stood calm. "It was the door completing its motion."

Ambrosius removed a common rock from his pocket and focused on it. Using his abilities, he placed intense pressure on it, causing it to glow. "If Darkmere is already here, time is against us. We must move with haste and caution." Levitating the now luminous liquid rock in front of him as a light source, he headed down the corridor.

Thorik placed the other Runestones back in his bag and followed him in.

Hunched over, Grewen was the next to enter the doorway. Brimmelle waited for the mognin to creep forward as the giant's body fit tightly into the available space.

Thorik stopped and turned around as he lit a torch. "Grewen, do you need help?"

"No, but don't let me slow you. I'll be there as soon as I can."

Ambrosius looked back at the giant mognin scraping his shoulder blades across the ceiling. "If there is no time to wait for you, I will not. I would expect the same from you, my old friend."

Grewen nodded. "True enough. Get going."

With that, Thorik and Ambrosius raced up the long corridor.

$$\text{❧ } 33 \text{ ❧}$$

DEL'UNDAY AMBUSH

Draq watched as Grewen attempted to force his bulky body through the doorway. Sniffing the air, the dragon lifted his long muzzle upward. Something wasn't right. His instincts were warning him of danger. Searching the platform, he saw that all was calm, and Avanda and Gluic had wandered back to the water's edge. "Brimmelle, get Grewen back out here."

Brimmelle didn't like the tone of the dragon's voice, let alone Draq himself. "He's almost through the doorway. What do you need?"

"Now, Fesh!" Draq yelled. "Get him out here, right now!"

"Fine." Tossing his hands in the air, the Fir worked his way under the giant to relay Draq's message.

Draq scrutinized the landscape for anything out of place. Again, the only activity was the two female Nums at the platform's edge.

Avanda could see in Gluic's face that something was wrong. "Gluic, are you ill?"

She did not reply. Lowering herself to one knee, Gluic softly touched the ends of her fingers to the tile platform.

"What is it?" Avanda asked.

Gluic waited a few seconds as she tuned into the vibrations she felt from her fingertips. "Here it comes." Then, unexpectedly, she pushed the youth toward Grewen and the doorways. "Run child! Run!"

Avanda was confused and turned after only a few steps. In doing so, she watched in horror as an enormous snake-like tail reached out of the lake, grabbed Gluic, and pulled her underwater.

"Gluic!" Avanda yelled as she stepped forward a few paces with arms stretched out in a wasted effort to save her.

Draq had seen the assault and was in the air and past Avanda before she realized what had happened. After a sudden rotation of his body to fly upside down, he arched his head back to dive aggressively into the water after the elder Num.

Avanda took another step and stopped before looking back at Brimmelle, who was running toward the water to save his mother. Behind him, Grewen had finally backed out of the doorway.

Missing the event, Grewen searched for Gluic and Draq as he followed Brimmelle. "Avanda, get to the doorway," Grewen yelled across the platform.

"But Gluic was pulled into the water. We must do something," she replied.

"Get away from the water, right now!" he demanded.

It was very uncharacteristic of Grewen to order her in such a manner. Knowing she had to follow his words, she struggled with the idea of just running away when Gluic was in trouble. She quickly met him halfway to plead for his help. In doing so, she could see that his eyes were fixated on something behind her, so she turned to investigate.

Along the shore was a soft outline of an object coming into view. It quickly materialized into a ship that had been docked on the opposite side of the platform from their rowboat. The illusion of invisibility faded and exposed a vessel with several Del'Unday standing on its top deck watching the new arrivals.

"The dragon is gone!" yelled a large white wolf-like creature with two long muscular tentacles extending from its upper shoulder blades. "Delvorian, you're with me. The rest of you prepare the boat for sailing. Darkmere should return soon."

Controlled movements of the thick tentacles were frequently interrupted by a loose snap, much like a bullwhip. But instead of just the sound of a crack, it gave off a strong electrical discharge that could be heard, seen, and smelled.

The mutated wolf-like creature jumped off the ship and onto the tiled platform. With strong shoulders that were taller than a Num, its tentacles rose higher than Grewen's head. This was a wolvian. Intelligent, calculating, and very dangerous.

A second Del'Unday leaped from the ship and landed next to the wolvian. It was a Brandercat. It landed with a slight favor on one side, and Grewen could see a deep scar on his right shoulder.

"I have a score to settle with your short companion when he returns. But I hope you'll entertain us until then." The chameleon cat limped forward from the injury Thorik had given him north of Woodlen. "Ka'Ru, you can have the Mog. I've got the taste for Num today."

Growls, barks, and cheers from the boat were quickly extinguished as Ka'Ru turned his head up toward them. This was not entertainment for him. This was a necessary removal of an obstacle. The Del'Unday on the ship quickly returned to their duties to avoid the watchful eye of the wolvian standing on the platform.

Grewen pushed Avanda behind him. "Run to Thorik. Tell him it's a trap."

She refused to run and leave her friends in such peril. She looked to the water and wondered what was happening under the surface.

Draq dove through the clear water behind the fast-moving sea snake. Wider than the dragon and three times as long, the serpent had collected its first catch for the day. Gluic was caught in its forked tail and was whipped back and forth. The snake could easily out-swim Draq if it was not for its cargo of Gluic.

Using this to his advantage, Draq simply stayed behind the sea serpent instead of trying to outmaneuver the creature. Trailing in its wake, he caught up and reached out to grab the snake, first with his claws on the front of his wings and then with his strong back legs.

His sharp nails pierced the snake's scales, causing a trail of blood to spill out, but it wasn't enough to cause it to let go of Gluic, who was going limp.

He knew her air was about out, and time was of the essence. Raising his sharp, red-tipped tail, he thrust it deep into the snake.

The snake went straight with pain, releasing Gluic. Her limb body floated lifeless. It appeared to be too late. But after a moment, she slowly regained her bearings and slowly swam toward the surface.

Draq started to follow her back to the surface until he realized that his tail was still lodged in the snake's body. He was unable to pull it out as he watched the Num float up and away from him.

∾

Brimmelle turned to Grewen. "Kill these deformed beasts. I'm going after my mother." He then prepared to dive into the water.

Ka'Ru took offense at the comment. His tentacles snapped in Brimmelle's direction, causing an electrical spark to shoot out from them, striking the Num in the head. Brimmelle stiffened for a moment before collapsing to the ground.

Avanda turned and ran for the doorway. She finally realized the need for Thorik's and Ambrosius' help.

Delvorian suddenly appeared out of thin air, blocking her path. His Brandercat abilities had allowed him to run around Grewen without being seen in his effort to block her entrance into the doorway.

The Brandercat purred, "You're too late to go for help, but not too late to be my next meal."

34

SIBLING RIVALRY

Thorik and Ambrosius reached a side entrance into a huge underground tubular waterway. Empty of water now, this new room looked like it could easily carry the flow of several King's Rivers.

Peering out from behind the entrance to the room, Ambrosius and Thorik surveyed the situation before attacking. They did not wish to fall into another trap of Darkmere's making.

Two massive metal doors rested at one end of the waterway. They were taller than the Dovenar Wall and as wide as they were high. Layers of artistically designed metal extended several inches into the room. A long continuous hinge ran along the doorway's stone sides as the closed double doors touched each other tightly. Torchlight reflected off the shiny metal doors into the room in wavy patterns. No rust or degradation was evident on the wet metal hinges or decorative door faces.

Wide stone locking pins extended several feet out of the floor and ceiling to cover the seam where the doors had met. One locking pin slowly slid into the ceiling and the other slid into the floor. The thick strong pins, which prevented the doors from opening, continued to disappear from their view. They were the only things holding back the doors and the massive amount of water from the reservoir on the other side.

Gaps between the doors began to release the water's pressure in powerful jets that shot in every direction, causing several inches to wash over the door level landing, down into the main part of the room, and then out through a long tunnel that ran to the lake.

Following the flow of water into the center of the room on the lower level, Thorik caught sight of several people rotating two of the four enormous valves as they walked around in circles, pushing the valve handles. Each valve apparently controlled one of the locking pins.

Looking at the group, Thorik gasped as he noticed Emilen and Wess, along with several others, working one of the valves. They all wore red cloaks similar to those of the Red Guards in Pyrth.

"It's Emilen and Wess! We need to save them." Thorik weighed his options to reach them undetected. "I think we can reach them if we go back and use that last branch in the tunnel." Thorik raced off to see if his assumption was correct. Upon turning down the side hall, he placed his backpack down as a signal to notify Grewen where to turn.

Ambrosius was not interested in the workers that rotated the large levers. He was glaring at Darkmere, who stood on the far side of the giant tube-shaped room designed as a spillway for millions of gallons of rushing water. He stood at the top of a far staircase, much like the one Ambrosius was standing on, and watched the door's locking pins continue to open. Ambrosius finally had his opportunity to confront his brother and, with a bit of luck, end his plans of destruction and domination.

With a flick of Ambrosius' finger, the stone steps fell out from under Darkmere's feet, causing him, and some rubble, to fall onto the ledge in front of the giant metal doors. He rolled and tumbled until he landed face down, covered with small pebbles.

Darkmere raised his eyes to see Ambrosius resolutely advance down the steps, along the wall, and then toward him. Returning to his feet, Darkmere stared contemptuously at his approaching brother.

Startled, the workers had stopped turning the cranks that were unlocking the doors to observe the conflict.

With a disrespectful glance to his side, Darkmere scowled at his crew. "Back to work!" Slowly and methodically, he returned his attention to Ambrosius. "Welcome, my brother. I was beginning to think you had missed the clues needed to get here in time. Bringing Gluic back to life paid off." He gave Ambrosius a devilish smile. "Surely you didn't think her return was pure luck?"

With only a slight hesitation, the workers returned to their tasks, pushing the rods attached to the valve in the center.

The water continued to pour out of the door seams, shooting in every direction. Stray waterspouts hit the workers, knocking some off their feet, and a few struggled to get back up.

Jets of high-pressure water occasionally slapped against the two E'rudites as they stood at odds with each other on the platform next to the doors. In addition, several inches of water rushed across the platform and then ran its course past them and into the rest of the room.

Ambrosius spoke first. "Before I destroy you, I want to know why. Why have you spent your entire life torturing me? Killing my wife, hunting my son, destroying everything I've created. Why?"

Arrogant, Darkmere looked shocked at the question. "How can you ask that after destroying everything that was rightfully ours? By our birthright, the entire Dovenar Kingdom was ours to rule. It was you who betrayed the kingdom by siding with the Ov'Unday, causing the Civil War. It was you who turned Ru'Mere away, and it was with his anger at you that he released these waters and flooded our great cities." Darkmere pointed his thin finger at Ambrosius. "You destroyed my Kingdom. Now I have destroyed yours, so we can make a fresh start."

Ambrosius looked down at Darkmere's outstretched arm. "Your perception of the truth has been poisoned beyond your comprehension and outside my ability to rectify." Reaching out with his mind, he crushed every bone in Darkmere's hand. "I banish you from this land, once and for all!"

Darkmere's hand imploded as fluids splattered in all directions. It was quickly followed by the snapping of bones in various locations of his arm, working from his wrist all the way up to his shoulder. Darkmere screamed out in pain.

~

MEANWHILE, Thorik exited the lower tunnel. To his side, he saw Ambrosius and Darkmere standing on the upper tier in front of the gigantic doors, which groaned from the pressure on the far side. In front of him, Emilen, Wess, and the others continued to rotate the valve that lifted the top locking pin. There were also eight more servants rotating the other valve for the bottom pin.

Both groups were wet and tired as they walked in circles, wading in nearly two feet of water. Even with the water running down the spillway, there was enough new water showering in from around the double doors to keep the levels high.

Thorik ran to Emilen. "Emilen, stop what you're doing. You'll flood the whole valley. We need to turn the valves the other way before it's too late."

"Thorik!" she yelled with excitement. "You've come. I'm so glad you decided to join us."

"No, not join. I'm here to save you and Australis." Thorik walked backwards, in front of her, as she continued to push forward.

"What are you talking about?" She continued pushing. "We need to cleanse the one to regain our Kingdom."

"I don't understand." He grabbed the lever arm of the valve and started to push back. However, the eight others pushing against him continued its clockwise rotation.

"You remember, from the Portent Scrolls. You've known it ever since you were a child. We all have!" she said prior to reciting the lyrics of the children's game.

> *"When all the jewels are in his crown,*
> *The mighty king will drop it down.*
> *All but one of the gems will break*
> *As it plummets into a nearby lake*
>
> *The treasure will again appear*
> *Striking disbelievers with great fear.*
> *But if the one is cleansed, you see*
> *Rebirth to the kingdom is foreseen"*

She continued, "It's Ambrosius. He is the one jewel that dropped from the

Mountain King's crown and landed in the lake. Returning to Woodlen, he caused great fear. Now all we have to do is cleanse him for the prophecy to come true, and our Mountain King faith will be reborn to new levels."

Thorik couldn't believe his ears. "No, you've got the wrong Kingdom. It's Darkmere's Kingdom that will be reborn. The Terra King is actually Darkmere in disguise."

Water was pouring out ever faster, and the level in the room had risen another half a foot.

Emilen grabbed Thorik's hands and locked them onto the handle with her own hands. "You're wrong, Thorik. This is our chance to make the ultimate sacrifice for our belief."

Thorik looked at her. Her red hood covered most of her beautiful curly hair, and her eyes were shallow and distant. It was Emilen, yet it wasn't. Her personality no longer was glowing, but the gem in the center of her new brass disk that hung from a leather necklace was.

"Em," Thorik asked, "How did you know what happened in Woodlen? And how did you know Ambrosius was coming here?"

"The Terra King already knew he was coming to Pyrth. I just needed to tell him where our camp was. He then gave Gluic's crystal the information needed to lead Ambrosius here."

Thorik was shocked. "How? Em, how could he have known we were coming to Pyrth? How did he know of Gluic's use of crystals?"

~

DRAQ WAS PULLED DEEPER into the water as he fought to free his tail.

The Giant Sea Snake dragged the Red-Tipped Silver Dragon along the Weirfortus wall in an attempt to kill him. Slapping Draq against the wall only embedded his pointed tail farther into the snake.

Draq's claws scratched at the stone, hoping to find something to grasp on the smooth wall. His air was limited, and he would need to escape soon to have any chance of surviving.

Without warning, the wall disappeared from his view, in what appeared to be a large opening into the Weirfortus structure. Draq prepared himself for the other side of the opening. When it came, he flung his body against the inside wall of the entrance and grabbed on with everything he had.

Slapping his body onto the inside wall of the tunnel caused serious pain, but the quick jar released the snake. Shaking it off as fast as possible, Draq quickly swam through the tunnel's entrance. The chase was back on, but this time Draq was the prey, and the snake was not encumbered with Gluic.

Draq realized that he had made a critical mistake. He had no idea if this tunnel would lead to air, something he desperately needed. "No point in second-guessing myself," he thought. Faster and faster, he sped through the water as the snake gained on him.

It was getting dark and difficult to see, even for his exceptional eyesight. Nothing was in view, and he was hoping he would not run into a wall at this speed.

The only benefit to the darkness was that, with any luck, the snake also was blinded.

Doubting his decisions, he considered making a sharp turn in the dark and then heading back out of the tunnel. But before he began the maneuver, he spied a slight light ahead. Racing with everything he had left, he breached the water's surface. "Air," he coughed after a large gasp.

Raising his head, he searched and found the source of the light down the tunnel. It was the last thing he saw before the snake attacked him from behind and swallowed him whole.

～

THE LARGE CAT, Delvorian, who once chased Thorik north of Woodlen, now blocked Avanda's access to the Weirfortus doorway. Instead of trying to get around him, she turned and ran to the mognin rowboat.

The cat slowly stalked her. He knew she couldn't get away. The idea of her running only excited him and increased his hunger.

Avanda grabbed her red purse of magical items that she had taken from Sharcodi, north of Pyrth. Turning with the sack in hand, she reached in and pulled out a vial of liquid. "Stay back or I'll turn you into a pig," she claimed, hoping he would accept her bluff.

He stopped for a moment and looked at the symbols on the sack. He knew it contained Sharcodi's enchanted items and came to a stop. "You don't know how to use them. Now put those down before you dissolve yourself, depriving me of my fresh meal." He proceeded toward her.

"I'm warning you. I'll use this."

"Then use it and get it over with. I'm hungry," Delvorian purred out at her while increasing his speed.

She threw the vial at him, which popped him on the nose before it bounced off and shattered on the tile floor. A purple liquid spilled out, causing a greasy stain on the ground.

The cat growled as he pawed his bleeding nose. Her attack had only annoyed him.

～

KA'RU BARKED as he showered Grewen with sparks from each whip of his tentacles. The tips of these flexible appendages fired small blue lightning bolts in every direction.

Electrical burns covered Grewen's forearms and hands while protecting his head. The giant tried several times to grab the powerful whips, but only received cuts and scorched skin to show for it.

"Why are you helping Darkmere flood the lands?" Grewen asked him as he defended himself.

"It is our time to take Australis back from the humans," he replied.

"But Darkmere is human. You would lower yourself to follow him?" Grewen pushed to cause friction from within.

"We will allow him to help us until we don't need him anymore," answered the wolvian.

"So, your alliance is not strong with him?" he prodded.

The muscular wolf-like creature was not about to tip his hand to the mognin. "It is strong enough." He lashed out and struck Grewen's chest with both tentacles at the same time.

Grewen's body straightened up and shook violently for several seconds before falling to the hard stone, landing with a thud.

AMBROSIUS and his brother continued their battle. Darkmere's crippled body was hunched over as he reached out and touched the ground in front of him. The stone at his fingertips changed into molten rock, and a river of it instantly raced forward upon the floor, heading toward Ambrosius. Steam rose as the water sprayed onto it.

Ambrosius jumped to the side, but his nemesis' power of alteration was strong; the shallow trench of super-heated stone followed his moves. He ran back up the stairs as the alteration caught up to him and melted the steps below his feet.

Launching himself away from the steps and through the air, Ambrosius landed near the seam of the doors. The powerful jets of water shot inches from his face as he gained his footing. Using nature's own water pressure, he angled the stream toward his brother.

The burst of water shot at Darkmere, who raised his arms the best he could. Not to defend himself, but to alter the air in front of him into an inferno.

The air between them changed to a furnace of flame and heat, evaporating the water instantly.

Ambrosius could feel the heat burn his skin and his lungs. Unable to breathe, he covered his face. His clothes and staff ignited in flames as he pushed more water toward Darkmere with no effect, except for the additional steam.

Resorting to his non-E'rudite powers, Ambrosius raised his flaming staff and launched it through the air like a spear. Darkmere had no time to react as the weapon emerged from the cloud of steam. Striking him on the forehead, it knocked him onto his back, breaking his concentration and ending the firestorm. Regardless, steam continued to billow from the magma on the floor, along with the cracking and popping of the water trying to cool it.

Before Darkmere could recover, Ambrosius tossed his brother in the air while reaching down and picking up his scorched wooden staff. After slamming into a far wall, Darkmere fell forward onto the floor. His body had been crippled and mangled by Ambrosius. Arms and legs were shattered at every joint. The only things functioning were his head and a few internal organs as he struggled on the upper terrace floor. Heavy waters splashed at him, washing him over the ledge and onto the main floor where his followers stood.

Emilen let go of Thorik's hands and ran over to Darkmere to pull his head above water while Ambrosius walked to the edge and looked down at his dying brother. Emilen cradled his head in her arms as his limp body swayed in the water's flow.

Ambrosius looked down at Emilen for a moment in her hooded robe with the brass disk and gem hanging from her neck. "It's you." It suddenly hit him. "You were Beltrow's assistant. You brought the gem to the council, but Volnic pushed you and broke the necklace that held it around your neck. Even so, you knew your father would eventually say the word to activate the illusion." His memories erupted as he looked at her. "I remember you pulling me into the boat and saving me. For what purpose? Just to lead me back into Darkmere's trap? Have you worked for Darkmere all along?" Ambrosius' mind raced as all the points finally connected. Beltrow had told him that he sent his daughter for the annual summer trade, yet Dare said they never arrived in Shoreview. She must have joined the Terra King as a Grand Fir during that trip. "Thorik, how long have you known Emilen?"

Fighting the current of the water, Thorik replied, "She arrived at Farbank about the same time I found you in the forest. But it can't be her; the spirits in Kingsfoot said that you killed them."

"The statues did not say that I killed them. They asked why the killer had returned. Emilen had returned to Kingsfoot and was in the city while we were talking to the spirits."

Thorik also started piecing it together: her comments to the Num merchant in Pyrth, her arguments with Brimmelle, her insistence on helping Ambrosius travel to Woodlen, everything.

"Why?" Thorik asked her.

"The Terra King speaks the words of the Mountain King. Listen to him. Realize what he could do for us. As a spiritual leader, they sent me on an important assignment, for our faith, to destroy the council and bring Ambrosius to Woodlen." Emilen touched Thorik's face softly to get him to understand. "We must help fulfill the Portent Scrolls and release the waters to cleanse him." She then looked up at the one she was referring to: Ambrosius.

Just then, Darkmere leaped out of the water as a shot of highly pressured water hit Ambrosius in the back. Darkmere's E'rudite abilities had mended his bones and tissues, just as he had done as the Terra King in Pyrth's amphitheater. Reaching up, he grabbed Ambrosius' left ankle and his right calf.

The skin, as well as the clothes that covered Ambrosius' lower body, mutated in form. Flesh and blood turned to soft, rotten wood with multiple cracks and holes. The transformation raged down into the stone floor as well as up his legs.

Ambrosius' right hand reached for the pain racing up his leg. Upon touching it, his hand and wrist became victims of the mutation as well. His now wooden hand was stuck to his wooden trunk, which rooted deep into the floor.

"You are not as bright as I thought, brother. I would have expected you to have already figured this out. By following my trail, you have made these people's prophecy complete, and rebirth of my Kingdom can begin."

Grabbing Darkmere's waist with his mind, Ambrosius squeezed tight, preventing any chance of escape for his brother.

Realizing he was captured with few options, Darkmere used his powers of alteration to change his form into that of Ambrosius' wife, Asha. She now stood where he once did, still being compressed with her arms tight at her sides. Her long, dark hair flailed about as she struggled to get free.

Asha screamed in pain from Ambrosius' grip. "Please, dear, no!" she called out to him. Her rich brown eyes and lovely lips begged Ambrosius to stop his attack.

Hesitation cut Ambrosius' focus as he saw his wife being crushed by his own powers. Understanding it was an illusion did not shield his heart from breaking at the sight of her in pain. Unfortunately, it drove deep into his emotions just long enough to allow Darkmere to break free.

Asha's face changed from a soft tan skin to a coarse white sand. The skin texture quickly expanded to the rest of her body and clothes. Afterward, her face changed back to Darkmere's bony appearance, still of sand.

Regaining control of his thoughts, Ambrosius squeezed with all his might.

The center of Darkmere's body rushed up and down from the point of the crushing grip. His body, now fully comprised of granular pieces, had easily been displaced. Each piece of sand fell back into its normal position once Ambrosius let go.

Ambrosius tried several more times to break or crush his brother's body, only to see the scattering of sand that moved back afterward. He unleashed a full wall of force, knocking Darkmere against the far wall. The body parts that had been displaced from the blast quickly reunited with his main trunk.

Still in pain, Darkmere laughed as he waved his minions to leave and then began to follow. Turning his head back toward his brother, he said, "It's too late. I have already won. Even if you were able to kill me, no one trusts you now. You have no friends, no army supporting you, and no voice of power. You're already dead."

The words stung more than the pain in his lower body. His mind replayed his brother's comments as he helplessly watched Darkmere begin to leave the room.

Ambrosius had to destroy his brother before freedom was lost forever. The only part of his brother's white granular body that he hadn't seen completely dissolve was his head. As he directed his E'rudite resources to crush Darkmere's skull, he heard a crack of unimaginable intensity.

Breaking off the remaining stone locking pins, water burst out of the doorway, slamming the metal doors to each side. A gigantic wave of water rushed out, the likes of which they had never seen before. Ambrosius rotated his upper body around to face the oncoming threat. Instinctively, he raised his staff with his free hand to hold the water back as hundreds of thousands of tons of pressure crashed against his invisible shield.

Quickly slipping out through a side tunnel with his minions, Darkmere escaped.

🕊 35 🕊

FLOOD WATERS

Grewen slowly regained his footing after being shocked by Ka'Ru's tentacles. Large scorched flashpoints remained red and tender on his chest from the most recent assault.

Brimmelle helped Gluic out of the water as Avanda situated herself between them and the prowling cat, Delvorian.

Beads, powders, strings, and seeds were scattered across the platform. A jar of eyeballs, box of thorns, mirror, and vial of blood were still intact despite Avanda's attempts to break them against the cat's face. So far, nothing that she had used from her sack of magic had done anything but slow the creature down. All that remained was a stick and a few dozen orange berries. The rest of the odd objects were scattered all over the platform, showing no magical ability. She simply didn't know how to activate them.

It was at this time that a crack rumbled the platform and the stone moaned from great pressure. The docking platform's right doorway rumbled open, and several Nums rushed out, followed by Darkmere. Emilen was among them and stopped long enough to remove the Runestones she had added to open the stone door for Darkmere. Wess exited the door and noticed his old friends on the far side of the platform as he was herded toward the ship by one of the Del'Unday.

Ka'Ru looked over his shoulder at Darkmere. "We will be there momentarily, my lord." He gave a slight bow of his head.

The Nums climbed aboard and were followed by the dark lord.

"Set sail," Darkmere ordered. "I want to be away from the wall when the water is released." Watching his servants Ka'Ru and Delvorian, he added, "Kill them and board at once."

With that, the ship started pulling away from the dock. They would have little time to finish their killing before they needed to make the leap onto the ship.

Wess could not stand by while Avanda was ripped apart. "No!" he screamed as he jumped off the ship and onto the platform.

Avanda pulled the handful of berries out of the sack and tossed them at the cat's open mouth. "Chew on these, you Fesh!" Half of them landed on the ground, rolling in various directions.

The cat chewed the ones that entered his mouth, swallowed, and smiled. Again, no results. "Delicious."

Avanda pulled out the stick, which was the last item in the sack, just as the Brandercat jumped on her and knocked her to the ground. Pinning her down, his head lurched forward to grab her throat.

Wess slammed his entire body against the cat, knocking it off of Avanda. She was free, but now Wess and Delvorian were locked together in a heated battle.

Wess used his strength to squeeze the cat's neck, cutting off his air. The Brandercat changed colors and shades as he bucked and tried to shake Wess off his back. The creature was weakening, but then again, so was the Num as he lost his balance. Wess fell to the platform with a thud, flat on his back, and the wind was knocked out of him long enough for the Brandercat to gather its wits.

Avanda ran to his aid, but Delvorian reached him first. With a quick bite to his neck and a twist of his head, the cat had snapped Wess' neck. The Num's body went limp, his head hung from the cat's mouth, and his arms fell to the platform like dead snakes. Delvorian dropped the lifeless Num from his blood-stained teeth and snarled at Avanda.

Avanda stood no more than an arm's length away. Shocked at the scene, she didn't know how to react. However, the Brandercat did. It took advantage of her fear and stepped up to her.

Opening his mouth and turning his head sideways, Delvorian placed his teeth around the frozen girl's throat. The cat's hot breath coated her neck as she stood in shock. It was over. There was nowhere else to run. Avanda winced as she felt a few of his teeth graze her skin, but instead of chomping down on her, he stopped and froze in his position.

Rumbling from deep inside Delvorian could be heard, causing his face to tighten and his side to flinch. It grew louder as the cat recoiled in pain and arched his shoulders forward. Short, deep breaths became loud and inconsistent. Losing his sense of balance, the cat spread his legs to keep from falling over. His very own actions had activated the orange berries.

Avanda snapped out of her trance and backed away from Delvorian, for it appeared the cat was going to be sick. Gluic grabbed Avanda's hand and made a dash toward the doorway. They would run for safety within Weirfortus, out of sight of the Del'Unday. However, Avanda attempted to pull away from Gluic to pick up her scattered unused magical items.

"Not now, Avanda. You can collect them later," Gluic instructed.

"But I can use them to save Uncle Wess," the youth responded as she looked at all the magical items scattered across the platform. Each had powers. She just needed to figure out how to activate them to save him. Tears ran down her face as she looked at her uncle's limp body lying among useless magical objects. She was desperate for a way to make things right.

Beyond his body, a ghostly dark shadow floated on the lake. Irluk moved toward Wess, preparing to take what was rightfully hers.

Gluic reached around Avanda and gave her a warm hug as she gazed at the Death Witch. "I'm sorry dear, but there's no way we can bring him back now. It was his time," Gluic confessed. "Be proud that he was there for you." She continued to escort the youth to the Weirfortus entrance.

Turning back toward the platform as they reached the doorway, Avanda saw dozens of giant larvae bursting forth from the Brandercat's midsection, consuming the cat from the inside out. Gluic covered her eyes and guided her into Weirfortus and up the long hallway.

Stunned at the scene, Ka'Ru lost concentration just long enough for Grewen to grab the wolvian's long thick tentacles, one in each hand.

Grewen stepped backwards, pulling Ka'Ru off his feet, before he twisted Ka'Ru's body and swung the creature around him. Leaning back, Grewen shuffled his feet and whirled around in a circle with the wolf-like Del'Unday swinging out above the ground.

Around and around, Grewen swung Ka'Ru, each time gaining more and more momentum.

As the initial shock wore off, Ka'Ru energized his tentacles. Sparks of electricity showered Grewen's face and burned the giant's wrists.

Grewen screamed as the overwhelming pain shot down his body. But he refused to let go as he continued to spin the creature around while making his way to the water near the ship that had already launched.

Every part of Grewen's body screamed in pain as Ka'Ru relentlessly drove electrical pulses into him. The burning flesh on his hands and feet smoked as sparks and discharges fired from inside his grip on the creature. "No more!" Grewen yelled. He was in agony as he turned one last time and released his grip with a massive toss of the wolvian toward the ship.

Ka'Ru was now a missile heading straight for the side of the ship offshore. He impacted the port side of the ship with a splintering of wooden boards and the sound of breaking lumber. The wolvian penetrated the hull before coming to rest on the far side of the ship.

The ship rocked violently from the attack, knocking a few of the crew overboard. Upon righting itself, the ship then began taking on water from the gaping hole in its side.

Staggering from the battle, Grewen turned to enter the Weirfortus hallway as the ship's crew struggled to keep it afloat as they continued sailing off into the lake.

~

AFTER BEING SWALLOWED whole by the giant sea snake, Draq had started his attack from within the creature's body. The snake's internal muscles tried to crush him to death, while its stomach acid began burning his eyes.

Using his spear-like tail, Draq punctured the snake from within. His strong back claws ripped his way out of the serpent's side. The snake thrashed about in pain as the dragon fought with everything he had to escape and find air to breathe. Ripping the snake's body apart, he worked his way out through the creature's ribs. Unfortunately, it was too late for Draq, and he slowly blacked out from lack of oxygen.

To his surprise, Draq woke up on the stone shore of the spillway, at the far end from Ambrosius. Half of his body was still stuck in the ribs of the dead serpent that had washed up. The sea creature's internal organs had spilled onto the stone floor and coated the dragon's body.

Weak from his battle, Draq needed time to recover. There simply wasn't enough strength left to free himself from his awkward position.

Draq looked upstream toward the torchlight. Clearing his eyes, he could see Ambrosius as the lights danced on a wall of water behind him. "Ambrosius!" he roared. But the raging waters that were flooding the spillway soaked up his words long before they reached him.

Struggling again with the snake's large rib bones, he couldn't free himself. It forced him to remain captive while watching his friend struggle.

~

AMBROSIUS COULD NOT MOVE his now wooden legs nor remove his attached right hand as he continued the nearly impossible task of keeping the water at bay. The water pounded against his invisible shield as it raced around him on both sides and across the top. He leaned his torso forward and pressed his E'rudite ability to its limits, causing the shielded area to grow slightly.

"Thorik!" Ambrosius yelled over the sound of the rushing water.

Thorik climbed onto the upper-level tier and worked his way to Ambrosius.

"Cut me loose," Ambrosius ordered.

"What do you mean?"

"Take your battle-axe and cut me free of my legs and hand."

The thought horrified Thorik. "I can't cut off your legs."

"They are no longer my legs. They are lifeless timber. Now cut me free of these wooden confines before it's too late."

"I can't! You'll fall and the water will crush you! You'll die!"

"It's too late to prevent that now. But you can let me save the kingdom before I go!"

"No! I can't do it! I can't be responsible for assisting you in your death!" Tears ran down his face at the idea.

"Thorik," Ambrosius yelled out in a commanding voice. "Anyone can be a leader when times are good. But to be a great leader, you must do what's right when times are hard, especially when you must sacrifice yourself and your loved ones." Struggling to keep the water at bay, he continued, "The lives of every man, woman, and child within the Dovenar Walls are at risk. Your fate is in your hands. Will you be the leader that is needed?"

Biting his lip, Thorik took a deep breath and reached for the axe, strapped to his back. It was the same weapon he had used to bust the lock on the wagon while freeing Brimmelle and Gluic. Raising it over his head, he realized that this would be the end of the E'rudite's life. He took a moment to steady himself, mentally and emotionally, for what he was about to do.

"Hurry!" Ambrosius yelled.

Standing motionless, he looked at the legs he was about to sever.

"Cut me free," Ambrosius demanded.

The wet double-bladed battle-axe swung through the air at an angle, slicing off the lower part of Ambrosius' wooden hand, his upper right leg, and his lower left leg.

The wood splintered and sent Ambrosius falling to the ground. His shield faltered for a moment, crashing enormous waves into the room. Quickly recovering, he pushed back with his one remaining hand.

"Yes!" Thorik yelled. His friend hadn't died from his actions. They were all still safe behind his powerful shield.

Ambrosius coiled his body from the pain. "Now close those doors and reset the locks."

Looking at the doors, Thorik was bewildered at how a Num could do such a task. "They are too large. Too thick. Too massive."

"Notarians designed them to move easily, as long as I can hold back the pressure from the water." Ambrosius' words were breaking up from his strain. "It will be hard at first, but you can do it."

"But the water extends past the doorway."

"I'm going to push the waters back into the bottom of the reservoir. You will have to close the doors behind me before I can't hold it any longer," Ambrosius instructed.

Thorik didn't believe his own ears. "No, you just cheated death. Why must you race right back to tempt fate again? This time you'll be crushed for sure. You'll be killed!"

"I told you, I'm already dead! I knew there was no escape this time. We must finish this."

"No! We can work together and rebuild Australis. Don't give up now!" Thorik shouted over the water.

"You don't understand. If I let go, we all die: you, your friends, and the hundred thousand that live within the Dovenar Walls."

Thorik pleaded with him. "There has to be a way."

"There is. Close the door behind me. Make my life worth something again." Ambrosius pushed with all his strength and slowly began driving the water back into the giant reservoir.

Tears ran down Thorik's face, mixing in with the water dripping from his hair. The thought of imprisoning his friend in a tomb of water was overwhelming. Thorik's questions of Ambrosius' true character were now answered, yet the answers were too late to act on and too late to acknowledge.

Thorik now questioned his own character. "I should have prevented this. Somehow this could have been stopped. If only I had been more supportive of him and not slowed his journey with my doubt."

His mind raced as he chose a path to take. "Now is not the time to dwell on what I should have said or done. Now is the time to act on what I know is right, regardless of how much I hate it."

"It's smaller than I remember," Gluic said as she stepped out of the corridor and into the larger room, followed by the other Nums.

Thorik turned around as the other Nums entered the spillway. "Quick! Up here! Help me close these doors!" He helped Avanda, Brimmelle, and Gluic to the upper level before giving them additional orders. "Brimmelle, take Gluic and Avanda to the far door and start pushing it shut." Seeing their expressions, he realized what he was asking seemed impossible. "Trust me, they will move if you push." At least he hoped it would be that easy.

Brimmelle was upset and not in the mood for Thorik ordering him around. "You don't know what we've been through out there! Where were you when we needed you?"

Thorik wasn't backing down. "You can tell me about it later. Right now, you need to run over and push that door closed!" he demanded.

"Are you insane?" Brimmelle was still shaking off the creature's electrical shock that had knocked him out earlier. "We need to get out of here before it's too late!" He grabbed Thorik by the back of his arm to escort him to the side tunnel.

Thorik had been overruled. His mentor had given him a direct order, and rightfully so. The chamber was quickly filling up with water, and the chances of them being able to close the enormous metal doors were slim to none. What had Thorik been thinking? Their only options were to run for safety or die trying to close these doors.

"No!" Thorik shouted. "Stop trying to run my life!"

"I'm not trying to run it, you fool. I'm trying to save it." He then added, "Once again!"

"I don't want you to save me. I don't want to feel in debt to you for saving my life when I was younger. Quit telling me how to run my life. That's not what I want from you."

Brimmelle stepped forward as he held back his anger at his ungrateful student. "And what is it you want from me?"

Thorik stood firm, looking Brimmelle square in the eyes. It was so simple a statement, yet so hard to say. "I want you to believe in my judgment. Support me."

Brimmelle looked up at the dome of water being held back by Ambrosius' powers. Water gushed out of the sides, splashing at the Num's feet. It took all of his willpower not to run for his life.

"Uncle, you once asked me when I would start seeing the greater view of life instead of just my insignificant piece of it. Well, I'm now doing this, and I need you to trust me and do the same."

"You sure picked a bad time to ask me to trust you."

Thorik replied, "You won't regret it."

"That's because I won't be alive to regret anything." He was obviously upset with his decision to support Thorik. "You better be right about this," Brimmelle mumbled as he headed to the far door.

Grewen had finally crawled his way out of the corridor. He stood up to see a giant wave of water arching over Ambrosius as he lay on the platform, holding it back with an invisible force. In front of the impending wave, Thorik looked over at him as he ran to one of the open metal doors.

"Grewen, stand between those large valve levers and get ready to start turning them," Thorik ordered. "You need to lock these doors the moment we get them shut."

Grewen looked over at Ambrosius and then back at Thorik. "We can't trap him in there."

"Grewen, I don't have time to debate this. Get between those levers right now." Thorik's voice had a strong sense of authority.

Ambrosius continued to drag his body deeper into the reservoir using the splintered stub at the end of his right arm, pushing forward as the water randomly sprayed out around the sides. He used the wooden appendages remaining on his legs the best he could for gripping the wet floor.

The crippled E'rudite had succeeded in moving one more foot into the reservoir and yelled back to Thorik, "Close the doors!" His body was trembling from the intensity of the water around and above him. With his staff overhead in his left hand, the vitality in his face was weakening as he looked up into the darkness. "There is no turning back for me this time. I can only hope that others will carry on in my place."

Thorik had already begun closing the huge left door as Brimmelle, Gluic, and Avanda started to do the same on their side. Barely inching forward at first, Thorik fought with everything that he had to get the door moving. Perfectly balanced doors and hinges allowed for friction-free movement; it was the sheer weight of the door that was causing all the issues. Once in motion, the doors moved slowly and smoothly around to their closed positions.

As the doors came close to one another, Thorik positioned himself in the center with one hand on each door, looking in at Ambrosius, who was lying on his back under the tremendous pressure of the water above. The staff that Thorik had made for him was still in Ambrosius' grasp, but no longer over his head. Instead, it was at his chest, still pressing up against the inevitable winner of this final contest.

Ambrosius peered over his shoulder at Thorik. His pale expression showed exhaustion and submission to his demise. "Find my son. Keep him safe." He struggled to get out each word from his collapsing lungs. "Tell him I love him." He finished as the doors closed in front of Thorik.

Thorik closed his eyes, firmly embedding the image of his last memory of Ambrosius. A sight he knew would haunt him to the end of his days. The once powerful man, who had lost his wife, fatherhood, and his Kingdom, was now being crushed to death trying to save those who would wish to see him die. They would never know his sacrifice for them as they continued to live another day and enjoy another meal in their illusion of safety.

He turned and yelled at Grewen, "Set the locking pins."

Grewen's hands were already on both valves as he sat in his rowing position between them. He began turning both at the same time so that one pin shot down from the ceiling and the other up from the floor, locking the doors shut.

Gluic had lowered herself onto her hands and knees. "Stones are rich with life." Her fingers fanned out over the granite floor as she closed her eyes.

Brimmelle fell next to her out of exhaustion. "Not now, mother."

A crash of water hit the doors and began spilling through the seams. The added pressure of the sudden implosion around Ambrosius caused damage to the doors, preventing them from holding all of the water at bay. The moaning of the metal doors echoed in the long tube-shaped room, while new leaks sprang forth.

Thorik moved everyone from the metal doors and ordered them to evacuate through the side caves before the doors gave way. But it was too late; the water's current was already grabbing the Nums and pushing them toward the lake. Gluic was washed away first, falling over the edge into the main level near Grewen, who reached out and grabbed her as she passed.

Brimmelle followed quickly after her and was whisked past Grewen on his other side, only to grab on to one of the turning rods on the second set of valves.

Thorik held on to the metal door by latching onto a few decorative insets.

Clinging on to the door's artwork, Avanda worked her way over to Thorik. Grasping on to him with both legs and both arms, she held on for dear life.

"Grewen," Thorik yelled over the noise of the raging water. "Grab Brimmelle and get them into the corridor. I'll hang on until you come back for us."

The water was not affecting Grewen. His weight was too much for it at this stage, but even he would quickly be swept away if the doors were to break. Hanging on to Gluic, he waded through the knee-high water away from the reservoirs to the second set of valves to collect the other Num.

"No!" shouted Gluic. "Grewen, drop me and allow us to be washed away."

"Not on your life," he replied as he made his way over.

"It's your only chance to save the kingdom from destruction. Those doors won't hold much longer," Gluic said as Brimmelle's fingers began to lose grip.

"Hang on. I'm almost there." Grewen rounded the large valve and extending rods.

"Turn those back two valves like the ones you did before and it will drop a stone wall in front of the metal doors to seal them tight," Gluic added.

"How would you know this?" Grewen asked.

"The stones tell us what we need to know," she said. "One must only listen."

Brimmelle looked over at his mother. "I trust her. Do as she says."

They were the last words Grewen's little ears heard from Brimmelle before the mognin watched the Num let go and get washed away. It was too late; Grewen could never run as fast as Brimmelle was floating away, even on flat ground. He looked back at Thorik, who was still hanging on to the door with both hands as jets of water from underneath it kept knocking him off his feet.

Grewen held tightly on to Gluic as he changed course to head toward Thorik.

"No! You heard me," Gluic said. "Turn the other valves! Close the door!"

Grewen looked up to see the bottom of the stone wall extending slightly from the ceiling, perhaps a foot above the metal doors. There were slots along the sides for the massive wall to be lowered into, for a snug fit. The floor had a shallow dip in it where the wall would rest, once dropped. Thorik attempted to stand in the shallow area as he struggled to hang on with his eyes closed to protect them from the spouting water.

The mognin reached down with one of his gigantic hands to crank one of the levers, only to find it stuck in place. He reached over to the other one with the same result. However, they did move when he turned them both in tandem. To do this, he would have to drop Gluic. He looked around for another alternative.

"It's okay, dear. You need to do this."

"I cannot let you go and send you to your death," he insisted as the water continued to rise around him.

"I know, dear. That's why I will have to help." She used both of her hands to stab his hand with the sharp end of a crystal, driving it far enough to draw blood.

Crying out in pain and surprise, he instinctively released her, only to attempt to grab her back once he realized what she had done. Again, it was too late, and she washed away.

The only ones left with Grewen were Thorik and Avanda. His only plan at this point was to drop the wall onto their location. He yelled out, "Thorik, let go! I'm dropping the wall. Get out of the way."

Extreme noise was pounding Thorik's head while he continued to be splashed from the various spouts. With eyes closed tight and rushing water covering his ears, Thorik heard nothing of the new plan and would continue holding on to the metal door until he felt Grewen come back to save them.

Water raged at Grewen's hips as he bent over and reached under the water to turn the large levers. In concert, they spun much easier than when trying to only turn one at a time. He could see the wall slowly start to lower.

Grewen was forced to sit down in a rowing position to speed up the process. In doing so, the waves lapped at his face while he pulled rod after rod on both sides, spinning them around in circles. Between splashes in his face, he could still see Thorik hanging on to the giant metal doors as the stone wall quickly moved downward.

The metal doors continued to bulge to their limits. Flooding from every direction increased as hinges began to snap apart. Grewen knew he only had seconds left and grabbed his last breath as he leaned under the water to pull with all his might. Faster and faster, he pulled until he heard the slam of the stone slab door hitting so hard that it vibrated the floor where he sat.

The valves were tight and would not move anymore. He raised his head out of the water, searching around the wall that was now completely lowered. The water was no longer pouring into the room. It was over.

He also noticed that Thorik and Avanda were gone, swept downstream or trapped between the rock wall and the metal doors. He looked behind him, down the long spillway outlet toward the lake, for signs of them. As the waters receded, he spotted Gluic and Brimmelle. Both had survived the flood. Draq had grabbed them both as they were being washed past him. The others were nowhere to be seen.

Grewen lowered his head. He had lost three great friends on this day.

Looking back at the lowered wall, he heard coughing, or perhaps choking. Thorik had been swept off into the side tunnel, where they had originally entered from. Clinging to him was Avanda, who still had her eyes shut.

Grewen stood up and ran over to them, plucking the Nums from the floor before holding them in his arms.

Thorik was not choking on water, nor crying in pain. Instead, he was bursting with the agony of losing his friend Ambrosius. He was devastated with a hurt worse than all of his other physical pains. A piece of him had just died, as though it had been cut out with a knife.

Avanda burst into tears, partly because Thorik was crying and partly out of shock from the events and loss that had just occurred.

It was clear in Grewen's eyes that he also was exhibiting the same pain.

"I've killed Ambrosius." Thorik trembled as he spoke.

"You've saved Terra Australis," Grewen replied.

✣ 36 ✣

RETURN TO FARBANK

It had been a long, quiet journey back across Lake Luthralum as Grewen paddled the boat up King's River, past Longfield, and to Farbank. As they approached the village, they could see several children playing along the shore while others, wrapped in warm blankets, fishing from the docks. Men and women were busy working as they finalized their preparations for winter.

Most of the trees had lost their leaves, and the few remaining had already turned brown from the freezing night temperatures. The fallen leaves had been cleaned off the roofs and raked out of the streets. Everything was neat and tidy.

The children near the river cheered with excitement as they saw a giant mognin rowing a boat toward them. It was carrying Avanda, Thorik, Gluic, and Brimmelle, toward the dock. The adults were more apprehensive about the sight of the giant, but came down to the dock all the same to welcome the travelers home.

Reaching the dock, Grewen held the boat steady as the Nums exited. It took several adults to keep the vessel balanced while Grewen vacated the rowboat without tipping it over. When he did, he stood up to full height to stretch his back.

The short Nums backed up at the sight of Grewen's enormous body. Fearing the giant, many of the villagers sunk deeper into their winter coats as they witnessed the odd sight.

One of the men shouted out, "Brimmelle, what is this creature you have returned with?"

Brimmelle raised his hands to calm everyone down. "This is a mognin, one of the Ov'Unday of the southern valleys." He looked up at the Altered Creature who he had once feared. "You will address him as Grewen. He is our trusted friend."

These were strong words for Brimmelle. He rarely used the words 'trusted friend', even among Nums in his village. In fact, no one in the village considered him as a friend, only as a Fir. A friend would put him at an equal level, which he would have never before accepted.

Avanda's parents ran down the slight slope to the river, arms stretched out as they saw her. Avanda met them halfway, jumping up into their arms and disappearing into their thick, wooly coats. The three hugged tightly.

Wess' brothers walked over to Brimmelle. The eldest, Hyphry, asked the Fir, "Where's Wess?"

Brimmelle's face and eyes lowered as his hands locked together behind his back. A moment later, he straightened his body up and looked at the three brothers. "I'm sorry to say that he didn't make it. Wess passed away during our journey."

Those in hearing distance quieted down to listen to Hyphry. "How did he die? Why didn't you save him?"

Brimmelle's eyes shifted back and forth, searching for a way out of this uncomfortable public scene. "Perhaps we should refer to the Rune Scrolls for guidance during these difficult times."

"No," Hyphry said. "You asked him to go with you. It was your responsibility. How could you let him die?"

Thorik stepped in, "Brimmelle didn't let him die. Wess was a hero."

"A hero? Our brother?" Hyphry asked in surprise.

Thorik replied, "Yes, without a doubt. He fought off thrashers and living stone statues. He saved us from freezing to death in the mountains and helped us save all human and Num life from a tidal wave of death."

Thorik watched as everyone listened in awe to the tale. "Along our journey, we discovered that a plot was unfolding to destroy all our lands. We traveled far to the south to stop it from happening. When we arrived, we were attacked, and Avanda would have been killed if it weren't for Wess. He sacrificed his life to save hers. Your brother should be remembered as a hero."

Wess' brothers smiled at Thorik's words. "I knew he had it in him," one said as they gave each other hugs and patted each other on the back. Grief would continue, but at least now it was with respect and honor of the tasks Wess had accomplished.

Thorik nodded with a sense of comfort at the sight of the brothers' reaction.

Several women, meanwhile, asked Gluic how she was holding up after such a long trek. She dismissed the questions and instead opened a sack to show them. "They have some wonderful stones in Pelonthal." They politely looked, but were not impressed as she continued to show them off.

Thorik was greeted with happiness by many, and he returned the sentiment. "It's good to be home." A sense of peace came over him, which he had not felt in a long time. He inhaled the comfort and easiness of the surroundings that he grew up in.

"We will throw a grand party for your return," Sorla shouted to the crowd, who cheered at the idea of it.

Thorik hadn't seen Sorla since the Harvest Festival, when she congratulated her husband Trumette for winning the foot race. She was always trying to make everyone happy and always willing to throw a party for any occasion.

"That is very nice, but we will not be staying," Thorik answered back. "We still have more to do to ensure your safety. The threat is still out there."

Sorla looked confused. "But you said you saved us already."

"We did, from one specific danger, but there will be more unless we are there to stop them from happening."

"You've done your part." Sorla nodded to Thorik. "Come home and relax. Others will take over where you have left off."

Trumette pulled her back. "The battle is over, but the war remains to be won, my dear."

Grewen looked down at the frail old Num. "Well spoken."

Trumette nodded at Brimmelle. "Where do I sign up for our next mission?"

Everyone chuckled at the idea before Brimmelle could respond. "I am not going on any more missions. I will be staying here to teach what I have recently learned," he announced to the shocked faces, knowing that they had never heard him speak of himself learning anything outside the words of the scrolls. "Thorik is the leader of this group. He knows what he's doing and carries my full support."

Silence followed as the Nums tried to rationalize this new Brimmelle attitude. It was still authoritative but showed feelings and depth to his words that had never been there before. It was a welcome change.

"But we must have a party before you leave again," Sorla again begged.

"There is no time for that," Thorik replied.

Grewen reached down and patted Thorik on the back. "Enjoy the blessings before you. It is these memories that we are fighting to keep alive."

Thorik smiled at his enormous friend. "All right, one night of festivities, and then we're off."

Everyone rejoiced and left to set up the tents and tables.

THE PARTY HAD RUN LATE into the night before Thorik finally headed home, up the path, which had not been kept tidy for a long while. Branches lay across the way as well as leaves, which needed to be raked. He would have to get up all the earlier in the morning to clean it up before they left.

He saw his cottage, small and simple. It was not grand like those he had seen on his travels, nor was it protected by any great walls. Yet it felt like the safest place in Australis. He couldn't wait to make a cup of tea in his own kitchen again and sleep in his own bed. No Del'Unday, Fesh'Unday, Coliseum battles, swimming corpses, or carved statues coming to life. It would be a welcome treat, even if it was only for one night.

Stale air hit his face as he opened the door. It wasn't overpowering, just unpleasant. He opened the flume in the fireplace and started a nice little fire. He rotated an angled metal rod over the top of the flame, carrying a pot of water for his tea.

When the water reached a boil, he poured it into a cup filled with tea leaves. He then grabbed a jar of sugar and scooped out a spoonful before stirring it in. Wrapping his hands around the large cup helped warm up his chilled body from the night's wintry temperatures. Blowing softly across the surface a few times, he took a sip to warm his insides.

His face pursed up as he realized that the scoop of sugar was actually salt. His tea was awful. Checking the labels on the jars, he confirmed that he had grabbed the correct one. Someone had switched the contents. His guess would be Wess, just before they headed upstream on their journey.

He had a soft chuckle and made himself a fresh cup of tea, this time with sugar. He sat back and listened to the approaching storm as the winds picked up and lightning could be seen in the distance. It was uncommon, but not unknown, to have thunderstorms this late in the year. All he could think about was how nice it was to be able to ride it out in the safety of the house he had grown up in. He washed up and prepared for sleep as the winds continued to howl through the trees.

Stretching out on his bed, he closed his eyes and thought back to the adventure he had recently survived. The challenges he had risen to. The challenges he had lost. Most important were the friends that he had met and lost along the way.

He still had deep feelings for Emilen, and he believed she also did for him. On one hand, he hated what she had done. The loss of life that she had caused and the feeling that she had deceived him burned in his mind. On the other hand, he wondered if she was a victim of Darkmere's control, carrying out his acts without the power to fight back. His heart still tightened when he thought of her lying with him in the tail of the dolphin statue while the warm mineral water of Kingsfoot Lake splashed up onto their bodies.

It was almost like being back there. He could feel droplets of water hit his body.

"Thorik, are you awake?" Grewen's deep voice broke his peaceful memory as he opened his eyes to see the roof of his cottage lifted off its walls by the mognin, who was looking down at him. Rain was starting to pour into his home and was saturating his bed sheets.

"What are you doing? Close the roof!" He sat up in bed and glared up at Grewen, who was leaning over the front wall. The fireplace shed enough light onto Grewen's upper body for Thorik to see that he was under attack. His shirt was half ripped off, and large bleeding scratches marked up his body.

A howl could be heard just as several thrashers jumped onto Grewen's chest and arms. An entire tribe had attacked, and Grewen fought to keep them off, falling backward out of sight, taking the roof with him.

A thrasher jumped from Grewen's falling body and landed on the front wall as it spied Thorik still in bed, shivering with fear and confusion. Thorik could see the scar of the three scratches over his eye. It was the silverhead. Sniffing the air, he remembered the attack on his tribe and Thorik's killing of his family. He jumped off and landed in front of Thorik at the same moment a second creature grabbed Thorik from behind.

Thorik screamed as he stood up and lunged at the creature attacking from behind. Holding the beast down with one hand, he began taking out his own aggression.

"Thorik! Stop it," Avanda yelled. "You're going to knock us off the boat."

Thorik jolted his eyes open to find himself on top of Brimmelle, in the mognin rowboat. The rain was coming down hard, and lightning lit the sky frequently to give him a clear view of Brimmelle's facial reaction from the unprovoked attack.

Avanda sat next to Gluic as they held a blanket over their heads to hold off the rain. The youth wondered if one of her magical items could stop the rain. She had collected most of them before leaving Weirfortus. However, sitting in a rowboat in the middle of the lake was not the best time for her to test the items for magical properties.

Grewen was still paddling the boat in the middle of Lake Luthralum with no land in sight, as Thorik helped Brimmelle back up and regained his own bearings. Swiping his face with his hand to clear the rain from it, Thorik was still disorientated as his dream of returning home was fading.

"Where are we?" Thorik asked.

Grewen spoke up first. "We just passed several rocky islands. We still haven't seen Draq, so we're sailing blind. The storm might have been too hard to fly in, and he may have stopped to wait it out. If I don't see him soon, we'll have to attempt to land on one of these islands until this storm blows past." Grewen continued to row. "And where exactly were you?" he said with a grin.

Thorik gazed out upon the waves on the lake as he gathered his thoughts. He was still coming to grips with the fact that he had dreamt the return to Farbank. "I was home."

The mognin nodded. "Things okay back there?"

A slight smile crossed the Num's face. "Yes, and I mean to keep it that way."

Grewen grinned. "Understood, little man."

❧ 37 ❧

ASSASSIN

The heart of the mountain churned with heat deep inside its cold exterior, only to be exposed by the occasional steam rising out of the center crater. Above all other mountains, this one stood amongst a range of non-volcanic peaks. It had fought its way up to its great height on its own instead of being carried up by the shifting of land.

So grand was its size that passing clouds were caught against it like fish in a net, unable to free themselves. Nearly a god among nature, it caused climate changes and shook the earth when it was angry. This happened more often now than it had in the past. In its youth, it had fought for great strength and had settled with age, but lately it was no longer at peace. No longer idle or content. Respect had been lost for the great power it had provided the creatures that lived upon it. Damage had been done to the mountain by those it had been protecting.

The heartbeat of the magma inside pounded away, rising and lowering with each passing emotion. It would explode; there was no doubt about it. It was just a matter of time. Just a matter of pressure, frustration, and anger. It would explode.

Steam escaped out of its various vent holes with gray smoke that contrasted with the glacier of white around the funnel's peak. Halfway down its slope, steam billowed out from caves under the deep snow. And below that, in a half-circle lake, smoke rose from the neck of a headless statue standing with its back against a sliced-out section of the mountain.

The statue only stood a thousand feet high, now that its head had fallen off and crashed near its feet in the heated mineral lake below. Dried streams of lava ran down the Mountain King statue's body, originating from the steaming vent at his neck. The once proud King now stood in snow-covered grief.

Excluding the warm steaming lake, the valley was blanketed with several feet of snow. It had been quite a while. Paths of deer and wild cats had been erased by the current blizzard that lashed out at the valley, perhaps brought on by the mountain itself.

Snow fell at an angle, and drifts built up like the dunes of the Kiri Desert. Only the lake fought to stay free of ice. The wind churned in the valley, down the mountainside, past the city of Kingsfoot, across the lake, and back up the southern mountain range before coming back for another pass. Like a wagon wheel, the storm rotated in the valley for days.

Through the windblown snow a figure moved down the mountain into the valley, against the flow of the storm to the north. Leaning forward on two powerful legs, the stranger fought for every step he took over the harsh landscape. Tall, thick boots of skins rose past his knees but still didn't fully protect his feet from all the cold. A long, bulky coat of furs covered the rest of his body. The hood of the coat was pulled down as tight as possible without impairing the traveler's vision.

Once he reached the valley floor, he worked his way from one white dune to another. Snow clumped onto his body, weighing him down all the more. It was as though the storm was fighting him, preventing him from entering the valley and keeping him from his destination.

As he neared the lake, the winds picked up even more and water sprayed the traveler again and again. The water instantly froze into layers of ice on his clothes and exposed skin within his hood.

Now nearly frozen, the traveler reached the bridge, in the center of the valley, which arched over the water outlet into the King's River. The bridge was coated with layers of ice and required him to pull himself across using the slippery arm rail. After passing the apex of the bridge, his feet began to slide down the other side. Using his right gloved hand for balance on the arm rail, he allowed the slide to continue until his hand hit a broken section and got knocked against the sharp edges of the stone railing afterward. He fell, but landed on one knee, a foot, and his left hand, protecting the bruised right one.

His hood had been flung off due to his fall and the wind, exposing a long snout on his face. Dark red in color, the skin sunk in around his bony features. His eyebrows lowered in disgust at fighting the storm. Exhausted from the constant attack, he rested a moment, looking at the last leg of his trip, the city of Kingsfoot. Growling a bit at the frigid wind pounding his face, he raised his frozen hood over his hairless blothrud head.

Picking himself up, he moved forward around the lake to the city. Plowing through snowdrift after snowdrift, he forced his momentum to increase as his body tired. He had to reach the city before his body gave out on him. Pushing with whatever strength he had left, he launched forward in a full run, busting his way across the last section of open land. Blasting through the last wave of snow, he reached the perimeter wall of half-exposed statues.

He stopped and leaned against one of the stone scroll statues to catch his breath and shield himself from the ever-ferocious wind. Reaching under his robes, he pulled out a small dagger covered with runes and gems along the handle. It was a glorious design of twisted blades as it shone with virginity. Not a scratch on it;

never used, never damaged. It was as fresh and sharp as it was the day it was made.

Holding the small dagger tight in his large fist, he looked at his reflection within the swirling blades. Still breathing heavily, he asked himself, "Are you ready for this? This could be your undoing."

Glancing around the statue, he saw a courtyard of half-submerged statues before the three vaguely distinguishable terrace levels up to the city's wall. Wind blasted him in the face as he looked about.

Placing the dagger back under his coat of ice- and snow-covered furs, he made his way up to the city in a slow gallop. The stairs in the center were useless under all the snow, but his large wolf-like legs on his eight-foot-tall body conquered them with ease.

He quietly pushed one of the two doors open and peered inside to see several vats of oil fires lighting the large room with yellow dancing light. Several doors and halls exited the room in every direction as he looked for signs of life.

Closing the main door behind him, a wave of warmth covered his body. He quickly removed his gloves and coat, the weight of which was more from snow and ice than furs and skins. He removed his shirt, which was soaking from the sweat of his trek. To have some body parts freeze while sweating to death in others was no way for this blothrud to travel. He hated the cold.

As he patted himself dry, a large scar could be seen on his back from his upper left shoulder blade to down below his belt. It had been a deep gouge that had never fully healed. It scarred much wider than the rest of the whip marks on his back. Several wide blades extended from his spine a few inches, many chipped and damaged but dangerous all the same. Spikes could also be seen on shoulder blades, knuckles, and elbows. They also were rough from battles of the past. He was a seasoned veteran with many a battle to his name.

Checking the blade once again, he rotated the dagger in his fist a few times to make sure he had a good hold on it.

He then spied a green light coming from a room at the end of one of the many hallways. The door was shut, and the light trimmed the bottom with shadows moving in front of the sickly light.

Standing up tall with his chest out firm, he proceeded down toward the closed door, dagger to his side. He walked with confidence and composure as he reached the door and opened it.

The room inside was half the size of the first room. Two vats, one in each corner on the far side, gave off a smoky green light that danced on the walls, which were covered in stone carvings of wilderness. The flickering light made the ceiling's carved tree leaves and the walls' ferns appear to sway in the breeze. Several small stone and crystal statues stood in the room. On the far side was a throne, midway between the two large vats. The throne was solid crystal and carved out to look like the base of a tree with roots reaching out for the seat and arms.

Sitting on the throne was a cloaked figure. It looked to be short and standing on the seat, seeing that no legs came forward and then down in front. The other possibility was that the figure was sitting with its legs crossed. The blothrud did not care either way.

As he advanced into the room, blade in hand, he noticed the animal statues moving and walking about. He slowed his pace as the stone and crystal animals followed.

A large black marble panther stood in his way just before the throne. It growled and prepared to pounce on the blothrud, who stood defiantly. A wave of a hand from the figure upon the throne caused the panther to back down and sit next to him.

The blothrud lifted his precious dagger and pointed it at the cloaked figure. "This is Varacon, the blade you requested. Countless lives have been lost to bring this to you."

The cloaked figure sat up slightly from its previously hunched over position. In doing so, the cloak moved and exposed his upper legs that had mutated into cracked and fragmented wood, splintering and decaying. His left hand reached out to take the dagger from him as the blothrud turned the handle for him to grab.

Lifting it from the red creature's hand, he inspected the blade. Polishing it on the right arm of his cloak, he exposed his deformed right hand. It also had been turned into shards of rotten wood. "You have done well, my old friend." His voice sounded raspy and tired.

The blothrud could see excessive burn damage along the cloaked man's neck. "What shall you have me do with it?"

The cloaked man looked up from his hood. "Santorray, you shall kill my son, Ericc."

SACRIFICE OF ERICC
THORIK DAIN SERIES BOOK II

PROLOGUE

———

Thorik's Log: 9th day of the 4th month of the 650th year.

After months of being stranded on an island after our boat crashed, we have been rescued by the captain of a seaworthy vessel. Yet I sit here on my seventeenth birthday filled with remorse over the death of my friend, Ambrosius. But with the captain's commitment to help find Ericc, I plan to tell Ambrosius' heir of his father's fate in an effort to prevent the boy from succumbing to the same end. The prophecy of his sacrifice on the 21st day of the 6th month must be avoided, for he is the last E'rudite who can stand up against Darkmere.

———

THE PROPHECY

"Your survival leads to my death," Lord Bredgin said as he cautiously approached Ericc in the center of the city while the midday sun shone brightly overhead. "I am here to reverse this dilemma and pen a new future in your stead."

Colors faded to gray shadows as the young lord muted the spectrum of light to his liking of shades of black. Light and darkness carried great power, which affected all living things. Light provided life as well as heat when focused intensely. Dark provided coldness, and if used properly it yielded death.

Ericc shuffled his feet backward, staying just outside of the grayness which loomed around Lord Bredgin. "Who are you?" Ericc demanded as his foot felt the icy cold of the impending shadow. Refusing to turn and run, the teenage boy defied the stranger's threats while keeping a safe distance.

"I am the one foretold to fall from the strike of your blade." A shadowy sphere extended from Bredgin's body as his presence muted light and colors several yards in every direction. Flowers wilted and clay pots cracked as he followed Ericc down the street in the center of town. People who failed to heed the ominous warning screamed from the pain given once they fell within his vicinity.

Southwind locals ran from the cloud of darkness after witnessing the life-sucking effect on those who had accidentally strayed into its path.

Ericc refused to turn his back to the young bald man, for it was best to keep him within his sights. "I have no quarrel with you. Why would I strike you down, aside from defending myself from your hostile actions?"

"It's not a matter of why. It's a matter of when, which haunts my days. Ever since I was a child, my father has been training me to prevent you from ending my life. For years I have searched for you in an effort to end this curse against me. Today is the day I have long awaited to change the future."

Ericc turned down an alley to protect the residents from the man's wrath, and the young lord left the main street to follow.

The red brick walls turned black, and the mortar cracked and crumbled as Bredgin smoothly entered the back alley. They both could hear screams from the far side of the walls as the darkness penetrated the interiors of the buildings.

"Why are you doing this?" Ericc asked as he listened to the pained cries for help. "How can you possibly convict me of a crime I have yet to even consider performing?"

"Don't play this game with me," Bredgin shouted. "You have the powers of the E'rudite. You are the son of the eldest of the twin brothers of war." He followed Ericc out of the alley and into a stable. "You are the one talked about by the Oracles. Two paths lie before you; one reveals your murder of me, and the other involves your sacrifice at Surod. I have chosen the latter."

Darkness rushed from Lord Bredgin toward Ericc in an attack to incapacitate him.

Ericc jumped out of the way, rolling into one of the animal stalls for safety.

The animals howled in pain as their bodies took the full load of the absence of light. More than just darkness, it drained the living flesh and dried up their bones while consuming all the warmth from their body.

Ericc watched as the tan hay on the floor took on a sour gray hue. Pushing his back up against the far corner, he watched the darkness increase with each loud step of his attacker. Wooden floorboards seemed to age decades before his eyes, and ropes lost their strength, dropping tools and a lantern onto the floor. Even the sound was distant as the darkness subdued all aspects of its invasive assault.

Lord Bredgin reached the stall and prepared his final attack on his trapped victim, only to find the stall empty. There had appeared to be no possibility for Ericc to escape, yet he had done just that.

Furious, Lord Bredgin yelled with rage, extending his grayness over two city blocks without care of whom or what he decimated.

✿   2   ✿

HIGH SEAS

The fury of the storm brought pain to all in its wake and would continue to do so until its own demise. No army could attack it, no fortress could defend against it, and no creature could outrun it. It was the king of all storms, with an unforgiving hand of pain and death. It reached out to smite all in its path.

Waves struck the side of a ship, forcing it to lean steeply, as thunder roared from flashes of lightning striking the water nearby. It was a sturdy caravel vessel, but it was too far out to sea to make port and too slow to outrun the giant swells.

A crew of over twenty members fought to save the ship, *Sinecure*. Sails were tied down and goods were stored. But the competency of the ship-hands did not accomplish this, for they were still green to the ways of the water.

It was the fiery captain who commanded critical life-saving orders. The *Sinecure*, its crew, and its passengers were all dependent on his abilities as he played a deadly game against the storm and sea.

It wasn't the first time he had saved these passengers. Stranded on one of the small Palm Islands for months, they were fortunate that he had spotted them. Then again, if the ship were hit any harder on the starboard side, their rescue may turn out to be their undoing. The captain had to turn the ship's bow into the waves before they capsized.

Avanda flung open the door and ran out onto the deck. The young lady's hair whipped at her face as the wind drove the rain hard against her. "Ralph? Ralph?" she continued to yell as the busy crew ignored her.

"Ralph?" the captain asked as he fought to steer the ship. "Who's Ralph?"

Thorik Dain stood near the captain, carrying out his orders and relaying them to his crew. "Avanda's lizard that she found on the island."

"Damn be it for the Fesh, get her below before she's washed overboard," the captain ordered.

Thorik left the captain's side and made his way down the steps to the main deck. He waited for a flash of lightning to see where she had gone. But when it struck, she was no longer where he had last seen her. Instead, she was on the *Sinecure*'s bow, reaching for the pole that hung over the front of the ship.

The thunderstorm released its worst at them. Lightning struck the water near enough to the ship for those aboard to hear it at the same time they saw it, vibrating the ship with its mighty force.

Avanda climbed out onto the ship's bowsprit as the waves lashed out and pounding rain drove hard into her back. As if holding onto the ship's front pole wasn't hard enough, her legs kept getting wrapped up in the lowered forestay sails. One wrong move, tall wave, or strong gust of wind could easily knock her off the horizontal pole and send her to a watery grave. In spite of the severe danger, she continued to climb toward the end.

Ralph had climbed out onto the bowsprit. It was normally a safe location for him, out from under the crew's feet as he so often basked in the sun's warmth. It was now the most dangerous place the lizard could be as he clung for his life.

Defensive instincts kicked in, causing Ralph to spit out a gob of saliva onto the pole between him and Avanda. Even with the pole saturated with water, the deadly acid in the lizard's spit began to sizzle away, eating through the wood.

"Avanda, come back!" Thorik yelled as he reached the front of the ship.

"Not without Ralph!" she yelled back over the noise of the howling wind and crashing waves.

Thorik reached out and grabbed her ankle. "He's not worth your life."

She attempted to scoot farther out, as her legs wrapped around the bowsprit. Lying on her stomach on the pole, she pulled with her hands and pushed with her feet. "I took him from his island, so I'm responsible for him now."

Thorik pulled her back toward him. "He's only a lizard!"

"He's part of our family!"

In the pitch black of the night, the captain turned the wheel hard, viewing what he could when lightning allowed. It was a small window of time to determine what was playing out. How far he had turned the ship and where was the next swell rising?

Both questions were answered as lightning struck the crest of a towering wave as it approached, illuminating the wave from within. It was clear that they would not survive.

Avanda and Thorik saw the wave light up as well, just as the bowsprit broke off right in front of Avanda. The lizard's acid attack on the pole had chewed its way through, and now it swung wildly in the air, hanging from the lines that connected it to the foremast.

Ralph clung tightly as the pole spun out of control, dangling over the water.

The ship began its climb up the swell, leaning back as the bow lifted into the air.

The bowsprit swung backward, nearly swatting Thorik and Avanda off the ship. Ralph leaped off the bowsprit and onto Avanda's head, just as Thorik pulled her back onto the ship's forecastle deck. Tumbling to the foremast, they both watched the wave prepare to bear down on them.

"Hold on!" the captain shouted to his crew, knowing full well that the ship had little chance against such a wave.

Ralph scurried into one of Avanda's pouches while Thorik held onto her with one arm and a secured rope with the other.

Always on the offensive, Avanda grabbed for her purse of magic. Pulling out a handful of small crystals, she broke free from Thorik and dove for the deck's railing, throwing them overboard and shouting words to activate her spell.

The crystals hit the water and instantly turned it to ice. Spreading fast, a magical iceberg grew beneath it, lifting the ship.

Water crashed from above as the top of the wave struck the ship. But instead of going through the wave and drowning, the ice had lifted them up and over.

Avanda jumped away from the railing and back into Thorik's arms. "It worked this time!" she yelled.

The swell broke off chunks of the iceberg and turned them into flying debris, hurling them back toward the ship. Large ice fragments pelted the men on deck, knocking several off.

One large shard pierced the hull and crashed into the upper deck's bulkhead. Water spilled in from the wave as the crew tried to board it up and bail out the water.

"I'm not sure your magic made things any better." Thorik held her tight, protecting her from the storm's wrath.

But it had helped. The iceberg had grown large enough to allow them to ride out the storm. Nevertheless, they were unable to steer the vessel and were now completely at the mercy of the waves.

❦ 3 ❦

SOUTHWIND

Thorik's Log: 15th day of the 4th month of the 650th year.

In spite of our needed ship repairs, we traveled up the Stained River and docked at Rava'Kor, where Captain Mensley has heard word of Ericc's capture. I leave my Runestones and logs of our trip here on the ship, for this may be my last opportunity to see them. The risk I take to find Ericc leads me into the city as well as into its prison.

Thorik sat by himself looking into his mug of ale, feeling sorry for himself. Months earlier, he had watched his friend's death, whose last images of suffering were etched into Thorik's memories forever. "Save my son" was Ambrosius' last request before Thorik had condemned him to his final demise.

Thorik's short Polenum body and soft facial features were hidden by the shadows of the pub. The evening sun was setting, and only a few lanterns had been lit. Humans sat in the broken-down structure. A cat ran across a sleeping man at the bar and chased a rodent across the floor and out of one of the openings in the walls.

The city of Rava'Kor had been destroyed by a series of major storms, including the latest one that nearly took the life of everyone on Captain Mensley's ship. Most buildings lay flat, or at best leaned to one side. The pub stayed standing due to pure luck, although it looked as if it could collapse at any time. Flying debris had punctured holes in the structure, and the hot, humid air of the surrounding tropical forest saturated everything. Even Thorik's mug was clammy to the touch.

Calls from tropical birds and monkeys could be heard in the distance, while local insects and frogs had ventured into the broken city to make their presence known. The city had evolved within the forest over a period of many years. However, the hot and humid climate and thick vegetation still remained in control of these parts.

The city reminded Thorik of himself: tired and depressed. He took another sip of the drink he had been nursing for over an hour.

"Thorik!" Avanda shouted as she noticed him through an opening in the wall, close to where he sat. The youthful Num sprinted around the outside of the pub before entering through an area that once held a large window. Her long straight hair was dirty, but still showed hints of flowery colors.

Three thick lines of darker skin interlaced around her neck and wrists. A similar pattern coiled up from the top of her feet, around her ankles, and up her calves before the three lines separated and continued their spiral up her legs.

All Polenums had these dark lines, except for her friend and former teacher, Thorik. The markings changed slightly as the Polenums grew older, becoming more detailed or bold, or flourishing in length and pattern.

This was the case with Avanda. She had matured quickly since they had left their hometown of Farbank. Her markings had grown in length on her legs, and two dark paths had extended from her neck and tightly twisted their way down her front to surround her navel.

Soft, sensitive skin lay in the dark lines and patches, causing her to shiver when traced. Coined as soul-markings, it was believed that these lines touched a Polenum's inner soul because of their tender nature.

Avanda had also matured physically; her height had increased, and her body had begun to fill out. It was obvious she was crossing the bridge from child to woman.

She walked past the humans in the pub as they looked down at her, some with disgust and others with catcalls and rude comments.

Bouncing up to the table, Avanda peered into Thorik's half-full mug and scrunched up her nose at the smell. "I don't think you should be drinking that."

Obviously uncomfortable about seeing her, Thorik watched as three military guards entered the pub. "Avanda, you shouldn't be in here. You need to get back to the group quickly." His eyes never looked directly at her.

"I've been looking all over for you. They've finally fixed the ship." Taking a piece of bread from his plate, she sniffed it and took a bite. Setting her purse of magic onto his table, she pulled out a few items to show him. "Do you want to see what I did? I was able to enchant this mirror. It now reflects the true you. Want to try it?"

"Not now. Maybe later."

"And I also remembered Sharcodi's magical phrase to activate this string of beads." Without even a pause, she changed the subject. "I don't think Captain Mensley appreciates how hard it is to learn magic all by myself. You'd think he would've been more grateful that I saved his ship."

"Great. Hurry back, and I'll see you when... Just get moving." Nervous inflections could be detected in his voice as his hands tightened into fists.

"I still don't understand why we had to come all the way up the river for repairs when the bay's port cities looked a whole lot more fun to explore."

Thorik kept his eyes on the guards as they sat down at a table near the main doors. The barkeep had their drinks ready in an effort to hold true to their daily routine in spite of the storm's destruction.

"Don't question the captain. We... He knows what he's doing." At least Thorik hoped the captain did. Thorik was about to embark on a dangerous venture based on Captain Mensley's plan. If the captain was wrong, it could be Thorik's end.

Ripping another chunk from the small bread loaf, she ate the soft inside and tossed the crust back on the table. "Did I tell you I made a wish to the lights over Lu'Tythis Tower last night? As soon as I finished, lightning raced across the sky. It must have heard me."

"More likely a distant thunderstorm."

"No, it was a clear night. It came from the center of the night lights, where the tower is."

"Captain Mensley should have never told you that folk tale. It's only a distant ancient structure."

"No, it's more than that. It answered me. You'll see."

"I'm looking forward to it. But for now, hurry back to the docks." Nervous, he took a sip of his liquid courage. He was on edge and not in the mood to talk.

"What's gotten into you?" She would continue to pry until she got her answer.

Thorik's voice was now fast and agitated as he stood up to address her. "It's going to get dangerous in here very soon. Go back to Gluic and Brimmelle, now! Gluic can explain to you why."

Avanda grabbed her purse and whipped her head around to see the oncoming danger. "Where? What's going to happen?" Her voice caught a few ears and then eyes.

"Avanda! Get out of here!" His voice was loud enough to wake the man sleeping at the bar before he took a drink and put his head back down. The other patrons turned as they watched the loud Num try to control himself.

Thorik slowly sat back into his chair, while Avanda crossed her arms. It wasn't like him to yell at her, and she didn't appreciate it, especially in public.

Most of the customers went back about their own business. A few of the men at the bar, however, kept their attention on the two short Nums.

"Hey, little girl. That guy bothering you?" one man said. "I'll take care of you and make sure no one hurts you." Eyelids at half-mast, the drunken man gave off a creepy smile while gazing at her.

Thorik watched as all three of the men, who had turned around from the bar, were eyeing her. This was no place for a young teenage girl, regardless if they were human or Num.

Thorik needed to prevent any conflicts. "Sorry to bother you. We'll keep it down." Avanda had been his student for many years, and he felt very protective of her. He desperately wanted to avoid conflict.

The widest of the three men continued to smile at Avanda. "Sure is pretty. How'd ya like to sit on my lap and share a drink with us?"

The tallest one grinned at the thought. "Maybe you could do a little dance up on the bar for us, seeing that you have our attention." The three laughed at the idea as one of them began clearing off a section of bar for her.

Turning to face the men head on, she glared at the drunks as they continued toying with her and laughing among themselves.

Trying to prevent any issues, Thorik slowly reached over and grabbed the back of Avanda's shirt to prevent her from charging them. "Don't do it," he said softly.

Still a little annoyed about Thorik ordering her to leave, she needed to make a point. "I can take care of myself." Pulling out of Thorik's reach, she stepped toward the small group of men teasing her.

"Avanda, don't," Thorik ordered without shouting.

She didn't listen. Walking the last few steps, she looked up at the hairy and dirty drunks. All of them stood at least a few heads taller than her. Swaying and belching from the alcohol, they waited for her to respond to their invitation.

"Do you have something you'd like to say to me?" she challenged.

The three men laughed at her boldness. "Yes," the thin man said as he pushed his grimy and untrimmed blond hair out of his face. "I've heard that Num females have the softest skin of any species." His buddies laughed out of support without knowing where he was taking the conversation. "So, seeing that we don't see too many Nums, I thought you could show us if it were true." He finished and provided a tooth-missing smile as his eyes glazed over from intoxication.

"Avanda," Thorik said softly as he stood up to walk over to her.

She was a girl in a young woman's body, coming of age and knowing just enough to be dangerous. She didn't like these men and quickly responded before Thorik could arrive. "If you want to feel something soft, try reaching between your own legs."

Avanda had overheard her Uncle Wess say the sarcastic remark to one of his brothers. It had been followed with a round of laughter by all. However, she did not receive the same response as he once did.

The blond recipient of this barb stopped smiling. His friends became silent as they waited for his response. Tension immediately elevated as all of the patrons now waited for a reaction. Even the seated guards turned to see what would unfold.

"I'd rather feel what's between yours." He then lunged at her, grabbing her by the shoulders.

Avanda screamed as the other two men helped by holding her still while their friend stood in front of her. She had prepared for a verbal battle but never would have expected it to become physical. No one had ever physically assaulted her for speaking her mind. But this wasn't her home village of Farbank, and they played by different rules here.

The guards looked at the drunks and turned away, avoiding any view of their doings.

Brushing his long, oily hair out of his face again, the thin man gave off an evil smile. He stood over her and cupped his palm behind her head as she looked up at him. "First, I want to see how soft your lips are. I'll work down from there." He held her head tight as he leaned down to kiss her.

"Stop!" Thorik yelled from behind the men. His battle-axe was held up and over his shoulder, ready to be swung. "Let go of her before you feel the blade of my axe."

Being a head shorter than the men meant very little as the sharp weapon prepared to swing and take someone's life. The men stopped, and one of them stepped toward the battle-ready Num.

He swung the axe, grazing the man's leather vest, triggering the realization that Thorik was serious.

Placing the battle-axe back into swinging position, Thorik stepped forward. "Let go of her!"

They conceded as they all turned to face Thorik while spreading out to surround him.

Stepping up from the table, the guards had decided to get involved, until the thin drunk waved them back. "I'll take care of this. Sit down and enjoy your drinks." And to the surprise of Thorik, they did just that.

"Avanda, get out of here," Thorik yelled as he watched them slowly complete the circle around him.

Instead, Avanda reached for a red and gold purse within her cloak and pulled out a string of red beads. She chanted a few words before dropping the beads onto the ground.

Incredibly, her spell worked, and a rainstorm of fireballs fell from the ceiling, hitting the three men. The illusion was weak, and those not intoxicated from ale could tell it was a hoax. Fortunately, the three men could not.

The men covered their heads as they screamed, for they believed their clothes and flesh were on fire. They bolted out of the pub in an effort to put out the flames in the local river.

Thorik lowered his axe and returned his attention back to his young student. "Why do you have to do that?"

"I don't like being bullied," she answered as she picked up her string of red beads.

Thorik put his weapon into its holder on his back. "One of these times you're going to wish you had just let it go and ignored the situation."

She looked at him square in the eyes. "You should take your own advice. How many times did Brimmelle try to tell you to let it go? Instead, you had to get involved with Ambrosius, and next thing I know, I'm on the opposite end of Terra Australis from my parents and you're sitting here feeling guilty about Ambrosius and sorry for yourself."

Thorik knew the locals had overheard the conversation, but her statement sliced deep. "I did what was needed. I had no choice," he said softly with all the intensity as he could muster.

"Grewen says we all have choices," she said sternly, looking into her former teacher's eyes. Pulling out a hexagonal stone that hung from her neck by a leather string, she continued in a soft voice, "You taught me to take responsibility for my actions. Was that all Fesh talk?"

"Watch your tongue." Thorik didn't like some of the habits she had picked up. Her use of inappropriate words and undisciplined magic were two of them.

Tracing the rune in the center of the hexagonal Runestone with her finger, she remembered the day he had given it to her before leaving Farbank. Thorik seemed so content and easier to talk to back then. "What happened to you, Thorik?" she asked.

"What are you talking about?"

"In Farbank, you kept all of us happy, and we loved being around you. Now you're grumpy and distant."

"I've grown up a lot."

"You're only three years older than I am."

"Growing up has little to do with your age."

Avanda nodded her head. "I see. So now you're more mature, like Fir Brimmelle."

Thorik did not like to be compared to their spiritual leader in such a manner. The Fir was always negative and closed-minded, opposite of what Thorik considered himself. "You don't understand," Thorik spoke firmly. "I killed a man... a good man." He paused. "A friend," he finished softly.

"If you hadn't, Weirfortus Dam would have released its water, and this city would be under Lake Luthralum." She looked around at the disastrous state of the pub and recalled the devastation of the city. "Of course, that might have been an improvement."

"It's more than that. I have a lot of responsibility now."

"I'm not sure I want to grow up if it means I can't have fun anymore. I'd rather be like my Uncle Wess."

"And look what happened to him."

"But Thorik, he lived life to the fullest. He enjoyed every minute. Never did I see him pouting or sulking like you. What a waste of time. Why can't you let this go so we can move on with our lives?"

Thorik sat back down at his table and looked at the half-empty mug of lukewarm ale. This was not the place, nor the time, to explain his plan to be arrested. Captain Mensley's contacts had located Ericc in the nearby prison mines, and the only way in to see him was to get thrown in himself. Not a mission he looked forward to, but a simple altercation with local officials should get him incarcerated for a few days.

"It's complicated." Thorik bit his lip after making the statement. He hated being on the receiving end of that phrase and never thought he would be on the other side of it.

"Sure it is. I'm not mature enough to understand," she said, dramatically pointing to herself. "Well, I'll let you do your grown-up soul searching while I head back to the dock. Brimmelle sent me here to let you know the ship is fixed and we can set sail in the morning." She stared at him before continuing. "And now you know. I'll see you back at the dock, unless you have time to walk me back."

"Time?" Thorik began to panic again as his eyes looked at the guards, who were finishing up their drinks. His window of opportunity to address the men was quickly closing. "No, I don't have time. Head back quickly."

Turning on the balls of her feet, she crossed her arms and stomped through the pub, out the exit, and into the street.

Most of the streetlamps had been broken from the storms, many of them bent over like withering plants against the thin haze hiding an unseen moon. Walls of buildings pitched to one side or another, and smoke billowed from distant fires. The smell of rotten food and sewage filled the thick, damp air while sounds of wild animals were heard from the nearby tropical forest.

Avanda turned and noticed a silhouette of a man standing at the corner smoking his pipe. Uncomfortable, she turned the other way instead.

Walking down the street, she looked back to see the unknown man following her. She quickened her pace, knowing she only had a few blocks to go before reaching her group at the dock.

Turning the first corner, she looked back to see the man gaining on her. Her heart raced as she realized she was in trouble. Charging forward into the dark alley, she bumped into a man standing in her way.

"Hello again, little Num," a man's voice said.

She reached for her sack of magic but was quickly nabbed from behind. Panicking, she screamed and kicked as the two men picked her up and moved her into the light of a distant streetlamp.

A large, rough hand covered her small mouth as they held her tight in wait for the approaching stranger who had been following her.

"About that kiss." The stranger pushed his long stringy blonde hair out of the way and over his shoulder. "I think I'll start lower this time."

❧ 4 ❧

ASSAULT

Avanda twisted and bucked as one drunken man held her captive and a second one stood behind her, covering her mouth and holding her head still.

Sweat ran down her neck and back as she fought for freedom. Nevertheless, the men were able to easily control the small Num.

"Take her cloak off," ordered the blonde leader as he stood before her.

One of the men grinned as he removed it. "I get her next, Lucian."

Lucian leaned down and looked into her enraged eyes. "There may not be anything left after I'm done with her." He removed her belt and tossed it to the side. His breath was thick with ale, making Avanda recoil to avoid the smell.

Her garments were saturated with sweat from the struggle in the hot, humid night air.

Enjoying every reaction he could get out of her, Lucian began unbuttoning her blouse as he whispered to her. "I bet you are so soft and pure." His rough and dry index finger touched between the buttons on her chest. "Silky," he said from his first encounter with her skin.

Avanda was helpless. Disgusted by this man who was removing her clothes, she turned her head so she could distance herself from the situation. His continued touch made her stomach churn as tears flooded her face.

Lucian watched her reactions to his touch. "Gentlemen, you'll be happy to know that she is soft. So very soft." Lifting her shirt, he exposed her navel and placed his dirty, dry palm against her bare stomach.

Leaning down, he placed a kiss on her belly as he moved his hands to her legs. Slowly, he moved them up to her knees. "Softer than a newborn tigra," he purred as he leaned the unshaven bristles on the side of his face against her exposed body.

"And now, my friends, we will know the answer to our question." Lucian moved his hands on her legs to the inside of her knees.

Avanda squeezed her eyes tight as she felt the horror of Lucian's touch.

"RELEASE HER!" a deep voice ordered from the darkness of the alley.

Stepping out into the soft hazy light, a giant Blothrud towered over the group. Veins pumping across the tight red skin on his hairless wolf-like face and across his enormous chest and arm muscles made it clear that he was ready for a fight. Blood dripped from his lip as he clenched his teeth in anger over the scene before him.

Lucian's face turned white, as though he was seeing a ghost. "Santorray? You're dead. I... I... I killed you myself," he stammered.

"Apparently not, but I've returned to repay the favor, and I don't intend to fail like you did."

But Lucian was not one to be intimidated, especially in his drunken state of mind. "Blades!" he shouted at his men, who quickly placed daggers at the young Num's neck and stomach.

Lucian shielded his position behind his two men and Avanda. "Back off, Santorray. This is not your business."

"I'm making it my business."

Avanda stood still as the men's blades pushed up against her, stretching her skin.

Lucian smiled at his position. "Leave, or we will kill her and blame it on you. My word against an Altered's word is no contest."

In one swift motion, the Blothrud grabbed a saber from his side and swung it in front of him with such speed that the metal blade couldn't be seen in the dim lighting. He then stepped forward, right in front of Avanda and her captors.

"Cut her!" Lucian ordered.

But the men stood motionless.

Lucian stumbled back a few steps in his inebriated state, confused as to why they weren't following his orders. "I said, cut her!"

Reaching down, Santorray removed the blades from both of the men's hands and abruptly pulled her off to the side. The men collapsed where they once stood, as their heads fell from their necks and rolled toward Lucian. The lightning-fast strike of Santorray's saber had cleanly severed them both.

Lucian pulled his own dagger out and threw it at Avanda, hoping to distract the beast long enough to make an escape.

Jumping toward the flying weapon, the Blothrud broke its path with the spikes that grew from the back of his hand. When he turned back to confront the man, Lucian had taken the opportunity to run.

Santorray's thick and hairy wolf-like legs sprang him from his position and into hot pursuit of the soon to be victim of a tragic, brutal murder. Lowering his upper body, the blothrud used the thick-skinned palms of his hand as front feet, racing on all fours.

Without a backup plan, Lucian instantly panicked. His arrogance had turned to fear once he had lost the upper hand.

It didn't take long for the blothrud to catch up to him. But as Santorray leaped for Lucian, the man turned abruptly and barreled his way through the doors into the pub. The creature missed his prey and skidded to a halt.

Thorik had been standing near the door, arguing with the local guards, when

Lucian crashed his way in. The two collided, sending them to the floor, knocking over a table and several chairs.

Noticing it was Thorik, Lucian tried to justify himself. He could only assume that the Num was a friend of the beast in pursuit. "I didn't hurt her! We didn't rape her!"

"Rape her? Avanda? What happened?" Thorik grabbed onto the man to get answers.

Lucian struggled to get free. "He'll tell you we hurt her, but we didn't."

"Only because I stopped you. You Fesh scum!" The voice came from outside the only wall still fully intact, until Santorray plowed his way in with a crushing blow from his shoulder. "Playing with helpless Nums? How about playing with me for a spell?" He flexed his already oversized muscles on his eight-foot sculptured body.

Thorik never turned around to see the ominous red creature that knocked a hole in the wall. He focused on preventing Lucian from getting up and escaping. "What did you do to Avanda?"

Thorik lost his grip on the man, who stood up to run. Jumping forward, the Num hit Lucian in the back. Falling, they both crashed through the table occupied by the local guards, who were in the midst of grabbing their weapons.

"Get him off me," Lucian ordered the men.

"Let them fight it out!" roared Santorray, assuming the girl was a friend of the Num.

Two of the three guards turned to look up at Santorray, blocking his ability to stop the third guard from breaking up the fight.

"I said, let them fight!"

One of the guards raised his sword to keep the creature at a distance.

Santorray grinned, making the man's forehead and hands begin to sweat.

The second guard raised his own sword as he grabbed a whistle and blew it hard.

Santorray's grin increased in size, exposing his long upper canines all the way to the gum. "All right, if you want it to be that way." Reaching both hands forward, past their swords, the blothrud grabbed the men by their uniforms and tossed them over his head into the air and through the wall behind him.

The last guard had just separated the two fighters as he turned to see what had happened. Grabbing a chair, he crushed the wooden furniture against the blothrud's exposed side before Santorray could lower his arms to protect himself.

Splinters flew as the chair struck hard against the beast. Nothing remained except the chair's back, which the guard still clung to. A stone statue would have moved more from the attack, as Santorray's grin never faded.

Dropping the wooden remains of the chair, the guard pulled his whistle to his lips to call for help.

A swift red fist to the mouth stopped the noise, as well as the man, before Santorray turned back to see the fight he was missing.

Thorik had fallen onto his back with Lucian above him, stabbing a broken stool leg down at the Num. Still inebriated, he missed several times as Thorik rolled out of the way. Finally, he thrust his weapon directly into Thorik's chest, and a crack from the Num's ribs could be heard upon contact.

"You pathetic peasant." Lucian stood over his victim, who held his arms over his chest. "You outsiders come into our province and think you are better than us!" Kicking Thorik in the side helped Lucian vent his frustration. "You don't know who you're messing with."

"No, but I do," Santorray said.

Looking up at the beast, Lucian was still breathing heavily from his brawl with Thorik. The less than sober man was cut and bleeding. Eyes darting from side to side, he planned his escape as the enormous Altered approached. There were plenty of holes in the walls to escape through, but all were short-term victories, seeing that he couldn't outrun a blothrud.

But then a venomous smile slowly crossed Lucian's face. "I hope you have this much energy after a few weeks in the mines."

"If they can catch me after killing you, they can have me."

"Unfortunately, you'll have to go there on assault charges, instead of murder."

Santorray could sense something was wrong. Peering out the holes in the walls, he could see several dozen guards taking position around the pub, ready to attack from all sides. They had heard the alert whistle.

"If I'm going to the mines, I might as well make it worth my while." Santorray leaned forward and grabbed Lucian with both hands, lifting him up in the air, slapping his body against a ceiling rafter. It was difficult to know if the crack that followed was Lucian's back or the already weakened timbers holding up the roof. Again and again, he used the man as a sledgehammer against the wooden beams.

Shaking from the fight, the building creaked and moaned as it struggled to remain standing. Sections of the roof were now caving in and falling to the floor.

Bleeding from his thrashing, Lucian swung the stool leg he still clung to at the beast's face, only to have it captured in the blothrud's mouth. Santorray's teeth snapped down on the wood along with two of Lucian's fingers, cutting them both from his hand.

Shaking Lucian like a rag doll above his head, Santorray heard the military ordering the attack. He turned his attention to the group rushing in at him, dropping Lucian hard to the ground behind his back for effect.

The guards rushed at him with spears from all sides, only to stop a few yards from him. They had a tight circle around the beast.

Spitting out Lucian's fingers, Santorray growled and showed his teeth stained with Lucian's blood. He waited for the first fool who wanted to test their courage as he slowly rotated around.

It wasn't long before a young strapping lad with a chip on his shoulder needed to prove himself to his peers. A lunge forward with his spear grazed one of Santorray's back blades. It was all the man recalled, for the beast's instinctive reflexes kicked his back leg into the man's forehead, knocking him out as well as into his peers.

A second man stepped forward with a two-handed broadsword ready for attack. He wasn't a guard like the rest. He was a giant of a man who stood nearly as high as Santorray's shoulders and wore armor with royal symbols on it. Blue and gold robes bore the kingdom's symbol of water, wheat, and a wall.

They sized each other up as the guards stepped back to give them room. "I am Asentar, supreme knight of the Dovenar Kingdom. You are now a prisoner of the Southwind Province. Come quietly, or I shall be forced to slay you."

Santorray was intrigued. He had fought many a man and Altered, but never a Dovenar Knight. In fact, he didn't think there were any left. "My issue is not with you, sir knight. It's with a man who takes pleasure in raping children. But if you come between me and my rightful vengeance, you will become my enemy as well."

Behind Santorray, Lucian had regained consciousness. Grabbing a dagger from one of the guards, he rushed toward the blothrud. Blood poured from his missing fingers, coating the handle with fresh liquid. With the blade in both hands, his face tightened in anger as he swung it over his head, down toward the creature's spine.

Santorray didn't see it coming as he focused on Asentar. The knight's eyes never revealed the pending attack. Not a twitch of the cheek or blink of the eye. There was no sign of Lucian's rear attack coming until he saw a blurred movement out of the corner of his right eye.

Jumping through the air, Thorik collided with Lucian, again rolling to the floor. The Num grabbed the man's wrist and pounded it against the floor, trying to break his grip on the dagger. After several failed attempts, Thorik pressed his fingers against the stubby ends of Lucian's missing fingers. The pain caused the man to release the blade as he lay on his back. Thorik grabbed the battle-axe from his back and held it over his head, ready to strike if Lucian made another move.

Asentar used this distraction to launch an attack. A step forward allowed a swift slice to Santorray's upper thigh, with an immediate move to his stomach. The blade held steady against the rough red skin of his abdomen, causing it to stretch and indent as he pushed slightly forward. Blood from the superficial cut ran down the blothrud's leg. The knight now had the advantage. "Surrender. I do not wish to kill you, but I will if I must."

Snarling, saliva and blood dripped from Santorray's mouth. "Now you've made yourself my enemy." His dark red skin brightened as fresh blood pulsed faster through his veins. His muscles appeared to grow before their eyes as his anger grew at the man who held a sword to his belly. The quiet tension hung in the air as the guards waited for the blothrud to attack.

Expressionless, the Dovenar Knight stood his ground, ready to do his duty. He didn't care if it was an Altered, whether it be Ov'Unday, Fesh'Unday or, as in the blothrud's case, Del'Unday. His only desire was to follow his oath to protect the kingdom.

The silence ended with the sounds of a legion of faralope hooves marching up to the building. Once there, a Southwind military official stepped down from his mount, followed by the rest of his armed men. The guards parted, allowing their general to enter the area.

In full uniform and colors, the general walked stiffly over to Thorik without saying a word. A large mustache trailed down below his powerful jaw. His ability to intimidate Thorik without speaking was remarkable. Stopping just shy of running into the Num, his hand snapped out like a viper and snatched the axe out of Thorik's hands before tossing it behind him onto the floor.

Thorik backed up as the wide-chested general stepped forward. Thorik had met wild boars with a more comforting demeanor than this man. His presence chilled the room with his disapproval of what he was seeing. Thorik instinctively wanted to apologize to him, even if he didn't know why.

Santorray didn't cower from the general, but his anger was subsiding. He had left Lucian a continual reminder of him, for he would never properly wield a weapon again.

Thorik felt the need to explain himself to the general. "He raped my friend, a mere Num child. He needs be locked away."

The general reached down with one hand and grabbed Lucian's hand. With one quick tug, the general lifted Lucian to his feet and then spun him around. He now had Lucian by the hand behind his back. The general lifted the hand a few times, causing Lucian pain, while pushing him forward toward the faralopes.

Following the general, Santorray and Thorik walked just outside the pub before stopping. They had given in to the inevitable; they were captured. Fighting was futile at this point as more military personnel arrived. Santorray dropped his weapon.

Sheathing his sword, the Dovenar Knight watched the proud blothrud outside the pub. "You were wise not to challenge me, Del."

Glaring over his shoulder, Santorray exposed his teeth while watching the knight grin at the Del'Unday's fate. With a forearm strike to the outer wall, the roof finally gave way, landing on the knight and many of the guards. "You were wise not to say that too close to me," he said calmly in the night air.

As the pub collapsed, the general and Lucian reached the faralopes. Letting go of Lucian, the general spun him around and pushed him backward. Still intoxicated with ale, he fell against the Faralope and cradled his hand with the missing fingers.

"Damn that beast! Did you see what he did to my hand?" Lucian said with obnoxious cockiness in his voice. "We were just having some fun. Santorray had no business getting involved."

Looking down over his beak of a nose at Lucian, the general grumbled, "Do you realize what you have put in jeopardy here? If the Matriarch finds out about this, she'll have our entire family put to death. You make me sick to be your father." He followed the comment with a loud and stern instruction to his second in command. "Take the blothrud and Num to the mines. I don't need word of this getting out."

The guard looked at the general with serious eyes for confirmation of actions to be taken.

Clarification came quickly from Lucian's father, "Make this problem disappear. It never happened."

❧ 5 ☙

SOUTHWIND MINES

Rats scurried away from the group as they walked down the dimly lit shaft of an old mine. Thorik's head hung low as he was pushed forward. "Are you sure Avanda is all right?"

Santorray continued to lower his head to avoid the beams that supported the rock ceiling. "Yes, I'm sure. I stopped them before they injured her," he said in his usual deep voice. "If you ask me that one more time, *you'll* be the one that's injured."

A group of bad-tempered guards moved the two deeper into the mountain. Each could blame their attitudes on their inhospitable working conditions and lack of hygiene, but the reality was they simply took pleasure in causing pain to others. It was the only power they had left in their lives. Even though they weren't prisoners, quitting wasn't an option, especially after what they had witnessed on a daily basis. An ex-guard telling tales didn't live long in Southwind.

Shaking his head, Thorik thought about his mistakes. "I should have walked her back to the ship. He wouldn't have touched her if I had been there."

Santorray ducked under a low ceiling beam as they entered a long corridor with cells on both sides. "You would have been killed at the start, to get you out of the way."

"You don't know that. I would have protected her."

"Even if you had the soul of a blothrud, you're still only a Num," Santorray said as one of the general's personal guards unlocked their cell.

Santorray's words only added to Thorik's grief. "This was a bad idea. This is entirely my fault."

"Yes, it is," the lead guard said. "And now it'a be my job to make sure ya pay for it." Laughing, he continued, "And you'll pay. Again and again."

Pushing Thorik into the cell, the guard moved out of the way for Santorray to be escorted in by several armed men. Locking the door behind them, the general's guard handed the keys over. "They're all yours, Da'Shawn. You have the general's orders. The blothrud loses one finger each day for his crime against Master Lucian."

Santorray tightened his fists as he stood firm in the center of the cell. "Just try." He then spit on the floor near the cell door.

The cell was dark with cold rock walls, floor, and ceiling and metal bars along one side. Flickering mining lanterns provided the only light from the corridor, which ran down the center of the dank detention units. Water dripped from cracks in the ceiling, creating puddles for the local insects to swarm and breed. Scattered remains of the prior inmates filled the cell with an overwhelming odor of rotting flesh.

Clutching the bars of the door, Da'Shawn looked through them at the blothrud. Chewing on tobacco, he allowed it to drip down his chin before finally spitting and leaving a string of brown saliva from his lower lip down the front of his soiled shirt. "Last inmate that tried ta escape made it up to da second level b'fore he was eaten by our Frudorian dragon. Duuke's always hungry for another meal."

Looking around the prison cell floor, he continued, "Seeing that he was quickly disposed of, we took his punishment out on his cell-mate." The guard reached his short spear through the bars into the cell and poked at the remaining torso of a human body before looking at Thorik. "I'd suggest ya talk yur big friend outta make'n a mistake that you end up paying fer."

Santorray ignored the dramatic speech as he moved to the back of the cell, kicking decomposing body parts out of his way.

"We don't want any trouble. We won't talk about what happened." Thorik attempted to get on the guard's good side. "We will serve our time for disorderly conduct and be on our way."

"Your time?" Da'Shawn's dirty face exposed several cracked and missing teeth as he smiled. "Better make yourself at home, Num. You stepped into a rat's nest when you crossed Lucian. During his bachelor party, no less. Soon to be wed to the granddaughter of the Matriarch, he is. She runs all the business in Southwind, and Lucian will be inheriting this 'ere mine once his vows are said. So, he makes the rules. You ain't going nowhere."

Da'Shawn chuckled to himself as he stepped away from the cell and walked back down the corridor.

The new inmates listened to the complaints of other prisoners as the guard walked past their cells.

Santorray spit in his hands and rubbed them together before applying it to the open wound on his leg. "It would have been easier to steal something."

"What?"

"You picked a dangerous way to get in here."

Thorik was shocked at the comments. "What makes you think that I would *want* to be in here, sitting in a disgusting prison cell?"

"I can tell by your speech that you're from the north. There are only three reasons people from the north come to Southwind. Either they are here to trade, sent to the mines as slaves, or journeyed here to save someone from the mines."

"How do you know I'm not here to trade?"

"Okay, who are you here to trade with? Be careful, I know most of the trading merchants in this area."

Thorik felt exposed, as though the blothrud could read his thoughts. "You wouldn't know him, he's new."

"Like I said, you picked a dangerous way to get in here."

"I didn't start the fight, you did."

"No, but I'm guessing you were sitting in the bar drinking up some bravery to do enough to get thrown in here. I've seen it before. It usually ends with your own death in the mines."

Frustrated, Thorik didn't like being on the defensive. "How about you? Who are you trying to get out?"

"I came back to Southwind to pay back an old debt."

"Was it worth it? Now you're just going to rot away in here."

"Yes, I've made my mark on Lucian to remind him of his actions. But no, I don't plan on rotting away. I'll be escaping from here."

Thorik recalled the guard's story. "Um, if you escape, they will take it out on me."

"Then I would suggest you escape with me."

"I can't."

"Why?"

"I can't tell you."

Santorray put his foot under one of the rotting bodies and kicked it toward the Num. "Then I guess you will become a permanent resident."

Decaying flesh flung off the pelvis and spine as it rolled up to Thorik. His stomach churned at the sight. He surely didn't want to end up like that.

Weighing his options, he considered what his next move would be. "Can you give me a few days before you escape?"

"No."

"Why not?"

"Give me a good reason why I should allow these humans to cut off a few of my fingers over the next few days. On top of that, we just accused Lucian of rape, which means we'll be lucky if they don't try to kill us before we get a chance to talk to anyone else." The blothrud reached down, plucked a slug up from the floor, and set it in the blood running down from his cut leg. "Why are you here? Who is so important to get out of here that you're willing to be beaten and worked to death?"

Thorik sighed. "I can't tell you. I don't even know you."

"San-tor-ray is the name." The blothrud emphasized each syllable and rolled the 'r' with pride. "And yours?"

"Sec Thorik Dain of Farbank."

"Okay, Sec, who is it you're after? Who should I put my fingers and my life on the line for by staying in here?"

"No, it's Thorik, not Sec."

"Yes, I know. So, who are you looking for, Sec?"

Thorik didn't have many alternatives. "This has gotten way out of control. I had planned on being thrown into here based on a verbal confrontation with some local guards. A two-night offense." Shaking his head in disbelief, he began to pace. "I never expected to have my life at risk."

Santorray was getting tired of Thorik's lack of forthcoming information. "Not my problem. I'm escaping with or without you."

"Give me a day. Just one day to see if he is even here."

"Who? Who is worth one of my fingers?"

Stopping his pacing, he walked closer to the Del'Unday. Thorik's lips tightened, and his voice lowered. "Ericc Dovenar."

This piqued Santorray's interest, and he sat up slightly. "And why would you be looking for the son of Ambrosius?"

"You know him? How?"

"Everyone knows the Dovenar family tree. It's just hard to tell the good branches from the bad ones. Are you working for Darkmere to assassinate the hidden son?"

Thorik looked shocked at the suggestion. "No, just the opposite. I've come to protect him from Darkmere."

A grand, yet terrifying, laugh bellowed out of Santorray. "You? You can't protect yourself, let alone Ericc from the likes of Darkmere."

"I stopped Lucian from ending your life," Thorik snapped back. He began to pace again, worried about how truthful Santorray's words could be.

Still chuckling, the blothrud fired back, "True, but I was also getting ready to fight thirty men at the time. All you had to worry about was one, a drunken one at that." Watching the Num's silhouette travel back and forth in front of the yellow lantern light was getting tiresome for the beast. "If you don't stop pacing, I'm going to break your leg off and eat it for my next meal."

Thorik's face flushed partly from embarrassment and partly from frustration as he walked over to the sitting Del'Unday. "Listen, I'm not *asking* for your help." Straightening his back, he lifted his chest. "I don't *need* your help. All I'm requesting is that you give me enough time to find him before you destroy my plans. One day. Two nights, tonight and the next."

Santorray looked at the little Num standing proud with conviction. "You have one day, Sec. I expect them to come for their first finger after I've given them a hard day's work, so get it done early so the second night is not needed. Do you know what he looks like?"

"I don't have a clue."

Santorray nodded, expecting no less. "Excellent."

❦ *6* ❦

FINDING ERICC

Morning came with the light and smell of burning torches as the guards opened up the cells and paraded the prisoners down the corridor toward the main mine shaft. Thorik and Santorray fell in line behind countless others, most of whom showed signs of starvation and unhealed lash marks.

The main shaft opened up into a large round room filled with men handing out mining equipment and daily rations. Above them, a catwalk encircled the room as archers watched for signs of misbehaving.

A thousand people slowly moved into and out of the large room. A layer of grayish brown dirt covered their bodies and clothes, making them all blend together.

"This will take more than a day," Thorik mumbled, realizing how hard it would be to find a young man he had never met before.

Santorray agreed. "If Ericc is here, and they know it's him, they wouldn't cage him with the rest of us. They would separate him to keep him alive and unspoiled for Darkmere's men to come for him. Someplace constantly under watch and with a private cell." The blothrud had been in the mines before and knew of only one place that met these criteria: the infirmary. Now the question was how to get in there.

They handed Thorik a pick and a chunk of dry bread. Placing the ration near his nose to smell something other than the sweaty prisoners, he found there was no aroma to it.

The prisoner in front of Thorik turned and snatched the bread from the Num. "This one's mine."

"Hey, give that back." Thorik looked at the guard to see if he had seen the incident. After seeing the guard roll his eyes at the issue, Thorik looked back at the blothrud. "Did you see that?"

"How did you ever survive on your own?" Taking a bite of his own tasteless bread, Santorray swallowed hard as it scratched his throat on the way down. "Trust me. It's not worth fighting for." Listening to his own words, the blothrud got an idea and tossed the rest of his meal to Thorik.

"Hey! Give that back!" Santorray roared at the Num before grabbing him and lifting him into the air.

Shocked, Thorik tried to kick free as he held the bread in one hand and the pick in the other.

"Swing your pick at me," Santorray said under his breath, before yelling, "I'll rip you apart!"

Thorik panicked from the unprovoked attack. "What are you doing?"

"I'm going to make you bleed! You'll be lucky if they can stitch you back together." Santorray raked his knuckle spikes across Thorik's stomach, ripping his shirt and skin. Any deeper and Thorik could have lost his internal organs.

Dropping his items, Thorik grasped his stomach as blood poured forth.

Santorray dropped the Num on the food table in front of the guard before picking up his bread. "It was *my* bread," he growled.

Guards rushed over while archers loaded their arrows and prepared to shoot, should the blothrud put up a fight against them. Several slaps from a short whip pushed the blothrud back into line and away from the Num.

"Worth keeping alive?" the food server asked a higher-ranking guard as they both looked at Thorik.

The guard assessed Thorik's cuts. "Wrap him up and send him to the infirmary. No reason to lose a good set of hands from nothing more than bleeding to death."

After having a filthy rag wrapped around his stomach and waist, Thorik was escorted down a different branch of the mine. The smell of fresh stew could be taken in as they entered a new open area, which housed the guards' mess hall and medical area on one side and several prisoner cells on the other.

Tossing Thorik into one of the cells, the guard yelled at a man in a long white cloak discolored with red blood who was enjoying his hot breakfast. Returning to his duties, the guard left this man in charge.

'What was Santorray thinking?' Thorik thought to himself. 'He nearly sliced me open.'

"Hey, are you okay?" came a voice from the next cell. Unlike the prisoners' cells, these had bars on three of their four sides.

Thorik looked over to see a young man about his own age. He had mahogany hair down to his eyebrows and over his ears, and a face that looked vaguely familiar. "Ericc?"

Sliding back into his cell, Ericc asked his own question. "Do I know you?"

Thorik was beaming. "It's you! I found you. Actually, you found me. But that doesn't matter right now. You're here, and now I can protect you from the prophecy being fulfilled with your death."

Ericc looked at the blood soaking into the cloth around the Num's stomach. "You're going to protect me?" he asked sarcastically. "Who are you? And how do you know me?"

"My name is Sec Thorik Dain of Farbank. Your father sent me."

"My father? I've been looking for him for months." Ericc stood up and leaned against the bars, hoping to see his father walk down the corridor and free him. "Where is he? Is he coming for me?"

Stress seeped into Thorik's voice as he tried to answer his question. "No, Ericc. He's not coming to save you. He asked me to."

"Why wouldn't he do it himself? Where has he been for the past eight years, and what will it take for him to see his own son?" His pent-up resentment mixed with excitement of the possibility of seeing his father again. He had been abandoned by his father and sent to live with friends of the family, away from civilization. He understood the risks of appearing in public, which had nearly led to his death when he encountered Lord Bredgin.

Nevertheless, eight years was too long to go without seeing his father. Ericc had run away and ventured into the cities to experience the life he had missed. But instead of finding the dream of freedom, he quickly became hunted by those who wished to see him dead. Escaping more than one attack, he was recently caught stealing food to survive. Thrown into the mines, he was recognized as Ambrosius' son and removed from the common labor only to be held in the infirmary until Darkmere or one of his assassins arrived to take him.

"He's not coming. He can't come," Thorik said.

"Why? What's the excuse this time? Another Grand Council meeting? A disaster in Eastland that only he can repress? I've heard them all over the years. Not this time. I'm in here until he personally shows up or Darkmere comes to kill me."

"Are you in here on purpose to force your father's hand to rescue you?"

"I'm in here on a charge of trespassing. But now that they know who I am, I'm going to put an end to this, whether it is by my father standing at my side or fighting Darkmere to the death. I refuse to live in the obscurity of shadows for the rest of my life."

"It won't work. You'll be killed."

"Then so be it. At least then I'll know my father's true colors."

"No, you don't understand. He asked me to come save you from Darkmere."

"Then you'll have to tell him to come himself."

"I can't. He's dead," Thorik blurted out. He hadn't intended to tell him in such an emotionless fashion. He had planned on a more respectful way to soften the blow.

Ericc shook his head. "Not possible. Not my father. No one can kill him."

"Ericc, listen to me. Darkmere and Ambrosius fought, and on your father's dying breath he asked me to save you, to prevent you from being sacrificed."

Now it sank in, and Ericc's body became cold and rigid. "How do I know you're telling the truth? How did you find me?"

"I traveled with your father in hopes of preventing Darkmere from flooding the kingdom. Draq traveled with us. My understanding is that he and his family raised you."

Thorik noticed no reaction from Ericc to his words, so he continued. "After the battle, our boat crashed upon the reefs of an island, and we were rescued by Captain Mensley, who helped us find your whereabouts."

Ericc stared across the hall. "Where is Darkmere?" He couldn't even look at Thorik as he talked through clenched teeth.

"Last I heard, he returned to Corrock to regroup, seeing that the flood was prevented. Why?"

"I'm going to kill him."

"No, you need to hide from him."

"I've been hiding my whole life. I'm going to Corrock to avenge my father's death."

"You don't understand. He wants you to come to him. He's baiting you, just like he did your father. Once he has you, you're to be sacrificed to prevent the prophecy from coming true."

"Prophecy? What prophecy?" asked the medic in the red-stained white cloak as he walked up to the two.

Thorik and Ericc suddenly became deaf and mute.

Receiving no answer, he opened Thorik's cell. "Fine. Let me see those cuts."

❧ 7 ☙

MATRIARCH

On raised steps, the Matriarch sat upon her throne of fear and deceit. She had no official authority, yet even the prominent of Southwind cowered to her demands. Ruthless tactics to obtain her power continued to escalate into her elder years. The little humanity she had in her youth had all been devoured by greed.

Her throne sat high enough to ensure everyone in the chamber looked up to her. Bodyguards stood at attention while servants attended to her every need. Her three advisors mulled over maps and decrees on a nearby table as she dictated new orders to them.

Visitors were welcome, yet the only ones she ever received were those who asked for her help. One would have to be desperate to do so, for the payment always outweighed the support she gave. This normally meant that they were indebted for the rest of their lives.

The only others that dared approach her were those whom she had summoned. To not drop everything and rush to do her bidding was a sure way to end one's life.

Lucian entered her chamber, limping in pain from his fight with Santorray and holding a bandage over his missing fingers. Lowering his eyes and head in respect, he addressed her. "Greetings, Matriarch. You called for me?"

Selecting a fruit from a servant's basket, the Matriarch waited for it to be cut and a piece to be eaten to ensure its safety prior to it reaching her own lips. She was in no hurry to respond to the filthy man who stood before her.

Lucian tried to stand perfectly still as he waited for her response. But the night of binging on alcohol still tugged and pushed at him, causing him to sway as his head pounded from his recovery. The injuries sustained from his beating didn't help any, either.

"What happened to you?" she asked in an indifferent tone.

"Santorray has returned, my grace."

"You told me he was dead. You told me that you had killed him yourself."

"Yes, you are correct. I saw him fall. I don't understand it myself."

"What else have you failed to understand? What else have you lied to me about?"

Lucian stepped forward and dropped to his knees. "Nothing, I swear. The blothrud must have had help, like he did last night."

"You lied to me."

"No, my grace. I witnessed his death."

"I trusted your words, and therefore have proliferated this lie of Santorray's demise. My words are now in jeopardy of being questioned." Taking a bite of her fruit, she pondered her options as she watched Lucian ask forgiveness at the first step to her throne. "Remove his tongue," she ordered a bodyguard, "so he can't tell any more lies."

Lucian screamed for mercy to anyone who would listen.

"And castrate him, his father, and any nephews. I don't want them breeding any more untrustworthy kin." She had little change in her voice. "Inform my granddaughter that her wedding is off. She shall not be married to a man of dishonor."

"I've captured Santorray," Lucian shouted as her strongmen grabbed him. "He now sits in the mines near Rava'Kor. I will travel back to the mines and finish my task, returning to you with his heart in my hands. Your words will be pure again, and my debt to you will be endless."

Overpowered by her personal bodyguards, Lucian's tongue was grabbed and pulled out to be sliced off. The edge of the shiny blade drew blood just as the Matriarch stopped them.

"You shall bring me his head so that I know it was him."

Lucian slowly nodded in agreement, considering he still had a blade to his tongue.

"By doing so, you save your life, one that is at my disposal forever."

"Thank you, Your Grace," Lucian uttered once they released him.

"If you do not return with it, your father and all your kin shall be hunted down and drained of their blood prior to your own painful execution. Do I make myself clear?"

The guards pushed him back down to his knees in front of her. "Yes, Matriarch, I am at your command. Santorray's head will be cut from his body and returned to you."

Footsteps could be heard approaching from behind Lucian. Asentar entered the hall with a strong, confident stride. His height allowing him to look directly at the Matriarch without raising his head. "Greetings, Matriarch. I am Asentar, high knight of the kingdom. The Doven Province sends words of unity to Southwind," he announced.

She sat up very straight, trying to keep his eye level beneath her own. "You are the *only* knight of the kingdom, from my understanding."

"Perhaps. I have not seen any of the others since the destruction of the Grand Council. I don't know of their well-being."

"They have all fallen. You are the last of their kind."

"All the more reason that I must speak to you about the reunification of the provinces."

"Why speak with me? I am not the Prominent of Southwind."

"Even the beggars on the street know that he is but a mere puppet on strings which you govern. You are in control of this region, and therefore I am petitioning you to stand with us. Reunite the Dovenar Kingdom and rebuild a unified council to stand against our enemies."

"Our enemies may not be the same. If you are referring to Darkmere, I have already settled this issue. For our support in his endeavors, he will be granting me full power over everything south of the Volney River. Your words of giving power back to the kingdom are wasted upon my ears. I have no interest in what you have to say."

Asentar took in a deep breath, raising his chest. "What tragedy has caused the words of a Dovenar Knight to not carry the attention and the authority to those that live in the kingdom?"

"Since the king relinquished his powers to the Grand Council, and then the council was destroyed. The kingdom is broken and you have no authority any longer. Peace can now only come about by joining with our prior enemies."

"I would submit that these efforts to appease your enemies will lead to your disposal, once they have what they want."

The Matriarch stood up and raised her voice in a demonstration of authority. "No one can dispose of me! I decide who lives and dies. I decide whom we attack and who we are at peace with. This will never change."

"Even if you are right, you can't live forever. They will eventually attack, for they live to destroy all that do not follow them. I have fought for peace for many years and have learned that we must enter talks with leverage. It is not too late to regain this advantage. We can rebuild our kingdom and still reach out to our enemies for peace. But as long as we stay fractured, our enemies will see us as vulnerable and will launch attacks upon us."

The Matriarch smiled at Asentar as she sat back down on her lavish throne. "I fully understand the capability of leverage. As we speak, the prince of your beloved kingdom prepares to complete my next transaction." Taking another bite of fruit, she enjoyed watching Asentar's curiosity. "A prisoner in the Rava'Kor mines was recently identified as Ericc Dovenar. The son of Ambrosius will soon be given to Darkmere in exchange for his E'rudite powers in rebuilding my old, crippled body. This will double my life and my ruling days. Your kingdom will soon have no heir; it will no longer exist. I am now the power to contend with."

"I find it doubtful that the son of Ambrosius could be captured by your people."

"You question my power?"

"I question your people's ability to pull off such a task. To do so would be a tremendous feat."

"We are a more formidable force than your bureaucrats give us credit for. They have never given me the respect that I deserve."

"I will inform them of such, if you can prove to me that you have actually captured the son of the rightful king."

"Lucian," she ordered as she turned to the cowering man. "Travel back to the mines by daybreak to show Asentar what we are capable of doing here in Southwind. Ensure that Ericc is properly handed over to Darkmere's servants when they arrive, and then kill Santorray for his crime of living."

8

CIVEJ

Returning to his cell after a day of stitches and herbal ointments, Thorik was frustrated with his conversation with Ericc. He had gotten nowhere with the young man. In fact, Ericc refused to even discuss the issue any further with Thorik.

Pushing Thorik forward down the corridor, the guard from the medical area noticed that his services were needed elsewhere. Dozens of guards were being dragged away from Thorik's cell.

Da'Shawn helped escort a few guards out of the doorway. "Damn you, beast!" he yelled. "Damn you all the way to Della Estovia!" Limping away, he gave instructions to his men to retrieve the remaining men still unconscious inside the cell.

Thorik looked through the bars as he approached the door. Santorray was standing in the center of the cell, covered in blood, and panting hard. Stab wounds and fresh whip marks covered his body, his left hand cupping his right fist as bright red blood poured from it. They had come for payment, to remove one of his fingers.

The guard pushed Thorik into the cell before helping remove his comrades.

Stumbling forward, Thorik felt responsible for the loss of the blothrud's finger. Even more so, seeing that he was unable to convince Ericc to escape with them. He wondered if he had the right to ask Santorray to lose another finger while attempting to persuade Ericc again.

Da'Shawn returned to the cell and slammed the door. "We'll beat you down, we will. We'll just end up taking two of them fingers tomorrow." He cursed the beast as he helped another guard down the hall.

Santorray opened his fist to reveal one of the guard's ears in his palm, surrounded by all of the blothrud's digits. Throwing the ear to the ground, the blothrud collapsed against the far wall from the exhaustion of the fight.

Thorik was pleased to see all of his fingers were intact. "You're okay!"

Still breathing hard and bleeding from his open wounds, Santorray shot the Num a serious look, which for the first time gave Thorik cause for alarm. Reflections from the lanterns and torches made the Blothrud's red eyes glow brightly. His heated breath looked like smoke against the cool, damp air.

Suddenly, Thorik felt like he was caged with a wild, starving animal. He froze, waiting for the beast to leap from his spot. Listening to his own heart race, he made no sudden moves. Instead, he lowered himself to pick up a slug from the floor. Cautiously approaching the wounded beast, Thorik placed the slug into the blood that dripped from Santorray's arm. Not knowing the significance, he had seen the blothrud do this several times the prior night and hoped the gesture would be a show of good faith.

Santorray responded. Respect had been given to him, and the blothrud relaxed his facial muscles, covering his teeth. A slight kingly nod of approval gave way for Thorik to continue the gesture several more times while the beast healed his own gashes with handfuls of his own saliva which bubbled and sizzled upon placement.

❧

THAT SECOND NIGHT in the cell with Santorray was worse than the first one. Hunger challenged Thorik's already tender stomach, but it was the dehydration and the bugs that were bothering him the most. He curled up in a ball on the damp floor, brushing off the flies that were trying to get at the blood-stained dressings covering his stomach.

"I can't sleep," Thorik moaned.

Santorray was still leaning against the wall, watching the dark corridor. "It's wise that you don't. I'm surprised we survived this long without an assassination attempt. There must be something more pressing going on than to rid themselves of our voices."

"I've got to get back to Ericc and convince him to come with us."

"I'm not sure your stomach can take another cut. You Nums have soft skin."

"There has to be another way."

"We'll have to see what presents itself."

"Any chance you could let me know prior?"

"There wasn't any time to discuss it. If the guards had seen us whispering before the fight, they would have assumed it was a ruse."

The two large doors at the end of the corridor crashed open, echoing through the cells as a strong narrow beam of light pierced the darkness.

Thorik sat up and watched the light turn into each cell and then back down the corridor as someone shouted questions to inmates, followed by screams of pain. The process continued cell by cell, advancing toward the Num and Blothrud. A deep, ominous cat growl resonated behind the yelling.

Nerves overcame pain as Thorik looked to Santorray for comfort.

Santorray's thin black hairs on his head and face stood on end as he exposed his teeth and squinted his eyes to focus on the coming terror. Drool dripped from his exposed gums as his instincts prepared him for battle.

If Thorik's skin could glow from turning sheer white, it would have done so at that moment. Edging past the cell wall was the nose of a giant black panther whose mouth could almost swallow the Num whole. Riding the cat was a young baldheaded man with thick tattoo designs running from his forehead, behind his ears, and down past his neckline. His quarterstaff illuminated his way, changing focus and strength at the rider's will.

Flashing a sun-searing light into the face of Santorray, the rider stared at the blothrud.

Thorik watched as a second figure emerged. A man-sized shadowy figure walked through the bars, entering their cell. Even the intense light from the staff couldn't shine upon or penetrate the figure. A cold chill ran up Thorik's back as he watched the silhouette of a man walk up to Santorray and reach inside the blothrud's chest with one hand.

Santorray bucked, arched his back, and swiped at the invader with his knuckle spikes, which passed through the shadowy figure without disruption. "What do you want?" the blothrud asked, gasping for breath.

Light from the end of rider's staff focused tightly on the Altered's eyes as the rider answered the question with one of his own. "What do you know of Ericc Dovenar's escape?"

"I don't know what you're talking about," Santorray forced out.

The bald rider didn't like the answer. "Civej, refresh this Del's memory."

Responding to his master's orders, Civej placed his second ghostly hand up into Santorray's skull.

The Blothrud screamed in pain, swinging wildly at the dark shadow in front of him. "I don't know where he is!"

"Do you know where he would be going?"

Civej's hand created a pain a hundredfold of any headache. Every sound and bit of light seemed to intensify the issue. "I haven't seen him. I don't know." His words were choppy as he struggled to get them out.

"Civej, that's enough with him. See if the Num knows anything," the rider said, pointing the beam of light onto Thorik's face.

Thorik cowered back up against the prison wall, knowing full well that if Ericc had actually escaped, he would be heading for Corrock to attack Darkmere.

Civej released Santorray, whose body went limp from the torture, and stepped over to Thorik. The thick vaporish figure's feet never actually touched the ground as he floated to his next victim.

"I don't know any more than Santorray," Thorik exclaimed, trying to prevent the same fate as his unconscious companion.

"Santorray?" Civej's master replied, turning the light back onto the blothrud, who had collapsed onto the floor. "It is you. What has become of the hero warrior that you would end up in such a place?" he asked Santorray, knowing he couldn't reply. "Once I find Ericc, I look forward to returning so we can catch up on some unfished business."

He shifted the light back to Thorik, and the Num could see the silhouette of Civej standing in front of him, ready to apply pain.

"Are you a friend of Santorray?" the rider asked.

Thorik quickly considered his options. Yes or no? One of these answers may prevent them finding out where Ericc is headed. "We have saved each other's life. I don't know if you would say he's a friend." Thorik took a deep swallow, hoping he had worded the answer properly.

"You saved the life of the mighty Santorray? An Ergrauthian Elite? The only blothrud to stand up against the immortal Ergrauth himself and live to tell about it. You saved *his* life?"

Thorik sheepishly replied, "Yes."

A subtle chuckle came from the rider of the giant panther. "Then you are truly a legend to be talked about. Unfortunately, legendary Num, today I must see if you have any knowledge about Ericc's escape." Nodding his head, Civej went to work, placing one hand into Thorik's chest, grabbing his lungs and squeezing them tight.

Thorik screamed out in pain. "Please! No!" is all he could utter before the air in his lung was exhausted.

The rider's light focused thinly on the Num's eyes. "Tell me what you know about Ericc Dovenar's whereabouts. Someone must have talked to him and heard his plans."

A second shadowy hand entered Thorik's head, shooting pain in an overloading capacity. Civej accessed Thorik's thoughts, allowing his master to absorb them through the beam of light. Pulling his memories so intensely, it began to leave parts of his brain hollow and without life. It would not take long for Thorik to lose all his memories, or even his life.

Thorik's childhood memories of his parents started to fade, as well as his months of being stranded on the Palm Islands. The extraction was painful, as though the thoughts were being burned out with a flame caused by the intense light from the rider's staff.

Thorik couldn't take it any longer. It was too excruciating. He'd tell him anything he wanted to know to stop the torture. So, he finally broke. "Ericc," His mind was becoming mush as he struggled to formulate words. "Ericc!"

The intense light quickly pulled away, followed by the removal of Civej's hands. Thorik overheard shouting about guards found dead and Ericc's escape path being discovered. One guard shouted to the man on the panther, "Lord Bredgin, he escaped through the east tower and was spotted heading north toward Swardfar."

The Num's eyes were blurry as he felt himself passing out. His last view, as he tumbled over to his side, was of the shadow demon being pulled into a box held by the rider, Lord Bredgin. Snapping the lid of the small box shut, the bald man tucked it away before racing away on his giant panther.

And then all went dark.

❦ *9* ❦

ESCAPE PLAN

The morning ritual of lantern lighting commenced in the prison corridor as though nothing had occurred during the night.

Rubbing his eyes, Thorik tried to shake out the cobwebs of his slumber. "I had the worst nightmare."

"It was no nightmare," Santorray said, resting his arm on one raised knee. Pressing his back against the wall, he pulled his shoulders forward to stretch his spine.

Squinting from pain as he sat up, Thorik was reminded of his stomach cuts. "Who was that? And what was that dark mass?"

"Lord Bredgin is the son of Darkmere. He rides the black cat, Shrii, and commands the dark vapors of a Wraylov."

"Darkmere's son? He's here to capture Ericc. We've got to warn him."

"He's long gone by now. Who knows where he's headed."

"I do. In fact, it's my fault that he's going there."

Santorray's eyebrows lowered. "What are you talking about?"

Getting to his feet, the Num walked over to the bars to make sure no one was nearby. The only person in sight was the lantern lighter as he made his way down the corridor. "I told him that his father was dead, killed after his battle with Darkmere at Weirfortus. He is now on a quest to Corrock to avenge the death."

"Darkmere has killed Ambrosius?"

"Yes." Thorik stumbled for additional words of explanation before correcting himself. "No. Darkmere set him up and left him to die."

"And how would you know this?"

"I was there. I watched it happen."

"And you couldn't do anything to help him?"

He bit his lower lip as the memories flooded back through his thoughts. Unfortunately, these memories had been untouched by Civej, and Thorik could remember every detail of the horrid event. "Yes, honestly, I could have. But I chose not to. I chose to seal him in his tomb to save the rest of us."

"So, you lied to Ericc, putting him in grave danger."

Thorik had thought this to be true, but he refused to say it out loud. "It sounds so much more menacing when you say it. As though I purposely set him up."

"A warrior does not hide the truth by finding a scapegoat for his own actions."

"Ericc and I had little time to talk. We were rushed. The medic showed up sooner than I had hoped."

"Spit it out, Sec. You were afraid of his reaction if you had told him the truth."

"Yes!" Thorik slapped his hands onto the bars. "I was afraid that he would hate me for what I've done. Hell, I hate me for what I've done. How could I look him straight in the eyes and tell him that I not only watched him die but also closed the doors, preventing his escape?"

Santorray stood up and walked over toward the Num. "Ah, this is why you allowed yourself to be thrown into the mines. To repent for your actions on Ambrosius, you wish to save his son?"

Thorik's head hung low between his arms, his cheeks flushed with emotion. "Yes. I can't live with myself until I can save Ericc from Darkmere. He plans to sacrifice the young man. I will not rest until I have prevented this from happening."

"It is a warrior's soul you have, Sec." Resting his large hand on Thorik's shoulder, he stood next to him, looking out of the prison cell. "I will help you on this quest."

Thorik wiped his face clear of tears, which had pooled in his eyes. "Why? Why would you do that?"

"Three reasons. First, you risked your life to save mine, although I'm not sure Lucian's attack would have been life-threatening. Second, if Ericc makes it to Corrock before you do, I can help find him. They do not allow Nums to freely walk about. And the third is a personal reason. I owe Ambrosius a favor. This seems like the perfect time to repay it."

"You knew Ambrosius?"

Patting his shoulders a few times, he sighed. "Fought alongside him in more than one battle, many years ago."

"He seemed to have fought most of his life."

"He never backed down to evil. We were proud to have him as a So'Er'Que Dooma Family member. A strong soul with the heart of a Blothrud."

Looking up at Santorray, Thorik questioned him. "Can you help me get out of here?" It wasn't what he wanted to ask him. It seemed unlikely that Ambrosius was a member of a Del'Unday family and also an Ov'Unday family member. But the idea of Santorray being willing to help him was too great an opportunity to start questioning such things.

"I can, but it will be dangerous. No guarantee. We'll have to fight our way up to the main exit, past the dragon, Duuke."

"I have a better plan. Can you get us to the supply entrance?"

"Yes, but it's a ship port, with a river that has taken the best swimmers' life and fish that will eat your flesh to the bones before you reach the other side."

"Can you get us there?"

"Yes, but it is foolhardy to venture to a dead end. I tried it myself the last time they imprisoned me in these mines, and it nearly killed me. There's no way you can escape safely unless we are fortunate enough to have a ship waiting for us in the port."

"Santorray, can you trust me?"

Looking down into the Num's eyes, Santorray searched for his own answer. "Trust has proven to be a vindictive temptress to me. How do I know this isn't a trap?"

Lifting the side of his shirt, Thorik exposed the slice marks from Santorray's blades. "I trusted you. Now it's your turn."

"Do not betray me, Sec."

"Just get us there."

~

Filing out of their cells, Thorik & Santorray fell in line with the other prisoners as they weaved their way toward the main room to collect rations of bread and mining tools. The eight-foot-tall blothrud held onto his side, and his demeanor was subservient. He needed the guards to lower their defenses against him for their plan to work. The cuts from their attempt to take one of his fingers added to the ruse.

Gathering his pick, Thorik grabbed his loaf of bread as he looked at the door behind the food table. It was a thick wooden door with a small peephole window, metal hinges, and a lock. He glanced up at Santorray, who gave him a wink of approval.

Santorray stumbled in line, grabbing his side. Falling to one knee, he rested from the fake pain as several guards came over to prod him back into line. He used the food table for support to stand back up, causing it to tip over as he fell, along with the bread.

He rolled out of line, grabbing his side as he crushed the loaves of bread.

"Get up!" a guard ordered, poking him with the end of his spear as the food server reset the empty table.

The blothrud complied and pushed himself back up on his powerful wolf-like legs.

Thorik helped his friend up, receiving the blothrud's large hand on his shoulder to provide balance.

Prodded by several guards, Santorray slowly made his way back to the line. It was at this time that the server unlocked the thick wooden door to acquire more rations.

As the key unlocked the door and the door began to swing open, Santorray single-handedly grabbed and tossed Thorik at the door. Flying over twenty feet through the air, Thorik was prepared to make their escape.

Hearing the commotion behind him, the server quickly darted through the doorway, hoping to shut and lock it behind him before any of the inmates arrived. But before he could do so, Thorik's body flew through across the way and hit the door, knocking the man back a few steps. Reaching for the door again, the server pushed it shut just as Thorik's mining pick entered the doorway and twisted, preventing the door from closing.

Santorray sprinted forward, knocking over tables and guards as he rushed the door. Arrows cut near enough to his head that he could hear the whistle of their feathers, but none pierced the skin.

Just as the guard gave a strong shoulder block against the door to keep the Num out, Santorray reached the door with his own shoulder, slamming the man against the wall.

Once they were through the doorway, Thorik turned and quickly locked the door behind them before racing after Santorray.

The short hall opened up into a cavernous dock area. The fragmented light danced around through the river's mist, landing on the crates along the docks. A large ship was docked at one side, where a few guards and several dockhands had converged, arguing about trade taxes and various other port regulations.

Stacks of supplies, barrels of ale, and crates of tools rested in various locations, many of them blocking the arrival of the prisoners as they raced into the dock area. The smell of tropical plants filled the air as vines hung from the upper mouth of the cave entrance.

After they rounded the crates, over a dozen men turned from the dock near the ship and noticed the escapees. Additional ship crew grabbed their crossbows and aimed them at the oncoming beast.

Thorik finally caught up to his cellmate and led Santorray to the men on the dock who had weapons drawn. Moving toward the guarded ship, there was no turning back.

A robust man in the center of the guards and dockhands convinced the guards to stand their ground. "Dat beast is look'n ta take the ship fer his escape. Stay togeth'r so he can't fight us one at a time." His clothes were different from the Rava'Kor Mine men, and he had a sense of authority about him. Shirtless, his large sweaty gut hung over his belt as he straightened his vest and combed his hair with a swipe of his hand.

Santorray approached the dock, with the Num next to him. He was looking for options as he counted the heads he would have to slay to escape, assuming he could do so before the other men aboard the ship launched their arrows at him. With over sixteen loaded crossbows aimed at the blothrud, the escapees' path seemed to have come to an end.

Thorik stopped and signaled Santorray to do the same. "Can we talk truce?" he asked the fat man in the center.

The man limped forward, using a Fesh leg bone for a cane. "Stay back by the ship, me lads," he said to the Rava'Kor guards. "I'll show ya how dis is done." Walking up to the two prisoners, he scratched his backside and laughed. "Looks like we got 'ere a few prisoners try'n ta escape."

Santorray growled and showed his teeth.

Wiping his nose on his arm, the fat man continued. "Ya know, there's never been a prison I couldn't escape from." He paused and looked back at the guards before nodding at the crew on his ship. The ship's name, *Sinecure*, could faintly be made out from the worn paint along its side. "Including this one," he shouted back to his crew.

Upon hearing his words, a large cargo net was tossed out of the ship by the sailors, landing on the guards below. Rising from the lower deck, a twelve-foot tall Mognin reached up and yanked a rope, pulling the net tight around the guards' feet. The entire group fell to the ground, entangling themselves more as they fought for their freedom.

"Come on, lad. We be waiting fur hours and is ready ta be leav'n dis place."

Thorik ran past him toward the ship. "Thanks, Captain Mensley. You were right. They had no plans of letting me leave, but your escape plan worked perfectly."

"I wouldn't say that. I see a blothrud where the boy Ericc should be stand'n."

"I'll explain once we're underway," Thorik yelled back.

Now realizing that they were safe to escape, the blothrud walked over to one of the netted guards and ripped off a patch of cloth from his coat. "Be glad that this is all that I'm ripping off you."

Santorray began to follow Thorik up onto the ship, but was stopped by the captain. "Captain Dare Mensley, I be, and this 'ere is my ship. Where does ya think you be going, ya Altered?"

Thorik looked over his shoulder at the captain. "He's with me."

"A Del, ya say? To board me ship? A bloth to boot, I add."

Santorray prepared to push the fat man out of his way until he noticed the captain's men aiming their crossbows at him again. He restrained himself. "You have something against the Del'Unday?"

"Of course I does, but that ain't the reason I stopped ya. I doesn't recall you paying for passage on me vessel. Perhaps a payment of that large crate over yonder would suffice." He pointed at a crate past a stack of barrels.

Santorray looked up at the captain's men. Hand-to-hand combat was one thing; but being showered with thick arrows was another. He agreed without acknowledging it and turned toward the crate.

With the guards and dockhands tied up in the net, there was no one to stop the Del'Unday from taking what he wanted. Lifting the entire crate with one strong heave, he walked it back over to the ship and up the ramp. Glass bottles clanked and chimed as they rattled around inside.

"Easy does it, ya beast," Mensley said. "Them aren't rum bottles ya be play'n with. She be Nectar of Irr." His mouth drooled and his eyes fluttered as he spoke the name.

Releasing the net's rope to the ship-hands, Grewen greeted Thorik. "Welcome back, little man."

"You're a sight for sore eyes," Thorik replied to the giant. "Where is everyone else?"

"Below deck," Grewen replied.

"Set sail dis 'ere ship before the workers come to der senses!" the captain shouted as he untied the ropes from the docks.

REUNION

Making his way down the narrow wooden stairs, Thorik was excited about seeing his family and friends. The other Nums had been waiting below deck until the captain gave them the all clear. They all stood up when they felt the ship launch into the river.

"Granna!" Thorik yelled with pleasure as he entered their room. She was the closest to the door and his first greeting. "I wasn't sure if I was going to make it out of there without your foresight." He hugged her tight before releasing her.

Smiling and nodding her head, decorated with various feathers and leaves, Gluic replied, "Sometimes when I grab for a stone, I drop a crystal." Wrinkles tightened around her mouth and eyes as she smiled, causing the soul-markings on her forehead to appear to change shape.

"Very true," Thorik said with a laugh. "I do so miss your view of the world."

"Not mine, child. Yours." Pulling one of the feathers from her hair, she placed it into his.

Confused, he didn't have time to respond, for a young female Num captured his attention. She had been standing in a corner holding onto her pet lizard. "Avanda, I'm so glad to see you're unharmed. I was so worried about you."

Reaching out to hug her, Thorik was cut short and grabbed by the front of his shirt and then pushed up against a wall by his uncle. "I suppose you're proud of yourself!" Brimmelle's face was tense, and he used his body weight to keep the boy where he was. Furious at his nephew over Avanda's incident, his thick eyebrows wedged together while he yelled at Thorik. "You let her be violated!"

"No, I didn't know about it until afterward." Thorik weighed half that of his uncle and struggled to pull his back off the wall. Even though they were no longer in Farbank, Brimmelle was still his Fir and rightful leader of the Nums. Thorik would never disrespect the position by taking a swing at him.

"On top of that, you didn't tell me about your idiotic plan to get into the mine. I had to find out from your grandmother."

"I knew if I had told you, you wouldn't have let me go."

"There is a good reason for that!" Fir Brimmelle yelled. "You could have been killed. And Avanda nearly was!"

Thorik's grandmother stepped up and placed a hand on her son's shoulder. "Brimmelle, the boy meant no harm to Avanda."

Thorik was thankful that she intervened. She had once again come to his rescue.

Brimmelle shrugged his shoulder, pulling away from her tender hand. "Not this time, Mother. You aren't going to mediate our problems anymore. I'll handle him like I should have long ago."

"You think I'm here to be a mediator and keep you from arguing?" she asked with a smirk.

"Not anymore. Take Avanda back to our rooms. Thorik and I need to resolve some issues."

Astonished, yet impressed, with Brimmelle's stance against her, Gluic gave him a devilish grin. "As you say, my son." Turning, she walked over to hold Avanda's hand and lead her out of the room.

Thorik's heart sunk. His grandmother had always helped him out of these types of situations in the past. Where was she going?

Gluic winked at Thorik as she left the room.

Pressed firmly against the wall, Thorik watched Avanda leave as well, lowering her head after sneaking a glance at him before closing the door behind her.

The moment the door shut, Brimmelle pulled his nephew from the wall and tossed him across the room.

Thorik landed on their supplies, breaking glass jars and spilling open bags. Thorik's sack of Runestones emptied across the floor as he watched his uncle cross the room toward him. "I'm sorry. I had no idea Avanda was in danger."

"That's no excuse," Brimmelle fired back.

Thorik pushed the supplies out of his way as he worked himself back onto his feet. "How could I have possibly known?"

Brimmelle kneaded his hands as he stewed about the incident. "You have to think ahead and be responsible for what could happen. She was in your care. She was your responsibility."

"You're one to talk. How could you let her walk into the city unescorted to find me? This is as much your fault as it is mine."

Brimmelle's face flushed with anger, and his Num soul-markings changed to a dark red. "That is enough! I am done with this. I've traveled across these lands for you, placing my followers and myself in constant danger. For what? Your disobedience? You're blaming these issues on *me*?"

"No. We did this for the saving of Australis, and the saving of Ericc."

Standing firm with an unpleasant scowl on his face, Brimmelle raised up one of his overly bushy eyebrows. "Where is Ericc? I thought the entire reason for us not returning home this last time was for you to free him. Surely this new fat friend of yours, the captain, hasn't led us astray."

"Actually, he didn't. Ericc was in the mines, just as the captain had said. I was able to find and talk to Ericc."

Looking around the room, as though he expected Ericc to suddenly appear out of thin air, he said, "Good, but I don't see him. Tell me that you didn't fail... again."

"I didn't fail."

"Then where is he?"

"He escaped before we could break him out."

"Why would he escape without you?"

"He escaped to travel to Corrock."

"You failed to recover him and fulfill Ambrosius' dying wish. You've given this a solid attempt, but, as you can see, it's futile. It is time we return to Farbank."

"We can't. He plans to hunt down Darkmere. He'll be killed."

"Sounds just like his father. The one who led us from our homes in the first place. The one who led the provinces and Altereds into a civil war that killed most of their people. We would be better off without the both of them."

"You don't understand. I have to go after him."

"No, you don't. You have no debt to that man. He's not part of your village, your faith, or your family. We, on the other hand, are your family, yet you continue to place us in danger to follow the desire of a dead man who isn't."

"But I owe him."

"Why? Why must you owe that E'rudite anything? He led us all to Weirfortus. He put himself in a position which would cost him his life when we all could have escaped. This is not your responsibility. It was his doing."

Thorik snapped back at his uncle. "My chest hurts every day from the memories and nightmares of allowing Ambrosius to die as I stood by and watched. You have no idea what I'm going through."

"No idea? You repugnant, ignorant boy. Do you not recall my saving your life during the storm that took your parents?"

Thorik was furious at the comparison. "You can't use that against me anymore. I've paid my debt to you!" His voice cracked with anger. "Besides, it's completely different; you *saved* me. You didn't sit by and allow me to die."

"No, even worse, I allowed your mother to die!" Brimmelle yelled back. It felt liberating for him to finally tell the boy of his mother's true fate, which had been bottled up inside him for years.

"What are you talking about? My mother and I were caught in the flooded river. She was able to help me up onto a tree before she was swept away. I watched as she sank. She died saving my life."

"No, she died while I was saving your life."

"That's not true." His face flushed with emotion over the traumatic topic. "I owe her my life and would pay it back if I could."

"But you can't," Fir Brimmelle snapped back. "When I reached you and my sister in that thunderstorm, she had been washed down to an exposed boulder. A section of the hill had just given way, and a large wave of debris was barreling down the mountainside toward all of us. I only had time to save one of you."

Guilt overcame anger as Thorik reflected on his existence, costing his mother her very own. "You made the wrong choice."

"I know." Brimmelle's teeth clenched. "She was a good woman. The only person I could ever fully trust. And *you* stole my sister from me."

Thorik wasn't expecting his uncle to agree with him, yet somehow, he wasn't surprised by it either.

Recalling the dreadful night, Brimmelle gazed at Thorik. "Turning my back to her, I escaped with you in my arms. I couldn't face seeing her eyes, knowing I wouldn't have time to reach out to the boulder and pull her to shore." Brimmelle's face twisted as though he had eaten a sour lemon. "Once you and I were safe, I looked back to see that she had made her way to the ledge and had crawled up on her own. Safe from the rushing river but not from the newly raging mudslide. It swept her away before my very eyes." Bowing his head, he wiped his nose. "All she needed was a few more seconds to reach safety. A few more steps. All she needed was for me to help her. But I failed her. My fear of running back down into danger killed her. My desire for our security. My fear. My selfishness."

"Why take it out on me?"

"I wouldn't have had to endure the sight of her death if you had stayed put. By following you into that valley, I saved your life and cursed my own. Every time I look at you, I hate myself for the cowardly way I let her die."

"Then why take me on as your Sec?"

"It's my way of paying my debt to her. Being a Fir and teaching the Mountain King's words is the only thing I know. What else could I give you?"

"How about encouragement and support for what I want?"

"That's what I gave my sister. By doing so, I encouraged her to take risks and search out her dreams, costing the lives of both her and your father. My endorsement to search for greater things set them off on their quest past Spirit Peak. I was such a fool to listen to Su'I Sorat. His tales of treasure enticed all of us to forget what was important. At least until it was too late. I learned a hard lesson about trusting outsiders which I will never forget, nor will I ever fall for their stories again."

✻ II ✻

STAINED RIVER

Filth from the mines tainted the river with slimy streaks of browns and reds. Vile flesh-eating fish fruitlessly attacked the sides of the ship while freshwater poisonous slugs fought the waves in a futile attempt to reach the deck.

Captain Dare Mensley's ship sailed quickly down the sewage-filled river. At times it was difficult to endure, but they had no time to dock and rest away from the water's smell. It was a chase down the river and to the bridge, which linked the cities of Krual'Dor and De'Ceit. Once beyond the bridge, they were free to sail Lake Luthralum.

The captain watched the riverside road for riders. "I can smell them at our heels."

"You can't smell anything over this foul river," Santorray said.

"Okay, then. I can sense it, ya big rud. I know they haven't just let us skip away. We just need ta make it past the Krual'Dor bridge before they get there."

"We'll need a lot of luck for that to happen."

"Luck ain't good enough. We need to beat them."

"Then we need to put luck in our favor." The blothrud grabbed a few pieces of wood chipped away from one of the crates and walked away from the captain. "One must ask the powers of life and nature for assistance or be content with failure."

"Hogwash. Nature ain't got nothin' to do with it. It's one man's mind against another," the captain yelled over to him.

"Then we are sure to sink in this ship with you at the helm."

"You ungrateful rud," the captain replied. "Go ahead and appease your spirits of luck for all I care. Makes no difference to me."

Santorray could feel the staring eyes of the entire crew as he sat down on the deck in the center of the ship. Ignoring most of them, he gave the giant a growl and exposed his teeth on one side before turning his back to them. It was a purposeful position to show dominance.

Grewen knew full well what his posturing was intended to do, but he wouldn't give the blothrud the satisfaction of an argument. There had been bad blood for thousands of years between the two Unday species, and the mognin could see that the blothrud had no plans to resolve such issues.

Removing his necklace, which held a large obsidian talisman, Santorray unbraided one of the many spherical beads along its leather path. Tapping the bead twice against the flat stone talisman, he placed the heavy sphere into the center of the cloth he had ripped from the guard's uniform. Two small sticks were snapped in half and then half again before being set onto the Southwind Province symbol that covered most of the fabric.

Wrapping the cloth around the heavy bead and the broken sticks, he opened a hanging lantern and poured a bit of oil onto the cloth before tying it off. "Vo'lar oondra beldortha," he said strongly to the newly created object. Lighting it, he allowed it to burn in his palm until he repeated his odd phrase a second time before tossing it into the Stained River.

Thorik looked on curiously at the event while sitting near the mognin, who was standing on the lower deck, but was still taller than Thorik. "Grewen, Santorray does a lot of unusual ceremonial rituals. In the prison it was with slugs and blood. Why is that?"

Grewen leaned back on the hatch opening and rested his arms on the deck of the ship. The mognin's twelve-foot-tall body caused the ship to be slightly top heavy when he stood on the main deck, so he avoided it when he could. "Most blothruds believe that all things have a life energy and when they come in contact with each other they have an eternal link."

"What does that have to do with the strange rituals?"

"The guard's cloth could be linked to the Southwind military, who most likely are searching for you. I would guess that the idea of sinking it could cause the guards difficulty in crossing the river or traveling by water to catch us. Seems a bit unnecessary to burn them."

"Magic? Is he some type of Alchemist?"

Grewen chuckled. "No, it's more superstition. You should see what they do before they go into battle." The hairless brown leathery skin, which covered his body, wrinkled even tighter when he laughed, and his small ears twisted from his smile.

Three large folds on the back of Grewen's neck bulged as he leaned his head back to look at the strong wind in the sail. "If we are successful in passing the bridge before they block us, he'll say it was because of his ritual or some hex he put on them. However, if we aren't successful, he'll excuse it as some twist of fate due to our not believing or the powers of nature not being pleased with us. There's always a way out of it for the devoutly superstitious."

Thorik always felt at ease when he was around Grewen. Calmness tended to roll off the mognin's shoulders and covered Thorik with a sense that all would work out well, even his issues with Brimmelle.

"All hands on deck!" Captain Mensley shouted from the upper deck. "They be in pursuit!"

Fifty riders galloped along the river's dirt road in an attempt to catch up to them. Arrows were already in flight toward the ship but simply didn't have the distance.

Brimmelle and Avanda rushed up from below, searching to see the reason for the captain's commands.

"Make yourself useful, rud, and grab an oar and 'elp us speed up this 'ere vessel."

Standing to his full eight-foot height, Santorray abruptly turned away from the captain and went below deck.

Captain Mensley couldn't believe what he was seeing. "Damn ya, Altered! We ain't outta da fire yet. Get yur red bulky arms up 'ere."

The captain's crew consisted of humans, all shapes and sizes. Some didn't look like they knew what they were doing. Others looked as though they knew, but in fact didn't have a clue.

Shaking his head in frustration, the captain watched the useless efforts by his men to speed up the ship. "Bottom of da barrel," he said in disgust. "Shoreview's finest recruits." He coughed out a laugh at his own joke before returning to the issue at hand.

The river snaked its way toward Lake Luthralum. On a straight river, they would have had a chance of escape, but the Stained River gave the advantage to the riders. Forging ahead up the next bluff, the riders prepared for their attack, while the ship followed the water as it weaved its way to the lake.

Rounding the bend, Dare spotted a wooden bridge high over the water, connecting the two bluff ledges together as the river narrowed tight. Covered with the jungle's vines and moss, thick old timbers held the structure firm as several dozen Southwind archers took positions across it.

"Down sails," Dare commanded, "Before they tear 'em apart with arrows and fire."

The crew began lowering the sails as quickly as they could, tossing them to Grewen, who stored them on the lower deck.

Loud cracks of thick timber came from below, with a pause between each. Santorray climbed the stairs from the lower deck carrying a cannon, minus its wooden base. Each step up the stairs caused boards to snap.

"What in the blazes are ya doing with me artillery?" Captain Mensley was stunned by the possibility of anyone being able to carry a cannon as well as the fact he was bringing it up at all. "We ain't got the powder to make 'em work."

Setting the cannon down, the blothrud ignored the captain and walked over to the crate he had brought on board from the mines. Grasping the lid tightly, he ripped opened the top in a single motion, popping the nails into the air.

Waving his hands violently to stop him, the captain couldn't believe his eyes. "Get yur hands off of me nectar!"

Santorray twisted around, grabbing Dare by his vest. Pulling his wolf-like snout tight to the captain's face, the blothrud's nostrils flared in anger.

Ripping off the front of Dare's vest, he growled as he released the captain and spit on the deck between them. Turning his back on Dare, Santorray ripped the vest into several thin strips before popping open one of the bottles.

"Take me whole damn vest if ya like, but leave me drink!" He pulled off what remained of the vest and launched it at him. "And don't you go marking your territory by spit'n on my ship."

Pouring the alcohol onto the torn cloths, Santorray saturated them before sticking one into the end of a fresh bottle. Proceeding to do the same action again demonstrated that he was building something.

Thorik looked at the bridge down river and then realized what Santorray was doing. Running over, he began opening bottles and sticking rags into the ends.

Dare jumped forward. "Ya criminals! Ya thieves! Use the bloody rum if ya need to, but leave the Irr alone." Grabbing as many bottles out of the crate as he could hold, he made a mad dash for his cabin, protecting his assets as he limped heavy without his cane. "Crazy beast. Doesn't ya know the value of what ye be wasting?"

Thorik tore some fabric from his own clothes to add to the dwindling stack. "I think I understand. We'll light the fabric as wicks and throw them at the bridge. Right?"

Santorray nodded as he popped open bottles and soaked more cloths.

Thorik pulled several more bottles out of the crate. "So, what exactly is the cannon for?"

A devilish look sparked in the Blothrud's eyes. "Backup plan."

"How do you plan to get us close enough to throw these bottles before they take us out with arrows?"

Glancing up at the approaching bridge, Santorray shook his head. "They'll be firing at us long before we get close enough."

True to his word, arrows flew, stabbing the deck with their sharp tips.

Reaching as far as he could from the open deck hatch, Grewen began gathering barrels and supplies. Taking them off the upper deck, he set them near his feet on the lower level, protecting them from the air assault.

Returning to the deck empty handed, Dare watched his crew duck from the missiles and successfully flee any harm. "Running for cover appears to be me crew's strength," he muttered to himself.

"Grab the wheel and ride the port side of the river," Santorray ordered Dare.

Reaching past Thorik, the captain loaded his arms with more bottles to salvage from them. "Not until ya give up on wasting me Irr."

"We're drifting the wrong way," the blothrud growled, irritated by Dare's lack of concern that no one was at the wheel. "Don't you care about your ship?"

"It ain't my ship, it's me lazy brother's. If ya stop kill'n me Irr, I can tend to her an' bring it back in one piece to the indolent cur."

Another wave of arrows hit the ship as Santorray grabbed the lid of the crate and used it as a shield to protect them.

Without any sign of appreciation, Dare limped back into the cabin, arms filled with liquor bottles.

Thorik looked back at his uncle, who held onto Avanda, protecting her under the stairwell from the oncoming attack. "Brimmelle, we need you to steer the ship."

Brimmelle looked up from under the stairs at the unprotected area at the wheel. "I've never steered a ship. Get someone who has."

"I'll do it!" Avanda shouted. Escaping Brimmelle's hold, she darted out and then up the stairs to the wheel.

Brimmelle clumsily worked himself up the steep steps in an attempt to catch her.

"Where to?" Avanda shouted. "How close do we need to get to shore?"

Few crewmembers were still on deck as the arrows from the bridge were landing more frequently and with better aim. Injuries were now being sustained, and most of the crew had fled to lower decks.

Santorray took command. "As close as you can without running aground."

Little time was left to make such adjustments before reaching the bridge. Avanda pulled hard on the wheel and quickly realized her excitement had caused a misjudgment in the effort required.

The ship pulled hard to port, nearly tipping the vessel over in doing so. Two men were flung overboard, along with ropes and other supplies which Grewen hadn't collected yet. Loud crashes of glass and metal could be heard from supplies below.

Grewen closed his eyes and moaned as objects on the lower deck came crashing into the lower half of his body.

Thorik held onto the crate, preventing himself from falling and rolling overboard along with some supplies.

Santorray gripped the deck with his wolf-like claws on his feet while hanging onto the crate of bottles. Nearly half of them had been converted to weapons and would be needed very soon.

Brimmelle had reached the top of the stairs and stumbled toward the wheel, which Avanda clung to. Latching onto the large wooden wheel, Brimmelle made an effort to stop the ship from running into the riverbank. Spinning the wheel in the opposite direction, Brimmelle overcompensated for her first turn. Never having steered a ship before, the Fir struggled to properly make up for the direction change.

"Watch out for the cannon," Grewen announced, watching it roll out of control, out of reach of his own long arms.

The cannon tumbled along the deck, just missing the blothrud, only to be stopped by the ship changing its bearing and swaying in the opposite direction.

Realizing she didn't have control over the wheel, Avanda slid out from under Fir Brimmelle's outstretched arms. Sitting back behind him, she opened the red and gold purse at her side.

Her lizard jumped out of her side pouch and ran over to the red purse to spy on what it held.

"Watch out, Ralph! You don't want to eat anything in there," she warned him.

The ship bumped hard against the shore as Fir Brimmelle grappled with the wheel to keep it under control.

Captain Dare Mensley whipped open the door and rushed out. "What ya be doing to me ship?"

Holding the crate firm to prevent it from crashing to the side, Santorray was less than impressed with the captain and crew of the *Sinecure*. "Saving it. Get over here and make your mark."

Rolling back, the cannon crashed into the crate, nearly taking off one of Thorik's legs. Translucent red liquid poured onto the deck from broken bottles of Irr.

"Destroying is more like it." Using his cane, Dare worked himself along the tilted deck back to the crate. "Years I've dreamt of such a bounty. Damn the moment I let a beast on me ship." Grabbing a third armful of bottles, he left his cane and hobbled back into the cabin just as Brimmelle attempted to correct the ship's direction again.

Grewen had lifted his massive body out of the deck hatch to help compensate for the deck's uneven plane. Using his enormous Mognin body, he shifted his weight from side to side to help Brimmelle keep the boat heading the right way.

Another volley of arrows pierced the deck's surface as well as the Mognin's thick skin. The few arrows in his arms and legs had no effect on his tough skin as he stood on deck, grabbing the main mast for balance.

A well-aimed arrow blazed past Grewen, nicking Santorray's arm and striking the bottle he held, pouring the liquid onto a coiled rope near his feet.

"That's close enough. First blood has been spilled," Santorray barked. "Keep us in near the shore!" he yelled to Brimmelle, who was struggling to do just that.

Grabbing a lantern's flint, Santorray sparked the drenched rope. A flame quickly grew as he grabbed two bottles and leaned the saturated cloth wicks over the fire. Once they were ablaze, the blothrud leaned back like a javelin thrower and launched one of the bottles high into the sky. The second one was shot from his mighty arm before the first had even arrived at its destination.

Striking the side of the bridge nearest to the boat, the bottle shattered and ignited. Flaming liquid splattered across the surface of the bridge and the vegetation that grew on it. The second bottle struck within a few yards of the first one.

Retaliation, in the form of flaming arrows, dotted the sky. Over a dozen oil-dipped missiles were now headed for the ship. Captain Mensley had been wise enough to ensure the sails were not up, but that wouldn't stop the ship from catching fire from this bombardment.

Grewen stood up to his full height on the front half of the ship, thus causing its nose to tilt forward and the aft to rise slightly out of the water. Reaching out with his arms, he tried to make himself as big of a target as possible, so that the majority of the fiery weapons struck the thick brown skin on his back. The few arrows that passed him by landed on the deck, starting the floorboards on fire.

Thorik quickly removed prepared bottles from the crate and lit them, handing them to Santorray as quickly as he could.

The blothrud's aim was more accurate than that of the archers on the bridge, and he strategically ignited both ends of the bridge with fire. Once they were fully engulfed, the archers in the middle abandoned the attack and attempted to escape.

Ignoring the surrounding battle, Dare Mensley limped his way back to the crate on the far side from Santorray to gather his next armful.

Grewen plucked out a few of the arrows and easily snuffed out the flames on his hide before the next attack of flaming arrows arrived.

A wave of cold air shot from the back of the boat toward the bridge. Avanda's attempt to activate the magical items from her purse had gone wrong again. Her endeavor sent a crystallized mass of moisture racing for the far side of the bridge. Upon impact, it suppressed the fire created by Santorray's bottle missiles.

"Sorry!" Avanda shouted.

"Damn, ya girl! I told ya, no magic!" Captain Mensley ordered. "Does ya not remember the hole you put in the side of me ship last time?"

"I was trying to put out the fire on the deck," Avanda said. "I think I've got this figured out now."

"No! No more," the captain ordered. "I'll make ya a deal. I has a small book on how ta control magic. It be yours if ya get below deck and never again perform magic on me ship."

Eyes growing to perfectly round circles, she was ecstatic. "Deal!" She gathered her items and ran below before the captain could change his mind.

Archers quickly ran back onto the bridge, hopping over the section of slick ice on the surface.

Santorray was furious that his attack on the bridge had been hindered by a little Num. There wasn't enough time left to re-ignite the far side of the bridge, especially now that it was covered with ice. After throwing the last few bottles at the under-support of the bridge, he reached down and pulled the cannon out of the base of the crate.

Unknown to those on the ship, the ice spell released by Avanda was continuing to work as it froze the bridge to such a degree of coldness that it began to crack and break apart. Stress from the weight of the bridge, along with the Southwind military, caused fractures as shards broke off and fell into the river.

Another volley of flaming arrows shot straight down at the ship. This time they passed Grewen, because of the vertical angle. Flames erupted all over the ship. The *Sinecure* couldn't withstand a second attack of this magnitude once it emerged from the far side of the bridge.

Santorray worked his way to the port side, carrying the heavy cannon, as they traveled underneath the bridge. Finding a railing area without flames, he waited until they started to pass the main support column for the west side of the bridge.

Swinging the cannon like a club at the column, splinters flew in every direction upon impact, yet the column held. Santorray had one last chance; he attacked the column from the other side with another mighty swing of the cannon.

The column shattered, and the bridge dropped, but only a few feet. The other support beams groaned as they took on the extra load. Vines snapped as they also attempted to hold the bridge in place.

Thorik noticed shards from the frozen bridge tumble down to the river as Avanda's enchantment continued to expand and freeze more of the bridge's base. "Santorray, can you throw something at the other end of the bridge? That frozen section," he shouted, pointing upward.

"It would take something the size of this cannon to do enough damage. And it's not possible to throw it that far."

"Nothing is impossible. Let me try." Grewen had moved closer to the others. Several dozen arrows now protruded from his back, most surrounded by oily flames.

"Mognins have the aim of a blind mole," Santorray said. "Wouldn't you prefer to hide someplace until this is over?"

"Don't confuse defensive logic with hiding," the giant said. Grabbing the cannon from the blothrud with one of his oversized Mognin hands, Grewen turned and tossed the heavy object high into the air as though it were a toy.

The giant's aim was not nearly what the blothrud's was, and the cannon bounced against the vine-covered bluff before falling back down. To everyone's disappointment, he had missed.

"I knew it," Santorray growled.

Falling back to the river, the cannon then slammed into the base of the main support column. It was enough to jar the column, snapping it away from its icy crystallized top, which connected it to the bridge.

The entire frozen section of the bridge shattered into shards of ice, dislodging it from the top of the bluff.

Swaying back and forth, the bridge finally collapsed once the main support beam gave way. Military personnel attempted to flee as they ran and jumped off to the sides while the bridge moaned and cracked.

Lucian and Asentar arrived at the scene just as the bridge crumbled. The Dovenar Knight quickly dismounted his ride to help the men off the remaining bridge, while Lucian stared bitterly down at the ship, and specifically at Santorray. The beast had escaped, but Lucian would not give up the chase so easily.

Sailing out from under the bridge, the crew of the *Sinecure* watched as the structure above them tilted forward. It raced the ship downstream as it fell, only to splash behind the vessel by a few yards.

"You were right. My aim is poor." Grewen grinned at the mishap gone right.

12

LAKE LUTHRALUM

Santorray burst into the main cabin to find Dare hiding the last bottle of saved Nectar. "You fool! Saving our skin is more important than a few bottles of liquor."

"Watch what ya say about the Irr. She don't take kindly to insults." Protecting the last bottle from hearing such words, he nuzzled it between his arm and chest. "There ain't been a drink that has come near her. Ta call her liquor is like call'n ya a Fesh."

Eyes widened and lips raised on the blothrud. "No one gets away with calling me a Fesh."

"And that's why I didn't. But now ya understand my meaning." Dare worked his way across the room to the blothrud. "Ta violate such grace with such loathsome words is not only pure evil, but it also sours the taste of the drink."

Blothruds had an exceptional sense of smell, and Santorray was already overtaxed with Dare's body odor. The man apparently didn't believe in the health benefits of cleaning himself.

"I don't care how much you praise your drink. If you jeopardize my life again for something as dry as your Irr, I'll rip you apart."

"Not dry, my Del friend." Stepping up to the fierce creature, he leaned against the beast and looked up at him from under his chin. "Nor sweet. Perfection can only be explained with a taste. Then ya'll understand."

Popping the cork, Dare embraced the fragrance rising from the open bottle before lifting it toward Santorray's muzzle. "Inhale."

Keeping his stature straight, he couldn't help but smell the perfume of the drink as he grabbed it. Powerful enough to remove Dare's vile body odor from the air, yet not overstated. It was a perfect blend of fruits and barley, which could be tasted by his palette before putting any in his mouth. His curiosity had been heightened.

Dare smiled as he watched the Del'Unday on his virgin voyage into ecstasy. "Go on. Take a sip. That's all ya need."

Santorray looked down at the captain. "You seem awfully eager for me to drink this. Is this some type of poison?"

"Watch ya words, beast! Give her back if ya ain't gonna partake!"

Pulling the bottle higher, out of reach from Dare, he opened his mouth and poured a swig in. Swirling it around in his mouth for a bit, he sighed with relaxation. "Why the hell did you let us throw the rest of those bottles off the ship?"

"That's what I been say'n." Reaching up for the bottle, Dare felt quite justified by his actions during the battle.

"Get your own," the beast said. "This one is mine."

"Ya can't drink a whole bottle of Irr by yourself."

"And who's going to stop me? You?"

"Na, it ain't that. It's just that it ain't ever been done before. Too much of a good thing will kill ya."

"I've drunk my share before. I think I can handle one bottle."

Dare slapped the sides of his firmly stretched stomach, which hung out before him. "I've been known to do me share as well. But never an entire bottle of the mistress Irr."

Hearing the celebration from within, Thorik opened the door and entered the room as Santorray gently poured the liquid across his long tongue. "Captain Mensley, the fires have been extinguished, and it looks like smooth sailing ahead."

"Aye, lad." Dare Mensley opened a second bottle and raised it in the air. "We all be safe and healthy now."

Shrugging his shoulders, Thorik didn't fully agree. "Well, Brimmelle's under the weather. I don't think sailing sits well with his stomach. I helped him to his cabin, and Gluic is watching over him until he feels better."

"Ya did well out there today, young Num."

"Thank you. I appreciate your help in rescuing us from the mines."

"We be needing a toast to celebrate your escape." Licking with anticipation, he placed his dry cracked lips over the outside of the glass and used his tongue as a plug inside the neck of the bottle to control the flow of the nectar.

"Enjoy. I'll leave you two to celebrate." Thorik turned to exit.

Gasping with pleasure after his first drink, Dare waved the Num back into the room. "Thorik, lad, come celebrate with us." Raising the bottle, he grabbed Thorik's hand and pushed the two together.

"I don't think my uncle would approve."

"Bloody hell, did ya not just escape from the Southwind Mines? The notorious Rava'Kor prison mines at that?"

"I did. But I—"

"But noth'n. Ya be a wanted Num now. High on the list of outlaws. You're famous to all them that hate the Matriarch and her thugs that run dem mines." Dare pushed the bottle up toward Thorik's face.

Thorik could see residual wetness and oily marks on the outside of the bottle's mouth. Dare's facial hairs collected near the end, while small pieces of food stuck on the inside of the bottle, left over from the captain's tongue.

Thorik looked up at Santorray, who was opening his mouth for another trickle of raindrops from his own bottle. The blothrud's red eyes were at half-mast and rolled slightly back into his head.

Looking at a few floating specks in the bottle he held, Thorik questioned the safety of drinking it. "I'm not sure…"

"Drink up!" Dare demanded.

Lowering it quickly, Thorik cleaned the neck and open end of the bottle with his shirt. As dirty as his clothes were, he still felt it was cleaner than Dare's leftovers. A quick swab of the inside of the bottle's throat was an attempt to get the visual image of Dare's tongue inside the bottle out of his mind. It didn't work.

Closing his eyes, Thorik lifted the bottle to his lips and poured a sip into his mouth. His taste buds came alive with this newfound experience. The toxic liquor went immediately to his head, providing a sense of euphoria. All fears immediately vanished. Life was wonderful. Not a care in the world existed. Vanished were the negative emotions and the regrets he had relating to Brimmelle and Ambrosius, as his mind focused on his senses of taste and smell.

Dare reached for the bottle, but Thorik was too quick. He took another swig, this time twice the amount as the first time.

"Not so fast, Num. Ya be lay'n flat if yur not careful." The captain grabbed the bottle from Thorik, who was attempting to wipe his mouth on his sleeve but missed and wiped his chin instead.

Santorray's glassy-eyed gaze led him over to the table in the center of the room, where he fell into one of the chairs. "This reminds me of the celebration after the Humoric victory."

"You be at that celebration, ya say?"

Santorray nodded and raised his hand. "Front line. Couldn't walk straight for a month afterward. But my arm allowed me to drink."

"It be me inn where ya all celebrated. Festive time it was. Even Ambrosius stored his staff that night and enjoyed the entertainment."

Thorik's ears perked up, but his eyes struggled to do the same.

Sloshing his head the wrong way, Santorray couldn't find Dare as he talked to him. "Really? I thought we celebrated in a tattered, run-down, rodent-infested, abandoned castle keep."

Falling into the chair next to Santorray, Dare's backside tooted in a low rumble. "Yep, she was one of a kind. Could hold the lot of ya and still have room fur more."

"You met Ambrosius?" Thorik asked.

Dare was in the middle of a chug on the bottle, causing him to spit some of the liquid onto his chest. While wiping it back up with his fingers and licking them off, he answered, "More than met him. He's a close friend. He trusts me with his life, he does."

Thorik took the bottle from Dare and wiped it clean with his other hand before taking a sip. "Not anymore."

"Why ya go saying that?"

The room spun as Thorik struggled to stand up straight. Looking at the center captain of the several he viewed, he handed the bottle back to him. "Because I killed him."

Silence added to Thorik's vertigo, allowing him to focus on the spinning.

Laughter roared within seconds as Dare and Santorray couldn't contain themselves.

Dare tried to stand, but quickly fell back into his seat. "Are ya listen'n to the little Num? He says he killed the mighty Ambrosius!"

"Has he told you how he saved my life yet?" Santorray asked.

"Really?" Laughing so hard, it was difficult to get the words out. "I hope dat I don't fall on him and 'urt him before he gets a chance ta save my life too."

Shaking off the effect of the nectar only created a headache for Thorik. "It's true." For a second, he forgot what he was going to say next. "I killed Ambrosius to stop a flood that would have wiped you out." Thorik tried to point at them, but was lucky to be in the general area. "So, you see, I have already saved your life once."

Laughter continued by Dare and Santorray while the captain kicked a chair over to the Num. "Have a seat, ya mighty flood stopper."

"No thank you. I'll stand." Thorik sat down, not associating his actions with his words.

Dare leaned forward to give Thorik the bottle after his own sip. "So, tell me da truth. Is me old friend Ambrosius truly gone from the earth? Darkmere has no one to stop him now?"

Without cleaning the mouth of the bottle, Thorik took a swig. "Yes, and it's my fault that Ericc is now in danger. Ambrosius was right to do whatever it took to try to kill Darkmere when he had the chance. But I stopped him. And now Ericc's days are numbered because of me."

Santorray belched. "No, it's my fault. The prophecy of Ambrosius' son taking Darkmere's son is my fault. I put Ambrosius' son into this situation in the first place, back when he was a child. I'm the one that owes Ambrosius."

Dare removed the bottle from Thorik's grasp. "No, it be my fault. I owes him."

Thorik's body swayed as he waited for the captain to go on. "Why? What did… you do?"

"I ain't done nothin'. Just felt left out of the conversation."

All three roared with laughter until Thorik fell off his chair and crawled his way to the cabin's exit. Using the door handle to lift himself to his feet, he opened the door and stumbled out.

Seeing Avanda looking over the railing, he swaggered over to her. When he placed a hand on her back, she jumped and pulled away.

Thorik was surprised at the response, and he quickly retreated and lost balance, landing on the railing. "What's the matter?"

Avanda could smell the alcohol on his breath as the vapors filled the area. His words were slurred, and his eyes struggled to stay open and focused. It reminded her of Lucian at Rava'Kor. Her instincts kicked in; her shoulders went up, her heart raced, and her back went tense. A flood of emotions ran through her as she struggled not to flee.

"Get away," she ordered. "Don't touch me."

Confused, Thorik reached out to touch her arm. "It's me… Thorik. I'm not going to hurt you."

Flinching away, she wiped her skin where he had touched. "You've been drinking. I told you I don't like it when you do that."

Thinking he had straightened himself up, he was actually leaning slightly backward at an odd angle. "You can't tell me what I can and can do… can't do. You don't know what I've been through."

Tight-lipped, she gave two controlled nods. "Nor do you." Turning, she walked away.

"What does that mean? I don't understand."

"Remember that." She then walked through the doorway to the steps below.

Attempting to follow her, he tripped and landed hard onto his shoulder. "Remember what?" Trying to stand, he toppled over onto his other side, where he rested as the cool evening breeze felt refreshing against his face. "Nor do you!" he exclaimed, repeating her words back into the air.

Grewen raised his head up from the lower deck. "Troubles, little man?" The giant leaned against the open hatch's corner and rested his arms on the deck on two sides of the hatch trim.

"No. Why do you ask?"

"Avanda just came down here in tears, and you're curled up on deck, under the stairwell."

"I'm sleeping out here, where I can breathe fresh air."

"I can smell you from here. Are you going to be sick?"

Attempting to stand, Thorik bumped his head under the stairs to the ship's wheel deck. "I'm fine."

"You'd be better off if you kept your distance from your two new friends."

"Santorray… Captain? Why? They're nice to me. Having a toast to our escape."

"Just keep alert around blothruds."

"What do you have against Santorray? He reminds me of… that blothrud that helped you escape… from the Coliseum… last year."

"That's because he is the same one."

"I knew it! He's of good nature. He helped you, and then he helped me flee from the mines. We're lucky to have him."

"Seems a little too fortunate for us to have the only well-mannered blothrud in all of Terra Australis."

Thorik worked his way over to Grewen, before falling against the giant's shoulder, and sliding down to the deck. "What do you have against Santor… torray? Why are you so standish… standoffish with him?"

"Lessons learned, little man. In general, the Del'Unday are difficult to understand. Tensions between our two species go back before the great Unday War."

Cuddling his back up against the warmth of Grewen's arm, the Num relaxed. "The Tri-Species War?"

"No, this was at a time when the Ovs and Dels first parted paths. When Hessik and Trewek ruled the lake valley. In youth, they were close allies, but everything changed when Ergrauth launched his forces past the Guardians and into our valley."

"Grab some paper and ink from my coffer. I haven't written in my log for several days," Thorik mumbled as he closed his eyes and backed up tighter against the giant's arm.

Grewen sighed as he recalled the ancient story. "The blothrud Hessik ruled Corrock. He wished to take Ergrauth head on. A foolish notion. Corrock didn't have the resources or strength to take on such an endeavor."

Calmness embraced Grewen's face as he changed the focus of his story. "Trewek the Wise, a mognin, ruled over Ovla'Mathyus. He was the architect of our current beliefs. He offered salvation in his city's stronghold, an impenetrable fortress with endless resources to survive."

"Unfortunately, blothruds would rather race toward death than walk away to safety." Grewen reached below and lifted up a covered basket of melons. Removing the cloth, he emptied its contents into his mouth, causing juice to splatter upon the deck with each bite. "Many events followed that caused the friction to increase between our species and our clans. Blothruds have always blamed the Mognins for the downfall of Corrock and will continue to use it as a reason to see us suffer."

Soft snoring resonated from Thorik. It was difficult to know how much he had heard.

Wiping his face with the blanket, Grewen snapped it clean and stretched it out over the Num.

"Safe dreams, little man. You can add to your coffer of notes in the morning."

❧ 13 ☙

RUMALDO'S PORT

———

Thorik's Log: 21ˢᵗ day of the 4ᵗʰ month of the 650ᵗʰ year.

Captain Mensley has docked our ship in Thasque for trading, but our travels by water will end at our next stop in the city of Rumaldo. Ericc has escaped the South-wind Mines and is headed toward Corrock to take revenge on Darkmere. We will gather supplies and attempt to cut him off before he reaches the Del'Unday city.

———

Avanda clutched a book tightly to her chest before leaving Avanda clutched a book tightly to her chest before leaving the ship to enter the city of Rumaldo. "Thank you so much for this."

"A deal is a deal, tadpole. Ya didn't perform any more of yur magic on me boat. Ya lived up to yur word, so I does as well." Scratching his backside, Dare didn't enjoy giving away one of his collectibles when there was still potential profit to be made from it. Nevertheless, the profit he would have acquired from its sale would have been much less than the cost of having to fix another hole in the bow of his ship.

Captain Mensley pulled up his trousers, moving his rolls of fat so they wouldn't get pinched by his belt as he adjusted it to the next notch. "Be careful with dat book, lass. Them words may help ya figure out how some of yur magical objects work, but spellcasting can become dangerous. Take 'er slow."

Avanda thanked him again and scurried down the ramp to the dock as Thorik approached the captain. She had evaded Thorik the entire trip, his questions falling on deaf ears and her eyes never making contact. Occasional answers over her shoulder were the most he could get out of her.

"Thank you again for helping us out," Thorik said. "It's good to know that there are still people that help others without expecting anything in return."

A few of the crewmembers scoffed at the comment. Preparing the ship for a few days at dry dock, they were anxious to get the passengers off the ship.

"Expecting anything?" the captain coughed, as though the words hit hard against his stomach. "It's been a pleasure help'n ya all out. But now I must be on me way to make plans to feed these 'ere jaw flappers. A crew without any grub can turn ugly." Several of the shipmates scowled at the captain. "Or should I say uglier," chuckled the captain.

Shaking hands farewell, Thorik straightened his backpack and joined his party on the boat landing. Grewen and the Nums followed Santorray off the docks and into the city of Rumaldo. Rounding the first corner, they disappeared from the captain's sight.

"Freeloaders," one of the shipmates said. "We did our bit, now where's our payment?" He was quickly joined by others who had stopped working as they gathered around the captain.

Captain Mensley picked up his large Fesh-bone cane and wielded it like a war hammer. "Get back, ya dirty sandrats. Did ya think I dragged ya out to sea for months to rescue them just fur me kind heart?"

"You ain't got a heart."

"Exactly, coins keep me blood moving," the captain said.

"We don't see no coins from this trip."

"Ah, look closer. Did ya not see the crate of Irr we collected?"

"That ain't coin. Plus, the beast tossed most of it out."

"Aye, he did. But I saved enough to sell, given ya all a full belly until we finish our job."

"When does this charter end? First, you told us it was to rescue some Nums from a deserted island. You failed to mention anything about a Mog being with them. Then you added a trip to Southwind and up to the mines, where most of us already have a price on our heads. And then we take on a blothrud who nearly destroys our ship. Now you tell us this journey isn't complete again?"

"Get off me ship if yur gunna whine! I'm lead'n ya all to a lifetime of wealth, and yur complain'n about have'n to be away from yur momma for a little longer. Get off me ship or close yur trap!"

The crew grew silent as they weighed their options. Finally, one spoke up. "This is the last voyage with you. No more after this."

"So be it," Captain Dare Mensley replied.

~

It wasn't long before the crew had finished their duties and made their exit from the ship to venture into town for the nightlife.

Dare stood alone on the ship, gazing over the open water, watching the waves come into port. The unique spicy smell of longtail redfish captured the harbor as several boats unloaded their daily catch.

A thin layer of low clouds defused the sunset of the humid evening. It would have been the kind of day Dare would pull out his fishing pole and fall asleep in the breeze, if it weren't for a winged beast heading his way from the north. Its reflective scales made it difficult to see at a distance, but Dare knew exactly who it was.

The red-tipped silver dragon dove down to the ship, expanding its wings only at the last second to stop his descent.

"Draq," Dare said. "Ya never mentioned anything about a blothrud. He destroyed me entire crate! You'll have to come up with a new payment for my time and loss of me valuable crewmen."

The dragon folded his glossy wings and perched on the railing. Slightly taller than Dare, he had the additional advantage of the railing as he looked down over his long snout. "The only things you value are the coins in your purse and the drink in your bottle. Regardless, neither are my problems. You asked for a case of Irr as your payment. I provided it. Your inability to outwit a stupid blothrud is not surprising, although it's still not my issue."

"Think of me crew. I got noth'n for 'em. They won't help me anymore unless I can show them something of value at the end of this trip." His head sagged as he tried to look pathetic.

"Listen, you fat, repulsive human, I don't care about your problems. Besides, Ambrosius knows you stocked away armfuls of your nectar after partaking some with Santorray and Thorik."

Dare's neck cocked to the side so he could look directly at Draq. "What? You been spying on me? Ya no good Altered!"

"I have better things to do than watch you. Ambrosius, on the other hand, is watching everything."

"Really? My sources tell me he was killed in Weirfortus. Closed behind the dam walls he be, under an ocean of water. Crushed. Yet you say he's still pull'n the strings. How do ya fancy he be doing that from under that weight?"

"He managed to float his way up to the top of the reservoir, where I found him fighting off the Death Witch's grasp for his soul."

"Why didn't you save him from being trapped by the Num in the first place?"

"I was detained."

"So, how about that? The Num was right. He damn near did kill the old E'rudite. But how did ya save him from the witch?"

"Let's just say I didn't go unscathed."

"I can just see it. Ambrosius sit'n on top of the world as he looks down from Weirfortus, bark'n orders for you to carry out."

"He's not at Weirfortus, and you are not to discuss the fact that he lives with anyone."

"Then you shouldn't have told me in the first place. It's gonna cost ya to keep me quiet."

"I told you because Ambrosius knew you wouldn't do as I asked without knowing he was backing it. I have further orders for you from him as well. You're going to keep his existence quiet or he will make sure you can't talk to anyone. Do you recall the battle of Lirsha Mare? Are you sure you want to go through that nightmare again?"

Dare scratched his backside as he recalled the event. "That little Num killed Ambrosius as far as I know."

"I thought so."

❧ 14 ☙

MYTHICAL FOREST ARCHWAY

Thick twisted timbers, cut from the edge of the nearby forest, outlined the shops and houses of Rumaldo. Solid architectural designs with subtle details and changes to color tones gave the city a sense of strength and prosperity without glitter or glamor.

Thorik led his group along the brick streets in search of final provisions for their trek past the Mythical Forest, across the Kiri Desert, and through the O'Sid Fields. The evening light had faded, and lanterns had been lit. Pubs and shops lined the main street all the way to the very north end of town where it abruptly ended, marked by two tall, twisted, leafless trees.

"The entrance to the Mythical Forest," Santorray said. "Not a place you want to venture."

"Yes, I know," Thorik replied. "I was captured by the Myth'Unday once."

Crossing his arms, Santorray looked down at the Num. "Not possible. No Num or human has been captured and lived to tell about it."

"That's what I've heard." Thorik smirked at the comment. "We'll need to leave first thing in the morning."

"We don't have that option," Santorray said. "The captain's side trip to the city of Thasque to sell his goods cost us valuable time that we cannot spare."

Thorik adjusted his pack. "It's his ship. Be thankful he came to Rumaldo to drop us off."

"He has foolishly allowed the Southwind military time to travel north. We must leave immediately to avoid being here when they arrive, if they haven't already."

Fir Brimmelle had kept quiet long enough. He didn't like the creature's attitude toward his Sec and needed to make a point of it. "Now you listen here; don't you start telling us what to do." His nose was in the air, and his tone was condescending. "We don't need your help, so either fall in line or leave."

The blothrud lunged at the Fir with both hands out, ready to grab him. Teeth showing, he growled hard enough to make Brimmelle's knees buckle from fear, causing the Num to fall to the ground. "Don't ever talk down to me, Num. I'm trying to save your pathetic life."

"Save?" The question came from a slight distance.

A large group of humans had stepped out of a pub to witness the blothrud in their city. It was uncommon to see Ov'Unday in town and rare to see a Del'Unday.

The man near the center, who had spoken up, continued. "We would all be better off without your kind. Words of saving our people have only led to battles which caused us to suffer."

"Perhaps we should leave," Grewen said calmly.

Santorray stepped toward the group of men. "And I suppose humans had nothing to do with the battles of this land."

"Only to fight for the survival of our kind." He then pointed at Grewen. "And his kind."

"Santorray, don't waste your time." Thorik stepped out in front of him.

"Santorray?" the crowd gasped. Whispering bled through the group.

The blothrud stood up tall and straight. He knew the stories of his past had been salted with half-truths and outright lies.

"We heard you were dead, killed in Southwind," said one man.

"I get that a lot."

"You're a murderer. You've taken part in many battles against us, killing our people and destroying our cities," said another man.

Santorray flexed his massive muscles and pounded his fist into an open palm. "Who's to say I'm not here to take out yours right now."

Thorik waved his hands in front of the blothrud. "No, wait! Don't let them provoke you."

The first man stepped forward, waving his finger at the blothrud. "You're as bad as Ambrosius and Darkmere. They've destroyed this kingdom."

Thorik spun around on the balls of his feet to face the man who had just spoken. "How dare you talk ill of such a great man? Ambrosius sacrificed his life to save you, your family, and your city."

"He's dead? That calls for a drink. No more bloodshed."

Thorik was aghast. "How can you say that after everything he's done for you?"

"He's never done anything to help me or my family," the man replied.

Fists tight to his side, Thorik stepped closer to the man. "Just because you don't know what he's done for you doesn't mean it hasn't been done."

"What has that old diplomat ever done for us, aside from launching a civil war that broke our people?"

"He prevented Darkmere from ruling and destroying your lands. He founded the Grand Council to establish peace among different cultures. He sacrificed his life to save you!" Thorik screamed, his fists now up by his sides.

The crowd backed away from him. Unbeknownst to Thorik, Santorray had stepped up behind him, ready to attack the crowd.

Thorik's face was flushed with anger, and his hands shook with rage. "He gave up everything for you to have the ability to sit in your pubs and drink your life away while complaining about him and others who have fought for you." Never before had he been so angry at someone he didn't even know.

Fearing the long reach of the blothrud, the men quietly backed off and grumbled to one another, returning to their pub for safety.

Santorray lowered his arms to his sides. "You've done well, Sec." He then walked back to the rest of the group.

Thorik stood silently, shaking with frustration. These people didn't understand how wrong they were. They didn't know the full story, yet they had already made their judgment. If they had known Ambrosius the way he had, they wouldn't believe the lies being told. The man should have been honored, not ridiculed. If Thorik hadn't condemned him to death, others might have discovered this truth.

Ambrosius had been like a father to Thorik. He had taken the Num under his wing and inspired him to be more than he thought he could be. The old E'rudite had trusted the Num to use his judgment, yet guided him when he veered off course. Ambrosius was a mentor that few fathers could aspire to become.

Grewen stepped up behind Thorik. "You have to let this go. It's been months. Ambrosius is gone. You made the right choice, but you have to move on."

Thorik turned and pounded his fist hard into Grewen's massive leg. He then hit a second time, a third, and then a blur of quick shots as he vented his frustration. His knuckles became bloody from hitting the hard, thick skin of the Mognin. "I can't forget what I've done. I see it every night in my dreams, and it drags me down in the days. It fills me with anger and regret."

Grewen looked down at the Num. "No, don't ever forget. You can't learn if you forget. You can't teach others if you recall only the good times. But you do need to forgive yourself, little man. Regret and anger will only compound themselves and make things worse."

Three more punches into Grewen's leg hit hard before Thorik broke down and wrapped his arms around the giant's leg. Tears streamed down his face as he gasped for breath from his own personal pain. "I miss him so much, Grewen. So very much."

"I know. We all do." Grewen patted Thorik on the back. "But it is time to free your heart from hate, including the hate you feel for yourself. It is time to move on."

Santorray interrupted their conversation. "Moving on is exactly what we need to do right now." He was pointing down the main street while talking.

A distant group of torches and flags headed their way, behind merchants and customers who filled the street. The holders of the flags could not be seen from their position behind the locals, but the colors of the flags were distinctly Southwind as they popped up and down from their Faralope mounts.

"Lucian has caught up with us," Santorray said. "No time for supplies. We need to head out of town right now."

"Through the Mythical Forest at night? I don't like the sound of that. Can't we hide in town until they leave?" Brimmelle asked.

"Do you really think the locals will cover for us?" Santorray responded sarcastically.

"Not after the greeting you and Thorik gave," Brimmelle spit back.

"We'll be safe if we stay on the road. Hopefully Lucian isn't aware of that fact."

Thorik wiped his eyes dry and regained his composure. "Santorray's right, we need to escape immediately. Onto the River-Green Road, everyone."

The four Nums led the charge out of town, quickly passing between the two large, twisted trees. Under the natural arch, caused by the limbs from each tree intertwining, a sudden chill befell them. A background moan could be heard from the tree trunks, along with distant screams from deep within the forest.

"Are you sure it's Lucian? We could be running from nothing," Brimmelle said.

Grewen followed the Nums under the arch, but couldn't hear the odd sounds that they did. "It's a risk either way." He reached up and softly touched the limbs of the arch.

Santorray watched the group's back, standing on the edge of the city with his nose high in the air, sniffing. He inhaled the smells from Rumaldo and its citizens, before taking in a familiar smell. "It's him. He's here. I can smell his stench a mile away. We need to hurry."

But it was too late.

A horn sounded, and the hooves of the faralopes charged forward. Locals had provided Lucian with descriptions of the party who had just passed through.

"Grab the older Nums!" Santorray raced under the arch and scooped up Gluic, who immediately became limp in his arms.

Grewen lifted Brimmelle and awkwardly ran out from under the arch onto the River-Green Road, which cut directly through the center of the Mythical Forest.

Thorik and Avanda easily outran the Mognin and Blothrud, leading the charge down the road.

Lucian emerged from the crowded street to see the criminals escaping. "They're heading for the forest. Quickly, seize them!"

Forty riders tore through the city's streets after the prison escapees, knocking locals out of their way. Banners high, the horn sounded again, this time with more energy.

"I want the blothrud alive. I wish to kill him with my own blade. Kill the rest if you must, burn the forest if you have to, but do not fail me," Lucian shouted as he and the riders reached the tree arch.

Deep voices came from the two trees. "Burn us?" The ground rumbled, and the limbs swayed violently. "Threats against the Myths, do we hear?"

Fear struck all the men and faralopes as they entered the archway. Myth'Unday whispers and shouts came from all directions as the armed men searched for a source. Then suddenly, the ground buckled as roots raised up and wrapped around faralopes' legs, tripping them and knocking off their riders. The attack forced most of them to escape back to the safety of the city streets.

Chaos filled the archway with the remaining Southwind men. They fought to contain the faralopes as they kicked at each other and attempted to buck their riders off.

Lucian went on the offensive. Dodging the attacks from the rising roots, he rode up to one of the trees and stabbed his torch deep into an open knothole.

The old, dry wood quickly caught on fire as an earsplitting scream came forth. Fire erupted up the hollow trunk to the arch.

Two Southwind riders followed his lead and lit the second tree in flames, causing the same effect.

Within moments, both trees were burning bright and hot. An arch of glowing yellows and reds filled the skyline at the north edge of town for all to see. Feeling a small sense of victory, the riders quickly returned to their mission and made their way underneath the arch and onto the River-Green Road.

"Here they come!" Brimmelle held tightly onto Grewen's shoulder.

"Get off the road! They won't follow us into the forest at night," Thorik ordered.

"There's a good reason why," Santorray replied. "I'd rather fight off a legion of Southwind's finest before taking on the Myth'Unday."

Thorik considered his suggestion until he turned and saw Lucian and his men racing up the road toward them. "We've survived it before. We'll have to take our chances on doing it a second time."

Grewen struggled to keep within hearing distance as he lumbered along. "Thorik, we were on the outskirts of the forest at the time, and we got lucky."

"We haven't made it too far into the forest this time, either," Thorik said.

A volley of arrows shot from behind, with several sticking into Grewen's back. The strong legs of the faralopes closed the gap as the men pulled out swords for the attack.

"We stay and fight," Santorray ordered.

"Then you fight alone." Leading the charge, Thorik turned to his right and disappeared into the dark forest. "Quickly, everyone, this way."

Following Thorik, Avanda jumped off the road behind him. Visibly irritated about the decision, Santorray followed him in as well.

Still carrying Brimmelle, Grewen had tired and slowed to a comfortable walking pace. It wasn't long before there was a full circle of riders around them.

"Thorik, help!" Brimmelle screamed from the road into the thick forest. "We've been captured!"

Lucian cupped his hands to his mouth and shouted in the same direction. "We have your friends. Either you surrender yourself and we let them go, or you hide like cowards, and we take them back to the mines in your place." Panning the dark, he waited for an answer to his bluff. He had no intention of leaving without Santorray.

Protecting Brimmelle from the soldiers, Grewen continued his slow walk down the road, interrupting the circle of riders. As much as the riders wanted to feel they had the giant under control, the reality of the situation was the mognin forced them to move with him if they didn't want to get pushed out of the way.

"Hold your ground and stop the mognin," Lucian shouted to his men.

The riders came to a complete halt, giving the giant no more path to walk.

Reaching forward, Grewen calmly separated the men and faralopes in front of him so he could continue on his walk. "Excuse me." He attempted to peacefully step out of the enclosing ring.

The men swung their swords at his thick arms. Panicking animals made it difficult to aim, let alone stay on their mounts. Nevertheless, a few swipes made their cuts, but they didn't stop the Mognin from slowly breaching their barrier.

Before the riders could obtain control over the giant again, Grewen stepped off the road to join his friends.

"After them!" Lucian ordered his men, none of whom responded. Instead, they looked at each other. "I said, go after them. They couldn't have gone far. Get in there and drag them back out." No response. "Those that do not obey will go in front of the Matriarch, for it is her order to return these prisoners."

It was the name of the Matriarch that finally caused them to venture forth, slowly and cautiously, into the dark forest, leaving the safety of the open road.

Lucian held half of his men back. "We'll wait here, just in case the prisoners try to escape back to the road." Lucian had no plans to personally enter the deadly forest.

A rider approached Lucian and his men after passing under the burning trees arching the road. It was the Dovenar Knight.

"Asentar!" Lucian shouted to him as he slowly approached. He knew that not even Santorray could stand up against the likes of the knight. "They have taken refuge in the forest. With your skills, you can flush them out so we can capture them."

The knight said nothing until he had reached Lucian. "You idiot! You burned down the sacred entrance to the Mythical Forest, a landmark that this kingdom promised to keep intact. In return they have historically allowed us safe travel on the River-Green Road. Not only have you jeopardized our trade route, but you may have also started a war with the Myth'Unday."

"It's about time we burn down this entire forest and rid ourselves of these pests. Besides, we shouldn't be tied to agreements made by those who we no longer follow. Those men died long before we were born, and their ways no longer work."

"The kingdom made a commitment to the Myths to stay out of their land and only use the road for passage. Does honor mean nothing to you?"

"When it serves my purpose." Lucian stopped as he heard screams of pain from his men within the woods. "And right now, my purpose is to retrieve those criminals. So, enter that forest and bring them back to me."

"I don't take orders from you. I only agreed to travel with you in hopes of finding Ericc. But if you deviate from my path to Eastland and Corrock, then we part ways. I never consented to hunt escaped criminals."

"These orders come from the Matriarch," Lucian said with authority. Just mentioning her name struck fear in Lucian's men.

"The Matriarch does not rule the Dovenar Kingdom or its knights." Asentar turned his mount around and galloped back to the city.

15

MYTH'UNDAY

R acing through the forest, Thorik instructed Avanda not get too far ahead of the rest. "We don't want to be separated in here."

She slowed and then eventually stopped and waited as the soft moonlight coated her with a pale blue light.

Grewen slapped his heavy feet down onto the forest floor as he awkwardly ran behind the group. He was exhausted and eventually slowed down until he heard screaming from the soldiers behind him.

The screams were not the soldiers' battle cries. Instead, they were yells filled with fear and pain, and the noises eventually died off one by one, followed by silence.

Santorray stopped and spun around, sniffing the air to see if they were still being followed by the Southwind military. Motioning for everyone to stop moving, he listened for any followers. "I don't smell or hear anything behind us."

Brimmelle struggled free from Grewen, stepped over to Santorray, and then reached up to help his mother down from the blothrud. "Good. They must have turned back."

"Not so," Santorray replied, peering deep into the thick forest. "Nature only sits this quiet when it has something to fear. I hear nothing, not even the leaves in the trees. We are being hunted, and not by men."

Gluic smiled with great pleasure. "Oh my, what wonderful life exists here." She quickly collected feathers and decorated her clothes and hair with the treasures from the forest floor, such as stringy moss, long red grass, and colorful mushroom tops. A bright orange feather was the final touch to her hair décor.

A soft voice came from above them. "You are not wanted here. Trespassers must be punished."

The quiet that followed added to the eerie feeling, and the group twisted their heads to look at each other for confirmation that they had heard the voice as well.

Avanda stepped closer to Thorik for protection as Brimmelle held onto his mother's hand to prevent her from wandering off.

"Stick together." Thorik looked back up into the trees for any movement. "They prey on those who stray off."

Without warning, Avanda's scream rang out and echoed throughout the trees.

Thorik turned to find her gone, when only a moment earlier she had been standing next to him. No footsteps were heard, nor footprints seen; she had disappeared, dissolved into the air and shadows.

Not only had she vanished, but so had the rest of Thorik's party, as he now stood in the forest alone.

Cupping his hands near his mouth, he shouted for them. "Grewen? Avanda? Granna? Santorray?" Soft muffled voices could be heard in response, too distant to understand. "Brimmelle?" Thorik yelled in a different direction, receiving no answer.

Shaking with fear, Thorik was deserted and assumed he would now stand trial in the forest by the Myth'Unday for the crime of entering their dwellings.

A crack of a stick eventually broke the silence. Fallen leaves shuffled, and footsteps could be heard. More than a few beings walked these woods in the dark of the night, none of which could be seen.

"Chop him up for a stew," a voice from the shadows said.

"No, I want to taste him raw," replied another.

Thorik's movements were slow, trying to determine what to do as he caught glimpses of shadows out of the corners of his eyes.

"I want his ears for my necklace," said a whisper.

Loud pounding on the ground shook the forest floor, kicking up leaves and twigs. The massive invisible steps moved directly toward Thorik.

"His eyes are mine," came another voice.

A second set of slightly softer footfalls moved in his direction as well, kicking small rocks as it raced forward.

Soft voices argued about his body parts as several smaller footsteps scurried about, running in various directions. "He's mine, leave him alone."

The two large invisible creatures stirred up dust as they approached, as though they would collide right on top of the Num.

Thorik leaped out of the way, only to feel an enormous invisible hand grab him around the waist and lift him up.

A great noise rang in Thorik's ears as the two large unseen creatures crashed, releasing him into the air, only to fall back to earth on his own.

"Don't bruise him. It makes the meat taste bad," said a voice inches from Thorik's ear.

With the wind knocked out of him, Thorik watched as sand and leaves were kicked up by the two large unseen attackers as they surrounded him. Each time one moved toward the Num, the other would do so as well.

Thorik was again grabbed and lifted into the air. He screamed for help as he struggled to escape. Having encountered the Myth'Unday once before, he hoped that his familiarity with one of their kind would carry some weight. "I am a friend of Theodore Hempton, a Myth'Unday such as yourself. I have passed his test and have been granted the approval to enter the forest."

The voices increased as the bushes and trees rustled more violently.

"My name is Sec Thorik Dain of Farbank. I'm a friend of the Myth'Unday!" he shouted out to them.

All movement stopped, though he continued to float in the air in the grasp of an unseen assailant.

Whispering could be heard from the forest floor as it traveled up the tree trunks and into the foliage before vanishing completely. The voices were gone.

Thorik stayed idle, expecting his release. But nothing happened; only the whispering had retreated.

Perhaps the name of Mr. Hempton was not liked in these parts and made things worse.

"Sec," a deep, distant voice called out.

"Yes?" he yelled back.

"Sec, can you see me?" The voice came through more clearly this time. It sounded like Santorray.

Thorik searched the woods. "No, where are you?"

"I'm holding you in my hands."

Thorik reached out and felt the invisible attacker. The hands and arms did feel like his friend, and once he realized this, the blothrud came into focus.

Not only did Santorray come into view, but so did the rest of his party. Each Num was moving around the forest without the ability to see one another. Even Grewen stood still, looking around for his companions. Gluic seemed to be the only one too busy collecting items to notice the events unfolding around them.

"Can you see them yet?" Santorray asked.

"Yes. Where did the whispering voices go?"

Santorray set the Num back on the ground. "The Myth'Unday all scampered off once you announced yourself. Perhaps you have been granted clearance."

"I don't understand what happened. Why did you attack me?"

"Grewen was going to walk right over you. I had to get you out of the way so you wouldn't be stepped on."

"You weren't affected?"

"Until I met you, I thought I was the only one to ever escape the Myth'Unday. The Great Oracle, Ovlan herself, sent me on a quest for her cause. In doing so, she granted me immunity from their games and tricks."

"How were you able to wake me from their spell? And why didn't you wake Grewen before he reached me?"

"The close voice of one you trust can break the Myth'Unday spell, allowing you to see what's real. I tried to wake the others, but apparently, they do not trust me."

"It will come with time. You have to earn it."

"That is your salvation, Sec. Trust has never been my ally."

"In this case, it was critical." Thorik moved over to Avanda, who continued to call out for help. Her abandonment in the forest had spooked her, but her desire to see the Myth'Unday had trumped those emotions.

Avanda watched leaves shuffle as Thorik walked up to her. Unable to see him, she called out to the approaching creature, "Hello? Show yourself. I won't hurt you."

Thorik leaned in toward her. "Avanda, it's me, Thorik. Can you see me? I'm standing directly in front of you."

Slowly, Thorik materialized in front of her once she trusted his words.

Thorik could see in her eyes that he was now visible to her.

"You're not a Myth'Unday," she said with disappointment.

"You're welcome," he responded before turning to free the rest of the group from the spell.

He quickly broke the curse on Grewen and his grandmother, but it took Gluic to break Brimmelle from his visual deficiency. Upon doing so, they all agreed the River-Green Road was still too dangerous, so they decided to continue to skirt the southern part of the forest.

Still frustrated, Avanda pouted as she fell in line for the trek east. "How come I couldn't see them? Last time I was in the Mythical Forest, I was able to see what they looked like."

"Innocence lost is such a tragic thing." Removing a bracelet made of weeds from her own arm, Gluic tied it around Avanda's wrist before they continued on their way.

16

ORDERS AND WEAPONS

After traveling through the forest for several hours to put some distance between them and the road, Thorik gave in to Brimmelle's complaining and stopped for the night at the shore of a large lake.

The clear night gave a spectacular view of the Lu'Tythis lights over the water. Wavy sheets of green and blue lights danced in a sky filled with crisp starlight, which reflected on the soft ripples along the lake's surface. A series of lightning bolts sprang forth from the center of the light presentation, and then they were gone.

"Make a wish," Thorik said to Avanda.

Avanda put her head down, paying more attention to Ralph than to Thorik. "This one is yours," she replied in a timid voice. She had avoided eye contact with him as much as possible ever since they rescued him from the Southwind Mines.

"Make all the wishes you want," Santorray said, "but we need a fire tonight, and that takes collecting some dry wood."

Grewen raised his hand slightly. "I'll take care of it."

Santorray nodded. "I'm going to scout ahead for a path."

"You should take someone, just in case the Myth'Unday return."

Hesitant to the idea, Santorray replied, "I'll go alone. The Myth's have nothing on me."

"Don't go too far. It's easy to get lost in here."

Santorray ignored the last statement and ventured in the opposite direction of the lake, over a small hill. He walked for a mile until he found an opening in the woods.

Stepping up on the highest point in a small glade, Santorray pulled a bead from his necklace and tapped it onto the talisman, which also hung from it. He placed it in the center of his palm. The round bead had the weight of lead and the texture of bark.

Tightening his grip on the bead in his right fist, he repeated a phrase several times. "Illume dula fara'du." By the fourth time he had said it, a red light glittered from between his fingers.

Twisting his body, he pulled his arm back into position before firing the glowing bead high into the air, over the treetops. The missile of light gave off enough luminescence to be seen from a distance, but not enough to brighten up the area. After the apex of its flight had been achieved, the light flickered out as it fell to earth.

Crossing his arms, he stood silently, waiting impatiently.

The sounds of the tree leaves seemed loud against the backdrop of near silence. A stray chirp from a bird occasionally broke up the bland white noise.

"Where are you?" Santorray said into the night air.

Frogs croaked softly in the distance as he stood firm, peering into the night sky.

A breeze blew through the trees in front of him and then to his left before coming back behind him to complete the full circle, and then it receded. Silence again followed.

Santorray sniffed the air, ripe with a fresh scent. "Come forth. Show yourself."

The woods did not reply.

Regardless, the blothrud could feel himself being stalked as though he was the prey. It was not a feeling he was accustomed to.

Deafening silence interrupted nature's music as the crickets cowered, frogs froze, and birds broke off their songs in mid-chorus. Absolute quiet had a way of making the night seem darker and chillier.

A sudden gust of wind raced out of the woods and rushed up to slap at the red Del'Unday's back, pushing him forward.

Rotating quickly, he swiped his knuckle blades at the object, only to find nothing was there.

A second powerful blast of air pushed up against his back. Twisting, he nearly made it all the way around before he was struck by a large black mass, knocking him to the ground.

Preparing to leap up, he saw a wave of distorted lights and reflections leaning over him. It arched over his body, from the ground on his right all the way to the ground on his left. The colorless mass reflected the blothrud's faint image several times across the archway.

"Get off me!" Santorray ordered.

"I think you've forgotten your place, assassin. You work for me," said the creature.

Growling at the comment, Santorray stood up as the reflective wings folded up against the sides of the twelve-foot-long creature. "I'd fight my way through Della Estovia before I'd ever work for you, Draq."

The red-tipped silver dragon tightened his wings and stretched his neck out to increase his height, which still only came to Santorray's shoulders. "Powerful words from a creature I'm giving orders to."

"Relaying orders. You're nothing more to me than a carrier pigeon."

The dragon stretched his wing out in anger. It was a natural instinct to demonstrate his size with his huge wingspan. "Don't you dare compare me to a Fesh."

"If you sneak up on me one more time, I'm going to beat you down like one."

Draq stretched his neck, fanned his wings, and slapped his tail about in anger.

Lowering his chin, Santorray pressed his forehead hard against Draq's and pushed downward.

Draq raised one of his large back legs to strike the blothrud's midsection.

Grabbing the dragon's leg before it could land a severe attack, Santorray held it at bay with both hands.

They both pushed hard against each other, neither making any headway. Growling and cursing each other's name, they locked horns in a show of dominance.

"Give me my weapons and let me perform my duties," Santorray ordered.

"I don't believe you're capable of this mission. Have you even found him yet?"

"Yes, now give me the damn dagger so I can kill him and get it over with."

"Not so fast. You must do it in public. Visible to many of Darkmere's allies. The dark one himself, if at all possible."

Santorray pushed the head of the dragon down by several inches. "I accepted this mission and know what needs to be done. Don't tell me how to do my task."

Draq whipped his tail and slapped the blothrud's legs out from under him. The attack forced Santorray to toss the dragon's leg high into the air, causing the winged creature to land on his back.

They both crashed hard against the moss-covered mound.

Calmly, the two slowly stood back up, leaving a generous distance between them.

Draq was tired of the confrontation. "Your supplies and Varacon are just beyond that thorn grove."

Santorray nodded his head in acceptance of the information. "Tell Ambrosius that Ericc will soon be dead."

"Where do you have him tied up?"

"I don't. I found him in the Rava'Kor mine. He escaped and is heading toward Corrock. I'm traveling with a group of fools who think Ambrosius asked them to save Ericc."

"Yes, Dare Mensley informed me of your meeting with the Num, Thorik, and his friends."

Santorray walked behind the thorn bush and collected his weapons and supplies. "Don't worry. I won't let any of them get in my way." Partially unsheathing the virgin dagger, Varacon, he looked at his reflection in its interworking spiral blades before storing it. Gems were embedded in its hilt, and rune markings told of its powers. "Their deaths will only add to the list that this journey has created."

"As annoying as these Fesh can be, you are not to harm them. Ambrosius provided me with instructions if you were to run into them. Follow Thorik. He is clever and will lead you to Ericc and, most likely, Darkmere as well."

"We are heading to Corrock. I can't ensure that Bredgin or his father will be there."

"Then stab Ericc in the Del'Unday city for all to see, including Thorik. This should take care of this mess. Bring the dagger back to me with Ericc's blood, and your debt will be paid."

$\mathscr{H}$ 17 $\mathscr{H}$

AVANDA

Flames from the campfire turned various colors and faded away as the air smelled of rotten eggs from the poorly executed magical spell. This continued for a few more seconds as Avanda flicked liquid from her fingertips while reading a passage from the book she had received from the captain. Each phrase was spoken with more authority, as the flame finally doubled in height and twisted like a tornado before returning to normal.

Grewen leaned back on his elbows and held a foot into the magical flame. It was hotter than normal, and he savored the therapeutic feeling between his toes and on the sole of his foot.

Brimmelle was disgusted at the sight of the giant's ugly, callused foot hovering over the fire and was not shy to complain about it.

Ralph was unimpressed with the magic as he stalked insects close to Gluic, who was setting out the crystals and stones she had collected on her trip. Each item had a specific place in the sand where she gently set it down. Racing around her, the lizard somehow knew not to step inside her circle of stones.

"Avanda, Ambrosius warned us about the dangers of magic," Thorik said.

She ignored him and tried her spell again, this time with more control and longevity.

Brimmelle's thick eyebrows pulled tight as he looked at Thorik while pointing at Avanda. It was obvious he expected Thorik to resolve this growing issue.

"You heard me." Thorik was visibly irritated.

Avanda stopped and challenged his stare. "Ambrosius isn't here, is he?"

This was the first time she had challenged him with such boldness. He had to respond firmly. "Well, in his absence, I am warning you."

"Warning accepted… but not taken."

"It's not a request. Stop using magic." Thorik knew he was being watched by the group to see if he could handle the situation.

"Why?"

"Because it's dangerous," Thorik said with more force than planned.

Ralph felt Avanda's tension and turned toward Thorik, raising and lowering his body with his mouth wide open to intimidate him.

Avanda tucked her magical items back into her purse. "It was an accident. One time. The captain was able to fix his ship."

"Not just from that standpoint. You're too young to understand the power that you carry."

"Who says?"

"I say."

"Who are you to say what I can and can't do?"

Snatching the purse of magic from her hand, his anger showed in his sharp voice and movement. "I can say it because I'm responsible for you."

"Really? It didn't seem like you felt that way in Rava'Kor, while I was being touched by those drunks. Standing there helpless. If I had understood magic better, I could have taken care of them myself. I obviously can't rely on you to be there for me."

Avanda ran out of the camp. Her hands covered her face to prevent exposing her emotions.

"Avanda, wait!" Thorik stepped forward to reach out to her. But it was too late; she had escaped the campfire light, into the shadows of the trees which hung over the lake's shoreline.

Brimmelle smirked at Thorik as the young Num left the group. "Not so easy to raise someone, is it?"

Leaving the perimeter of the camp, Thorik followed Avanda along the lake's grassy banks for several minutes, until she finally stopped and leaned against a tree.

Thorik approached cautiously, as though she were a viper ready to strike. "What's with you? Why are you always mad at me? You won't even look me in the eyes anymore." He attempted to comfort her by placing his palm gently on her shoulder.

Flinching hard from his touch, her eyes filled with anger. "Don't!"

"What happened to you? Why won't you tell me?"

"I shouldn't have to tell you. You should have been there to prevent them from…" Searching for a word she could speak without feeling ill, she continued, "… groping me."

"I'm sorry about what happened, but I had no idea they were outside the pub waiting for you."

"You should have. You promised."

"I promised? When?"

"After Uncle Wess left me. You promised you wouldn't leave me alone and that you'd protect me."

"That's not fair. I didn't leave you. *You* left the pub."

"That's because you wouldn't leave with me. You told me to go."

"I couldn't leave. I had to get into the mine to save Ericc."

"His safety is more important than mine?"

"No, of course not. You would have been fine if you hadn't upset Lucian in the first place."

"I see, this is all my fault. Not yours, not Lucian's, but mine. I'm the one that caused all of this."

"I didn't say that."

"You didn't have to. I can tell by the way you and Brimmelle look at me. Your disappointment in my actions that caused it to happen."

"Well, if you hadn't—"

"See, right there. You blame me for this. I deserved it because of the way I behaved, or the way I stand up for myself, or the way I live my life."

"Avanda, we're not in Farbank anymore. You can't get away with doing the same things. The way you act directly affects how strangers respond to you. They haven't grown up with you to know how good a person you really are. It's your responsibility to make a good impression on them at your first meeting."

"Have you noticed that not once have you told me that this was Lucian's fault? I thought you loved me for who I was and would always be there for me. Not to lecture me about what I'm not."

"I care for you greatly, and I hate Lucian for what he did," Thorik said.

"You didn't care enough about me to stop their heckling in the first place."

"It wasn't that important. They didn't bother me."

"It was important to *me*. It bothered me a lot. I've never cowered down to bullies like you do. And now look at me. I can't stand to even be looked at by a man, let alone be touched." She cleared the tears from her face. "Thorik, I trusted you. I believed in you even when others didn't. You promised to take care of me, and you didn't. And then, when I need you most, you blame me for what happened."

There was truth to her words. His focus on reaching Ericc had consumed him so much that he had ignored his companion's feelings. "I dropped a crystal trying to pick up a stone."

"What?"

"Nothing. It was just something Gluic was trying to tell me."

Turning his back to her, he gave her some space. His hands tight behind his back, he pondered how to settle the issue so the bickering would stop and the tension would ease. "I'm tired of being so careful of what I can say around you, afraid that it may upset you. What do we need to do to resolve this?"

"Resolve? You can't just fix this like you mend a cut. You have to listen to me."

"But I have listened to you," Thorik said. "And I still don't know how to help you move on."

Avanda shook her head in disappointment. "You heard what I said, and you want my pain to go away. But you haven't listened to me and understood my feelings. I never asked you to solve my problem, only to understand how I feel about it and be there for me."

Thorik picked up a few pebbles and started skipping them one by one across the lake's surface. "I'm sorry, Avanda. You're right. I just..." One of the small rocks stopped in midair and then fell straight down to the ground, prior to leaving the shore and hitting the lake's surface.

"Ouch," a tiny female voice said from the lake's shoreline.

He didn't see anyone. "Hello?" he asked instinctively, before realizing that he might be speaking to a Myth'Unday.

"Close your eyes," Thorik said to Avanda. He spun around and jumped back to her.

"Too good to look upon me?" the voice asked. It wasn't a whisper like the faeries from before. This voice sounded more solid.

Avanda peered past Thorik in an attempt to see what he was blocking. "Thorik, what is it?"

His hand reached for her eyes, covering them only for a second before she sprung away from his touch. "Don't look at it. It will cause you great fear."

The voice closed in behind Thorik. "Are you saying I'm ugly? A face that could turn you to stone? Is that what you think of me?"

"I want to see!" Avanda yelled, pushing Thorik aside.

Thorik heard silence as he kept his eyes shut. Reaching out, he couldn't find the younger Num. "Don't look at it. Close your eyes."

Avanda had stepped away from Thorik. "She's beautiful."

"Did you think Ovlan would create something hideous for her forest?" the voice replied.

"Run, Avanda!" Thorik shouted. "Get out of here while there's still time. Get back to camp."

Avanda ignored him. "I've never seen anything like you before. You're not like that faerie I caught last year."

Thorik's words became background noise to Avanda as he continued to shout to her.

"Yes, I'm unique in all the world."

"There isn't any other of your species?"

"Only one. But my brother is deformed and grotesque. Only I carry the beauty of our species."

"I'm so glad I can see you. You're amazing."

"Yes, I am."

"I'm Avanda. What's your name?"

"Raython the Ethereal."

"Thank you for letting me see you. I can't wait to tell everyone in camp."

"I'm afraid that won't be possible. I can't let you spin tales about my beauty," Raython said. "No words could possibly do me justice. No matter how hard you tried. Even if you could, it would just cause others to seek me out to gaze upon my brilliance."

"I'll only tell a few."

"No one must know."

Avanda gave a large sigh and shrugged her shoulders. "I won't tell anyone when I get back."

Raython laughed. "Honestly, how could you not let my secret out after seeing such a magnificent creature as myself? The truth is, no one could restrain themselves. That's why you can't go back."

"What? I have to go back. They're waiting for me."

"Then they will be waiting a very long time."

Avanda's shoulders rolled back as she crossed her arms. "They'll come looking for me, and they won't let you keep me."

"You will be long gone by that time, assuming you exist at all anymore."

Avanda felt uneasy about what Raython was saying and sought to regain the upper hand. She grabbed for her purse of magic, only to find she didn't have it with her.

An evil smile crossed Raython's face. "Say goodbye to your friend." She indicated Thorik, who was still shouting at Avanda to run away while covering his own eyes.

Avanda finally took heed of his words and bolted for Thorik, grabbing his hand on her way to camp.

The escape was short-lived as she was jolted backward, spinning Thorik around as he held her tight with both of his hands.

"You've looked upon my grace. You must pay the price."

Thorik held his eyes closed. "She's hideous, Avanda. You've failed her test, and now she will take you away."

"What test?"

"You saw what she wanted you to see, what you wanted to see, instead of what she really is, a repulsive, ill-looking creature."

"How would you know?"

"Her brother, Mr. Hempton, told me about her after I defeated him in his game and won our freedom."

"Theodore?" Raython shouted, scanning the forest for her brother. "Wicked is he who lies about me. He's the ugly one."

"No, it's you." Thorik opened his eyes and stared hard at Raython. He saw her as a hunched over beast with wart-covered skin, a long nose, bony arms, pointed ears, and crooked teeth.

"How dare you look upon me without my permission," Raython said. "Your eyes diminish my beauty. Like footsteps across a stone floor, every step you take wears at its luster. Who gave you the right to see me?" She lunged forward at him.

Thorik lifted a mirror, which he had taken out of Avanda's purse of magic, successfully stopping the Myth'Unday's attack. "Your brother did." Fortunately, Thorik had kept the purse after he took it from Avanda back at camp. He had recalled Avanda telling him about enchanting the mirror to only reflect the truth.

Raython looked at her reflection and screamed, seeing the same creature Thorik had envisioned. She backed away from the sight. "What have you done to me? You evil Num. You've made me hideous."

Stepping forward with the mirror held firmly in front of him, he worked his way closer to the Myth'Unday.

She finally released Avanda to cover her own eyes from the horror of her own reflection.

"Avanda, run back to camp. Get help while I hold her off," Thorik ordered.

Avanda eagerly ran off to alert the others of their danger and return with help.

"I had a mirror once," Raython cried from her own reflection.

"I know, your brother told me he broke it."

"Yes, that's what caused this abomination before you."

"You weren't always deformed?"

"No, not until that day. I once truly was the most beautiful life Ovlan had ever created. I admit that I let it go to my head. Especially after Theodore first gave me the mirror. I went insane with power over my own looks as I gazed at my reflection for years. The mirror and I became one and the same. And when my brother broke it, it took my looks with it."

"I'm sorry to hear that. But it sounds like he was trying to save you from yourself."

"Perhaps," she admitted. "But if only you could have seen me back then. Long silky black hair, perfect complexion, a soft Num-like nose, and bright purple eyes. I was amazing."

As she spoke, Thorik envisioned her body looking like it once had. Before he knew it, she was once again beautiful and amazing to behold.

Raython grinned. "And now, my dear Num, you are mine for failing the test."

☙ 18 ❧

THE GREAT ORACLE

Thorik hung from the branch like an icicle. The game had been lost, he had been captured, and his options were slim.

Raython danced in front of her prisoner, enjoying her victory, until she heard a noise from within the woods.

A tall, thin woman emerged from the trees and approached them. Her hair was made of golden wheat interlaced with long, thin, green grass, flowing down to her lower back. Her dress was a mixture of leaves and moss, and her silky white skin gave off a slight glow.

Raython turned and bowed toward the woman. "Ovlan, my lady. To what do I owe this greeting?"

Ovlan's walk was more of a glide, as her feet never disturbed the leaves she stepped on nor left a footprint in her wake. "What have you captured, my dear little Luchorpan?"

Rubbing her hands together, Raython turned her head to look back at the Num without ending her bow. "Dinner. He failed my test, so he's mine to eat."

"Indeed." Ovlan's voice was soft and airy, but was heard as though she were whispering into the Num's ear. "My children told me of one named Thorik who they met earlier today. Is this him?"

"I caught him without their help. He's mine. He will be a tasty meal for my starving body. I get so few outsiders."

"Not this one, my love. This one is special. My children have captured several men near the River-Green road. You may select any of those for yourself."

Disappointed, Raython knew better than to argue, so she nodded in agreement and rushed off into the forest.

Ovlan then approached Thorik and softly brushed a finger against his cheek. "I have been looking for the Polenum named Thorik Dain of Farbank." Ovlan's glossy dual-ringed eyes tightened their focus on the Num's eyes. "It's good to see you again. It has been a very long time."

Thorik's confines released without warning, dropping him to the beach. Confused, he looked at the woman before him. Her body flowed like water under a flawless, silky layer of nearly transparent skin. "Do I know you?"

Her smile was warm, like his mother's. So much so that it made him uncomfortable.

"Have we met?" Thorik asked.

"I have met you, but you have not met me."

"I think I would recall if I had seen you at some point."

Her smile continued. "You have done what I asked of you and risked so much for me. It is my turn to repay you."

"I haven't done anything for you," Thorik said.

"Not yet. But you will."

"I don't understand."

"What is it you need from me?" Ovlan asked. "Where are you traveling?"

"I'm traveling to Corrock to save a young man from being sacrificed. Darkmere, his son Lord Bredgin, and his Wraylov are hunting him. I need a way to fight them off and protect him."

"Ah, a weapon you seek. Perhaps the Spear of Rummon." She smiled with a distant look in her eyes. "Seems fitting to bring Rummon back into the land, and by you, of all people."

"I was thinking more of a sword or an axe. Something I can fight with to get in and out of Corrock. A spear seems so limited. I need something that will help me out a little more."

"No, Rummon will serve you well. It's the least he can do."

"He? The spear is a he?"

"Yes, he is the one who took the life of the one your people call the Mountain King. This would be a good opportunity for him to make amends with the Polenums."

"The Mountain King? You want to give me the spear that killed the Mountain King?"

"No, of course not. I'm only going to tell you where he is. It will be up to you to retrieve him."

"No! I don't want to wield the weapon that killed the greatest Num who ever lived. If I were to find it, I would destroy it."

"I don't think you would."

"Why?"

"Because Rummon has suffered enough. He wishes to help you on your journey."

"I would have to be insane to use such a weapon. Fir Brimmelle would never let me even carry it."

"Rummon agonizes the days away beneath the water-carved vats of boiling water and mud. He will remain imprisoned in the heart of the Carrion Mire until the end of time, unless you save him. He waits for you to revive him. He wishes to be strong again. He needs you to find him."

"I don't even know where the Carrion Mire is."

"Your companion does. Santorray will help you. But Rummon is destined to be yours."

"But we don't have time. We must catch up to Ericc before he tries to attack Darkmere. He'll be captured. He'll be sacrificed."

Ovlan gave him another gentle smile. "You may only choose one path. Do you wish to prevent him from being captured in Corrock or sacrificed in Surod? I do not foresee you being able to do both, and the latter cannot be accomplished without Rummon."

19

CHOOSING A PATH

"Absolutely not!" Santorray crossed his arms and spit on the ground between Thorik and himself. "We still have a chance to intercept Ericc before he reaches Corrock. Hunting down a weapon requires time we don't have."

Stepping forward onto the blothrud's saliva, Thorik rubbed his foot on the ground and accepted the challenge. "Ovlan said it was the only way to save him, so that is what we do."

Santorray flexed his muscles and let out a roar. "Dare you challenge me on this? I've risked my fingers and life for you, then you trust a stranger who claims to be the Great Oracle over my proven judgment? How do you know it wasn't another Myth'Unday trick? I would need to see her for myself."

"You can't. She's gone."

Brimmelle stepped up to be heard. "Thorik, we've had enough of your adventures. You promised to find Ericc and then bring us back to Farbank. Mother and I can't take much more of this. I'm with the Altered on this."

Thorik looked at his group, reading their faces in doubt about Thorik's story. "It was the oracle, Ovlan. I know it. I trust my instincts on this."

"How do you know for sure?" The booming voice of the giant Mognin came as a shock to Thorik.

"Grewen, don't you, of all people, believe me?"

A compassionate grin crossed the huge face of the mognin. "It's simply a question, not an accusation."

Thorik panned the group. "I think it's *more* than a question from the rest of you."

Walking over to her grandson, Gluic placed two black stones in his hand. "People say I also see things that aren't there. But we know better." She winked at him in approval and then thinned out the dead grass from her belt to make room for fresh foliage.

Her words didn't make him feel any better.

Grewen pulled a flaming log from the fire and began pressing it into the arch of his foot to relax his muscles. "To be honest, Thorik, we didn't see anything."

Thorik pointed at the youngest of the group. "Avanda did!"

Lowering her eyes, she shook her head. "I only saw Raython, and you turned her into a hideous creature with my magic mirror."

Gluic lifted up a thin crystal. "Ovlan's as lovely as the forest itself. I so miss her." By now, she had collected and was wearing at least one item of every plant type they had passed. Grass, flowers, leaves, and sticks were garnishing her hair or tied to a part of her body or clothes.

"Well, it doesn't matter what you saw," Thorik said to Avanda. "You must believe me. Our only option to prevent the sacrifice is to obtain the Spear of Rummon in the Carrion Mire."

Santorray shook his head. "In the Carrion Mire? It's the wrong way, which will cost us critical time."

"I don't care."

"Do you even know where it resides?" the blothrud asked.

"No. Ovlan said you would know."

"I do, but I refuse to tell you for your own safety."

"Santorray, if you're too afraid to travel there, then give me the directions we can go on without you."

"Fear has nothing to do with it. Certain death I can face, for a noble cause. Risking our lives for a weapon, when we should be catching up to Ericc, is a fool's journey."

"Allow me to be foolish. Tell me where it is, and you can be on your way."

"No. Even if it was truly Ovlan, her quests are usually more dangerous than they sound."

Gluic stepped behind the blothrud. Grasping her thin, long, clear crystal in one hand, she reached out and touched the side of his arm.

A fraction of a second passed as she saw his thoughts with the aid of the crystal. She viewed the trail he had used to travel into the mountains and the cliff wall he had climbed to the Carrion Mire. Seeing through his eyes, she looked out from the mountaintop and assessed his location.

But before the visions ended, the pendulum swung from past to future. Santorray raised his weapon and thrust it deep into Gluic's body. She watched herself fall to the ground; the blade had struck her heart.

The moment of contact with Santorray was over, and Gluic fell to the earth in much the way she had seen herself do in the vision.

"What did you do?" Brimmelle yelled at the blothrud. His fists prepared for an attack but were ignored by Santorray's focus on Gluic.

Thorik ran to his grandmother and cradled her head in one hand. "Granna, are you hurt?"

After a few breaths of recovery, she opened her eyes. Peering at the beast that still stood over her, she lifted her crystal to display it. "I know the way. We don't need your guidance."

The Fir's fists twirled around, ready for combat. "You heard her. Be gone."

Like a flash of lightning, Santorray reached down and scooped the crystal from her. "You obviously didn't see everything, old lady, otherwise you'd realize how dangerous it is."

"I've seen enough. Past. Future. The crystal carries more than you know."

Using his mighty strength, Santorray crushed the crystal into several pieces and threw them to the ground. "Don't ever play that game with me again."

Shocked, Gluic screamed as if she had just seen her own child die. Greenery fell from her body until she regained her composure.

"Enough!" Thorik was tired of the arguing, which was rushing toward physical violence. "Gluic, can you take me to this Carrion Mire?"

"Yes."

"Good. Are the rest of you coming with us?"

"If Mother is going, then I will not be left behind." Fir Brimmelle helped her up.

Avanda nodded her head in agreement, as though she had an option. Thorik and Brimmelle would have never allowed her to be left behind.

"I promised I would help protect Ericc from Darkmere," Grewen said.

Thorik's group all turned to see the blothrud's lips ride up and expose his teeth with anger.

Thorik accepted the snarl as a no. "Then we part paths here."

"I will go with you," Santorray growled.

"We can't trust him," Brimmelle said.

"Do you need him?" Gluic asked Thorik.

It was Gluic's words that concerned him the most. *What had she seen through the crystal?* Thorik thought as he turned to address the Blothrud. "Why? Why should we take you with us?"

"You'll never make it on your own."

"We've made it across this land without you."

"Not into Corrock to save Ericc and never through the Carrion Mire."

"Why the sudden change? Why do you want to join us?"

"Get this straight, Sec. It's not my passion to see that you survive. Ambrosius himself asked you to carry out this task. I owe the man and vow to pay it off by supporting his request."

Thorik looked at his grandmother for wisdom.

Picking up the crystal shards, Gluic spoke to each of them. "Not an ending, just a fresh beginning in a new form. We will be carried to a greater purpose."

Making his decision, Thorik made clear his rules. "Guide us, Santorray. As you have said, time is critical, so we must make haste. But understand that I lead this quest."

Santorray barked out commands, despite Thorik's words. "East to Swardfar. We'll gather provisions there for our trip into the mountains."

20

SWARDFAR

<hr>

Thorik's Log: 2ⁿᵈ day of the 5ᵗʰ month of the 650th year.

Ovlan suggested that I find a weapon to help me on our journey. It's off our planned path, but who am I to question the Great Oracle?

<hr>

Days had lapsed since they left the forest as Days had lapsed since they left the forest as Santorray led them just south of the mountain-sized humps of the Solann Ridges. Rounding Faralope Peak, the group descended toward the city of Swardfar. Greensbrook's easternmost city side-saddled the Lax River, which slowly weaved through the endless crops and pastures.

Freshly turned soil filled the air with sweet fragrances of the rich, dark red earth. Surrounded by tall wildflowers, fertile fields were plowed in unnatural patterns across the valley. Warm temperatures and afternoon showers kept the southern side of the Solann Mountains in a state of accelerated growth, perfect for the farmers' crops.

It had been an uneventful week of hiking over soft hills and around the Solann Mounds, which stood like gigantic toes out of the earth. Fruit-bearing trees littered the way, providing plenty to eat, even for Grewen.

Approaching the city from the north side of the river, they crossed a wide, sturdy bridge. A large open area presented itself on the south side of the river as the tall Dovenar Wall curved inward toward the city. The wall bordered all of the provinces to keep out the Altered Creatures and had a similar design throughout, but used different materials in its construction based on materials available.

Guards watched from above as two faralope-driven wagons headed out from the large gates. Supplies filled one of the wagons, while the second carried several noisy children. Their parents held the reins on each.

Gold nuggets and a single pinecone were dropped into the toll man's bucket by Gluic as the group reached the city. After pulling one nugget out to verify its authenticity, the toll man nodded to the guards above. They were uneasy about having a blothrud stride into their town; nevertheless, they approved the group. It was not illegal for Altereds to enter Greensbrook. The wall was there to prevent an invasion by an army of them.

Santorray ignored the looks and stares. Shoulders back and firm steps forward made it clear he was not to be disturbed by the locals, including any city law officials.

In spite of that, onlookers came from every door and window to behold the massive size of the Mognin and the evil-looking blothrud. A young boy poked his head out from under his mother's arm and waved at the Unday from his second-floor window.

Grewen waved back and smiled, scaring the mother, who quickly shut the window shutters.

Approaching a watering hole, a young girl carrying a large basket of flowers was startled by the odd group. The outsiders quickly surrounded her.

Santorray tossed a water bucket down the well. He quickly hauled it back up with fresh water, which he drank. Lowering it from his mouth, he noticed the entire community had come out to the large courtyard to watch them.

Santorray tossed the bucket back down the well. It seemed louder this time as it splashed into the water below. The inhabitants of Swardfar were ghostly quiet, making his actions very noticeable.

Pressing the back of her legs against the well wall, the flower girl tried to break the tension by holding up her basket of goods as a gift of peace.

"I don't mind if I do." Grewen reached down with his oversized two-thumbed hand, plucked the basket from her, and pitched it into his mouth. "Thank you. I'm famished. Salt-lilacs are one of my favorite flowers."

Screaming from the sight of the giant's enormous mouth crunching down on her basket, she ran from the group and raced down the street and around the corner, out of sight.

Santorray pulled the second bucket up but felt resistance when he lifted it to drink. Thorik was holding on to it.

"You've had some. It's Gluic and Avanda's turn," Thorik said.

The thought had not occurred to him. It had been so many years since he had had to work within a group that his natural response was to only look out for himself. Fighting his instincts to rip the bucket from the Num's hands, he shoved it slightly toward Thorik. "Go ahead; I've had my fill for now."

One by one, they quenched their thirst before passing it on. Grewen added a few handfuls of wheat from a nearby wagon load to satisfy his stomach's needs.

Locals hadn't spoken a word. Not a sound, aside from the shuffling of feet. The silence became eerie as they stood staring with their blank faces.

Eventually, a middle-aged woman approached from the main street, led by the young girl whose flowers were eaten by Grewen. The woman had a natural attractiveness about her without any frills or glamorous accessories. Her clothes were of earth tones, and mud from the fields had stained the ends of her dress.

"Welcome, travelers, I am Pawnel Fenwood. What is your business here?" she asked.

Thorik stepped forward. "I am Sec Thorik Dain of Farbank. We are just passing through. We wish to purchase provisions."

"We have none to sell you. Please be on your way."

"We require little. Surely you have some bread, blankets, and ropes."

"We have them, but have none for you."

Santorray growled at her, showing his distaste for her lack of hospitality.

Thorik showed no signs of anger. Instead, he was curious as to the reason. "Why? Have we done something to offend you?"

"War is approaching between Darkmere and the provinces remaining loyal to the kingdom. We wish to be left out of it and will not select a side, nor support those on either side, until the victor is known. We have seen many outsiders, such as yourselves, pass through here as of late, and we wish to avoid any relationships or transactions with any of you."

"You approve of whoever wins?"

"We are isolated from all others in our province and will see no support if we join their cause. It is better for us to stay distant and tend to our fields. Once it is all over, the conquering army will purchase our crops for their men. If we take sides and favor the losers, we could be destroyed."

"If Darkmere's army wins, they will take more than your crops. You'll become his slaves."

"Perhaps, but he will still need us to tend the fields. Little will change for us."

A loud, distant drumbeat hit hard twice before pausing, followed by a series of three beats.

The crowd screamed and ran in every direction. Total chaos had erupted from the deafening quiet as they ran for their houses, locking the doors behind them.

Pawnel sent the young girl home before turning back to Thorik. "What have you done? Who has tracked you down to our city?"

The distant silence was broken by a crashing of wood at the far entrance. Something was destroying the southern gate.

Pawnel turned and ran toward the sound before Thorik could answer.

Santorray stretched his chest and unsheathed his sabers. Spinning them a few times in his hands, he prepared for battle. A quick cut to his leg drew blood on purpose.

"What are you doing?" Thorik asked about the wound.

"I draw my own blood to show my enemy that I do not fear his attempt to injure me."

"No," Thorik said. "You're not here to fight anyone. This is exactly what Pawnel doesn't want to happen."

"I've evaded enough conflicts for you and your plans. I'm not going to run any longer."

"Santorray, you're neither a coward nor a fool. But let's at least find out what this threat is before we take aggressive measures against it."

"Agreed," Santorray said hesitantly.

"Grewen, find someplace for everyone to hide until we get back," Thorik ordered.

Grewen smiled as he looked around the open courtyard. "I'm a little big to play this game."

Thorik began running with Santorray toward the sound of destruction. "Be creative, Grewen. Come up with something."

Grewen looked at Avanda as he placed a large basket upside down on his head. "Can you still see me?" His shoulders shook as he laughed with Avanda.

Santorray and Thorik raced across the town, catching up to Pawnel as she entered the large southern marketplace. Just then, the south wall entrance exploded, ripping the mighty doors apart.

Entering the destroyed doorway, Lord Bredgin rode in on a large black panther. An intense burst of light shot out from the man's staff, as though he were looking through the walls of homes and businesses. Colors faded to a dull gray from his presence in all directions, and screams could be heard from the direction of his staff's light.

Thorik, Santorray, and Pawnel stood out of Bredgin's view, on the backside of the market.

Santorray growled. "Why is he here looking for us?"

Pawnel glared at Thorik. "I knew you brought us trouble."

Thorik pushed off her comment. "Or has he followed Ericc here? He may not know we're even here."

"True," Santorray said. "But if Bredgin is looking for Ericc, he's going to rip this town apart to find the boy, whether or not he is here. So, we're going to have to fight him eventually, and I refuse to run this time."

"There are no strangers in Swardfar aside from you," Pawnel said.

Bredgin stored his staff and then used his power over darkness and light as he entered the main street. He and everything around him were a shade of gray; no colors could be seen within twenty feet, including his own clothes or skin.

Reaching out with his left hand, he created darkness to encapsulate a surge of local guards running toward him. Absolute emptiness of light sucked the warmth out of the men as they stumbled over themselves to find their way. Coldness, fear, and depression rapidly set into all in the dismal dark.

Bright light sprang from his right palm, blinding all those who would look at it. Heat from the light could be felt from a block away, except in the dead zones of darkness.

Releasing one guard from the veil of darkness, Bredgin advanced. "Where is the son of Ambrosius? Where is Ericc Dovenar?"

The man shivered from his short time in the dark, and the light from the sun now made him squint. "I don't know of such a boy."

An intense light shot forth from Bredgin's hand, hitting the guard with such force that it knocked him backward as it burned his face.

Heat blisters covered his face and neck, cracking and oozing out pus as the man reached for them. He screamed in pain as his eyeballs exploded from the heat, and then he collapsed onto the dirt road.

Lord Bredgin pointed his palm at one of the taller buildings, releasing a focused light which ripped through its wall and started the structure on fire.

"Your attempt to hide the boy will only get you all killed," Lord Bredgin yelled to the people of Swardfar. "Hand him over. Now!"

Thorik thought about the challenge as he watched the destructive power of Darkmere's son. "I think I know how we can save your city."

"We refuse to get involved," Pawnel said.

"You're already involved," Thorik corrected before turning to address Santorray. "Go back to the northern courtyard entrance and make sure everyone is still in hiding until we need them."

"You expect me to hide?"

"No, I expect you to fight Lord Bredgin and prevent him from capturing Ericc, should my plans fail. Trust me on this."

With some hesitation, Santorray returned to the rest of the group.

"Follow me," Thorik said to Pawnel as he ran into one of the local shops.

As Thorik and Pawnel burst in to the closest shop, they found two families huddled together. Terror covered their faces as they had expected the attackers to rush in, but relaxed once they realized it wasn't them.

Pawnel kept away from the window and approached them. "It will be all right. Just stay down until it's over."

"He's not after us," Thorik explained to the locals. "He's after Ambrosius' son, Ericc. Do you know where he is? Have you seen him?"

Frightened, the locals shook their heads.

Meanwhile, Santorray returned to the north entrance to find the Nums vanished and Grewen stacking crates, wagons, and baskets around him to hide behind.

Grewen waved to the blothrud. "Will this do?"

"Pathetic," Santorray announced.

"Yeah, I'm not good at this game." Grewen looked at his temporary wall. "Where's Thorik?"

"The fool is trying to get rid of Lord Bredgin on his own. We need to prepare to attack Darkmere's successor when he enters the area."

"Attack? I'll help you restrain him, but I will not take part in a murder. Especially when we can walk out those gates and avoid the conflict in the first place."

"Listen, your friend Thorik has just put his life on the line to stop this man. Odds are he's already dead. Do we not at least owe it to him to slay his killer?"

"Revenge killing? Never." Grewen said. "I don't believe Thorik would put himself in such danger on purpose. But even if he did, he knows the risks. Plotting to murder his killer will not bring him back. It only makes us killers."

"This is what's wrong with you Ovs. You want justice, but you're never willing to fight for it."

"An eye for an eye?"

"Yes!"

"No!" Grewen replied. "It perpetuates the issue and gives each side more reasons to continue to advance the conflicts."

"Instead, you would cower down and be subservient to every threat that arises?"

"No, but defending oneself is a far stretch from plotting murder. Have you ever tried to use your mouth to solve an issue instead of your fists?"

"I find my fists have been very effective in resolving problems," Santorray said proudly. "Talking is fine if your enemy can be trusted. But in my travels, I have found many speak only to deceive you. Lord Bredgin is one of them. To bargain with him would be to reach inside a dragon's mouth on his promise not to bite down. His instinct forces him to chomp down on your arm."

"Quiet, you two." Thorik ran into the open area. "He'll be here any moment."

Grewen and Santorray looked over at the Num with surprise.

Thorik's hasty arm movements showed his concern over their hiding spaces. "Santorray, hide behind Grewen."

"Hide?"

"Yes! Or you'll ruin everything." Thorik pushed the massive blothrud behind Grewen's wall and then behind the Mognin. "Be still. Here he comes."

A deep cat growl preceded the sighting of the black panther in the courtyard. Longer than Grewen was tall, the cat ran smoothly into the area, ridden by his master.

The pace was fast. There was passion in Lord Bredgin's face as he bolted through the area, leaving a trail of death in his gray wake. Bricks crumbled, wood aged and cracked, and plants withered and died from the immediate exposure to his presence.

The wagons and baskets that made up Grewen's wall lost their strength and tumbled down as the panther raced by, exposing the giant. Nevertheless, the rider was too focused to even notice those that he killed, let alone those he passed by.

Out through the gates, over the bridge, and down the road sped the panther and Lord Bredgin.

Santorray exited the makeshift wall. "Why did he leave? Did he find Ericc and kill him?"

"Yes and no," Thorik answered.

"No games, Sec. Out with it."

"I ran from shop to shop, telling everyone that Lord Bredgin was after Ericc and that Ericc had recently been captured in Rumaldo by Lucian," Thorik explained. "After Bredgin gathered this story from multiple people, he believed it and headed out to Rumaldo."

"Clever," Grewen said.

"Lucky," Santorray added.

Thorik adjusted his backpack. "We're lucky he didn't destroy more than he did. What matters is that he's gone, which is what we need to be, so let's head out toward the Carrion Mire before we lose any more daylight."

Pawnel walked up behind him. "I believe you will need some provisions."

"Yes, but I do not wish to make you my enemy by forcing you to do business."

"You could have escaped out the north gates. This was not your problem. Instead, you stayed to help without causing a fight, while saving many lives. It is the least we can do for you. What do you require?"

DOR'AVELL RANGE

Dor'Avell's western range was sprinkled with small hot springs pouring from cracks in the steep mountainside. Mineral deposits stained the rocks below the flumes, painting artistic murals across a canvas a thousand feet high and tens of miles across.

The soft green hills of eastern Greensbrook clashed with the steep cliff face of the mountain range as though the land had suddenly broken free and lifted to a new level without any natural progression. Scattered chunks of the fractured cliff had fallen and embedded themselves into the soft soil below.

Venturing along the bottom of the natural divide, Thorik's party discovered ancient black marble walls leaning against the base of the cliff. They were from a lone building, long forgotten and damaged by several of the fallen rocks.

Santorray led them toward the roofless structure, and then stopped several yards shy of reaching it. "Closer to the cliff we are, the more in danger we are by falling boulders. We'll camp here for the night and climb in the morning."

Thorik set his pack on an empty statue base and began unpacking his cooking utensils. "How are we going to get beyond the cliff face?"

"Straight up."

"Not likely. It's too dangerous for Avanda. Gluic and Brimmelle don't have a chance."

"You asked me to take you to the Carrion Mire. It's up there. Your poor choice of traveling companions is not my issue."

"You joined us to help save Ericc. We come as a package. It's all of us or none of us."

Growling at the comment, Santorray hated taking the long way to do anything. "I'll see if I can find an easier path."

Brimmelle was breathing hard as he finished the last hill and reached the campsite. Watching the blothrud explore the wall for a way up, he threw his gear down. "There is no way I'm climbing up that cliff."

Santorray was nearing his breaking point. His patience with the constant complaining and issues of the Nums had been taxed. He knew if he reacted, he might not be able to stop himself from ripping someone's head off, so he grumbled to himself instead.

Finding a fallen boulder surrounded by the lush grass of the area, Gluic climbed up on top and began her daily ritual of sorting her stones and gems. Each stone would be set in the pattern one at a time after she spoke to it and listened for a response. Afterward, she would close her eyes and let nature speak to her.

Brimmelle sat down near Thorik's backpack to perform his daily reading of the Runestone Scrolls, despite not having the actual scrolls anymore. Thankfully, he had them memorized, so he began reading them out loud.

Santorray could not stand Brimmelle's monotone reading, which often went on for an hour or more. "Quiet. I'm not in the mood for your spiritual preaching."

"The preaching you refer to is the words of the Mountain King himself. They command respect," Brimmelle replied.

Santorray scoffed. "By who?"

"By all. If it weren't for him, you wouldn't be free."

"Not likely."

"Do you not know of the Mountain King War against the Notarians? He freed your species from slavery. By winning the war, he freed all species."

"Winning the war? No Num won the Sovereignty War!"

"The what?" Brimmelle questioned.

"The war where the Del'Unday rebelled against the Notarians and destroyed their civilization, freeing all slaves."

"Your facts are skewed. It was the Mountain King who freed them. A Polenum."

"Your people may have had their own leader at the time, but it was Ergrauth himself that led the war and defeated them."

"Sacrilege! How dare you disgrace the king and his actions with your false tales? Leave it to an Altered to decimate the truth for his own bidding."

"Are you calling me a liar?"

"Absolutely!"

Grewen walked over between them and said nothing, in hopes of calming the two down by simply separating them.

Santorray stepped to the side to see past the giant while addressing the Num. "Then how do you explain the fact that we won the war?"

"You didn't. We did."

"The Del'Unday ruled this land for thousands of years following the war. How do you call that a win for the Nums?"

"The Mountain King won the war by freeing the slaves. It was only after this that the Altereds assassinated our king and our people to take over the land. We fought for your freedom only to be cowardly back-stabbed by you Altereds."

Santorray bit his lip to draw blood as he prepared to do battle.

By this point Grewen was having difficulty holding Santorray back from reaching the Fir and ripping him apart. "I think this debate is over," Grewen said.

Thorik agreed with Grewen. "Brimmelle, can you help Avanda and I collect something to eat so Santorray can concentrate on tomorrow's travels?"

"I haven't finished my readings."

Thorik helped the Fir to his feet. "Yes, I know, but Avanda and I will be down the hill collecting berries and won't be able to hear you from up here. Please join us."

"Of course. I'm planning to read the Rune Scroll of Truth today. You should listen especially closely to this."

Down the hill the three Nums went, two picking berries and wild roots while listening to the third talk with little variation in his voice for nearly an hour. As always, his memory was perfect, but he lacked the ability to keep anyone's interest.

Grewen waited for the Nums to leave before approaching Santorray. "Why are you doing this?"

Santorray continued eyeing the cliff for an easier passage. "Doing what?"

"First of all, why did you save my life in the Coliseum last autumn?"

"Is that an Ov's best attempt at appreciation?"

Grewen realized his clumsiness at how he approached the subject and corrected himself. "Truth be said, truth be heard. You saved my life, and I am grateful."

"Accepted."

"It's not common for blothruds to have such valor."

"Who said anything about valor? I needed your help to escape, nothing more."

Grewen nodded, feeling that it was closer to the truth than Thorik's assumption of gallantry. "I'm glad I could be of assistance."

They both stood there eyeing the cliff as Grewen continued. "Although I find it odd that the blothrud we ran into in Woodlen ended up being the same one Thorik met in Southwind. Your travels are quite extensive."

"I could say the same for you."

"Stop the charade, Santorray. Why are you here? Why would a Del'Unday care about helping a human boy?"

"I told you. I owe Ambrosius and wish to pay him back by saving his son."

"A very honorable story. The kind that Thorik loves to hear. But I've met too many Del'Unday to believe this is just for your own inner peace of mind."

"Think what you wish. I don't owe you any explanations."

"No, but you will owe one to Thorik if you veer from the path you have told him. He's counting on you. He relies on you, and I will not stand by and let you hurt him. I don't trust you, Santorray."

"I never asked you to," the blothrud said before walking away.

❦ 22 ❦

SYMBOLS

A soft hum could be heard over the crackling of the campfire. The musical hum was light and airy with specific tones, carried over the heads of the band of adventurers as they slept through the night.

Thorik was awakened by the noise and quietly stood to search out the source. Grabbing his backpack, he reached inside for a candle as he walked toward the ruins nearby.

The melody changed often as Thorik entered what was once the entrance to the black marble building. A large piece of cliff lay in the center of the first room, reminding him why they chose not to sleep inside the remaining walls built against the unstable cliff.

Flickers of another light danced against a wall, originating from the next room. Cold to the touch, the wall was smooth under his fingers as he leaned around the corner to see beyond it.

An area of the marble floor had been cleared of dust, pebbles, and weeds by the careful hands of Gluic. Tracing engraved lines on the floor with her fingers to clean out the remaining dirt, she continued to hum her tune. "Powerful, isn't it?" she said without acknowledging that her grandson had arrived.

"What is this?"

Free of cracks and damage, the engraved floor symbol designs interlaced natural vine-like lines with hexagons as they filled a circle the width of Thorik's old shack in Farbank. The designs were those of the ancient Notarians, who had created many structures across the land before the Great Mountain King War.

"The power of your Runestones applies here."

"Granna, the stones I have are sacred to our beliefs, but they have no power. In fact, I'm not sure how important they really are. The more I learn about other cultures, the less it seems we really need the stones or the Mountain King's words."

"We need him right now more than ever before."

"But what if Santorray is right about Ergrauth freeing the slaves, instead of the Mountain King? They inherited the land after the war."

"True, and yet not."

"Who do I believe?"

"The Runestones."

"Why?"

"They are the wind, the water, and your body. They existed long before the Mountain King War and have much to tell us. They have the answers to everything."

"Yes, I know. The Runestone Scrolls tell us everything we need to know."

"No. Not the scrolls, the stones. Your Runestones."

"Gluic, you're asking me to believe something that I've never heard you even talk about. You've never attended Brimmelle's readings or tried to teach me the king's words."

"His words should be said and heard. They are good words, but both of these acts are short lived. Living up to them is what is important. Your Runestones go beyond our lives and touch all things."

"Why haven't you spoken of this before?"

"There is less time now than there was before."

"Less time? What do you mean?"

"You must learn to understand the runes."

"I know what they mean. Fir Brimmelle pounds them into me every day."

Gluic walked over, reached into his backpack, and pulled out the pouch of his Runestones. Grabbing one, she slapped it into his hand. "What is this?" she asked.

Thorik tried to move his hand out from under Gluic's hand so he could see the symbol, but she refused to let go. "I can't see the symbol."

"You don't need to."

"Yes, I do."

"Trace it with your fingers and your mind."

Thorik agreed to his grandmother's request and began moving his fingers around. Thousands of years of wear had diminished all sharp edges and nearly removed some of the ridges altogether. The symbol on the gem in the center categorized the meaning, but it was the ridges on the stone itself that defined its individuality.

Gluic tightened her grip on him by slapping her other hand below his and squeezing. "No, not so fast. Slowly. Close your eyes. Touch the pattern. Feel the stone's power."

Pausing only slightly, he slowly traced one of the raised lines on the stone. Once it came to an end, he moved on to the second one, and then to the third. "Is it the Runestone of Kindness?"

"Stop thinking what you have been taught and begin understanding what it really is."

"I don't—"

"Keep tracing," she interrupted. "Only think what the stone tells you."

He traced another line that eventually split into two. "How do I know which way to follow? Are there rules to observe? I'm pretty sure it's the Runestone of Kindness."

Covering his hands from above and below, she closed her eyes and waited for him to continue.

He tried time after time with no results. Guessing would only upset Gluic, so he refrained from doing so.

After an hour went by, he began to get sleepy, relaxing his eyes, his shoulders, and his mind. It was at this point that he jolted from a sensation within his palm. A flow of light, energy, and information flashed on and then off again. He couldn't recall any details of it. It was just a burst of something deeper than reality.

Thorik opened his eyes to see his grandmother standing at a distance, in the center of the floor circle, smiling at him. His palm was very warm as the Runestone of Kindness rested on it. "What just happened?"

"More than symbols of our faith, they explain the fabric of our world."

"Even though Uncle Brimmelle never believed them to be the true Mountain King Runestones, I've always held out hope that they were. Do you know for sure, Granna?"

"Yes, dear. The original E'rudite masters had them hidden for you to find, understand, and use."

"For me? How would ancient people know who I am? And how would they know we would find them?"

"Shhh, son, I have a lot to teach you in a short time. Focus on the stone. Trace the lines. Understand what it is."

"But—"

"Trace the pattern."

He did as he was told. Over and over again he tried until he once again relaxed, allowing the stone to control him. The gem in the center of the stone began to give off a slight glow.

Tingling crept into his fingers, across his palm and up his arm. Streams of energy flowed from the stone as though miniature tadpoles raced inside him, warming his body.

As the sensation reached his head, he felt light of weight. His vision blurred. His hearing went deaf. Cut off from all outside disturbances, Thorik no longer thought of himself as a Polenum. Instead, he was one with the air, the wind, and the sky. The out-of-body experience was more than he expected.

Dropping the Runestone, he crashed back to earth as his legs gave way.

Gluic kneeled beside him and held his overly warm hand. "What is this stone's true nature?"

"Air."

"Ah, good. That's one of the three we need. Get up so we can find the other two."

❧ 23 ❧

THE CLIMB

Time had been wasted on breakfast as the morning sun climbed into the sky. Bags were now packed, and it was time to venture to the Carrion Mire.

"I'm telling you, Thorik, there is only one way up, and that is to climb. I looked for other options, and there were none to be had. So, you either have your friends follow my lead up the cliff, or they can stay behind." Santorray placed a large coil of rope over each shoulder as he prepared for his ascent. "Of course, we could just forget this foolishness and head to Corrock. There may still be enough time to intercept Ericc."

Thorik pulled on his own backpack. "Why won't you at least try what we found? If it doesn't work, we'll try something else."

"Sec, you are trying to revive life into a Notarian device. This can only bring bad fortune to our journey. I will not allow the nature of luck to frown upon me by touching such a thing. I'm going to climb up to that first outcropping and secure a line for those who wish to join me. Test your theory and then start your climb. We don't want to get caught on the cliff face after dark." The blothrud began to scale the steep rock wall. "Alone this would not be easy, but with the older ones and the Ov it may not even be possible."

Thorik watched the agility of the blothrud as he made quick work of the first dozen yards. "Have it your way."

Santorray grasped the small, exposed notches of rocks with his feet and hands as he moved upward. Boiling water from underground springs flowed from small cracks along the way, scalding his skin when touched. Loose sections of rocks gave way and fell to the ground when bumped or grabbed. Soon, the first three hundred feet were behind him.

A thin segment peeled away from the rock face as the blothrud pulled his body up with it. He let go with his left hand and swung himself to the right, so that the rock missed his body and tumbled down to the green grassland below, embedding itself into the lush grass and soil.

Hanging by his one arm, he swung himself back to the left just as steam blasted out from where the thin rock had once rested. The scorching humid air hit him square in the chest.

His skin instantly blistered and turned brown as he swung again to the right. But the steam left a scorched trail across his chest and shoulder. Any closer to his face, and he could have lost his vision.

~

THORIK SETTLED the rest of the group down.

Grewen sat cross-legged in the center of the engraved circle, which Gluic had exposed the night before. He took up most of the space, so the Nums had to sit on the Mognin's legs or, in Avanda's case, on his shoulder.

Ralph stood outside the circle, lifting his body up and down as he hissed at Grewen. Opening his mouth, he took on an attack stance toward the giant.

Grewen finally got the hint and lowered one hand to allow the lizard to run up his arm and over to Avanda. Perching on her shoulder, he hissed at Grewen in a display of dominance, while Avanda laughed at her little friend's unwavering bravado, and his belief that he was as big as everyone else.

Brimmelle squirmed for the fifth time and adjusted the blanket he sat on to ensure a barrier existed between himself and the giant's leg. "This is foolishness, Thorik. How embarrassing this will be for you when nothing happens."

"I don't know that anything *will* happen, but I'm willing to give it a try."

"I don't see why we need to be part of this experiment. Seems foolish to put us at risk. Let the Altered go by himself to test it," Brimmelle said.

Gluic rested her stomach against the folds of Grewen's leg to lean over the mognin's knee as she instructed Thorik. "Now, recall what you did last night. Listen to them. Once you hear them and feel them, place them where they belong."

Thorik tightened his backpack and held three of his Runestones out before him. Selecting the top one, he closed his eyes and felt the energy within it. The flow through his fingertips was no longer unidirectional. He could feel energy traveling into his arm as well as out of his own body to the stone itself.

The gem in the center of his Runestone gave a slight glow, and the stone itself became hot to the touch. Holding it as long as he could, he finally set it firmly down into one of the carved hexagonal symbols within the floor.

He quickly repeated the sequence two more times as he walked around the group. Sitting inside the circle when he released the third and final one, he held onto Grewen's foot just in case something major occurred.

Silence followed.

Brimmelle continued to sit up straight on the giant's leg. "Like I told you before, they are Runestones, not some sort of magical rocks from Avanda's purse of disaster."

Avanda perked up at the idea, grabbing her purse of magical items. "Thorik, I can help."

"No!" the entire group said in chorus. She reluctantly put it away.

Ralph spun around on her shoulder as he hissed at all of them for shouting at her, until she finally stroked the back of his head to let him know it was okay.

Thorik watched the gems in the center of the stones continue to glow and pondered his options. Eventually he closed his eyes and touched the carvings in the floor to perform the same process he had done with his individual Runestones.

Gluic smiled and nodded. "Hold on tight."

Suddenly, the entire circle, on which they were seated, blasted up in the air. A column of marble, from under the engraved circle, raced toward the sky. The outer carved ridge of the circle itself was now the edge of the column's surface.

The force knocked Brimmelle backward into the center of the circle, with his head wedged under Grewen's loincloth. Avanda and Ralph shot off of Grewen's shoulder, landing on Brimmelle's stomach.

"Wheeee!" screamed Gluic as the speed and force prevented her from lifting her head to see just how high the marble column had lifted them.

The force had caught Thorik off guard as well. Slipping at the onset of the upward blast, his head and shoulders leaned over the edge of the increasingly tall column while his arms wrapped around Grewen's toe.

Unable to pull himself fully back onto the surface, he watched as their camp from last night shrank into the distance. Speeding past Santorray, Thorik had no time to react as he watched the blothrud nearly lose his footing at the sight.

Rocketing up the cliff, Grewen struggled to move his jaw to speak. "Thorik." His loud, deep voice was only faintly audible even to the Num's ears. "Will this stop on its own? Or will you need to do something?" he shouted over the rumbling of the column.

The thought never even occurred to the Num. Thorik pulled on the giant's toe with all of his might in an effort to lift himself back onto the platform. He was unsuccessful until Grewen pulled his foot in tighter. This dragged Thorik in, but wedged Brimmelle even deeper into a position he had been trying to get out of.

Thorik lay flat on his stomach and reached out to the carvings. Feeling the energy, he willed the column to slow down.

Nothing happened.

"Gluic, I need your help. It won't do as I tell it to."

Gluic enjoyed the ride, resting on the crease between the giant's calf and thigh, just over Thorik's position. "I won't always be there for you. You can figure it out."

"Granna, this is not the time to learn."

"It's the best time."

He tried again to order the stone to stop. It did not.

"It won't obey me," Thorik shouted.

"Who gave you the right to order it?" she said.

They were reaching the top of the cliff at a violent speed. Thorik knew his forcing of the column to stop wouldn't work, so he compelled himself to relax and allow the stones to draw out his calmness and slow down. It was only a theory, but he had to try something different.

Reaching out his palms to touch the ridges in the platform, he thought of slowing down, but the fierce speed continued as they came into view of the cliff's plateau.

Thorik had to forget about what was going on. He had to recall a time when he was extremely calm, a time when he was at peace.

A vision finally appeared in Thorik's head. He was floating in the waters near the city of Kingsfoot. Back when they had first left Farbank. Back when life seemed so much simpler.

Thorik's arms stretched out at his sides as he and his beloved Emilen relaxed in the warm spring lake. The water tingled against his skin as it healed his cuts and battle wounds. A layer of mist coming off the lake made him feel like he was floating among the clouds.

The vision then changed to Emilen and Thorik embracing. Holding each other, they peered up at the thousand-foot-tall Mountain King carving as they rested in the half-submerged tail fin of a dolphin statue. He was at peace. He was content. Pulling her in tight, he knew it would be one of the few times in his life he would feel this way. Thorik turned to kiss her.

Thorik realized they had come to a stop, and he suddenly snapped out of his daydream state. Opening his eyes, he quickly pushed himself away from Grewen's toe, which he had been cuddling. While wiping his lips, after being pressed against Grewen's skin, he noticed the giant's grin at the event.

"Toe fetish?" the giant joked.

The column had stopped adjacent to the top of the cliff, where a lifeless crust of land stood before them.

A muffled voice could be heard. The group looked about, wondering what it could be.

Thorik jumped off the monstrously tall column and onto the plateau. Still hearing the voice, he spun around. "It's not coming from out here. It's coming from the column."

Grewen helped Avanda and Gluic over to the cliff before pulling Brimmelle out from under him by his legs. "I thought that muffled voice was you." The giant's smile was large as he uncoiled his legs, hanging them both off the column's ledge.

Brimmelle hung upside down from Grewen's grip, furiously wiping his face. "Put me down, you filthy Altered."

Grewen complied and set him down in front of him.

The Fir straightened up his clothes before wiping his face again. "The smell. I'll never get it out of my nose. It's horrid."

"Watch it." Grewen warned Brimmelle of the dangerous location where he stood.

However, the Fir took it the wrong way. "No, you watch it. Don't ever touch me again." Brimmelle backed away from the giant as he talked to him, unknowingly closing in on the column's edge. "How dare you put me, the seventh Fir in my family line, into a position that makes me look like an…" His voice trailed off as he finally noticed that he was on top of a column's platform, which was now a thousand feet in the air. He had missed the entire trip.

The Fir's knees buckled and ached. Light-headed, he swayed. Nausea kicked in as he envisioned himself falling. Unbalanced, his arms flailed erratically, tipping him over the edge.

Brimmelle fell from the column.

He tumbled several feet before the giant's outstretched hand caught him. Despite the safe landing in the mognin's palm, Brimmelle's body went limp as if he had crashed into the camp below.

Grewen carried the shaking Fir onto the top of the cliff, toward Thorik. "Don't forget your stones, little man."

Thorik agreed, removed his backpack, and jumped back onto the column. "The risk is that, by removing them, the column may go down just as fast as it came up. Or perhaps it can't move at all without the Runestones in it."

Grewen set Brimmelle down so he could get his bearings. "Or you could leave them and avoid the risk entirely."

"I've left my Runestones once before, and I vowed never to do that again." Thorik leaped back across onto the column's sturdy platform. Slowly, he placed his fingers on the edges of one of his Runestones to pull it up. Tilting the stone slightly, he was able to get his other fingers behind it and pull it out of the carved inset. The light from the gem in the center immediately went out.

Crash! The thunderous noise echoed in their ears. Thorik dove for the cliff, landing and rolling to a stop at Grewen's feet. Looking up, he could see a confused look by the giant, who had his hands together in a clap of excitement. The noise had come from the giant, not the column.

"Sorry. I was pleased to see the first one come out so easily," Grewen said.

Thorik placed the Runestone in his pack and jumped back over to grab the rest. Reaching down to take the second one, he turned to watch Grewen, who had his hands tucked firmly at his sides.

The second and third Runestones came out without issue, and the Num jumped back to safety as Santorray climbed up to the surface of the plateau.

Hot, sweaty, and exhausted, the blothrud pulled himself up onto the ridge and sat back to observe the rest of the party.

Brimmelle fanned himself to cool off his dizziness and regain his composure. "Let's get out of this place, away from this cliff."

Panting from the hard climb, Santorray continued to rest. "You're going to wish you were someplace as peaceful as this ledge once we enter the Carrion Mire Valley."

"At least we will be down in a valley instead of up here in mountains."

Santorray pointed away from the cliff toward the passage leading between the mountains. "Around that bend is the base of the valley. We'll have to look for another way down on the far side of the valley."

"We'll just get back down the same way we came up," Brimmelle said while pointing toward the column.

The column, however, had been forgotten for a few minutes and, in the meantime, had already slowly lowered itself nearly fifty feet as it continued on its way back to the campsite.

Santorray grinned. "I think your luck just ran out."

❦ 24 ❦

CARRION MIRE

Terraced pools of clear, steaming water created a layered landscape of naturally formed pyramid-shaped mound, some leaned against the mountainside while others stood independently. Crystallized minerals acted as dams for each step down to the next tier as water flowed over the dam walls of each level.

Colors rich in reds, greens, yellows, or blues coated the bases of various pools. Some were stained with syrupy red mud, which oozed its way down the terraced hillsides like a long snake of oil.

Sulfur burned the Nums' sinuses and caused their eyes to tear up as they watched the boiling water vomit thick bursts of liquid from exposed holes. The area tasted of death but still felt alive in a primitive-earthly way.

This was the Carrion Mire, a valley with no plants or animals.

There had never been any valid reason for anyone to enter the valley. But here they were, Thorik leading his mismatched group of oddities into the bowels of Australis.

Santorray took in a deep, full breath and savored the flavor of the sulfur before releasing it. "During the third age, the Va'Del'Unday used to send their young men up here to test their courage and fortitude. Those few who returned had to show the mark of the beast to prove they had stood against her in battle."

"You never said anything about a beast." Thorik looked at the valley walls with concern.

"Would it have mattered?"

Stumbling on his response, Thorik realized that it wouldn't have. "No, but your tendency not to disclose everything you know until the last minute is less than desirable. What does the beast look like?"

"Its body is of stone, and it spits boiling water. A heart pulses liquid rock through its arteries. An attack by the beast will either crush you or burn you alive."

A slight rumbling of the ground preceded a rush of water from one of the ponds, shooting thirty yards into the air for nearly a minute before ending just as abruptly as it started. A shower of mineral water fell back to earth, some of it drifting toward the group.

The smell sickened Thorik, so he held his hand over his mouth and nose. "What would happen if they fought the beast without receiving a wound?"

Chuckling, the blothrud pulled out a small, thin carving knife. "There is no fighting the beast without her leaving her mark. The question is whether she will leave enough of you intact to survive." Cutting his palm with the blade, he tightened his fist, dripping blood into one of the pools of water.

"What are you doing?" Thorik asked.

"Let's get this over with."

"You're calling out the beast?" The Num's heart raced. "Are you insane?"

"She knows we're here. She's waiting for us to get farther into her lair, where we have no chance."

"With our back against that cliff, I think she has us at a disadvantage already. Surely, we can sneak in and collect the Spear of Rummon before alerting her."

"Are you oblivious to what I've been telling you? She knows we're here. The valley and the beast are one and the same. The blood I bait her with will cause her to react and make mistakes. It's her desire to taste blood that is her downfall. Given the time to plan, she will devour us all."

Thorik looked across the valley walls for a creature to appear. "Where will she strike from?"

"She is the valley. These pools are her stomach."

"We're inside her?"

"Yes."

"How does this help me find the Spear of Rummon?"

"Did Ovlan tell you where it would lay?"

"She said he was imprisoned in the heart of Carrion Mire."

"Then it is there that you must travel while I distract her." Santorray pointed to a crack in the distant valley wall. "Run to the cave of the Carrion's heart once she attacks. I will detain her as long as I can."

The valley launched its attack on Thorik and his team. Geysers erupted from dozens of spouts, filling the air with hot, steamy air. The ground shook violently and heaved up under the group's feet. Water in the nearby pools turned from clear to a dark red.

Thorik struggled to stay on his feet as the ground continued to shake, waiting for Santorray to give him the approval to run for the cave.

Without warning, the ground stopped moving as quickly as it had begun.

"Run!" Santorray yelled.

The Nums launched forward from their stance, running as hard as they could before the creature attacked with more force. Grewen quickly fell behind them as he heaved his heavy body forward.

The earth cracked below Santorray's feet, spraying up searing steam.

Jumping out of the way, the blothrud fell to the ground.

The crack opened further, exposing a deep gorge with a magma river flowing through it. Vents sprayed their hot water at Santorray, pushing him toward the gorge's edge.

Unable to withstand the pounding of intense pressure and heat, the blothrud jumped across the gorge, allowing the pressure to help him across.

The victory was short-lived, for the pools on the far side began to churn and swirl. As the gorge increased in width, the ground buckled and rolled in an effort to push him back in.

Santorray grabbed onto one of the tier walls for support, burning the flesh on his hand.

A wave of fiery water roared down the pyramid of tiers, crashing against Santorray's body, knocking him off his feet and into the gorge.

Thorik reached the cave entrance and turned to ensure the rest of his group would make it as well. He had held onto Brimmelle the entire way to keep the Fir's pace up.

Avanda followed quickly behind as she assisted Gluic. All four Nums turned and caught their breath from the long dash.

Grewen lumbered along as quickly as his wide mognin body would allow him. His heavy feet pounded the ground as he swayed his massive weight back and forth.

The Carrion Mire changed its focus from Santorray to Grewen as the ground rose and a wave of earth rushed behind him. As the rolling earth caught up to Grewen, the pools began firing blazing hot water at him.

However, Grewen never lost focus. If anything, mognins enjoyed the heat of fire and boiling water. What he avoided at all costs was jumping over open crevasses, like the one that began to open in front of him.

The new crack in the earth spanned the distance between the tiers of hot sulfur water, blocking his route to the cave.

Without missing a step, Grewen turned and stepped into a nearby water pyramid. Climbing up the terraced levels of boiling water, he was able to avoid the ground fissures.

However, the Carrion Mire fought back. A thick geyser forced its way up under the Mognin, nearly knocking him off balance. The rush of water was so wide that only Grewen's legs and arms could be seen as water shot in the air and against his body.

The ground shook and buckled as geysers erupted one after another.

Stepping out of the mighty geyser's stream, Grewen managed his way down off the lowest tier of the mineral pools and into the mountain's subterranean entrance. Entering the cave, the extensive heat could still be felt from his wet clothes.

"Are you hurt?" Thorik asked.

"No, but I'm cleaner than I've ever been."

Thorik studied the valley as it reacted to its defeat with a tantrum of spraying water and cracking earth. "Where's Santorray?"

Grewen looked back. "I don't see him. I'm sure he's safe. I have the feeling that he's been here before."

"Why do you say that?"

"He has the mark of a Va'Del'Unday. He took that ancient Del'Unday test at some point in his life. I wonder if it was to prove something to someone else or to himself."

"I hope he knows enough to stay alive," Thorik said.

Grewen turned to enter the cave. "I hope he knew enough to steer us in the right direction."

The wide cave before them was filled with a myriad of stalactites and stalagmites. The dripping sounds from thousands of points on the ceiling could be heard echoing from deep within.

Thorik lit a few torches and handed them out as they proceeded forward.

Hot air flowed across Thorik's face and out into the valley as they ventured inward. He headed toward the origin of the heat.

Following Thorik one step at a time, the group worked their way across the enormous underground room and then down a twisting side cavern. The floor was rough with a series of holes and jagged protrusions, making their travels difficult.

Rumbling and the crushing of rocks could be heard from the cave in front of them as the heat continued to increase.

Down deeper and around another corner, the cave eventually opened up to an enormous underground river of molten rock.

Near the shoreline, a large red boulder lay in the river. Unlike most of the rocks that had fallen, this one was glowing from the inside, and a low tone resonated from it.

A long crack in the ceiling opened, like a gigantic mouth, only to slam shut again. The intensity caused rocks to fall, some landing in the river, some along its banks. Each time the ceiling opened, Thorik could see the sky as well as part of the Carrion Mire's valley walls.

We're under the valley floor, Thorik thought before noticing Santorray. The blothrud had fallen into the mouth of the beast and had grabbed onto ceiling rocks to prevent his fall into the magma.

"Santorray!" Thorik shouted, pleased to see he was alive while fearing for his life as he precariously hung on.

The rumbling of lava as well as the boulder's low tone stopped immediately after Thorik yelled. The sudden silence of the cave made everyone freeze with caution.

Brimmelle had never seen a river of magma before, but he knew enough that its flow shouldn't be able to stop in mid-motion. "Thorik! Find the spear so we can leave this place."

"It's on the heart!" Santorray barked as he moved to another rock for a better grip. "Pull it out while I make my way down."

Large masses of lava pulled together and lifted from below, stretching up toward the magma shoreline like headless snakes. Each of the fire serpents acted independently as they moved toward the group.

Unsure what Santorray meant by the 'heart', Thorik ran past the glowing boulder to look at its other side. There, sticking out of its side, was a red metal spear.

Thorik estimated the distance from the magma shore to the spear and knew he couldn't reach it. Grewen was his only option to reach far enough. "Grewen, help me grab the spear. The rest of you can start heading back out the way we came in."

Brimmelle grabbed Avanda's and his mother's hands as they made their way back up the cavern. Tremors slowed their progress as they escaped the fiery serpents. As they raced around the stalagmites and stalactites, the ceiling fell; the jaws of the cave were attempting to bite into their meal.

A sharp point scraped across Brimmelle's shoulder blade, while Gluic became penned between floor and ceiling rocks. Avanda had ducked to safety and returned to help them once the ceiling lifted back up. But there wasn't much time, for another bite from the cave was already underway. This time Avanda's arm was pinched and Brimmelle was knocked to the ground.

Lifting and dropping of the ceiling continued as the Nums tried to prevent themselves from being crushed by the rock teeth.

As the next lifting of the ceiling occurred, Brimmelle brought the two women back into the large room with Thorik and Grewen. Fortunately for the three Nums, they hadn't made it very far up the cave before it had tried to chew on them. It had also helped that Nums were short. A human or blothrud wouldn't have been so lucky as to squeeze between the rocks.

"We can't escape that way," Brimmelle yelled to Thorik, who was dodging the striking blows of the lava snakes. "We're going to follow the cave deeper into the mountain."

The Fir led his flock of two past the shoreline and back into another cave, this one without teeth.

Grewen arrived at the shoreline and reached for the spear, but it was just too far to grasp. "I can't get to it."

Thorik dove to the ground and rolled to his feet, evading another blow from the living lava. "I recall you once saying that anything is possible."

One of the flaming liquid snakes struck Grewen from the side, sending him onto the rock floor. His clothes burst into flames, and he tried to put himself out with his large hands. "I didn't say it was impossible, but I'm not going to wade my way through lava to grab it." He lifted himself back to his feet. He could withstand a quick tap from the molten rock, but any more than that would surely do him in.

Thorik jumped away from another liquid snake. "Throw me over onto the stone. I'll remove the spear and jump back so you can catch me."

"I've proven that I don't have good aim." Grewen blocked an attack with his large forearm. He recalled his poor judgment when he threw the cannon at the bridge.

"I trust you." Thorik wanted to avoid another attack. "Hurry!"

Grewen grabbed Thorik and tossed him over onto the glowing red boulder. This time, he hit his mark.

Hot, but not scorching, the boulder vibrated under Thorik's feet.

Grabbing the spear with both hands, Thorik yanked the weapon out in one mighty pull, causing a violent reaction from the cave itself.

The entire underground shook hard. Ceiling rocks broke free, lava sprayed up into the air, and chaos erupted.

Thorik lost his footing and slipped to the side of the boulder, hanging onto the

Carrion Mire's heart with one hand while the other clenched tightly onto the spear. He could feel the steam from the magma burn his legs. He would surely roast to death if he did not quickly escape.

All of the masses of liquid rock merged into one larger serpent which attacked Grewen, driving him back, away from the shoreline.

Thorik was alone, hung onto the boulder in peril. The sweat on his palm lubricated his hold, causing him to slowly lose his grip.

Thorik's hand slipped off the boulder and he fell backward toward the raging lava. His mind raced on all the things he should have done as well as the people he would miss. It was during that fleeting moment that he realized how precious his life really was to him. *I'm not ready to die*, he thought as he fell.

"Not so fast, Sec." Santorray latched onto Thorik's arm.

Santorray had finally made his way down and landed on the heart of Carrion Mire to help Thorik with the spear.

Pulling the Num up into his arms, Santorray used his strong back legs to launch himself into the air and onto the rocky shoreline.

The large lava serpent blocked the cave exit as it thrashed around, knocking Grewen to the ground.

Once the mognin was out of the way, the flaming snake turned to attack Santorray and Thorik. Their skin wouldn't take the heat that the mognin's could. Even a close call would burn Thorik's fair skin.

The snake hovered above them for a second as it studied its next two victims. Liquid rock dripped off its massive body like sweat, splattering fire onto the ground. Then it lurched forward to hit them dead on.

Thorik jumped one way while Santorray leaped the other. Neither made it out of the way far enough to avoid the heat of the creature's strike.

Covering his head, Thorik waited for the flesh-blistering pain. Waiting with eyes closed, he realized it must have somehow missed him.

Thorik looked up to see the lava serpent frozen solid. Beyond the frozen appendage from the river, Avanda stood with her book and purse of magic. She had frozen the beast.

Standing up, Thorik realized she had also frozen Santorray, as the blothrud lay stiff on the ground.

Avanda shrugged her shoulders. "I'm getting better," she said to Ralph, who peered out of her side pouch.

Grewen lifted himself back to his feet. "You did just fine, little one." Picking Santorray up, he groaned from the blothrud's weight. "But he's going to have words with you when he thaws out."

They could hear the cracking of ice as they left the main cavern. The beast had defrosted its limb and was thrashing about in anger. Its inability to extend any farther from the magma river prevented the desired chase.

～

It was a long and arduous hike filled with waterfalls and angled passages. The cavern cooled off quickly as they distanced themselves from the heart of Carrion

Mire. By following the flow of water, they avoided becoming lost in the maze of underground passageways. Stopping often to rest, they made poor time. Even Brimmelle was too exhausted to complain.

The caverns led the group under the northern mountains of the Carrion Mire's valley and away from the cliff that Santorray had climbed. It was the right direction, but the mountains were wide.

Torches were at a premium, and they limited themselves to only one or two to be lit at a time, for they didn't know how long it would take to reach the surface. Although they were burning torn fragments of their clothes on the ends of the torches, they had nothing to light for a campfire. No tree roots existed this deep under the earth. Nevertheless, they stopped to rest without a fire. Everyone was cold and miserable.

Santorray continued to shiver as he thawed out from Avanda's spell. Grasping tightly onto one of the torches, he found himself holding the fire too closely in an effort to warm himself up more rapidly, scorching his skin. Hating the cold, the blothrud frequently gave a low growl directed at the young spellcaster, and would continue to do so until he was warmer.

She ignored his snarls and posturing, which only agitated him even more.

Gluic reached into Thorik's backpack and pulled out his sack of Runestones. "Remember when we were trying to find the right stones to raise the column?"

"Yes… and one of the stones we tried ended up glowing and giving off a lot of heat." Thorik reached into his sack and pulled out several Runestones before finding the one he wanted. It didn't come into play then, but it should now.

Holding the Runestone of Belief out in front of him with both hands, he traced the worn ridges on the top and stared deeply into the crystal in the center. The sensation started. A flow of energy exited the stone into Thorik's right hand, up his arm, through his body, and back out his left arm and hand before completing the circle into the stone.

The red crystal in the center started to glow as he held his thumbs on the two small blue gems near the sides. The light and heat increased and decreased as Thorik willed it to, as long as he kept his concentration focused.

Once he raised it to a temperature he no longer could hold onto, he set the Runestone down and backed away from it. To his relief, the glow and heat continued to radiate without his touch, much in the way the column stayed up after he removed the stones, before it eventually returned to its normal position.

Red light shone on the cave walls and warmed the group as they huddled in a circle. Every so often, Thorik would lean in and rejuvenate the Runestone's intensity by holding it firm and allowing himself to be at peace with the object. This lasted an hour or so each time.

Once warmed, Thorik inspected the Spear of Rummon. The tip had layers of razor-sharp points, like rows of teeth working down from the point of the shaft. Incredibly light for its size, the shaft was covered with tiny dragon scales. The base had a hole where a longer rod once existed to give the spear its full length. But, for a Num, the extension was not needed.

It felt warm to Thorik's touch, and he could feel his own heartbeat in his palms as he grasped the spear's shaft. If Rummon had killed the Mountain King, it gave off no sense of wishing to do the same to Thorik. In fact, it made the Num feel safe and secure when holding it. He hoped Ovlan was correct about him needing the weapon. He also hoped Brimmelle wouldn't find out that Rummon was the one who killed the Mountain King.

After the inspection, Thorik added loops onto his backpack to store his newfound weapon, for his hands needed to be free to climb through the caves.

Fortunately for the group, the caves eventually leveled out, and they made good time through the underground passages as they followed the water, hoping it would lead them out to the surface.

~

AFTER WALKING on and off for nearly three days, the cavern finally opened up onto the north face of the mountainside, which was filled with lush vegetation. They would eat well today.

Tired and dirty, they walked out into the hot sun. Several trees hid the mouth of the cave, and the shade helped ease the party's transition from the cool, dark underground.

Grewen's arms were still black from the scorch marks received by defending himself against the lava creature. Some injuries were too deep to ever totally heal.

Burn marks and heat blisters scarred parts of Thorik's body as well, especially on his lower legs from when he held himself over the lava after grabbing the spear. He only hoped the spear was worth the effort and pain. "We made it," Thorik sighed as he blocked the sun to allow his eyes to adjust.

Santorray had fully thawed out by the time they saw the light of the sun but still shivered from the experience of being frozen alive by Avanda's spell. "We're out of the Carrion Mire. But we still need to travel through the Kiri Desert and O'Sid Fields before we reach Corrock. We also need to cross River's Edge during our travels."

"River's Edge?" Thorik gasped. "No, I do not wish to see that place again. The dead continue to roam the waters. Can't we go around?"

"No other option. Eastlanders kill Unday on sight, and Ovs won't let Dels through their land. River's Edge is our only path."

$\maltese$ 25 $\maltese$

CROSSING RIVER'S EDGE

Thorik led his party down the north face of the mountains, across a large, soft-hilly valley, and into the southern Kiri Desert. Dry grass terrain mixed with patches of small trees, shrubs, and cacti. Herds of horned estoos grazed on the foliage. Eventually, the Dovenar Wall bordering the River's Edge Province was in view.

At each campsite, Gluic had performed her healing rituals with her stones, making sure Thorik joined in and learned her techniques. Burn marks on Thorik and Grewen were still discolored, but they were less sensitive to the touch after each treatment.

As usual, Thorik logged the prior day's events before leaving camp. New species of animals and plants had been recorded, along with unique terrain. Thorik didn't want to forget anything, for he had grand plans of telling his students in Farbank about everything they had encountered. He tucked all of his notes into his scratched-up wooden coffer before placing his supplies in his backpack. Or at least what was left of his backpack.

Thorik gave a slight chuckle when he gazed at the sad pieces of fabric holding his pack together. It was once so clean and sturdy. *We've been through a lot*, he mused.

Much of the vegetation attached to Gluic was wilting quickly, and she spent time each day gardening and weeding her findings.

Pulling a handful of govi-weed out of the ground, Grewen tossed it into his large mouth as he squinted his eyes. "What's that?"

Turning to the west, the Nums could see a cloud of dust rising from the desert floor.

"Could be another herd, or a chuttlebeast," Thorik said.

Grewen tried to determine what could be making the dust. "I've never seen chuttles on the south side of River's Edge."

"Troop movement," Santorray said. "We need to reach the Dovenar Wall before they block our path."

Brimmelle sighed at the thought of another foot race. "Let's wait here for them to pass us by, and then we can go on our way afterward.

"If we've seen them, then odds are they've already seen us," Santorray said.

"Faralopes can only run for a few hours. They must then rest for an equal period of time," Grewen informed Brimmelle. "If what we see is Lucian's army, then they are in a short race for something important. With Eastland still far to our east, my wager is on us."

"Enough talk," the blothrud said. "Head out, now."

With a slight slope to their advantage, the group moved quickly toward the distant Dovenar Wall surrounding River's Edge. Each hill they crested provided a better view of what was heading their way. Santorray had been correct; it was the Southwind army, banners high and Lucian out in front.

Soft hills gave way to tan-colored sand dunes, slowing everyone's movement except Grewen, who quietly enjoyed the hot sand between his toes.

It wasn't long before Lucian and his thirty-four military escorts were nearly within firing range. Their steeds moved comfortably in the loose sand.

Reaching the twenty-foot tall Dovenar Wall, on the south side of the province, was both a bad and good thing for Thorik and his group. As it stood, it blocked their path until they could climb over it. But once they were on the far side, they had a better chance of escaping. With Lucian and his men approaching quickly on their faralopes, there wasn't time to plan.

Santorray and Grewen began tossing the Nums up onto the top of the wall, one by one. Despite Brimmelle's objection, he also was tossed by Santorray.

Racing up the dune toward the Mognin and blothrud, several Southwind servicemen removed their swords from their sheaths. Others loaded bows.

Brimmelle helped his mother down the steps on the far side of the wall while Avanda already stood at the bottom, waiting for them. "Don't give me that look, young lady. Get in that water and start making your way across," Brimmelle ordered the youth.

Holding her elbows, Avanda shook her head. "I'm not getting in that water." Her memory of the attack last time in River's Edge added to her prior fear of the water.

Bracing his right shoulder blade against the Dovenar Wall, Santorray squatted to extend his knee out to Grewen. "Climb up. Use me as your ladder."

The Mognin recalled how long it took him to pull his body up to the top last time he had scaled the wall. "We don't have enough time. I'll help you over," Grewen replied.

Looking at the quickly approaching attackers, he knew they didn't have the luxury of time to get Grewen up and over. "You sure?"

"Yes. All I ask is that you take care of those Nums."

Santorray stepped into the mognin's cupped hands and was lifted high enough to climb the wall. "I'll do what I can."

"Thorik trusts you, Santorray. They are good people. Don't let him down." Grewen pushed up the blothrud's leg to help him with his ascent.

"We can't leave without Grewen," Thorik shouted from the top of the wall. "They'll throw him into the mines."

Santorray finished his climb and stood up. Grabbing Thorik by the arm, he spun the Num around. "He's made his choice. The right choice. Hopefully, it will delay them long enough to get us out of arrow range before they scale the wall." Avoiding oncoming arrows, the blothrud scooped up Thorik and jumped off the wall into the flooded province.

The river valley was covered with water from wall to wall, and small islands were sporadically exposed. The water was shallow near the Dovenar Wall, and Santorray's feet drove deep into the mud beneath it. Dropping Thorik, the beast leaned back against the wall to free his legs.

Lucian's men raced to the wall and surrounded Grewen. There was nowhere to hide. It was a long walk for the mognin in either direction, and their swords would take him down long before then. There was no stepping into the Mythical Forest for protection.

"No escape this time, Ov," Lucian said. "Tie him up. The rest of you get up on that wall and capture his friends."

On the far side of the wall, Avanda hesitated for a moment before stepping off the final staircase riser into the water. Their last encounter with River's Edge was a terrifying attack by undead skeletons. It had taken place far to the west in deeper waters, but the memory still struck her with fear.

Gluic jumped in, followed by Brimmelle. The muddy water was only up to their ankles, but the soft mud made them sink deeper whenever they stood still.

After pulling his legs out of the thick mud, Santorray ran north, toward the far wall, only to turn around and see the fear in the Avanda's eyes. "Hurry, it won't be safe here for long." As the words left his mouth, he noticed one of the first soldiers work his way up onto the wall. Pointing at the man, the blothrud shouted, "Get out of there, now!"

Avanda saw the man gather his bearings and load his first arrow. She didn't have to be told again. Launching from the bottom step and racing across the mud, she quickly passed Brimmelle.

The first arrow whistled by Brimmelle's head as he struggled to keep up with the rest. He soon caught back up to Avanda, who had stopped to dig in her purse of magic. Grabbing her by the shoulders, he pushed the girl to keep her running.

Perching on Avanda's shoulder, Ralph hissed at the Southwind soldiers and pumped his body up and down, attempting to scare them off.

Thorik held onto Gluic's hand and was nearly dragging her across the thick muck.

Another arrow landed near them, and then another. Several men had scaled the wall and were adding to the firepower. Others, including Lucian, had made it over the wall and were now in a foot race with the Nums. Neither seemed to have the advantage as they sloshed their way across the sunken field.

Nearing the center of the mile-wide province, Thorik knew the deepest point of the original river would be just ahead, and they would have to swim across. But that wouldn't be an issue if they didn't even make it that far.

Brimmelle and Gluic couldn't keep up the pace, and the Southwind troops quickly closed the gap.

Brimmelle stopped to catch his breath, bending over and resting his hands on his knees. His feet continued to sink in the thick mud as he stood still.

"No, don't stop." Thorik raced back to help him continue their escape. But by the time he got the Fir moving again, it was too late.

Over a dozen troops had arrived and began creating a circle around the Nums.

Santorray stopped his run and looked back to ponder his options. He could still go across the river to freedom and have the potential to reach Ericc, or he could return to fight the Southwind guards with a chance of losing everything. "I'd rather fight than run, any day." Pulling out his sabers, he cut his shoulder to draw his blood to show his courage before charging at the group with the roar of a battle cry.

Additional troops arrived and created a firing line for the oncoming beast.

Lucian was not going to allow Santorray a chance to get too close. "Fire!"

Arrows flew at the beast, on target and ready to pierce the blothrud's chest and face. Santorray fell and crashed deep into the mud just before the arrows hit. However, it was not by design; something had grabbed his legs and tripped him.

Reloading their bows, the troops watched the blothrud violently swing his sabers at the mud. Rolling to the side, he stood up, only to trip and fall again. It was as though he was fighting the mud itself.

Cautiously moving forward, the archers prepared to fire if this was some type of trick. Unfortunately, they learned too late that it wasn't.

Skeletal hands reached out of the mud and grabbed the feet of the approaching archers. Surprised, they released their arrows, firing them in every direction as the men tumbled into the mud.

The group surrounding the Nums also felt the mud move beneath them. The Nums did as well. They felt fingers raking the sides of their boots. Half-fleshy faces appeared out of the mud before sinking under again.

One by one, the troops were pulled into the mud. Some fell forward, some back, and others straight down into the murky water.

Lucian made a dash back for the south wall they had climbed over. Muddy hands swiping at his feet struck several times but never hit hard enough to trip him. He could see the water churn behind him as what looked to be several of these unseen creatures raced after him.

Looking forward toward the wall, he could see a dozen more blocking his path. There was no way to escape, so he changed his direction in an effort to reach one of the lone islands.

The water churned on both sides of Lucian as he raced for a pocket of dry land. A grabbing of his boot caused him to fall forward into the mud, just shy of the island. A second bony hand reached out and grabbed his shirt. Rolling out of his garment, he crawled up onto the dry, hard dirt and collapsed.

The Nums had their own problems. They were also being attacked and would have to save themselves, seeing that Santorray was struggling with a dozen of his own mud-covered skeletons.

A semi-fleshy hand and arm reached up and grabbed Avanda's leg. She screamed and attempted to pull away.

Ralph leapt off her shoulder and onto the attacking arm. He spit on its bony wrist, causing the arm to break away as the acid from the saliva did its work.

Avanda called out a spell from her book as she pinched a powder from her purse. Despite her inability to focus while under siege, the spell activated and dried up the water in the area she stood. Mud, which covered the skulls and bony arms, became instantly dry, causing them to retreat for the moment.

Unfortunately, the moment wasn't long, for the dry area quickly filled back in with water, rejuvenating the watery attackers with more force than before. Reaching up, several grabbed her hard, pulling her entire body under water, along with Ralph.

The Nums and the soldiers screamed as they all were being pulled into watery graves.

Santorray's sabers broke bones, but the thick mud slowed his swing and minimized the damage he was able to inflict.

Grabbing his spear, Thorik thrust the weapon straight down, stabbing one of the skeletal arms holding Avanda under water. Shaking from the strike, the skeleton's arm instantly turned to ashes. A deep rumble followed the attack, and a shock wave of sound and water spread out from the spear, knocking over anyone who had been standing. Thorik was the only one able to remain on his legs, keeping his balance by holding onto the spear itself.

Vibrations resonated from the weapon and through Thorik's body. A deep undertone of a heartbeat pounded against the Num's chest. Each pulsation worked deeper into his body, toward his heart, until they both hit the same rhythm.

Heavy strokes of his heart flushed his skin with heated blood, causing the water around his feet to stir and boil. The dead-risen people of River's Edge sunk away from him.

The event was localized, and the rest of his group continued to struggle.

After he pulled the spear from the mud and water, the dead proceeded to move in again.

"Back!" Thorik stuck the first few inches of his weapon into the water.

The enemy retreated, this time farther away.

Keeping the tip of the spear in the water, Thorik helped Avanda from the muck and up onto her feet. She was covered with mud and scratches, but her concern was with finding Ralph.

Claws tight into her leather boot, Ralph hissed at the fleeing undead, protecting his friend.

Thorik didn't understand why the skeletons were afraid of the Spear of Rummon, although at this point he didn't care as long as it continued.

Holding Avanda tight, Thorik worked his way to Brimmelle. The Fir had been on his hands and knees, trying to prevent his face from being pummeled. Miraculously, his attackers retreated the moment his Sec arrived.

Fir Brimmelle grabbed onto Thorik's arm, using it to lift himself to his feet. "What took you so long? I was nearly killed. Where's mother?"

Screams from the Southwind army continued as the Nums searched for her, but she was nowhere in sight.

Cupping his hands, Brimmelle screamed for his mother.

No response.

"Come on." Thorik turned and began running to save Santorray, keeping the spear's point in the water.

Brimmelle stood his ground. Searching for his mother was his top priority. However, the water near him began to churn and proceed directly toward him. Backpedaling at first, he turned to keep up with Thorik and Avanda and the safety of the spear.

The blothrud had over a dozen of the partially flesh-covered undead attacking him. Some had pulled him into the mud up to his hips; others had clung to him as he thrashed about.

Two partial skeletons flew past Thorik, nearly hitting the Fir. Santorray was peeling them off and tossing them as fast as they advanced.

Nearing the blothrud, Thorik drove the spear through the water and into the mud. "Be gone!"

A wave of force rammed his enemy, blowing them off Santorray and causing the undead from under the water to disappear.

Relieved of his attackers, Santorray took a quick head-count and realized Gluic was not with them. "Only one casualty. It could have been worse. Move out."

Brimmelle was furious at the notion. "Casualty? We're not going anywhere without my mother."

"There's no way she could have survived. Skilled soldiers can't survive these things. Your decrepit old Num didn't have a chance."

"She's very resourceful," Thorik said. "Besides, we've already lost Grewen, I'm not letting go of Gluic as well."

Santorray pointed to the muddy battlefield. "There are only a few people visible above the surface, and even those are so covered with the walking dead that it's impossible to tell which one is her."

Thorik pushed through the mud back toward where the initial attack occurred, still angry about leaving members of his party behind. The rest of his group had no choice but to follow him if they wished to stay within the spear's circle of safety.

Racing to the first pile of undead, the spear did its job by making the unwanted crowd scatter into the mud. What remained was the ripped open back of a Southwind soldier. His ribs were broken and his internal organs were exposed.

Santorray used the gruesome sight to make his point. "Finding Gluic may not be a wise idea. You don't want your last memory of her to be something like this. We've lost one. We could have lost more."

Thorik ignored him and moved on to the next, only to find this one without a head or arms.

One group of fleshy skeletons still stood above the surface. These last ones, however, stood silently in a circle.

When Thorik ran to meet them head on, they turned to block and defend what stood behind them. Thorik charged forward, placing the spear in both hands, ready to strike. His friends raced behind him.

As he reached his attackers, Gluic stepped out from between them.

Thorik pulled the spear quickly to the left and up in the air to avoid stabbing her in the stomach. The move cost him his balance, and he tumbled into the water, splashing with the full force of his body.

The undead scattered from the near proximity of the Spear.

Tears covered Gluic's face. "So sad, their story."

Avanda jumped forward and hugged her.

Brimmelle was less than impressed. "Mother, do you realize what you put us through?

Gluic ignored him as she addressed Avanda. "So many in endless suffering. They just want to be released."

Pulling himself back to his feet, Thorik was somehow not overly surprised that she would have a group discussion with the dead. "Unfortunate as it is, we can't help them."

"I know. I told them we couldn't help them today, but that you would be back."

"I will?"

"You're not going to let them continue to suffer, are you? How can you live with that?"

"I don't have the power to unravel ancient Alchemist magic."

"I know, dear. That's why I told them it wouldn't be today."

As usual, Santorray was tired of Gluic's conversation. "We must travel north with haste," he said to get everyone moving.

Thorik turned back to the south wall and then glanced down at his spear. "Maybe we can still save Grewen."

Archers stood on the wall waiting for the opportunity to get the Nums back in range. The chances of running through the thick mud and reaching the wall before being killed were slim to none.

Santorray scoffed at the foolish notion. "Not even a dozen blothruds would hold up against them. They have the advantage. The high ground, arrows, and plenty of time. We have no shelter from their attacks nor speed in our advancement."

Thorik held his weapon firm. "I don't care. I have the Spear of Rummon. It has to count for something."

"Excellent plan. Leave your family here to be killed by the skeletons while you attack," the Blothrud said sarcastically.

"I'll take them with me."

"Your weapon may scare away the undead, but how will it protect us from arrows?"

Thorik was becoming frustrated as he heard the logical argument. "I don't know."

"No one wants to leave one of their men in battle, but no good will come from your plan."

"I can't just allow him to be captured and tortured because of things I've done."

"He made a choice. Accept it."

"So did I with Ambrosius, and I still regret it."

Spitting in his palm, Santorray held it out to Thorik. "I'll make a pact with you, Sec. I will help you save Grewen after we find Ericc, as long as you give up on trying to save him right now and accept that he made this choice for all of us to succeed."

Thorik spit in his own palm, trying to conform to the blothrud's ritual, and shook his large hand. "Agreed. I trust you, Santorray."

Turning, the entire party headed north across the river. Everyone clung onto Santorray as he treaded the deepest sections, and Thorik kept his spear poised for any potential attacks.

Fortunately, none occurred.

❧ 26 ☙

O'SID FIELDS

———

Thorik's Log: 1st day of the 6th month of the 650th year.

We've made it past the dunes of the Kiri Desert and across River's Edge, but we have lost Grewen in doing so. My heart and prayers hope that he stays alive until I can return to rescue him.

———

Spring had made its presence known as the sun warmed the southern O'Sid Fields, turning the winter's green grasslands and rolling hills into golden brown grass that crunched when stepped on. Tall trees with long, thin leaves shaded small pieces of the open plains.

Flocks of traccu birds perched in isolated trees, watching for field mice and other rodents. Their sky-blue color made the trees appear to be bearing fruit.

Prides of tigras and packs of beardogs were often seen resting in the shade of the trees when they weren't hunting the local macrauchenia or other grass-feeders.

Herds of chuttlebeasts could be seen roaming the land, devouring anything dead or alive, as the small koa birds picked ticks and other insects off their backs. Spooked easily, the herds would stir up a spiral of twisted wind and dust which was sometimes as high as the Lu'Tythis Tower.

With most of her decorative plants dead, Gluic began replacing them with feathers of local birds. It wasn't long before they were in her hair and shoes, and around her neck and wrists.

Santorray watched from the top of a hill as a distant herd split in two, just before the group walked down into the next small valley. "Keep your eyes on the herds. Always assume chuttles are ready to attack. They change direction without warning. Never let your guard down. They are a powerful Fesh."

Lips dry, skin burnt from the sun, and eyes sore from squinting from the glare, the Nums had little interest in the distant chuttles. They didn't even acknowledge the advice.

Thorik walked up front with Santorray. "Santorray, I have to ask you, what exactly is the prophecy of Ambrosius' son?"

"Ambrosius' son will slay Darkmere's son if he is not sacrificed on the Eve of Light."

"Yes, I know that part, but there has to be more to it."

"It was foreseen by the Dark Oracle, Deleth. It was then told to his student, Darkmere, who has lived with the threat over his son all his life."

"When we were on the captain's ship, did you say you had something to do with the prophecy?"

Santorray glared down at the Num. "The Nectar of Irr affected your hearing."

"It's possible. I don't recall a lot from that night," Thorik said with a laugh. "So Darkmere has been hunting down Ericc since he was born. What a terrible life for him."

"If it was so terrible, why did Ericc leave his safe haven?"

"Valid question. But what I don't understand is why he needs to be sacrificed at a specific time and place?"

"The Eve of Light is a sacred time. It only lasts for a few moments on one day of the year, when the sun finally reaches high enough in the sky to cast light over the Shi'Pel Peaks and onto the Surod Temple."

"Again, why sacrifice Ericc? And why does it need to be at a specific temple on that day?"

"Do you know nothing about Surod?"

"No, I don't," Thorik said honestly.

"How have you Nums survived with such little knowledge?" It was a rhetorical question, which he knew Thorik would try to answer if he gave him time, so he didn't. "Surod is the birthplace of all species. The Notarians forged the first of each of our kind in that temple on that day, during that small window of time. It is a gateway to life beyond the Fesh. It is a portal to the souls we carry inside us. Without this temple, all creations by the Notarians would have been mindless beasts reacting instinctively to their environment instead of having free will to create something more."

"Rubbish!" Brimmelle announced from behind them, displaying the soul-markings on his arm. "Nums are the only ones who have souls. Each unique. Each given by the Mountain King to give us purpose. Altereds may have the ability to crudely communicate, but they don't have souls."

Santorray glanced over at Thorik. "Perhaps not everyone received the full level of soul and thought that was provided."

Thorik grinned before returning to the topic. "I now understand about the emotional tie to Surod for embedding souls into new species. But what does that have to do with Ericc?"

"It's an opening for souls to pass through, regardless which way they travel.

When the Notarians created a new species it was void of any soul, so one would flow into it. Sacrificing someone with a soul at the Eve of Light allows the soul to pass back to the beyond, never to return."

"Isn't killing him enough?"

"No, you can kill a man's body and leave his soul aloft You know not where it will revive itself, whose new child will be taken over with it, whose ailing body it can capture, or where it may linger and haunt. To kill someone as powerful as an E'rudite you must make sure you do it correctly."

"Ericc's not an E'rudite…is he?"

"He has the lineage, so he has the potential. The question is if he knows his powers."

Reaching the top of the hill, the group stopped. The herds they had seen before had split up and now were collected into several smaller groups which encircled the hill where the party now stood on.

Chuttlebeasts always became chaotic this time of year. Shedding of their thick wool left trails of coarse, dark brown fiber across the fields, which prompted their mating season. In addition, they were getting anxious to migrate north before the summer heat swept the plains.

Aside from narrow gaps between the gatherings, Thorik's party didn't see any other options available to leave the hilltop.

"We should wait them out," Brimmelle suggested.

Santorray looked up at the sun as sweat poured down his body. "No shade, little water, and the Nums' sensitive skin do not bode well for your plan. It could be hours or even days before they move on."

Thorik pointed toward the largest of the gaps between herds. "Chuttles can't see well. If we quietly and calmly walk in the larger openings, we could make it without them knowing we were here."

"Have you smelled one up close?"

"Yes, so let's not get too friendly."

"Agreed."

The group moved lightly down the hill into the next shallow valley. Dry grass cracked under their feet, causing them to move at an extremely slow pace to minimize the sound.

As they entered the passage between the herds, the ceaseless shifting of beasts continuously reshaped their path. Snouts blew and hooves scratched the ground when the beasts sensed something amiss.

Covering their faces with their clothing didn't stop the stench from the chuttles, which burned the group's eyes, noses, and throats. Tolerable for a short period of time, it wouldn't be long before the headaches would begin, leading to fainting. It was fortunate that they still had distance enough not to smell them up close.

Halfway through, the passage closed completely, merging the two herds into one.

The travelers stopped, signaled by Thorik, who then pointed for them to return the way they came. But they weren't more than a few steps back before their retreat was closed off as well. They were trapped.

Each member looked around for options, afraid to speak since it could alert the chuttles. The smell was getting worse as the chuttles closed in on them. Headaches began to affect them, followed by dizziness.

Thorik had fallen to his hands and knees as he watched Gluic pass out, followed by Brimmelle and Avanda. Santorray was down to one knee, swaying, ready to slap his upper body hard against the ground. Thorik had to try something. He was willing to try anything.

Jumping out of Avanda's side bag, Ralph ran up on her shoulder. Mouth wide open, he turned his body around in a circle, hissing at the chuttles to fend them off. He was the only one not affected as he pumped his body up and down to ward off the creatures.

Taking the Spear of Rummon out, Thorik stabbed it into the ground before him. A wave of pressure rushed out in every direction, knocking over Santorray but leaving the chuttles standing on their four sturdy legs. A loud roar from the spear could be heard by the entire chuttle gathering, as well as distant herds. A deep pounding in the ground followed.

Chuttlebeasts for tens of miles around stopped in their tracks, feeling the pulsing in the ground. Instincts took over as the mating call of the female chuttle drummed on the O'Sid Fields. The distant chuttles charged in the direction of the origin of the sound.

The local chuttles, on the other hand, began battling each other for the rights to what they believed was a female in heat. Massive heads knocking up against each other resounded across the landscape as hundreds of beasts exploded into a show for dominance.

Strangely enough, the dirt being kicked into the air reduced the potency of the chuttles' smell, giving Santorray and Thorik a slight reprieve from their reaction.

Ralph scurried back into Avanda's pouch as he saw Santorray approach.

The large, cube-shaped heads of the chuttles crashed together as the seven- to eight-foot-tall wild beasts ran over anything in their paths. Many of the creatures fell to the ground after being knocked unconscious from such head-to-head strikes.

Picking up Brimmelle with one arm and throwing Avanda and Gluic over his other shoulder, Santorray fought his way across the landscape. Swinging his free arm, he pounded hard against the woolly Fesh'Unday in his way.

A full body block was needed at one point to move the tail end of a chuttle far enough for him to force his way through. Nearly dropping his companions during the move, he avoided performing it again. Instead, he used his bony, razor-sharp blades across his back and elbow to inflict enough pain to make the crazed creatures steer clear.

Thorik removed the spear from the ground, but the earth continued to shake from the chuttlebeasts in heat. Since they stood at twice his height, Thorik was more likely to be stepped on than rammed. Rolling under wool-matted stomachs and between kicking legs, the Num dodged the best he could with his head spinning from the fumes. Reaching the edge of the turmoil and seeing Santorray, he dove under the last beast, only to be kicked in the head, knocking him out cold.

❧ 27 ❧

CORROCK

The Hessik and the Fount Rivers merged together to form the Squalid Waters. Behind this joining of waterways stood a city of ruin as well as renewal. Damaged walls and new towers shared the same locations. A backdrop of sharp-pointed mountain peaks gave the sense of the land's mouth opening to devour the city.

Ancient outer walls of sturdy granite now stood with gaping holes, revealing centuries of construction and destruction. No recent attempts had been made to repair any borders; defensive measures were few.

Multiple bridges crossed both the Hessik River to the south and the Fount River to the west. Some had been destroyed from past battles and never restored.

Thorik woke and looked about with weary eyes, his head still painfully aware of the chuttlebeast's kick. "Where are we?"

"Welcome to Corrock, Sec," Santorray said.

Santorray had taken control and brought them the rest of the way to the city during Thorik's chuttle-induced slumber. The blothrud had kept the group of travelers far enough back from the city to prevent detection.

Thorik retained a shallow headache and a red bump on his forehead, despite Gluic's healing techniques. Shaking off the lingering pain, he got straight to business. "Santorray, how do you propose we get inside?"

"I'll walk in."

Thorik slowly stood up to test his legs. "How about the rest of us?"

"You're not coming with me."

Already in a bad mood from the pounding still in his head, Thorik's face flushed to match the lump above his brow. "Yes, we are. This is our journey, which you joined, not the other way around. We will go in together."

The blothrud crossed his arms. "You're going to make a very simple event into something complicated. Let me do what I need to do, and I'll bring Ericc out to you, assuming he ever made it to Corrock and that he's not already dead."

"Then I guess we're going to make it complicated. I haven't come all this way to just sit back and wait for you to find out what has happened to him. What was the point of obtaining the Spear of Rummon if I'm not even going to attempt to save Ericc? Ovlan wouldn't have told us to get it if we didn't need it."

"Give me the spear if you think it's needed. Nums aren't welcome in Corrock except as slaves. You're a liability."

Thorik pulled the spear in tight. "No."

"Seems odd that a Num would cling to a weapon that killed their king."

Brimmelle scoffed at the comment. "It's more likely that an assassin's dagger held by a blothrud killed our king."

"Ovlan told me that I was the only one to wield him," Thorik added before Santorray could respond to the Fir's verbal jab.

"Him? It's an object. Metal, leather, skins." Santorray bent down to grab it out of Thorik's hands.

Thorik backed up, gripped the weapon firmly in both hands, and pointed the spear at the blothrud. "We're going in together to save Ericc."

Santorray instinctively grabbed the spear out of Thorik's hands before the Num could react. "Don't ever point a weapon at me. I've killed people for less."

The moment became precarious as a low distant growl emanated from the weapon Santorray held to his side. Fragments of words could be heard, but not understood, as the spear started glowing red. Sounds like those from an echo in a tunnel raced forward as though they were going to leap out of the object.

Santorray threw the spear to the ground, kicked dirt on it, and stepped back with caution. "It's possessed. The spirit of Rummon still lives within it."

"And apparently doesn't like blothruds, for some reason," Thorik said.

"There's a reason. The dragon Rummon was killed during an attempt to harness some of his energy for the most powerful weapon ever seen. Apparently, they captured the dragon's life force as well."

"For who?"

"Ergrauth, the mightiest blothrud Deleth ever created. He was unstoppable with the power of Rummon at his side, equal to that of the Oracles themselves. He dominated the land, air, and water. At least until the spear was stolen and hidden, only to be unearthed thousands of years later by a little Num named Sec Thorik Dain."

Thorik bent down and gently picked it back up. The ghostly voice subsided, as did the red glow. "Like I said, only I am to wield him."

"Even if that old relic has that dragon's soul, it is too old and weak to take on the entire forces of Corrock."

Changing his grip on the spear, Thorik stood with confidence. "If this was such a powerful weapon for Ergrauth, perhaps it will do the same for me."

"The heart of a blothrud you have, Sec. But you fail to understand that you are just a Num, a Num without any soul-markings at that. What makes you think you can take on such a task?"

Soul-markings showed maturity and characteristics of Nums. Not having them made others question Thorik's right to be taken seriously. He sighed while straightening his shoulders. "Ambrosius once told me that I was intended to be more and achieve great things in spite of my lack of markings. I believe he meant that I have an honorable lineage and that I have abilities passed down through generations. I was meant to be more than just an average Num."

Santorray could appreciate his pride, but he understood all too well the dangers inside the city. "And you will be. The average Num does not travel to Corrock to die."

BOUND AND CHAINED

Thorik led the Nums into Corrock. Each Num had their hands tied with a rope that linked them to the rest of the Nums. Santorray walked in front, holding the rope, which controlled them all. It was the only way that the Nums would be allowed in the city: as slaves.

The Del'Unday species ranged from the small rico rodents to the blothruds themselves. Some looked like man-sized insects, while others hid behind cloaks and hoods.

Corrock was built with numerous types of architecture erected over thousands of years. New construction consisting of mud blocks built on millennium-old foundations and half-walls of marble or granite.

Houses and shops expanded upward over the years as tenants used lighter materials such as wood to add additional floors. Rooftops pierced the skyline like cracked rock spires, in visual harmony with the mountains just to their east.

Fresh Fesh meat hung in open windows of a few shops, waiting for a customer to scrape off the flies and purchase. Shops of weapons and slavery shared street corners with shops of jewelry, fruit, and baskets, and blacksmiths. The streets were busy with customers and merchants.

Santorray occasionally struck up conversations with merchants to find information about the son of Ambrosius. As he had predicted, they were too late. Ericc had recently been apprehended and held for justice for his father's criminal acts against Corrock.

"Your quest to find your spear has cost us our chance to prevent Ericc's capture," Santorray said to Thorik as they walked along the streets.

Shoulders drooping with the feeling of defeat, Thorik did the only thing he knew how to do: come up with a new plan. "Can you find out what prison he is in? There must be a way to free him."

Santorray chuckled. "The Del'Unday don't have prisons. We give the victims of your crime an opportunity to take vengeance upon you. If severe enough, we put you to death afterward. Why would we spend time and effort housing and feeding criminals who had little care for our well-being?"

"That seems extremely harsh."

"Not at all. If you broke into my home and killed my child, I would have the right to take my anger back out on you in any way that I see fit."

"What if I only stole an item? Do you still have the right to torture or kill me?"

"Yes. You took your chances when you illegally entered my home. Our laws make you think twice about committing a crime."

Thorik grew slightly tense at the thought of accidentally breaking a law unknown to him. His best bet would be to keep his head down and stay close to Santorray. "So, if Ericc's not in a prison, where would he be?"

"On display for the locals to taunt and take out their anger over Ambrosius' legacy. He will be tied up in an open area until he dies or Darkmere's men come for him."

After several hours of wandering through the streets, the travelers entered the fourth district of the city. Each section of the city had all streets end in a central gathering place. The fourth district had been known as the lower quadrant ever since it was partially destroyed nearly a decade ago. Depressed even more than the rest of the city, less new construction and commerce were seen as Thorik and his team walked into the center of the district.

Standing in the middle of the courtyard, Ericc had his hands bound in chains above his head. Whipped and bloody, the young man had passed out from the torture he had taken. Blood dripped down his body and pooled at his feet, but not enough yet to cause his death.

The boy was displayed for all Corrockians to take out their anger at Ericc's father. Ambrosius had single-handedly destroyed the fourth district eight years prior. Killing innocent Del'Unday and crushing ancient temples had outraged the locals against Ambrosius and his family, as well as the entire human race.

Thorik froze in his tracks. "Santorray, it's Ericc."

Del'Unday walking through the open area stopped to mock the human. Some would throw sticks and small rocks at the prisoner while others approached him to give him more personal pain.

Santorray waited until no one was standing on the platform where Ericc hung like a piece of Fesh meat. "Let's approach."

Thorik tugged back on the rope, which held all the Nums. "In broad daylight? With hundreds of Del'Unday in view?"

"We need to at least let him know we are here, so he hangs on to life long enough for us to save him."

"Agreed."

Santorray led the way, pulling the Nums behind him. As he approached Ericc, the blothrud inconspicuously pulled out his small virgin dagger and held it between his hand and the hair on his leg. The blade glistened with a polish never tarnished with the blood of a victim, at least until this day. Varacon's twisted blades came to a sharp point, and the gems within its hilt glowed with the anticipation of a first strike.

Walking up the steps to the chained boy in the center of the crowded courtyard, Santorray continued to change his hold on the dagger to make sure he had a firm grip on it. Designed for a smaller hand, it never felt quite right.

The ideal location for this assassination would be in front of Darkmere at Surod. Regardless, Santorray was ready. It was time to stab Ericc in front of plenty of witnesses and in front of Thorik. It was time to end this mission and to repay his debt. It was finally at an end.

Stepping forward to Ericc, Santorray pulled the blade away from his hairy leg and quickly shoved it forward.

"Ericc!" Thorik shouted, jumping between the young man and the Blothrud. His focus on the young man blinded him to the potential attack on his life.

Santorray nearly stabbed the blade into Thorik's back before he halted the weapon.

Ericc's swollen black-and-blue eyes opened. His vision was blurry, but the Num's voice triggered his memory.

"Ericc, it's me, Thorik, from the Southwind Mines. We're here to rescue you."

"Rescue? Where's Darkmere?"

Santorray pulled the weapon back into hiding, waiting for Thorik to move out of the way.

"We haven't seen him yet," Thorik answered. "We'll come back after dark and rescue you, so don't give up."

Santorray sheathed the dagger before it could be spotted. "Yes, stay alive until we return."

One of the local blothrud guards stepped toward the platform. "Get your slaves away from the prisoner. You know better than that."

Santorray pulled back on the rope to get Thorik away from Ericc, before dragging the group of them out of the open area and into a side alley.

Thorik was thrilled that Ambrosius' son had not been killed. "All we need to do is wait for dark, and then we can grab him and sneak him out."

Santorray snarled. "You fool, you nearly got us caught. Your little conversation with Ericc may have drawn more attention to us than the single guard who told us to leave."

"What's the issue? We did as we were told."

"Any attention to us is not wanted. We were fortunate he didn't recognize me."

"Do you know him?" Thorik asked.

"No."

"Then why would he?"

Santorray paused before answering. "My reputation tends to precede me. If I'm noticed, our plans may be at an end."

"Okay, then find a place for us to hide for now. We'll return after dark when it isn't so obvious who you are or what we are doing."

~

As promised, the adventurers returned to the open courtyard after dark fell. Dozens of oil lanterns circled the platform, casting light onto their prisoner and the apparatus that his chains hung from. Against the dark of the night, Ericc looked like a glowing star for all to see.

Brimmelle folded his arms and grimaced at Thorik. "Yes, much better after dark."

Thorik nodded in agreement that conditions had not improved.

Santorray focused less on Ericc and more on the surrounding windows and alleys, which could view him. "Wait until the howl is over, and then follow my lead."

"Howl?"

A single howl could be heard from the mountain foothills outside of the city. It echoed throughout the now silent city.

Once completed, a return howl began within the city, this time made up from every resident within Corrock. From every direction, long emotional howls fired back to the mountain from where the first one originated until it slowly wound down to a few stragglers before ending.

Dead quiet followed.

Thorik waited for Santorray to explain, but received nothing. "What was that?

"Praise to Ergrauth for sparing their lives." Santorray continued watching for locals who passed by windows and doorways. "Corrock and Ovla'Mathyus agreed to stand up against the powers of Ergrauth during the Unday War. However, the Ovs refused to stand alongside the Dels of Corrock when the attacks began. The Corrockians who survived the attack are forever in debt to Ergrauth for sparing their lives."

"It's my understanding that the Ovs offered refuge to the Dels."

"And forfeit their homes, land, and honor? What kind of offer is that?"

"One of survival."

"Anyone can survive. Dels must live. We must thrust ourselves into every new day with vitality and ferocity as though it may be our last, for some day it will be. We would choose to live a short life of grand excitement and triumphs over a long life of serene dullness."

"Your people chose certain death against Ergrauth's forces over certain life behind safe walls?"

"My people?"

"Corrockians."

"Sec, I am not a Corrockian."

"Oh, then what are you?"

"I'm not a Corrockian." The point was made for Thorik to drop the subject.

"I found it!" Avanda had been searching for a spell in Dare's book of magic that could help them with the situation at hand. Digging into her red purse of magic items, she pulled out a small vial of clear liquid. Etchings of small frogs surrounded the mouth of the glass vial. "If we give Ericc some of this with the right words, we can make a temporary illusion of Ericc while freeing the real one."

Silence fell on the group as they stared at her as though she was speaking a different language.

Lifting the vial up to show the group, she removed the cork. Sticking her tongue out, she placed one drop of clear liquid on it before Thorik or Brimmelle could stop her.

Smiling at first, Avanda started choking and coughing, as she pushed the cork back on.

Thorik slapped her back. "Spit it out. It could be poison."

Brimmelle told her to relax and breathe.

Pushing them both away, Avanda caught her breath. "I'm fine. It just tastes terrible."

Reading in her small book, she spoke the verbal piece of the spell. "Lavare'Repla'Hospes." Still choking on the taste, she tried the words again a few times. By the fourth time, the words were spoken correctly, and Thorik and Brimmelle stepped back from her.

Avanda's body blurred for a moment in the torchlight before a second Avanda stepped forward out of the original's body.

Two Avandas now stood in the group and spoke at the same time; neither could be heard over the other.

"Defying the Mountain King's limits, this is." Brimmelle backed away from the replica.

"Avanda, that was dangerous. You don't know what it could have done to you or how long it will last." Thorik reached over and touched the new Avanda. She was damp and tacky to the touch.

Santorray finished his scouting of the area. "We'll have to sneak out there, give him the potion, say the words, and then switch the chains from the real Ericc to the magic one."

Thorik sighed. "I'll do it. It's my responsibility."

"No, I'll do it." The new Avanda grabbed the vial out of Avanda's hand.

"Give that back!" Avanda chased her likeness into the courtyard before wrestling her to the ground.

One of them finally stood with the vial in hand, only to be pulled back down by the other.

Santorray held the other Nums back in the alley as two krupes and a brandercat left their dark posts that were hidden from the light. Dark spiked armor covered the two-legged krupes from head to toe as they walked toward Avanda and Avanda.

The brandercat's scales faded in color and blended into the dark courtyard, making it practically invisible to the observer. It took concentration to keep its scales in tune with the light and colors, preventing it from attacking while doing so.

Seeing the krupes approaching, both young Nums made a dash for the center of the yard. Jumping up onto the platform, one of the girls was caught by a krupe, who held onto her leg.

Screaming, she tossed the vial up to the other Avanda, who then raced over to Ericc.

A brandercat appeared out of nowhere, leaping at Avanda across the large platform.

Diving out of the way, Avanda rolled and jumped to her feet.

The krupe below had the other Avanda in his clutches, with no hope of escape.

Turning around, the brandercat smiled at the Avanda who was still on the stage, knowing he couldn't miss at this close of a range.

Avanda knew she only had one chance. It was time to act like a Del'Unday and live life to the limit as though it would be her last, for today appeared to be so. Opening her vial, she lunged at Ericc, placing the mouth of the bottle to his lips and tilting back his head.

Leaping through the air, the brandercat's dislocating jaw opened and took Avanda's entire midsection into his mouth before he landed to the side of the chained prisoner.

Avanda's body went limp in the large cat's mouth as he carried her to the edge of the platform before snapping his jaws shut and tasting the fresh Num blood. Violently crushing the prey in his mouth, the brandercat was surprised to find a wave of water gushing out from her body as though it was only a bag of nauseating oily water.

"Lavare'Repla'Hospes," yelled the Avanda who was captive.

Ericc had swallowed nearly the entire bottle. His body blurred to all that watched. Shaking, his body appeared to pull itself into two. A second Ericc now stood on the platform; however, this one wasn't chained up.

"Restrain him," ordered the , still trying to get the wretched taste from his mouth.

But before the krupes moved, a third Ericc appeared, followed by a fourth and a fifth. It continued until the yard was filled with Ericcs, each beginning to make their own escape plan down the many streets and alleyways.

Ralph climbed out of Avanda's side bag and leaped onto the krupe's arm that held her. The lizard spat on it, and the armor sizzled away, while some of the acid worked its way underneath, onto the creature's skin.

Avanda was dropped as the krupe swatted the lizard off his wrist.

Mass confusion erupted and continued to get worse. The krupe turned his attention to the Ericc in front of him, plunging his sword into the boy's chest. Ericc popped like a thin sack of water, pouring his sour liquid onto the ground. It wasn't a moment later that two more Ericcs jumped off the platform and took his place.

Thorik and Santorray raced into the crowd of Ericcs to cut free the real one, while Brimmelle and Gluic found Avanda picking up Ralph and trying not to be stepped on during the stampede.

Santorray approached the real prisoner and had a free opportunity to stab Ericc in the heat of the battle, but it could easily be missed from the public's viewing.

One slice from Santorray's saber and the chains holding Ericc up were compromised. Lifting the semi-conscious young man, Santorray led the group toward the southern gate. With hastened speed, they stormed out of the city as sirens of alert could be heard from behind. The blothrud would uphold his original plan to stab the boy when all could see. The mission required it to be in public and in front of Darkmere, if possible. This was not the time or place.

"Darkmere?" was all that Ericc could get out before passing out from starvation and loss of blood.

Lanterns were lit and horns blared as the city awoke to the news of Ericc's escape and his running amuck in their streets.

29

UNDER SIEGE

Exhausted from the hours of running, Brimmelle and Gluic fell hard to the ground, spraying dirt into their faces.

Brimmelle spit dirt back out into the darkness and yelled, "Far enough! We can't run any farther."

"See those torches in the distance?" Santorray pointed behind them across the flat land. "They're tracking us and gaining on us."

Avanda sat down to rest as well. "My legs hurt, and I'm thirsty. I need a break."

"I can't carry you all, so get on your feet and keep moving," Santorray growled.

"Santorray, set Ericc down and give us a few moments to drink and rest." Thorik kneeled down and handed his grandmother some water. "We'll move all the more quickly afterward."

The sliver of moon gave off just enough light for them to see general shapes. Thorik was unable to see the pleasure across Gluic's face as she sipped the water, but he could hear it from her sigh of relief.

"We have no time. They are nearly upon us."

Thorik slowly got to his feet. "We have a bigger issue."

Several dozen men approached on three sides of Thorik's group.

Santorray saw the figures as well. They had unknowingly run directly to the men's camp. Lifting his nose, he took a deep breath. "Eastland military." Growling, he squinted in the darkness to see his enemy, but his eyes just couldn't validate his words.

Thorik stood over the Nums on the ground to protect them. "We're trapped."

Both sabers from Santorray's belt were immediately unsheathed for an attack. "Not without a fight." He allowed blood to drip from a fresh bite of his lip. The pre-battle ritual let their enemies know they don't fear being injured.

"They have crossbows. Put your weapons away before you get us killed."

"I'll die fighting before I let them capture us."

"And how will that help any of us? We will have failed Ambrosius and lost our own lives just to slay a few of their men."

"Better to die trying than not to try at all."

Thorik moved in front of the blothrud. "There's a time to fight and a time to back down. This is one of those times to understand we can't win. We must save ourselves for a time when we can."

Hesitating, Santorray heard the stress of additional bowstrings being pulled back and locked in place. He could only assume they were pointed at him. Even if he charged forward, he would most likely perish before he even reached the first few Eastlanders.

"I trusted you at River's Edge when we left Grewen. Trust me now. I know what I'm doing. Put your weapons away," Thorik said in an order laced with compassion.

Slowly, Santorray sheathed his sabers.

They stood motionless as they waited for the men to speak.

Instead, the men made an opening for them to pass forward. They knew better than to approach a blothrud to remove his weapons. They would wait to do so back at camp when they had more reinforcements.

Thorik helped the Nums to their feet. "Come on. They're leading us someplace."

Santorray picked up Ericc and followed the Nums. "Most likely their base camp."

"Fine mess you got us into, Thorik." Brimmelle complained. "Walking us right into our enemy's camp."

"More likely your annoying voice was overhead by scouts," Santorray said to Brimmelle.

Over the next few hills, torchlight illuminated an area with tents and wagons. Flags from Southwind and Eastland were prominently displayed throughout the camp, where several hundred men prepared for the night.

In the center of the camp was a thick post to which Grewen was chained. Sitting down, he leaned against the post, his wrists and ankles bound by the same chain.

A fleeting moment of exhilaration came upon Thorik when he saw his mognin friend. Just to know he was still alive was enough, but to have him within sight was remarkable. Nevertheless, this quickly passed as the Num realized that he also would be shackled and all of them were most likely headed for the Southwind Mines.

The scouts quietly led them down the hill and into camp, while one of them rushed ahead to alert their commanders.

Stopping at the main tent, Santorray set Ericc down on his feet. Seeing that he wasn't able to stand on his own, he moved him next to Brimmelle for support.

The injured young man held onto Brimmelle before the Fir had the option to push him off to another. Ericc's weakened knees wobbled, and his vision blurred.

"Where's Darkmere?" Coughing, he had no idea where he was or what was happening around him.

Exiting from one of the larger tents was an older man, ripe with scars from many battles. His red robes covered metal armor across his chest, which bore the symbol of Eastland, the symbol of bloodshed and hatred to all Altereds. Three swords crossing blades, forming a triangle, with blood pooling in the center from each weapon. "Well done, men. You've recovered Ericc," the general said to his scouts.

A second figure emerged from the tent. It was Lucian. Pushing his long blonde hair out of his face and behind his ear, he bestowed a smile of devious enjoyment as he watched Santorray stand before them. "General Hatch, these are the criminals I've been looking for, especially the blothrud. I knew they had something to do with Ericc's escape."

"Remarkably, you were correct," the general said. "As agreed, I'll give Ericc to Asentar. Do what you wish with the others." He then turned to his commander and added an order. "Remove their weapons and tie up the blothrud and Nums."

Santorray grabbed for his sabers with lightning speed, causing the archers to prepare to fire.

"Wait!" Lucian yelled before addressing the general. "I don't want the Matriarch cheated out of seeing Santorray's death. I will address this."

The general had little respect for Lucian, but he needed to keep the Matriarch from becoming an enemy. "Commander, keep an eye on our Southwind friends in case this gets out of control." Then the general returned to his tent.

Lucian turned to address the captives. "It's over, my friends. You've been captured, and we didn't even need to use your Mognin companion for bait."

Stepping forward into the street in front of them, Lucian looked directly at the blothrud. "Santorray, I thought I had killed you once, but I won't underestimate your resolve this time. Instead, I shall behead you in front of the Matriarch herself. Then I shall mount your head to decorate her chamber's wall to ensure you never come back to life and haunt my streets."

Raising his hand with two missing fingers, Lucian made sure Santorray could see the stubs. "Seeing that you bit off my fingers, I plan to cut up your mognin and Num friends and feed their meat to our hungry troops who worked so hard to track you down. Only fair, wouldn't you say? Of course, what would you care? Blothruds never get along with other species."

Santorray slowly cut his own shoulder before pointing his bloody sabers at Lucian. "I'll teach you what is fair."

Over thirty men pulled back and locked their crossbows. The same number readied their swords.

Lucian nodded his head at Santorray, trying to convince him to take a swing at him, giving the archers reason to fire their arrows. "As much as I prefer to kill you in the company of the Matriarch, I can live with your death occurring right now. So I strongly recommend you and your followers drop your weapons before my good nature is taxed, and I decide to kill you *all* right now."

"Santorray! No!" Thorik shouted. "Not now. This is not the time." Removing his spear from its holder on his back, he prepared to drop the weapon to lead his party in their surrender.

Lucian laughed at the statement. "The mighty blothrud, Santorray, taking orders from a Num? And a small meek one without soul-markings at that."

Thorik's grip tightened around the spear instead of releasing it to the ground.

Santorray's hands shook as he fought off the temptation to finish the job on Lucian regardless of what would follow.

"He's baiting you. Don't give him a reason to order our deaths." Thorik tried to relax his own hands.

"Your deaths have already been ordered." Lucian continued with a cocky wink. "You might say that I'm just playing with my food. Bringing it to a boil before I eat it."

"Hold back," Thorik ordered Santorray.

Lucian enjoyed the game and decided to continue it down a different path. Eyeing one of his men, he gave him the signal to grab the girl from the back, which he did. Avanda was pulled from the group and brought around to the front.

Avanda squirmed and bucked against the man until he finally released her in front of Lucian.

Helpless, Thorik looked on with fear and anger. Would he once again not be able to protect her? Would he be forced to watch her pain this time? "Leave her alone!"

Lucian leaned down to her height. "I never got a chance to see just how soft your skin really was."

Reaching for her red purse, Avanda was going to take care of the man here and now.

Lucian pulled out a crooked blade from his side and slapped the flat side of it against her hand, cutting her hand near the thumb, causing her to drop the purse.

She immediately clutched the injury with her other hand and cradled it near her chest.

"Not this time, little witch. No magic to help you out." Dripping with her blood, Lucian's blade moved to her neck and pushed against her skin. He then peered toward the blothrud and said, "And no one here to save you this time."

Waves of Rava'Kor memories flashed in her mind. Helpless, they would soon violate her. They weren't alone this time. A crowd would watch her being assaulted. Her arms and legs went rigid, tense from the memories. She wanted to run, or attack, or anything other than stand there and relive his repulsive touch to her body.

Ralph had climbed out of her backpack and onto her shoulder. He leaped onto Lucian's hand, biting down hard onto his wrist. In doing so, his acidic saliva poured out onto the man's skin.

Lucian screamed and reached out to grab the lizard off him, but the spines on the little creature's back poked deep into his palm.

Ralph coiled his body around Lucian's entire wrist, chewing on the flesh as the acid softened it.

Unable to get the critter off, Lucian smacked the lizard's head with the hilt of his blade, knocking it out cold.

Ralph fell to the ground, exposing a severe red ring of torn flesh around Lucian's wrist.

Lifting his leg high in the air, Lucian smashed his boot onto the lizard, crushing it into the hard ground several times. He made sure the creature was dead before wiping the bottom of his boot off with his knife.

Avanda was in shock from watching the slaying of her little friend. No longer did she wish to run. Now her only desire was to see the man pay. Her body filled with rage over her companion's death.

Lucian turned back to her and placed the knife back to Avanda's neck. Lizard flesh and blood dripped from the blade onto her chest. "For crimes against me, you are now legally my slave, to do with as I wish. And I wish to feel your soft skin, all of it, every night, until I get tired of you and sell you off to slave traders."

Reaching out with his other hand, Lucian dragged her injured hand toward his face. "But until then, you will please me and fulfill my desires." Slowly, he dragged his tongue across the open wound on her hand to taste her blood.

Pulling her hand back, she slapped him hard across the face. She no longer feared the man who once haunted her dreams. In some way, he had just freed her from her internal torture.

But her slap had only heightened his desire for her, and he smiled at her tenacious spirit. "I'm glad you like it rough…" Lucian slapped her back across the face, knocking her to the ground. "Because so do I." Lucian lifted his blade to stab her.

"NO!" Thorik screamed in violent rage, his fist squeezing tight around the shaft of his spear.

A roar erupted from the Spear of Rummon, launching a magical flame from its point, which engulfed Lucian's head. Fire coated the man from his neck up as he screamed in pain, dropped his dagger, and placed his hands over his eyes to protect them. But it was insufficient. His eyes had been seared, and the skin on his face continued to burn.

Avanda watched as white flames stirred between his fingers as his hands caught fire. She witnessed the flames coil inside his mouth as he yelled for help. However, there was no help to be given or time to give it. The flame ended as fast as it had begun, leaving Lucian's face and hair charred and blackened, and he gasped for breath.

As the reality of the assault took hold, the archers switched their aim to the Num.

Thorik quickly drove his spear into the ground.

A mighty shock wave emanated from the weapon, violently crashing outward, followed by a rhythmic pounding in the ground. The blast wave covered the valley. Soldiers fell, tent stakes snapped, faralopes panicked, and campfires flared from the fanning of the flames. The Eastland army took a few moments to collect themselves from the shock of such an unexpected force.

"Now, Santorray," Thorik ordered, even though the blothrud was already pursuing his first victim in the same motion of getting back on his feet.

Lucian fell to his knees, begging Avanda for mercy. The burns in his lungs made him gasp for air.

"You're evil and vile." Avanda's stomach tightened as she looked at the destroyed face of the man who would have raped her. Picking up his dagger, still dripping with Ralph's blood, she held it to his neck. "It's one thing to fight for your morals, even if they are skewed. But you have none. The world will be better without you."

"Then kill me." His pain was overwhelming as he searched for an end. "Or I'll hunt you down."

She looked at Ralph's dead body and pushed the blade forward, only to stop just before slicing his neck. "That's too good for you. I prefer you live to feel the pain that you inflict on others."

Avanda stood up with a new strength as she watched Lucian collapse before her.

A tight circle of men continued to fight Santorray with long swords and flails, leaving the archers only a periodic open shot to his head. An unfortunate miss of the blothrud could end up hitting their own men, so no shots were fired.

Thorik pulled out his throwing daggers and entered the fight. He attempted to stay out from under Santorray's feet and away from the swinging of his sabers. The few men that reached in to pull Thorik away from the blothrud were met by the stinging of the Num's blade.

Brimmelle and Gluic were captured, but they put up little resistance, for they were both held at knifepoint.

Avanda reached for her red purse with new enthusiasm.

Pulling out her red beads, she chanted, but was bumped during the commotion of the men fighting Santorray and Thorik. She dropped and lost the beads in the process. Stirred-up dust quickly covered them, and they fell out of sight.

Reaching back into her purse, she removed several small bones. "Bellfin'Pec." She waved her arms about. The ground near her turned to thick mud and spread out past Gluic and her son. The expression on her face was the same surprise and disappointment that came over Brimmelle. As all three sunk up to their waist, the mud made it nearly impossible for them to escape.

They were caught.

Lucian's men pulled them from their predicaments and carried over to the mognin. Avanda, Gluic, and Brimmelle were quickly chained up to the same post as Grewen.

Fir Brimmelle's eyes searched about the camp. "What happened to Ericc?"

Gluic smiled. "He decided not to join our battle."

"I wish he had taken us with him."

~

BACKING UP TO SANTORRAY, Thorik watched as the mighty blothrud tossed men in the air. Weapons, shields, and helmets shot in every direction from the fight behind him. His haste to assist his friends had led him away from the Spear of Rummon, so Thorik put his tiny daggers away and grabbed a fallen sword and shield. He then proceeded to hold off the men attempting to grab him and tie him up with his friends.

Santorray continued to take man after man down, but there were simply too many of them. He would exhaust his strength long before they ran out of men. He knew the odds of survival were unlikely, but at least he would go down fighting.

Fighting his way forward, Santorray carved an opening for Thorik to escape and free Grewen and the Nums. It wasn't long-lived; still, it was enough for the small Num to twist his way through. Unfortunately, the clever moves cost him his newfound sword.

Thorik reached Grewen and the Nums. "Where's Ericc?"

His grandmother replied, "He left."

"We'll search for him as soon as I set you free."

The locks on the chains around their ankles and wrists were too large for Thorik to break with the small daggers, and his spear was lodged in the ground on the other side of the Eastland troops. He had nothing to break the locks with, so he futile attempts to bend them with his small dagger.

"Thorik," Brimmelle said.

"Just wait, I might be able to…" Thorik's voice trailed off as he noticed what his uncle was alerting him to. A dozen men, with swords and arrows pointed his way, stood poised for battle. The fight was over. They had lost.

Two high-pitched horn blasts sounded, causing the men around Santorray to stop fighting and back up, while Thorik was captured and added onto the chain of prisoners.

Santorray was breathing hard from the fight. Human blood was splattered across his face and chest, but he was not harmed.

General Hatch had his troops back under control. "Spears ready!" he ordered.

The circle of men encompassing the blothrud were handed long spears from behind.

The general demanded synchronized movements from his troops. "Spears down."

His men spiked the wooden end of their spears hard against the earth.

"Spears aim."

Leaning the front blades of the spears forward to waist level and keeping the back ends of them on the ground, soldiers behind them placed their boots on the base of the weapons to ensure they didn't slide backward.

Santorray was now in a prison of two dozen spear blades. Smiling, he licked the human blood from his face to intimidate the men. He wondered how many he would take out before he fell.

"Front lines down." Hatch watched his orders performed in perfect movement as the men around the beast squatted down without moving the spears.

"Archers ready."

Standing behind the squatting men, a circle of archers lifted their crossbows in unison.

"Archers, aim."

The archers pulled back on their strings and locked them in place; the arrows were lined up to fire.

Refusing to go down without a fight, Santorray attacked.

"Fire!"

30

DEL'UNDAY ARMY

A loud howl from the hill caught everyone's attention, as an army of Del'Unday charged into the valley. Some at a run, others riding Fesh'Undays, they descended toward the camp with murderous screams of war. The Corrockians had caught up to Ericc and they launched their attack without any warning.

General Hatch immediately reassembled his troops against the Del'Unday, an enemy he had fought many times. "Fall in line. Two tier front. Archers at center and side points."

The first to attack were the entelodont hogs, with shoulders taller than Thorik and long snouts with two large lower saber-like teeth. As the hogs jumped down onto the Eastland troops, the men lifted their spears in the air to skewer them as they landed. Spears snapped in half as the beasts hard underbellies withstood most of the blows. Only a fourth of the hogs' first attack wave were seriously injured.

The crushing weight of the hogs flattened many of the men as they proceeded past the front lines. With their heads down, the hogs charged the second line of defense with their thick frontal horns.

The general gave his orders to a well-organized battalion. Archers fired, taking out the majority of the hogs before they could reach the second line.

The front line held fast against the remaining hogs and prepared for the oncoming brandercats who blinked in and out of visibility. The Eastland men tossed handfuls of white powder in front of the battle line to help spot their arrival. Large invisible cats raced forward, running through the powder, which clung to their feet and legs, allowing the men to see them.

Eastland guards thrust their spears forward at the locations where the painted feet shone bright in the torchlight. Hitting their marks more often than not, the men prevented most of the Del'Unday from breaching the first line of defense.

Krupes finally crested over the hill and surveyed the scene. A single blothrud was barking out orders to the stocky creatures coated in black metal armor. The krupes were the foundation of the Del army, defensively tough, with excellent battle skills and a robust constitution.

The general pulled his frontal defense line back into an arch to capture the krupes in the center. Ordering his archers into new positions, he walked toward the center of the front line's arch. He knew the drill. He knew once the Del'Unday had sent their preliminary forces into battle, the leading blothrud would be open to talking about a surrender. General Hatch had no plan on surrendering, considering he was winning the battle, but it was an excellent opportunity to size up his opponent.

Krupes lined up straight across the hill, unwilling to bend to the men's arch, as the blothrud walked forward into it.

Taller than Santorray, this blothrud wore decorative jewelry created from pieces of his prior victims' bodies. A few skulls clanked together on a rope over his shoulder, threaded eyeballs swung from a necklace, and rib cage and finger bones created a helmet.

"I am General Hatch from Eastland. We have the right to travel the O'Sid fields."

The blothrud spit on the general's boot. "You have our prisoner and the criminals who helped him escape."

"We have them in custody. But they will be held in our kingdom for their crimes against our people before we consider if they are to be given to you. What be your name, beast?"

"Bellfor."

For the first time, the general realized he was dealing with a seasoned veteran, a legend among the Del'Undays. "Bellfor the Savage? Your reputation precedes you. I am surprised you're willing to come forward and offer us a chance at surrendering, even though we obviously still have the upper hand."

"I'm not offering anything. I've come to take back what is ours and punish those responsible."

The shuffling of the general's troops caught Hatch's eyes. A legion of krupes appeared on each side of the valley. He had underestimated the number of creatures at the blothrud's disposal.

"Do you honestly expect us to stand by and let you take our prisoners?"

"No, I expect you to die trying to stop me."

Uncharacteristic of these types of talks, a second human approached the center ring. Easily a head taller than most men, his muscles were well-defined, and his legs were the size of tree trunks. A long sword in one hand and a short sword in the other, he made it clear that he was not afraid of the blothrud.

General Hatch welcomed his companion. "Sir Dovenar Knight Asentar, please meet the legendary Bellfor of Corrock we've heard so much about. I believe this was the blothrud you were in search of."

Asentar stood solid at the general's side, sizing up the creature. "I have no bad blood with you, Bellfor. It would be wise for both of us to keep it that way, for I have come to speak with your leaders about an alliance of power to prevent Darkmere's approaching war. I implore you to prevent this fight from escalating so we can discuss our potential future."

Bellfor snarled and spit at the general.

A flash of a short sword panned in front of General Hatch, catching the blothrud's saliva. Asentar then wiped the spit off on his boot. "You will not intimidate us."

"Then we will just kill you." Howling high into the air, Bellfor signaled his army to attack. Lunging forward to rip the general's head off, he was blocked by Asentar, who quickly became engaged in a heated fight with the blothrud.

General Hatch was confident in the knight's ability to hold off Bellfor, so he returned to command his troops to ensure a victory.

The sound of a hundred krupes running in metal armor from all sides was ominous and terrifying. Reversing the front line's arch, General Hatch now had three of his four sides protected.

The battle had begun.

More brandercats arrived under the sporadic illusion of invisibility. Enormous terra grubs broke through the earth and pulled men underground, eating them whole. Krupes deflected the arrows and most blades with their strong black armor, while more hogs charged the lines. The Del'Unday were designed to fight wars.

Organized and disciplined, the men fought back. Close range bow attacks allowed arrows to enter krupe helmet eyeholes and kill whatever existed inside the mass of metal. Brandercats were stabbed and entelodont hogs were attacked from both sides. Sacrifices were made, while minor victories were achieved by coordinated efforts.

The blades of Bellfor and Asentar clashed again and again. The two warriors tested each other's strength only to find Bellfor had the advantage. However, Asentar's speed and skill with the sword was dominant.

Bellfor swung his mighty flail with one hand and a multi-pointed black blade with his other. Hammering hard against his opponent, he knew that all it would take was for one of his blows to shatter a leg or arm.

General Hatch was preoccupied with his troops and failed to notice his captives.

As the battle waged on, several of the krupes moved over to the prisoners to take them back to Corrock. Breaking the chains from the post, they pulled Thorik's group to their feet.

When pulled forward, Gluic fell to the ground, knocking many of her feathers from her hair. Spreading her fingers wide on the hard earth, she smiled before being helped up by her son. "Oh my. Here we go."

"Yes, mother, here we go again."

"No, my son. They have finally arrived."

Brimmelle dusted his mother's knees off. "Who? Who has arrived?"

The ground rumbled, lightly at first and then a rough, earth-shaking tremble.

A thousand chuttlebeasts stormed into camp, hooves beating on the ground. The constant thumping of the Spear of Rummon had called the beasts into heat. Lust had lured several herds into the valley for a display of dominance.

Chuttles ran over men and Del'Unday alike. Brandercats were flung in the air, krupes bounced off the cubic heads of the smelly beasts, and men were trampled. No one was safe.

A few hogs met their marks, biting hard into the chuttlebeasts, but the numbers weren't in their favor, and it wasn't long before the hogs had to run for their lives.

The krupes pulled harder on Thorik's chain, forcing his group to walk faster in an effort to get over the hill and out of the local anarchy.

Chuttles ran in front and behind the group as Grewen dug his giant heels into the ground, preventing a safe escape from the Southwinders, that would lead them right into the hands of the Del'Unday.

Gluic fell again from the tug-of-war between Grewen and the krupes.

Angered at the captive's resistance, one of the krupes pulled out his spiked mace and swung it hard at Grewen's head.

Just then, a chuttle crashed its way through the krupes, causing the mace to miss. A blur of thick wool passed in front of the mognin, leaving only the unattended ends of their chains. The beast had left no sign of the krupes.

Grewen was pleased at their luck until he himself became a victim of the rampaging herd. Hit hard on his back by a stray chuttlebeast, the mognin crashed to the ground, just missing the Nums. His chains prevented the Nums from seeking safety as they attempted to help him back to his feet.

Loud cracks of chuttle heads rocked the valley as the carnage increased. Tents had started on fire while men and Altereds screamed in pain, as the chuttlebeasts frantically struggled to find the source of the thumping.

A blade swung in front of Thorik, just missing his body. Instead, it crashed down, breaking his chains.

"Go get that damn spear so we can get out of here," Santorray said.

Thorik looked up at the blothrud. Santorray looked like a pincushion, with arrows embedded in his shoulders and chest. Blood poured forth from the wounds as he struggled to lift his saber again to free the next Num.

Thorik couldn't believe Santorray was still alive in such a dire state. "Are you—"

"Get going! Hurry!" the blothrud demanded.

Thorik took Santorray's order and raced down the hill toward the spear. The vapors of the chuttles were thicker in the bottom of the valley, burning his eyes so badly it was difficult to see.

Jumping and rolling out of a chuttle's charge, Thorik landed at the feet of an Eastland soldier, who quickly grabbed him.

"Got'cha," was the only thing the soldier said before a krupe's heavy mace crushed his forehead, releasing Thorik to the ground.

A quick, heavy boot to Thorik's stomach kept the Num from escaping as the krupe lifted his mace to bury it deep into his chest.

Another chuttle plowed over Thorik, taking the krupe with him.

Thorik was in the heart of the mess and knew the spear was close. Diving from one place to another, he finally spotted Rummon and jumped for him.

Pulling him out of the ground, he turned to find a large, square, wool-covered head bearing down on him. There was no time to move, so Thorik held the spear with both hands and braced for the impact.

A snarl from within the spear sprang toward the beast, hitting it in the head as though it had knocked up against another chuttle.

Pulling hard to the side, the beast charged forward as the side of his head hit Thorik, smacking the Num hard to the ground.

Lucky to not have been hit head-on, Thorik only had the wind knocked out of him. Standing back up, the Num spotted Ericc, who looked confused since he still had trouble standing and seeing.

The chuttlebeast that Thorik had avoided was now heading directly at Ambrosius' son at a full gallop.

Ericc looked over at Thorik just as the beast's head hit him. Ericc vanished instantly and reappeared next to the Num. "Where's Darkmere? They said he would come for me."

Thorik couldn't believe his eyes. He must have seen it wrong. People couldn't change locations in the blink of an eye. "We saved you from him."

Ericc struggled because of his health and fell to one knee. "No, I need to go back!" he demanded before he collapsed.

Thorik helped Ericc to his feet and led him back through the mayhem toward his group, with the spear out in front. A corridor opened for their escape in whichever direction he pointed the spear. The two scrambled over the hill and into the next small valley to catch up to Grewen, Santorray, and the Nums.

The Mognin ripped out the last few arrows from Santorray's back, and the blothrud screamed in pain. His own blood had coated his lower body and much of the ground.

Thorik watched the blothrud pass out after the last arrow was removed. "Is he going to make it?"

After wrapping Santorray's upper body in cloths to stop the bleeding, Grewen picked up the nearly lifeless blothrud and headed east, away from the camp and the chaos. "He's lost a lot of blood. Arrows penetrate deep at that close range. It's hard to say."

❧ 31 ❧

KIRI DESERT

———

Thorik's Log: 6th day of the 6th month of the 650th year.

In one fell swoop, the Spear of Rummon saved us last night from being captured by the Corrockians and the Eastlanders. It caused a herd of chuttlebeasts to storm the battlefield. Our escape during the chaos leaves us without knowledge of who won the battle, if it was completed at all. We escaped with our lives. However, Santorray is badly injured. Grewen is leading us to a safe place to heal him.

———

Gluic removed her hands from Santorray. They had spread his massive body out on the ground, with stones placed in specific locations on his body for her to heal him. They had sewn deep wounds up, but it was far too soon to know if he would ever recover.

Ericc rested nearby after his healing from Gluic had been performed. Water, food, and rest were all he needed.

Removing one of the stones from the blothrud's head, she handed it to Thorik. "Here's your Runestone back. Keep it safe."

"I will. I always do."

"Good." She removed one of her remaining feathers from her hair and placed it in his. "Now, did you watch what I did?"

"Yes, Granna. But I keep telling you that I don't have the ability to perform a healing."

"Me neither. I let the stones tell me what to do. You'll do fine." Reaching over, she straightened his feather.

Thorik pondered on how to interpret her last statement as he watched the blothrud moan from the pain. Gluic had suddenly started instructing him on various techniques, which she had never expressed interest in showing him before. "Granna, what did you see in the Mythical Forest when you held the crystal to Santorray?"

She recalled the images. "A murder, dear."

"Of who?"

Gluic smiled with compassion and nodded slightly.

"You? But why? Who would murder you?" Thorik asked.

"Don't fret, Thorik. Worrying about it won't change anything."

"Santorray? He's the one, isn't he?"

"And what would it change if he was?"

"First off, we could go without healing him."

"And let him die, even though we can save him? Could you really do that?"

"Yes." Thorik spoke before thinking. Removing the bright orange feather from his hair, he poked the end of it a few times at his other hand. "No, but how can you heal him, knowing he will end your life?

"End my life? Dear, he's only going to murder me. I'm sure it will be for a good cause. But someone else actually ends my life."

"There's a difference?"

Gluic pinched Thorik's skin. "This flesh is only a host for our souls. I talk to people all the time that aren't restricted by these barriers."

"Yes, I know. As the Mountain King's words say, 'Our soul-markings show we have souls'."

"Not exactly, but close enough."

"I suppose you've talked to the Mountain King?"

"He's very nice. Even he would tell me the intent of the words is as you said, but there is more depth to them."

"If that is true, why is it I haven't received any? Am I without a soul?"

"No, my dear. Soul-markings display your personality, your mettle, and your idiosyncrasies. That much we can see. But they also hold truths about you and your purpose in life. Your purpose is so strong that it is holding back the rest of your traits from showing through your skin."

The thought never crossed his mind. "Is that possible?"

"Can you raise a column of marble a thousand feet in the air with your mind?"

Thorik hugged his grandmother for her constant encouragement. She always had a way of making him feel better. "Thank you, Granna."

"Don't ever doubt your value, my boy."

Grewen returned to the temporary camp with Brimmelle and Avanda. They had walked up to the top of a nearby peak to scout ahead. "Looks clear; just a stray small herd of chuttles. Did you get the litter completed?" Grewen had broken a few branches off the tree they rested under, before heading out to scout, to give Thorik material for the device that would haul the blothrud.

"Yes, and we just finished another healing of Santorray. Ericc should be ready to travel as well." Thorik woke Ericc and helped him to his feet. "We have a lot to talk about, starting with your little disappearing trick back in the Eastland camp."

The young man didn't reply as he grabbed some items to carry. He had been unappreciative and agitated ever since they rescued him.

Grewen reached down and picked up the semi-conscious blothrud.

Santorray woke from his haze and tried to push away. "I'm fine. I'll walk."

Setting him into the litter, Grewen agreed with him. "Yes, you will, just not today."

Attempting to sit up, Santorray instantly realized he couldn't. The pain was too great, and his muscles were too torn. "Watch out for chuttles." In his own way he was trying to lead the group and give them advice. "Always assume they are ready to attack. They change direction without warning. Don't let your guard down. They are a powerful Fesh."

Grewen snapped a handful of dry grass from its roots and tossed it in his mouth. "And they stink too."

Brimmelle couldn't let the opportunity go to waste. "You're one to talk."

Grewen strapped the blothrud in and lifted one end of the litter to drag him. "What? I kind of like my smell. Musky yet earthy."

"Unearthed is more like it. Your odor is of a plate of rotten eggs and raw fish after baking in this waterless land for a week."

"That doesn't sound so bad," Grewen said. "Now you've gone and made me hungry."

"I helped Thorik gut a giant stink beetle once, and its sack exploded all over both of us, yet even that smelled better than your feet."

"Why would you cut open a stink beetle?"

"To retrieve one of Thorik's Runestones, which he irresponsibly left on the floor."

"Do you really think my feet smell?"

"I've smelled better things pulled out of a pig's rectum," he replied as a joke.

"What were you doing pulling things out of pig's rectum?" Grewen countered with his own sense of humor, while they headed up the next hill and continued to banter back and forth.

Meanwhile, Thorik tried to get Ericc to talk. "Your father meant a lot to me." He received no response. "He saved our lives more than once. If it wasn't for him, the entire Dovenar Kingdom would be under water."

"Don't paint him angelic. I know better," Ericc finally said.

"He was a good man."

"A good man doesn't leave his son to be raised by others."

"He had no choice."

"That's a lie. He chose to leave me. He chose to never return to see me. He chose to let me grow up without him. And now to die before I could ever see him again."

"He was protecting you."

"To what end? To live a life alone, without a father? I would have rather died alongside him than hide in a cave all my life."

"He tried to do what was best for all of us. He was responsible for the Dovenar Kingdom, as well as the rest of Australis. He's saved hundreds of thousands of lives."

"Forgoing his family in his noble quests. How dare he bring me into this world if he wasn't going to be there for me? I hate him for it. His responsibility to Australis constantly put my mother and me in danger. It killed my mother, and it's his fault. Where was he? He promised to protect us."

"He couldn't possibly be there to protect you every moment." Thorik recalled his own situation with Avanda.

"Then he shouldn't have told us he would. Hidden away, I've missed out on my youth. Because of him, I'm being hunted down by the Del'Unday as well as the kingdom you talk so righteously about. Because of him, my life is in shambles."

"Listen, you need to stop blaming your father for all of your issues. He did the best he could for you. He loved you. He would have died for your mother if he could have. You need to accept who he was and take responsibility for yourself, your own actions, and your own future."

"That's exactly what I was doing before you came along. I was waiting for Darkmere to arrive at Corrock."

"To end your life?"

"To end his."

"Revenge won't bring your father back or give you those lost years of youth."

"No, but it will end this torment once and for all. I will continue to be hunted until one of us is dead."

Thorik didn't know how to reply. Ericc's last statement was correct, even if Thorik didn't agree with the boy's plans.

The two stopped talking about the subject. Aside from general communication around evening camps, Ericc isolated himself from the rest.

On a number of occasions, Thorik attempted to strike up a conversation about Ericc's E'rudite power to shift locations in the blink of an eye, but failed to get the young man to talk each time.

32

UNWELCOME

Days had passed before the terrain changed to include sporadic sinkholes filled with lush vegetation, surrounded by the desert rocks. Traveling along the southern slopes of the Ossuary Range, they frequently ran across small streams, which supplied water to the great Volney Lakes. Many of these streams were underground, only exposing themselves in these sinkholes before disappearing again.

Brimmelle stopped in his tracks. "Why are we traveling east? The Dovenar Kingdom is west, as well as Farbank."

"Ro'Volney Lake is east. It is a place of safety for the Ov'Unday." Grewen adjusted his grip of the two long branches on either side of the litter as he dragged Santorray up the hill. "Salvation for our people."

Brimmelle scoffed. "Your people? Haven't we had enough of cities filled with Altereds?"

"It's good to see how open-minded you've become," Grewen joked.

"This entire journey has done nothing but reinforce my belief that Altereds bring confusion and harm to this land."

"Yes, because the people of Southwind were so much gentler," the giant mused.

"Santorray attacked one of their leaders, and then he and Thorik escaped from their prison. Of course, they were going to come after us. I consider our meeting with them in the O'Sid Fields to be a blessing in our effort to escape those Del creatures."

Santorray squirmed in his confines as he awoke from his unconsciousness. He struggled to move because of the tight straps, a feeling he was not comfortable with. "Grewen, free me at once. I can't take this any longer. I'm going to crack someone's skull if I'm not unrestrained."

Brimmelle pointed at the blothrud. "See? Look at the violence inherent in their species."

Santorray tried to break free. "You're first, Brimmelle. When I get out of here, I'll—"

"You'll what? Show everyone that I'm right by attacking a defenseless Num half your size?"

"That's enough, you two." Thorik stood at the top of a hill as the rest approached. "Grewen, how much farther to safety?"

"We're close. Just over the next ridge and we'll be bathing our sore feet in the Ro'Volney Lake."

Reaching the next main hill opened up an oasis before them. In the center of the desert was a green-trimmed lake full of life. Small sand dunes occasionally rolled along the shoreline, hiding the trunks of trees and large vegetation, but for the most part lush tropical plants formed the outline of the lake.

Huts blended into the vegetation as Ov'Unday species went about their business. Horned cluppers filled their hollow ivory tusks with water to bring back to the settlement, while Mognins watered fields and harvested crops.

Giant sloth-like creatures slowly roamed the village as they went about their business. Known as gathlers, this species reminded Thorik of the elderly with their slow, methodical movements.

As they approached the first Ov'Unday settlement, the short, dark hairs on Santorray's neck stood on end. "They will not let us pass."

"They won't let you pass, is what you mean," Brimmelle said. "After what your species has done to them."

"Brimmelle, not now," Thorik ordered.

A few Mognins and one gathler had spotted the travelers and met them on the edge of the village. The gathler calmly addressed Grewen as the group's leader. "Truth be said."

Grewen responded to the greeting. "Truth be heard."

"I am Coova, voice of our village."

"I am Grewen, voice of our pod."

"How is it you travel with these species?" Coova asked.

"They are my family."

"Of what family are you?"

"I am Grewen of the Ki'Ov'Unday, but my traveling companions are my personal family pod."

"Pod members may dine with us, but they are not to pass through these lands. Only pure family can venture beyond to Trewek."

"We ask for sanctuary. All other paths are blocked by those who wish to see our companion dead."

One of the Mognins looked past Grewen at the blothrud tied to the litter. "A death sentence on a Del'Unday is not our issue."

Grewen smiled. "No, it's the human who is in this peril. He is the son of Ambrosius."

"Ambrosius? Why would you bring his tension to our land?"

"The boy is in need of safety. His father no longer can provide it."

"To invite him in would ask for outsiders to hunt him down in our lands. Why would we risk this?"

"Because we follow the compassion of Trewek. The innocent boy needs our help."

One of the local Mognins sized up the lad. "Do you request our security?"

"I don't ask for anyone's help," Ericc answered.

"Then none will be granted," the Mognin replied.

Disappointed in Ericc's response, Thorik stepped up front. "Just because he doesn't ask for our help doesn't mean he doesn't need it."

"Truth be said. Continue," Coova said.

"Ericc is angry at his father and Darkmere. He's willing to risk his life to vent those feelings. We need time to talk to him and work through this. Time we don't have out here in the desert."

Coova's brows moved slowly down in between his eyes. "We do not wish for you to bring anger into our land. No one will house it. Without shelter, you will be no better off."

Grewen got a thought and tried a new tactic. "Ambrosius used to live on the south side of the lake, just west of Lagona Falls. He was granted residency."

Coova methodically nodded. "Truth be heard, but this is not Ambrosius."

Thorik added to Grewen's path. "Ericc lived there as well when he was a child, so he is already a resident unless they revoked it."

"Not that we know of. But we are a long way from such places and would not know of such affairs."

"But you can't assume it has been revoked," Thorik said.

"Truth be heard."

"So, he should be allowed to travel to his home."

The Mognins looked at each other before waiting for the gathler to speak.

Coova mulled the discussion in his mind for a while before finally responding. "Truth be said."

"Excellent." Thorik gave a sigh of relief.

"But not the blothrud," Coova added.

Thorik couldn't believe the prejudice of such passive creatures. "He is injured. To leave him out in the desert would be no less than murder."

"You may travel with him back from where you came. We did not suggest you leave him here to die," Coova said without empathy for their plight.

"But that would split us up."

"Truth be heard."

Thorik's jaw tightened at the slow, emotionless gathler. "We won't do that. He's risked his life for us. He deserves to see this through as much as us. As Grewen said earlier, we're family."

"No, you're a pod. A subgroup attached to a family member, which has not been approved by the collective group. Few non-Ov'Unday are considered to be family. A Del'Unday as a family member would be a sight to be seen."

Once again, Thorik looked to Grewen for help in getting Santorray past this barrier of prejudice.

Adjusting his hands again on the litter, Grewen suggested an option to give them some time to think about the issue. "Can we partake from the lake's relaxing venue until we are at least rested?"

"With a blothrud walking free amongst our homes and children?"

"Of course not. He would stay confined to the litter."

One of the mognin's addressed Grewen directly. "Grewen of the Ki'Ov'Unday takes responsibility for his bindings staying taut?"

Grewen lifted his shoulders up at attention. "Truth be heard."

"Truth be said," Coova replied.

33

BLOTHRUD AMONG
OV'UNDAYS

Springing over thirty feet in the air, a Yularian snake flipped through the air in an acrobatic sequence of moves before splashing back into the lake. The aquatic Ov'Unday species had been entertaining the travelers during their feast as locals enjoyed getting to know the Nums, as well as Ericc and Grewen.

Several of the agile winged sea snakes coiled around Gluic as she stood up to her waist in the lake. Yularians covered her and flapped their brightly colored wings as the elder Num reached out with her arms.

Brimmelle sniffed at the food with hesitation. If it weren't for his stomach growling, he would most definitely have passed on the odd-looking fruits and vegetables. "Mother, stay away from those creatures. Who knows what they are capable of?"

Avanda cracked opened a nut to find sweet tasting berries inside. "This is amazing." She proceeded to try at least one taste of everything available and stuffed several of her favorites in her pouches for later.

Ericc bit into a sour melon and spit it out. "I can't eat this."

Thorik handed him a stalk of a local vegetable. "Try these. They have a spicy bite to them, but they're very enjoyable."

Tasting it, Ericc found it to be true. "Why are you doing this?"

"Doing what?" Thorik replied.

"You risked your life for me in the Southwind Mines and then again in Corrock. What do you feel you owe me?"

"You? Nothing. I made a promise to your father to protect you from Darkmere."

"Why?"

"Because of what happened. His death."

"If it was Darkmere who killed my father, why do you feel you personally have a debt?"

Thorik squirmed slightly. "Darkmere didn't actually kill your father, directly..."

"How do you kill someone indirectly?"

"Ericc, your father and I were deceived by one of Darkmere's minions and baited into the dark lord's trap. Once we met him in combat at Weirfortus, the dam broke and Darkmere escaped, knowing Ambrosius would do the right thing and try to hold back the waters from the dam's reservoir. In doing that, your father prevented a flood from destroying the kingdom."

"I don't understand. Holding back the water wouldn't have killed him; only letting go and being crushed by it would. But then the flood would have occurred."

"Not if the reservoir doors were shut to prevent it."

"How was he able to close them while holding back the water?"

"He wasn't." Thorik rubbed his strained eyes as he recalled the event. "I was responsible for closing the door behind him."

"You trapped him inside?"

"Yes." The answer was difficult for Thorik to say.

"You killed my father," Ericc said through clenched teeth.

"No, it's not like that."

"And now you feel protecting me resolves your transgression." By now, emotion filled Ericc's voice.

"You don't know what happened. You weren't there."

"If I had been there, I would have helped my father out instead of letting him die so you could survive."

"Ericc! Stop it. I loved Ambrosius as though he was my own father. He believed in me. He trusted me. I would have done anything to save him. But I couldn't. It destroyed me to close those doors. When he asked me to protect you from being sacrificed, I gave my word, and I mean to live up to it."

Ericc absorbed Thorik's words. "I don't know what to say." Standing up from the group, he began to walk toward the lake, but stopped and turned back for a few last statements. "Thorik, I envy you. You lived my life. My father treated you as his own son; you traveled together and fought together. He praised you and taught you, and in the end, he asked you to take his life to save others. I wasn't a part of any of it. The joys, the sorrows, the victories, the failures. I have no memories of my father like you do. I missed it all."

Turning, Ericc walked out by Gluic, who was now covered with Yularian snakes, all flapping so hard that she had been lifted up several feet above the water's surface.

"Feed me," bellowed Santorray from the side, still strapped to the makeshift litter.

The order went unanswered for the fourth time, but the blothrud was not going to lower his voice and ask nicely, regardless of how hungry he was.

Before he ordered food for a fifth time, he noticed a commotion among the Ov'Unday. Something was wrong.

A strong, low drumbeat pounded away, stopped, and then pounded again. It was their warning drum. An announcement to take cover for some, but a call to arms for others.

The Ov'Unday grabbed nets and rudimentary defensive weapons and raced for the edge of the village.

Santorray stretched his neck around to see what was happening. "They tracked us here."

Thorik looked at the first set of hills, waiting to see what would come over. "Who?"

Grewen watched as well. "Whoever won the battle that we escaped from."

A mass of figures appeared at the hill's crest as the army approached the village.

Waiting for a signal, the first line of attackers finally launched forward after a blaring howl was heard from behind them.

Racing down the hill, brandercats and giant hogs were followed by a line of krupes.

The Ov'Unday stood steady, wasting no energy on rushing toward them, conserving everything they could until it was required.

The Del'Unday front line reached its victims.

Mognins tossed out nets to capture brandercats while grappling with the hogs as they hit their defensive lines. In spite of their size and strength, the mognins couldn't contain them all. Several broke through and headed for the village, intending to create disaster.

The line of Ov'Unday was now broken as many chased the Del'Unday down, and others held the captive Dels at bay.

By this point, the krupes had a military line ready for an attack. A second howl was called out, summoning the first line of warriors to return to their posts. Those not restrained by the Ovs did just that.

Bellfor stepped forward to discuss the Ov'Unday's surrender.

Coova slowly approached the halfway point to meet the blothrud in hopes of determining how to avoid a bloodbath.

Even from a distance, Santorray could see the talk was not going well. "Cut me free. I can stop this," he said to Thorik.

"How?" the Num asked.

"Don't ask questions. Just free me."

Grewen shook his head at Thorik and Santorray. "Allow the Ov'Unday to take care of this in our own way." He then headed over to stand with his people.

The leader from the Ov'Unday returned to his council of leaders. "They want Ambrosius' son," Coova informed his council.

A clupper shook his head. "We granted him sanctuary."

"He has resident rights. Trewek promises protection," said a Mognin.

Coova listened to their comments. "They will attack if we refuse."

"They will most likely attack after we give them what they want."

"That would be characteristic of them," Coova agreed.

"We easily outnumber them ten to one."

Looking at the huts and families that lived in them, Coova sighed. "Even at those odds, we will lose family members. Are you willing to risk losing your wife or child over this boy we don't even know?"

The discussion continued among the leaders as Santorray argued with Thorik over his own freedom.

Thorik finally gave in and pulled out a dagger to cut through the straps but then stopped himself before doing so. "These are not your people. You told me yourself that you're not Corrockian."

"I'm not, but I have a better chance of stopping a battle than these mogs and gaths."

They watched as Coova returned to Bellfor and signaled that there would be no deal.

A sigh of relief came from Thorik until he saw Bellfor decapitate the gathler for refusing his offer. Coova's body fell to the ground.

The Ov'Undays gasped at the atrocity, as did Thorik and his family pod.

It was now the responsibility of the second-in-command to walk up to Bellfor and answer his offer. A clupper stepped forward on all four of his hooves. His large tusks could be used as weapons if need be.

"The offer has now changed," Bellfor told the clupper. "The boy must accompany by a dozen of your adult males. My troops crave fresh meat."

Appalled, the clupper snorted loudly. "We will not give in to your demands. Any attempt on my life or any of our people will be the end of these negotiations. You know as well as I do that your army is too small to take us on."

"We'll see about that." Bellfor raised his sword to strike, only to stop at the sight of the creature behind the clupper. He struggled to understand what he was seeing. A blothrud was entering the open land from the Ov'Unday side.

Thorik had cut Santorray free of his restraints without receiving permission. The Num could not stand by and see the slaughter continue. He needed to trust Santorray to resolve this.

Dealing with the severe pain of his wounds, Santorray tightened his jaw as he put on a façade of being fully healed. Strutting up to the clupper, he patted the Ov'Unday on the back. "I'll take it from here. Go back to your people."

Hesitating, the clupper eventually trusted Santorray and backed off, returning to the other leaders. He didn't see how it could hurt their efforts to allow the two blothruds to talk.

Bellfor spit on the ground near Santorray's feet. "A blothrud living among the Ov'Unday? What kind of Fesh are you?"

Stepping on the ground where the saliva landed, Santorray kicked the ground to cause dust to fly. "You question me? You will not address me until I ask you to!"

Infuriated at Santorray's condescending tone, Bellfor swung his weapon hard, only to be stopped by two sabers. "How dare you talk to me in such a manner? I am Bellfor, champion of Corrock." A second swipe of his weapon was stopped as well.

Santorray blocked two more quick blows before speaking. "Does Corrock no longer follow Ergrauth?"

"Damn those who speak Ergrauth's name while standing with his enemies. Corrock will defend him to our death and after."

Santorray's defensive moves to block the relentless attacks caused his wounds to open and bleed. The pain was overpowering as he fought to appear in control. "Then back down and heed my command. I am a messenger of his voice."

"You're a lying Fesh with no honor."

Ripping off the bandages from his shoulder, Santorray exposed an open wound next to a symbol branded deep into his red skin.

Bellfor was stunned at the marking, holding his sword firm against Santorray's sabers instead of placing another attack. "You are an Ergrauthian Elite? What would one of our lord's supreme defenders be doing in these parts?"

"To question me is to question Ergrauth himself."

Bellfor pulled back to listen as he eyed the mark. If this was truly an Elite before him, Santorray's words would demand authority. Anyone caught impersonating an Elite would be sentenced to an eternity of shame and torture in Ergrauth's city.

Santorray allowed Bellfor to get a long look at the branding on his shoulder. "I am here to take Ambrosius' son to Surod to put an end to this prophecy once and for all." He covered his wound up to stop the bleeding. "Your attack here is defying Ergrauth's wishes and my plans to carry out my mission."

Bellfor stayed silent and backed up a step. He realized the danger he had put himself into by striking an Elite. It was a potential death sentence.

Santorray stepped up to Bellfor. "Listen closely. I will have the Ovs release our people. You will then return to Corrock to put your efforts into rebuilding that pathetic city into something that is grand, something we are proud to call ours, like it once was. Do you understand my orders?"

Arms at his sides, Bellfor nodded. "Yes, Elite. But what shall I tell Darkmere when he arrives?"

"Tell him to meet Santorray in Surod on the Eve of Light."

34

FAMILY

The Del'Unday were released, and the entire army marched back over the hill. It was a sight no Ov'Unday would have believed if they hadn't seen it with their own eyes.

Thorik ran over to Santorray, who continued to stand in defiance in the center of the battlefield. "How did you do that? What did you say?"

Santorray's pain had taken its toll. His wounds had reopened, and blood had been lost to the dirt at his feet. The blothrud fell.

Santorray dreamed of days past as a child, when his sister and he trained to fight. Visions of later battles flowed through his mind, while Darkmere and Ambrosius faded in and out of view. The series of visions crossed his thoughts until he felt himself being stabbed in his right shoulder blade.

Waking from his sleep, the blothrud felt a sharp poking on his back. One of the local gathler women was tapping a hammer onto a long stick with a fine angled tip to it. She periodically dipped the tip into black ink.

"Congratulations," Grewen announced to Santorray. "You're the first Del to become part of the Ro'Ov'Unday Family."

The tattoo on his shoulder blade had just been finished. The symbol of the family was now a permanent mark on Santorray's body. The decorative circle with a wavy line crossing it at the center was very similar to the one he had seen on Grewen's back. Each line was actually made up of tightly placed symbols.

Grewen helped the blothrud up off his stomach to a sitting position. "You are now free to walk our land and help us protect it from outsiders."

Santorray looked at the audience who had watched the tattooing. The entire village had come out to participate. Tears in many of their eyes, they smiled softly at the new member.

"Grewen, what's this all about?"

"They have all come to give you a part of themselves. You will now be responsible for their lives as much as they are for yours."

One of the Mognins stepped up to Santorray. Pricking his finger, he placed it up against the fresh tattoo, pressing his blood against the red skin of the blothrud. "I trust you with the lives of myself, my wife, and my children." Moving off, he let the next Ov'Unday have his turn.

Santorray realized that the entire village was standing in line to do the same thing.

Next was a young clupper with tears in his eyes. Leaning his face against Santorray's back, he brushed his tears against the tattoo. "Thank you for saving my father's life. I'm in your debt."

Santorray looked up at Grewen. "Are they all going to…"

"Yes."

"This could take hours."

"Usually does."

By the time the last Ov'Unday pressed her lips against the tattoo, the ink had smeared down his back as it mixed with blood, tears, and saliva. The original circle and wavy line still held strong as the smeared trail faded the farther down it went.

Santorray was emotionally drained. He had never witnessed such an outpouring of love and trust. Spending most of his life on his own had made him immune to such needs. Or at least he thought he was immune.

For the first time in a long time, he felt welcomed. Not being on edge and ready to fight was an odd feeling. So odd was the emotion that he didn't know if he liked it or not. But he wouldn't have time to find out; they needed to head south.

Santorray stood and walked over to Thorik, who was watching Avanda and Ericc play in the lake. "We must leave."

"Why? This place is peaceful. Avanda has finally opened Ericc up. We're safe here."

"For how long?"

"Until we decide to leave," Thorik said.

"Sec, we are placing these people in danger. Don't you think Darkmere will find us here? And when he does, he will kill everyone in his path."

"We should at least wait until the Eve of Light has passed."

"No, the Corrockians know he is here, so this is the first place Darkmere will look. We need to leave before he arrives. He'll know right away that the son of Ambrosius is not among them and leave them be."

"Where could we go that is safer than here?"

"We shall retreat to the mist of Lagona Falls. My understanding is that it's the Ovs' safe haven for their afterlife."

"A graveyard?"

"No one lives there, so no one will be placed in jeopardy."

Thorik breathed in the calmness of the village. Even Brimmelle was getting comfortable on the shoreline. "Are you sure?"

"Yes."

"I'm trusting you with our lives, Santorray."

The blothrud looked at each of Thorik's family pod members and sighed. "I know."

35

LAGONA FALLS

Thorik's party left the village and followed the shoreline to the east, occasionally stopping to rest in the shade of the palm trees that grew along the sandy beaches. Passing the outskirts of Trewek, they marveled at the size of the towers and architectural grace of the massive city. Santorray had no desire to enter and convinced the group to continue south, away from the Ro'Volney Lake, to the larger Ki'Volney Lake.

Days went by with general chatter, mostly from Brimmelle about how he felt they should have stayed in the safety of the village a little longer.

As they walked along the north shores of the Ki'Volney Lake, the eastern cliffs became more apparent. Harsh mountain ranges lined the region, with the grandest being the Shi'Pel Peaks to the southeast. They were the highest points in all the lands.

A wide waterfall, several times the height of the marble column they once traveled on, broke free from the mountain landscape, spilling so much water so far down that it became mist before hitting. The mist filled the valley along the cliff line and out to the lake.

Thorik appeared concerned as they proceeded to travel deeper into the misty vapors as they continued to thicken. "Grewen, is it safe to travel past the falls?"

"Safe, yes; recommended, no."

"Is that because it is sacred land where you bury your dead?"

"No, Lagona Falls is where we go to die. It is where we make our final pilgrimage to seek enlightenment and endless wisdom. It is the end of our journeys and the beginning of a higher level. We don't normally plan on coming back out."

Ericc looked skeptically at Grewen. "But we can, can't we?"

"I don't see why not. I know of some who have passed it, staying out of the eternal lands. We just need to stay along the lake's shoreline."

The plants in the thick fog grew taller than normal. Thick mushrooms and moss coated wide tree trunks, and colorful flowers opened up large enough to sit in. The overgrowth made it difficult to see very far.

Grewen watched as several hummingbirds licked sap running off a mound of large fungi. Breaking off a piece of the mound, he took a bite. The sap was sweet to the taste and smell. "The good news is we won't go hungry."

It was at this time that soft music from somewhere in the distant misty woods sang in the Nums' ears. Elegant and enchanting, the music tugged at their gentle emotions and relaxed them.

Even Brimmelle was put at ease by the tone. "Where is that coming from?"

The Nums moved away from the beach and into the forest, light-footed as they searched for the source. Avanda held Gluic's hand to help her through the heavy foliage.

Ericc and the two Unday followed the Nums, unaware of what the little ones had heard.

"This smells like a trap," Santorray growled as he finally started hearing the music. "We should stay near the lake and continue heading south."

Nevertheless, east was the direction of the two Unday and Ericc as they tried to keep up with the Nums. Thick vines spanned the trees, acting like crude nets against the large bodies of Santorray and Grewen. Ericc and the Nums, however, had no problem walking between and under them.

"Thorik! Get back here. We need to stay by the shoreline," Santorray yelled without getting a response.

Ericc was the next to hear the sounds, causing him to race ahead and catch up to Thorik.

Grewen eventually heard the music, stopping to listen without the noise of his heavy footfalls. "Aw, Trewek's Aria. The call to enlightenment. It's more exquisite than I had been led to believe."

Deeper and deeper they went into the forest as the mist, plants, and vines became denser. Soon the Nums and Ericc were out of the Undays' view.

Santorray cupped his hands near his mouth to focus his voice. "Thorik? Ericc? Where are you?"

There was no response.

"Enlightenment?" Santorray snarled at Grewen. "This is one of the reasons your people are weak. You allow these types of places to exist without knowing anything about them."

Grewen kept moving the vines out of his path as he continued forward. "What would you suggest, an invasion into these fertile lands to wipe out all dangers?"

"Absolutely."

"Barbaric. Can't you coexist with nature? Why do you have to destroy it?"

"I'll coexist with it once I know its strengths and weaknesses."

"You talk like it's a potential enemy."

"Sometimes it can be."

Passing by large mounds of fungi and through thick leafy vines, the two stopped to listen for the rest of their party.

Grewen hummed with the tranquil sounds of Trewek's song. Swaying with the music, he moved forward, deeper into the forest.

"Grewen, snap out of it," Santorray ordered.

But the Mognin's grin said it all as he relaxed his eyelids and sauntered away under the music's spell.

Santorray continued to call for the others as he followed Grewen through the forest and eventually into a clearing.

A motionless pond rested in the center of the open area, and the Nums and Ericc sat along its misty shores. Peaceful silence was only interrupted by the soft song of the local hummingbirds, which hovered over the lake and around the new guests.

"It's amazing." Avanda lifted her hand out for one of the hummingbirds to land on.

"Beyond words." Brimmelle rested against a rock, watching three birds sing inches from his face.

Gluic sat near Brimmelle as she watched his enjoyment. "It's good to see you smile." Turning, she enjoyed the song from several birds inches from her own face.

Santorray did not share their enjoyment. "So you discovered the source of the music. Now we need to head out."

Grewen sat down. "Why? This feels safer than anywhere else we've been."

"A little too serene for my taste," Santorray spit back.

Thorik nodded. "Yes, serene. It is a wonderful place to hide from Darkmere."

"No, this is not a place to hide. We must travel south."

Desire and other worldly issues started fading from their minds. The concepts of fighting and revenge mellowed as they relaxed in the safe haven.

Ericc looked at the blothrud. "Sit down and enjoy yourself."

"Ericc, I thought you were tired of hiding from Darkmere. Yet you sit there now and do just that."

"Hide?" Ericc questioned. "If anything, I feel free. Free to enjoy life for the first time."

"You're not free. You're hiding in a forest," Santorray argued.

"I feel like I can do anything right now. I could remove all evil from the world with a wave of my hand."

"But you choose to sit there and do nothing instead."

"This is a glorious place." Ericc ignored his last statement.

Thorik looked over at his agitated friend. "Santorray, we will camp here for the night."

Santorray stood silent, watching the group enjoy the serenity of the music and smells. Each member was in their own world as they gazed at the hovering birds.

The blothrud continued to try to get them moving, even to the extent of lifting them to their feet, only to see them sit back down again.

Frustrated at the situation, he walked out of the pond area to vent his frustrations by slamming his fist into trees, logs, and anything else in his reach. After punching a mound of fungi, a large section of it cracked off, exposing a body underneath.

Encapsulated in the fungi sat a gathler, leaning against a tree with a contented smile on his face. He appeared to have been enjoying the same sounds as his friends.

Several hummingbirds swarmed the blothrud, attacking him from all angles. He had destroyed one of their food sources.

While swatting away the birds, he ripped off more fungi, further revealing the Ov'Unday. One of his wrist spikes accidentally grazed the creature, cutting it open, and causing it to bleed.

"It's still alive?"

More birds showed up to attack the blothrud. Their powerful beaks poked hard at the blothrud, trying to get to his eyes. Whispers from every direction replaced the beautiful song with threats of death. "Get out!" they shouted.

"Myth'Unday! I should have known," Santorray barked, while protecting his face from them.

He ripped off the top of the fungi mound and exposed the gathler's brain, which had fungi growing from within it. Sections of the gathler's chest were also open cavities as fungi grew inside him.

There was no way to pull the gathler out of the mound without ripping out the fungi which appeared to be keeping him alive.

Santorray ran back to the pond to alert his friends. All of them had the same blissful expression as the gathler he had just discovered.

Gripping Grewen on the shoulder, he shook him hard to pull him out of his distant thoughts. Looking down near his hand, Santorray noticed small outcroppings of fungi across the Ov'Unday's back. It had already begun.

Hours went by as Santorray tried unsuccessfully to wake the crew from their trance. Fungi continued to grow on them, though the blothrud desperately tried to remove it while fighting off the Myth'Unday birds.

Night fell, and his ability to see new patches of the fungi became difficult. The less effective he was at removing the fungi, the less the hummingbirds bothered him.

Santorray removed his talisman necklace and untied one of the beads in it. After tapping his talisman, he squeezed it tight. Once it turned a glowing red, he threw it high into the air.

The red glow rocketed into the night sky before returning to the earth and extinguishing.

Santorray lit a lantern and continued his removal process for several hours before attempting a second bead. It was this second attempt that brought help.

The red-tipped silver dragon dove down between the trees and into the opening, scaring the Myth'Unday away. The lantern light reflected off his scales, giving him a glistening effect as he landed.

"What have you done? Were the instructions too difficult for you to understand?" Draq asked in an angry voice.

"What took you so long? You're going to put everything at risk," Santorray countered.

"Why didn't you kill him at Corrock?"

"Hold your forked tongue. We need to get them out of here before they become part of the forest." The blothrud shone the lantern on Thorik's neck, which was now covered with fungi.

Draq looked around at the party members as they gazed into nowhere. "How could you let this happen? He trusted you."

"Don't tell me what I already know. Help me get them out of here."

"Do it yourself."

"I can't lift them all."

"All you need is Ericc. Leave the rest."

"From what you have told me, I doubt Ambrosius would want me to abandon Thorik."

"We don't have time to ask him, do we? We both know the dangers of not accomplishing our mission. Grab Ericc and finish your task. Come back for the others later, once the sacrifice is complete."

"There's a good chance that they won't be alive when I return," Santorray argued.

"There's a greater chance they won't survive at Surod!"

Santorray looked around at the faces he had come to know. Recalling the trials they had been through and the camaraderie they had shown caused him to hesitate to take such actions. He had built friendships and become part of a family unit. Even memories of nearly ripping Brimmelle apart brought a smile to his face.

"No," Santorray said. "We must save them all."

"Listen, blothrud, you have a mission to perform. Stay focused and carry it out. Killing Ericc in front of Thorik and the Corrockians would have ended this. But now that you're this far south, sacrificing him in Surod is your best option."

"I'm not leaving without my entire team."

"Team? They aren't part of your team. If they really knew your mission, they would skin you alive. So don't get emotional about friendship and trust. They trust you only because you haven't let them know who you really are and what you're trying to do."

Santorray would have rather had a physical fight with the dragon than this verbal one.

Draq watched as the blothrud struggled with his decision. "Would Thorik save you if he knew you were an Ergrauthian Elite, vowed to carry out Ergrauth's every order?" Draq pointed at Santorray. "Murderer of Kasa, beheader of ChoFon, and traitor to Ergrauth himself. I know your past better than most, and loyalty is not your forte."

Santorray tightened his fists as he listened to this trial by his peer.

Draq continued to drill his point. "Would they risk their lives for you if they knew you've worked for Ambrosius and Darkmere? Face it; you've broken every alliance you've ever had. You have no friends, no team, and no companions unless you lie to them about who you are. Once you strike Ericc down, they won't trust you anymore anyway."

Santorray took a deep breath. Draq was correct, but it was a chance that he would have to take. "We take all of them or the mission is over. It is now your decision that will determine Ericc's fate."

Draq flapped his wings hard and thrashed his tail, pounding it against the mossy ground. After letting off some steam, he finally gave in. "I will carry Ericc to the Volney Shore. No more."

"You will carry him last, after the Nums."

The two Dels stood firm, ready to lash out at each other as the tension mounted.

"This is the last time I'm coming to your aid," Draq said.

"This is the first and only time I've asked for your help."

"You owe me."

"Get in line! I owe a lot of people, including these Nums."

Draq grudgingly accepted the terms and lifted the first Num up and out of the forest.

Santorray lifted Grewen's enormous arms over his head and began dragging the mognin to the lake shoreline while Draq took care of the rest. The fungi quickly flaked away once they were out of the forest and into a safe location.

It wasn't until sunrise when Santorray reached the Nums at the lake. He had been lugging Grewen all night long, and he finally fell onto the beach from exhaustion.

The Nums had been lying near the shore for several hours after Draq had flown away. Waking up, one by one, they stretched from their marvelously refreshing dreams, ready to hit the day hard.

Grewen also awoke, and noticed that his clothes were filled with moss, branches, leaves, and everything else that could be scooped up off the forest floor. As he stood up to stretch, a pile of forest debris fell from under his robe onto the beach. "Well, that was unexpected."

"How did we get here?" Ericc asked as he sat up on his knees.

Shaking it off, the mognin was also extremely refreshed and exhilarated. "Last thing I recall was walking through the forest."

"I never even set up camp." Thorik stretched and yawned.

Brimmelle stood up and stretched his back before walking over to Santorray. "Get up, you lazy beast." He kicked sand onto the back of the blothrud to get a reaction.

Santorray rolled over after only being asleep for a few minutes. His fatigue was obvious in his dismissal of Brimmelle's comment.

"And what do you know of our getting to this place?" Brimmelle asked bitterly.

Santorray slowly rose to his knees. "I saved your life by carrying you out of the forest and onto this beach."

"Dragged, is more like it," Grewen chuckled as he pulled another branch out of his robe.

"Oh." Brimmelle showed little appreciation. "I don't recall being in any danger in the forest."

Thorik and Ericc agreed with a nod.

"Regardless, daylight is burning. We can't sleep the day away," the Fir said as everyone collected their gear and headed south.

Exhausted, Santorray slogged his way to his feet and followed. "You're welcome," he sarcastically said to the distant group of travelers.

❧ 36 ❧

AMBROSIUS' HOME

Thorik's Log: 14th day of the 6th month of the 650th year.

We have left Lagona Falls and need to keep hidden until the 21st day of the month, when the threat of the Eve of Light sacrifice has passed. We are almost there. Just one more week.

As they traveled southeast, the mist-covered terrain abruptly changed back to sunbaked lands, west of the Shi'Pel Mountains. A thin strip of short bluffs along the shores remained fresh with life. They followed this shoreline oasis for most of the day until they noticed an abandoned cliff-dwelling settlement.

Several shacks were built up against the smooth, rock-faced bluffs overlooking Ki'Volney Lake. Randomly placed on the short bluff, all were the size of one-room homes without paths or ladders to get to them.

Only one of the shacks rested by the bottom of the bluff, so the group investigated it.

"I know this place." Ericc was astonished at the sight. Running up to the lowest door, he looked back at Thorik with a wide smile. "This is my home."

"Too small for Ambrosius," Santorray replied.

Thorik walked up to the door, next to Ericc. "You remember living here?"

"Vaguely. It's been eight years, but I do recall that symbol." Ericc pointed to the bluff wall near the shack. Three overlapping circles, each with a single rune within it, were etched into the rock. "My father designed that to represent my parents and myself. I remember him teaching me that all would be safe when I found this symbol."

"Apparently he was wrong," Santorray said.

Pushing the door open, they revealed a large, dust-covered room. The shack walls were nothing more than a façade for an enormous home carved out of the bluff itself.

The large, round room domed up to the center. Thick roots from trees on the bluff worked their way down the walls and into the floor. Etched-out shelves provided locations for art, which now lay broken on the floor. Furniture lay askew and dormant from the attack which once terrorized Ericc and his mother.

Several hallways exited the room, all with stairs leading up to reach the other shacks they had seen wedged onto the bluff.

"This is where I grew up." Ericc moved about as fragments of memories flashed in his head. "Mother was working in the kitchen when they arrived. She hid me over there just before the door was kicked in. They dragged mother out of the house, kicking and screaming. I never saw her again."

Thorik stood near Ericc and tried to envision the horror of a child's view of the crime. "What happened to you?"

"They grabbed me and tied me up. We traveled for days on Notarian roads and bridges before they took me up the mountain."

"What mountain?"

"Shi'Pel."

"Why?"

"To bring me to Surod."

"Surod?"

"Yes, it's halfway up the mountain, in the Go'ta Gorge."

Thorik turned and stormed out of the house, straight up to Santorray. "This is your idea of a safe place? Within sight of the very mountain where Darkmere plans to sacrifice Ericc?"

"Yes." The blothrud eyed Ericc standing in the doorway watching the confrontation.

Thorik didn't plan on such a casual response.

Santorray leaned over and dipped a cloth into the lake. He was tending to his wounds again, which were scarring over nicely. "Thorik, Ericc can't be on the run his whole life. He'd never be able to trust anyone for fear that they would turn him over to Darkmere."

"What's his other option, confront him?"

"Exactly."

"Are you crazy? Have you ever met Darkmere? He has powers we can't even begin to understand. He can change the air into fire or poison. He can manipulate the form of his body and alter the makeup of those he touches."

"Yes, I've met him. And yes, he is powerful."

Ericc stepped closer. "So are we. Santorray is a great fighter, and Grewen has strength. Thorik, you have the Spear of Rummon, and I have some powers myself."

Avanda refused to be left out. "My magic can help."

"No," Thorik and Brimmelle said in unison.

Ericc wasn't backing down. "Thorik, you may have saved me, but you are sentencing me to a lifetime of hiding. I'm going with Santorray to take care of this once and for all."

Thorik looked to Grewen for advice. "And will you be traveling with Ericc to his death?"

"I told you I would do whatever I could to protect him from this fate. It would be very hard to do that from down here when he is on the mountain."

Thorik looked around for support to find only Brimmelle on his side. Gluic's grin told him that she was waiting for him to decide his own fate. "This is wrong. You're walking into a trap," Thorik announced.

Brimmelle wrapped his arms tightly across his chest. "This is the end of the line, where the Nums and the Altereds separate. It is time for us to go home. We can do no more."

Thorik panned from Fir Brimmelle to Grewen. "I have to agree with Brimmelle. I've done everything I can to save Ericc as promised. But I cannot willingly go into what I believe is a trap when we have other options." Thorik's eyes swelled with water as he looked at Grewen's face. "No matter how hard I try, I cannot save someone who does not wish to be saved. This is where our journey ends and we must part ways."

"So be it." Santorray finished cleaning his injuries. "You will be safe traveling along the shoreline to Eastland. Blend into the crowd and get transportation to Woodlen. I've never met a Num with a heart of a blothrud before I met you. Never lose that quality." Spitting in his hand, he held it out to Thorik, who spit in his own hand and slapped the two together.

Ericc collected his items before walking over to Thorik. "You honored my father's wishes. I give you credit for that. Remember him fondly; you were the son to him which I always wanted to be."

Grewen watched the first two begin their walk toward the mountain. "Thorik."

"Grewen, no, please don't go." Thorik's heart pounded hard against his tense chest, and his voice cracked with emotion. "I lost you once, and it about killed me. I can't lose you again."

Grewen's smile warmed the Num's heart like it always did. "Little man, you have your own journey and life ahead of you. You must do what feels right and then live with the ramifications of those actions. This feels right to me, but it's okay that it doesn't for you."

Thorik wiped his eyes. "I'll go if you tell me to."

"I would never do such a thing. Even with these broad shoulders, I can't carry that much weight of responsibility. You know that."

"At least tell me if I'm making a mistake."

"Only time can tell that." Grewen lifted the Num up for a last hug. "It takes courage to do what you feel is right, especially when those you love don't support you."

Setting Thorik back down, he waved at the group. "Goodbye, my friends. Safe journey home."

Thorik stood motionless as he watched Grewen turn and walk away, slowly catching up with the other two, heading for their potential end.

"I'm going with them," Avanda finally said, running past Thorik.

But it was short-lived; Thorik grabbed her and stopped her escape. "Avanda, this is not your fight. We've done our part."

"You've done yours, but I haven't done mine. I'm finally starting to understand how to use my magic. I can help."

"I know you can, but it's over. We promised to save Ericc and did just that with your help. Now it's time for us to go home. We can't spend the rest of our lives watching after him."

"He's part of our family now. It's our responsibility to be there for him when he needs us most."

"Sometimes you have to let go of family to let them travel on their own path and do things you don't believe in."

Disappointed, Avanda stood with Thorik and watched their friends disappear over the first hill.

It was over, and it was time to make plans to return to Farbank. In some way it was a relief to know they were going home. If they hurried, they could be there in time for the sounds, smells, and tastes of the harvest festival and all the food and contests that went along with it.

It felt good to start their return home after doing what they had set out to do and more.

As Thorik set up Ambrosius' old house for the night, he thought deeply about how much he missed his cottage and the people of his village. It was nice to be inside again with shelves to stack items and chairs to sit on. He forgot how much he missed the little things.

After his chores were done, Thorik sat down and pulled out his coffer of maps and notes. "It's been a long journey," he muttered at the drawings as he reminisced before adding new notes.

———

Thorik's Log: 15th day of the 6th month of the 650th year

Ericc leaves his parents' abandoned home near Lagona Falls as a free man. No longer a captive of men or beasts, he travels to confront his enemy in the temple of Surod. He leaves with Santorray and Grewen, but not me. It is time for us to return home, to Farbank, for I cannot save someone who does not wish to be saved.

———

As he neatly straightened up his papers and returned them back to their wooden case, Gluic walked into the house.

"It feels good to give up the fight and just rest," she said peacefully as she walked past him.

Thorik was shocked at the comment. "Granna, I'm not giving up. I saved Ericc from being captured. I did what I set out to do."

She nodded at his words as she dug in his sack of Runestones. "Yes, you are right. You only promised to free him, not to save him from his plight."

His shoulders raised at the underlying sarcasm. "I can't prevent him from going to Surod at some point in his life, I can't stop Santorray and Grewen from helping him, I can't stop the Eve of Light from occurring each year, and I can't stop Darkmere from hunting him down. I'm only one Num, a small one at that, without even a soul-marking for respect."

"And that is why you do not have them."

"What?"

"Dear grandson, you show great courage when under stress. But when you have time to plan, your faith in yourself falls behind all others."

"What are you saying?"

"Would you travel up that mountain if Ambrosius were here with you?"

Thorik straightened up. "Of course. We would stand a chance with him at our side."

"So, it is only worth fighting for a good cause if you are guaranteed a victory?"

"No… but it is foolish to walk into a trap, even for a good cause."

"Isn't that what Ambrosius did?"

Thorik realized she was correct. Ambrosius sacrificed himself to save many, even though he knew he was entering a trap. "I just wish I was something more than what I am. I have no powers or strength to achieve such a lofty goal."

Gluic walked back to the table and set his Runestone of Belief on the table in front of him. "Physical strength and magical powers are no match for someone who never gives up and continues to believe in himself. It is the will to succeed and a relentless drive to accomplish that which makes the difference in this world, not the birthright of power."

Thorik held the Runestone in his palm and stared at it while absorbing her words. "Granna, Ambrosius once told me I was special and reminded him of the Mountain King. I guess I secretly hoped to find out that I'm a descendant of the king himself."

"If you were, would you suddenly have more belief and faith in yourself?"

"I would be prouder." He took in a deep breath and swallowed hard. "Yes, I would have more faith in myself. Tell me, Granna. Am I his heir?"

"Thorik, you are not the offspring of any nobleman or king. And your pride should come from within, regardless of such. You are Thorik Dain; the one who prevented the great flood, the one who rescued Ericc from Corrock, the one who stood up against much stronger men when they attempted to lead us, and the one whose desire to do good overshadows his own well-being. I am very proud to be your grandmother. It is about time you start being proud of who you've become. It is this very conflict within you that prevents your soul-markings from showing themselves."

"But Granna, I was happy when I lived in Farbank. Why didn't the soul-markings show then?"

"You were content to pacify Brimmelle and the other villagers. You haven't been proud of yourself since your parents' deaths, which happened just before your markings were to show themselves. Ever since then, you have questioned every decision you have ever made instead of doing what you know is right and being proud of yourself for doing it."

Thorik was silent as she left the table and walked to the front door, holding it for Brimmelle as he entered the home carrying firewood. Closing the door behind her, she left Thorik to do some thinking.

Brimmelle walked to the fireplace. "It's about time you came to your senses and let these humans and Altereds work out their own problems. I can't wait until we get back to the comfort of our own village."

"I'm not going back yet. I need to help Ericc get past this point in his life. No one should have to live in fear of being seen alive."

Fir Brimmelle dropped his wood hard to the floor. "Oh no you don't! We agreed to let them go. We've done our part."

"Yes, you've done your part. You need to take Gluic and Avanda back to Farbank. I must catch up with Ericc to help him."

"You? What can you possibly do to help them? You'll be stomped on."

"I will do whatever it takes to succeed."

"Against Darkmere?"

"If he is there, yes."

Brimmelle walked over and grabbed his Sec by the collar with one hand while pointing harshly at Thorik's face with the other. "You listen to me. We are done with this."

Thorik took the Fir's wrist and pushed his arm away, freeing himself. "No, I'm not."

"What are you trying to prove?"

"Nothing. I believe I can make a difference, and Ericc needs me."

"If you leave, I'm done with you. You will no longer be a Sec of Farbank."

"If that is your decision, then I accept it."

"If you leave and die up on that mountain, you'll make your mother's death worth nothing. She will have sacrificed her own life to save you, and you will repay her by just tossing it away. How can you disrespect her with this futile attempt?"

Thorik moved his Runestone into the exact center on the surface of his coffer, tweaking the rotation to make it perfectly align with the box's corners as he thought about how to respond. "It is because she gave up her life for me that I know I must use every ounce of my being to make this world a better place and do what I believe is right."

Brimmelle turned his back to the boy in anger before tossing logs into the fireplace. "Under no circumstance are you taking Avanda! I've watched her and know she has deep feelings for you, but this is not up for a debate."

Thorik knew his uncle was done discussing it. "Agreed. But I need to tell her I will be leaving without her. Is she still out front?"

Brimmelle brushed his hands clean from the wood bark. "I don't know. I haven't seen her."

"Wasn't she outside helping you?"

"No, I thought she was in here with you."

Thorik instantly became anxious and uncomfortable. "You don't think she went after them, do you?"

"She wouldn't dare." Brimmelle raced out the front door to confirm his doubts.

Thorik ran upstairs, only to find it empty. Leaning out one of the upper windows, he could see Brimmelle ask Gluic where Avanda was. Gluic pointed down the path where Grewen, Santorray, and Ericc had traveled.

The path was empty, and it would be dark soon. Their only chance to catch up with her and the others was to start fresh in the morning and hope Grewen kept at a slow pace.

Brimmelle stared down the lonely path in disbelief. "Mother, when did she leave?"

"A few hours ago. Right after Ericc and the others left," Gluic said casually. "I guess that means we'll be going after her."

"Why didn't you stop her or tell us that she had left?" Brimmelle asked in frustration.

A devious grin grew on her face. "I'm sorry, dear. But back in Southwind, you asked me to not mediate your problems anymore."

❧ 37 ❧

ROAD TO GO'TA GORGE

Thorik, Brimmelle, and Gluic walked east along the dirt path, which ended at an ancient road leading up the cliff, and hopefully across a plateau, through the Go'ta Gorge, and up to Surod. Finely carved street stones now lay slightly askew from the ground underneath giving way. Column bases bordered both sides, some with columns still standing on them.

Thorik envisioned what it must have looked like when the road had first been built and thousands of people paraded on its grand path.

Every few hours, the road expanded into a round open area, often providing stone roofs for shade and wells for water. The Nums took pleasure in both, whenever they were available. However, many of these structures had fallen from battles long past, as well as some that looked more recent.

Snaking its way up the first steep cliff, the road reached the top of the plateau where Lagona Falls fell from. That said, they had just begun their hike up into the mountains. But before crossing the plateau, they needed to rest for the night after the day's long trek. Avanda and the others were still not within their view.

Gluic cleared a section of stone road to make way for her gems, crystals, and stones she had picked up along the way. "Come out of those stuffy purses and get some fresh air." She then placed the items on the road in flowing patterns. "Enjoy and revitalize."

Thorik set down his backpack and removed his wooden coffer so he could access his flint for Brimmelle.

Camp duties had changed over time. Thorik could recall when Fir Brimmelle wouldn't lift a finger to help; now he was in charge of the fire. Gathering wood and stoking the fire somehow gave him a feeling of importance that he missed from his days in Farbank.

Brimmelle got the fire started just as Thorik returned with roots and a few small prairie gophers for dinner. "It's not much, but it will keep us going."

Brimmelle set another log on the fire. "It will do."

Thorik nodded and prepped the food for dinner. "Brimmelle, can I ask you something?"

"What is it?"

"It's about my mother."

Brimmelle's shoulders tightened, but he did not reply.

"Did you mean what you said about making the wrong choice and saving me instead of her?"

Using a thick stick, the elder Num poked at the beginnings of the fire. "Yes."

"Oh." Thorik pondered the answer. "Do you really hate me?"

"I never said I hated you."

"Then why have you treated me the way you do?"

"I've been trying to make a responsible man out of you. Someone that your mother would have been proud of me having raised in her absence."

"This isn't about me, is it?"

"What do you mean? That's what we're talking about."

"No, I think we're talking about you, your guilt, and your living up to my mother's expectation of how to raise me."

Brimmelle broke his stick and tossed it into the flames.

Thorik watched the fire coil into the air. "You've been so fearful of making decisions about me of which she may or may not have approved. In doing so, you avoided making any decisions outside of the Mountain King's words."

"The king's words are wise. All should follow them."

"True as they are, they could never provide me with the warmth or guidance I needed from a father, or in this case, an uncle."

"Where is all this coming from?"

"I was just thinking about Ericc. He never had the opportunity to grow up with his father. Whereas, I grew up the past several years with you, yet it felt like you weren't there."

"I was always there for you."

"Physically, not otherwise."

"A village Fir is busy. I didn't have time to play games with you all day."

"I never asked for that. But from time to time, it would have been nice to have been praised for what I accomplished."

"You're fortunate to have what you did. My father passed away when I was eleven. I had no father figure after that."

"Yes, I am fortunate. But that doesn't mean you couldn't have told me I did well now and then, or congratulate me after a successful hunt, or even allow me to show you the maps and notes I've taken on this journey so we can teach others about what's beyond our valley's mountains."

Fussing with the fire, Brimmelle sighed. "Fine, show me your sketchings."

"Really?"

"Yes, under one condition."

"Name it."

"You close that box of notes up and stop wasting time with them."

"Forever?"

"At least until we have safely retrieved Avanda. You need to keep your focus on her until then."

"Agreed." Thorik opened his coffer and pulled out a stack of paper from within. Notes from over a year filled the pages. Maps of their travels with journals from events brought memories back to them both, causing even Brimmelle to chuckle a few times.

It had been the first time in Thorik's life that he felt a positive bond with his uncle.

Brimmelle, on the other hand, recalled what he loved so much about his sister: her sense of adventure.

Time passed quickly and the mountains appeared to grow as the Nums moved southeast across the plateau. The ancient road eventually crossed and then followed the thin river to the base of the gorge before riding up the north face of the Shi'Pel Range.

The river they followed had etched the sandstone gorge out to a smooth shape. Jagged red rocks had fallen from higher elevations and had embedded themselves across the canyon floor and in the river, causing violent rapids. Solid black outcroppings looked like tumors among the various reddish hues of the surrounding soil, and the water dripping from melted snow far above them looked black in the shadows of the mountain.

The south side of the Go'ta Gorge was also the north side of the Shi'Pel Peaks. It was a cold, dark, and lonely place, even at midday. The mighty peaks continuously shaded the road from direct sunlight, which explained why the columns that normally bordered both sides of the road had been replaced with stone vats. Though they were empty now, Thorik assumed the vats had once contained oil, lighting the road up the mountain to Surod.

Glaciers melted from the high peaks in the summer heat. But instead of giving life to the valley, like it did near Farbank, the water carved out rough grooves in the mountainsides. And instead of large flowing rivers, water perspired from the rocks themselves, dripping constantly as it worked its way down into the base of the gorge.

Up the mountain, in the peak's shadows, an off-white building was seen hanging onto the side of a cliff. But it was more than just a building with walls and a roof; it resembled an enormous ribcage protruding from the mountain. Each rib bone connected to the rest with a thin dark skin, like the chest of a man who had starved to death. Nearing the neckline of the structure was a light shining through a round, flat crystal nearly the width of Santorray's arm span.

Above the main building was a smaller one in the shape of a skull breaching the mountain's side. Above them, a third thin and tall structure appeared to be an enormous forearm and hand pointing to the sky as it held another large crystal embedded in its palm.

The entire structure reminded Thorik of the Mountain King statue, only stripped of robes and flesh and more encased in the mountain itself. The body size was approximately the same, but it didn't give off the feeling of tranquility that the one in Kingsfoot did.

The road that lay before Thorik and his family crossed a bridge and worked its way up the mountainside before ending at the skeletal building. "This must be Surod," Thorik said to himself.

Brimmelle stopped to rest, placing his hands on his knees as he breathed the cold, thin air. "We didn't make it in time to stop them before they entered. They've been captured."

"We don't know that. They may have snuck in."

"Santorray, Avanda, and Ericc?" Brimmelle said. "They most likely screamed war cries as they charged the place."

"Grewen may have talked them into a plan."

"Not likely."

Thorik looked at his resources for the siege on Surod, which consisted of his uncle and his grandmother. "We don't have enough for this. We've only succeeded this far because of Grewen and Santorray."

Brimmelle's face turned red. "After all I have done to help you survive on this venture to our deaths, you don't see me as an asset? I know I don't have the omniscient attitude of Ambrosius, or the smell of a Mognin, or the uncontrollable temper of a blothrud. But whether or not you know it, I have been constantly protecting you and our family."

"That's not what I meant." Thorik hadn't planned on starting a fight.

Brimmelle walked toward the bridge without him.

Gluic put her hand on Thorik and smiled. "He's grown a lot since we left Farbank. I'm very proud of both of you."

It was an odd statement to come from his grandmother. "Thank you, Granna. Are you well?"

"Remember, strength comes from within you, and you have a lot yet to give." She escorted him down the road, behind her son.

The stone bridge before them crossed a deep ravine, which opened up into the Go'ta Gorge. The long bridge had eroded over the years and was missing some stone floor tiles. Those that remained were worn-down, soft, and wet by the moisture given off from the melting glaciers.

Thorik stepped out onto the bridge. "Careful, it's slippery."

Nearly halfway across, Thorik noticed an odd smell getting stronger as they proceeded. Following it forward, he found the source. Some type of acid had eaten away a large section of the bridge. "What could have done this?"

Brimmelle held his mother's hand tightly as he walked across the bridge, trying not to look down over the sides. "Nothing natural. Looks like something from Avanda's purse of catastrophe."

Thorik realized his half-joking comment could be correct. "There could have been a battle here, but how long ago?"

"Not very, seeing that it's still spreading."

The acid was still dissolving the stone at the center of the bridge. Several of the keystones were gone, with only one remaining. If it continued to spread to the last keystone, the bridge would collapse, assuming it would last that long.

"We need to get off this bridge." Thorik helped his uncle and grandmother over the remaining narrow block. "Run for it."

It wasn't as simple as that. Many of the floor tiles had fallen, leaving holes in the bridge. Those that remained were uneven and difficult to run on without tripping in the shadowy darkness.

Gluic tripped, taking Brimmelle down with her.

Thorik turned back to help them, tripping himself in the process. Rolling forward, his lower half fell into a hole where a stone tile was missing. Grasping at the slick floor around him helped very little. Thorik slid down into the hole up to his chest, with his legs dangling below the bridge.

Brimmelle helped Gluic to her feet before he noticed Thorik. Running over, he tripped and slid toward Thorik, too fast to stop in time.

Brimmelle plowed headfirst into Thorik, pushing him farther into the hole.

Thorik knew he had a choice of grabbing his uncle or allowing himself to fall. If he were to grab Brimmelle, he most likely would drag him down the opening with him, killing them both. Gluic would be on her own. He couldn't do that to her. She needed Brimmelle, even if she didn't think so.

Falling backward after butting heads with his uncle, Thorik reached his hands out to grab the sides of the surrounding bridge tiles. Unfortunately, he missed.

Brimmelle reached down and grabbed his Sec's wrist, causing his own body to pull forward into the hole until it abruptly stopped.

Gluic had grabbed onto Brimmelle's leg and anchored her own feet in the unleveled section of the bridge, which Brimmelle had tripped over.

Thorik opened his eyes and looked up at his uncle's strained face. Their hands grasped each other's wrists. It looked too far to climb, and he could see the agony on Brimmelle's face from holding onto him. "Brimmelle—"

"Shut up and grab my other hand." Reaching down with his second arm, he met Thorik's other hand by the third swing. "Now climb me."

"I can't. I don't have the strength."

"I'm not Grewen. I can't lift you. I'm not Ambrosius. I can't use E'rudite powers to just push you up here. All I am is your fat, old uncle, so use me as one and climb up on my back."

"I don't have the strength. I can't."

"Yes, you can."

"But—" Thorik began before being cut off by Brimmelle.

"Get yourself moving. Now!"

Thorik didn't question him again. He knew that tone, and when it was released Thorik had learned to do as he was told regardless of anything else going on, so he did. Hand over hand, he struggled to climb his uncle's outstretched arms until his hands clasped around the back of the older man's neck and under his armpits.

Brimmelle strained from the pain as he cradled his neck up to give whatever support he could. Clasping his own hands together, he gave Thorik a foothold, which allowed his nephew to climb the rest of the way with much more ease.

With Thorik now out of the way, Brimmelle had an excellent view of how high they were, causing his body to start going limp as he began passing out.

Rolling off of the Fir, Thorik helped his uncle out of the hole before Brimmelle fell unconscious. "Ambrosius and Grewen have nothing on you, Uncle." Lying on his back, he panted for air.

Also on his back, Brimmelle rubbed the back of his neck. "That's Fir Brimmelle."

Thorik laughed. "I'm glad you were here for me, Fir Brimmelle. Thank you."

"I've always been there for you. But it was stupid for you to have us running across this slippery bridge in the first place."

Thorik grinned at the closest thing to emotional appreciation he would ever receive out of his uncle. 'You're welcome.'

Gluic closed her eyes as her hands spread out on the stone tiles. "They say we should leave. We don't have much time."

"Agreed." Thorik stood and helped them up before they quickly walked to the far end of the bridge and onto the cliff side road.

Crossing his arms behind his back, Brimmelle stopped and turned back to the bridge. It still stood firm despite the warnings from both of them. "Apparently, you two aren't always right about these things."

Nearly on cue, the center of the bridge crumbled down before both ends ripped from the ravine's sides and tumbled inward, crashing into the shadowy darkness.

Brimmelle sighed at the sight and then turned back to his family. "Not a word, Thorik. Not *one* word."

38

TEMPLE OF SUROD

The road ended in the center of the lowest rib of the primary structure. Unguarded, it looked unused for many years.

Black granite filled the courtyard, as well as all the walls between the off-white marble ribs. Life-sized statues lay broken on the ground, and cracks in the foundation offset the once flat platform.

Thorik and his family walked cautiously up to the open entrance. Soft wind streamed out from the structure, rustling their clothes, before stopping and reversing its direction back inside the massive statue's chest.

A low thumping could be felt in the ground, like a heart beating in slow motion.

As Thorik stepped into the enormous skeletal statue, his boot crushed an object beneath it. Thousands of black beetles scattered from the area, up walls, and into cracks. The sound of their shells slapping against each other made Thorik's arms nervously tingle and shake.

The beetles had been feeding on several large, human-sized creatures that were lying on one side of the first room.

Thorik reached into his backpack and pulled out his sack of Runestones. Holding the Runestone of Belief, he traced the worn ridges and thought of nothing but the Runestone. Red light illuminated from the gem in the center of the Runestone, casting shadows of the three Nums up onto the walls. The oval room of red stones bled, dripping onto the floors, pooling, and trickling down the open cracks.

They knew it was only water from the glaciers above, but that made it no less unnerving.

Similar in style to the city of Kingsfoot, the walls and ceiling had been carved into specific shapes. But instead of plants and animals, corpses littered the surface of every wall and arched ceiling.

The red light added to the effect of blood pouring from the bodies and out of the skeletal mouths.

The entrance breathed out again and then back in as the ground's heartbeat continued.

Thorik walked over to the bodies the beetles had been working on. They were half devoured krupes with their heads sliced off and tossed across the room. "Santorray's work?"

Brimmelle scoffed. "Who else?"

The beetles crept back into the room after their initial fright, drawn back by the smell of the dead body. It was time for the Nums to leave the room.

Deeper into the chest they walked. Skeletal arms and legs hung off the walls and ceiling as though they were making an effort to escape the stones in which they were embedded. The sizes ranged from mognin to Num, if not smaller.

The corridor stopped at a spiral staircase going up as well as down from the floor they were on. The staircase wrapped around what appeared to be a giant spine, matching the size and placement for the exterior of Surod's structure. They could hear water flowing down inside the spinal column, while torches lined the staircase.

"The heart of this place is up." Wrenching his neck to see anything up or down the well-lit stairwell, Thorik placed his Runestone back in his pack. "I would venture to say the heart is where the sacrifice would take place."

Air rushed down the stairs at them and then returned upward.

A scream from below rang out just as Thorik had started his way up the stairs. A second scream confirmed that it was Avanda.

"Wait here, where it's safe." Reversing his course, Thorik made his way down the wide spiral staircase.

The staircase coiled around the giant spine, and Thorik followed it down several flights until it finally opened up to a basement filled with structural columns and room for storage.

Avanda screamed for help again as Thorik ran past crates, old supplies, and cages stacked up in unorganized aisles.

"Avanda?" he called out.

"Here!" she screamed with delight at the sound of his voice. She was locked into one of the smaller cages, only half her own height. "I can't believe you came for me."

Thorik took out his tools and started working on the lock. "I would never leave you behind."

"Never?"

"Avanda, I'm sorry I wasn't there for you that night in Rava'Kor." His voice was humble and soft as he worked the lock. "The only thing I could think about was Ericc, and that was shortsighted. I was a fool not to see how important you are to me. I wasn't listening to anything you had to say that night. I just wanted you out of my way. I was wrong. I'm sorry for not being there for you."

"It wasn't your fault. I knew better. Brimmelle had told me to be back before dark, but I spent longer than I had planned to explore the city. Then you tried to stop me from picking a fight, and I should have listened."

"This isn't your fault. Lucian was behind this. He is the one to blame for his actions against you." Thorik tried a different tool to pick the lock.

"But you can't always watch over me. Someday you'll let me go, like you did Ericc."

"Perhaps. Perhaps not. But now I have learned to be there for you when you *are* here. I trust you and believe in you." Picking the lock, he removed it and opened the small door. Pulling her out, he lifted her to her feet and looked straight into her eyes. "You are now, and always will be, my dearest friend."

The two hugged at the reconciliation of their emotional issues. The weight from their tension dropped, freeing them to look fondly at each other once again.

Thorik was the first to break the gaze. "You know, you never told me what you wished for on the Lu'Tythis lights." Still overjoyed to find her alive, he allowed himself a moment of peace before he would remind her of the danger they were still in.

Squeezing him tightly, Avanda caused him to embrace her back just as deeply. "You just made it come true." She had fantasized about him ever since she became his student, many years ago. Her desire for him to want to be with her was unfolding.

Smiling at the thought of him fulfilling her wish, he finished the hug and collected his tools, knowing they needed to get back upstairs.

"How did you find us?" she asked.

"You're the only one we've found. Where is everyone else?"

"We got split up when we were attacked. I dropped my purse of magic as I made a run for it. How did you get rid of Bredgin's panther?"

"His panther?"

"Yes, the one that has been guarding me."

"I haven't seen it."

Without warning, the crates from behind the two Nums burst forward, exposing the giant black panther, Shrii. Her mouth was large, and her teeth were so white they nearly glowed from the lantern lights.

The Nums ran but were quickly cut off by the cat, preventing their escape to the stairs.

Thorik pushed Avanda through the metal bars of a large cage to protect her from the cat. He followed once she was in, but it was a tight fit for him.

Shrii pounced, claws ready to rip him into pieces.

Over halfway through, he became stuck. His backpack was too large and could not fit between the bars while being worn. But there was no time to take it off. Shrii had arrived.

The straps tightened as he pulled forward, and Avanda pulled his arms toward her.

Shrii attacked, biting at the Num. Grabbing Thorik by his pack, she lifted him up to the top of the cage, knocking Avanda backward.

Thorik spread his arms and legs to prevent himself from being pulled back out of the cage.

Shrii shook her head to dislodge him. Placing one of her huge paws against the base of the cage for leverage, she began pulling him out.

Thorik struggled to hold on as the straps from his pack dug deeply into his skin. The cat's strength was vastly superior to his. He simply could not win this.

Avanda reached up and pulled one of Thorik's legs with no luck.

Pushing forward, Shrii then snapped her head back to rip him out of the cage.

It worked. Thorik lost his grip. His pack ripped from his body, and Thorik tumbled to the floor outside the cage.

The cage had also been impacted by the final pull, and it tipped forward toward Thorik.

Shrii shook the pack for a moment before tossing it aside, returning her attention to the fallen Num. As she swiped her paw at him, the cage finished its tip and crashed onto her front leg.

The panther shrieked from the pain and recoiled her leg, causing the cage to fall onto the Num.

Thorik had rolled into position between the approaching bars but misjudged the angle, and it crushed his left forearm. Thorik let out a murderous scream as he felt his arm break. In addition, he was now pinned under the cage, with its weight far too heavy for the Num to budge.

Avanda had fallen forward with the cage and quickly jumped up to help him, but the weight was too much for her as well.

Shrii resumed her stalking, watching the captive Nums. Nudging the cage with her nose caused great pain for Thorik, and he yelled with each movement.

Placing a paw on top of the cage, the panther prepared to leap up onto it. Its added weight would easily sever Thorik's hand from his arm.

Thorik and Avanda twisted and pulled his arm with no success. Lifting the cage was just as futile. They were out of options.

A second paw reached up as the panther prepared for the leap. Shrii's eyes focused on the helpless Num as she sprang up off the ground.

As Shrii's weight transferred onto the cage, the bars pressed deeper into Thorik's arm, which would soon snap off as if a dull bladed meat cleaver were cutting off a chicken leg. Thorik's only hope would be a clean enough cut that would at least allow him to escape.

The weight of the cat never fully materialized because the panther was lifted up into the room. While it clawed the air in front of it, Thorik could see two enormous arms wrapped around the cat. It was Grewen, standing behind Shrii, holding her tight. The panther twisted and clawed as it tried to free itself from the Mognin's bear-hug.

"Escape!" Grewen ordered as he leaned up against the cage to tilt it enough to free Thorik.

Thorik pulled his arm in close to protect it as he moved safely between the bars before Grewen dropped the cage. "What can we do to help?" the Num asked, pushing past his own pain.

Grewen fell to the side as he grappled with the cat, destroying various wooden crates and supplies while maintaining his hold on Shrii. "There's no time. Run to the high chamber to stop the sacrifice before it's too late."

Avanda assisted Thorik out of the cage. "I need my magical items."

Thorik followed her comment with, "And I need my spear."

Grewen struggled to keep his control of Shrii as the two tumbled around the room, breaking everything in their chaotic path. "I can't hold her much longer. Get going!"

The two Nums fought to stay clear of the two giants as they randomly twisted and rolled around the room. Thorik tried to retrieve his spear twice before realizing that he would be flattened or ripped apart.

Grewen and Shrii rolled on the ground as the cat tried to break free, crashing into support columns and breaking metal cages.

Upon Grewen's last order, they ran for the stairs, Thorik's broken arm tight to his stomach. "Where are Ericc and Santorray?" he asked Avanda.

"It's not good. Ericc has been captured."

"And Santorray?" Thorik asked.

She paused for a moment. "He's the one that captured Ericc."

"He wouldn't do such a thing. He gave me his word."

"He lied to you. He lied to all of us."

"No, not Santorray. I don't believe it."

"Then you'll see it for yourself," she said as they raced up the spiral staircase.

Leaping from every other step, they climbed several flights before reaching the main floor where Thorik had left his grandmother and uncle. But the room was empty.

"Where did they go?" he asked himself before seeing a few odd-looking stones and gems on the steps leading up. "They went up." He retrieved the stones along the way.

Porous walls provided vent-ways for the rushing of air in and out as the Nums made their way up.

The trail of gems led up onto a level with a round loft and several doors, only one of which had additional stones near it. He collected the rest and placed them in his pocket before listening to any sounds coming from the far side of the door.

Faint voices could be heard but not comprehended.

Avanda began to slowly open the door, allowing a sickly green light to escape from the room on the other side. "Isn't that the Notarian light which affects the stone carvings?"

Thorik stopped her with a finger to his mouth before swinging the door open enough to look inside at the large open chest cavity of a room. The inside of Surod's ribs filled the walls in an abnormal oval-shaped room.

The flickering green light caused the stone walls to slowly expand and contract, as if lungs actually existed inside the massive room, pushing against the structure's ribs and body. The air rushed past the Nums and down the stairs and then returned upon each gigantic breath.

In the ceiling, on the far side of the room, was an enormous clear crystal; the same one they had seen from outside near the neckline.

In the center of the room was a shallow pool of water. Next to it, away from the entrance, sat a sacrifice altar formed in the shape of an upside-down spider lying on a solid block. Its legs reached into the air as it waited for its next victim.

A single copper vat was positioned opposite the altar. Resting on a metal base, the oils within the vat gave off the enchanting green light, causing the walls surrounding the main level to be alive with magical energy as small stone creatures entered and left the stone murals.

Several large, porous stones were embedded into the floor around the perimeter, each giving off steam and causing the room to be warm and moist.

Holding his broken arm, Thorik leaned in past the door to see farther, but snapped back when he heard a voice from a side passage.

"Is everything prepared?" an older man's voice asked.

Thorik had heard that voice before but was unsure where, so he poked his head in again.

"Yes, Father."

Thorik recognized the last voice as that of Lord Bredgin, making the first voice Darkmere. Knowing this, his heart raced, and his breathing became heavy with fear. Without a plan, he could do nothing until an opportunity arose, so he watched and waited while wrapping up his broken forearm to minimize its movement.

Darkmere and his son walked into the main chamber. "Bring in Ambrosius' heir."

Bredgin signaled to a krupe guard at the far doorway, who in turn opened two large doors.

Ericc was led into the room by Santorray. The young man's wrists were tied, and he wore a necklace with a large translucent brown gem in it. Brimmelle and Gluic followed Santorray; their hands were tied up the same as Ericc's.

The krupe guards, armored in their standard black metal, accompanied them toward the center of the room, pushing Ericc forward with their thick spiked maces.

"Santorray," Darkmere said as a greeting.

"Darkmere." He replied with a nod.

"You have done well." Darkmere turned and visually inspected Ericc. "He has been delivered in full health, I see." It had been a long time since he had seen Santorray, and he had wondered if he was still fighting for his cause.

"As you requested." Santorray looked at Ericc and sneered. "However, I wish to change our terms for delivery."

"Our terms were final. Your payment will be provided. Don't get greedy."

"To Della Estovia with the payment. I want the right to sacrifice the son of Ambrosius and end this prophecy once and for all. I wish to end the lineage of Ambrosius."

Darkmere grinned. "Terms accepted."

39

THE SACRIFICE

Thorik stood in the doorway with Avanda, furious at Santorray's betrayal. It took all of Thorik's mental fortitude not to scream out his anger as he watched the events unfold.

Two krupes grabbed Ericc and picked him up off the ground before setting him onto the altar. With the power of the green flames, the stone spider legs came alive and instinctively pulled in, holding the young man down flat on the table.

Santorray kneeled near the shallow pool and performed a ritual to prepare for the sacrifice while Darkmere and Bredgin went back into the other room as they discussed the ceremony.

Refusing to miss out, Avanda pushed her head farther into the doorway to see what was happening, bumping Thorik's arm in the process.

Tensing from the pain, Thorik moved to give her room. "Santorray's weakness is his back. He struggles to see rear attacks until it's too late," he whispered as he unsheathed two small blades from his belt and handed one to her. "I'll take down Santorray while you free Brimmelle and Gluic. Whoever is done first can free Ericc."

She looked at the small blade. "What if one of us gets caught?"

"Then it is up to the other to free Ericc and escape."

"But—"

"This is not up for discussion." Giving her a kiss on the cheek, he winked and said, "I trust you."

The two Nums ran out of the doorway in different directions, hiding behind the large steaming rocks as they made their way to their targets.

Thorik knew he needed to attack before he was seen, but he had failed to mention this to Avanda. Running out from behind a rock, she made her way to the elder Nums.

Spotting her instantly, Santorray broke off his rituals and sat up straight.

Thorik had to strike before Santorray could alert the others. Charging out from his hiding place, with his bad arm tucked to his side, Thorik leaped at Santorray's back, hitting his target. His blade cut deep into his shoulder blade, causing the blothrud to arch back and howl.

Thorik's body landed hard against Santorray's back blades, slicing his face and chest before he fell to the floor. There was a reason blothruds weren't attacked from the rear, and Thorik just found out why.

Santorray reached back and pulled the blade out, releasing a trail of blood down his back, before turning to see Thorik lying on the ground in pain. The Num's clothes were drenched with his own blood from several deep cuts.

Attempting to crawl away, Thorik was quickly stopped by Santorray. "You're not going anywhere," the blothrud said, reaching down and lifting him by one leg.

Meanwhile, Avanda had cut Brimmelle and Gluic free and they ran over to release Ericc. But no matter how hard the Nums pulled, the stone spider leg constraints would not budge.

Thorik could see that it was futile for them to continue. "Run! Get out of here."

Several krupes were already entering the room to see what the commotion was about. Time for escape was minimal.

Avanda and Brimmelle continued to pull at the legs to free Ericc, while Gluic stood silently, smiling at Thorik, happy to see him still alive.

"Run!" Thorik screamed again, realizing that their window of opportunity had already passed.

Krupes now blocked every doorway, while a few entered the room to gather the Nums.

Santorray dropped Thorik near the pool before tending to his own wound.

"Why?" Thorik asked the blothrud. "I trusted you."

Santorray pulled a bandage tight to stop his own bleeding. "I told you that trust is not my ally."

Avanda, Brimmelle and Gluic were quickly captured by the krupes, who then stood silently at attention as they waited for their master to arrive.

Darkmere entered the room to appraise the situation. The E'rudite's white clothes and skin didn't bother the Nums as much as his solid white eyes, for no one could tell where he was looking. "Welcome, Nums. I'm so pleased you could attend our ceremony. Nevertheless, your etiquette leaves something to be desired."

Overcoming his pain, Thorik sat up in defiance to the dark lord. "I defeated your plot in Weirfortus. I plan to do the same here."

Darkmere was amused by the strength of the Num's tone. "Defeated? My dear Thorik Dain of Farbank, I've been watching you for some time now. Not only was I not defeated, but *you* made it possible for me to prove that Ambrosius was a war monger when you led him to Pyrth. Then *you* killed him for me inside the Weirfortus reservoirs while saving my valuable kingdom. And now *you* have led his son, Ericc, to me just in time for the Eve of Light. I honestly don't know how to thank you enough."

Struck with grief, Thorik sat in silence, pondering his actions and response.

Darkmere was correct on all accounts. What had he done? How could he have been manipulated so easily?

A chill in the air could be felt as Lord Bredgin entered the main chamber, waiting for orders from his father.

"Bring out Bryus," Darkmere ordered.

Bredgin walked over to the living stone wall and literally stepped into the mural. Walking deeper into the inch-thick stone wall carving, Bredgin opened a door. Inside stood a weather-beaten old man, shivering in his ripped-up rags.

Pulling Bryus out through the door, Bredgin dragged him out of the wall carvings and into the main room before tossing him against the raised stone lip surrounding the shallow pool, opposite Thorik.

Bryus had been beaten. Blood dripped from his lips, while bruises covered his exposed arms and chest. Ripped and frayed clothes exposed additional injuries as he leaned over and scooped up some water to quench his severely dry throat.

"It's time for you to conduct the ritual," Darkmere said to Bryus.

Bryus looked up at the Nums and then over to the blothrud. Standing up, the battered man looked down at Ericc's face. "You have your father's looks." His voice was warm and calm before he turned to face Darkmere. "As I've told you, I won't be a part of killing the son of Ambrosius."

Darkmere nodded to Lord Bredgin before addressing Bryus. "I was concerned that I wouldn't be able to persuade you to change your mind, so I've invited my son here to extricate what we need from you."

Lord Bredgin opened a small box at his side, releasing a black vapor, which molded into the shadowy form of a faceless man. It was the wraylov, Civej.

Bryus watched as the thick shadow drifted over to him. Reaching out to push it back, his hands felt only the thickening of cold air. "Keep it away!"

Civej leaned down, grabbing Bryus' head with both hands.

Bryus screamed in terror as Civej's fingers worked their way under his skull, probing for thoughts that would allow Darkmere to complete the sacrifice without him. Critical words were needed to ensure it was done correctly. It was all in Bryus' head, waiting to be extracted.

The end of Lord Bredgin's staff lit up like a star before it focused tightly onto Bryus' forehead. "Give us the words. Show us the spell!"

"NO!" Bryus screamed. His body went rigid in pain. His face started to twitch.

Civej reached deeper into his head, pulling his memories and leaving pieces of his mind dead.

Soft at first, a light began to creep through the enormous crystal in the ceiling. The sunlight had been working its way over the Shi'Pel peak, reflecting through a crystal in the outstretched hand of the structure above them and then down into the room. The Eve of Light soon would begin.

Darkmere motioned to his son. "We don't have time for this. Take it all from him. Kill him if you must."

Lord Bredgin pushed harder with the light from his staff to access the thoughts that Civej was releasing from the man. "Pull it all. Now! Leave nothing."

Bryus' body convulsions erupted from the unthinkable pain. It was only a matter of seconds before he would be dead and Lord Bredgin would have what he needed.

The light from above increased, shining down through the giant crystal in the ceiling, warming the altar as well as Ericc.

"Lux Specere Vocare Mori," said Bredgin. "I have extracted the words needed to conduct the sacrifice."

Santorray acknowledged the phrase and repeated it to himself a few times to memorize it.

Civej pulled his hands back from the man's head and waited for Lord Bredgin's next order.

Bryus collapsed on the floor, stiff as a board except for the twitching of his left cheek and eye.

Pointing to Ericc, Lord Bredgin gave new orders to his wraylov. "Now, find out what he knows before we kill him."

Ericc panicked. His knowledge of Ambrosius' friends and hiding places would soon be exposed. The family who had protected him for so many years would be exposed, and their lives would be placed in danger.

Following orders, Civej floated over to Ericc and prepared to strike.

With an unexpected crash, the main doors broke free of their hinges as Grewen and Shrii tumbled into the room. The Mognin was covered with scratches and bite marks from his continued attempts to restrain the giant panther. They had been in a relentless battle since Thorik and Avanda had left the basement, except for one free moment when Grewen collected their gear and tried to break away. It was short-lived, however, and the attempted escape cost the Mognin large cuts down his back.

Rolling to break free, Shrii pushed Grewen into one of the porous rocks, breaking it in half. Steam burst from a large crack created by the impact, filling the room with a slight haze.

Releasing the cat for a moment, Grewen tossed Thorik his backpack and Avanda's purse of magic. In doing so, he gave Shrii the upper hand, and she pounced on him, knocking him onto Santorray.

Ignoring his personal pain and tucking his broken arm to his chest, Thorik leapt for the items and grabbed his spear from his backpack. In one motion he drove the spear into the floor, setting off a shock wave that knocked everyone except Civej off their feet.

Tossing Avanda her purse, Thorik was required to free his hand from the spear, for his other was still useless.

The wraylov quickly moved and attacked Thorik before he could regain his weapon. With full ferocity, Civej drove one hand deep into the Num's chest and the other into his skull.

Tremendous pain exploded within the Num as every part of his body convulsed from the attack. The encounter was brutal and could not be withstood for long.

Shrii attacked Santorray as well, and Grewen, for she liked neither. In doing so, she caused the blothrud and Mognin to work together to stop her assault.

As they fought, Santorray focused more on protecting the dagger, Varacon, instead of slaying the giant panther.

Brimmelle ordered his family to escape during the distraction, and he ran for the main exit with them.

Instead of running, Avanda reached for her purse and began casting spells, causing krupes to freeze in place before they could grab the Nums. This opened a momentary path for Brimmelle and Gluic to escape.

Brimmelle had reached the main doorway when he noticed his mother was no longer with him. She had stopped to help Ericc. Thorik, on the other hand, was in the final moments of life, and the young man reached out to Brimmelle for help, just as Brimmelle's sister had several years prior. But the Fir had no way to stop Civej. The creature was too powerful, and to run back into the room ensured both of their deaths. He looked upon Thorik's face as he once had his own sister's before he watched her death, dreading his options.

Gluic reached the altar. "It's time," she said to Ericc.

Ericc struggled to move. "Gluic, pull this amulet off me. It's preventing me from using my powers to help."

As she tried to do so, the table's spider legs tightened, preventing her from being able to move the amulet and chain over his head.

While she continued in her attempt to pull the legs back from Ericc, the light from the crystal in the ceiling continued to increase, intensifying its light on the altar.

Avanda turned her attention to Lord Bredgin and Darkmere with a volley of fiery rain and spells of freezing temperatures.

The illusion of fire didn't faze either of them, and the light from Bredgin's hand melted her frost spell before it could reach them.

Darkmere, on the other hand, easily altered the air around Avanda into a poisonous gas, causing her to stop her spells and gasp for air.

Meanwhile, Brimmelle could not allow the memory of Thorik's death to forever haunt his days. Pushing away from the doorway, he rushed over. Reaching Thorik, he tried to push Civej off his nephew, but his hands slid right through the shadowy form. Civej's attack could not be stopped, so instead Fir Brimmelle positioned himself between the wraylov and Thorik in an attempt to save his sister's child.

Civej changed victims and began his assault on Brimmelle with the same tactic he was using on Thorik. The same results occurred, and Brimmelle went into seizures.

Thorik began to revive from the torture and realized that Civej was hovering over Brimmelle. His uncle had saved his life. But by doing so he had jeopardized his own. Thorik couldn't allow this to happen.

Rolling to his side, and on his broken arm, Thorik yelled in pain as he grabbed the Spear of Rummon with his free hand and then used it to pierce the shadowy form.

The heat and flame of the dragon's soul extended past the metal of the spear and into the wraylov, vaporizing it in a series of wisps which broke free from the creature's dark center.

The blood-curdling scream from the shadowy beast resonated against everyone's body.

The darkness then faded away. Civej was no more.

Furious, Bredgin held up his staff, focusing an intense light directly at the Num.

Still holding the spear, Thorik held up his broken arm to block the light, only to find that its strength was so intense that he could see right through his own flesh, allowing him to see the broken bone beneath the surface. The burning of his skin could be felt on his face and arm as the light narrowed its width and focused its energy.

Thorik turned his back to the light, only to feel the heavy pressure on his shoulders pushing him down to the ground. Twisting back around, he released the Spear of Rummon to assault the attacking lord.

Rummon took flight directly at Bredgin's head. A battle cry came forth from the spear as it flew through the air.

The power of the sun paled in comparison to the light from the end of Bredgin's staff. The light hit the spear with such force that it knocked the embedded soul of the dragon unconscious. The spear fell to the floor as any other metal rod would, for its power had not been enough to take on an E'rudite.

Around the altar, an intense light from above created a cylinder of white so bright it could not be seen through.

Darkmere ensured that Avanda would perform no additional spells as she fell to the floor, gasping for air. "Santorray! It is time for the sacrifice."

At the far end of the room, Shrii broke free of Grewen again and leaped at Santorray, pinning him under her. The blothrud had had enough. Reaching behind him, he grabbed a large chunk of rock, which had broken free during their battle, and slammed it into the cat's head. Knocked out, the panther fell onto the blothrud.

Shocked at the failure of the spear's attack on Bredgin, Thorik didn't know how to react until he saw the light of Bredgin's staff move toward him. Diving out of the staff's focus, Thorik tucked in his broken arm, rolled to his feet, and ran into the living wall mural. Although the carvings were only inches deep, he was able to move around inside the mural, for it had its own magical depth. Once there, he dove behind a carved boulder.

Bredgin turned in pursuit, following the Num into the stone landscape. Staff in hand, he exploded the carved scenery with intense light as he quickly went deeper into the wall, searching for the Num.

Thorik backtracked and leaped out of the mural. In doing so, he ran to the copper vat of flaming oil. Slamming his body against it, he caused it to fall.

The vat tipped over and landed upside down in the pool, extinguishing the green light, which was keeping the wall mural alive.

The mural froze in mid motion as a distant cry echoed from within it. Lord Bredgin was trapped.

Darkmere was startled by the scene of his son becoming trapped in the rock wall. Releasing Avanda, the dark lord turned to the mural and touched it with flat palms. "What have you done?"

The fierce white column of light from above made it difficult for anyone within a yard of the altar to see anything.

Free from the panther, Grewen saw his opportunity and made his way over to the altar. Feeling around inside the column of light, he found the altar's restraints. He quickly began snapping off the table's spider legs to free Ericc.

Santorray raced over and attacked, hitting Grewen with his entire body, knocking the Mognin backward and off his feet. Grabbing the virgin dagger, the blothrud rushed back to the table to finish the job while the light was still strong.

Keeping his eyes shut to protect them from the overpowering light, Ericc removed the amulet from around his neck. It had been preventing him from using his unique abilities. He was now free to show everyone what E'rudite powers he had and take vengeance on the man who was responsible for his parents' deaths.

But without warning, Varacon, the virgin dagger, was thrust forward by Santorray, piercing flesh for the first time. Never had it tasted blood or felt the warmth of the inside of a body. Varacon was finally alive, at the cost of another's life.

"Lux Specere Vocare Mori," Santorray shouted from within the curtain of light.

Stepping back from the column of light, Santorray's hand was now stained with blood, his dagger no longer virgin.

A momentary flash illuminated the room as the column of light took on a nearly solid form, pulsing like a heartbeat against the altar and the surrounding area.

As fast as it had begun, the pulsing ended and the column of light returned to normal, still bright within a yard of the table.

The silence that followed was almost deafening.

Santorray lifted the bloody dagger, showing Darkmere the deed had been completed.

"The prophecy has finally come to an end," Darkmere stated with a sigh of relief, hands still resting on the mural he was trying to revive to save his son. Without the aid of the Notarian flame, it was questionable if even Darkmere could perform this task.

"No!" screamed Thorik. He had failed to keep his promise to Ambrosius. He had failed to atone for sentencing Ericc's father to death. He had failed a new friend as well as himself. Ericc had been sacrificed.

Brimmelle had regained consciousness enough to see the raised bloody dagger. "Never trust an Altered," he muttered.

Then the room suddenly began to shake. Cracks appeared in the walls, widening and dropping chunks of debris to the floor. Lord Bredgin was attempting to escape the solid rock he was encased in.

Darkmere's focus on saving his son increased. Fractures raced out from his hands as he pressed them hard against the wall. Blocks from the upper walls began to fall, and the crystal in the ceiling was knocked out of its holder, ending the column of light before it fell and crashed down in front of the altar.

Shards shattered in every direction, and the Nums jumped for cover. Santorray and Grewen turned their backs to the crash, allowing the fragments to embed in their backs instead of their fronts.

With minimal focus, Darkmere turned the crystal pieces into water before they hit him. His attention was on freeing his own son. He would deal with the Nums later.

Returning to his feet, Thorik grabbed the Spear of Rummon and headed to the altar to collect Ericc's body before the rest of the roof collapsed. But to his astonishment, Ericc's body did not lie on the altar soaked in blood from the stabbing of the dagger, Varacon. Instead, Gluic's body lay in his place.

"What have you done?" Thorik screamed at Santorray.

"Mother?" Brimmelle screamed in horror, racing over to her.

Santorray's eyes grew wide, exposing his astonishment at the accident. The blood dripping off his dagger was that of the old Num instead of the young man. "What? This can't be!"

Ericc appeared out of nowhere, just behind Darkmere. A blade in his hand, he stabbed the thin man in the back.

Shocked, Darkmere fell forward against the wall mural. He hadn't anticipated this. However, he wouldn't submit easily.

Reaching behind him, Darkmere grabbed his attacker's hand and used his powers to burn the boy's skin. By the time the dark lord had turned to see who his attacker was, Ericc was gone.

Ericc had vanished, but he appeared behind Darkmere again, stabbing him a second time, this time below his shoulder blade.

Expanding from the wall mural, a veil of darkness covered the area as Bredgin attempted to crumble the wall from within. In doing so, he unintentionally surrounded Darkmere and Ericc in the deep shadows as well.

Darkmere fell onto the ground from Ericc's assault as well as his son's darkness sucking his life from him. He could overcome the dark but doubted his attacker could. Rolling onto his side, he changed the air between him and the wall into poisonous gas, hoping to prevent his assailant from escaping the dark dread.

Ericc choked from the poison and vanished again, this time appearing near the altar. Grabbing a fallen piece of ceiling block, he threw it into the dark void, hoping to hit the dark lord.

Momentarily suppressing his grief at Gluic's death, Thorik turned to Ericc. "We need to get out of here before the entire building comes down on us."

However, Ericc had only one thing on his mind, and that was revenge.

The shaking of the floor woke Bryus from his earlier attack. He gathered what thoughts he still had, stood up, and then stumbled about as he made his way for the exit. Several krupes had arrived and blocked his path. A quick wave of his hand and some verbal commands set off a spell which caused every krupe in the room to scream in pain as they attempted to cover their ears.

"Avanda, follow him while the krupes are occupied," Thorik yelled, pulling Brimmelle off his mother. "There isn't much time. We need to flee!"

"I'm not leaving Mother in this unholy place."

"Save yourself and Avanda," Thorik ordered as he pushed Brimmelle from the scene before waving the giant over. "I'll get Ericc while Grewen carries Gluic."

Brimmelle looked up to make sure the Mognin was on his way before grabbing Avanda's hand and racing for the exit.

Thorik tossed his pack over a shoulder and moved to grab Ericc. But before Grewen could reach Gluic, a large section of ceiling fell onto her body, crushing it and sending rock fragments in every direction.

Several pieces hit Thorik, knocking him to the ground. By the time he regained his footing, Ericc had disappeared and Grewen was lifting the large stone off Gluic's body. To Thorik's horror, her torso had been crushed. She was beyond all hope.

The sight etched itself into Thorik's memory. She had always been there for him. Her healing ways went beyond her abilities with stones and crystals. She had given him so much and had advised him so often that he didn't know how he could go on without her.

As hard as it was, his emotional tribute to his grandmother would have to wait. More ceiling sections began to fall as Thorik waved Grewen instructions to leave his dear grandmother's body and escape while he still could.

Thorik wasn't even sure if he would have time to exit before the room crumbled apart. But he had to look for Ericc one last time. And there he was, on the far side of the room, beyond the heavy dust and falling debris, being held captive by Santorray.

"Santorray!" Thorik screamed in anger as he charged toward them. But his movement was stopped by a section of the wall giving way, falling on top of Ericc and the blothrud, covering their bodies with several feet of stone blocks. They, like his grandmother, had been crushed.

Thorik knew he didn't have time to move the fallen wall, even if Grewen was still in the room to help. "I've failed", he said to himself as the other walls began to give way. "What have I done?"

Rushing to the exit, he stopped for one look back to see some signs of life from Ericc, but instead he saw more rock crumble down from above.

Reluctantly, Thorik finally raced down the stairwell, quickly catching up to his group as they returned to the first floor.

The skeletons in the walls and ceiling swayed back and forth from the collapsing building, many of them falling onto the floor.

Grewen hunched over to block the majority of the debris from falling directly onto the Nums as they ran for safety. Blocks pounded hard against his back, and the structure's entrance was beginning to cave in.

Running across the large main foyer, time was not on their side. Blocks plummeted in front of the exit, far too fast to dodge while making an escape.

Grewen pushed his way forward. Bending over, he made a safe area for the Nums to pass, while his back took the beating of his life as he held up the doorway.

Brimmelle helped Avanda under Grewen and over the fallen blocks to safety. The two Nums rushed over across the open courtyard to where Bryus stood watching the structure collapse in upon itself.

As Thorik moved under Grewen, the doorway's keystone snapped and the structural wall fell upon Grewen's shoulders. He was trapped, and Thorik would be as well if he didn't leap to safety.

"Jump, Grewen!" Thorik tugged on the giant's arm.

Grewen's legs trembled from the weight. His back cracked as he moaned from the pain. "Get away from the building," Grewen said in a deeper than normal voice.

But Thorik refused to leave, even as the upper levels rained down on the court-yard outside. "No, I'm not losing you again."

Grewen knew this Num far too well to argue with him, so instead the Mognin removed one hand from his knee long enough to swat the Num out into the court-yard and out of danger.

Thorik rolled to a stop before looking up to see his dear friend hold the doorway open long enough to say goodbye.

Grewen released the blocks on his shoulder, allowing them to collapse on him.

"Grewen!" screamed Thorik.

As the blocks fell down on him, Grewen was propelled out of the doorway and into the courtyard. Santorray, who had slammed his own body up against the Mognin's backside, had pushed him out.

Grewen and Santorray rolled across the yard to a safe distance from the building.

Thorik rushed over to Santorray and pointed his spear to the blothrud's head. "I don't know if I should thank you for saving Grewen or kill you for betraying Granna and Ericc. Perhaps both."

Santorray brushed the dust and debris from his face as he growled, "You fool! You nearly ruined everything!"

❦ 40 ❦

TRUTHS REVEALED

Surod imploded with a crash that echoed throughout Go'ta Gorge. The ribs of the structure were gone, as well as the upper section that had looked like a hand reaching to the sky. It was all destroyed, now nothing more than a pile of rubble.

Brimmelle held Avanda tight as he grieved in disbelief of losing his mother. The shock of her death left him unable to speak as he attempted to cope. Grewen's approach to console him wasn't even noticed by the dazed Num.

Firmly controlled by his good arm, Thorik's spear was still within striking distance as he pointed it at the blothrud's face. "What do you mean by blaming me? How did I ruin anything when it was you who deceived us?"

Santorray sat up, brushing more dust off his shoulders. "First of all, if you don't get that spear out of my face, I'm going to break it over your head."

Knowing Santorray's quick reflexes and long reach, Thorik backed up. "You killed Ericc!"

"No, he's not dead."

Thorik was stunned by the comment. "I saw you. Ericc died in your grasp as you held him for Darkmere. You've betrayed us all."

"I grabbed him to pull him away from his attack on Darkmere. To help him escape, whether he wanted to or not. But he vanished as the wall fell onto us."

"I don't believe you!"

"I don't care!" the blothrud barked back.

"I know you killed my grandmother! That I saw with my own eyes. How could you? After everything we've been through?"

"If you hadn't shown up, this wouldn't have happened, and she would have been fine."

"Then you would have murdered Ericc. How is that less of a betrayal?"

"No one would have died if you had kept your Num nose out of it."

"You don't consider sacrificing Ericc as a death?"

"Not if I had stabbed him with this!" Santorray pulled out the once virgin dagger, still covered with Gluic's wet blood.

"Varacon," Bryus said from the back as he approached the blothrud, stopping once as a facial twitch froze up the rest of his body. "Is it truly her?"

"Yes."

Thorik looked back and forth between Santorray and Bryus. "What's a Varacon?"

Licking his lips, Bryus' fingers wiggled in the air with the anticipation of touching the dagger. "Varacon, the virgin dagger," he said to Thorik. "You know the song. *Created for his love, hoping to never see the day, when his blade is used, life won't fade away...*" Humming the next chorus, he smiled as he waited for them to sing along.

Thorik was not in the singing mood. "My grandmother is dead, and we're talking about a dagger that has its own song?"

Looking at Santorray, Bryus laughed and slapped the blothrud on his backside. "You fooled everyone, didn't you? Even Darkmere. Pretty clever for a blothrud, I must say."

Thorik turned the spear toward Bryus. "Who are you?"

"Bryus Grum is the name. Prominent of EverSpring. Well, former Prominent." His outstretched hand to Thorik went without being shaken.

"What do you know about Santorray's betrayal?" Thorik asked.

"Oh, yes, very clever. Nearly pulled a fast one on everyone." Bryus' words were slightly slurred, and he breathed hard as he tried to get them out correctly. The attack from Civej had done more damage than he was letting on.

Thorik pushed the spear up toward Bryus. "Enough with the games!" he yelled, gripping his weapon tightly, waking the dragon's unconscious soul from the attack by Bredgin.

Hot dragon's breath slowly poured off the end of the spear, with a slight sulfur smell to it. A low growl came from deep within the spear. Thorik knew the creature inside had returned.

Thorik made sure he had Bryus' attention as he poked the end of the spear near the man's face. "What are you two talking about?"

Bryus Grum's eyes crossed as he looked at the end of the spear, now only inches from his nose. "By the powers of Ergrauth, I never thought I'd live to see with my own eyes such a sight. Is this the Spear of Rummon?"

Thorik held it firmly, ready to strike. "Yes."

"Amazing!" Bryus was overjoyed at the Num's answer. "Tell me, where did you find it? Who had it all these years? What powers does it possess? Do tell, do tell."

Thorik was getting more upset as Bryus became more overcome with excitement. Not getting anywhere with his conversation, he turned the focus back to the blothrud. "Santorray, I demand to know what's going on!" Thorik shouted.

Santorray stood up, holding the dagger before him. "This is Varacon."

"Oh, yes, it certainly is," Bryus said with excitement as his facial tick spasmed throughout his entire body.

Santorray ignored Bryus' commentary and continued. "I came here to stab Ericc with it, in front of Darkmere, to ensure the dark lord saw the boy's death."

Thorik shook his head. "No, you've been working for Darkmere all this time."

"It is true that I worked for the dark lord once, a long time ago. However, I led him to believe I was still loyal to him. It was the only way I could execute my plan."

Bryus slapped his knee at the joke. "What a ruse."

Thorik found no joke in the blothrud's words. "You were planning this the entire time."

"Yes, I was."

"That's why you stayed with us, because you knew we'd lead you to him."

"Correct." Santorray's answers were sharp off his tongue. He was not pleased about Thorik ruining his plans.

Bryus swiveled his head back and forth with excitement as he watched the volley of words being passed between them.

"You used us." Thorik's hand, which held the spear, trembled with anger.

"I did."

"Everything you told us was a lie."

"No, everything I told you was true."

"How can that be? Why would a friend of Ambrosius try to kill his son?"

"For the sake of Ericc," Santorray grumbled as he clenched his teeth.

"Killing him would save him?"

"That's correct."

Bryus clapped. "Keep going, lad. You're almost there."

Thorik's focus was so intent on Santorray that he didn't even hear the man's words. "How is Ericc's death considered to be the same as saving him?"

"I was only going to kill his body, not his soul."

"And how did you plan on accomplishing this?"

Santorray lifted the dagger higher. "With Varacon, the soul snatcher."

Bryus screamed with delight that the secret was out as he danced around and mumbled the song again to himself.

Thorik looked at the bloody dagger as he pieced his thoughts together. "Your plan was to stab Ericc in front of Darkmere to make him believe that Ambrosius' son was dead and the prophecy had ended. Darkmere would then stop hunting Ericc. But what kind of soul deserves to be trapped in a weapon?"

The Spear of Rummon grew hot for a moment in Thorik's hand to remind its master of its own fate. Tempted to change hands, he quickly felt the reminder of deep pain when he moved his broken arm.

Santorray shook his head. "This was only to be a temporary exile; his soul would eventually be placed back into a new body. One that Darkmere would not see as a threat."

"How did you plan to do this?"

"I don't have that kind of power. I did my part; it would be up to…" Santorray realized he spoke more than he had planned.

"Your part?" Thorik asked. "Who are you working with? Who was to complete the second part of this mission?"

"We are friends of Ambrosius. We look out for his affairs."

Thorik demanded to know more. "Who do you refer to? Who sent you on this mission?"

Pulling back his shoulders, Santorray looked into the Num's serious eyes. "My contact is Draquol."

"Draq? He's alive?"

"Yes."

"We are friends with Draq. We traveled with him while venturing with Ambrosius. Why didn't you come forward and let me know what you were planning?"

"We couldn't trust you knowing. It was too large of a risk. Darkmere and his son have many ways of getting information out of people. Which is why you must never discuss this or write of it in your journals. No evidence must exist of his escape. Your journals in the wrong hands could be dangerous. The boy's life would be at risk if Darkmere found out."

"But by not telling me, you've killed my grandmother."

Bryus stepped in between them. "No, no. Only her body, not her soul."

Looking the blade over, the Num wondered if it could be true. Could his grandmother's soul be trapped inside the weapon? Reaching back with his good arm, he placed his spear in the loops along the side of his pack to store it. He then pulled his grandmother's broken crystals from his pocket and recited the phrase she said to him. "Not an ending, just a fresh beginning in a new form. We will be carried to a greater purpose."

The words broke Brimmelle out of his intense trance of grief. "That's what Mother said about her broken crystal."

Thorik disagreed. "No, she was telling us about what she had seen for her own destiny. This dagger provides her with an opportunity to move into a new body to fulfill a new purpose." After dropping the crystals back in his pocket, Thorik reached up for the dagger, and Santorray allowed him to have it. "We will take the dagger back, and you will extract her, just as you had planned to do for Ericc," Thorik said to Santorray.

Santorray picked rocks out of the hair on his legs as he shook his head. "I'm not going anywhere until I find Ericc and make sure he is safe. In spite of your interference, Darkmere still thinks I killed Ericc, for he knows not who attacked him. His search for the boy should end, unless Ericc resurfaces again. Therefore, I must to reach him before that happens."

"I thought Darkmere was dead."

Santorray looked back over his shoulder at the rubble. "It will take more than that to end an E'rudite's life. Ericc disappeared as the wall collapsed. So, he could be anywhere."

"How far can he travel like that?"

Santorray was irritated that his search was starting all over again. "Depending on how far his E'rudite abilities have progressed, he could potentially have shifted locations to anywhere he has already been. He could have returned to the home along the Ki'Volney Lake, or to Rava'Kor in Southwind. Who knows, perhaps his ability only allowed him to jump past the next mountain ridge."

"But what about Gluic?"

"I have my priorities, Thorik." Stress of failing in his own mission came through his voice. "She'll stay safe in Varacon, as long as you don't draw new blood with it again."

"Why?"

"I don't know. Just don't do it. I'm not an Alchemist!" Santorray barked.

Bryus jumped in with excitement. "But I am! I can tell you why it shouldn't draw blood, how it should be handled, how to keep her soul at ease, how to—"

Thorik interrupted the man from going on and on. "Can you tell me how to release my grandmother from this dagger so she can live among us again?"

A strong twitch held his face tight for a moment before he could speak. "Well, of course!"

"Excellent." Thorik held out the dagger toward Bryus. "Please do so," he ordered with some urgency in his voice.

"Not here." Bryus laughed. "We need to go get Vesik first."

"Who is Vesik? Another Alchemist?"

"No, no, silly Num. Vesik is a book. The book, for us in spell-casting. Vesik is the master book of spells, created by Irluk herself.

"The Death Witch?"

"Yes. Well, no. Before she became the Death Witch. When she was young and ruled magic across our lands."

"You have this book?"

Bryus laughed. "No one *has* Vesik. It is of its own cognizance."

"Do you at least know where Vesik is?"

"Of course I know where it is. I'd have to be daft to even bring up the idea if I didn't know where it was."

Thorik tucked the dagger away and turned to Santorray. "I've fulfilled my promise to Ambrosius. I've prevented Ericc's sacrifice. In fact, no one will ever be sacrificed at Surod again. It is now time for me to take care of my own family."

"Understood, Sec," Santorray replied. His tone had lowered as his temper faded. "You truly have the heart of a blothrud. Fight for what's right, and you'll do just fine."

"Are you sure you won't come with us?"

"No. I need to find out if Bredgin survived the collapse before I return to the valleys below."

Thorik nodded before spitting in his hand and holding it out to Santorray. "Good luck in finding Ericc."

Santorray smiled, spit in his own hand, and shook the Num's little hand. "May Ovlan walk your path."

With that, they parted ways. Santorray climbed onto the rubble to start his dig, while Thorik led his group down the mountainside. The destroyed bridge was no longer an option to leave the area.

"Where is Vesik located?" Thorik asked Bryus.

"Govi Glade."

"That sounds nice."

Bryus nodded his head with a smile and twitch. "Yes, I wish that were true."

❧ 41 ❧

STRATEGIES

Draq flapped his red-tipped wings hard to crest the Haplorhini Mountain Range and enter the King's Valley. It had been a long flight for the dragon with news of Santorray's quest.

Diving into the valley, he soared past the thousand-foot-tall Mountain King statue, its head and hands lying in the lake near the king's feet. The statue and the mountain it was carved from stood in contrast to the rich greens of the surrounding trees and grass. The atmosphere was always spiritually uplifting.

Vapors from the warm mineral water of the lake filled Draq's lungs as he flew just feet above its surface on the way to the carved city of Kingsfoot. The water had special properties that rejuvenated and healed. Just being in its presence caused one to feel fresh, calm, and clear-headed.

Passing the docks, Draq approached the terraced open garden area preceding the city's main entrance. A wide staircase connected each terrace from the base stone courtyard up to the carved city walls.

On the top terrace was a man sitting among the plants. His untidy mahogany hair flowed down past his shoulders, and his once trimmed beard was now scruffy. The cloak he wore was weathered, and half his face showed signs of a nearly healed burn.

Draq landed near the man, perching on the ledge of the terrace wall. "Darkmere and his son have witnessed Ericc's sacrifice. Surod has been destroyed; therefore, the prophecy has ended."

The man sat in the dirt near the plant he was tending to. He was missing both feet and the fingers from one hand, but it did not prevent him from pulling the weeds and cutting off stressed branches. "Where is Ericc now?"

"He was not captured by Varacon. He has escaped."

"Has Santorray located him yet?" the man questioned, never turning from his duties.

"He is in pursuit."

"I see." He dusted the rich soil off his hands. "I believe it is time I got to know my son again. Have Santorray bring him here once he has found Ericc."

"Ambrosius, do you think this is wise? You are not fully healed from Darkmere's attack. What if they are followed by his minions or the dark lord himself?"

"As powerful as this lake is, the waters are slow at bringing back my limbs, but we cannot wait any longer. The hunt will start over again if Ericc is found to be alive." Ambrosius stopped to ensure his work was complete as he recalled helping Fir Beltrow cover this very plant to protect it from a past harsh winter. "Besides, I have protected him long enough. It is time he stood at my side with pride instead of in hiding with fear and anger."

"He will not be as warm to the idea as you may hope."

"We have no choice. War is coming, and we must prepare. Grab the wooden box next to my chair and bring it out to me."

"Yes, my master."

Draq had difficulty walking; his body simply wasn't designed for it, with his arms built into his wings and his back legs designed to perch and attack. Regardless, he still had all of his parts, unlike his friend Ambrosius, so he ventured into the city and collected the box.

Upon returning, Draq found his master sitting on a bench near the city's entrance. "Here you are, my lord," he said, setting it in his lap. "Is it wise that we rest so much on the shoulders of a Num without him even knowing we are depending on him?"

Ambrosius opened up the wooden coffer to find a pile of papers with notes and maps drawn on them. Scanning through the sheets, he pulled one out. "He can't know. We must trust his judgment."

They watched as the blank paper in his hand began to show new markings. It was filling in notes before their very eyes, as though an invisible scribe sat with them.

"When did you realize Thorik had the other coffer?" Draq asked.

"I noticed it just before we reached Weirfortus. But it wasn't until after my battle with Darkmere that I realized what it was."

Draq leaned over to view the new writings. "If Thorik ever found out that the journals he places in his wooden box are recorded in the coffer's twin, he would never trust you again."

"It's imperative that he doesn't find out."

"The Num trusts you and continues to mourn your death."

"Which is exactly why he must not find out the truth."

❧ 42 ☙

LUCIAN'S RETURN

Four Southwind soldiers marched down the corridor at a pace shy of a run. Their boots echoed in unison like the beat of drums preparing an audience for the arrival of the protagonist in a play. Their steps continued to increase in speed until they stopped abruptly at two large wooden doors.

They waited in silence for the doors to be opened from the inside. Once they did, the four soldiers advanced to the center of the large room and tossed their cargo onto the floor.

A groan came from within the large sack that they had deposited. Moving slowly, a man from within kicked his way free. His hands and legs were tied with rope. He struggled to speak, for his tongue and lips had been severely burnt. His eyes had been damaged so extensively from a fire that he could only see shadows with one eye. Hearing was the only sense that still functioned properly.

"Welcome back, Lucian," the Matriarch said. "Did you kill Santorray?"

Lucian lowered his head. "He still lives," he slurred out with great pain in his throat.

"Ah." She rested on the back of her chair as she crossed her ankles. "And Santorray was able to burn your face with a troop of Southwind's finest at your side?"

"He had help. A Num named Thorik Dain helped him escape from the mines. It was this same Num that did this to me." He coughed several times as he tried to answer.

Amused, she asked him to elaborate, knowing the pain he received each time he talked. "Your squad could not fight a blothrud and a Num?"

"We were attacked by an army of Del'Unday. Corrock is on the move again."

"What happened to Santorray and Thorik?"

He lifted himself up onto his knees. "Escaped."

"How could you let them escape?"

"They had help. Other Nums as well as Ericc."

"Ericc? You saw Ambrosius' son and didn't die trying to bring him back to me?"

"Santorray and Thorik are protecting him."

Stepping down from her throne, she exclaimed, "You fool! You've cost me my youth!" Grabbing one of the copper plates of food from her servant, she swung it hard, hitting him in the head and knocking him to the ground. "Ericc was my gift to present to Darkmere. I need Ericc!"

Furious, she pounded his head with the plate several more times before tossing it onto the ground.

Waiting for her to end the assault, Lucian kept his hands over his head to protect himself, while everyone else in the room waited for her tantrum to be over.

Snatching a lantern from the nearest column, she began pouring the oil onto his legs. "It saddens me, for I ask for so little," she reasoned with herself. "I give simple orders and priorities so you can understand them. You just don't listen."

Lucian could smell the oil and rose to prevent her from setting him alight, but he was stopped short as she stomped down hard onto his leg, breaking it with a loud snap.

With the oil now soaked into his pants, she lit his feet. "Don't you dare move," she ordered.

Others in the chamber looked on, fearful of appearing as a sympathizer if they would turn their heads from the torture.

The flames lapped at his lower legs. "Please, no. I promise I'll do whatever you want."

She was cold in her response. "I *want* you to stay still. Stop moving."

He continued to try to appease her. Perhaps she would put out the flames if he did as she asked. But the heat was unbearable, and his skin was catching on fire. The smell of burning flesh filled the hall as the flame engulfed his legs up to his knees.

Trembling to prevent any movement, he asked for forgiveness. Not receiving it, he screamed and began trying to put the flames out with his hands.

"You just don't listen." She cracked the bent-up metal plate against his head one more time. "You don't trust me enough to do as I tell you. I take care of your family. Is your trust too much to ask in return?"

"I trust you!" he screamed, stiffening his body to prevent himself from moving.

"Do you?"

"Yes!"

"Are you sure?"

"Yes!"

"Then don't move and don't speak."

The fire spread up his thighs and waist. The smell became repulsive and the sight revolting. The man stayed straight as an arrow, trusting that the Matriarch would put out the flames any second. The pain had passed the threshold of understanding as he shook and convulsed from the trauma.

The Matriarch glanced at her audience of guards, servants, and advisers. Many couldn't take the sight any longer and had closed their eyes or turned their heads. The smell of burning flesh added to the horrifying scene. She had proven her point as to what it meant to fail her.

"Put him out," she ordered and waited for her men to fetch buckets of water before finishing her sentence, "… on my command."

Lucian heard the words and continued to live the torture. His body started shutting down. He no longer could feel anything or smell his own flaming skin. Only his brain remained active as the Matriarch waited until his entire body was ablaze.

But before his heart stopped, she had her men dowse Lucian's body.

"Remove him from here. String him up on the street to send others a message about not obeying my orders," she said calmly. "And clean up this filth."

Her men removed Lucian immediately while other servants began to clean up the mess left on the floor.

"Hire a bounty hunter and two assassins," she told her lead bodyguard. "I want Ericc captured, but I want Santorray and Thorik Dain killed."

ESSENCE OF GLUIC
THORIK DAIN SERIES BOOK III

PROLOGUE

Thorik's Log: 22nd day of the 6th month of the 650th year.

Our attempt to stop Darkmere from sacrificing Ambrosius' son, Ericc, at the Temple of Surod has ended in tragedy. It was far worse than I could have expected and more distressing than just the temple crumbling down upon the feuding parties. The soul of my grandmother, Gluic, has been captured inside an enchanted dagger. In addition, my arm was broken during our battle, but our new companion, Bryus Grum, used one of his spells to repair it. The only positive outcome of this venture is that the relationship between Avanda and me is finally on the mend. However, I'm concerned about Bryus teaching her magic and what she will do with such powers. Nevertheless, we require his talents to find the spell which will free Gluic.

I

END OF THE LINE

"She's dead, Thorik!" Brimmelle's fists shook uncontrollably. "My mother is dead because she followed your lead. This is all your fault," he accused his nephew.

Thorik lifted the dagger, Varacon, out toward his uncle. The small dagger had multiple blades that twisted to a sharp point. Two red gems in the hilt swirled from beneath their surface and gave off a slight glow. "No, she's not. Gluic has been captured inside this spellbound dagger."

"I saw her lying on the floor, dead. Her life's blood was pouring from her body. Her eyes had rolled back into her head!" Brimmelle shouted. "You told me Grewen would save her!" He firmly pointed at the giant who accompanied them.

Grewen lowered his eyes at the verbal jab; even though the giant mognin stood nearly three times the height of Brimmelle, he came across as much less threatening than his size would indicate.

"There wasn't time. The ceiling collapsed and crushed her body." Still facing him, Thorik stepped between Brimmelle and Grewen. "Uncle, you must understand that her body has gone, but we've saved her essence."

"Says who? Who knows this to be true?"

"Bryus Grum," Thorik replied. "Haven't you been listening to him? He's been explaining this ever since we left the temple."

"You trust this buffoon?" Brimmelle jerked his head toward a lanky man in old torn clothes. "We don't even know him. For all we know, he could be working for Darkmere."

"I seriously doubt that, seeing that he was Darkmere's prisoner when we arrived. We even heard the Dark Lord give the order to kill Bryus."

"Sounds like one of Darkmere's tricks to fool us."

"Tricks?" Thorik was perplexed at the thought. "Darkmere doesn't care about us. He seeks revenge on Ambrosius and his family for preventing his conquest of

Terra Australis. He cares not of Nums from Farbank and a few traveling companions."

Brimmelle scoffed. "He's been using us to get to Ambrosius, his son, and whoever else he wishes to destroy."

Thorik shook his head. "Darkmere didn't even know we were going to be showing up at the temple. In fact, we wouldn't have gone there at all if it hadn't been for our attempt to prevent Avanda from reaching the temple to save Ericc. How could he have prepared for such unpredictable actions?"

Brimmelle scowled at Avanda, who was a few years younger than Thorik. "That's very true. She's constantly out of control."

Thorik watched Avanda recoil from Brimmelle's threatening posture. "Hold on, Uncle. This is not about Avanda, nor is it about Grewen or Bryus. If you want to blame someone, blame me."

Brimmelle stepped up close to his nephew and placed his face inches from the young man. "I do." The cold, harsh words made it clear to Thorik that his uncle, Fir Brimmelle Riddlewood the Seventh, the spiritual leader of their community of Farbank, had reached his limit.

Thorik knew that ever since they had left their small village of Farbank, Brimmelle had begrudgingly followed him in an effort to protect his mother, Gluic, from harm. But now that she was gone, his uncle had no incentive to follow him one step further.

Thorik's initial reaction was to back down. Years of training to yield to Fir Brimmelle influenced his judgment. However, this time he composed himself and stood straight and firm against his uncle's stance.

The two stood on the rocky mountain, halfway between the demolished Temple of Surod high above them and the base of the Go'ta Gorge. The bridge had been destroyed, so they were forced to travel down to the bottom of the gorge. Subterranean vent holes slowly released clouds of steam, which lifted just over their heads before dispersing out into a ceiling of fog-like clouds.

Grewen, Bryus, and the young girl, Avanda, stood nearby and watched the altercation. Bryus' intense curiosity was focused on Thorik's dagger instead of the two arguing Nums. His facial tic pulled his cheek back and his eye closed. It had been doing so ever since being attacked by Darkmere's minion. Bryus' own magic could not prevent it from pulling uncontrollably on his face.

Grewen shook his massive head in disappointment at Thorik and Brimmelle's struggle to get along. Clasping his hands together, each one half the size of Thorik, the giant sighed at the sight before him.

Avanda stepped forward and spoke with concern and respect in her voice. "Please, Fir Brimmelle, don't blame Thorik. It was my fault as much as it was his." The swirling dark lines on her skin, also known as soul-markings, faded in color as she held her breath waiting for Brimmelle's response.

Brimmelle's deep stare never left Thorik's eyes.

Standing his ground, Thorik waited for his uncle to speak.

Fir Brimmelle took in a deep breath before responding. "We left Farbank with six Nums. Emilen betrayed us, Wess died trying to save Avanda, and now my mother, your grandmother, is dead." His tone was dry and intense. "I'm heading back to Farbank with Avanda. You are no longer welcome there. Do not return."

Thorik's eyes gave away his heartache. Brimmelle had previously taken away his responsibilities as one of the village's hunters. He had also threatened to strip his spiritual title 'Sec' from his name, which would bring shame to him upon returning. However, to forbid the younger Num from returning to the only home he had ever known was beyond Thorik's belief.

"No!" Tears instantly filled Avanda's eyes. She lunged forward and grabbed onto Thorik's arm as though he was being torn away. "I won't return without him."

Thorik continued to stand strong with his face just inches from his uncle's. "Gluic is still with us." He held up the dagger near their faces to visualize his point. "We can still save her."

"Stop it!" Brimmelle grabbed the dagger from Thorik and backed away several steps. "This is a dagger, not a living being!"

"Brimmelle." Thorik's voice vibrated with great fear. "Please… hand me the dagger, Varacon."

"No. You need to stop believing these illicit tales of the supernatural." Brimmelle waved the dagger about as he talked. "The Mountain King gave us the words to follow and nowhere did he sanction such nonsense."

Thorik's right hand moved out into a begging position. "Please, Brimmelle. Don't wave that about. It was a virgin dagger before striking Granna Gluic. If it strikes again, we may lose her!"

"Hogwash!" Brimmelle claimed, still waving it about. "These are the kind of fables which have caused you to forget your roots and your faith."

Watching the dagger nearly slap the side of a boulder, Thorik panicked. "In the name of the Mountain King and everything he stands for, give me that dagger before you kill my grandmother!"

Brimmelle was shocked. "How dare you use the King's name to serve your personal needs?" With that, he purposely slapped the side of the boulder with the dagger, causing sparks to fly from its blades.

"NO!" shouted everyone as they all rushed toward Brimmelle. But a second slap of the weapon hit before Thorik could leap across and knock his uncle to the ground.

Avanda was the next to jump on as she grappled Fir Brimmelle for the dagger. The three Nums stumbled in their reaching for the item, and they began to tumble down the mountainside. Cooking tools and travel gear flew from Thorik's pack, as well as his spear and his wooden coffer. Avanda's entire pack was ripped from her body as the Nums barreled in a tangled mess down the steep incline.

Bryus yelled at the sight. "Be careful!" The thin old man rushed after them before stopping at Thorik's spear. Picking it up, he quickly inspected it for dents with his brown eye, and then scratches with his blue one. "Are you damaged?" he asked the weapon as he brushed the dirt from it.

Grewen lumbered past Bryus and attempted to follow the trio, but he couldn't keep up with the out-of-control Nums, who whirled and bounced off boulders and loose rocks until they rolled into one of the vent holes and out of view.

Grewen trudged his bulky mass toward the small entrance as quickly as his body would allow him. He wasn't a fast runner on a flat surface, let alone down a mountainside. That said, he was going fast enough to cause him to skid past the hole while trying to stop.

Once he returned, he peered over the brim of the hole, only to find Brimmelle partially blocking the entrance. He had hit his head and been knocked out from a short fall to a small ledge as his legs spanned the hole, resting on the far wall. The enchanted dagger was still firmly in his hand, but the other two Nums were nowhere to be seen.

Straddling the steaming vent hole, Grewen leaned over and used his oversized dual-thumbed hand to pluck Brimmelle off the ledge and set him on safe ground before returning to the hole.

"Hello?" Grewen yelled into the vent, hoping the other two Nums had only fallen to a lower ledge.

There was no answer.

Grewen cupped his hands on both sides of his mouth and called a second time down into the vent hole. "Can you hear me?" Again and again he tried, but the giant's tiny ears couldn't hear any response.

"No respect!" Bryus eventually approached Grewen, who was now lying on the ground, reaching deep into the hole. "Did you see what jeopardy they put the Spear of Rummon into?" He spied the dagger still clutched by Brimmelle and added, "As well as Varacon."

"Right now we have more important matters to deal with," Grewen replied.

"Surely you jest," Bryus laughed as he held up the spear. "Do you realize the sacrifices that were made to create such a finely crafted piece of art?"

"They pale in comparison to one of these Nums' lives." Grewen strained to reach his hand deeper into the dark vent in order to feel around.

"Nonsense." Bryus walked over and pulled the dagger from Brimmelle's hand. "The Varacon dagger was forged out of love. A tragic story of two people who desired to be together, but only in death would they achieve this." Holding the dagger in front of his own face, he admired it. "It's a shame they never used it." His cheek twitched a few times as he gazed at the sight. "We have two of the most amazing enchanted items ever created, and you're worried about Nums."

"Your lack of humanity toward the living is amazing." Grewen continued to stretch his arm as far as he could. "Your precious weapons are safe. Now, how about helping me save Thorik and Avanda?"

Bryus nodded in agreement and waved a hand, shooing Grewen out of the way so he could look down. While the giant mognin dislodged himself from the hole, the Alchemist stored his newly acquired items.

Kneeling next to Brimmelle, Bryus began searching through all of the Num's pouches until he found some fishing line and a hard nut. He quickly removed the items and walked over to Grewen, who had finished rolling the rest of the way out of the hole. "Slap me up," he said to the mognin.

Grewen was confused. "What's that?"

"You know, back side of the head. Give her a tap." Bryus then turned his back to Grewen and began tying a knot into the fishing line.

Grewen blinked a few times, unsure of the reason for the request. "I don't believe in hurting others."

"Just a nice solid tap. Nothing bone-crushing. Perhaps a nice thump on the back side."

"But I—"

"Come on, you big lug, do you want my help or not?" Bryus placed the nut in his teeth, cupped his hands below his chin to catch the nut pieces, and then waited.

Hesitantly, Grewen finally reached over with his massive hand and thumped Bryus on the back of his head.

Bryus' head violently snapped forward. His teeth slammed shut, crushing the nut into hundreds of small pieces. At the same time, the jolt from the powerful thump caused his left eye to pop out of its socket, break from the skin that held it, and flop into his hand.

Bryus screamed in pain as he turned to show the mognin what damage he had done. "Why so hard?" he yelled. "I said a tap!"

A chilling wave rode up Grewen's back as he realized what he had done. The idea of purposely hitting someone and then knocking their eyeball out was horrifying. "Bryus, stand still. We'll figure a way to fix this."

Bryus held his brown eye out in front of him with straight arms. "How? How can you fix this? What have you done to me?"

"I'm sorry, Bryus. I didn't realize I hit you that hard."

"Oh, come now, I've had little puffins hit harder than that." Bryus didn't attempt to hide his sarcastic tone.

Perplexed at the comment, Grewen stopped suddenly as he tried to understand what was going on.

Bryus started laughing at Grewen's bewildered facial expressions. "What a ruse." The man chuckled again before chewing up the nut pieces in his mouth and swallowing with a sigh of enjoyment.

Then, ignoring the giant, Bryus tied his detached eye onto the end of the fishing line. "Shall we have a look-see?" His voice was back to its normal tone.

Dangling the line over the vent hole, the eyeball twisted and turned as it prepared to see what was below. A patch of muscles still clung to the backside of the eye and hung limply below. Bryus proceeded to slowly lower his own eye into the hole. "I can see a second shelf below."

"Are they on it?" Grewen asked.

"No." The Alchemist continued to feed more length to the line.

It was a long and slow process as Bryus had difficulty seeing out of his detached eye in the thick mist of the vent. But eventually he was able to find something. "Ah, there it is. Right there." He then gave a sigh of closure.

"What do you see?"

Twirling up the line quickly, Bryus was silent about what he saw. Once it was fully removed from the vent, he untied the knot on the line to free the eyeball, and then carefully placed it back into his eye socket.

"Well? Did you find them?" Grewen asked.

A twitch pulled Bryus' cheek to the side. "No."

"Then what did you see?"

"The mark." He struggled to get his eye in straight.

"What kind of mark?"

Resolving his eye corrections, he chuckled at the mognin. "Do you not know where we are? We are standing above the underworld, Della Estovia. You know, where the dead roam. The demon Bakalor's realm." His laugh had turned slightly insane in tone. "Bakalor's mark was in that vent hole. Who else would mark his territory with the skulls of the ancient Notarians?"

Grewen sat quiet at first as he began to plan. "I doubt that Bakalor would even know they have entered his domain. There is still time."

"Time? Did you get thumped on the head as well? Bakalor doesn't take kindly to visitors from the surface. People don't casually enter his lair and return to be with the living. It's not a vacation spot. They're gone. There is no escape for them."

❦ 2 ❦

DELLA ESTOVIA

The vent hole slowly curved to the side as Thorik slid and tumbled his way down the tunnel. Rolling head over heels at times, he fruitlessly attempted to protect his head and face from any injuries.

Avanda rolled and bounced behind him until a fork in the tunnel split them up. Her path, down a new tunnel, was longer than Thorik's and finally opened onto the floor of a large cavern, where she skidded to a halt on her stomach.

Thorik's travel through the tunnel ended with a short drop onto the top of an enormous pile of loose grains coated with a thin layer of small pebbles. Pulling his arms in tight, he rolled his way down the massive pile for what felt like minutes before reaching the bottom.

Once he had come to a stop, his first duty was to determine where he was and where Avanda had landed. He was coated with debris from the pile, and his body now itched, as though a thousand tiny pins were pricking him. His arm, which Bryus had recently repaired, was throbbing in pain and needed attention as well. He immediately began brushing off the debris while his eyes slowly adjusted to the low light.

Thick crystals were embedded into the walls and lit the caverns with a soft, bluish glow. Scraggly vines covered large sections of the light-blue crystals, absorbing light and warmth from them as well as moisture from the thick, humid air. It only took a few seconds for Thorik's eyes to adjust to the darker surroundings.

The pile that Thorik had tumbled down was in fact a pile of guano from the tens of thousands of bats hanging from the ceiling. Bats, however, were the least of his issues. The pile's outer layer, which he had assumed was pebbles, was instead a layer of predator roaches and centipedes eating the guano.

As hideous as the sight was, the realization of his own body still covered with the them finally sunk in. Guano was in every pocket and had stained his clothes, while the roaches and centipedes crawled up his pant legs, under his shirt, and into his hair.

Panicking, he began to quickly disrobe in an effort to get the insects off of him. He felt millions of little feet moving up his legs and across his back. Frequent bites pinched Thorik as the insects attempted to burrow their heads into his skin.

Ripping at his clothes as quickly as he could, he screamed from the pain as he stumbled away from the pile of guano and bugs. But the pain was just beginning. Now that he had removed the free crawling insects, he needed to uproot the ones that had latched themselves onto him.

The first one he pulled off his stomach snapped in half, its head still buried in his skin and working its way deeper. There wasn't much left to grab on to; he would need to dig into his own skin to grasp the head for removal.

Thorik pinched his skin around the head and forced the head back out, but the insect's pinchers still held tight. Using his other hand, he grabbed the insect's head and yanked it out of his body. Skin tore, blood spilled, and the poison from the insect burned like acid under his flesh, but at least it had been removed.

It was at this point that he realized the severity of his situation. Dozens of these insects had burrowed their heads into his stomach, arms, and legs. Each one was eating its way through his body as though it were in a race. Each one was extruding an acid-based poison into his system. Each one was looking for a nest to bury its offspring in this fresh new host.

The Num screamed from the pain as he grabbed one after another in an attempt to rid himself of them. His face was covered with tears as well as a few of these insects, one of which burrowed its way through his cheek, falling into Thorik's mouth.

An instant gag reflex caused the Num to spit up the insect along with a shower of vomit. Thorik fell forward to his hands and knees as fluids dripped from his mouth. The insects on his chest and stomach hung like fish on hooks, flapping back and forth as they attempted to grip his skin with their feet.

The poison from the bugs caused him to be lightheaded and dizzy. He pinched another insect out of his arm and screamed from the pain. He then pulled another from his leg. But his eyes were giving him visions of the insects flying and changing shapes. Reality blurred into a hazy unreal world where there was no pain.

Thorik collapsed onto the cavern floor as he viewed what appeared to be a giant insect, nearly the size of him, approach from the distance. He watched helplessly as it ran past his backpack and stood up on its back legs before it pounced on him.

Thorik tried to kick. He tried to roll away. But it was no use. He had lost control of his body. He would now lie powerless as he watched himself being eaten alive.

❄ 3 ❄

AVANDA

Avanda looked into Thorik's fearful eyes, as though he saw her as some type of beast. "Thorik! Can you hear me?" she asked as she quickly began removing the insects from his limp body. "Don't you dare leave me!" she shouted, turning him over to see a dozen more insects buried in his back.

Instead of his friend, Thorik's imagination saw her as a giant insect attacking him. Fear and poison raced through his body as he started to fade away.

The sight of the clinging insects caused a wave of emotions through her. They were literally devouring her friend and companion, let alone the Runestone teacher she had emotionally fallen for. These vicious bugs were harming the one she loved, and her fear of his death intertwined with an uncontrollable revengeful rage against them.

Her anger at the insects drove her to aggressively dig out every last one of them. Her hands bled from the insects fighting back and biting at her. At first, she tossed them to the side, but it wasn't long before her fury caused her to squeeze and crush their heads after taking them out. The popping sound gave her satisfaction in repayment for their attack on Thorik.

One after another, she ripped the insects from his back, legs, arms, stomach, and chest. She continued to increase her speed as her anger grew and her concern for self-injury disappeared. Again and again, she cursed them as she plucked them out.

Before she knew it, she had removed them all. She searched his body one more time to ensure she hadn't missed any. Standing up, she then stomped on any full or partial insects within a few yards of Thorik. She didn't know how to stop her desire to fight something, anything, just to relieve the anger that had built up inside her.

Frustrated, she turned to Thorik. His naked skin dripped blood from small holes throughout his body. His injured arm was twisted under his chest, and his legs were wrapped around each other. His face, normally ever so sweet to Avanda's eyes, was now locked in a state of pain and fear.

Her heart melted at the sight, and her anger soon faded. Avanda's feelings for him had grown ever since he became her Runestone teacher several years ago in Farbank. Back when life was simple and fear of death was not a daily concern.

Thorik's body trembled, snapping her out of her momentary daydream. Avanda quickly covered him up before creating a safer place for them to rest.

After dragging Thorik's unconscious body into a side cavern, near one of the soft, glowing wall crystals, which had vines clinging to them, Avanda gently set his head on a pillow she had made from his backpack. She had removed the contents from the pack and filled it with guano to create a soft resting place.

Grabbing his flint and a handful of vines, she started a small fire. Afterward, she collected his clothes and placed them on the pile of his pack contents.

Avanda had also found fresh water dripping down through the walls and ceiling. Using Thorik's only remaining cooking pan, she collected enough for them to drink and for her to wash out the insect bites.

Once he was cleaned up, her concern turned to keeping the campfire going. This was their only source of heat and light, although a very faint glow emanated from the thick crystals.

Exhausted, she took a moment to lean up against one of the crystals, only to find it caused her to relax. Even though it gave no heat, it warmed her insides and washed away any remaining aggression from the event.

Hours passed as Avanda cradled Thorik's head, and she gave him sips of water each time before she took a sip for herself. She repeatedly washed his body to keep his wounds clean. When she became tired, she cuddled up against his back under his blanket, sharing her body heat with him. Then her hand wrapped around his side and lay upon his chest so she could tell if he was still breathing.

This went on for days as she waited to be rescued. Never wavering and rarely sleeping, she constantly checked his breathing and fed him water. She became obsessed with keeping him alive.

Over time, she had learned that the centipedes could be eaten, and the roaches burned like pieces of coal, so she made frequent trips back to the guano pile to keep the fire bright. Each time she did, she rushed back as quickly as possible, always fearful that something would try to harm Thorik while she was away.

Her imagination began to get the better of her as she became convinced that the little critters were plotting to take him. She could hear them whisper in the distance. Knowing they were watching her, she staggered her timing to collect water and roaches so they couldn't plan properly.

She had dreams of fighting off creatures to save Thorik's life. In her state of malnutrition and sleep deprivation, she struggled to tell the difference between dreams and reality. In her mind, she had saved his life a dozen times. She was losing her sense of reality.

On the other hand, Thorik slept. He breathed and his heart continued to beat, but he did not wake.

Preparing to sleep, Avanda pressed her chest up against his back and softly played with his hair. "Thorik, I promise to take care of you. You're safe with me here."

After so many days with no one to talk to, she had become used to talking to Thorik while he slept.

She pulled him in tight and sighed. "I know you've been alone since your parents died. And I also know how Emilen tempted you with love and then used it against you. I knew she was never right for you, anyway." Avanda scowled at the thought of Thorik's prior love and how she deceived him into falling into Darkmere's trap. "Emilen is the reason Ambrosius is dead, and why you are here fighting for your life."

"But I'm here now. I've always been there for you. I..." she paused and reached her lips near his ear before whispering, "... I love you, Thorik Dain of Farbank."

And with those words, Thorik blinked and his lips began to move. Still in his sleep state, he managed a single reply before passing back out. "I love you too, Emilen."

Avanda froze. Her body went stiff, and she felt her heart miss a beat. Her body instantly broke contact with his as she rolled away. She then stared at him in disbelief. "No," she muttered. "NO!" she shouted.

"It's not fair," Avanda argued with the sleeping Num. "I've always loved you. Emilen pretended to love you, only to use you." Standing up, she wobbled from lack of sleep and food as she glared at Thorik. Her head was foggy and her thoughts were a mess as anger built up inside. "Emilen left you for dead, while I stayed at your side to keep you alive!

"Why? What's so special about her?" Avanda waited for an answer, which she knew she wouldn't get.

"Would you prefer if I was ruthless and conniving? Perhaps if I lied to you. Or is it her looks? Is it?" Her voice was loud and angry as it echoed throughout the caverns. "Why won't you love me instead of her? What's wrong with me?"

Avanda's mind raced from topic to topic, trying to make sense of it all. "What did I do to you that was so wrong, making my love for you so distasteful? I deserve to know that! Don't you think you owe me an answer?" Tears poured down her face as she yelled at him.

Thorik continued to be silent.

"Emilen. Emilen? How can you say her name, yet be unable to say mine?" And with that, she grabbed the pot of water and flung the liquid out toward him in an emotional outburst.

The water splashed against his face, causing him to start choking.

Avanda immediately realized that she had let her self-pity get the best of her. She quickly snapped out of it, dropped the pan, and ran to his side, hoping she hadn't drowned him. "Thorik! Can you breathe?"

"Yes," he said as he coughed.

He was awake! He had made it through the insect's poison and had regained consciousness.

"Oh, Thorik, I thought I had lost you. You've been passed out for so long that I didn't think you were going to come back to me." She leaned over his face with a smile that verged on becoming a cry.

"Avanda, you pulled me through. You did it. You saved my life."

"You would have done the same for me."

Thorik looked deep into her tearful eyes and nodded. "Yes, I would."

❧ 4 ❧
PACKING

Realizing that no help would come for them and the vent shafts were too steep and smooth to climb back up, Thorik rested and recovered as long as he could until the need for food overwhelmed the desire to wait. The little protein they had obtained from eating the nearby centipedes simply was not enough to survive on. They needed more.

Thorik created an arrow on the ground out of rocks, which indicated which way they would travel. He still held out hope that Grewen, Brimmelle, and Bryus were on their way to save them.

Untying a pouch filled with Runestones, which had survived the fall into the caverns, Thorik removed the Runestone of Belief. Taking in a deep breath, he traced the ridges on its surface and closed his eyes as he allowed himself to fully relax.

Tingling along his fingertips worked its way up his hands, arms, and then his chest before completing the circular flow of energy that moved between him and the stone. As he did so, the red gem in the center of the Runestone began to glow and light up the cavern. With additional concentration, he could also cause the Runestone to give off heat, but it was a taxing endeavor and required more focus than Thorik was willing to give at the moment. Light to guide the way would be good enough for now.

Over the past few months, he had become quite skilled at activating this Runestone, although he hadn't yet determined the powers of most of the others.

Thorik opened his pack. His head dropped and he sighed at the sight of the guano within it.

"It packed in nicely." Avanda grinned at the idea of him sleeping on bat droppings for the past week. "It was the best pillow you've had in months."

"I'll never get the smell out of my hair." He gave off a slight chuckle as he dumped the guano out of his pack.

"How's your arm?"

Thorik scooped out the guano so he could use his pack again. The thick consistency clumped between his fingers and on his forearm. "It still hurts." Finishing the unpleasant task, he tried to shake the rest off of him.

"I know that. I was just wondering if it feels broken."

"It hurts bad when I use it, but Bryus' spell to fix the break seems to be holding. The insect bites are currently more sensitive." He scratched at the sores on his neck. "They still itch as well."

"I'm sorry I couldn't heal you. I did the best I could."

Stuffing his items back into his pack, he glanced up at her. "Avanda, you did great. You kept me alive. How could I ask for anything more… especially at your age?"

"What do you mean?" Her voice had turned cold and lower than normal.

Thorik continued to pack with his stronger arm. "Nothing."

"I'm not a child anymore."

"I didn't say that you were." He tried to end the conversation by standing up.

"I'm less than three years younger than you."

"I know. Are you ready to head out?"

"My parents have nearly six years between them."

"That's wonderful."

"So we are close enough in age to be together."

Thorik was realizing where this was going, but didn't feel that it was the proper time to discuss it. "Yes, we are. It's a fine observation, but right now, we need to be talking about getting back to the surface."

Avanda wasn't willing to let it go that easily. "What are you afraid of?"

"Afraid? I fear many things. Those predator roaches for one, bad tempered blothruds for another. But most of all, right now, I fear where this conversation is leading."

"Why? Why can't you talk about us?"

Thorik finished with his pack and lifted it up on his shoulder. It still smelled terrible. "Avanda, now is not the time."

"Now is the perfect time. It's only you and I. No one else is here to disturb us."

"Let's start walking."

Avanda grabbed his sore arm to stop him.

"Ouch!" he yelled from the pain of her grasp, even though it hadn't been more than a squeeze. It did, however, get him to stop and listen to her.

She looked him square in the eyes and waited for him to return the eye contact. The gentle light from his Runestone gave her soft pale skin a glowing appearance. She would never be as beautiful and voluptuous as Emilen, but Avanda had a strength about her that softened when she looked Thorik in the eyes. "Thorik, I need to know if you have feelings for me."

Thorik shrugged his shoulders. "Of course I do."

"No. I mean genuine feelings. Like you did for Emilen."

She had caught him off guard, and he stared while blinking at her. Just Emilen's name made his heart flutter.

"I see," she said softly.

"Avanda, I love you… like a little sister."

She pulled her eyes away, followed by her head and shoulders. Grabbing her items, she kept her back to him. "You must think I'm a fool to expect you to desire me."

Rubbing his brow, Thorik sighed at the situation. "I don't think you're a fool. In fact, I think you're the brightest Num I've ever met. You're courageous, intelligent, and honest. Perhaps even too honest for your own good. But I love that about you."

Turning back to Thorik, she studied his face. Her eyes appeared to be searching for the truth in his expression. "Then what is it about me that prevents you from being mine?"

Thorik bit his lip for a moment as he tried to muster the words. "Emilen…"

Avanda's shoulders drooped again once she heard her rival's name.

"Emilen," he started over, "stole my heart. I would have done anything for her. I practically did. At times, I forgot who I was just to satisfy and please her. In a way, I compromised my core values to please her. And then I came to find out that she was deceiving me. Leading me on, like some grazer on a rope."

Avanda relaxed her shoulders and posture as she listened to him.

"I don't know what kind of spell she had over me, and my concern is it was no spell at all, but instead, it was nothing more than love. If that is all it was, then I fear falling in love again, for I may lose who I really am, what I stand for, and most importantly, the mission I am on to free my grandmother."

"But Thorik, I would never—"

"I know," Thorik interrupted. He stepped up to her and placed his hands on her shoulders. "I know you wouldn't intentionally do this to me. But that is not to say that it wouldn't happen anyway. And right now I can't afford to take that chance. I have to maintain my focus on keeping you alive as well as saving Granna." Looking deeply into her eyes and thinking about more pleasant times, he smiled. "Once we get back to Farbank, I can let my guard down. Not until then."

Although Thorik could tell that she still disagreed with his concerns, he watched her softly nod in agreement.

❦ *5* ❦

TUNNELS

Crystals as thick as Grewen's waist jutted up at awkward angles from the cavern's floor and up through the ceiling. Just like the crystal they had set up camp next to, these occasional pillars gave off a faint glow, helping the two Nums negotiate their way through the maze of tunnels.

They were lost, and no matter which turn the Nums made, the path always led to further subterranean depths. Hope of finding a way back up to the surface was giving way to a desire for an underground river which would lead them out of the Shi'Pel Mountains and to the Volney River.

It had been days since they had eaten. "Even an insect would taste good at this point." Avanda's lips cracked as she spoke. Her body was bruised and cut from the various sharp rocks she had bumped against and fallen onto. Dark circles were now around her eyes from lack of sleep. She was exhausted. "Is there no end to these caves?"

"We'll get through this." Thorik's voice and mannerisms were always optimistic, even when he wasn't. "Just a little farther." He shone the light from his Runestone deeper into several tunnels to decide which one to select.

"You said that yesterday."

"It was only a few hours ago."

"No." Her voice was agitated, and her stomach moaned from lack of food. Insects simply weren't enough to survive on. "We've slept since then."

Thorik tried to recall, but the hours and days were all blending together. Without seeing the sun rise and fall, it was difficult to know just how long they had been away from the surface.

Avanda shook uncontrollably from the cold, damp air of the caverns. This seemed to happen more frequently as time went on. It always started lightly and then became uncontrollable for what felt like an hour before it subsided.

Thorik pulled her in tight to share his body heat. He was worried about her and knew he had to save her from these cold, dank caverns before she became ill. "It'll be all right." They continued to walk together down a new tunnel. "We'll stop soon so I can activate the Runestone for heat."

"Why can't you do that now?"

"Because we'd have to stop."

"Then let's stop so you can warm us up. The Runestone stays warm long after you get it going."

"True, but I don't think you understand how much it takes out of me. I'm already struggling to keep this one activated to shine our way. I'd have to rest after focusing my thoughts enough to generate heat from within it."

"Then let's rest."

"Soon. Just a little farther." Thorik knew that the more often they stopped, the more likely they would die in the caves from lack of food and water. "Besides, I have a good feeling about this tunnel. It smells fresher."

Avanda raised her nose to sniff before disagreeing with him. However, she noticed something different. "Is that water I hear?"

Thorik stood still for a moment. "Your ears are better than mine. I think you're correct." Focusing his thoughts, the gem in the center of his Runestone brightened the path before them as they began walking down it. It wasn't long before they approached a fast-paced underground river with a glowing crystal rising from it in the far wall.

Racing over to its shore, they both began scooping up handfuls of water to their dry lips. The icy water nearly burned as it went down their throats. Handful after handful filled their stomachs until they felt refreshed.

Standing back up, Thorik nodded his approval at the river while helping Avanda back up to her feet. "This is our best option." He had a renewed sense of hope, which came across in his voice. "This river will take us out of here."

Avanda's soul-markings turned nearly white as her heart pounded and her head shook back and forth. "I don't see a path along its side for us to walk." Nervous cracks in her voice were heard over the rushing water.

Holding back a chuckle at the idea of a conveniently placed path alongside the river, Thorik knew they wouldn't be that fortunate. He also knew her fear of the water was overwhelming her. "I'm an excellent swimmer. You can hold on to me."

The idea of drowning paralyzed her in her tracks. In the past, he had talked her into crossing rivers, but at least in those circumstances she could see the river-banks. This river forced its way into a tunnel with nothing more than a small air gap at the top. "No."

"Avanda," Thorik said warmly. "This is our only option."

"No, it's not. We can try another path."

"For how many days?"

"For as many as it takes."

"We don't have many days left. We're starving to death. Waiting for the perfect situation is not an option for us."

"You know I can't swim."

"I'll do all the swimming. All you have to do is hang on to me."

"And if you go under?"

"Hold your breath."

"WHAT?"

"We're going to hit a few areas in any river that will pull us under for a few seconds. Just hold your breath until I can get us back up to the surface."

Avanda's arms were crossed as she stood in defiance.

"Listen, we're lost down here, and this is the only opportunity we've seen to get to safety. I need you to trust me."

"I trust you. I just don't trust the water." Avanda watched the river lap at the rocks as it sped past them.

Thorik stepped between her and the water and softly held her hand before looking square in her eyes. "Avanda, trust me."

She looked at him and back at the water several times before closing her eyes and nodding her approval. But it was obvious that she did not like it.

Thorik took advantage of the moment and quickly secured everything in his backpack, and then pack onto his body. He tied her to him with a few yards of twine, to make sure that they didn't get too far separated in case she was to let go.

Leading her over to the water, he gave her very little warning, fearing that she would back out. "Here we go! Take a deep breath!" He grabbed her and jumped into the water.

The cool water engulfed them and immediately knocked them against sharp rocks near the bottom, where they tumbled out of control, unable to determine which way was up.

❧ *6* ❧

DARK RIVER

Caught in the violent swirls of the lower part of the raging river, Thorik and Avanda rolled head over heels in different directions until they both were jolted to a stop. The twine that connected them together had become snagged around a rock at the base of the river.

Like two kites on a windy day, the Nums flapped around in the rushing waters. The pitch-blackness of the cavern prevented them from seeing each other, but Thorik knew Avanda would be panicking by now. He had promised to hold on to her, and he currently wasn't. The jolt had pulled them apart.

Thorik fought off the instinct to panic and fight his way free. Instead, he reached for the twine and climbed it. After a few very difficult pulls upstream, he reached the area where the twine had been lodged. Reaching around the sharp rock, he attempted to lift the twine over, but the twine's pressure against the rock was far too much for him to overcome.

Thorik then pulled himself against the river to climb around the far side of the rock. But once there, the water pressure forced his chest firmly against the rock, preventing him from easily getting his hands in place to remove the twine. After working his fingers down along the twine to locate the point of the snag, he realized that the twine was wedged far too deep into a crack for him to jar it loose. It was stuck.

His air was depleting, and he knew Avanda may have already lost hers. His actions needed to be swift.

Reaching past the rock, he grabbed the taut twine, which held Avanda. Kicking off, he allowed himself to be taken by the river straight toward her. He tumbled forward.

Thorik's body slammed into Avanda. They both flopped about at the bottom of the river. Immediately unbuckling his leather belt, Thorik fed the leather through her belt, and buckled it back up. Then he removed his hunting dagger and cut both twines which held them captive.

The two Nums flew like a cork popping off a bottle. They spun, and rolled, and twisted until they finally reached the surface.

Thorik gasped for air, not knowing how long it would last. Fortunately, they were now riding along the surface of the river.

"Avanda!" Thorik yelled, realizing she hadn't taken a breath yet.

Her head was limp on her neck, and she showed no signs of life.

Moving her into a position to ensure her head was above water, he began working his way to the side of the river. He hoped to find a ledge at some point to pull her to safety.

It was then that an unseen rock from the low ceiling cracked against Thorik's head. Lights flashed in Thorik's eyes, and he felt himself pass out.

HE DIDN'T KNOW if it had been seconds or minutes, but when he regained consciousness, Thorik noticed the river had slowed. It had widened as it entered the side of a large, hot, dry, boulder-filled cavern with a few glowing crystal columns. The faint blur of the crystals' glowing light in an open area was all he needed to escape the river.

Finding a handhold, Thorik rolled Avanda and himself out of the water. His head bled from the cut created by the unseen rock, but he wasn't concerned about himself. Avanda wasn't breathing.

"Don't you dare die on me," Thorik ordered the lifeless girl before him.

Still unbalanced and dizzy from his own wound to the head, he spun Avanda onto her front and began pressing on her back to get the water out of her mouth. His grandmother, Gluic, had taught him many healing techniques, which he had hoped he would never have to use.

She still wasn't showing signs of life, causing Thorik to shake with fear of losing her. "Avanda! We made it out of the river. Wake up!"

Grabbing his sack of Runestones, he reached in and selected the Runestone of Health before flipping Avanda onto her back. Gluic had also taught him how to know what each Runestone felt like, so he could tell them apart without requiring light to see them.

Setting the Runestone of Health onto her forehead, he placed his hand on it and allowed himself to become one with it. This was difficult to do in his dizzy and panicking state of mind. Focus, he told himself.

The gem in the center of the Runestone glowed as he felt Avanda's thoughts. She was still in there. She was still alive. But for how long? He could tell she was drifting away. She couldn't pull any air into her lungs. She was dying.

"NO!" he shouted in anger.

Thorik knew he had to get her to breathe. Holding the Runestone firmly on her forehead, he took in a deep breath and placed his lips against hers and tried to breathe life back into her. His thoughts still focused on the Runestone to understand what she needed as he took another breath for her.

"Please don't leave," he said between breaths. "I need you."

The Runestone allowed him to know that she was coming back with each breath he gave her. The process was slow, and by no means was she safe yet. He resolved he would breathe for her for all of eternity if that was what it took to save her, and he began with the conviction to only stop when she could do it on her own.

"Come on, Avanda!" he yelled before the next breath. "I know you can do this. Come back to me." Another breath was given. "I believe in you."

Avanda's body jerked once and then a few more times before she rolled onto her side and began coughing up the rest of the river water, which had clogged her lungs. She was alive.

Thorik comforted her and patted her back while she continued to be sick. The rush of anxiety from nearly losing her suddenly kicked in, and his heart beat so hard that it hurt his chest. It overwhelmed him with the joy of her survival, and he dropped his forehead against her shoulder.

Avanda eventually turned over and leaned up against him, resting her head in the crook of his arm. She looked up at him with exhausted eyes. "I told you the water was a bad idea."

With tear-filled eyes, Thorik chuckled and nodded as he wiped his face clean. "I should listen to you more often." He then hugged her tightly, knowing how close she had come to leaving him forever.

And with that, it was decided to rest for a while before determining the next course of action of their escape plan.

Thorik created heat and additional light from one of his Runestones. Because of his depleted strength from malnutrition, the Runestone never lasted long after he let go, so he would frequently pick it back up to recharge the stone with his own energy.

Once rejuvenated, Avanda ripped some cloth from the base of her dress and tied it around Thorik's head to stop the bleeding, before she started exploring for alternate routes out. She refused to get back into the river. "I think this is our way out," she said to Thorik over the noise of the river.

Thorik looked across the boulder-filled room and spotted Avanda's silhouette standing in front of an angled crystal column. "Why do you say that?"

"Because I don't see any water this way."

Thorik grinned. He knew she would taunt him for years to come about his great escape plan, which had been a disaster. But he gladly accepted her teasing over her not surviving the river. "This time it's your decision."

Impatient to get out from the caves, she walked back to the warmth of the Runestone and crossed her arms. "Can't one of your Runestones just show us the way out of here?" Her tone was slightly agitated as she wished for a door to magically appear to allow them to leave the dark underground.

Thorik thought about it for a few seconds. "I'm not sure. I only know what a few of them do. I really haven't had time to try the others."

Even in the hot, dry air, Avanda's shivers raced across her body because of the wet clothes. "See if one of those will conjure up something to eat as well." A smirk crossed her face before she walked about the cavern again.

Sitting cross-legged, Thorik pulled the Runestone of Trust from his sack and closed his eyes. Relaxing the way Gluic had taught him, he closed his eyes and focused his thoughts and energy to allow the Runestone's powers to work their way up one arm and then back down into the other arm before returning to the Runestone. It felt as though miniature electric eels were coursing through his body as he waited for something to reveal itself.

He patiently waited as the sound of the river lowered in his ears before ending his intense focus. Opening his eyes and looking up, Thorik watched Avanda move at a fraction of her normal speed as she walked around the cavern. On the other side of him, Thorik watched the river move at a pace far too slow for water and too fast for ice. Standing up, he moved closer to the river, reached out, and then scooped up a handful of the odd moving water, only to find the liquid he touched suddenly move normally. After flowing out of his palm, it slowed in its descent back to the sluggish river.

Time appeared to be affected by this Runestone when activated. However, time was not the only thing affected. Thorik's body was being depleted of strength as his legs wobbled and his head spun. Unlike the other Runestones he had used, he could not use this one for more than a few moments at a time.

Allowing his thoughts to return to the real world, the rush of the river's noise returned along with the movement.

"Didn't that one work?" Avanda asked as she glanced back at him. "Try a different one."

Giving himself a few moments to shake off the effects from the event, Thorik put the first Runestone away and pulled out the Runestone of Courage, hoping again that this would be the one they would need to help them escape the caverns. He took in a deep breath before relaxing his shoulders as he exhaled. The Runestone texture slowly faded from his fingertips as he felt past the smooth rock and into its internal powers. Closing his eyes, he became an extension of the Runestone and acted as a conduit for it to release its energy.

Avanda gasped, causing Thorik to open his eyes and look at her.

There, in the caves, were hundreds of ghostly figures. Shoulder to shoulder, they walked through the cavern as they all headed in from a passage and then out the other side. More filed in behind them in a continuous, slow and steady march. Sounds of footsteps and moaning filled the room, even though most of the apparitions' feet never even touched the cave floor.

Standing up, Thorik moved over to Avanda and then turned toward several semi-transparent figures coming toward them, while Avanda pushed her shoulder blades against his to watch his back.

The spirits walking toward the Nums proceeded past them, keeping their distance from the Runestone, which Thorik held out in front of him. Their faces sagged like candle wax in the hot sun, yet it was apparent that there were spirits of multiple species in the group. Human, Polenum, Del'Unday, Ov'Unday, and even Fesh made up the slow-moving crowd.

Avanda watched the procession move past them. She eventually reached out with her hand and softly touched the arm of a female gliding past. A tingle ran down Avanda's arm as though the energy of her own body was flowing out of her and into the spirit.

The mist of the ghostly woman's arm turned dark and solid. Her skin became visible and warm as it spread up her arm and toward her chest. Gasping suddenly, the woman turned and looked at Avanda in astonishment.

But the energy needed to bring this woman back to life was being stolen from Avanda, who felt sick and looked pale. Lightheaded, she removed her hand from the woman.

The ghostly lady, with one solid arm, immediately panicked. Feeling life again for the first time in so many years, she wasn't about to let it slip away so easily. Reaching out, she clutched onto Avanda's wrist to absorb the energy she so desperately needed.

Avanda fell to her knees as she felt drained of her life. Her skin turned a light gray, and even her normally colorful hair lost its luster. She was being depleted of all her life forces.

Thorik's shock at the sight of the oncoming ghosts had worn off before he had realized Avanda had fallen behind him. In turning, he witnessed the attack of the semi-solid woman on Avanda. There was no time to spare as his young friend mouthed the word help, unable to make a sound.

Kicking the woman's arm away from Avanda, Thorik stood between them and held out his Runestone to get a good look at her.

But the woman craved what the Nums had; life. Reaching out to touch Thorik, she suddenly stopped. The Runestone prevented her from passing. She tried to touch either of the Nums again and again, each time being blocked by the Runestone's power.

As the woman proceeded, the solid structure of her arm slowly bled out into the rest of her body, causing the ghostly image to become more visible. Along with that, her arm softened and became transparent again. She hadn't received enough life force to keep her with the living; however, she had already stepped out of the realm of the roaming souls.

Her body struggled between the two worlds as parts of her body attempted to become solid, depleting other areas. She let out a hideous scream of pain as the vapor-like parts of her vanished and the solid parts fell to the floor before they quickly dried up, cracked, and crumbled apart.

The woman's spirit continued to change from white vapors to a solid mass as she gave off a high-pitched shriek, which echoed within the caverns.

Both of the Nums covered their ears to minimize the sound, but upon doing so, all the other ghosts disappeared. Thorik's concentration on his Runestone wavered, breaking their ability to see them.

However, the woman and her scream were still present. She looked at Avanda as her face became solid and asked one simple question before it was over. "Why?"

Avanda didn't have time to respond before the woman's head cracked and crumbled into grains of sand before falling to the floor.

Avanda sat in shock. Her body was weakened from the assault, but she slowly regained the color in her skin and hair.

"Are you hurt?" Thorik asked, reaching down to help her up.

Lightheaded, she grabbed his hand, carefully stood back up, and shook her head.

"What happened?" Thorik asked.

"I don't know." Avanda felt terrible. She had not intended to cause the woman any pain. "I just wanted to see what a ghost felt like."

"Well, don't do that again."

Ignoring his comment, Avanda swiveled her head and searched the cavern. "Do you think they are still around us?"

Peering around, Thorik nodded. "I would assume so. We just can't see them without the glow of the Runestone."

Avanda shivered and wrapped her arms around herself. "Do you think they can see us without the Runestone being used?"

"I don't know."

"Can they grab us again?"

"I don't think so. Somehow, the Runestone allows us to see and touch each other. But they can't touch the stone itself." He looked down at the stone still in his hand. "Without the Runestone's powers being activated, they could be walking right through us."

They both stood silently to listen for any noises or to feel any sensations. An occasional footfall or moan was heard, but always at a distance, and the direction was difficult to isolate.

Avanda continued to tremble from the ghostly woman's assault. "Do you think they can hear us without the Runestone being used?"

"I don't think so." Even with that said, Thorik felt a cold sensation on his arm and shoulder. Shivers immediately ran up his spine and then over his head to his temples.

"You don't belong here," a voice whispered into Thorik's right ear.

Thorik quickly covered his ear with his hand and jumped out of the way, expecting to see someone, but he didn't.

"I heard it as well." Avanda's eyes became excessively wide as she scanned the room.

"Bakalor will come for you," the voice said again.

Avanda grabbed onto Thorik's arm as she searched for whoever was talking.

Thorik began to activate the Runestone again, but his nerves prevented his ability to concentrate.

"Who is Bakalor?" Thorik asked.

"You will become one of us, Dain," the now familiar voice announced.

Shaking his head to dismiss the idea, Thorik continued in his attempt to become one with the Runestone. "We will heed your advice. Can you show us the way out?"

Without warning, the cavern shook from a tremor deeper down into the cave. A soft, ill-green light emerged at a distance and exposed the silhouette of a ghastly giant beast stepping into the mighty cavern.

Avanda's grip on Thorik's arm increased as she watched the events unfold.

"It's too late," the voice said as it trailed off.

Thorik ignored everything except the Runestone as he felt its energy flow through him. Knowing it was working, he looked up to see the spirits running the opposite way from where they had been walking earlier. The one who had been talking to him presented a distorted smile on his melted face.

Before they could talk again, the spirit in front of them blended into the rest of the misty vapors that were hurrying away from the approaching yellowish green flaming beast, as it grabbed handfuls of spirits and tossed them into its mouth. Its touch caused them to instantly become solid masses filled with life, and they screamed in pain from his sharp teeth biting down on them. Their sudden return to life was abruptly over.

The screams of horror were deafening, and the crunching of bones, along with the tremors of the beast's movement, put Avanda into a state of panic.

She grabbed Thorik and pushed him into a safe hiding place surrounded by boulders. But by doing this, she broke his concentration on the Runestone. The ghosts were now gone from their sight, but the beast remained.

❦ 7 ❦

BAKALOR'S LAIR

Bakalor, the demon of the underworld, advanced toward Thorik and Avanda from the far end of the cavern. Rock and mud made up the demon's bones and muscles. Crystals filled in for teeth and long, sharp nails, and diamonds the size of Thorik's head were inset in his eye sockets. Standing on two legs, he shoveled handfuls of the dead spirits into his mouth. Once swallowed, their souls were lost forever, never to have the chance to reincarnate into a body of a future person or creature.

Thick flaming oil dripped off the demon's body, acting as a lubricant to allow his various parts to work together. Subtle, oily flames rippled out from every crack as they illuminated his entire body.

Thorik and Avanda peeked out from the confines of the boulders they hid among. They were silent, but their blood pulsed through their bodies at a fast pace as they realized that the new threat was more than they felt they could deal with.

Towering in size, the demon stood at a height easily twice that of their giant friend Grewen. But this was no clumsy moving creature. He moved within the cave as if he were an extension of the rock and earth. Walking into a cavern wall, he would be absorbed into it before exiting the far side.

After shoveling several more handfuls of the dead into his mouth, he finally came to a stop and searched about for something amiss. Feeling the cave's vibrations through his feet, he could sense something was wrong. "Heartbeats? Here, in Della Estovia?" The voice was booming and coarse.

Thorik and Avanda ducked back down behind the boulders, hoping to evade detection.

"This place is not for the living," Bakalor announced, shaking the walls with his voice. "You have trespassed into my domain. Who are you? And why have you come?"

Thorik and Avanda tried to communicate to each other with hand signals, attempting to plan an escape from the cavern. Neither did an adequate job in relaying their message.

The cavern floors acted as extensions of Bakalor's feet, and he could feel the warmth of the Nums' bodies behind the boulders. Reaching an arm down into the rock below him, his palm sprang up out of the rock across the cave directly below the Nums. Oil quickly saturated the ground near the Nums' feet as the boulders they hid between transformed into Bakalor's fingers.

The giant hand, which had emerged from the cave's floor, closed onto the Nums and encased them in rock before lowering back into the cave's floor.

On the far side of the cavern, Bakalor pulled his hand up out of the ground near his feet and then opened it up near his face. Rattled by the abduction, the Nums in his palm looked back up at him in awe.

The center of the demon's face sagged down over the front of his mouth. His steamy breath smelled of sulfur, and the texture of his skin was abrasive and composed of several types of minerals.

"I am Thorik Dain of Farbank," the Num announced as he held his hand out to deflect the burning hot air from the demon's nostrils. "We fell into your caves by accident. We are here only in search of our way out."

Bakalor's hand lifted them closer to one of his diamond eyes as he inspected his captured prey. "Your name sounds familiar. Thorik Dain of Farbank?"

"Yes," Thorik answered hesitantly. The giant diamond rotated inside the demon's eye socket as it studied the Num. The thick, flaming oil drained out of the socket and into the beast's mouth.

"After all these years? Could it be? Yes, I believe it is. I know you," Bakalor finally announced.

"You know of me? Has someone told you about us?"

"Don't toy with me," the demon growled. "I know you, just as you know me!"

"But how?"

"You are the reason I am here!"

Avanda shot a look at Thorik, who was just as perplexed.

"Me?" Thorik asked sheepishly.

Ignoring the question, Bakalor closed his fingers around the Nums again, sealing them in tight before walking into a nearby wall. The wall absorbed the majority of the demon's body, while a few stray rocks slapped against the wall and rolled to the floor.

The Nums could hear the grinding and slamming of rock as the demon traveled through the earth's solid crust between each cave. Bakalor traveled in a straight line. Cavern walls were just as easy to pass through for him as open caves, much like a Num walking from one room of a house to another through walls made of rice paper.

The difference, however, was that the demon's body transferred from rock to rock along the way instead of pushing a solid form all the way through. This was also the case for his hand within which the Nums sat. The rocks continued to move past them, opening up and separating at just the right time to maintain a consistent shape of the inside of the demon's palm. The only part of Bakalor that traveled with him was the thick oil, which seeped through cracks and acquired new rocks for his body.

Thorik and Avanda bounced around inside the giant fist for quite some time before it finally stopped and the rock fingers opened up. Once their eyes adjusted, they surveyed their surroundings.

A cavernous terrain, miles in every direction, lay before them with a maze of tall pumice walls and several ancient buildings constructed on bridges that spanned the rivers of lava. The cavern's ceiling was nearly a quarter mile high and covered with arching rows of stalactites where cracks in the limestone had existed. Flames shot up from rivers that tumbled down various falls and rapids throughout the open cavern.

In contrast to the red flowing magma rivers, giant light-blue crystals jutted up from the floor at odd angles, reaching up and embedding themselves in the high ceiling. Resembling columns of sunlight breaking through dark and dangerous clouds, the crystals gave the Nums a sense of hope that there was freedom just beyond this hideous place.

But their attention needed to be on where they were and not where they wanted to be. This mighty cavern was a hot and dry landscape, which smelled of sulfur and acid. Even if the demon set them free, they would struggle to survive in such a place for long.

"The underworld," Thorik said under his breath to Avanda. "This is where the dead roam in their afterlife." They had both heard the fables of such a place, but had never given the stories any validity until now.

Bakalor tilted his hand, dropping the two Nums onto the flat top of a rock column, which he had silently called upon to grow from the floor just moments prior. The demon then sat down in his enormous throne and reveled in his accomplishment.

Screams of pain could be heard; however, the bodies they came from could not be seen. The Nums searched in every direction for the owners of the voices, but they found none.

"This..." Bakalor opened his arms, "... is what I have created from my humble beginnings. I nearly perished during my first century down here. Eventually civilizations grew above ground and brought corruption, greed, and malice. These were the tastes I learned to enjoy."

As he listened to the demon, Thorik pulled out the Runestone of Courage, which he had used earlier to see the dead souls. "Avanda, keep him occupied," he whispered.

"It wasn't long before my children began to bring the essence of the dead to me in droves. I no longer need to hunt on the surface during the dark of night." Bakalor straightened the enormous spear and mace next to his throne. "Bitter to my taste were their souls at first, but I learned to tolerate them. The sweet taste of the noble and pure of heart is so rare. However, the crystal columns usually take most savory before I find them."

Avanda trembled as she followed Thorik's instructions. "Bakalor, is it?"

"It is."

"What happens to the souls down here?"

"I eat most of them and they are forever lost. A few are pulled into the crystal columns and whisked away to some higher plane. The rest walk endlessly in my caverns, at least until they are called upon to live again." Bakalor coughed at the idea. "Doesn't seem to make sense. They live life after life, making the same mistakes and always ending up back down here. There are only a few that actually learn from prior lives and are granted access to the columns."

Thorik had been ignoring the demon. Instead, his focus was on the Runestone. It wasn't long before the gem in the center glowed and the light illuminated the hundreds of thousands of ghostly figures which moved among the giant cave's maze.

The dead walked the underworld in an endless search for peace. All species and all ages slowly paraded in lines, hoping they could find any end to their fruitless existence.

"We do not belong here," Thorik said to Bakalor.

"Nor do I," the demon said spitefully.

"No, you don't understand. We aren't dead yet. Only those who have died are allowed in Della Estovia."

Bakalor leaned forward and reached out to poke Thorik with one of his enormous fingers. "You are correct. But I will resolve this issue, slowly, for livestock is a rare treat for me. Your plump, juicy flesh is much to my liking, regardless of your innocence or sins." Bakalor firmly pressed a single giant finger against the Num and held it there.

Thorik's body went rigid as he felt the heat rush away from his body. The gem in the center of his Runestone instantly dimmed and the view of the ghostly inhabitants disappeared.

Bakalor's body jerked at the influx of fresh life-force. "So sweet is the taste, I nearly forgot." He arched his head back as he sucked in the warmth. "You will come to fear me... every minute of every day."

Waves of warmth flowed from the Num, each slowly removing months and even years from his life as his body showed the signs of the attack. Thorik's youthful face was quickly becoming a man's as each year of his life was raped from him. In addition, the process induced muscle seizures and stinging sensations across his skin. His heart quickened, his lungs squeezed tight, and his head felt as though it was being drained of blood.

Bakalor breathed in with quivering lips, as though the sensation of receiving the Num's life-force was erotic in nature. His eyes rolled back in his head as a grin of pleasure crossed his face.

Confidence and courage drained from Thorik's body as well, leaving doubt and fear to fester in his mind. Bitter thoughts from his past sprang forth to suppress the times of joy and love. Good was slowly being devoured by hate and fear.

Avanda grabbed Thorik to pull him away, only to find herself caught in the vacuum effect caused by the demon. Heated waves of energy now pulled from her chest and flowed out of her body and into Thorik's before they continued out into the demon. Thorik's pain was now Avanda's, and they screamed from their suffering.

The agony was stifling for Avanda. She could feel the demon's presence on her, in her, and within her own thoughts. It felt as though the demon had climbed into her body and was using it as a toy as he selected the best parts of her memories to pilfer.

Bakalor was now breathing heavily with ecstasy from his tasty treat of energy from non-dead life forms. His enjoyment caused him such pleasure that he eventually fell back and collapsed into his throne, releasing his contact with the Nums.

A burst of flame erupted from the oil that covered the demon's body. The heat fanned against the Nums as intense fire shot high into the air for several seconds before dissipating to its prior soft flame. Upon returning to normal, Bakalor sighed with pleasure and closed his eyes. The ordeal had literally exhausted his own body, causing him to pass out from a pleasure he had not enjoyed for decades. The spirit of the Nums had been more than he had expected.

Sobbing from the pain, the Nums held onto each other as they dropped to the surface of the column. Fear of another attack caused them to shake and cry, for they had never felt so helpless to defend themselves.

Thorik looked for a way to escape as he held Avanda tight. Her body continued to tremble, and her skin was cold against his. "I'll get you out of this."

Avanda's lungs hurt so much that it was difficult for her to speak while crying and gasping for breath. "We aren't going to make it this time."

Thorik instinctively agreed with her before realizing that the thoughts placed in his head by Bakalor were clouding his judgment. Looking directly into her eyes, his now aged face gave her a stern look. "Don't talk like that. Never give up hope."

She shivered uncontrollably. "It's over, Thorik. We can't beat him."

The words made emotional sense, but Thorik fought off the temptation to give into Bakalor's thoughts of defeat and fear. "Don't say that!" Thorik searched frantically for a way down off the column where they sat. There was no way to climb down, and the jump would easily break their legs. However, there was another option.

"Avanda, stand up." Thorik helped her to her feet and turned her toward the sleeping demon. "We can jump over to his throne and climb down from there."

Shaking her head as she regained her strength, Avanda had no desire to jump toward the demon. The horror he had implanted in her mind swayed her thoughts. "He'll wake up."

"Not if we land on the throne's armrest without touching him."

It was a risk, seeing that Bakalor's arm covered over half of the throne's armrest. On a good day, Thorik would feel very comfortable about the leap, but in his current state, he wasn't sure he could do it. He knew Avanda stood even less of a chance.

Bakalor snarled and growled in his sleep, causing both of the Nums to cower slightly. But the demon's noises only lasted a moment.

Thorik rubbed his hands up and down on Avanda's arms to warm her up. "I'll go first, then I'll catch you when you jump." It was easier to say than to do. The demon had embedded such fear inside him that it was difficult for him to look directly at Bakalor's face.

Avanda stared in a terrified trance at the demon instead of replying.

"Here I go." He stepped back to get a few steps of a running start. Crouching down, he paused before launching himself forward and stretching his body out to make the distance.

Flying through the air, his legs kicked a few times before he landed on the armrest and rolled toward the demon, sliding to a halt just before touching the sleeping giant. He had landed so close that the oily flames on the demon's body dripped onto Thorik's back. Thorik scooted away and rolled on his back to put out the flames before rising to help Avanda. He dared not look over his shoulder to see if the demon was aware of his presence, for fear of cowering once he saw Bakalor's peering eyes.

Avanda had cringed as she watched Thorik's near-fatal leap and roll. Now she paced on the small surface of the column, trying to gain enough confidence in her ability to jump the span. It was uncommon for her to doubt herself, but the demon had struck a nerve she had only felt once before, when she was nearly raped in Southwind. Both aggressors had both made her feel vulnerable and violated, a feeling she hated.

"Jump!" Thorik held out his hands, ready to catch her whenever she jumped.

The sight of the demon caused Avanda to lower her head and her feet to back up. She didn't know why the sight of him caused her such tremors of fear down her spine, but she eventually realized that she wouldn't be able to make the jump if she looked at him. Even the thought of him caused her to become unsure of herself.

Thorik watched her pace. He knew their window of time was limited and Bakalor could wake up at any moment. They had to move quickly and quietly. If caught, a second attack would surely drain them of any energy or desire to attempt such a daring escape. "Hurry!"

Focusing on Thorik's face, a bit of strength came back into her body. "I can do this." She then stepped back before making a three-step jump.

Bakalor coughed and swung his arm off the armrest and onto his stomach while in his dream state.

Thorik fell flat onto the armrest to avoid being hit by Bakalor's arm, but Avanda panicked while taking her last step in leaping across.

Avanda flew across with arms and legs flailing around before landing on top of Thorik. Grabbing him the moment she landed, her out-of-control tumble pulled him off the armrest and onto the seat of the throne before rolling off and landing on the cavern floor.

Thorik landed first, on his back, while Avanda's strong clutch of his shirt kept her on his front.

Lying face to face on top of each other, they moaned softly from the pain of the fall, still hoping to escape before the demon was awoken. The silence that followed convinced them they hadn't woken Bakalor up.

Avanda knew she couldn't have done it without Thorik. She needed him. He had saved her more than once. Without giving it another thought, she gave him a quick, unexpected kiss. "Thank you."

Thorik was slightly unsure how to respond. "Not now." The serious jeopardy they were still in required their full attention. Looking at her disappointed response to his words, he realized he could have said something more tactful. "We're not out of this yet. I'll give you that kiss when we're actually free."

"Agreed." She rolled off of him, and they immediately ran from the demon's throne and into the maze.

8

ESCAPING FROM THE UNDERWORLD

Della Estovia was a vast terrain of rivers and falls of flaming molten rock with ruins of ancient stone buildings and bridges. The dry, bitter air was hard to breathe, and predator roaches periodically covered the ground. Worn trails looped around the entire open cavern in an endless maze of sharp-edged pumice walls preventing the short Nums from climbing up to see a way out.

Running on and off for nearly an hour through the rock labyrinth, Thorik pulled Avanda around yet another corner. "Keep moving so we don't have bugs climbing up our legs."

"I am," she replied as the crunching of insects under her feet made it obvious that she was keeping up a quick pace. "But we're going around in circles. We'll end up right back where we started."

Thorik made a quick decision on the approaching junction as they ran toward it. "No, it just seems that way. We're getting close to one of the bridges I saw before we escaped the top of the column."

"Don't you have a Runestone that can help us find our way out?"

"We don't have the time to try them all right now."

"Then use the Runestone of Courage so we can see the ghosts."

Thorik led them around the bin at the junction. "What good will that do us?"

"We can ask them how to get out of here."

"If they knew that, they would have already used it to escape."

Avanda realized he was right, but she also knew they couldn't keep running forever. "Then let's ask them what path leads back to the caves so we can hide until we figure out a better plan."

"It's too risky."

Avanda pulled her hand free of his. "The risk is mine to take as well. I haven't eaten in days, and I can't run forever. We can't go on like this, Thorik. We have to try something else."

Turning, Thorik watched her slow down to a fast walk. He knew she wasn't going to run any longer. "You're right. It could take us days just to find our way out of this maze, and possibly weeks to get to the surface. We can't survive that long without food and water." He then slowed to allow her to catch up. "Staying here won't help either. Let's at least keep walking."

"Why does it always have to be your way? Didn't the river teach you anything?"

"It's not always my way. Besides, the river would have worked if the undertow hadn't dragged us on the bottom and snagged our line."

"Stop justifying your actions. You always think you know the best way to do things. You don't take my suggestions seriously. The ghosts might be able to help us."

Reaching his hand out to her encouraged her to keep moving. "Once we get to the bridge, we'll be able to see over these walls. If we can't determine a path at that point, we'll try talking to the local souls."

She nodded in agreement. "My ideas are just as valid as yours, Thorik. You need to take them seriously."

"I know. I'm trying."

"Well, try harder." The sharpness in her tone was clear.

Thorik didn't respond. Instead, he led her around several more bends in the labyrinth before it opened up to a raised stone bridge which spanned a wide river of flowing red liquid rock. In the center of the thick bridge was a circle of tall marble columns holding up a heavy, and once impressive, roof structure. It appeared to be the remains of a large temple, with most of its walls now rubble. Only a few internal walls still stood, as well as several columns leading up to the building.

Both Nums showed signs of fatigue as they climbed the tall steps leading to the bridge. The lack of food was taking its toll as they dragged their feet while they passed several freestanding columns on their approach to the center structure.

Thorik noticed carvings in the columns, which he had seen before. They were the markings of the Notarians. These were the original species of this land that created all Altered Creatures. And they were the ones that the Mountain King had fought against to free all species and races from them. Only a few of these extremely powerful Notarians survived. They were known as the three Oracles.

Blocks had fallen from the ceiling of the center edifice, hiding the writings and symbols along the floor tiles. A thick metal ring had been placed in the center of the floor, surrounding a hole a few yards in diameter. Within the hole, flowing lava could be seen.

Thorik stepped up onto the highest block of fallen debris to see as far as possible. In the distance, he could see the mighty Bakalor passed out on his enormous throne. In the opposite direction, he could see the edge of the cavern. Its walls were littered with tunnel openings, but which one would grant them access to escape?

Leaning one way and then the other, Thorik attempted to see beyond one of the large ceiling-high crystals, which blocked his view. It stood just beyond the other side of the bridge, at the base of the steps, and was as wide as the Bakalor's shoulders.

Avanda looked for an escape route as well. "What do you see?"

"A maze with no obvious end." He felt slightly defeated. "But if I could just see past that crystal, there might be something I'm missing."

"Thorik, you promised to try asking the spirits."

"Only after I've tried this first."

"You tried. Now let's move on."

"But I can't see past the crystal. Maybe if I climb over to the side," he said to himself.

"Thorik! Why is there is always one more thing you're going to try before you do what I suggest?"

Snapping him out of his thought, he knew that tone in her voice. She was about to become unmanageable. "Don't get upset. I was just thinking out loud. I was getting ready to try your idea."

"Sure you were." Her arms were folded tightly in front of her.

Thorik climbed back down off the fallen ceiling blocks and removed his sack of Runestones. The close proximity of the glowing light-blue crystal column made it easy to find the Runestone of Courage. With few distractions, he was able to merge his thoughts and energy with the Runestone, causing the center gem to light up. However, his lack of nutrition, water, and sleep made it difficult to keep the link between them under control.

It had been over a week since they had eaten anything other than bugs, and sleep had been in the form of passing out for a few minutes at a time due to exhaustion. If it hadn't been for nearly drowning in the river, they wouldn't have had any water either.

Avanda had moved closer to Thorik, to ensure none of the spirits would touch her. However, she had nothing to fear, for though thousands of spirits appeared throughout the surrounding maze, none were on the bridge.

Thorik opened his tired eyes from his meditation. "Avanda, hurry! Find out if they can lead us to an escape tunnel."

Avanda knew that meant leaving the safety of the bridge and returning to the pumice walls. "Why do they all avoid the bridge?"

"I don't know. Perhaps spirits can't climb steps." He forced a smile.

"But insects can, and they aren't up here either. Everything seems fearful of this bridge. Perhaps we shouldn't be on it."

"It's the safest place we've found so far. Avanda, I don't have the strength to hold this all day. Find out what they know."

Avanda pulled at him to follow her, but his weakened condition caused his movement to reduce their ability to see the spirits. She was only able to move him to the top step before he sat down from exhaustion.

"Just go to the edge of the steps. If they can't approach us, then you'll be safe from their touch. I need to sit and rest if I plan to keep this Runestone active." As difficult as it was to keep a Runestone performing its task, it was mild compared to the initial activation. Thorik wasn't sure if he had the capacity to reactivate it closer to the bottom step if he were to lose his connection on the way down.

Apprehensive about heading down the steps alone, even if this was her idea, Avanda slowly moved toward the passing semi-transparent figures.

"Hello?" She looked for a kind word in return. Instead, she noticed a look of fear in their eyes.

"Get off the sacred aerie!" one spirit shouted. Another repeated the warning.

"I don't understand," she replied.

"He'll see you!" one of them yelled.

"The birthplace of his children cannot be disturbed," moaned another.

Avanda shook her head. "I don't care about that! I need to know how to escape. We shouldn't be here. We need to return to the surface."

"Leave the sacred nest before it's too late!" another spirit warned. "Crystals are the only freedom."

"What does that mean?"

"The bridge is his children's birthplace. Stay clear!"

Avanda refused to leave without an answer, so she continued to ask them for assistance.

Meanwhile, Thorik sat on the top step as he concentrated on the Runestone before him. It seemed like he had been focusing on it for hours, even though it had only been a few minutes. Craning his neck back and then to the side, he stretched it a few times before opening his eyes, hoping to see his companion returning with the information they needed.

Instead, what he saw caused him to lose full concentration on the Runestone.

The spirits disappeared.

Avanda looked up the steps at Thorik, who now had a horrified expression on his face. Climbing the steps as quickly as she could, she reached the top step and turned around to see what had struck him with fear. "What is it? I don't see anything."

Thorik pointed out in front of them. "There, beyond that third crystal column, is Bakalor's throne."

"Yes, I see it. So?"

"He's not in it."

It took a moment for his concern to register in her mind. "He's awake!"

"And looking for us!"

Both of the Nums immediately stood up and started racing across the bridge in hopes of hiding in the far maze before the demon made it this far.

A thunderous crack exploded from behind them as rocks scraped against each other and snapped under tremendous pressure. Bakalor lifted out of the ground at the bottom of the steps to the bridge, as rocks flew in every direction. "Get out of the nursery!" he yelled with such force that it shook the bridge.

The Nums evaded the falling debris from the eruption of Bakalor's entrance as they headed into the structure in the center of the bridge to hide from him. As fruitless a plan as it was, their only other option was to jump over the edge into the molten lava. Hiding was obviously the preferable choice.

Bakalor gave chase, stepping quickly up onto the stone bridge. Flames increased across his body as he approached the building in anger. "Get out!" he demanded, swinging his arms in frustration.

Thorik realized the demon couldn't reach up through the ground and grab them as long as they stayed on the bridge. In fact, it appeared that he couldn't manipulate the stones of this bridge at all, perhaps because it was built by the Notarians. Then again, that wouldn't matter much if the demon knocked the structure down on top of the Nums.

Bakalor was outraged at the Nums' invasion of his sacred place. The columns were just close enough to each other to prevent the demon from coming inside without destroying it. Grabbing one of the stone columns, which led up to the temple, he ripped it from its foundation and swung it like a club at the roof. His intent was to scare the Nums out of his sacred place. However, he had underestimated the remaining strength of the building.

Cracks spread like lightning across the ceiling, and chunks of stones fell near the Nums. The structural integrity of the building had been compromised, and a second attack could finish it off.

"Run!" Thorik yelled to Avanda, pushing her toward the far side of the bridge.

She did what he asked, as the bridge shook from the demon's feet pounding on the other side. Racing across to the far steps, Avanda turned, only to realize that Thorik hadn't followed her. He was standing just inside the building, taunting the demon in an effort to keep Bakalor's focus on himself.

Nevertheless, Bakalor noticed Avanda's escape beyond the building's walls. Instead of hitting the roof again with his column club, he leaned over the side of the bridge and threw it at her. The stone column twirled through the air toward the young Num.

Leaping off the top step, she dove and rolled down the bridge's staircase just as the weapon struck. Crushing the top of the stairs, it cracked and bounced before one end crashed near her as the other side slammed into the thick crystal just beyond the steps.

Fragments of crystals sprayed in every direction. Light blue shards coated Avanda's body as she covered her face to protect herself. Then the stone column broke into several large pieces before coming to a rest near the base of the crystal column.

Slowly opening her eyes, Avanda looked at the damaged glowing crystal, which went all the way up through the cavern's ceiling. The inside of the crystal was hollow and gave off a pleasant and inviting light. Brushing off the dust and crystal fragments, she rushed toward it.

Peeking her head up inside, she saw a bright light which, surprisingly, didn't hurt her eyes. In fact, it felt good and refreshing as she sensed family within the light inviting her in. Her hair flapped in her face as she gazed upon the light. A stiff breeze was pulling her into it. So much so that she had to brace herself in order to prevent herself from being sucked up into the crystal.

"Thorik!" she yelled over her shoulder. "I found our way out!"

Thorik couldn't hear her over Bakalor's growling, which caused the walls to quake and the Num's body to vibrate.

"If you want me out of here, you're going to have to come in here and get me!" Thorik taunted. His hopes of riling up the demon could pay off if the heavy ceiling crashed down on Bakalor and killed him, or at least knocked him out long enough for the two Nums to get away.

Not used to anyone threatening him, the demon took the bait and entered. His shoulder hit the columns instantly, and debris rained down from the ceiling.

Bakalor stopped and watched the sight before glancing over at Thorik, who was poised to leap out the other side of the building once it began to fall.

Slowly pulling back, the demon gained control of his anger. "Clever. I forgot how deceptive you can be."

Thorik was so close to his plan working that he refused to give up on it. "What? Has a mere Num outlasted the mighty Bakalor? How will you ever live with such a defeat? Come and strike me down now, or are you too much of a coward?"

Bakalor paused, took a deep breath, and then laughed. "You have no idea where upon you stand, do you?"

"It doesn't matter where I stand. What matters is that I stand, defying you and laughing at your inability to defeat a Num."

The demon fully composed himself and then grinned, knowing he had the upper hand. "Let me show you where you are." Reaching down, he grabbed one of his stone toes and, with a quick twist, he snapped it right off. The demon screamed in pain for a moment before recovering. He then took the toe, about the size of Thorik, and rolled it into the structure.

Thorik moved back behind a column. He assumed the demon was rolling the giant toe at him, but it quickly became apparent that he was not the target.

The boulder of a toe rolled into the center of the building and into the open metal ring. As it fell into the hole, the metal ring flashed a molten red and gave off a misty vapor that settled across the floor. The toe fell through the ring and into the flowing river of magma.

Thorik looked up at Bakalor's pleased face, unsure what the demon was planning.

"I have just given you the privilege of seeing my son's birth. I shall call him Grub. Isn't that what you Nums call your meal? Because that is what you are about to become. So, in a sense, I've named him after you."

Thorik felt he had lost the upper hand and slowly started backing away. His timing was wisely planned.

Spraying up from the river and back through the metal ring was a large glob of glowing magma. Bakalor's toe had been heated into a molten ball. Landing just to the side of the ring, it started to form.

The round glob of molten rock began to cool and form common features. Soon, he stood the height of a Num, on two massive legs, with long, sharp claws on his feet. Four thick, muscular arms extended from his round torso, one pair set at his shoulders, the other set just above his hips. Nevertheless, his arms were not his oddest feature, for he had no neck or head on his shoulders. Instead, an enormous gaping mouth opened up in his stomach. Dozens of sharp teeth extended from outside his mouth while a second set could be seen inside the creature's mouth. "I am here for you, Your Grace," it announced to Bakalor as its teeth from a significant underbite formed.

The heat emanating from the demon's son was so intense that Thorik felt the hair on his arms burn despite his distance.

Thorik turned from the sight and ran toward Avanda, knowing that once the creature received his orders, he would burn him alive.

"Grub, kill the Nums!" Bakalor pointed at Thorik before stepping away from the structure and back down onto the ground where he had originally erupted from.

Rolling forward, Grub set off in pursuit.

Avanda had pulled herself away from the broken crystal and was on her way up the stairs when she saw Thorik jumping down them. "The crystal!" she shouted, turning herself around to head back down.

Grub arrived at the top of the steps, and Thorik could feel the creature's heat on his back as he grabbed Avanda's hand to pull her to safety.

Avanda pulled back. "No! Climb into the broken crystal. We'll be safe there."

Thorik had no time to argue. He followed her lead toward the large, hollow crystal.

Grub rolled down the stairs with ease as he caught up to them.

The Nums leaped from the bottom step and landed on the ground long enough to make one last jump to safety inside the broken crystal column. As they flew through the air, they knew that this was their only chance of survival. Fortunately, they were on course to land inside the hollow column and succeed.

Just before the Nums landed inside the crystal, a giant stone hand sprang up from the ground. Bakalor's hand reached up and caught them both in midair before closing its rock fingers around them. Again, the Nums were back in Bakalor's palm.

Their escape had failed.

The Nums bounced around inside the demon's hand until Bakalor eventually pulled his arm out of the ground while standing on the far side of the bridge. Opening up his palm, the demon grinned at his prisoners before closing his fingers again. "Grub! Cover that hole in the crystal with some molten rock before any more souls escape. Afterward, introduce yourself to your siblings before returning to my throne."

Bakalor sank into the rocks and traveled below the cavern floor, carrying his cargo of two Nums. A few minutes later, the demon's palm reopened, dropping Thorik and Avanda onto the column near his throne once more.

"Your courage will be removed and you will learn to fear me," Bakalor announced. "This I can ensure." And with that, he pressed them both down under his enormous fingers and started stripping years of life from their youthful bodies.

9

BATTLE PLANS

Thorik and Avanda's bodies had aged over a decade from the two attacks. Muscle spasms and aches filled their bodies, while their minds were groggy and confused. This time Bakalor had made certain to hurt them enough to prevent a further escape.

Lying limp on the top of the stone column that stood before the demon's throne, the two Nums reached out to each other to let the other one know they were still alive. Their bodies had betrayed them and left them without the strength to sit up. A handful of fingers interlacing would be all the physical reassurance they could give one another as they watched Bakalor sit on his mighty throne.

"You are not to be consumed like the meal of a frenzied thrasher." Bakalor produced an evil grin. "I will savor you two, enjoying each and every moment of life you have to give me."

"I can't try again," Avanda coughed out between cries of pain.

"One more time," Thorik said through his teeth, tightening his fingers entwined with hers. But her fingers loosened. "Avanda, don't leave me. I'll get us out of here."

"Not this time." A tone of defeat was in her soft voice.

"It's not over." Thorik spoke despite the pain he felt in his lungs every time he did so. But his body was not living up to his words as his fingers slowly unraveled from hers.

Avanda could feel him slipping away. Unsure if this would be that last time she would talk to him, she attempted to move her head in order to look into his eyes. Fatigued, she was successful on her third attempt. She could now see his face as his eyes struggled to stay open. Knowing what her last words needed to be before she closed her own eyes and drifted off, she said, "I love you."

A loud crack of thunder came from above as storm clouds rolled along the ceiling of the cavern and an intense white light grew from the center of the cloud.

Lightning flashed again as thunder snapped hard enough for Thorik and Avanda to feel the powerful vibrations against their bodies.

A dark mass emerged from the center of the cloud, followed by a trail of nearly transparent figures. The long train headed down and then toward Bakalor.

As they approached, it became apparent that the long procession line was a parade of new souls, brought down to be enslaved by the demon. But it wasn't clear what was leading them down. The dark mass was more of a swirling of ash and debris, constantly changing its shape and form.

Bakalor leaned back and relaxed in his throne as the new souls were dropped into the already overcrowded cavern, turning completely invisible to the Nums as each spirit distanced themselves from the dark form which had led them there. The demon waited patiently as the dark mass floated down near his throne after dropping off its cargo.

Avanda's face went rigid, staring at the object descending toward them. She had finally recognized who the mass was.

"What is it?" Thorik felt the pain of each word in his chest.

"The Death Witch," Avanda said in a somber tone.

The swirling mass advanced until it hovered over the arm of Bakalor's enormous throne. Once stopped, the shape of the witch became obvious. Her long hair and flowing robes continued to blow from an unseen wind, and her body was a whirlpool of floating burnt debris, but Avanda could identify her, nonetheless. The Num had witnessed her once before when she, Irluk, had taken her uncle, Wess.

"Irluk." Bakalor's right rocky eyebrow raised. "You continue to keep my halls filled and my stomach full."

"These days are soon to end," Irluk replied.

"Really?" The demon leaned forward with interest. "What news have you heard about our plans?"

"The living are fragmented. Bonds between cities and species have broken down. There is no cohesion nor unification."

"Excellent." Bakalor's thin eyes looked into the distance as he plotted his next move. "When will this opportunity be taken advantage of?"

"War is mounting. Ergrauth's armies are on the move to attack the west."

Bakalor grinned at the thought. "I wish I could be on the surface to watch the end of days. So little remains before my triumphant escape from this prison."

"Our kingdom is near," she said.

"When will Lu'Tythis Tower be ready to fall?"

"It is a strong tower. Everyone you have sent is working on it."

Bakalor looked over the side of his armrest, as an area of rock flooring transformed itself into a replica of Terra Australis. Miniature mountains rose under Bakalor's powers as the grand Lake Luthralum Tunia sank down a bit.

Hanging his finger over the lake area, Bakalor allowed the thick oil from his body to pour down until the lake bed had been filled. Aside from color and clouds roaming over it, the miniature landscape was a perfect replica of Terra Australis. Triangular in shape, the replica ranged from Farbank in the northwest, to the Southwind Mines in the south, and back up all the way through the Ergrauthian Valley of the Del'Unday in the northeast.

Snapping his rock fingers, he produced sparks that flew down and ignited the pool of oil. The sickly green flame from the miniature lake caused the entire map to come alive with colors, clouds, and blue water in the other lakes. It appeared to be Australis in every way except size and the life that lived there.

Thorik and Avanda craned their necks to see the cause of the new bright light. But once they managed to, they couldn't believe their eyes. The oil they had once used from the Mountain King Temple had also been used to create Bakalor. Or was it the other way around? Perhaps the ancient Nums had retrieved the oil from Bakalor's body. Regardless, both Nums had seen this rare oil bring stone objects to life when it was lit as it gave off its ill-colored greenish illumination.

Bakalor and Irluk scanned the map. The tip of Lu'Tythis Tower gave off tiny bursts of lightning, and the demon nodded his approval. "It appears you have already fractured it. This needs to be ready when the war is underway."

Slowly nodding in agreement, she watched the lightning flair out from the crystal on the top of the tiny tower. "Understood. However, we need more forces to make sure it falls down in time."

"Agreed." He then turned his attention beyond the living map. "Grub!" he called out to his youngest son.

Silence followed until the rocks near the landscape replica began to quake and bounce, followed by the surface blasting up and out of the way to reveal the demon's son, Grub.

Cooling quickly on the surface, the glob crusted over before four arms and a mouth emerged from its headless round body. Dirt and rocks rolled off Grub, displaying his crusted skin, which exposed internal hot magma between the cracks. "Yes, Your Grace," Grub said to his father.

"Have you met your siblings yet?"

"Yes, as you instructed."

"Good. How many can we send to Lu'Tythis Tower?" Bakalor asked as he studied the moving map.

Grub had no eyes to see what his father was looking at. The vibrations in the rock led him to where he needed to go. "They have informed me that most of my siblings are already at the tower. There are four of us here in Della Estovia. We await your call, Your Grace." Heat exited his mouth each time he talked, as though the door of a furnace opened.

Bakalor glanced up at Irluk to see if four more of his servants would be enough.

Irluk was also reviewing the map, plotting her own moves. "Three for sure. Four would guarantee it."

"Grub?"

"Yes, Your Grace."

"Take the rest of your siblings to the Lu'Tythis Tower. You are my guarantee."

Grub leaned forward in a bow and held it, waiting to be dismissed.

"No excuses, Irluk, I have given you everything you requested. This had better be precisely executed."

Irluk bowed her head in respect, but quickly released it and looked the demon in the eyes. "With these additional resources, I will be ready by the time Ergrauth leads his army beyond the Guardians and reaches River's Edge. They prepare to leave as we speak."

Focusing on the living map, Bakalor caused a small red-colored ripple within the miniature Ergrauth Valley to move out of the City of Ergrauth and toward the peaks of the Guardians.

Plotting each move out again to ensure he hadn't missed anything, he questioned her about each task she was to perform. "Have you revealed the location of the Winds of Conquest?"

"Not only revealed, but the demon Ergrauth has awoken them."

"Well done. Where is Darkmere?" the demon asked.

Irluk pointed at the map. "He has left the Temple of Surod and is heading toward Corrock."

Under the demon's influence, a small dark point jutted up from the map, located near the city of Corrock. Bakalor wanted to see where each of the pieces were sitting in his game of war. "Will Darkmere have the human armies of Doven moved to north Woodlen when Ergrauth's army attacks Doven's wall?"

"He will. The southern Woodlen walls will be unprotected." Her voice was calm and confident. "He will also have Corrock ready to destroy the city of Trewek."

"Excellent, Irluk. Now, I must know, what did you do with Ambrosius after you killed him?"

Irluk did not answer.

"You did kill him, didn't you?"

"We fought at Weirfortus but I was unable to take his soul. Now he is in hiding. Something prevents me from finding him."

"How many attempts will it take for you to finally remove him?"

"He had unexpected help. I will not underestimate him again."

"Perhaps he is still more powerful than you. You obviously can't contain him," Bakalor jabbed, peering over at her body of flowing burnt particles. "He did turn you into what you are. Perhaps he has regained what he once had." Nodding in agreement to his own words, he added, "I believe he is still stronger than you."

The speed of her whirling debris immediately increased. "Perhaps once, but not anymore! I will take his soul before the end of this war!"

"You had better," Bakalor said bluntly. "Otherwise, he could destroy everything we've worked for."

Irluk pondered her plight. "I must find his weakness." She glanced over at the Nums, still lying on the rock column, dazed and half-conscious.

"You!" The Death Witch floated over to Avanda and Thorik. Her charcoal hair flailed about over the Nums' heads as her face continued to break apart and reform from the ashes that made up her skin. "I've seen you before. You're friends of Ambrosius." She moved in closer for a better look. "Avanda? Is that you?"

The Nums didn't know how to respond, so they held onto each other's hand without saying a word.

"Bakalor," Irluk said in an unusually canny way, "I would like to take these two back up to the surface."

The demon sat up and looked away from his map. "No. This Num holds responsibility for my imprisonment down here. He needs to suffer!"

Thorik was confused and failed to reply before Irluk did.

A devious smile grew upon her face and then she spoke in an ancient language the Nums couldn't understand. "I only mean to borrow them. I need worms for the end of my hook. Besides, I'll bring him back down here afterward whether they live through it or not. They deserve the suffering you plan to unleash upon them."

"The Num needs to suffer for what he did to me. I want to be the one who sucks the life from him."

"Understood. But you've waited many years for your revenge on him. I think you can wait a little longer. He's not going to leave Terra Australis, and he must die eventually. If all goes well, you will rule the land above the caves soon enough, anyway. So he will be yours no matter how you look at it."

Bakalor sighed at the witch's logic. "What is your plan?"

Irluk gathered her thoughts before replying to him in a foreign tongue. "Have Grub follow them back to the lake valley. Once these two Nums are in jeopardy, Ambrosius will come out of hiding to save them. And once he does, I'll be there to end his life."

"What would you have me do to them if no jeopardy strikes on its own?" Grub asked.

"I don't care. Kill the ones they travel with and put these two in peril. Once it's serious enough, the old E'rudite will show himself to save his friends. It's his weakness."

Grub bowed his body forward and turned to the demon. "I await your orders, Your Grace."

Bakalor contemplated his options and licked his lips at the idea of having another taste of Num. But in the end he agreed with Irluk. "Grub, send your siblings to the Lu'Tythus Tower. You, on the other hand, will follow these two Nums until Irluk's trap snares success."

"Yes, Your Grace."

Unsuccessfully, Thorik and Avanda attempted to understand what was being discussed. But even if they had had a grasp of the odd language, they were in no condition to intervene. Nodding at Avanda, Thorik assured her that everything would be fine as he held her hand tight. What else could he do but give her hope, even if he didn't have any himself?

Swirling her ash-filled body above the column, Irluk quickly surrounded the two Nums before lifting them into the air toward the cavern ceiling. Thorik and Avanda's bodies met, and the two Nums gathered enough strength to grab onto one another. Again, clouds formed in the center of the cavern's highest point, while lightning flashed and thunder boomed around them.

Wind tossed them back and forth, but they continued to hold each other as tight as possible, even locking their legs together to prevent them from being torn apart. All was pitch black aside from the blinding bright flashes of the lightning.

Rain drenched the Nums as they continued to roll and spin out of control until they had lost any perspective of time. Their sense of balance was skewed, and they had no concept of which way was up. The rain became so severe that it nearly drowned them.

It was at this point that a large set of hands grabbed them and tried to pull them apart. Their grip was nearly impossible to break as they clutched onto each other even harder. But again, the hands pulled at them, this time breaking their tight bond.

10

REUNION

"What are you two doing?" Thorik and Avanda heard from a familiar voice. "I'm telling you, they look older," a deeper voice said.

"Nonsense, they are just weathered by their journey," replied the first voice.

Both Nums opened their eyes in the cloudy evening sunlight. Thorik's uncle, Brimmelle, was standing with his arms crossed while their giant friend, Grewen, was holding the two younger Nums in his hands after plucking them out of the river.

Brimmelle spoke up again. "We've been searching endlessly for you, only to find you two playing in the water." He could now see that their faces looked older than he remembered and Avanda's soul-markings had expanded around her neck, but he quickly dismissed it as poor sleep and nourishment. "And apparently you two need a reminder of the Mountain King's words on personal health. You look terrible."

Thorik didn't care what Brimmelle had to say. They had traveled to Della Estovia, been attacked and nearly eaten by insects, and then captured by Bakalor who had the intention of keeping them in damnation for all eternity. Thorik grabbed Avanda's head, pulled it in, and kissed her hard on the lips, giving her the passionate kiss he had promised after their fall from Bakalor's throne. Pulling back just as quickly as he had pulled her forward, he shouted, "We're alive!"

Brimmelle was stunned at the unexpected kiss, while Grewen grinned at the sight. Pleasantly surprised, Avanda took it with much more meaning than was intended.

They were free from the underworld, and Thorik couldn't recall a time he was more relieved. Jumping down with excitement from Grewen's hands, his weakened legs nearly buckled under his weight before he hugged his uncle. Thorik's soaking wet clothes squished against Brimmelle's already dirty robes, turning them into a muddy mess.

Brimmelle quickly pushed free and attempted to brush the water off of him. Slightly taller than Thorik, the robust Num's thick soul-markings running down his arms and across his body were darker than normal, due to his emotions. Standing firm, he was proud of his markings, because of their wide and long patches, unlike the whimsical lacy markings on Avanda or the lack of soul-markings on Thorik. "Have you gone insane?"

"Acting a bit batty, are we?" Bryus Grum walked up to inspect them. "I like you a lot better this way." Thin and lanky with messy hair and torn clothes, Bryus was the opposite of Brimmelle when it came to personal care and hygiene.

Avanda sat calmly in Grewen's oversized hand as she watched Thorik smile and laugh like the teacher she had fallen in love with back in Farbank. Tracing her lower lip with her finger, she played back the kiss he had just given her. It was more than she had hoped it would be.

Grewen watched her reaction as she fell softly onto her back against his forearm. He could tell that she had taken the kiss seriously. His thick, leathery skin wrinkled on his bald head as he smiled at her with wide eyes. Cupping his dual-thumbed hand, he cradled her around her waist and wondered what he had missed while they were underground. "Your age, as well as your relationship, has advanced since we've seen you last."

It wasn't long before Thorik began telling the story of Bakalor, but then he stopped so he could start the story from the beginning, when they landed in the cavern of Num-eating insects.

"Wait just a minute." Brimmelle strummed his fingers a few times. "Demons? Death Witches? It's more likely you fell down that vent hole, landed in an underground river, and washed up on shore. Della Estovia may truly exist, but I don't believe you have what it takes to escape from such a legendary place."

"Uncle, I'm not making this up."

Fir Brimmelle puffed up his chest and felt his nephew's forehead as though he could make a medical diagnosis. "You're burning up. You must have a fever, causing you to hallucinate. In addition, you have a bump on your noggin where you were hit fairly hard. You're lucky you survived the fall after attacking me the way you did."

"Attacking you?" Thorik couldn't believe what he was hearing. "We were trying to save Gluic. Is she harmed?"

Brimmelle was appalled by the question. "Of course she is, Thorik. She's dead!"

"No, I mean the dagger, Varacon. Is the dagger intact? Has it been damaged?"

The name of the enchanted weapon caused Bryus to perk up. "Varacon damaged? Fortunately, no." Pulling it out from a pouch, he carefully removed the cloths he had wrapped it in. "You see, Num, Varacon can't be spoiled so easily. The most experienced tradespeople created this masterpiece from the finest metals. I would assume its birth was in the sacred city of Derivate."

Bryus was a skinny human who wore rags for clothes and an old leather belt with a talon from a claw on one end. On his feet he had thin leather sandals, which exposed his crusty dry heels and cracked wrinkly skin between his toes. He had a personality that flopped back and forth between a jester and a bitter old hermit, neither of which was enjoyable to be with, nor was there any warning of the shifting of attitude. It was a far cry from what Thorik expected from an Alchemist. His two different colored eyes didn't help, nor did the awkward-looking woven pack Avanda had made for him before she had fallen into Della Estovia.

Bryus walked on his bony legs like a drunken bird, and he constantly bumped into the others as they traveled. Thorik assumed the attack by Darkmere's forces had scrambled his brain so much that he was fortunate just to be alive. And lucky for Thorik he was, for he needed Bryus to locate the book of Vesik, which held the spell required to save his grandmother.

Thorik approached the Alchemist and reached for Varacon, but Bryus pulled it away as he spoke about the dagger's assumed birthplace with great enthusiasm. "It is the original home of the Notarians, you know. Pwellus Dementa was the first city created. The original plans for our world were made there."

Nodding, Thorik thanked him for the information and reached for Varacon a second time.

Pulling the dagger away again, Bryus continued to tell his story after a twitch in his cheek. "Plans were developed to make this land into a heaven like no other. I believe the Great Oracle, Ovlan, ruled over the Notarians at that point. She created the Myth'Unday, you know. They are dangerous little critters. Stay clear!" Bryus' arms were straight out at his sides as he warned Thorik of such dangers.

Unclear how his question of the dagger turned into a warning about Myth'Unday, Thorik interrupted as he reached out toward the item held by the Alchemist. "The dagger, Varacon, may I see it?"

"Of course you can see it," he shot back with surprise. "We can all see it. It's no figment of our imagination. It is a genuine artifact. It is a piece of art, most likely crafted by Horib himself. Oh, but Horib was a wicked one, wasn't he? The way he always placed more into his art than what was requested. Never did they suspect what was really lurking in his masterpieces."

"Bryus!" Thorik shouted. He was getting tired of the tangents that Bryus continued to go on. "Please hand me the dagger."

"Well, of course, dear boy." Smirking, he hesitated before giving it up. "Why didn't you just ask?" Spinning the dagger around in the cloth, which still lay in his hand, he handed Varacon to Thorik hilt first.

"Gluic?" Thorik asked softly as he pulled the dagger from the man and lifted it near his own face. "Are you still in there? I hope so. We've survived Della Estovia and have come back for you. I'm going to prevent you from having to see that place."

Brimmelle crossed his arms as he glared at Thorik. "You've gone absolutely insane, Thorik. Are you even listening to yourself anymore? You're saying that your grandmother is trapped inside an old dagger and you fought off a demon and the witch of death to climb out of the underworld where only the dead can go."

"That's only partially true." Thorik held the dagger near his chest, trying to feel any energy inside. "We didn't fight our way to freedom. They let us go. I don't know why."

"Well, that sounds more reasonable." Brimmelle's words were thick with sarcasm. "You stumbled upon a mythical place forbidden by all living beings, and the ruler of the dead just returns you to the surface because you are the almighty Thorik Dain."

Thorik thought about his uncle's comments as he looked the dagger over for any scratches. Realizing there weren't any, he began wrapping it up to place it in his own pack. "You know, I think you're right."

Brimmelle was stunned by the answer. "What?"

"I don't know how, but Bakalor knew me. In fact, he hated me and blamed me for his rule over the underworld. To add to my confusion, I don't understand why he would free me if he loathed me so?"

Brimmelle muttered to himself in disbelief. "The boy's fall must have caused more damage to his head than what is visible."

Thorik continued to talk over his uncle's words. "And then we learned that there's a war coming. It hasn't started yet, but it will."

Brimmelle sighed as he sat down. "Wonderful, Thorik can now see into the future."

"And the only one that can stop it is Ambrosius."

"Well then, why didn't you bring him back up with you? His soul should have been wandering around down there someplace."

"Because he's not dead," Thorik said.

"Of course not. Even though you watched him die."

"Apparently, he still had enough strength to fight off the Death Witch."

Brimmelle dropped his face down into both of his hands as he chuckled at the insanity of it all.

Thorik looked past his uncle and spotted his weapon, the Spear of Rummon, tied to Bryus' pack. He hurried over to it. "Thank you for finding Rummon."

"Wait one minute, Num." Bryus turned in a circle to keep his back away from the Num. "This is no toy. This is the Spear of Rummon."

"Yes, I know." Thorik continued to chase the spear on the man's back, frequently reaching for it without any luck.

"Do you understand that the life force of the most powerful dragon that ever lived is trapped inside of it?" Bryus kept spinning to keep it out of Thorik's reach, causing himself to get dizzy. "He is a demon! Fear him, for he will try to communicate with you and conquer your willpower." His words were getting loud and theatrical, with large gestures of his arms. "He is our enemy, Thorik. He's the murderer of your sacred Mountain King. Do you have the internal strength to handle Rummon's words, should he choose to speak them to you?"

"Yes, we've communicated more than once." Thorik's voice was flat and serious.

Bryus stopped spinning around and became slightly disappointed as well as very dizzy. "You have? Could I have a word with him? I've been trying to communicate with Rummon for days without any luck."

"Perhaps later." Thorik removed the spear from Bryus' back and placed it into the loops of his own pack before looking around at his surroundings. "Where are we?"

They were no longer in the Go'ta Gorge. Instead, they stood near a large river, upstream from an ancient marble bridge spanning it.

"I think I'm going to be ill." Bryus sat down from all his spinning as he fought off the self-induced nausea.

"Volney River." Grewen was still amazed by Thorik's stories. "The Lagona Falls drops off just past the bridge. Where did you think you were?"

"I would have assumed we were still in the gorge." Thorik quickly pulled the facts together. "You gave up on us in the gorge. You left us for dead?"

Brimmelle instantly shot Grewen a look of irritation. "If it was up to me, we wouldn't have left!"

In his usual calm baritone voice, Grewen corrected the husky Num. "If it was up to you, we would have starved to death up on that mountainside staring down into a vent shaft, which we couldn't fit through."

"Bryus was thin enough to fit through it," Brimmelle protested.

Bryus' cheek twitched. "I told you, as plain as the ugly is on your face, that I'm not willing to pass the barrier into Della Estovia to save a few Nums. It's a death sentence. Once I saw the markings, I stopped, and if you were intelligent enough to understand their meanings, you would have as well."

"But this wasn't a request to find treasure," Brimmelle protested. "And these weren't just a few Nums. These were members of my village."

"Listen, you self-righteous little toad, I might have considered going down there for the right historical artifact, but I had only met your companions a few days prior to the incident. The incident where you put their lives in danger and then turned around and expected me to risk my life to save them. I think not!"

"They've been at each other ever since Brimmelle regained consciousness after being knocked out from your tumble," Grewen told Thorik and Avanda as Brimmelle and Bryus continued to spar back and forth. "I tried to lower your uncle down several times, but was unsuccessful. He became stuck on several attempts, and at one point, he was jammed in a spot for several hours. We weren't sure if we were going to get him back out."

Thorik turned his back on the quibbling travelers as Brimmelle puffed up his chest and stood his moral high ground while Bryus cut him off at his knees with logic and sarcastic remarks. "Grewen," Thorik said, "we tried to climb back up, but it was too slick and steep. I was nearly killed by insects. We were starving and freezing to death, and yet we waited for you. You never arrived. We couldn't wait any longer."

Grewen nodded with a slight smile. "You did the right thing, little man. There are times you must look after yourself, for as hard as I tried, we couldn't reach you. Eventually, I agreed with Bryus to seek out others that could help us. We thought it would be best to head to Trewek, where there are Ov'Unday who can search underground much more effectively than we can."

Thorik didn't know how he felt about being abandoned when he had been so sure that they would come after him.

"We never gave up on you, Thorik," Grewen handed the Num his wooden coffer and other items that had been flung from his pack before he fell down the vent hole. "We only changed our plans once we realized we could do no more. To his credit, your uncle never wished to leave. However, following his lead most likely would have killed us as well."

Thorik nodded as he looked over the items while returning them to specific locations in his backpack. "Thank you for your efforts. Fortunately, Avanda and I had each other to get us through." Thorik turned and winked at Avanda. "It was an experience I wish never to repeat, but we pulled together, and now we're free of that place."

Avanda realized how right he was and smiled at his last statement. "We're better Nums for it."

Tossing the backpack on, Thorik tightened his pack's straps and stood up straight with confidence. Not overconfidence, but after seeing certain death, life was such a welcome adventure. He looked ahead at the open road before them with an enthusiasm he hadn't felt since they left Kingsfoot.

"So," Grewen said, "where are we off to?"

Bryus stopped his bickering with Brimmelle in mid-sentence once he heard the question. "Govi Glade, of course, to find the spell book Vesik. The spell within is your only hope to free Gluic from Varacon."

Thorik looked over the bridge and toward the northwest. "We must save Granna, but we must also notify others of Bakalor's pending war along the way. They will be destroyed if they are not alerted and prepared."

"And who is going to believe a Num such as yourself?" Brimmelle puffed up his chest as his soul-markings turned nearly black. "Who do you think you are? The Mountain King?"

"I think that's what I've finally come to realize," Thorik said over his shoulder. "I don't need to be the Mountain King to get things done. I just need to believe in myself and take action. Others will listen to my words and see my confidence in what I say."

Grewen grinned. "Well said, little man, but just because they will listen does not mean they will act."

"Grewen, if I've learned anything from you, I've learned that I can only control my own actions and reactions, not those of others. I must do what it takes and hope that others will do the same."

Brimmelle's markings faded back to their normal hue as he shook his head in disgust. "I know the end of the world is near when Thorik becomes responsible for saving it."

II

CAMPSITE

———

Thorik's Log: 4th day of the 7th month of the 650th year.

Avanda and I have returned from the fiery depths of Della Estovia, yet we do not know for what purpose. Bakalor had us at his command and was showing no mercy as he stole over a decade of our lives. Regardless of why he released us, we are just thankful to be out of there and back on our way. Before we head to the Govi Glade to find the spell book to free Granna, we'll head north to Trewek to alert them of the pending war. But for tonight, Avanda and I plan to eat, drink, and rest. Three simple pleasures that we have desired for so many days. May tomorrow bring us opportunities, and may we never forget how fortunate we have been, even if those opportunities are not to our liking.

———

After sunrise, the group collected fresh water for their trek across the desert. The water was warm but drinkable. It was a mixture of Shi'Pel glacier runoff, the rains along the Spirit Tower Range, and hundreds of small desert valleys along the eastern Volney River Valley. It was old water that had slowly traveled through thousands of miles of rough, dry lands, and it tasted of every mile.

In order to head northwest, they first had to cross over an ancient stone bridge which spanned the mighty Volney River. It had held up well for thousands of years, with only minor damage and erosion. Once the water traveled under the bridge, it fell thousands of feet into the Ki'Volney Lake valley. The mist from this mighty Lagona Falls transformed the lower desert into a forest of life, breathing oxygen back into the water before it traveled west to Lake Luthralum.

While crossing the bridge, Thorik and Avanda stopped for a few moments and looked over the falls and across the open land below. The scene was majestic and filled with the colors of life as various rivers ran into clear blue lakes. Beyond the initial forest, tan sand dunes spread across the lower desert like waves on an ocean. Desert lakes were trimmed with green vegetation, as were the mighty mountains, often rising to white peaks.

Taking in a deep breath, Avanda clung to Thorik's hand and absorbed the vastness of the entire landscape. "I never realized how beautiful our land was until we almost lost the chance to see it forever."

Thorik squeezed her hand. "I couldn't have done it without you, Avanda. You saved my life."

"And you mine." She then let go of his hand. "Don't move," she requested as she searched through her pockets. The rest of the travelers had already crossed and were continuing on their way.

Thorik gazed out onto the miraculous scene while waiting for her. It felt wonderful to be alive.

"Here." Avanda handed him a light blue crystal shard.

Thorik looked at it for a moment before realizing where it had come from. "This is from Della Estovia. Is this one of shards from the crystal that Bakalor shattered?"

"Yes. When the crystal was hit, it showered me with debris of small pieces. I want you to hold on to it and think of how we feel right here, at this moment, as we look over the valley and realize how bad it could have been, and how we worked together to make it through alive."

"Thank you, but this is too important of a memory for you to give to me."

"I'm not."

"You're not?" He was obviously confused.

"No. This is ours to share. When times are difficult for one of us and we need strength and support, all we will need to do is hand this to the other." She closed her palm over his, covering the shard before cupping her other hand below his. "No words will be needed; we'll know what it means. Even if we become angry with each other, this will be the symbol of how we felt about one another while standing here on this bridge. It will be the symbol of our true feelings."

"Thank you," Thorik said softly. "But—"

"I know. You need to stay focused on saving Gluic." She nodded. "You'll know when it is time to give me the crystal back, and I will be there for you when you do."

A silent nod followed as the two scanned the horizon for a few more minutes before leaving the bridge and catching up to the others.

~

THE TRAVELERS FOLLOWED THE LONG, sharp edge of the plateau north for the entire day. Looking down over the western valley, the plateau and the valley below slowly merged into the same elevation far to their north, near the southern base of the Ossuary Mountain Range. They still had a long trek ahead of them before this joining of terrain, but night was settling in, and traveling in the dark could lead them right over the cliff. It was time to stop and rest after a long day's walk.

Words from the Mountain King's scrolls quickly filled the air as Brimmelle recited them as he did every night while Grewen cleared the area for camp.

Thorik prepared camp bedding for the night with the help of Avanda at his side. Although he was still in slight denial, a special bond had been created between the two during their time together. They had saved each other's lives, they had warmed each other in the freezing caverns, they had suffered violent pain, and they had nearly died together. It was only natural that deep emotions would come from it. But he questioned if there was enough depth of emotion to last outside of Della Estovia, in the real world.

Grewen moved several large rocks into place for fire containment, as well as some for sitting upon, while Bryus established a secondary campfire for himself.

Helping the Alchemist set up his campsite, Avanda noticed his belt. "What kind of animal talon is that which holds your belt tight?"

Bryus looked down at his leather belt and the clasp made from a claw. "It's just from a Fesh'Unday's claw. A pet of mine." He talked in a low tone and turned his head, making it obvious that he didn't want to discuss it. "I can finish up my camp; you should help with your own."

He wasn't in a talkative mood, so she shrugged her shoulders and left just as Thorik approached Bryus. The two Nums winked at each other as they passed ways.

"Why don't you sleep near our campfire?" Thorik asked Bryus.

"I prefer my own space. Gives me time by myself to think," he replied.

"Time to think? You spend all day by yourself, never adding to any of our discussions. How will you ever get to know us if you don't join our conversations?"

Bryus' eye and cheek twitched at the comment. "Who said I wanted to get to know you?"

"Well, no one. But since we're traveling together, it would be nice to know a little about you."

"Is that necessary?" he replied with a grimace.

"Yes. The only conversations you've had with us are about enchanted relics and ancient symbols. It seems to me that you care more about things than you do people. Surely that's not true."

"It might very well be. I don't know you. And to be truthful, you don't really know each other as well as you may think. Given the right circumstances, most people are willing to abandon or double-cross each other."

"I don't believe that to be true, especially with us. We are what the Ov'Unday call a family pod. We aren't related, and we may bicker from time to time, but we are a family of sorts, nonetheless. We are there for each other and always will be. Do you have any family?"

"Family?" The word seemed to have struck an emotional cord.

"Yes, family or close friends." Thorik's hesitation was caused to the man's reaction.

"Do you not understand who I was? I was the Prominent of EverSpring, until that..." He paused as he placed a hand over his eye to keep it from twitching. Emotionally and powerfully, he let loose on Thorik with his background. "...I ruled EverSpring until my friends' fear of Darkmere was greater than our own relationships. Those that I trusted conspired against me and helped the Dark Lord overthrow my power. They turned me into an enemy of my own province, enslaved my family, and imprisoned me in an effort to force me to help him sacrifice Ambrosius' son."

Dropping his head for a moment, Bryus regained control of his facial tic. "Friendship is based on convenience and the need for something from someone else. Once that need is gone, so is the relationship!"

"Surely they didn't all just turn their back on you," Thorik said to Bryus before turning to Grewen for conformation. "People wouldn't give up on their close friends so easily, would they?"

Grewen tilted his big, bald, leathery head. "It is an unfortunate truth for many. Trust takes years to embed in the hearts of others, but only moments of doubt to rip out, regardless of any proof being provided."

Bryus nodded in agreement with the mognin while looking at Thorik. "And people like you have the nerve to question why I care more about enchanted items than people. It's because I know where I stand with these objects. They don't discriminate or judge or change based on threats of greed or cowardice."

Thorik was not expecting the lecture and wasn't sure how to respond.

"Tell me, Num. Do you feel better knowing that I have lost everything and don't even know where to look for the ones I love? My family is locked away, not knowing of my fate or their own. I don't know of my wife's health or my daughter's pain. Have they been tortured? Have they been violated? These are the thoughts that fester in my mind when you say the word family. So, are you pleased with yourself for bringing up such a painful issue?"

"No, of course not."

"Then why the hell do you want me to set all that aside and become one of your happy family pod members so we can save your grandmother? Again, the hand of friendship is reached out to me, as long as I help you get what you need. Tell me that I'm wrong!" he said skeptically.

"Well—"

"Well, what's my other option?" Bryus flung his arms in the air as he spoke in a loud, demanding voice. "I can't return home to my province without being captured again, and I don't know where my family is being held, so I might as well help you until I figure out what I'm going to do next."

Thorik nodded, as though he was accepting Bryus' request to stay with them.

"But I'll tell you this, Num. You need me more than I need you. Therefore, if I want a second camp set up so I can keep to myself, then I expect to have one."

Agreeing with him, Thorik stood there silently as he watched Bryus return to his private campsite.

Grewen leaned forward and grabbed Thorik's head from the back in order to stop his nodding in agreement. "Is it me, or do you get the slight impression Bryus wants to be left alone?" The mognin let out a slight chuckle.

~

DARKNESS ARRIVED, leaving the rising moon as the only light source.

Brimmelle had continued to recite the Mountain King's Runestone scrolls from his memory. Thrashers had destroyed his actual scrolls when they had first left Farbank, but his exceptional memory and a lifetime of teaching them enabled him to recall each scroll to the very letter.

In the soft light, Thorik stood silently and watched his companions. He noticed that Brimmelle's telling of the sacred scrolls had changed since they left Farbank from his once dull and dry monotone readings. His presentation skills had improved as he now added examples and short stories to teach the laws, according to the Mountain King. He was slowly becoming interesting to listen to and much easier to understand.

The night was relatively calm aside from Brimmelle's readings and Bryus whistling to catch beetles.

Grewen sighed in relief as he plucked stones from the bottom of his enormous feet. The thick hide on his soles took a lot of abuse, seeing that he didn't wear any sandals or other protection. Then again, most mognins didn't.

Flicking stones out of his skin, the mognin made a game of it and shot them out in the desert to hit various objects. He missed more often than he hit, but he had nothing else to do other than feeding his face with whatever shrubs he could find.

Thorik chuckled at the sight of his giant friend. He never seemed to have a care in the world. Nothing ever got under his skin, figuratively or literally. There was only one other person in his life that lived so carefree.

"Granna," Thorik said softly to the dagger Varacon, which was completely wrapped up for protection and tied solidly to his belt, "I'm going to bring you back, no matter what it takes." Placing his hand firmly on the dagger's hilt, he thought about her. Thorik missed her deeply as he recalled the many times when she got him out of trouble or into trouble, as so often happened with her. He closed his eyes and smiled at the memories.

A second hand was placed on top of his, which still held the dagger's hilt. This one was soft and slightly smaller. It belonged to Avanda. "Can you tell if she is well?" she softly asked Thorik.

He shook his head as he opened his eyes. "No, I can't tell anything."

She slid her fingers in between his so she could touch the cloth covering the dagger. "I'm sure she is fine."

The palms of his hands began to sweat, and his ability to form basic sentences seemed to be impaired by her soft touch. "What makes you... um... say that?" His voice was soft, as it cracked with nervousness.

"Do you know anyone more likely to be trapped in a dagger and still survive?" A shy smile grew upon her face.

"No," was all he could muster.

"Close your eyes." She moved in closer to him. "Breathe softly and call to her in your mind." Watching him for a few minutes, she finally asked, "Did you hear anything?"

"Yes."

"Really? What?" she asked quickly in a soft voice.

"Fir Brimmelle's words from the scrolls, Grewen chewing on local weeds, and your breathing in my ear."

Avanda laughed sweetly at his response. "Come on, it's time to cook some dinner."

Brimmelle opened his eyes and looked up from his absent congregation. "Haven't you started working on lighting a campfire yet? What have you two been doing?"

Thorik shrugged his shoulders like a child would when asked about missing treats that resembled crumbs on their face. Avanda's soft touch and voice had affected him more than he had expected.

Avanda squeezed his hand, stopping him from answering before she did. "We were so taken with your readings, Fir Brimmelle, that we failed in our duties."

"Duties need to be maintained." In spite of his words, Brimmelle easily accepted the excuse and returned to his hour-long sermon.

Avanda winked at Thorik, giving him permission to exhale and move. Even he had to chuckle with her. She knew how to make him feel good and smile.

"Sorry I kept you from your responsibilities," she said.

"It's all right. It doesn't really matter." Not willing to receive a second warning from Brimmelle, they both laughed it off as she left to collect more brush for the fire.

Bryus Grum interrupted their soft laughter as he walked into the main camp to collect a handful of leaves and twigs for his own fire. He was still struggling with the twitch he had acquired during Darkmere's attack on him in the Surod Temple. "It's good to see that you finally understand."

Slightly confused, Thorik started pulling out his cookware. "Understand what?"

"That it doesn't matter," Bryus replied.

"What doesn't matter?"

Bryus chuckled as he looked at the young Num. "Anything."

"Nothing matters?" Thorik asked Bryus to clarify as he attempted to light the fire.

"Exactly."

"Why do you say that?" Thorik started his duties while they talked, before Brimmelle looked over at him.

"For it will all end in disaster, anyway. So why even try?"

Thorik didn't like the sound of that. "You mean Bakalor's War? We may still be able to stop it from happening."

Bryus laughed. "It's already written. There are no other options. We are at the end of this cycle. The fourth age of Australis will come to its climatic finale in this war."

Opening his backpack to remove his cooking spoon, his face crunched up from the Alchemist's comment. "We are? By whose words? The Mountain King never wrote about such things."

"Wyrlyn. The greatest E'rudite of all time. His ancient prophecy speaks of these last days, when the dead rise from Della Estovia and return to the land of the living."

"Sounds dreadful. How would he know of these events to come?" Thorik took a moment to think about the name. "Who is this Wyrlyn? I've never heard of him."

Bryus looked shocked at the news. "How is it possible that you don't know of him? He has influenced everything in everyone's life. Aside from the Oracles themselves, he was the supreme architect of our world."

Removing the wrapped dagger from his belt, Thorik placed it snugly in his backpack before attempting to light the campfire. "I'm a little surprised at your respect for him. It was my understanding that Alchemists and E'rudites have been at odds for thousands of years. However, you have nothing but praise for an E'rudite that has informed you of our doom."

Avanda returned with a handful of dead shrubs for the fire. But before she could toss them near the future campfire location, Bryus grabbed specific plants from the bundle within her arms.

"Clovik Ty," Bryus told her as he held up the first plant. "Dungelier." He held up the second plant as his face twitched.

Avanda stared at him, confused as to what he was doing.

Bryus turned back to Thorik as he began ripping the branches into long, thin strips. "I used to be a single-minded spellcaster."

It was an opportunity for Thorik to understand him better, so he kept pressing the conversation forward. "What caused you to be single-minded?"

"Higher magical academics," he spit back. "They gave me the basics, but along with those lessons they planted seeds of their own vision of how the world should work. Their own version of what truth really is."

Thorik continued to struggle to light the campfire. Prior to their arrival, the mountain rains had bled over into the desert valley and drenched the land, so nothing was dry. "Isn't that why you went? To understand how magic works?"

Bryus laughed as he ripped more strands off of Avanda's plants. "That's not what I'm referring to. It's the philosophies of those who are right and wrong in our world that were inserted during our normal lectures."

Thorik was confused again.

Bryus handed the strips of Clovik Ty branches to Avanda. "Tie them end to end." He then ignored her as though she wasn't even there.

Avanda didn't appreciate being ordered around, but, with a wink from Thorik, she began tying the ends together. The branch strips were coarse and rough to her touch, but she learned how to handle them without cutting up her hands.

Again, Thorik tried to create a spark for the fire, but failed. "Why is identifying wrong and right actions bad?"

"What?" Bryus asked while tearing strips from the Dungelier plant.

"Your academic seeds of right and wrong," Thorik repeated.

"Who's to say what's right?" Bryus looked confused as a series of twitches erupted on his face.

"I thought you said you had single-minded thought when it came to spells."

"Oh, not anymore. Not since I accepted the words of Wyrlyn. Once that happened, the headmasters of Alchemy tossed me out on my ear. Lucky for me, they didn't strike me down where I stood. Brave are those who search for new truths, but fools they are called by the educated leaders, for the brave put in question what the leaders have taught. Therefore, they put into question those who have taught it."

Thorik thought it was comical how candid Bryus was about the fact that they could have killed him. His contained laughter worked against him as he crouched on his knees while attempting to ignite the wild grass. "How did you get involved in the teachings of Wyrlyn?"

"Ambrosius Dovenar told me about them," Bryus said to Thorik before addressing Avanda. "Now, tie these Dungeliers from end to end like you did on the Clovik Ty and then weave the two plants together."

Avanda had just finished the first set and wasn't looking for more work to do. Nevertheless, she grudgingly took them from him and began her next task, although she didn't know what he was trying to accomplish.

Bryus turned back to Thorik. "Once I accepted the science of Wyrlyn, everything seemed to fall into place."

"Let me get this straight, you gave up on being an Alchemist, and now you are an E'rudite?"

Abruptly, Bryus sat straight up stared at Thorik for several uncomfortable seconds as one long twitch shook the side of his face. "An Alchemist does not just give up spell casting. It is my faith. It is what I believe in." His voice was loud, and his words were sharply pronounced. "Can I not just add the teachings of the E'rudites to what I already know to be true? Why must it be one or the other and never a combination of the two?"

Thorik suddenly felt like he was under attack from something larger and more menacing than the frail man who sat next to him. The man's change in demeanor was always so sudden that Thorik could never prepare for any extensive discussions.

Bryus roared with anger over Thorik's original question. "I am proud to be an Alchemist! How dare you assume otherwise? I studied my entire life to achieve and master the most complex spells of our time." Pointing at Thorik, he continued in a thunderous voice, "Do you have faith in your Mountain King? Have all new ideas ripped away at the fabric of your beliefs, or are you capable of adding to them?"

"I don't know. I've been questioning my faith for quite some time now. The stories we've heard from other cultures tend to be in conflict with the writings of the Mountain King. Instead of being so quick to dismiss my own culture, perhaps I too need to be proud of what we have, while accepting what others have as well."

Thorik looked at Bryus for some level of approval.

A twitch on his cheek and a few blinks later, Bryus replied very casually, "Doesn't matter much to me. It's your life."

Bryus then looked directly at Avanda and smiled from ear to ear. "Excellent work." She had weaved the two long strips of plants into one thick one. Placing the ends in each of her hands, he had her allow the strips to sag into an upside-down arch. "Now spin them around like a barrel rolling down a hill."

Avanda did as she was told. She was concerned about Bryus raising his voice like he had to Thorik. Once she had the strips spinning so fast they were difficult to see, he told her to pull her arms apart, thus tightening the spin in front of her. The smaller radius of the spin caused the strips to speed up even more.

"Now loosen," Bryus instructed her. And as she did, the spinning strips slowed and became wider. "Now tighten again. Back and forth while saying the word 'Jungere' as you do it."

She did as she was instructed, pulling the spinning strips in tight and then back out again several times as she said the word he had given her. Her hands were now getting hot from the friction.

"Faster," Bryus ordered. "Yell it out!"

"Jungere!" She screamed as the heat increased and her arms tired. "Jungere!"

The strips ignited into flames as they spun around in front of her. "Jungere!" she screamed even louder.

Bryus laughed as he watched her. "The spell is over. You don't have to do it anymore."

Feeling foolish, she stopped the spinning and tossed the flaming strips onto the pile of campfire kindling, where they instantly ignited the rest of the shrubs that she had already stacked.

Bryus clapped his hands before rubbing them together. "So, what's for supper?" His demeanor was oddly light and friendly, as though he had been invited over for tea.

BRYUS' STORY

A distant red ember of light flickered in the wind a few miles from the Nums' camp. Bakalor's son, Grub, patiently waited for Ambrosius to appear. Half buried in order to feel every vibration made at Thorik's distant campsite, the lesser demon could track the footfalls of each individual in the camp. None, however, were created by the visitor he waited for.

~

WELL-PREPARED ROOTS HAD BEEN EATEN, and the travelers had got settled in for the night. Thick clouds rolled in over the desert, preventing them from seeing stars or even the location of the moon. Yellowish flames from the crackling campfires were the only light source, as shadows of the group flickered against the dry prairie.

Small gusts of cool air frequently blew down from the heavy clouds, fanning the campfire flames and kicking up dirt. The smell of fresh rain was present but not yet seen or felt.

Grewen regularly stoked the fire, Thorik cleaned up the camp, and Brimmelle complained about his lack of comfort. It was their routine, which took place every night at camp. In a way, it gave them comfort and a sense of security to have a predictable pattern, especially seeing that nothing else in their lives right now was stable or reliable.

After making notes about their journey and placing the papers in his coffer, Thorik closed the wooden box and walked over to Bryus and Avanda at a smaller second campfire. "Why don't you join us for a little while?"

Glancing past the Num at Grewen and Brimmelle, the Alchemist dismissed the idea. "Not in the mood for socializing," he said before noticing Thorik's coffer. "Nice prattle box. I gave a set of those to the king when the twins were born."

Thorik looked down at his coffer, which he had always thought to be unique, only now to find out that others had the same thing. "Thanks."

Bryus quickly returned to showing Avanda the insides of a large beetle he had cracked open. "This is his poison sac. It is especially useful for many charm spells on Del'Unday."

Avanda was very attentive to what he was teaching. She had been so limited in the past with only what she had taught herself using the magical items from within a found purse. It was extremely liberating to know she wouldn't be restricted to those enchanted objects any longer.

Thorik stood silently and watched the lesson. He was unsure which bothered him more; the concern that she was more interested in learning from the Alchemist instead of himself, the distrust that was building due to Bryus' lack of interest in becoming part of their group, or the fear of Avanda learning more magic. His former Runestone student had caused more problems than assistance when casting her limited spells. There was also the fact that Thorik had become enamored with her, whether he wished to admit it or not. And these feelings were affecting his judgment.

"Avanda, I'm not sure you should use magic." Occasionally, Thorik would speak in a fatherly tone, and this was one of them.

Tilting her head, her shoulders sank at the thought. "What? Why not?"

"It's dangerous," he replied, holding back his desire to give in to her needs. He battled his emotions to display himself as the leader he wished to become, instead of giving in to the kindness he wished to show to make her happy. Nevertheless, he knew this was the right thing for everyone.

"I've saved us several times with my spells." A sour look appeared on her face.

"You've also nearly cost us our lives twice as many times," he said sternly.

"But now, with Bryus teaching me, I'll be better." Her tone was solid, and her words were evenly paced. She was standing her ground.

Thorik knew her words to be true, and it concerned him that she would have such magical powers. "I'm sure you will, but I just don't think it's right for you to wield these types of forces."

"Why? Because I'm a girl? Because I'm younger than you?"

Danger signals flashed in Thorik's mind as he quickly determined how he was going to prevent himself from looking like the villain in this conversation. "That's not what I said. I mean you, as well as myself and all other Nums. We aren't supposed to be using mystical powers and casting spells. It's just not our way. I don't think we can control the elements of nature safely."

"Oh, I see." She abruptly stood up and brushed herself off. "We Polenums shouldn't be dabbling in things outside the norm… like using a Runestone to see the souls of the dead."

It was now Thorik's shoulders that softened and rolled forward. "That's different—"

Quick to interrupt, Avanda continued. "And we would never harbor weapons that have unnatural strengths and powers, such as the Spear of Rummon."

"I needed it to save our lives—"

Avanda walked toward him, forcing him around the small campfire. "Nor would any of our kind travel with Del'Unday or Ov'Unday, for that would be wrong as well."

Stumbling past Bryus, Thorik continued to walk backward as he kept a healthy arm's length from her. "You can't suggest that it was my idea that we—"

Smiling, she was confident she had the upper hand as she continued to stop him in mid-sentence. "And how safe would you say it is for us to be traveling to the underworld and back while in search of a magical book to give us the spell to free your grandmother from an enchanted dagger?" Stopping at the end of her long and pointed question, she stood rigid with her hands tightly on her hips.

Thorik tripped and fell to the ground as he continued to stare at her. "I'm just telling you what Ambrosius told me. He warned us that magic was dangerous and we should stay clear of it."

Crossing her arms, she stood at his feet, eyeing him down.

His words caught Bryus' attention. "Ambrosius?"

Thorik raised himself from his back up onto to his elbows as he caught wind of a way out of Avanda's verbal trap. "Yes, Ambrosius," he said to Bryus. "You knew him. His words carry significant weight, wouldn't you say?"

Bryus' cheek twitched at the name of the old E'rudite. "Powerful man. He has a lot of questionable ties. But when it came down to it, he could find the most elusive artifacts."

"Artifacts?"

"Ah, yes. The treasure of Joral, the pearl of Wespee, Hesek's belt, and many more were reclaimed by him. He was quite the scavenger when it came to rare antiquities."

Thorik squinted his face, perplexed by the comments. "He isn't like that. He had a larger look at the world. He had no time for trinkets, enchanted objects, or treasures from the past."

Bryus' grin made Thorik feel very uncomfortable. Nearly evil in appearance, the man's face seemed to morph before the Num's eyes as the light from the flames added to the effect. "Ambrosius is one of those treasures from the past."

Feeling uncomfortable, Thorik scooted away and stood up next to Avanda. Suddenly, she seemed safer to him.

"Don't you know who he is? Don't you know the story?" Bryus' voice was rougher and slower than normal, adding an extra element of strangeness to him.

"Of course, I do. He's Ambrosius Dovenar. The rightful king of the Dovenar Kingdom."

"He gave up that right!" Bryus corrected loudly, followed by a severe twitch to his cheek.

"Yes. I know. But only because he felt that he and his brother, Darkmere, were tearing it apart."

Placing his hand over his cheek and eye, Bryus pressed firmly to stop his facial tic. "They have been, ever since they were children."

"Yes, and Ambrosius didn't feel E'rudites should rule a kingdom. Hence, he created the Grand Council to rule the land in his stead. This council was—"

"Don't tell me about the council, Num," Bryus broke in. "I was once on the council. I know what really happened there, not you!"

"I wasn't implying that I did. You had asked me if I knew who Ambrosius was."

Bryus grunted. "What a weak attempt to describe a man who helped design this land and all the history that followed."

"I admit, he was… is," the Num corrected himself, "a great man to whom we owe many a gratitude, but he himself told me of his birth into the kingdom's royal line. He's far younger than you make him out to be."

Bryus jumped from his seat, grabbed a rock, and charged toward Thorik.

Thorik pushed Avanda back out of the way before crossing his arms in front of his face in an effort to block the rock from hitting him. But instead of being hit with the object, Bryus pulled Thorik's arm forward and slapped the rock hard into his palm.

"What is this?" Bryus pointed to the rock he had just given Thorik.

Bewildered at the emotional instability of the man, he cowered slightly as he looked at what lay in his hand. "It's a rock."

"And where do rocks come from?"

"The ground?"

"No, you fool. Larger rocks. That rock used to be part of a larger rock before time had its way with it. Perhaps it sat up high on one of these mountains before it broke off and rolled or washed down into the valley. Do you understand?"

Thorik nodded. "Yes."

Bryus smiled, for his point had been understood.

"But what does this have to do with Ambrosius?"

Bryus' eyes popped wide open with disbelief. "I just explained it to you."

"Well, maybe you need to do it without using a rock."

Bryus snatched the rock out of the Num's hand and held it uncomfortably near Thorik's face. "This is Ambrosius." He then pointed up toward the peaks of the mountains. "That is Wyrlyn."

"Are you saying that Ambrosius is a descendent of Wyrlyn?"

"You're getting closer."

"Surely you're not saying that he once was Wyrlyn?"

"Oh, you're a quick one, aren't you? Figure that out all on your own?"

Thorik ignored the condescending tone from Bryus. "How can one person who lived several thousand years ago become a man who was born a half a century ago?"

Bryus was stunned. "You honestly have never heard this tale?"

"Honestly!"

A grin of questionable intent gleamed across his face. He seemed mad with excitement over the opportunity to discuss such matters. "The story of Wyrlyn and Irluk." His hands waved about for effect.

Avanda got excited as well. She was enjoying the nonsensical ways of Bryus. "Irluk was involved?"

"No questions!" Bryus snapped, as he fluttered his fingers in the air while preparing for the story.

"Wyrlyn was the greatest E'rudite, as well as the first. Taught by the Notarians themselves, he was granted special privileges to help design Terra Australis once the ocean waters were removed from the valley. The Notarians had little interest in structures or devices outside of the Weirfortus Dam, the Lu'Tythis Tower, and a few others. It was Wyrlyn and his apprentice, Irluk, who developed the rest."

"His apprentice?" Thorik asked.

"No interruptions!" Bryus ordered. "Wyrlyn and Irluk created magnificent structures and enchanted items that survived long after the Mountain King War and the murder of most of the Notarians."

Thorik and Avanda were shocked at the comment but a swift open hand from the storyteller alerted them to remain silent.

"After the war, Wyrlyn and Irluk went their own ways and began teaching others in their own methods of controlling the forces around them. Irluk took on a spiritual view of these forces, realizing that nature's energy was not a series of random elements, but life-imbued sources to tap into. She created a new thought and practice of casting spells, which allowed those not as privileged to still perform E'rudite-style acts. Her followers became known as Alchemists."

Avanda smiled at the newfound knowledge. Thorik, on the other hand, was starting to understand where the story was leading, but was unsure how it would get there.

Flailing his arms around, Bryus continued. "Two separate cultures evolved. The E'rudites, who believed the powers should only be accessible to those few who have been taught over countless years to control them with disciplined techniques, and the Alchemists, who believed that all people should benefit from nature's powers. A deep chasm of disagreement and resentment grew between them until it exploded in a war between the two. But unlike any other war, this one affected time and space. It tore at the fabric of all things they had learned to control. The Govi Glade was never the same after that battle."

"The battle may not have lasted long in their time, but it lasted over a thousand years for the rest of Terra Australis. As far as I know, all were killed except Wyrlyn and Irluk. They continued to battle on, both being crippled and deformed from the magnitude of each other's attacks. Eventually, Irluk was removed from the living, but Wyrlyn could not fully eliminate her."

"Wyrlyn had suffered as well. Unable to mend his own deformed body, he traveled to the Dovenar Kingdom and found a host for his essence: a young princess with a child yet to be born. Wyrlyn allowed his broken body to die as his spirit implanted a second child within her."

Bryus finished his story. "And so, Ambrosius was born only moments prior to the original child, Tarosius, thus taking on legal rights to the kingdom."

Never one to hold back, Avanda blurted out her conclusion. "That's why Irluk talked Bakalor into letting us go. She wishes to finish her fight with Wyrlyn, who is now Ambrosius. They let us go so we could lead her right to him."

A moment of confusion crossed Bryus' face, followed quickly by a smile. He nodded approval at her comment, without giving away whether he had himself come to the same conclusion.

Thorik's eyes darted back and forth as he thought about the story and Avanda's keen observations. "Why didn't Ambrosius tell me?"

Relaxing his theatrical arm movements, the Alchemist sat back down in front of his campfire. "He has no memory of who he was as Wyrlyn. Only his powers prevailed in his leap into his new mother."

"Why didn't you tell him?"

"I did. He didn't believe me."

"If he didn't believe the story, then why do you believe it?"

Bryus' face twitched, and his half-formed smile made him look insane. "Because I don't have a better theory. Do you?"

❧ 13 ☙

BRIMMELLE'S ACT

Distant howls called to the thunderstorms and raging winds that hung tight along the northern mountain peaks, but the desert campsite was now still, all except for Brimmelle, who tossed and turned on the hard sand. The sleeping venue was bad enough, but what kept him awake was his mother's death and the disrespectful way of remembering her.

Thorik's obsession with the dagger, Varacon, was outrageous in Fir Brimmelle's mind. How could Thorik believe such fantasy? Especially about his own grandmother. Why couldn't the young man just accept her death? He had. Then again, Brimmelle still blamed Thorik for her death. Perhaps that's why the younger Num wasn't willing to accept her being gone. Thorik couldn't face the truth of his own doing.

Brimmelle finally sat up and looked around at everyone sleeping around the campfire. Thorik and Avanda slept quietly, unlike Bryus, who talked in his sleep. Grewen had fallen asleep while eating, as a handful of weeds still hung out of his mouth. All were oblivious to Brimmelle's insomnia.

"Thorik must accept the fact that she is gone," he muttered to himself as he spotted a set of small rocks placed in a swirling pattern near his feet. Assuming his nephew had placed them there to honor Gluic, he quickly disrupted the pleasant design. "Once he accepts this, we can return to Farbank."

Brimmelle sat and thought long and hard about his mother's death and what the right thing was to do about the situation. His conclusion always ended in returning home to let the villagers know of her plight. It never led down a path of telling his people that they had turned her into a hand-held weapon.

What a disgrace he would feel to tell other Nums that his mother was a twisted blade, which couldn't even carve up dinner properly. Gluic was a Num with a soul, not a piercing dagger. People would think he was out of his mind if he introduced them to his mother, the kitchen utensil. He might as well tell them his father was a spaded shovel and his grandfather was a doorknob. Where would this line of thinking end?

Brimmelle shook his head at the thought. "Unacceptable."

But what was he to do? "Thorik wouldn't give up on his quest to save her, unless..." Smirking ever so slightly, he constructed a plan to resolve the issue before him. "It's for his own good," he whispered, justifying his own thoughts. "Yes, this will be best for everyone."

With that, he tossed off the blanket and quietly walked over toward Thorik, stopping short near his gear. Reaching down, Brimmelle kneeled for balance as he slowly opened his nephew's backpack. Untying the top, he reached in and pulled out Thorik's coffer. Disappointed at the sight of the wooden box of worthless notes, he set it aside to reach back in for the dagger.

It wasn't long before he felt the cloths wrapped around spiraling blades. After ensuring Thorik was still asleep, he pulled out Varacon and unwrapped it to validate he had grabbed what he came for, and he had. Setting it aside, he stuffed the rest of Thorik's items back into his pack.

Lifting the dagger from the desert floor, he stood up and walked out of camp to find a place to hide it. He distanced himself from the camp, wanting to make sure that Thorik didn't find it while searching the area. Thus, he walked for a few minutes before stopping at the cliff, which overlooked a great void. During the day he would have seen the great Volney Lake valley, but the cloudy night made it difficult to see beyond the cliff's edge. This actually worked to his advantage, for the light would have allowed him to see how high he was, causing him to shudder with fear.

"He'll miss it at first, but then he'll come to accept that it is gone. We will then head home." Standing on the ledge, he raised the dagger over his head to toss it straight out into the blackness.

"It's about time." Bryus' voice resonated from the darkness before him.

The voice frightened Brimmelle. Losing his balance, he slipped and fell, dropping the dagger as his legs swung out over the ledge.

Bryus walked out from the darkness as though he was walking on an invisible glass which extended from the ledge. Calmly approaching, he watched Brimmelle kick and twist to pull himself back up onto the desert floor. "You obviously don't want Thorik to have Varacon, and I obviously want it. I suggest you stay quiet about giving it to me, and I'll forget that I saw you stealing it from him."

Brimmelle couldn't understand how the man was walking on air, but his immediate attention had to be on climbing back up on the ledge. "Don't you threaten me. I'll tell him what I want."

Bryus' cheek twitched as he thought about the Num's argument. "You are probably correct. So, to prevent that from happening, it would make sense to take Varacon from you and then allow you to fall off the cliff to your death."

"What?" Brimmelle panicked in his climb back up. Slipping in his haste, he caught himself at his armpits. He now hung onto the ledge with his arms straight out and his fingers grasping onto rocks, just inches from the dagger. "How dare you! I'll tell him everything."

Bryus walked directly over him and placed the bottom of his foot on top of the

Fir's head, slowly pushing him down off the cliff. "Thank you for warning me of your planned actions."

"If I go, I'm taking the dagger with me." Brimmelle quickly slid one of his hands out and grabbed the hilt of the blade. But in doing so, he lost his grip on the ledge and slid off the cliff.

Bryus stomped his foot forward onto the Num's free hand, which was scratching the desert floor as Brimmelle fell toward his death. The Alchemist's weight, however, was enough to hold the Fir's hand firmly onto the ledge as Brimmelle's feet dangled below. "We can't have that now. I really must have Varacon."

Hanging from one hand under Bryus' foot, Brimmelle held the other hand out with the dagger on display. "I'll make you a deal."

"Excellent! You're in such a suitable position to do so."

Brimmelle's hand was in terrible pain from being crushed, even though he knew he had to ignore it. "Help me back up to the surface... and then safely to camp, and I'll give you Varacon. I won't tell Thorik anything about the dagger. I haven't seen it. And to be honest, I never want to see it again."

"Deal." Bryus removed his foot, allowing Brimmelle to fall.

The scream and fall were short, as the Num fell to an outcropping of rocks just below his previously dangling feet. Falling flat and then taking in a deep breath, Brimmelle watched the Alchemist walk down steps that didn't exist. Once he arrived on the outcropping, he reached out his hand for the dagger, which was grudgingly given to him.

Brimmelle rolled to his knees and then stood up. "I don't understand. Why do you want it?"

"It's old magic. There is so little of it left."

"Old magic?"

Bryus inspected the dagger closely with his eyes and fingertips. "Yes, this is history. It is more valuable than any of us. We are but a blink of an eye. This, my little Num, is a true legend that is timeless. It will exist long after we are gone."

SEARCH FOR GLUIC

Thorik opened his eyes as the sun began to rise and turn the mountains to deep shades of red with veins of black. The mountain storms had moved on and left pockets of fog clinging to small valleys. It was a beautiful view to wake up to. All was peaceful and seemed right, except for an odd red light pulsing in the distance.

Rolling to his side, Thorik stretched his back and neck before preparing to investigate the red light. However, his plans changed when he noticed his weathered backpack. The sight caused him to sit up quickly and his eyes to grow abruptly large with concern.

Brimmelle stoked the fire in order to warm himself up. "What's the matter?"

Thorik grabbed his pack, opened it quickly, and looked inside. "Someone has been in my gear."

"What makes you say that?"

"It wasn't tied correctly."

"You have a specific way you tie it?"

"Yes."

"You must have just been tired last night and did it wrong."

"No, I've never tied it differently." Thorik reached into his pack to move things around. "And items are out of place."

"Thorik, things shuffle around as we walk."

"True, but I reset them every night before I sleep. I set everything I have in a specific place." Pulling out the coffer, he opened it up to ensure his notes from the travel were still inside. They were. Then he pulled out one thing at a time and inspected it. He found no damage, but something was missing.

Frantically, Thorik emptied the remaining contents and searched the surrounding ground. "Where is it?"

Brimmelle kept his eyes on the fire. "Where's what?"

"Varacon! Where's Granna?"

Never looking at his nephew, Brimmelle fired back a planned response. "We've been through this. Your grandmother is dead. She's gone. Accept it."

Thorik was rattled. "Uncle, I'm serious. The dagger is gone. Someone has stolen it."

"For what purpose?" his uncle asked.

Thorik didn't have an answer as he looked within every cloth and under his own bedding for the dagger.

"When was the last time you saw it?"

Thorik extended the search to the rest of the camp and around the bedding of Grewen and Avanda, waking the younger Num, but not the giant. "I know it was here last night."

Grewen stayed in his relaxed slumber while Avanda stretched and blinked her eyes in the morning light.

"How do you know?" Brimmelle asked. "I didn't see you take it out."

"Well, I did. And I recall having it last night. In fact, I remember feeling it under its protective cloths before I placed it in my pack last night."

Avanda yawned and rubbed her eyes as she began listening to the conversation.

Brimmelle made his way over to Thorik's gear, secretively tossed a few things inside of his backpack, and then walked over to Thorik, who was attempting to roll the sleeping mognin off his bedding to check underneath it. Brimmelle lifted the pack near Thorik. "Is this it?"

Thorik turned with excitement and grabbed at the pack. Inside, he felt a dagger's hilt and blade under several layers of cloth. "You found it, Uncle!" Pulling it out, Thorik tossed off the cloth layers to reveal one of his throwing daggers, which he used to hunt. The sight of it crushed him.

Brimmelle patted him on the back. "It appears that you lost it during yesterday's travels."

Thorik turned back to see the long desert path they had traveled. "Then we need to go back."

"Not likely. Even if we did, the wind has prevented us from retracing our footsteps. If we walked just a few yards from our original path, we would easily overlook it. It would be a wasted journey."

"No! We can't give up on her."

"We didn't. She is in a better place. We have to accept that fate has taken her from us, and now we must move on."

By this point, Avanda was up and looking for the dagger as well. Trying to push Grewen on his side to see if he was sleeping on it, she called over to Thorik. "I'll help. Don't worry. We'll find it."

Grewen eventually rolled to his side, allowing the Nums to check his bedding. A few live scorpions and a small lizard escaped from under his robe after the movement, but the mognin himself never fully woke up.

"I can't give up that easily." Turning from his uncle, he continued to pull the campsite apart in his search. However, after another hour of searching the camp and the surrounding area, Thorik eventually fell to his knees. He had failed to protect his grandmother. "I should have looked beneath the dagger's wrappings to ensure it was Varacon. How could I be so irresponsible?"

Fir Brimmelle puffed up his chest with a deep breath, much like he used to do before teaching his flock the daily sacred writings. "You and I have had this conversation before. You continue to keep your head in superstitions and unnatural beliefs instead of the solid and proven words of the Mountain King. Perhaps this will wake you up and force you to focus."

A slight grin crept into Fir Brimmelle's mouth as he watched the look of defeat grow on Thorik's face. Turning from his nephew in order to hide his satisfaction, he walked away to collect his own items for traveling. The sooner they left the camp, the less likely Thorik would change his mind and start looking for the dagger again.

Covering his face with his hands, Thorik was too deep in grief to fully pay attention to the Fir's words. The cool morning air finally registered on his body, causing him to shiver as he started to cry.

Avanda had listened to enough of his conversation with Brimmelle to understand what had happened. Seeing Thorik mourn the loss of Gluic, she approached him and covered his back and shoulders with a blanket before leaning over and hugging him. "I could have sworn you had it last night," she said softly to herself.

"I can't believe it. She's gone," Thorik finally whispered in disbelief.

"I know." Avanda's voice was kind and gentle.

"I'm responsible. She'll be forever entrapped in a dagger, lost in the desert."

Avanda thought about the issue as she leaned her head up against him. "What if she can help us find the dagger?"

A confused look crossed his face, warranting her to elaborate.

"What if she can venture a distance from the dagger? Last night, Bryus was telling me how souls are trapped in objects. Some enchanted items embed souls, while others act as portals. Because of Varacon's ability to absorb her soul on its own, perhaps this one is a portal. We know she was stabbed, causing her soul to be captured, and we'll need the dagger again to release her. But in the meantime, perhaps it's more of a home for her than a prison. Maybe she can wander away from it."

Thorik listened to the intriguing idea. "She always was one to wander off."

"Right," Avanda continued. "Perhaps she continued to walk with us after you dropped the dagger."

"And how do you expect me to ask her where it is?"

Avanda's right eyebrow raised, as if it was a foolish question to ask.

But Thorik was still fighting off the grief of losing his grandmother and needed a slight prod.

Walking over to his gear, which was uncharacteristically scattered across the ground, she picked up his pouch of Runestones and tossed them to him. "It worked for us when we talked to the spirits in Della Estovia. Let's see if Gluic can do the same."

Catching the sack, Thorik immediately understood the plan, but was less optimistic about it. "You realize that this will only work if your assumption is correct, and she followed us instead of staying with the dagger?"

Avanda smiled at him. "I know. But we won't know until you try."

"Agreed."

Thorik quickly dug into his pouch to remove the Runestone of Courage before setting the rest near his feet. Closing his eyes, he held the ancient stone out and touched two of the three smaller external gems.

"What's going on here?" Fir Brimmelle asked. He had been preparing to leave when he noticed Thorik standing at the edge of the camp with the Runestone in his hands.

Avanda blocked his path. "It's okay, Brimmelle. I've seen him do this before."

The Fir attempted to sidestep the young lady, but he was quickly cut off. He could knock her down if he wanted to, but his desire was to interrupt Thorik, not hurt Avanda. "Thorik, this is the foolishness we just talked about. You must not take part in these rituals. They are against the Mountain King's beliefs."

His words fell on deaf ears as Thorik lost himself in meditation, while Avanda continued to prevent the Fir from reaching him. But after only a few more attempts, Brimmelle stopped trying. In fact, he stepped backward in disbelief.

Avanda turned away from the Fir to see what was happening. Extending from the third small gem on the Runestone was a thin ribbon of vapor as the light in the center gem glowed brightly. The darkness of the Della Estovia caves had hidden the vapor's view, but its purpose was now apparent as it circled Thorik and prevented any spirits within the ring. This had been why the souls of the underworld parted ways when they saw them.

Thorik extended his arms toward the prior day's path in hopes of seeing Gluic standing in the distance. Unfortunately, there was no one there.

"Hold it high over your head," Avanda suggested. "So she can see it. Perhaps it will lead her here."

Thorik held the stone as high and far as he could, while facing it forward. But again, nothing was to be seen.

Avanda ran over to Grewen to wake him up. "Get up! We need your height. You need to lift Thorik high in the air as a beacon for Gluic."

Grewen blinked his eyes a few times and smacked his lips as leftover desert weeds fell from his mouth. "What happened?"

"Thorik needs to be high in the air in order to signal Gluic." Holding one of the mognin's eyes open, she peered into it.

"Right now?"

"Yes."

"Can I get something to eat first?" Grewen mumbled.

"No," the Num, a fraction of his size, ordered.

Grewen nodded, sat up, and shook the sleepiness out of his head before standing up and walking over to Thorik. Stretching one last time, he scratched his chest and asked for the purpose again. "Why am I doing this?"

Avanda was taking charge of this situation. "Just pick him up!"

"Whatever you say, little one." And with that, he grabbed Thorik with his massive oversized mognin hands and raised him high into the air as though he were a torch.

Thorik concentrated all of his efforts into the gem as the light in the center shined brighter against the sun's morning gleam. Prying one eye open, he looked out at the desert to see his grandmother or any other sign of her existence. If not her spiritual vapors, a reflected shimmer from the Varacon blade itself would more than suffice.

Avanda watched intently, changing views from the desert to Thorik, waiting for a sign from either.

Nevertheless, neither of the Nums could see anything out of the ordinary. It was nothing but dry lands and weeds.

Several minutes went by before Grewen spoke up again. "Avanda?"

"Yes?" Avanda responded quickly with renewed excitement. "Do you see her?"

"I believe so."

Avanda tried to force her eyes to look harder. "How can that be? Nums have much better vision than mognins."

"That may be true, but sometimes it's less about your eyesight and more about where you look."

Looking at the giant, she followed his line of sight toward the smaller second campfire where Bryus was still sleeping. Sitting near him was the translucent figure of an elderly lady placing small rocks in swirling patterns."

"Gluic!" Avanda screamed with delight.

Thorik quickly panned down from Grewen's hands to Avanda and then to his grandmother. He was immediately overjoyed, and in doing so, he lost his complete concentration on the Runestone. She was suddenly invisible again.

"Set me down!" Thorik yelled as his excitement got the better of him.

"Up, down, make up your mind," Chuckling, he set Thorik back on the ground.

Running over to Bryus' camp, Thorik held out the Runestone to allow them to see her once more.

"Stop!" Fir Brimmelle ordered. "This is wrong. It is blasphemy to bring the dead back to life. We cannot do this without corrupting our morals."

"She isn't dead!" Thorik fought back.

"She is!" Brimmelle yelled louder. "Even if her soul is adrift and here with us, it is not normal to be conversing with it. This is to be shunned and feared, and not attempted. This is wrong!"

"Why would we fear Gluic?"

"It's not just my mother. You have no idea what you are unleashing with that Runestone. Demons and other evil might be freed to cause us harm in your efforts to speak with the dead. These are not trivial things we talk about, for your knowledge has no more wisdom than mine on what gateways you may open and what dangers can come of this."

"Then let's ask Gluic if it is safe."

"If it is your grandmother. When you start playing with the unknown, you are easily misled into believing what you want, even if it's not real. She could be a beast from Della Estovia in disguise."

"But she isn't."

"How do you know, Thorik? Prove these facts to me, right now."

Thorik started several sentences to do just that, but stopped each time during the first words. "I can't prove this any more than you can."

Brimmelle's face showed signs of being fatigued from the fight. No longer did he attempt to intimidate. Instead, he begged Thorik in a genuinely sincere manner, which was uncommon for the uncle. "Then why take the chance? Why risk this? My mother is dead. Let her rest in peace. I'm asking you to respect your grandmother, as well as her son. If this was your mother, I would grant this to you if you so asked." Brimmelle shook his head slightly as he continued. "Don't contact her again. Please. I can't bear it."

Thorik's natural instincts were to stand up to his uncle. But memories of Bakalor tugged at the Num each time he summoned the courage to say something. It was as though he were fighting against both Brimmelle and the demon. All the fear and self-doubt that he had worked so hard to rid himself of suddenly reappeared. Bakalor's wrath and curse were still affecting his judgment, despite being free of Della Estovia.

Avanda looked at Thorik and waited for him to activate the Runestone, regardless of his uncle's words. But he lowered the stone and glanced at the newly awoken Bryus before turning from the sight. Reaching around his waist, Avanda accompanied Thorik back to the mess he had made at the main campsite.

"Thank you," Brimmelle said softly to Thorik as he watched them walk away. Turning back to Bryus, he could see the man was impressed with the Fir's ability to prevent the finding of the dagger in the Alchemist's gear.

�֎ 15 ✎

PYRAMIDS

————

Thorik's Log: 10th day of the 7th month of the 650th year.

Gluic is gone. I have lost her in the desert, and now our journey has come to an end. Today we will reach the City of Trewek, home of the Ov'Unday, and rest before we make our long trek back to Farbank. War is coming to this land, and we should leave before it sweeps us away with it. The only thing we have left to offer the kingdom is the Spear of Rummon, which I would gladly give to Ambrosius if I should ever be so lucky to see him again. Perhaps he will visit Farbank a second time, but this time under better conditions.

————

Thrusting up out of the center of a massive sinkhole along the dry desert mountainside, a city of rich brown and green bamboo towers appeared before them. Deep below the desert, surface water rushed out from underground caverns into the sinkhole, flowing past the many green vegetative islands that connected the city towers together through a series of creatively engineered bamboo bridges. Plant life grew with vitality in the humid environment that filled the sinkhole and the surrounding caverns.

Even though the recessed waterway was several hundred feet below the desert floor, the city was prominently displayed above the surface with dark brown towers covered in thick vines. The towers were giant bamboo stalks nearly half a thousand feet high, and multiple holes in the sides allowed light into the hollow center.

Above the city, on the desert floor, were nearly a hundred white tetrahedron pyramids placed in a circle surrounding the sinkhole opening. Each of these three-sided structures was set several hundred feet from the opening and stood twice the height of Grewen. All had markings of the Ov'Unday and a doorway on the only completely vertical wall, which faced the center of the sinkhole. The other two walls of the pyramid angled down into the desert floor, much like a two-sided tent would if the front side was raised and the back side touched the ground.

Grewen approached the closest structure along their path and started reading the carved markings. For several minutes he inspected the door, which was large enough to drive a wagon through. Stepping back away from it, he shook his head. "This is not our way in."

Bryus walked up to the sand-pelted doorway. "Well crafted, although I've seen better. It wouldn't take too much to unlock it."

"No, it's only a distraction." Grewen calmly turned away from the door and glanced back and forth at the other pyramids on either side of the current one. "We'll find the actual entrance. I suppose it doesn't matter which way we work our way around. The odds of finding the right one are the same."

Brimmelle scoffed at the comment. "I thought your people were open and trusting. Why the locked doors and all these games?"

"Trewek is isolated out here, and it's only a few days from Corrock. It is wise to keep the Del'Unday from being tempted to attack."

By this point, Bryus was working on a spell to cause the stone slab of a door to slide open. His interest was less about entering and more of testing his own knowledge.

After giving the door a half-hearted push, Brimmelle dusted his hands free of sand. "Why didn't they construct a wall instead of these games of misrepresentation?"

"Walls have a way of working both ways. They keep others out, and you can also become your own prisoner. It simply isn't the Ov'Unday way."

"The Ov'Unday way? You say that as though it is superior to all other ways. From what I've seen, you are far from it. Your hygiene, for starters, is far less than exemplary."

Grewen grinned at the Fir's misguided perception. "It's not surprising that you would take it that way. You tend to fear what you don't understand."

"Fear?" Brimmelle challenged the notion. But before he could continue, Bryus interrupted him.

Bryus had just stepped back away from the pyramid. "Success! It's unlocked." He was obviously pleased with his skills of deduction. "Ingenious design. It took me several attempts to crack it. I would assume most Del'Unday wouldn't have a chance."

"This is not a good door to enter Trewek," Grewen informed them. "We must be patient and find the proper one, which is connected to the ramp below, leading us down to the city."

Pushing the heavy stone double doors open with a wave of his hand and a few verbal magical commands, a ramp appeared before Bryus. It led down under the desert floor and then turned to the left.

Curious, Avanda grabbed Thorik's hand and led him down to the bend in the ramp. They found that the underground hallway abruptly ended with a fall hundreds of feet to the cavern's floor.

"Grewen, I'm confused," Thorik called back to Grewen, who remained at the doorway.

The giant grinned. "What doesn't add up this time, little man?"

"Why would they build this pyramid if this wasn't a real entrance? It's only a decoy, with no safe way down."

"But it is an entrance." Grewen chuckled at the Num's confused look.

"You told us this wasn't our way down to the city," Thorik replied as Avanda and he walked back up and exited the pyramid.

"That is correct. As you can see, this path ends with a fall to our deaths."

"Now I'm more confused than before. Why am I not understanding you?"

"Thorik, you're going to find out in life how important it is to ask the right questions, not just the first one that you think of. Most people ask questions and resolve that the answer they get is the answer they were looking for. But, in fact, it isn't. If you're confused about the answers, perhaps it is best to ask a more specific question."

Thorik thought about this for a few moments. "What is the purpose of these pyramids?"

Grewen grinned. "Excellent question, little man. All of these pyramids are an entrance to Trewek. However, only one of them is used at a time. This prevents outsiders from quickly approaching and attacking. And to ensure the secret of which one is the valid entrance, a different pyramid is periodically selected."

"How do they change from one pyramid to the next?"

"The ramp in the cave below us is frequently moved so that it fits up tightly to the bottom of a ramp inside one of these pyramids."

Thorik glanced back down the ramped hallway. "So this is an entrance, just not our entrance at this time."

Grewen nodded as he headed to the next pyramid. "So we need to find out which one is attached to the movable ramp. It will take some time to review each and every pyramid, but patience is a virtue."

"How can we help?" Thorik asked.

"Can you read ancient Ov'Unday script?"

"No."

"Then I think you'll have to be patient with me."

Avanda didn't care for the idea of slowly walking all the way around the city, checking each of the nearly hundred pyramids one at a time. There had to be a faster way. "How about if we went to the edge of the sinkhole and looked inside to see where the lower ramp fits up to the pyramids?"

"Be my guest, little one. It might just keep your urge to be active under control. And who knows, there is always a chance it may help." The giant gave her a slow wink to send her on her way.

Avanda smiled proudly at Thorik. She loved being the developer of a great idea. Grabbing Thorik's hand again, she led him toward the rich brown and green towers rising from the distant sinkhole. The hard, flat, tan desert of the immediate area was an extreme contrast to everything in the sinkhole.

Meanwhile, Bryus had climbed up toward the top of the pyramid as he looked for additional writings. "Ovlan," he yelled back down to the party. "She helped create these structures."

Grewen looked up into the blistering sun before replying. "The Nums are heading toward the sinkhole. I'm going to investigate more pyramids to determine which one leads us safely down."

Bryus squinted out toward the sinkhole and the spires rising from within it. "Nothing of interest out there. I'll go with you. I've read these writings before."

The idea of looking down into the sinkhole was far from appealing to Brim-melle. His ankles and knees tingled and became weak at just the idea of looking down over the sinkhole's ledge. "Agreed. I'm not heading out there. I'll stay here with you."

"Excellent," Bryus fired back sarcastically. "Your complaining will surely improve our effectiveness."

THORIK'S FATE

Brimmelle rested his back against the side of yet another pyramid while Bryus attempted to determine if it was the way into the city. Grewen had already moved on to the next structure to speed up the process, as he and Bryus were taking every other one. The Num had stayed near the pyramids due to his fear of heights. Just the thought of approaching the sinkhole made his stomach churn.

Hot and bored, Brimmelle closed his eyes and recited the ancient words from the scrolls he had lost so long ago. Standing in the pyramid's shade, he envisioned his followers back in Farbank all listening with great interest, hanging on to each and every glorious word he spoke. The Mountain King would have been so proud of him to see how he protected his writings. Oh, how he wished he could have met the king in person.

Over time, Brimmelle had started actually listening to the stories within the Mountain King Scrolls, instead of just reading the words. This revelation inadvertently caused his voice to fluctuate when he told it. It no longer was dry and monotone; then again, he was far from being a great bard. His pacing remained that of a drummer playing a death march.

The readings agitated Bryus, who was already struggling to concentrate on the ancient language. It was more difficult than he had let on. Working on a vertical side wall of the pyramid, he finally called out around the corner to Brimmelle, "Hold your tongue, Num, or I'll cast a spell to prevent you from using it."

The comment was inappropriate in Brimmelle's mind. "These are not just any words. These are the exact words handed down from the Mountain King. They are the foundation of the Rules of Order."

"I don't care whose words they are."

Brimmelle was astounded at the lack of respect. "How can you not care?"

Bryus never looked away from the glyphs he was working on. "Because I don't need you preaching to me about something I have no interest in."

"Well, you should. The Mountain King saved our land from the Notarians." Brimmelle walked around the corner to confront the Alchemist.

Bryus ignored him. "Good for him." His response was flat and unemotional.

Shocked at the candor, Fir Brimmelle puffed up his chest to defend his king. "Good for you, as well! If it were not for him, you wouldn't be free. We would all still be slaves."

"So you say."

"No, these are the facts!" Brimmelle corrected. "They were recorded and handed down generation after generation. He fought for freedom. He did this for all of us, including both you and I."

Bryus had hit his limit. "Listen, you pompous little fat Num. Don't stand there on your moral high ground and tell me what's right and what's not. You weren't there, nor was I. I don't owe him anything. He doesn't even know me, so how could he possibly have done anything for me?"

"This…" Brimmelle's hand shook as he pointed it at Bryus. The thick soul-markings across his body turned a deep shade of red as his blood accelerated through his veins. "This is why your land is at war. This is why you humans, Dels, and Ovs can't live in peace. You disrespect the one who has granted us all free-dom. You disregard him and shun him from your beliefs. Even when we freely give you his words to live by, you ignore them. Your species will never survive. Eventually, you will all end up killing each other, and I hope you all end up in Della Estovia, assuming it really exists."

Bryus finally turned from his glyph. "You ignorant Fesh-faced blow-hard. Don't cram your beliefs down my throat and expect me to thank you for sweet-ening the dung you fed me. Your thoughts are old and outdated. They don't serve our land any longer. Your perfect world of the Mountain King doesn't fit into real-life situations."

"It did in Farbank!"

"Then go back to Farbank and leave us alone!"

"That's exactly what I've been trying to do!"

"Then we agree!" Bryus' voice was still raised and agitated.

"Yes, we agree," Brimmelle announced as though he had won the discussion.

A long silence followed as the two didn't know how to move forward from the point they had ended. Eventually, Brimmelle added onto his thought. "And because we agree, we need to get rid of the dagger."

Bryus' face twitched at the comment. "Listen up, little Num. By the fate of some odd fortunes, Thorik ended up with the enchanted Varacon dagger as well as the mighty Spear of Rummon. Either of which I would give my right arm for. But yet, the naïve Num doesn't tap into the powers of either of them, nor does he wish to give them up, while you wish to toss them away as though they are trash. It makes no sense!" Shaking his head quickly, he attempted to unscramble the thoughts in his head. "I will wait for the opportunity to take Rummon off his hands. Until then, I plan to keep Varacon well hidden."

The thick and messy eyebrows on Brimmelle's face moved inwards and down. "I may have convinced Thorik to stop trying to reach Gluic for now, but my nephew is known to change course and strive for his original plans. And if he tries to reach my mother again with his Runestones, he will again find a potentially deadly vaporish spirit next to you. The boy can be foolhardy, but he is not stupid. He will quickly realize that you have the dagger."

With eyes thinning, Bryus glared at the robust Num. "I plan to keep Varacon. You'd have to be ignorant or stupid to not realize this by now."

Brimmelle puffed up his chest in defiance. "Are you calling me stupid?"

"No, I gave you two options to choose from," Heavy arrogance filled his tone.

Flustered, Brimmelle didn't know how to respond.

Bryus grinned at the Num's frustration. "The key for both of us to succeed is to prevent Thorik from using the Runestone."

"How?" Brimmelle was apprehensive of the Alchemist's plans.

"I could make a spell to break his fingers so he couldn't hold them. Or I could just poison him and resolve the entire issue."

"I think those are a little drastic."

"That means so much from a Num who recently wished my entire species would go to Della Estovia. We're talking about one insignificant little Num, one that never grew any soul-markings. What's wrong with him, anyway? Is he diseased or something? I've never seen one of your species without your markings."

"He's odd, but not ill." Brimmelle was slightly embarrassed about one of his family members looking or acting wrong. He felt it was a reflection on himself.

"Pity, I thought he might pass away on his own, resolving our issues. And honestly, who would miss Thorik?"

Brimmelle didn't say a word. He never thought he'd be in a conversation where he would have to defend his nephew. As much as he grumbled about Thorik, he knew the younger Num was always trying to do good, even if it wasn't within the words of the Mountain King's writings.

Bryus continued after a surprised scoff. "You would miss him? You complain about him all the time. Your life would be so much better off without him. You could return home and all would be well. This sounds like too easy of a solution."

"You're not going to kill my nephew or any other Num if I have anything to say about it. Nor will we hurt the boy. It's wrong to even think about it. Your solutions are extreme. Does morality escape you completely?"

"Listen, most people are just in the way of progress. They're either idiots or naïve and exist only because they have a framework of civilization that allows them to. If they do their job, they can survive. Few can survive without it. Fewer still have the capacity to establish the framework in the first place."

Brimmelle crossed his arms. "Where are you going with this?"

"The masses are expendable. They are easily replaced and are a waste of my time. There are really only a few of us that make life livable for the rest. This Num folklore Mound King of yours—"

"Mountain King," Brimmelle quickly corrected.

"Yes. Fine. Whatever. He sounds to me like one of those few who could establish the framework needed for your people to live. But let's be honest, beyond this king of yours, there haven't been more than a few Nums that have made any serious contribution to these lands."

"I have!"

"You have spoken his words and tried to enforce them." Bryus chuckled at the thought. "If you hadn't done it, someone else would have been there to do it. You're just one more drone in the Mountain King's framework, doing what you were told."

"I'll have you know I play a key role in the upbringing of Farbank's children."

"Really? Do they all look up to you and come running down the street to thank you for changing their lives? Do they go out of their way to be with you and learn more from you? I seriously doubt that."

The words hit hard. Fir Brimmelle had always been very distant from the villagers. In fact, it was Thorik that would have met Bryus' description long before Brimmelle. "This conversation isn't about me. It's about preventing Thorik from finding the dagger."

"Really? I thought we were discussing the mating rituals of the Chuttlebeast." Bryus turned back to the glyph on the pyramid wall. "Get rid of Thorik and we solve the problem."

"I'm not going to allow you to kill my nephew."

"Well, I'm not getting rid of Varacon. Therefore, you'll have to destroy the Runestones so he can't use them."

Brimmelle had never considered the idea. "Destroy the Runestones?"

"Yes, unless they are ancient and powerful. In that case, I want them."

"They were found by his parent. It doesn't matter how old they are or who owned them, they represent the Mountain King symbols, which we live by. The idea of destroying anything in the form of a Runestone is sacrilegious."

Bryus shrugged his shoulders. "Then eliminate Thorik. There you have it. Two great options to keep that little brain of yours thinking for the next few days."

Brimmelle had no comeback. He had been outsmarted on every verbal assault he had tried. So, to avoid any further abuse, he slowly walked quietly away from the Alchemist and around the corner of the pyramid.

"Idiot," Bryus mumbled to himself before shouting out instructions to the Fir. "Brimmelle, bring me my water. I need a drink." He was confident that the Num was beaten down enough to take orders. Bryus always enjoyed adding a little salt into the wound.

Dazed, Brimmelle walked over to Bryus' gear and reached in for a water skin. But in doing so, he accidentally uncovered Varacon. Staring at it, he considered stealing it. But he hesitated as he thought about the Mountain King's words against such acts. Then again, he had already stolen it from Thorik, and then Bryus had blackmailed it away from Brimmelle. Perhaps this act was not stealing, but was instead an act of reversing Bryus' unethical act. The Fir's own ethics were in turmoil as he studied Varacon and questioned Thorik's and Bryus' thoughts about the dagger. "Do two wrongs make a right?" he asked himself. "I started this, and I need to end it." Snatching the weapon, he covered it with a cloth and hid it inside his shirt.

Eventually, Fir Brimmelle returned around the corner and handed Bryus his water.

"It's about time," Bryus said.

Brimmelle nodded and moved out of view with a slight grin on his face. "Fool," he mumbled under his breath.

"Idiot," Bryus said again as he finished deciphering the glyph. "Well, this isn't the correct entrance. At this pace, we should have it figured out by the time they change the ramp to a new pyramid."

"Bryus," Grewen shouted from two structures away. His baritone voice rumbled across the desert as he called out to the Alchemist. "I found our way down."

❧ 17 ❧

SINKHOLE

Avanda had led Thorik to the edge of the sinkhole's rim before realizing how thin the ground was near the desert's boundary. Below them, the ground tapered back underneath them and thickened as it approached the countless caves in the sinkhole's walls.

Thorik quietly absorbed the enormous size of the hole and the city within it. Built in the center of the opening, which was easily over a mile across, the towers were out of reach from any attack. The cavern below the opening went back several miles in every direction and was comprised of homes and farms.

"Amazing," Avanda commented as Thorik approached from her side. "It reminds me of the hollow insides of a gigantic pumpkin, but instead of pumpkin guts, it has green vines clinging to the cavern walls and ceilings."

Thorik chuckled at her assessment. It was crude, but mostly true.

They could see a long ramp under the far ledge as it extended in a wide arc around the exterior of the city. Creatively engineered bamboo columns held the sturdy bamboo ramp as it worked its way up from the cavern floor in an enormous spiral underneath the Nums. Towers and bridges between them prevented the Nums from seeing where it finally reached up and hit the surface of the desert.

"Hold my feet," Avanda quickly dropped down on her stomach and leaned over the edge of the sinkhole.

"Wait!" Thorik jumped for her legs to ensure she wouldn't slide too far over.

Grabbing the edge of the desert floor, Avanda stretched her neck down to see what was below them.

She found that the desert was only a few feet thick at the very edge but increased in thickness the farther it was from the edge. "Thorik, lower me to my waist so I can see where the ramp leads to."

"I don't think that would be safe."

"Come on, Thorik. Where's your sense of adventure?"

"It was pushed aside by my responsibility to ensure your safety."

Pulling her head back up, she shot Thorik a look of disapproval. "I want to go lower."

Thorik's instincts told him to stand his ground, but his ability to tell her 'no' seemed to have vanished. He suddenly felt fearful of causing conflict if he didn't do what she requested. It was a relationship that he had slowly been allowing into his heart and he didn't want to damage it.

Avanda changed her expression from a pout to a smile and coyly batted her eyes at him. "Please? It will only be for a few seconds." She didn't have to wait long to determine if her game had worked.

With a deep sigh, Thorik gave in and repositioned himself behind her to ensure she couldn't fall. Sitting down, with his legs straddling hers, he gripped the ground with his boots and held her ankles with his hands. "I've got you. You should be able to lean over far enough to see the top of the ramp now." He prayed that he would not have to use his left arm to pull her back up, for it hadn't fully recovered yet from being broken at the Temple of Surod.

Spinning around, she leaned over at her hips to see beneath them. Avanda allowed gravity to stretch her down as far as she could go. And there it was; the top of the ramp ended on a platform surrounded by two tall guard stations. These were the only military-looking structures in the entire city. They appeared to be designed to stop invaders.

"I can see it!" Avanda began pushing herself back up. Unfortunately, the ground she pressed against gave way, sending a shower of sand to those below her in the city outskirts.

"Time to come back up," Thorik shouted as he clung to her ankles.

Avanda grabbed a firmer hold and pushed herself upward. Again, the rocks and sand loosened up and fell away. "Thorik, you're going to have to pull me up. I can't get a solid grip."

Thorik repositioned his feet to pull her back up. "Try to push while I pull," he instructed. "And... Push!"

Thorik pulled as Avanda pushed, only to find she had loosened a large rock on which she had been lying. Her hands fell free along with the rock, just as Thorik pulled her up to safety on the desert floor. He then let go of her ankles in order to grab his own arm in pain. The sudden jerk to save her had shot thousands of tiny painful spikes through his injured limb.

But the safety was short-lived, as the ground under her began to break away. The fallen rock had caused the ground under them to loosen, and it was all starting to crumble apart.

Avanda screamed and swiveled around toward Thorik. However, she was too late, and her body fell from the ledge.

Reaching out, Thorik grabbed her wrist with both of his hands, causing her fall to snap to a halt. His legs were now spread out around the new opening, braced firmly on the desert floor that remained after the center section of ground had broken free. Thorik screamed in pain as his left arm took the brunt of the jerk.

Dangling below him, Avanda gazed hundreds of feet down toward the city.

The only thing preventing her from certain death was Thorik's grip. "Help!" She reached up with her free hand to grab Thorik's arm and kicked wildly.

Residents of the city were starting to notice Avanda's high-pitched screams above and several rocks had fallen into a garden, just outside the islands and city towers.

Adrenaline raced through his body as Thorik dug his heels into the desert on both sides of her. He leaned backward and pulled her up slightly.

Avanda desperately reached out in an attempt to pull herself up. Her hand scratched and clawed at anything she could reach as she continued to thrash about and scream.

"Stop kicking!" Thorik struggled with her movements, as he himself was fighting his own pain. Her violent behavior was causing him to lose his grip as she jostled about.

Unfortunately, she was beyond reason. Her only thought was to grab anything to prevent her from falling.

And as Thorik had warned, her kicking caused her to slip out from his grip. It was a moment of horror for him as he felt each of her fingers slide away from his own fingers. The moment was devastating. He wished it away, hoping it hadn't really happened. But, unfortunately, it had.

Free of his grasp, Avanda's other hand grabbed onto Thorik's belt, nearly pulling it down below his waist. Thankfully, his legs had been spread out to span the gaping hole, where she still hung.

Thorik instantly grabbed her wrist with one hand and used his other to help pull himself away from the ledge. Pressing with his heels and pulling with his free hand, he slowly moved himself to safety while dragging Avanda out of danger. Again, pain shot through his previously injured arm as he used it without caution to save her.

Once they were a few yards from the opening, she released his belt and he released her wrist.

"I knew this would happen!" Thorik's agitated voice was shallow as he gathered his breath and clutched his arm in pain.

"You did not!" Avanda replied, struggling with her own breathing. Her emotions were still running very high, even though she was on safe ground. His agitated words caused her to reply in the same tone.

"Yes, I did! I shouldn't have let you talk me into it." Thorik was upset about the situation more than at her. In fact, he was furious at himself more than anything for doing something so foolish. He knew better.

Avanda had crawled slightly farther away from the sinkhole before picking her head up enough to question Thorik, who was now resting next to her. "I talked you into it?"

"Why do I let women affect me so?" he scolded himself, for he knew better than to attempt such a foolhardy act, especially with a bad arm. He had stood up to dragons, the undead, and other various beasts, but he struggled to stand up to those who he loved, always afraid of losing them in an argument. Nursing his arm, he continued, "I need to learn to stand my ground."

"Stand your ground? All I did was ask for your help. You could have said no if you felt it wasn't safe."

"I couldn't. Once you gave me that look and that smile..."

"You put my life in danger because I smiled at you?"

"No, you didn't let me finish." The adrenaline from the event was fueling both sides of the conversation.

"I don't have to. I love you, Thorik Dain, and you love me whether you're willing to admit it or not. I expect you to protect me from anything that can harm me, even if it's from myself."

Thorik blinked in confusion. "I tried to stop you!"

"Not very hard. I can't believe you allowed me to risk my life when you knew I shouldn't."

"Hey, this isn't my fault," he fought back. "You're the one that felt the need to lean over the ledge in the first place."

"Fine! This is all my fault." She abruptly rolled onto her side with her back to him.

"That's not what I said."

"You were very clear. It isn't your fault. Those are your exact words. Therefore, it must be mine."

Thorik bit his lip in frustration. "Avanda..."

"No, I will never coax you with my smile again. I don't want to be accused of causing you any more pain. I'll continue to learn enough magic so that I don't need your help, or anyone else's, for that matter."

Thorik sighed and rolled on his side, facing away from Avanda. "I don't need this. This is why I can't have a relationship right now."

"What relationship?" Her words were bitter and to the point. She had just severed any relationship that had been started.

"What happened to 'our love'?" he fired back at her.

"I'm questioning the same thing."

BRYUS EVENTUALLY MADE the trek over toward the sinkhole in order to notify the Nums that Grewen had not only found the entrance, but also been granted clearance for all of them to enter the city after speaking with the guards at the top of the ramp.

When the Alchemist arrived, he found the two Nums lying on the desert floor, back to back.

Bryus chuckled at the sight. "Must be some kind of Num ritual." A series of face twitches followed before he continued. "Either of you Nums want to join us? We're heading down to the city."

❧ 18 ❧

TREWEK

Passing the guard towers at the entrance, Grewen led the group down the long ramp, which rotated around the perimeter of the city. Easily twice the width of Grewen's wide shoulders, the ramp and its railing were designed for simplicity and functionality, as well as subtle elegance.

Despite its width, Brimmelle struggled with the ramp's height and fell twice from disorientation. During one of his bouts, he fell and landed against the trim of the walkway. Taking advantage of the situation, he pulled out the cloth-covered dagger and dropped it over the edge. The Fir watched Varacon unravel from the cloth and plummet to the muddy fields below as his stomach rolled and his head spun from the height. The deed was done. The dagger would be lost forever.

Bryus watched Brimmelle just lie on the ramp and stare down at the fields below. "Stand up, you old fool, and keep your feet about you."

Avanda eventually assisted Fir Brimmelle to his feet and then with the rest of his descent down the ramp.

The base to the entire lower ramp rested on a pontoon-style bamboo platform that floated in a wide and very deep water-filled ditch among the city's farms. This ditch had been dug out in a perfect circle around the city and through the cavern-filled farms and fields so that the ramp could be rotated in order to line up with any of the pyramid ramps above them. A dirt path followed the exterior side of the ditch, as horizontal bars were embedded in the base of the ramp every few yards. It appeared to take hundreds of Ov'Unday to work together and push these bars in order to rotate the ramp to a new pyramid.

The fields reached back miles from the city toward the dull cavern walls. Various crops were in season, while other land was being plowed and seeded. They had carved trenches out to carry water from the underground river into the fields to water the land.

"Did you have any issues getting permission for us to enter?" Thorik asked

Grewen as he gazed out at the festive city below them as the high water levels ran slightly over its banks.

"No. I have been here before. Nums are not feared, and Bryus looks too old to cause much trouble, even for a human. Had he been a Del'Unday, we surely would have been rejected."

As the travelers made the long walk down, they observed the city and its surroundings. The city itself was a marvel to behold. Grand bamboo towers rose hundreds of feet in the air; several even extended above the desert floor in the center of the opening. Walkways between them resembled branches, while bridges between the islands contained creative open and covered bamboo designs.

Rising out through the openings and above the desert surface, the tallest towers had been designed to capture the sun's rays and send them down the center of the enormous shafts below the desert floor before dispersing them to meet the city's needs. Bright arrays of light beamed out of well-planned holes within the towers, coating the subterranean fields with the rich sunlight they needed.

Farther away from the sinkhole opening, fewer plants existed. The far walls of the sinkhole were bare, aside from a littering of cave holes, some carrying water into the city area, some carrying the water out. Many of the caves did neither.

The aroma of freshly baked goods and sweet fruits filled the air. Low-pitched water-chimes gave the entire city a background noise that put everyone at ease. These pleasant, soft-sounding metal water-chimes were periodically accompanied by a few higher-pitched wind-chimes. The native music was calming and relaxing. Even Brimmelle was able to walk the lower section of the ramp without gripping tightly onto Avanda's hand.

Once they reached the bottom, they worked their way through the farming community toward the central city. The Ov'Unday were a collection of gentle races. They consisted of many different species; some on four legs, some on two, and others with none as they slithered or flew. An endless variety of colors and skin types covered the many different types, which ranged from the giant mognins down to the mouse-sized quix with their six legs and large eyes.

Passing a garden, Avanda noticed a large rock had crushed a row of plants. Explaining the ordeal that had taken place above with Thorik and herself, she easily convinced Grewen to reach into the garden and remove it.

Children ran up and down the streets and played various games of tag, enticing Avanda to play as well. The adrenaline rush from her near-deadly fall from above had subsided, and she had slowly begun talking to Thorik again. Her interest in playing with the locals was deferred with a soft nod from him to keep up with the group as they traveled inward toward the towers.

Thorik watched the playing as they walked along before making any reference. "Grewen, these children seem very happy. It reminds me of Farbank."

Grewen nodded and grinned. "Yes, they are happy. But they are raised far differently than the children you know."

"Why do you say that?"

"You have restrictive ties to your children. Parents oversee and control their raising."

Thorik thought that it was an odd observation. "Yes. So?"

"Once Ov'Unday are capable of moving about, they become the community's children. All adults are now their parents, and they must protect all young and help guide them."

"That's ridiculous," Brimmelle spoke up. "They couldn't possibly all give the same advice. The children would become confused. They would have no foundation."

Grewen stopped a child running in the street. "Don't run near the river. It's overflowing, and the streets are slick."

The child looked out toward the river and then at Grewen. "I'll be careful." He then headed off to catch up with his friends.

"You see," Grewen continued, "We believe if young minds are exposed to many ways of thought, it stimulates their ability to reason and judge for themselves what is right and wrong."

Avanda was amazed. "I want to live here."

"Oh, no you don't." Fir Brimmelle grabbed her by the hand to ensure she didn't wander away. "This kind of thinking leads to chaos."

Thorik naturally wished to prevent any arguments. "If that was true, then it would already be chaos."

"To a degree, it was at first." Grewen recalled historical stories of the time. "A wise mognin named Trewek started our culture believing that a level of chaos would be required for us to gain the internal salvation we needed."

"That makes no sense." Brimmelle scoffed at the idea.

"You must be willing to be open to all thoughts and ideas before you can select the ones you wish to adhere to. If you only know of one option, you can never be enlightened enough to know if you are following the right path."

Brimmelle shook his head. "This is wrong and confusing for children. It is the parents' duty to have them understand the truth."

"Isolating them in Farbank to give them only one point of view prevents them from knowing if it is the right one." The mognin smiled with anticipation at the expected response from the Fir.

"But it is the right one. Why fill their minds with things that are wrong?"

"Wrong in your mind, but not to others."

"Are you suggesting we should teach our children in ways that we don't believe, even when we know they are harmful?"

"I'm not suggesting that you do anything. I'm only stating that we Ov'Unday allow our children to question everything and make their own decisions."

Avanda continued to watch the wonderful sights. "If I lived here and did something wrong, who would discipline me if everyone is considered to be my parent?"

Grewen chuckled. "I can understand why you would want to know such a thing before moving here. However, we do not provide discipline or punish others. Trewek did not believe in it."

Even Thorik was surprised by the answer. "So you can get away with anything you want?"

"Acting out against your fellow Ov is a sign that something is wrong. We come together as a community to try to help these individuals. We counsel them so they understand what they have done, how it has affected others, and how they could handle the challenges better in the future."

Brimmelle scoffed. "You mean to tell me if someone committed murder, you wouldn't throw them in prison?"

"We have no prisons. This is a concept that only the humans and Polenums share."

"Don't be lumping us in with humans." Fir Brimmelle puffed up his chest. "The human we have with us should show you our differences."

Looking back in order to see Bryus, the group realized the Alchemist was no longer with them.

"We need to find him." Thorik was disheartened that they would need to take the time to do so.

Grewen softly nodded to Thorik to ease his concerns. "He will find his way. We are nearing the bridges to the city. He knows you will plead your case to the elders to warn them of pending war. I'm sure he will catch up to us."

Crossing a bridge to the first island, Thorik was impressed by the craftsmanship and attention to detail on the railing. Not nearly the detail of the Kingsfoot carvings, but definitely more artistic. Nothing had been constructed haphazardly; it was all done to provoke thought and awareness of the surroundings.

They walked across island after island, linked by the bridges, until they arrived near the center where the tallest of the towers rested on one of the largest islands.

Grewen then approached a large sloth-like creature known as a gathler. This specific gathler stood before the entrance of the tower and wore forest green robes. Grewen's conversation with him continued for several minutes as he pointed at Thorik while explaining what they came for. With an official nod from both of them, Grewen turned around and walked back to Thorik.

"The next meeting of the elders is not scheduled for another month."

"What? We don't have a month," Thorik argued.

Grewen held up his hand to stop the Num from getting upset. "However, they will be making a special meeting here in a week."

Brimmelle was skeptical. "That seems a little too nice for them to do for a few unknown outsiders."

"True. However, we are the second request they have received in the past two days to speak to the elders of pending war. Apparently, there are others who know about this."

19

OV'UNDAY ELDERS

Thorik's Log: 18th day of the 7th month of the 650th year.

Today we will meet with the Elders of Trewek to warn them of Irluk and Bakalor's plot to take over the land. It has been a slow, restless week, as I can't for the life of me figure out who else could be here to warn of the same matters. The only advantage of this past week was the care I received for my injured arm from the locals. It's never fully healed from being broken at the Temple of Surod and is a constant reminder of the event and the stabbing of my grandmother. Bryus, however, is still missing. Then again, what do we need him for now that the dagger has been lost?

"Hurry up, Avanda." Thorik wished to be on their way to the elders' meeting. After impatiently waiting days for the event, he certainly didn't want to miss his opportunity to speak.

They were already running late due to Avanda's new interest in playing a local ball game. She had been playing the game for nearly a week and had become very good at it. As always, she became obsessed with the idea of becoming the best at it.

A large circle of brown and white pins was near the perimeter of the field of play. Most of the white pins were still standing up, while only one brown one remained upright. Normally played as a defensive game, where each team member stood near their pin to protect it, Avanda had bewildered her opponents by playing an aggressive offensive strategy. Leaving her pin unprotected, she ran around the field knocking over her opponents' pins with the ball. The one-on-one ball play worked to her advantage, as the rest of the players feared to venture away from their own pins, in spite of the fact that they had already fallen.

Keeping her eye on her next opponent, Avanda prepared for her next shot. "We're almost done," she shouted to Thorik. Then, taking her final shot, she kicked it past a young mognin and knocked over the pin behind him. "Yes!" she cheered with her hands in the air, followed by her team members quickly congratulating her.

"I'm leaving without you. I'm not going to miss the entire meeting," Thorik warned.

"I'm coming, I'm coming." She finished up the last few congratulatory hugs with her new friends and then ran over to Thorik. "Why the rush?"

"The elders' meeting has already started."

Keeping up with his pace, she ignored his concerns and skipped along in a carefree manner. "So? You're not scheduled to be the first to talk, anyway."

"I'm curious as to who else brings warnings about war and what they have to say about it."

"Why? This isn't our war."

Thorik shrugged his shoulders. "It might very well become our war."

"Why would anyone want to fight Nums? What have we ever done to them?"

"They don't think that way. They want to rule everyone, regardless of whether we have issues with them or not."

Walking past a market, Avanda stopped for a moment to take in the sweet smell of the freshly baked bread. "We could always live here. We're safe in Trewek."

"No one will be safe as long as Bakalor and Darkmere wish us harm."

Avanda turned from the bread and quickly caught up to him. "But if we leave them alone, they'll leave us alone."

"I wish that was true."

"You don't know that it isn't." Stepping up to a vegetable and fruit stand, she smiled and looked over the produce. The Ov'Unday tending the stand winked at her and handed her a small bunch of grapes. She thanked him and ran over to Thorik.

"There are others that wish to see us dead if we don't follow their ways."

Pulling a grape from the stem, she popped it in her mouth and enjoyed the sweet, rich taste. "Then we'll just follow their ways."

Thorik stopped and looked at her. "How can you say that?"

Plucking another grape, she held it out to Thorik. "These are fantastic. You should try one."

"Avanda, I'm serious. How can you say that you don't care?"

Realizing he didn't want the grape, she ate it herself. "Easy. I didn't follow Fir Brimmelle's rules most of the time, and nothing ever came of it. What do I care what rules others put in place?"

Thorik grabbed the grapes from her. "What if I said that you could no longer have grapes?"

"That would be mean. Why would you do that?"

"I'm not. Our new rules may say you can't have them."

"That's just silly." She quickly reached out for her grapes.

Thorik pulled them back. "No, you are no longer authorized to have them. Now, what are you going to do?"

Trying to grab them again, she missed as he moved them away. "I'm going to take them, anyway."

"Such acts under our new leadership could cost you your freedom or your life."

Avanda grabbed his arm in an effort to pull the grapes toward her. "Stop it, Thorik. I'm hungry."

"The new rulers don't care. You have one purpose, and that is to serve them."

Avanda let go of him and crossed her own arms. "I don't serve anyone." Her lips tightened, and a hint of a scowl appeared.

"You will have to if we don't all stand up and help fight this threat to our freedom."

Avanda stood silent as she gave Thorik an evil eye. The grapes were now high enough above his head that she couldn't grab them. "Enough with the lesson. I'd like my grapes now."

Thorik smiled. "See, it doesn't feel good to have others in control of you."

Avanda felt he was pushing the point too far. Stepping out, she quickly stomped on his foot, causing him to drop the grapes, which she caught in mid-air. Popping a grape from the stalk, she crushed it in her mouth. "I'm guessing that you would know how that feels better than I do." A sly smile faded onto her face.

After a few hops from the sore foot, Thorik laughed. He only wished that he were half as self-assured as she was. "Okay, you have your grapes, this time. Let's hope that I can always be allowed to give them to you. But for now, we must hurry on to the meeting."

"After you." She nodded with a silly smile, showing him grape juice between her teeth.

~

A FEW MINUTES LATER, Thorik and Avanda reached the tall tower where the elders were meeting. A crowd of Ov'Unday stood outside in the foyer discussing the various issues that had been slowly leaking out of the meeting chamber.

Grewen and Brimmelle were waiting for Thorik to arrive so they could all walk in together. Grewen calmly chatted with several Ov'Unday as Brimmelle impatiently leaned against a far wall, wondering what was taking the young Nums so long.

"Sorry we're late," Thorik said to Brimmelle.

"Wouldn't surprise me if you end up being late for your own funeral." Brimmelle moved from the wall and walked with them up toward the main door where Grewen stood.

"I don't understand why you even attended this with us, Uncle. You have no interest in Ov'Unday affairs."

"True, but I do have an interest in us leaving here so we can start our journey home. And you tend to say things that get us involved in events that we shouldn't be in. So, I'm here to remind you to keep your words to a minimum. Say what you need to and then let us be on our way."

Rolling his eyes in protest, Thorik shrugged his shoulders innocently. "That's all I plan to do, dear Uncle. I have no plans to get involved."

"Just like all you planned to do was help lead Ambrosius from Farbank to Kingsfoot. That ended up with us here, on the far side of Australis, with two dead Nums and a bounty on your head for escaping the Southwind mining prisons."

"Understood. I've learned my lesson," he said as they approached Grewen at the tower's entrance.

Just outside of the building's main doors was a faralope with reins and a saddle strapped onto its back. Only humans rode the two-legged faralopes, so this was an odd sight in the Ov'Unday city. It was then that they entered the building to address the elders.

The main hall was filled with various species of Ov'Unday disagreeing with one another with a civil temperament. In the center of them stood a tall human with blue robes and a Dovenar crest on his chest plate.

Thorik was amazed at the strength in the man's voice. The speaker didn't need to be loud or aggressive in order to be commanding. Inching his way through the crowd, the Num finally poked through and realized who the man was. Thorik had seen him before, once in the coliseum in Woodlen, another time in Southwind's city of Rava'Kor, and then again in the O'Sid Fields when Thorik and his party were captured by the Eastlanders.

"Truth be known, Asentar, high knight of the Dovenar Kingdom." The leader of the Ov'Unday elders spoke loudly, attempting to clear the air of side conversation so they could focus. This specific Ov happened to be a gathler, which resembled a giant hunched-over sloth in its form and slow movements. "Have you walked in here as a self-appointed liaison to your kingdom? Am I to understand that you don't even have approval from all the kingdom's provinces to speak on their behalf?"

Asentar's rugged facial features didn't flinch at the obviously devastating words of truth. "That is correct. But I do speak on the behalf of the kingdom's people."

"And for these people, you are asking for our assistance to fight against an aggressor who has neither threatened us nor caused us harm?"

"I'm asking for your support to unify our land. We are fractured and easy prey for those who wish to see us fall. And make no mistake; our aggressor is cunning. He only makes enemies with a few of us at a time to reduce his battlefronts."

One of the elder mognins entered the conversation. "But to support your efforts, we would have to go against our very beliefs. We shall not shame the teachings of Trewek, especially here in his namesake city."

"I am not asking you to give up your culture; I only ask that you be willing to fight for the freedom to continue to have it."

The mognin shook his head. "We will not fight."

"Then you will be killed or enslaved. Your civilization will be washed from this land, and your enlightened ways will be forever lost."

"You cannot possibly foresee this," the mognin replied. "You only speculate based on your fears."

"The Grand Council members have been murdered, the provinces within the Dovenar Kingdom have been taken over by local leaders, and communications with the Del'Unday have all but ended. We are now broken as a civilization." Asentar's voice was firm and powerful. His conviction was relentless.

The Grand Council had been the one hope for all species to work in peace. The notice of its destruction was grave news to the Ov'Undays. Their sense of safety within the city of Trewek suddenly was in question.

After allowing the elders time to absorb the severity of the situation outside of their enormous sinkhole, Asentar continued, "Tremors of war have been heard from the east side of the Guardians, Darkmere rallies the Corrockians, and the Terra King breeds hate into the hearts of mankind. We are on the verge of the fight for our lives, whether you care to participate in it or not."

"No, you have it wrong." Thorik had been so caught up in the moment that he had spoken up before even realizing it.

In spite of Avanda's smile at Thorik's outburst, Brimmelle shot Thorik an angry look for speaking up out of turn.

Thorik held up a soft hand and nodded at his uncle to assure him he would not go any further than needed, but his self-confidence wavered once he looked away from his uncle and over at the other faces in the room.

All eyes had moved to the Num, who now stood in the front of the crowd. It was enough to make Thorik feel unnerved, but it was the reaction of Asentar glaring down at him that made his knees weak.

"Truth is in question. Step forward and speak your name," commanded the head elder.

Thorik stepped cautiously forward as he waited for Asentar's approval as well. The Dovenar Knight was intimidating because of his size as a man, but more so because of the self-confidence that emanated from him.

Asentar nodded to the Num, giving him the floor to speak.

"Thorik Dain of Farbank."

The gathler elder leaned forward. "Greetings, Thorik Dain of Farbank. May truth be your ally. Do you have knowledge to discredit what we have heard here today?"

"Yes. I mean no."

"Well, which is it?"

"Asentar is correct about Darkmere and the Terra King. But what hasn't been told is that they are both the same person."

A moment of confusion rolled across the crowd and elders before the Num continued.

"Darkmere has been preparing the Del'Unday army to attack the Dovenar Kingdom, which will be very easy seeing that he is also swaying the kingdom's tactics from within the Dovenar walls disguised as the Terra King."

"How do you know this?" Asentar asked.

"We traveled with Ambrosius after the destruction of the Grand Council."

"Impossible. All of the council members were killed."

"Not all. Ambrosius survived, barely. I nursed him back to health. Then we traveled to Woodlen, where we met the Terra King. He escaped, but we caught back up with him later and prevented him from destroying the entire Dovenar Kingdom."

"If this is true, then why have we not seen Ambrosius?"

"Because he sacrificed his life to save the kingdom. I was there."

The gathler's voice came across sad when he spoke. "Truth be heard, he is truly dead."

"Well…" Thorik was uncertain how to reply. "Maybe not."

Brimmelle dropped his forehead into his palm as he hid his eyes from the embarrassment.

"Thorik Dain of Farbank, do you enjoy confusing the situation?" the gathler asked.

"No sir, just the opposite. I prefer things to be nice and orderly, but I'm finding out that real life isn't fitting into this mold."

"Then spit it out and tell us why you now question his death," Asentar said.

"I overheard Irluk saying that he still lives."

"The Death Witch?"

"Yes."

Another elder spoke up with a condescending tone. "Do you have conversations with Irluk often?"

Several in the crowd snickered until the gathler elder raised a hand to silence them.

"No sir. In fact, I've never talked to her," he replied to defend himself. "She was talking to Bakalor."

After a fraction of a second of quiet, a roar of laughter quickly erupted from the crowd. Grunts and snorts and the sounds of hooves hitting the stone floor monopolized the hall.

By this time, Thorik was feeling very sheepish. However, he noticed that Asentar hadn't changed his demeanor toward him. The man stood respectfully as he waited for him to continue.

"I hope you can support these claims," Asentar spoke softly to the Num before the elders began the discussion again.

An elder mognin stood up tall and clapped his enormous hands together to silence the crowd and regain control. The impressively loud single clap did its job, and the gathering quickly came to a hush. The mognin remained standing as he gazed down at the little Num. "You, Thorik Dain of Farbank, have had acquaintances with Bakalor?"

"You might say that, sir."

The elders cautioned the crowd to control their noises based on his answer before continuing.

"Little Num, do you know where Bakalor resides?"

"Yes, Della Estovia."

"That is correct. You obviously couldn't have met him unless you traveled into the underworld."

"I know. That's where he had his conversation with Irluk."

"Honestly, do you expect us to believe that you have traveled to the underworld and back without getting caught by Bakalor?"

"No. We were caught." Thorik was getting tired of this line of questioning. "And I overheard them saying that Ambrosius was alive. They're also working with Darkmere to cause hostilities among our people. They plan to have Ergrauth's army attack our weak defenses. And most importantly, Bakalor himself plans to return to the surface."

Thorik had everyone hanging on his every word until the final one.

Asentar shook his head. "Bakalor can't return to the surface, even if all creatures would perish in such a war. He simply can't survive in the sunlight."

"Apparently, he doesn't believe that to be true. Irluk and Bakalor are playing us like pieces in a game, and we're going along with it. So, the question is, do we allow them to continue, or do we take control of our own movements?"

The hall fell quiet as the crowd waited for the elders to ponder the Num's concerns.

Asentar watched Thorik as the Num stood firm to his words. Smirking slightly from one side of his face, the Dovenar Knight patted the Num on the back and winked at him. Regardless of whether he had convinced them or not, Thorik hadn't backed down.

One of the mognin elders finally spoke out to Thorik. "Proof! Evidence is needed. This is superficial conjecture. We don't know that any of this is true."

Thorik sighed. There was no way to validate his story.

Asentar realized that the elders had finally opened up to discussing the idea of taking a stance, if he and the Num could provide something more. "Tell me, then, if I could bring proof to this chamber, would you consider joining with us?"

The elders looked back and forth at each other before the gathler replied. "Truth be said."

Asentar was pleased with their answer. He knew the odds of having the Ov'Unday on the side of the Dovenar Kingdom were slim, but the likelihood had just increased. "Excellent. Then we shall return with proof."

"We?" Thorik and Brimmelle both said, confused about the knight's statement.

"Thank you for honoring my request to speak with you today." Asentar bowed to the elders. "I can only hope that I am wrong about the pending war, but it is a good sign that you are willing to discuss the option if I should unfortunately be correct."

"Willingness to discuss this topic does not ensure our support in your efforts," the gathler said.

"Understood, high elder. We will bring evidence back to substantiate our story or put an end to it once and for all. Is this acceptable?"

"Truth be heard, truth be said."

Nodding his head one last time in courtesy, Asentar turned from the elders and guided Thorik out of the main hall and into a busy foyer. Once there, he stopped and sighed as he peered down at the Num. "You had better be right on this. I'm taking a risk that your story holds water."

Brimmelle was stuck next to Avanda and Grewen in the crowd. It would take them a few minutes to fight their way through the crowd and follow Asentar and Thorik. "He better set that man straight!" Brimmelle complained.

"He'll do just fine," Avanda replied as they followed Grewen out of the meeting room.

Meanwhile, Thorik pulled on his pack's straps to straighten it up. "Why would you rest your success on me?"

"Because…" The knight struggled to admit the truth behind his reasoning as he pulled him farther from the room. "Because I have no other options at play here. I need the Ov'Unday to join with us before it's too late. You are the first one I've met that has overheard the planning of this new war. Seeing that I need evidence to convince the elders, you will help me find it."

"But I have no evidence. I only overheard parts of their plan. I am of no help to you."

"You were in Della Estovia?"

"Yes."

"Then take me there so we can acquire the proof we need."

"I won't be going back to that place! Why would I do such a thing to help you?"

"Are you not the same Num who I held at bay in Southwind along with the blothrud, Santorray?"

Thorik wasn't pleased that the knight recalled his face from that night in Rava'Kor. "Yes."

"You travel with dangerous companions."

Chuckling lightly at the observation, Thorik straightened out his pack again as he watched his companions arrive. "You have no idea."

"The two of you were arrested and placed in the prison mines, only to later escape."

"Again, you are correct. Are you wishing to arrest me?"

Brimmelle was shocked at the discussion he came upon. "Don't let him intimidate you," he said to Thorik, who ignored his uncle's comments.

"Perhaps, if I have to. But, more importantly, I will tell you that your life is most likely in danger. The Matriarch controls the province of Southwind, and she does not take kindly to prisoners escaping, and she took even less kindly to you killing her men, those she sent out to retrieve you."

Thorik shot a look at Avanda. "Lucian?"

Avanda recoiled from just hearing his name, recalling the man who had killed her pet and attempted to rape her.

"Yes, Lucian was taken back to the Matriarch. I know not of his fate, although if he still lives, it is a meager existence for survival. His return without Santorray and yourself most likely caused heated emotions. I'm sure the Matriarch has sent out a platoon of her best men to capture you, or even worse."

Thorik's pale skin faded to an even lighter shade as he realized his past was catching up to him. "Worse?"

"Yes, she may have hired assassins to eliminate you."

"If I understand your offer correctly, you'll protect me from the assassins as long as I take you to Della Estovia. If I don't, you'll turn me in?"

"Thorik, this is not about me or you. This is about saving an entire kingdom. We need to find some evidence to back up our claim that war is coming."

"I cannot lead you to Della Estovia." The Num glanced over at his uncle. "I couldn't even if I wanted to. We were lost when we were captured by Bakalor, and I have no idea how we escaped."

Asentar crossed his arms and scowled at the young Num, uncertain of Thorik's integrity. He had based his case on the Num's story, which was starting to lead to dead ends.

Thorik cocked his head to one side as an idea came to him. "However, there might be another way we can gather what you need without traveling there."

"And how is that?"

Thorik glanced at the crowd of Ov'Unday walking past them. It made him uncomfortable continuing the discussion with so many ears around. "Let's take our leave of this place before we discuss it."

20

ASENTAR'S MISSION

Asentar reached over and grabbed the reins of his faralope and led Thorik and his friends out of the congested part of the city.

As they paraded away, Avanda hid a few grapes just inside Brimmelle's pack. She was curious to see if the faralope could sniff them out. To get things started, she bit one grape in half and fed it to the Fesh'Unday beast to tempt its taste buds.

Once they had left the main public market area, Thorik explained his thinking to find evidence. "You see, going to Della Estovia will only allow Bakalor and Irluk the opportunity to capture us, and even if we eluded them, they would know we know about their game. We will have tipped our hand and allowed them to change plans, if needed."

"Let go!" Brimmelle complained as he tried to shoo the faralope's snout away from the back of his neck.

Avanda snickered at the sight of the slobbery mess the Fesh'Unday was leaving all over the Fir's pack.

Asentar tugged on the reigns of his faralope to keep it from bothering the Nums. His mount returned to following the knight but occasionally veered off to chew on Brimmelle's pack. "What's your suggestion?" the knight asked Thorik.

"Would it not be better to let them play out their plot so we can be a step ahead of them?"

"It would. But I lack sufficient information to carry this out. The facts you have provided seems too general to establish a plan. Is there more that was said by Bakalor and Irluk?"

Thorik taxed his brain to recall everything he could from the terrible ordeal. "They talked about trying to take down the Lu'Tythis Tower."

Asentar shook his head. "Concerning, but I don't know how that remote tower plays into launching a war."

Warm, moist air blew across Thorik's face as he continued to reenact the scene in his head. "Ergrauth has started moving his troops to the Guardians, and then he'll move them to River's Edge."

"Already?"

"Yes. Ergrauth has also awoken the Winds of Conquest."

Asentar slowly removed his gloves and folded them while in deep thought. His movements were now slow and methodical. "Then he has found them."

"The Winds of Conquest? Do we really need to fear wind?"

"What? No. They aren't really wind. They are lesser demons. Twins, in fact, with the birthright to rule the skies above the battlefields."

"Why have I not heard of them before?" Thorik asked.

"They were captured a long time ago by a great hero, who magically burnt them down and placed their ashes in an urn. They were condemned to an eternity of sleep, never to be released or awoken. A spell was cast on the urn to prevent it from being opened. It was then hidden in order to prevent anyone from trying to revive them. It has long been said that they would be brought back to life in order to fight in the final war of Australis."

"So, they found the urn and have brought them back to life?"

Brimmelle fell back as the faralope grabbed his backpack again.

This time Avanda burst out laughing as the Fesh'Unday ripped a chunk of fabric out of the pack, exposing the grapes.

Asentar tugged hard on his Fesh'Unday's reins, freeing the Num and ignoring him at the same time. "Yes, they may have been revived, if what you heard was correct."

Thorik sighed at the lack of planning he was able to bring forth. "But this again changes nothing. We still need evidence to prove they are on their way."

"This changes everything," Asentar announced. "They will rule the battlefield skies when they attack us. Our arrows and catapults will be useless. Our air attacks will be for naught. We will have to fight them hand-to-hand. And without the strength of the Ov'Unday, we will be quickly overtaken."

"But..." Thorik quickly began to create an alternative plan. "What do you suspect happened to the urn after they were released? Would they have kept it?"

"What? The urn would be useless. It's possible that they may have saved it as a reminder of their imprisonment, perhaps as a symbol of Ergrauth's power to release them. Dels tend to be superstitious about those types of events. Why?"

"If we were able to find the urn, would that not be valid proof that war is coming?"

Asentar nodded in agreement. "You are correct, Sir Num. I must travel to the city of Ergrauth to retrieve this."

Thorik reached out and shook the knight's hand. "I hope our paths pass again someday."

"If we don't cross paths again in life, the stories told of our triumphs will pass long after we are gone. For it is not how long you live, young Num, but what you have done to change the world in the time you were given."

Asentar mounted his faralope, waved farewell, and rode off down the street.

Thorik watched the Dovenar Knight ride around the corner as he wondered if they would truly ever meet again. "Grewen." He then glanced up at his friend.

"I'm assuming this is where we part ways as well. With Gluic gone, we must return home to Farbank."

Grewen smiled. "Nonsense, little man. I'll at least accompany you to the safety of the King's Valley before we say our farewells."

It warmed Thorik's heart to know he was not on his own to make the long trek. However, his thoughts quickly changed as he spotted Bryus walking down the street toward them.

Carrying a large pouch filled with items that bulged the fabric at its seams, Bryus was covered with mud up to his waist, and it appeared he had made no attempt to clean any of the clumps off. His sleeves from the elbow down were also coated with the brown soil. Despite that, the old man strolled down the street as though there was nothing out of the ordinary.

Brimmelle's face turned shades of red and his soul-markings darkened as he watched the Alchemist leave a trail of mud clumps down the street.

Thorik half laughed at the spectacle. "What happened to you?"

Bryus walked up to the group, handed Avanda his pouch, and then proceeded to shake his hands and sleeves clean of mud as the Nums covered their faces from the thick flying brown specks. "Nothing. Why do you ask?"

"Maybe because you look like you've been rolling around in the fields for the past week."

Bryus stared at Brimmelle instead of Thorik when he answered. "Why would I do something that insane? Can you think of any reason, Brimmelle?"

Thorik watched his uncle's face continue to turn a brighter red. "Why is he asking you, Uncle?"

"Yes." Bryus scooped mud from his side and tossed it onto the street. "Why would I be asking you?"

Brimmelle's response was cold and emotionless. "I don't know."

Bryus laughed at the response. "Hypocrite."

With tight lips, Brimmelle said nothing to his defense.

That wasn't going to stop Bryus. "What happened to your Rules of Order and sacred words to live by? Does that only apply when it's convenient for you or works in your favor?"

Avanda stepped forward and asked the obvious question, "What are you two talking about?"

Seeing Brimmelle stiffen at her question, Bryus stepped up next to the elder Num. Reaching over behind his head, he placed his arm over Brimmelle's shoulders before pulling him in tight against him. Mud slid down off of his sleeve onto Brimmelle's back, neck, and shoulders. "You see, Avanda, when people make promises to me while explaining how righteous they are, it annoys me. But when they go back on their promise and take it back away from me, then I get upset. And then when I notice them throwing it off a ramp into a muddy farm where it could take months to find, then I get outright vengeful."

Avanda looked at Fir Brimmelle for a response. "What did you do?"

"Yes." Bryus was overdramatic as he pulled him in tighter. "What did you do? Why don't you explain it to everyone?"

Mud continued to drip down Brimmelle's neck, under his shirt, and down his back. His clothes were stained with the brown mud, and Bryus made sure to wipe his boots off on the Fir's pants. "I made a promise which I realized I couldn't keep."

Moving his muddy hand off Brimmelle's shoulder, he placed it on top of the Num's head and wove his filthy fingers through his hair. "Yes, that is what happened."

To the surprise of the others, Brimmelle allowed the Alchemist to cake mud in his hair, as the Num steamed from the disrespectful and embarrassing event.

Brimmelle growled through his tight teeth and lips before speaking. "But the question is, did you find what you had lost?"

"I found mud, you fool. Endless rows of wet mud."

Bryus stepped away from the Num in order to scoop up a clump of mud from his leg before preparing to press it into Brimmelle's face.

Grewen had watched the scene with great interest, but the humor of it all was about to turn violent. Reaching down, he blocked the smashing of mud into the Fir's face. "Not here, boys. We will not bring violence into the home of Trewek."

"We're not done with this," Bryus snarled at Brimmelle as he took his large pouch back from Avanda.

"You are for now." Grewen grinned. "Our stay here is at an end. We'll pack our gear while you two clean up. As soon as you're ready, we'll head up the ramp and out of the city..." He paused and thought about it for a moment before continuing. "... after we eat one more meal."

Avanda laughed. "Always thinking with your stomach."

"Not always... Just when I'm awake." His baritone chuckle echoed down the street, leading their party forward.

＊ 21 ＊

ASSASSIN

With the city of Trewek behind them, the travelers walked west for days along the vegetative desert, which bordered the mountains to the north. Small flashes of red light flickered from the sparse tree- and brush-covered foothills. Always appearing as a single light near a hilltop, the red glow seemed to follow the travelers to the west.

"Do you see that?" Avanda asked Thorik.

"Yes, I've seen it several times since we left Trewek."

"What do you suppose it is?"

Attempting to see farther, Thorik squinted without any luck. "I don't know. I think someone might be following us."

Avanda followed his lead and squinted at the distant light. "Do you think so? Could it be one of those assassins Asentar told you about?"

"Possibly, but they are traveling in a very difficult way. It appears they are climbing up and down those sharp ridges in order to go from peak to peak."

The two Nums continued to watch the light until it faded from one location, only to show up at a distant hilltop moments later.

Avanda shook her head in disbelief. "How are they doing that?"

Waving the mognin forward, Thorik kept his eyes on the distant red glow. "Grewen?"

Slapping his huge bare feet onto the scorching desert floor, Grewen was enjoying the walk. "What do you see, little man?"

"It's a light up on the foothills that seems to jump from peak to peak in only a few moments. But I never see it leap. Instead, the light fades and then reappears at the next location. We're being followed, although I don't know what it could be."

Grewen glanced out toward the mountains. "A dragon? It could be flying from foothill to foothill and then give off a fiery blast upon the crest of each."

Thorik agreed with the logic. "Scout? Or is it spying on us?"

"It's more likely to be a scout, seeing that we have nothing to do with the pending war. And even if we did, Del'Unday are more likely to attack us and get it over with instead of watching us from a distance."

The flame faded as they all watched and waited for it to reappear. But this time it did not.

"Odd." Avanda kept searching the distant landscape. "It's as though it knew we were talking about it, so it stopped following us."

Brimmelle showed little interest as he walked past them to the west. "Coincidence," was his only comment.

The other Nums followed Brimmelle as they continued to peer off to the side to see the red glow again. Their interest quickly died off as the foothills showed no signs of life.

Bryus followed Grewen, who was following the Nums through the desert as it slowly became littered with cacti, short desert trees, aloe plants, and jagged rock outcroppings. Wind had carved horizontal designs and holes into the unearthed large rocks. Even with a slight breeze, the holes caused an eerie whistling sound.

"Do you hear that?" Thorik turned his head to hear it better.

Avanda stopped to listen to the wind flowing through the holes in the rocks. "I think it sounds nice."

"No, not the wind." Thorik motioned his hand for everyone to stop moving. This worked for everyone except Brimmelle, who continued to lead them home as he walked around the next outcropping. Thorik waited for his uncle's footsteps to fade off so he could listen for the sound once again. "I thought I heard a rustling from an animal or something."

Grewen thought little it. "These parts are covered with snakes, scorpions, and rodents."

Shaking his head, Thorik didn't accept the explanation. "It sounded bigger than any of those."

Grewen's tiny ears couldn't hear anything moving. "How big would you say it sounded like?"

"I'd say the size of a man," Thorik answered as a man in black clothing stepped out from behind the rocks where Thorik had heard the sounds.

"Thorik Dain?" the uninvited guest asked.

Thorik immediately felt intimidated by the stranger's knowledge of who he was, but also by the weapons he carried. "Who wants to know?"

Sliding two thin, short swords from their sheaths, the man spoke in a bitter tone. "The Matriarch. She has a score to settle with you."

Thorik slowly stepped backward. "I've never met her. You must be mistaken. What is my crime?" Contradictory to his own words, he knew that escaping the Southwind Mines would eventually catch up with him. In addition, the Dovenar Knight had warned him about the Matriarch's assassins.

"Crime?" the man said. "I could not care less. The Matriarch ordered your capture. That is enough for me."

Glancing over the man's shoulder, Thorik searched for the man's ride. "You should know that we have seen you following us for days. We've had time to prepare for your attack. And, as expected, you've fallen into our trap." Thorik stood up straight and firm, hoping to bluff his way out of the confrontation. "I will give you only but a moment to turn and leave on the dragon you flew in on before we release our plans."

"Dragon?" The man chuckled at Thorik, causing the Num's square shoulders to soften. "I know not of who you have been watching, but I travel by land, which is how I plan to return with you." Stepping forward, he raised the tips of his swords toward Thorik in order to caution the Num from any unexpected movement.

Not his dragon? Thorik's demeanor sank as he questioned what he saw. Is there a second assassin tracking us?

"Leave us alone!" Avanda valiantly jumped in front of Thorik. "We won't allow you to harm him."

Now, with both of his blades near the female Num's face, the assassin grinned. "Extra casualties are not a concern of mine."

Her eyes watched the sharp points of the swords circle her nose and lightly touch against her cheek. Swallowing hard, she realized that her move may have not been her best option to help Thorik.

Grewen stepped closer to the Nums to intimidate the assassin with his massive size. But the act only caused the man to bolt forward, push Avanda to the ground, and then grab Thorik. In the same motion, he swung himself behind the Num and placed one of his sharp iron blades on the Num's neck and the other near his gut. The man was incredibly quick.

Avanda shot back up, only to see the blade pull tight against Thorik's skin as she approached.

"Stay back," Thorik told her to prolong his life long enough to find a way out of the situation.

She did as he asked, but it wasn't easy. Her instincts told her to lunge forward and knock the man on his backside. Nevertheless, she followed Thorik's instructions.

Bryus looked the man over, only to find nothing intriguing about his attire or weapons. The risk of losing Thorik from the party actually resolved the issue of the missing dagger secret, plus it provided an opportunity for him to retrieve the Spear of Rummon. Therefore, Bryus stood idly by to see what would unfold.

Vowing not to harm others, Grewen had only hoped to scare off the intruder. Instead, he had escalated the issue. This vow had often put him at a disadvantage, for a quick bit of violence from a giant his size could easily change the outcome. One advantage Grewen had was his height, and with it he could see Brimmelle working his way back around the outcroppings toward Thorik and the assassin. Grewen needed to keep the man's focus away from Brimmelle's path long enough for the Fir to show up and grab him from behind, assuming he had the courage.

"Do you plan on killing all of us?" Grewen asked the assassin.

"If you choose to protect Thorik. However, the Matriarch's purse of gold is awaiting only one head, and apparently I was the first to find you, so it will belong to me."

Grewen's eyes focused on the man, even though he was tempted to glance behind him at Brimmelle's approach. "Are there more coins for your purse if you should bring him back alive?" His voice was loud enough that the Fir should have been able to hear the conversation.

"There are, which is why I've allowed him to live this long. But if any of you try to stop me, I will gladly accept fewer coins for his dead carcass."

Grewen patiently waited for Brimmelle to jump out from the outcropping and tackle the assassin, but he hadn't seen any movement out of the corner of his eye. Raising his voice, he again tried to tell Brimmelle what was about to happen if he didn't act quickly. "So what you're telling us is that you're going to kill Thorik right here in front of us... right now?"

Darting his eyes between Avanda, Bryus, and Grewen, the assassin thought it was odd that the only one showing any interest in saving Thorik was the female Num.

"If you'd like to watch." An evil little grin rose from one side of his face.

It was at that time that Brimmelle finally jumped out from behind the large rock and grabbed the assassin from the back. The act nearly caused one of the blades to slice Thorik's head off, leaving a long cut along the side of his neck to remind him of just how lucky he was.

All three fell to the ground and rolled toward Bryus. Brimmelle clung to the man's back as Thorik turned to face the assassin and grab the man's wrists. Thorik's arms strained and shook in an effort to push back the sharp iron blades from piercing his face.

Avanda never thought twice as she ran over to help subdue the assassin, but she found it difficult to reach him since she was sandwiched between the two other Nums. This issue didn't stop her from trying. Collecting a hand-sized rock, she grasped it as a weapon and began swinging it. Unfortunately, most of her attacks hit Thorik and Brimmelle by mistake.

The three continued to wrestle as Bryus stepped closer and watched with concern. "Watch out for the spear! It's irreplaceable!" As he tried to avoid Avanda's wild swings with her rock, he attempted to pull the spear out from behind Thorik, but the incessant rolling prevented him getting proper access to it. "Brimmelle, hold him still!" he yelled as he made another unsuccessful attempt to grab the spear.

Grewen had stepped over to the chaotic mess of flailing body parts fighting for dominance. Wishing to pull the assassin off Thorik, the mognin realized he would have to peel away Bryus, Avanda, and Brimmelle first. It wasn't an easy task to do while trying to avoid injuring them.

Wrapping his three fingers around Avanda's waist with one of his mighty dual-thumbed hands, he pulled her out of the mix.

She responded with one last attack on the assassin as she threw her rock at his head. This, of course, hit Brimmelle square in the back.

Setting her off to the side, Grewen grabbed Brimmelle with his left hand while moving the Alchemist away with his forearm. His other mighty hand swung forward to scoop up the assassin. Before he could do so, however, Avanda jumped back toward the fight, causing the giant to reach out and stop her. Inadvertently, this allowed the assassin time to make an attempt on Thorik's life.

Rolling Thorik onto his front, the assassin swiftly pulled his sword over his head to make a fatal cut into the Num's back.

Eyeing the Spear of Rummon as it sat in jeopardy of being damaged during the attack, Bryus lunged forward to push the assassin off of Thorik as the hired killer swung downward.

It was too late for Grewen to stop the motion, too fast for Avanda to conjure a spell to disable him, and too close for Brimmelle to not visually remember this tragic end to his sister's son with his non-forgiving memory. It would assuredly play in his mind every day for the rest of his life.

Just as the sharp blade began to puncture the Num's skin, the unthinkable happened. Bursting out of the ground, a crusted-over molten mass flew up, striking the assassin in his torso and arms. The heat from the object instantaneously vaporized his flesh upon impact as it arched over Thorik's body. The assassin hadn't even had time to scream before he was devoured by the heated rock.

The trajectory over Thorik led the molten rock through the assassin as well as one of Bryus' arms. Falling to the same fate, the Alchemist's right arm dissolved into steam and liquid from the flying mass. The nerves and arteries were instantly cauterized, and Bryus' mind had yet to comprehend the pain as he tried to jump out of the way.

Landing and then rolling to a stop, the heated mass paused for a moment. As it did, Thorik and his party watched as the spherical magma-filled-mass opened its enormous mouth, spewing inferno-temperature heat as it surveyed the damage it had done. Long, thin teeth extended from the outside as well as the inside of its mouth, as the red fiery blaze inside dried the surrounding air. Its underbite allowed an enormous amount of heat to escape his mouth even when it was shut, causing the view of him to look blurred through the vapors.

"It's you!" Thorik attempted to block most of the heat from his face. The Num was only shocked and not seriously harmed.

Upon that one comment, the mass lowered itself into the solid rock below, leaving a black scorch mark on the desert floor. It departed as quickly as it had appeared, taking the heat along with it.

"What was that?" Bryus asked as he stood in awe from the experience, having one less arm than he had a few seconds prior.

"Bryus!" Avanda shouted as she stared at the stub of an arm remaining. "Your arm is gone!" She rushed to his side to help, but once there, she realized there was nothing to do.

The Alchemist looked down at his missing limb. "Damn!" The pain from the unexpected amputation began to overpower him. Falling to his knees from the wave of agony, he started giving Avanda instructions to help him reduce the pain. His words were hard to understand as he tightened up his jaw from the horrific sensations he was now feeling from the remaining stub of his arm.

Avanda quickly grabbed the needed components and followed his instructions. Slicing off a leaf from a local aloe plant, she collected an iron bowl from his pouch. "Bryus, where did you get these things?" She looked into his pouch filled with an hourglass, empty jars, blades, and metal plates, just to name a few of the items.

"Who cares!" he screamed. "I got them at Trewek, if it hastens your pace!"

Avanda ignored the items and quickly mixed the plant's juices with some pollen that they had collected earlier on their journey, per his instructions. She then quickly began applying paste mixture to the burnt flesh on the end of his remaining arm, just below the shoulder.

"Awww!" Bryus screamed as she applied it, causing her to stop. "Don't stop! It will be worse for a moment, but then it will quickly subside."

She did as she was told and continued to apply the aloe juice as he yelled from the liquid's touch. However, within moments, she could see the agony in his face quickly drop, and he began breathing normally again. Avanda sighed. "Bryus, your arm is gone. What are we going to do?"

With the pain reduced to a tolerable level, the Alchemist looked at his now stub of an arm. "Actually, my arm has been gone for years. The one I just lost wasn't mine to begin with, and it surely wasn't the best one I've had." A clenched teeth light-hearted chuckle over his obvious pain showed he was fighting his way through it.

"Not yours?"

"It once belonged to a blacksmith from Spiritwater." He glanced over at his still intact arm. "Why couldn't that beast have taken the one I retrieved from River's Edge?"

Brimmelle had finished dusting himself off from the fight as he watched Avanda and Bryus. "Your arm is missing, and you're upset about which one it is?"

"I'm not missing my arm. It was destroyed," he spit back as a facial tic pulled hard on his cheek. The aloe continued to reduce the pain, but Bryus' temper was starting to show through as he began to fully rationalize that he had lost a body appendage. "If I was missing my arm, then we'd all be walking around looking for it. Or I'd be having sentimental memories about it, causing me to miss it. The arm is gone, and now I need to look for a new one again."

Avanda tilted her head at his last statement. "Again?"

"Alchemy is a very dangerous profession, my dear." He stood back up and readjusted his balance, now that he was missing a limb. "You'll learn that the only way to succeed is to try, and sometimes that means causing a few painful attempts until you get it right."

Brimmelle coughed. "She's had plenty of painful attempts, for sure."

"It hasn't been that bad. I just need practice and guidance."

"Guidance?" Fir Brimmelle pointed at Bryus, who was looking for objects to temporarily replace his arm until he located a new human one. "You want to take guidance from a man who has blown both of his arms off?"

Bryus spoke up without looking toward the Nums. "Not true. I only blew one arm off twice. The other one was eaten away." Bryus shivered at the memory. "Nasty story."

A sickly look crossed Brimmelle's face at the thought.

Avanda, on the other hand, was intrigued. "How do you put on a new arm?"

Bryus picked up one of Thorik's cooking spoons and held it up to his stub to see how it looked, but he wasn't impressed, so he tossed it back down. "The same way you put on a new leg or eye."

"A new eye?"

Swiveling abruptly toward her, Bryus pointed at his eyes, one blue and the other one green. "You don't think these are my originals, do you? I lost my first one while casting a spell to achieve my mastery of enchantment."

"I'm sorry it didn't go well."

"What are you talking about? The spell went perfectly. In fact, I received special commendations for ingenuity."

❧ 22 ❧

PRATTLE BOX

After ensuring Bryus was going to live, Thorik and Grewen approached the scorched circle of earth left by the molten rock creature. Tenderly stepping out onto it, the area under the toe of Thorik's boot cracked and sank down an inch. It was unstable, much like how Thorik felt at the moment.

They both stood there and stared at the ground for several minutes before Grewen broke the silence. "Do you know what that was?"

Thorik had been holding his hand to his neck in an effort to stop the bleeding from minor cut caused by the assassin's blade. He also favored one leg because of the injury during the ordeal. "Yes, I've seen it before in Della Estovia. It's most likely the red light that we've been seeing following us."

"I see, our assumed dragon following us from distant hilltops is really a glob of lava," Grewen said.

Thorik corrected him. "Grub."

"A grub of lava?"

"No, Grub. I think it's the creature's name."

"You've met it?"

"It's Bakalor's son. He was born while we were trying to escape." Thorik rubbed his fingers against his forehead. "It's difficult to recall the details. It happened so fast."

Bryus continued walking around the area to find a temporary arm which would last him until he found a live donor. Meanwhile, Avanda bandaged Brimmelle's cuts from his confrontation with the assassin.

Grewen pushed one of his toes down onto the location of Grub's exit, only to find the ground brittle. The pressure broke off shards of glass-like fragments for several inches deep. "Why would Grub be following us, and why would he be saving your life?"

"Saving my life? He nearly killed me," Thorik replied.

"No. It was an obvious attack on the assassin. Bryus happened to be in the way. And once you showed signs of being alive, he vanished."

Thorik hadn't even considered the idea. "I have no explanation."

"Thorik, did you make some type of pact with Bakalor to save the lives of Avanda and yourself?"

"What? Why would you say that?"

"Well, I don't know anyone who has ever escaped from Della Estovia, yet you did without any powers of an E'rudite or an Alchemist. And then, when your life was threatened, one of Bakalor's servants shows up and saves you. It's a question that needs to be asked."

Thorik was shocked. "Grewen, how can you imply such things, after what we've been through?"

"I'm not implying anything." The mognin grinned. "It's a fair question, which you are now avoiding."

"Avoiding? I'm not avoiding anything."

Grewen's response was light-hearted and slow. "Then answer the question."

"I shouldn't have to. You're my friend. You should trust me."

"I never said I didn't. It's only a question, Thorik. You're reading too much into it."

"If you must know, we didn't make any pact with Bakalor, nor Irluk. I have no idea why they let us go or why they have Grub following us. I can't for the life of me understand why they would protect me. I'm no one special. I have no way to help them, even if I wanted to."

"How about if you didn't want to help them?"

"What?"

"What if you're correct and they don't expect you to help them?"

"Then they are fools to let us go."

"No. Think about this. What can you do that others cannot?"

"Activate my Runestones?"

"That's good. Anything else unique that you do that most others don't?"

"I record our travels in my coffer...or prattle box." He quickly corrected himself.

The term caught Grewen's attention. "Prattle box?"

"Yes, that's what Bryus said it was. He informed me that he gave a set to the king's twins."

"Ambrosius and Tarosius?" Grewen asked. "I would assume he would have given it to them before Tarosius changed his name to Darkmere."

"I don't know. Are those the only twins in the king's line?"

"As far as I know," Grewen answered after a moment of thought. "Is your coffer similar to the ones he gave them, or is this actually one of them? Does it have any magical abilities? How did you acquire it in the first place?"

"Slow down. I have no knowledge of any magic it may have. Years ago, a stranger to Farbank gave it to me during his visit. His name was Su'I Sorat."

Grewen looked up from the Num to the Alchemist who was tugging on a limb from a short, dead desert tree. "Bryus?"

"Not now." The man tried to snap off the trunk of the tree with his one arm. "I'm busy."

Grewen approached the Alchemist, reached down, and snapped the base of the stiff plant from its root system. "There. Now do you have time?"

"No." Bryus' candid responses often came off arrogant. "Break off all the side limbs so it's a single stick."

Grewen complied by snapping the limbs off a handful at a time.

"Be careful!" Bryus shouted. "That's my future arm you're recklessly ripping apart."

Grewen grinned at the statement as he continued trimming.

"A little more off from that side," Bryus instructed. "No, you fool. Leave that one alone. Take off the one next to it. I don't want to look like a freak with an odd curled limb at the end of my arm."

"Sorry. What was I thinking?" Grewen spoke with a straight face but in a humorous tone.

"Apparently you weren't."

"Here." Grewen handed the modified tree trunk to the spellcaster. "Now, we'd like to ask you about something you told Thorik, regarding a prattle box."

Bryus pushed the end of the thick stick up against his stub of an arm. The width of the stick was perfect, but it was made for the length of a mognin's arm as it dragged on the ground eight feet in front of him. "Hey, you big buffoon. Do you see an issue here?"

Grewen chuckled at the sight. "No, is there a problem?"

"Perhaps not, if I wanted to use my arm to plow a field! Listen, baby-ears, if you want my help on something, I suggest you shave a few feet of trunk off my arm."

Grewen began doing just that as Thorik arrived with his coffer. "I hear you gave the king's twins prattle boxes," Grewen said.

"Smooth out the base," he instructed the giant. "Yes. So?"

"Are prattle boxes common?" Thorik asked, hoping he would say no.

"They once were, but you don't see them much anymore."

"How about this one?" The Num held up his coffer.

Bryus reached for the wooden box with his right arm, only to recall not having a right arm. His left hand did a much better job in taking it. Opening it, he dumped the contents onto the ground before looking inside. "Ah, yes, here it is."

Grewen set the wooden arm near Bryus as he waited to hear his assessment.

"Here what is?" Thorik frantically picked up his papers and writing utensils from the desert floor.

"This is one of the prattle boxes I made for Ambrosius and Darkmere."

"This is one of those boxes? Are you sure?"

Pointing inside, at the base of the box, he noted his name carved into the base.

"Um," Thorik mumbled. "No, this says Suyrb."

Bryus chuckled. "I know. It's an old game, but you know how tradition plays a role in games."

"What are you talking about?"

"Surely you know. It's the same for prattle boxes as it is for prattle bottles or prattle clay pots."

Grewen and Thorik looked at each other with confused faces before they both replied, "No."

"Alchemists have used prattle devices forever. I just thought it would be fun for the twins to each have a prattle box. It's all fun, you know."

"What's fun?"

"Writing a little note and tossing it inside."

"Yes, and then what?"

"Then the person with the other prattle box opens it up and the words flow onto their paper. That way, when the twins were separated, they could write back and forth from anywhere."

"So anything I write will be available to be read from any other prattle box?"

"No, of course not, only from its mate. They are made from the same material, and the spell is cast on both at the same time."

"It's always two at a time?"

"Well, doing one by itself seems pointless."

"What I meant was, are there some prattle boxes with three?"

"Perhaps, but I only made two of these."

"But again," Thorik was still confused, "it doesn't say your name."

"Sure it does. You see, the original inventor of the prattle spells signed his name backward as a joke so others wouldn't know who created it. Ever since then, it has been a tradition to do so. Call it an inside joke."

Thorik looked at the name carved inside the box. "Suyrb is Bryus backwards."

"You're a genius. How did you figure that out on your own?" the Alchemist sarcastically mocked.

Thorik had learned to ignore Bryus' patronizing tone. It was somewhere on the border of lighthearted teasing and condescending truth. Thorik brushed it off like normal. "Where is the other one?"

"How would I know? It was a child's toy. Most toys are destroyed or lost by the time their owners grow up."

"But what if someone has the other one, such as Ambrosius or Darkmere?" Thorik asked, now concerned about someone reading all of his logs.

Without any passion in his voice, Bryus told it like it was. "Then you have been telling them everything we've been doing: where we are going, when we expect to be places, and what we have done."

Thoughts rushed into Thorik's mind of all the information he had recorded since they had left Farbank. "It would make sense if it was Darkmere. That's how he's known how to always stay one step ahead of us."

Grewen agreed, but he gave another point of view. "Or perhaps Ambrosius has the other one, and Bakalor and Irluk are hoping you will call him into their trap. Maybe that is why Grub is following us, to keep you alive long enough to lure Ambrosius to you."

"How would we know?" Thorik asked. "Bryus, are there any markings on these to say which one you gave to whom?"

"Are you serious? I gave them to the king as toys for his children. Did I not already say this?"

Frustrated with himself over the information he had written down and placed in his coffer, Thorik wondered what to do with the wooden box going forward. "If I write something to bring Ambrosius out into the open, and he does, then we fall into Bakalor's trap. But if Darkmere has the other box, then we've alerted him that Ambrosius is still alive."

Grewen added an additional scenario. "You're also under the assumption that the other box still exists and that it is being used by someone."

Thorik nodded. "There's only one way to find out."

❦ 23 ❦

AVANDA'S MAGIC

Thorik's Log: 23rd day of the 7th month of the 650th year.

An assassination attempt has been made upon my life, and my understanding is there will be more. The Southwind Matriarch has ordered my death for crimes against her. I was lucky to survive this first attempt with only minor injuries, but Bryus lost an entire arm. I fear that we will not make it past the Squalid Waters as we seek safety beyond them in the Chuttle Fields. The next four nights will be sleepless until we pass this waterway. It's imperative that we survive, for I must deliver critical knowledge, which I obtained from Della Estovia, to Ambrosius. All will be lost if this information falls into the wrong hands.

The stage was set. Whoever would meet them at the Squalid Waters would be the one owning the twin to Thorik's prattle box. However, there were still assumptions being made, such as if they would take the bait, or if they could arrive within the time given.

If no one arrived at the destination, nothing would be learned. The other prattle box could be lost or destroyed just as easily as it may not be opened and checked within the next few days. This scenario would be the worst case, for it left all questions still open.

∿

THE TRAVELERS HAD SET up camp within the rocky terrain to minimize the exposure of their campfire. As usual, Grewen collected the brush and limbs, Brimmelle stoked the fire, and Thorik set up the camp and beds. Avanda tended to spend the evenings with Bryus to learn as much magic as he could teach her.

"Hold still," Avanda said to Bryus. Her attempt to attach the arm-sized tree trunk onto the stub of his arm was not going well.

"You're still not pronouncing the words right," Bryus complained as he tried to keep the stub of his arm lined up with the moving trunk. "If you cast that spell while my arm isn't lined up, you're going to cause it to be lodged in my chest."

She balanced the new wooden arm on her shoulder, but the trunk swayed from side to side and up and down as she tried to keep up with Bryus' own corrections. "I'm going to lodge it into your chest without the use of any spell if you don't stop fussing!" Her words were firm but without anger.

With one arm steadying the thin trunk, Avanda grabbed the stump of his arm and forced the two up against each other. "There! Now, what's next?"

"I've told you three times already." Bryus reached up to cut a handful of hair from the side of his head, but despite the blade's sharpness, he simply couldn't cut it with one hand. "I don't know why you're making this so difficult. Both my wife and daughter have performed this spell on me many times with ease."

Avanda's arms and back were getting tired as she watched the old man attempt to cut off some of his hair to activate the spell. It was pointless. "Why didn't you tell me you needed some of your hair before we got your arm fit up?"

"Because you asked me to only give you one step at a time."

Grinning at the sight of Bryus wrestling with a blade in his hair, Avanda wondered how he ever became a master in Alchemy. "What else do we need besides the verbal commands and your hair?"

He looked at her with great confusion. His face twitched and his good arm lowered. "Are you daft? We'll need my new arm."

"I know that." She pinched the skin of his stub to emphasize her reaction to his ridiculous response. "I meant what else besides that?"

"Those are the only components."

To the relief of her back, she dropped the yard-long trunk on the ground, let go of his stub, grabbed the blade from his hand, and cut off a handful of hair from the side of his head. Tossing the blade to the side, she slapped the wad of hair in his hand before she picked up the trunk again and pressed it up against his stub.

"There." She thought for a moment before moving on. "Now, what do we do with the hair while I'm casting the spell?"

Impressed at her brashness, Bryus gave it away in his facial expressions. "Well, after we boil the hair for a while, we will—"

"Boil the hair?" Avanda interrupted.

"Well, of course. You always boil the hair to ensure it's pure for the joining of the arm, otherwise it may not take. Every third level student of magic knows that."

"How could I possibly know such a thing?"

Bryus' face twitched. "How do I know what you do and don't know?"

"Didn't you find it odd that we hadn't boiled up some of your hair prior to us lining up your new arm?"

"No. I assumed you would have already had some."

Avanda was perplexed as she dropped the tree trunk back to the ground. "And why would I have some of your boiled hair?"

"I have no idea. I wondered the same thing."

Not knowing how to respond, Avanda slapped her hands on the sides of her head and began shaking it as she talked to herself. "This is the person who's going to teach me magic? I'd be better off on my own."

He nodded. "You're probably right. But then again, how far are you going to get without even knowing about the basics of preparing your spell components?"

"Preparing? I've never had to prepare anything before casting spells."

With a smug look, he nodded again. "True. And how has that been working for you?"

Embarrassed by the obvious answer, she skirted the question. "We've done just fine with what I've taught myself."

"I'm glad to hear it. Then you won't be needing any of my help then."

Sighing, she knew this might be her only chance to learn the skills needed to cast spells that wouldn't cause Thorik and Brimmelle to run in fear. She grabbed the wad of hair out of his hand and headed over to the campfire to boil some water.

Bryus was quite pleased with himself as he watched her walk away. There was a satisfaction he received when he manipulated people into doing what he wanted without using any magic.

Sitting near the campfire, Grewen had taken a flaming limb out of the fire and began scrubbing the bottom of his feet, while Brimmelle took his usual nap before the evening meal.

Thorik had finished his camp chores and had begun working on something to eat. Pouring some of their water into one of his pans, he hoped to make a stew with the roots and fruit Grewen had collected from the desert plants.

Placing the pan over the fire, he looked down and noticed a grouping of small rocks in a smooth artistic pattern near his feet. It reminded him of his grand-mother. She had a tendency to make various designs in the sand with her collection of gems and stones.

While he was smiling at the thought of Gluic, Avanda walked up next to him and tossed a wad of hair into his pan. Thorik glanced up in disbelief. "What are you doing?"

Avanda crossed her arms and stared at the fire with a pout on her face. "I'm fixing Bryus' arm."

"You just wasted good water for our stew." Thorik looked into the pan to see if it could salvaged by picking the hair out.

"Leave it in there. It needs to boil for a while."

"What's a while?"

Avanda hadn't asked. "I don't know. Could be a few minutes to an hour. Bryus will have to let me know."

"An hour? That will boil off most of the water. We can't afford to waste it."

She shrugged, accepting his statement as fact. "We'll get more tomorrow."

"I don't know if you've noticed, but we are in a desert, and there aren't a lot of fresh streams handy."

She turned to look directly at him. Her face was serious and her hands were firm against her hips. "Bryus is missing an arm, Thorik. Don't you think that is a little more important than us eating tonight?"

Grewen's eyebrows raised as he looked up from tending to his feet. "Can we vote on this?"

Thorik glanced over at Bryus, who was reaching for things with a hand that no longer existed. "Avanda, do you think it's a good idea for you to be spending so much time with him?"

"Why not?" A frown grew upon her face. "He can teach me how to be a great Alchemist."

"And why would you want to do that?"

"Why wouldn't I? The ability to cast spells to help all of us has to be a good thing."

"Is it?"

"Yes," she answered quickly. "Just think, Thorik, what if I could wield the power to stop people from hurting us, such as that assassin?"

"Or like Lucian?" Thorik frowned with concern. "Is this your way of preventing someone like him from ever taking advantage of you again?"

"It sure wouldn't hurt. I would have cleaned the world of his scum, and no one would have missed him."

"Avanda, I know how hard that was on you, but learning magic won't erase the past."

"But it can prevent it from happening again in the future. The next time a stranger lays a hand on me, I'll be ready."

Thorik sighed. "Don't go down this path with the intent to harm those who threaten you."

Realizing that she was painting herself into a corner, she tried a different angle. "Learning magic is more than protecting myself. Think of it. What if I could cast spells that could ensure we had plenty of food to feed everyone in Farbank? We wouldn't have to spend all year fishing, hunting, and farming."

Looking sad about the idea, Thorik paused before he responded. "Then what are all the farmers, hunters, and fishermen going to do? What would be the point of the Harvest Festival if we didn't have to work hard in the first place?"

"They could just enjoy the festival instead of having to slave all year long to prepare for it."

"But that's part of the festival. It provides us with a time to feel good about all the hard work we've done."

"But what harm is there in making life easier?"

"None. But if people don't struggle to achieve, then they also don't appreciate what they have once they receive it. There's a personal satisfaction that comes along with overcoming hardships. Never giving up and forging ahead to accomplish your desires, regardless of the obstacles, is one of the most powerful feelings in the world. I would never want to give that up."

Again, she felt he was cornering her, so she turned the conversation in a new direction. "Yet you have done just that."

"What?"

"Are we heading back to Farbank?"

Thorik's shoulders drooped a bit. "You know we are."

"Well, we're heading back there because you gave up on Gluic."

Thorik's face turned red at the accusation. "I didn't give up on her. Brimmelle asked me to leave his mother at peace."

"She's at peace? Gluic is trapped in a dagger which is lost in the desert."

Thorik's throat tightened. He couldn't respond.

"Would you have left me in the desert?" she asked.

"No. Of course not."

"Then why did you leave her?"

His eyebrows pulled in tight. "I already told you."

"Because Brimmelle told you to." She wanted to confirm his reason.

Thorik nodded.

Avanda asked her questions casually and without malice. "What happened to 'regardless of the obstacles' in your lecture to me? It looks to me like your biggest obstacle is Fir Brimmelle, and you gave up instead of forging ahead."

Using his own words against him hurt. His heart tightened at the thought of abandoning his grandmother. She had helped him in so many ways, and he gave up on helping her without much of a fight. But every time he needed the courage to stand up and fight for his beliefs, visions of Bakalor flashed through his mind and caused him to lose his edge.

He turned and stared at the fire as he crucified himself for his actions. He had abandoned Gluic and he no longer possessed the courage to fight for her survival. How would he ever live with himself?

Avanda realized she had gone too far in her efforts to turn the issue away from herself. However, she stood by her comments, even though they could have been conveyed with less sharpness.

Standing behind him, she reached up and placed a soft hand on his back. "I'm sorry. I didn't mean to hurt you."

"No, you're right. I shouldn't have given up on her. Now it's too late."

Her hand slowly traced his spine up and down as they softly chatted. "I didn't think I would ever hear you say that anything was too late to be fixed."

Thorik drew in a deep breath in response to her comment. "We can't turn back now. We have to be at the Squalid Waters in a few days. Hopefully, Ambrosius will be waiting for us. He can help us find Granna."

"Avanda!" Bryus yelled from his side campfire.

Turning her head slightly, she responded. "Yes?"

"That should be long enough. Let's get this over with."

Turning back to Thorik, she ran her palm across his back one last time. "I've got to go."

"I know." His voice was soft and appreciative of her comfort.

Avanda collected a fork to scoop the hair out of the boiling water, but when she peered over the pot's rim, she was surprised to find a dozen roots floating in the water along with the hair.

Grewen noticed her displeasure. "What?" Giving her his wide grin, he hoped to soften her obvious issue with his actions. "I figured we could do both things at once. It's getting late, and I'm hungry."

Avanda glanced back at Bryus to make sure he hadn't seen anything before she quickly scooped out the majority of the hair. She didn't believe the roots would affect the spell. At least she hoped they wouldn't.

⁂ 24 ⁂

SQUALID WATERS

Two rivers merged into one at a city of filth and depression. The Fount River from the north and Hessik's Blood River from the east bordered the city of Corrock before joining. The northern river was fresh and drinkable, while the Hessik's Blood was stained red and caused illness upon consuming. Sewage from the city added disease and poisons, which would take over a hundred miles of river to clean out.

It was down this river where Thorik and his team had planned to cross. Nearing the only remaining bridge that still stood intact over the river, they slowed their pace as they watched for anyone emerging to meet them.

The bridge was many hours south of Corrock but still considered the property of the city. As the only safe crossing outside of the city's bridges, it had become a source of revenue for the city as it collected tolls from those who crossed. In addition, it allowed the Del'Unday to monitor all who traveled from the O'Sid Fields to the Volney Lake Valley.

Constructed of stone blocks, columns rose out of the water every dozen paces and arched up to a keystone. Long, thick timbers had been crudely placed along the row of wide columns to replace what had originally been built at the crossing. With the multitude of battles that had taken place in the area, it was surprising that the bridge was in as good a shape as it was.

Spanning over a half a mile long, the bridge included two-story guard towers on each side of the river, where guards were posted for taking tolls and protecting their land. The tops of the towers allowed for an easy view across the bridge to see if anyone was crossing.

Thorik looked up at Grewen with concern after spotting a blothrud standing on the tower closest to them. "Will he allow us to pass?"

The giant looked at the lone guard posted on the upper floor. "We won't know until we try."

"What if he doesn't?" Thorik asked.

"Then we will be forced to find another way across."

"Assuming they don't capture us and throw us in prison," Brimmelle grumbled.

Grewen grinned. "No such luck. Remember, Dels don't believe in prisons for criminals. The victim has the opportunity to retaliate with whatever force they feel necessary, or you will be tied up in public to have the locals decide your fate. Hopefully, if we pay the toll and quietly move on, this guard won't accuse us of any crimes."

"That's not their only option for crimes, you know," Bryus interrupted. "They've been known to hold your family responsible for your crimes against them. Blackmail is not against the law to the Del'Unday. In fact, it's an acceptable part of their culture."

Avanda kept an eye on the blothrud who was standing firm on top of the guard tower, watching the outsiders chat about their approach. "I think we're making him nervous. We should either approach or leave before he calls for assistance from the far tower."

She was correct. The blothrud stood like a statue, overlooking the eastern desert as the mognin, human, and three Nums stood just minutes from the crossing. Changing his grip on his long spear, the blothrud squinted his solid red eyes as he wondered why they had stopped.

Like most blothruds, the guard on the roof stood several heads taller than the average human, with thick wolf-like legs, muscular human arms and torso, and a head that resembled a hairless wolf crossed with a dragon. His attire was heavy and bulky to increase his size even further, while leaving open slots for his spikes to extend out of his skin from various locations on his back and arms. The metal helmet he wore had holes for his eyes and ears as well as studded leather strips running down his thick neck. The blothrud was in battle gear, making the simple guard shack seem more alarming than it should have been.

Bryus collected a few items from his small pack and began grinding them up in his hand. Once he had it massaged into a thin paste, he began plastering it all over his face, neck, and chest. "Shields my skin from the sun, as well as other things." He gave a wink to Avanda, who had watched him create it.

Even though Avanda had attached the tree trunk onto Bryus' arm, he continued to struggle with it. If all had gone right with the spell, he should have been able to control it and bend it by now. Instead, it was just a weight hanging from his shoulder. The spell had only been partially successful.

"There's only one way to find out what he will do." Thorik then started his walk toward the tower.

But before arriving, a second guard walked out from the first floor of the stone building. This one was a krupe, a two-legged human-size creature completely covered in thick, black, spiked armor. Krupes were the foot soldiers for the Del'Unday, obedient and silent.

In some way, the krupes made Thorik more nervous than the blothruds. At least he knew where he stood with the latter. Krupes never showed their faces or talked, so they were impossible to read.

Thorik approached cautiously. "Hello. We wish to cross."

The krupe stood silent as he watched the rest of the Num's group arrive.

"What is the toll for the bridge?" Thorik asked firmly, not showing any signs of being intimidated.

Again, the krupe was mute.

It was apparent that the creature was not going to talk, so Thorik decided to walk past him. He figured that he would enter the bridge without issue, or he would be stopped and then a toll would be discussed.

He was half right. The krupe's long spear sliced down inches in front of Thorik, stopping the Num in his tracks. But no instructions followed.

"Name your purpose," the blothrud guard said as he stepped out from the lower level of the tower. He had made his way down as the travelers had approached.

A shiver of fear ran up all the Nums' backs from the loud, rough voice. "Thorik Dain of Farbank." Thorik's voice was quick and in a higher pitch than he had intended to be.

The blothrud used his impressive size to walk up near the Nums and look down over his wolf-like snout at them. "I asked for your purpose, not your name."

Even though he had Grewen, Bryus, and the other Nums with him, Thorik felt extremely vulnerable and at a disadvantage. "We're traveling back home to Farbank."

Pushing his way through the group, the blothrud eyed each one to ensure each member had fear in their eyes. This was true until he found himself looking up into the eyes of Grewen, who was grinning at the posturing that so many Del'Unday do.

"Something amusing, Ov?" the blothrud said sharply.

Grewen knew all too well that a bad tempered blothrud could take down just about any foe, so he didn't wish to provoke him. "Just pleased to see that the Del'Unday are still the masters of intimidation and brutality."

Thorik closed his eyes at the comment, wishing he hadn't irritated the Del.

Lifting his shoulders back and his chest higher, the blothrud eyed the mognin hard. "We will always be the masters of such admirable traits." Grewen's comment had actually been a compliment to the Del'Unday, so the guard allowed the grin to go without ramifications.

Next, the guard eyed Bryus, who was busy scratching his skin where the flesh of his arm was attached to his wooden appendage. "You disrespect me by ignoring me?" the guard barked.

Bryus glanced up at him. "Listen, you sickly dog-faced mutant, right now my arm is more important to me than watching you boost your ego."

"Perhaps you will think differently after I rip your head off."

"Not likely," Bryus snapped back. "If you ripped my head off, I wouldn't be thinking anything, would I?"

"You would long enough to know you were defeated by the hands of a superior species, instead of a mutant."

"Nice retort. Did they teach that kind of misguided sense of importance in some arrogance lesson as a child?"

The blothrud's patience had run out. "Here's a lesson you should have learned a long time ago." His arm swung out at Bryus, clobbering the man square in the chest. The sound of cracking bones rang out.

Bryus was pushed back from the impact, but not as far as the others would have assumed.

The blothrud's fist had been destroyed upon the attack against the shield of magical lotion Bryus had applied earlier. Bones were snapped in half, and some were poking through the blothrud's skin. His fist was a mass of loose flesh instead of the weapon it had once been.

Howling in pain, the blothrud used his other hand to grab Bryus by his tree trunk arm in order to pull him close enough to bite his head off. Not an uncommon tactic for blothruds.

Bryus snapped his fingers and spoke a short phrase just prior to having his head encased in blothrud teeth. The spell which Bryus had cast was based on the beetle poison he had collected earlier in the desert. The snapping had released a spray into the air and into the face of the Del'Unday, causing extreme burning in his eyes and on the surrounding tissue as well as in his nasal cavities.

The blothrud reared back as the spray instantly blinded him. Swinging violently, he proceeded forward to attack Bryus, who had already calmly stepped off to the side. It wasn't long before the poisonous spray had made it to the blothrud's lungs, causing them to constrict and burn.

The blothrud coughed and struggled for air as he fell to his knees.

Bryus put his magical components away. "Brains will always win over brawn." His brazen attitude was apparent.

Avanda was in awe of his ability to take on such a powerful creature. In her mind, it validated the need to learn as much from this Alchemist as possible. He could teach her how to protect herself from all enemies.

Seeing the attack, the krupe lunged forward but was quickly stopped by one of Bryus' spells, which locked the creature into a frozen position before it crashed to the floor, stiff as a board.

"That's amazing!" She was visibly pleased.

Bryus, on the other hand, was disappointed. "That's not right. He should have gone up in flames. This new arm of mine is proving to be detrimental to my spells."

"Why did you have to do that?" Thorik shouted at Bryus while looking at the Del'Unday guards.

"Unfortunately, they won't die," Bryus responded. "In fact, they'll be healed in a matter of days. If my spells had worked properly, they would have been dust by now." Inspecting his wooden arm, he looked perplexed. "What went wrong?"

Thorik was visibly upset about his actions. "We could have made it past these guards without incident."

"He was a loud, pompous fool. I just taught him a lesson. No harm was done."

"No harm?"

"They're just a few stupid Dels. What's your issue?"

"One minute you're jumping all over the place with excitement about a rare insect or plant you found, and the next minute you're treating people like lesser beings."

"I treat people appropriately for what they deserve. Don't blame me if most are idiots."

"Why couldn't you have been respectful long enough to allow us to just pay our toll and move on?"

"Paying a toll on this bridge is ridiculous. They didn't even build the bridge. They use this as an opportunity to intimidate others and to collect finances for war. I have no interest in supporting either of them."

"I don't care if you have an interest in them. One of these days, your arrogance and personal interest are going to get someone killed, if you're not careful."

Bryus laughed. "Then be advised right now to stay out of my way while I'm helping you."

Thorik was frustrated and knew he wasn't getting through to the man. "I don't want your help!"

"Oh, yes, you do. You simply don't realize it."

"No, you aren't listening. You're making things worse for us. You treat us as fools and don't even try to get to know us and what we really need."

"I don't need to get to know you. Nums, humans, Del'Unday, Ov'Unday, you're all the same. You're all annoying. Most are unpredictable, savage, under-handed, and of false words. They talk of petty issues and fill their lives with menial work. However, enchanted items, such as the great Spear of Rummon you carry, are intriguing." Bryus' face lit up as he looked at the spear hanging on Thorik's back. "They are part of the larger scope which changes the world."

The unpleasant words bothered Thorik, even if he knew there were threads of truth in them. "You're entitled to your thoughts, but as long as you travel with us, you don't take action unless we menial people ask for it."

Bryus laughed again. "And you will eventually come asking."

＊ *25* ＊

THE CROSSING

Thorik led his followers onto the long bridge toward the distant bluffs just beyond the second tower. Sturdy and functional, the wide bridge had seen better days. Many armies had crossed here at some point since it had been built, and it appeared that some had actually fought directly on the bridge.

Avanda walked up front with Thorik and Bryus as she continued to question the Alchemist's knowledge of magic. She wanted to know everything that there was to learn about the subject.

Fidgeting with his wooden arm, the Alchemist continued to test the new limb with minor spells to no avail. "This arm is simply no good," he muttered to himself. "Why won't it take?"

Wanting to avoid the conversation about what went wrong with the spell used to attach his arm, Avanda changed the subject. "How did you know to cast a spell ahead of time to shield your chest from the blothrud?" she asked.

"It's a typical blothrud approach to issues. They strike out at anything that denies them what they want. It's usually respect." His tone was condescending and rubbed Thorik the wrong way.

"You don't have a lot of respect for most species." He had given up trying to be nice to the Alchemist.

Attempting to bend his wooden arm, Bryus realized that his spellcasting would be limited until he found himself a new arm to replace it. "That's not true at all. I find all species equally inept and annoying." He smiled, enjoying his own validation of thought.

It took Thorik a few seconds to accept what he thought he heard was really what was said. "How can you say that?"

"Simple, Num. It's easy to tell the truth when it's painfully obvious." Bryus smiled. He enjoyed a hardy disagreement with someone who stood up for themselves, and his respect had begun to grow for Thorik.

"Have you no admiration for the great accomplishments our people have made? The ability to create great cities, music, and art can't be dismissed."

"True, but they are few compared to the damage we have all done. The wars we have fought, the blood we have all spilled. We are like roaches that are slowly destroying the land. Your approval of great, beautiful cities is just another example of the destruction of nature. Music is played from instruments made only by the death of plants. We are all guilty of this. However, you wonder why I lack reverence for our own kind?"

Thorik responded quickly. "As much as I agree with you that war is usually counterproductive, using what the land provides to improve our lives doesn't seem wrong, as long as we only take what we need."

"But we don't follow that, do we? Unlike the Fesh'Unday, we take more than needed. We become greedy and careless." Bryus cleared his throat. "And because of this, I have more respect for Fesh'Unday than I do for the rest of us."

"And yet you marvel at objects of old."

"Without question, Num. You see, they don't create war or destroy resources. They can be utilized to do such things by us barbarians, but not by their own volition, for they are pure. Embedded into them are the raw powers that were used to create this land, untarnished by men, Dels, Ovs, or Nums. Good and evil do not apply to them. They are what they are, even if we label them as cursed, while others label them as a grand gift. Oh, we are a fickle lot, aren't we?"

"Although I do not share it, I can surely see your point, but you act as though these objects are more valuable than us."

Bryus nodded. "More valuable, and more trustworthy. I would easily give my life to prevent the destruction of Rummon's Spear, Varacon, or others with such a rich history and background."

"And yet," Thorik spoke slow and sharp, "you had no issue with us leaving Varacon in the desert, unprotected from the elements or future careless people who may stumble upon it."

Bryus stopped in his tracks, motionless and silent, staring forward instead of looking Thorik in the eye.

Turning to face the Alchemist, Thorik assumed there must be more to his statement than he had thought. "Do you care to explain why you left this enchanted dagger so easily?"

Bryus was staring at the bluff on the north side of the river. The grasslands, across the top of the bluff, broke away to layers of hard rock before leveling out in a dry flood plain next to the river. His eyes squinted while he focused on his thoughts. "I think there is someone waiting for us on the other side."

Thorik turned to verify. The prattle box had worked... but on whom?

26

RETURN OF THE E'RUDITE

Beyond the bridge and guard tower stood a cloaked man hunched over as he rested his weight on a wooden staff, while his left hand held his cloak tightly in front of him, keeping his identity concealed. He stood alone on the far side of the bridge, as though he had been waiting for hours for them to arrive.

A fully armored blothrud stood high on the second guard tower, watching the travelers cross the bridge. His muscles strained against the confines of the restrictive metal, leather uniform, and headgear. He was even more massive than the blothrud they had met at the first tower.

Standing on the end of the bridge were two krupes, one keeping a trained eye on the travelers and the other staring at the cloaked man beyond the bridge. Weapons in hand, they gave the impression that there would be trouble.

Cautiously, Thorik led his team toward the end of the bridge as one krupe kept his focus on them. The blothrud focused on the strangers as he modified his grip on the long, thin spear before him.

It was odd to Thorik that the man concealed his identity. If it was Ambrosius, why did he not just step forward and hold the Del'Unday at bay with his powers? Or had he lost some of his abilities in his fight for survival from being crushed in the Weirfortus Dam?

If it was Darkmere, why the façade? The Del'Unday from Corrock were at his disposal. Why not just allow the guards to capture the travelers and then step out of the tower for his attack?

Thorik's lips tightened as variations of these thoughts raced through his head. Why the charade?

Avanda walked alongside Thorik and noticed his pacing had changed as his body became tense. "What's the matter?"

"I don't know. I just feel like we're walking into a trap."

The feeling was spreading to the rest of the group. Something definitely felt amiss. Bryus was the only one not paying attention, as his focus was on repairing his wooden arm.

Stopping several yards short of the guard tower, Thorik scanned his environment one last time. From what he could feel, all eyes were on him to make the next move. Although he had never seen the actual eyes of a krupe and the helmet on the blothrud made it difficult to see its face, Thorik could sense their stares.

Avanda grabbed Thorik's hand and squeezed it tight.

He squeezed back to assure her that all would work out. But he had misunderstood her hand gesture.

Releasing and squeezing his grip several times, Avanda was alerting Thorik to a new threat, one they hadn't noticed yet. A subtle red flame appeared behind the cloaked man, up in the bluffs.

The tension in the air was thick as everyone waited for Thorik's next move.

Following Avanda's line of sight, Thorik instantly realized the pulsing light in the bluff was the lesser demon, Grub. He was here to attack Ambrosius. Thorik had played into Bakalor and Irluk's trap and had lured the E'rudite out from hiding and into danger.

Her voice stayed calm and soft. "He's here to attack Ambrosius."

Bryus finally looked away from his arm and noticed the man in the distance. "Ambrosius? Is that you?" he yelled.

Grub's light immediately vanished. The krupes quickly turned toward the cloaked man as the blothrud above them left his post and ran down the tower steps to join them.

The cloaked man removed his hood to show his face. And there stood the man Thorik had thought he had sent to his death so very long ago. His mahogany hair and beard covered his tanned face as he displayed his blue robes by tossing off the old cloak. Standing up straight, it was obvious that his arm and legs had been repaired since his battle with Darkmere.

Knowing that Grub would be attacking, Thorik raced forward to warn his old friend. "Watch out! It's a trap!" he screamed as he sped past the unsuspecting krupe guards.

His warning was just in time. Ambrosius leaped forward as the ground opened up and Grub shot out to hit him.

Thorik charged ahead, with the krupes on his heels. "Ambrosius! We're under attack! You've been set up."

Avanda ran behind the krupes as Brimmelle stood his ground on the bridge. "Avanda, get back here! You'll be killed!" he yelled. "Ambrosius can take care of himself."

Grewen made his way off the bridge to help but was slammed along the side by the blothrud, who had raced out of the tower to enter the battle. The impact knocked the mognin over and his bulky body hit hard onto the ground, stirring up a cloud of dust. The blothrud dropped his spear, fell to one knee, shook off the unexpected collision, and then bolted toward Ambrosius.

Bryus, standing near Brimmelle, pulled out several items from his pack and began casting a spell from the safe distance of the bridge. Brimmelle had seen enough spells go wrong that he instinctively moved back away from the Alchemist.

Meanwhile, Ambrosius and Grub were in a heated battle. The E'rudite held off the heat of the creature as it relentlessly attacked him. At one point, he literally caught the crusted-over glob of magma in his hands to prevent it from slamming into his face. He then used his powers to throw the creature high into the air over the bluffs.

Keeping his distance in front of the krupes, Thorik arrived to see Ambrosius' hands still smoking from his touch of the lesser demon. "Ambrosius!" the Num yelled as he tossed his body into his old friend for a strong hug. "I'm so glad you're alive. The Death Witch said—"

"Irluk? What does she have to do with this?" Ambrosius asked as he pushed Thorik back to look him in the eyes.

But there was no time to answer. Two krupes were arriving fast.

Reaching out with his right hand, Ambrosius used his powers to cause the ground at the two guards' feet to crumble away. With no time to react, one immediately fell and broke his neck on the far side. The other had enough momentum to launch himself over the hole, only to miss his footing and fall backwards into the deep pit. Krupes were sturdy front line attackers but had little talent for jumping and climbing.

Avanda arrived and made the leap over the crack in the ground with ease. "Ambrosius!" She quickly jumped into his arms.

Again, there was no time for a reunion. The blothrud had been on Avanda's heels and jumped over the hole without missing a stride. He was in a full attack run toward Ambrosius and had unsheathed his bastard sword for the pending brutal battle.

Raising his staff in his right hand, Ambrosius froze the air around the blothrud, causing the beast's lungs to restrict airflow. The blothrud grabbed his chest and tumbled to his side near the E'rudite's feet, stirring up dust from his crash.

"Thorik, tell me about Irluk," Ambrosius said quickly, knowing the blothrud would soon be back on his feet. "What does she have to do with this?"

"It's too late." Avanda watched a black mass of floating debris in the sky approach. Irluk was arriving to take Ambrosius once and for all.

"NO!" shouted Ambrosius. "What have you done?" he asked, looking directly at Thorik.

"I didn't know if you had the other prattle box."

Crashing out of the earth behind them, Grub flew into Ambrosius' back, knocking him forward toward the pit where the krupes had fallen.

Spinning around and using his powers, he held the magma creature at bay while screaming in pain from the fresh burns on his back.

Free of the E'rudite's powers, the blothrud rolled to his feet to return to his attack on Ambrosius.

Thorik grabbed the Spear of Rummon from his back and blocked the blothrud's path. "Get back!"

In one quick slap, the blothrud knocked the spear out of Thorik's hands and sent the weapon flying. He then quickly pushed the Num aside to make his attack on the E'rudite. Stepping forward, he thrust his sword into Ambrosius' arm.

The Death Witch slowly closed in on the battle, waiting for her revenge. "Grub, I want him alive. In pain, but alive. I will deal the final blow in front of Bakalor himself." Her airy voice sounded distant but clear.

Grub opened his mouth, displaying the fiery furnace within. The heat would have instantly killed any mortal, but this was an E'rudite. The lesser demon had hoped it would at least cause him to pass out from the pain.

Removing the thick blade from Ambrosius' arm, the blothrud kept as much distance from Grub as he could as he drove the metal tip of the weapon into the E'rudite's side.

Thorik returned to the battle with the Spear of Rummon in hand as he leaped into the pit and jammed the weapon into the back of the blothrud. "Leave him alone!"

The Del'Unday guard screamed in pain as he arched his back. The spear hadn't gone deep, but the essence of the dragon within it fought for his Num master and inflicted great pain on his victims. A mighty roar emanated from the spear, and the blothrud fell.

Thorik then turned the enchanted weapon to Grub. Wondering how it would affect a lesser demon, he had no other option but to plunge it into the creature if he had any hope of saving Ambrosius.

This time, there was no roar when Thorik stabbed Rummon into Grub. Instead, the spear shook uncontrollably, and Thorik could not hang on to the weapon as it violently thrashed about. Grub also began to vibrate and swirl recklessly. Heat blasted in every direction. The spear slapped against the ground and through the air as the two continued their fierce attack with one another.

Ambrosius was unconscious from the attack, so Thorik leaped on top of him in order to protect him from any more harm as Grub and Rummon fought to the death. "I'm sorry I pulled you into this." Thorik looked the man over.

The E'rudite's skin was swollen and blistered from Grub's attack. His right hand still firmly clenched the wooden staff, which Thorik had made for him so long ago. He noticed the Runestone of Health was proudly carved near the top of the now-blackened burnt wood. Thorik recalled the day near Kingsfoot when Emilen and he had originally etched Runestones into the staff.

The memory caused Thorik to jump up to his feet and race off to the blothrud, where he proceeded to steal the guard's wide bastard sword.

The Death Witch quickly approached, floating just feet from the ground.

With the guard's sword in hand, Thorik stepped back to the E'rudite and raised it over his head, positioned to plunge the blade straight down into the E'rudite's chest. "You want him dead, then you shall have him!" he yelled at Irluk. "But I will not allow you the satisfaction of bringing him to Della Estovia alive to be tortured."

Thorik drove the sword straight down into the unconscious man's chest, causing the E'rudite's body to jolt from the pain.

Both Avanda and Irluk screamed, "NO!" as they rushed forward to stop the attack on Ambrosius. But they were unable to prevent it in time, and the sharp tip penetrated his chest and wedged itself deep inside of him.

Avanda pushed Thorik out of the way and uprooted the sword before being shoved to the side by Irluk. She could see that the E'rudite was still alive but fading fast.

"Thorik, what have you done?" Avanda turned to fight off the Death Witch.

Thorik grabbed her from behind and pulled her away. "I did what I had to do."

Without warning, an explosion rocked the ground and stopped all conversations as pieces of pumice rained down on them. The sound of the Spear of Rummon dropping to the ground followed. Grub had been defeated.

The swirling charcoal debris that made up Irluk's body intensified at the scene. With a quick unsettling gaze at Thorik, she increased the speed of the debris that made up her body and robes. Accelerating, the debris spread out and began collecting the steaming rock fragments of Grub.

Once all the lesser demon's parts had joined her chaotic mix of spinning fragments, Irluk lowered herself onto the E'rudite before lifting him up into the air and away from the bridge, back toward Della Estovia. Her mission was finally complete, in spite of the fact that Thorik tried to take the honor of the last blow from her.

Avanda was furious at Thorik. "How could you do that?"

But an explanation would have to wait, as he noticed the blothrud guard standing back up. Thorik ran past the blothrud to collect the Spear of Rummon.

"Thorik, hurry!" Avanda yelled.

Thorik quickly wrapped a cloth around the enchanted spear's handle and picked it up. Smoke rose from the cloth as it singed against the heat of the metal remaining from its battle with Grub. Swiveling around, he expected to see the blothrud attacking Avanda. However, he was surprised to see the Del'Unday right behind him.

Slapping the spear out of his hands for a second time, the creature twice Thorik's size roared at him in anger. "Sec, don't you ever strike me with the damn spear again!"

The words struck a moment of fear into Thorik before he abruptly thought it odd that the blothrud knew his spiritual designation was that of Sec.

"Next time you do that, I'll break Rummon over your head!"

The voice was familiar. Could it be? "Santorray?" Thorik asked.

Removing his helmet, the blothrud displayed his true identity. It was, in fact, Thorik's dear friend.

27

A BLOTHRUD'S POINT
OF VIEW

Santorray pulled off the rest of his restrictive Corrockian guard uniform. Scars covered his body, and some scars, such as the angled one on his back, covered the entire length of his torso. Few areas were without wounds from swords, claw marks, arrows, dagger stabs, and countless other items. The freshest was, of course, the gash Thorik had given him with his spear.

Thorik put the Spear of Rummon in the holder of his backpack. "It's so good to see you." He couldn't help but give his friend a tight hug, even though the num was in the blothrud's way of tending to his own injury.

Grewen approached, limping from the earlier knock down by Santorray as the blothrud had raced out of the tower. "What just happened here? Did my eyes deceive me, or did Irluk finally gain Ambrosius' body?"

Avanda was still in shock. "How could either of you do this? Ambrosius is part of our family."

"True," Thorik said. "But Darkmere is not."

"Darkmere?"

"Yes, without question."

"How do you know?"

"I didn't at first, but then I noticed he was holding his staff with the wrong hand. But what gave it away was the staff. I carved a Runestone symbol into it myself, but it was the Portent Runestone, not the Runestone of Health. Darkmere wouldn't have noticed the subtle differences in the designs."

"And that is all you went on?"

"Yes." Pulling out some cloths to help bandage the blothrud, Thorik glanced up at Santorray. "How did you know?"

Santorray had been holding his palm over the bloody injury. "I was sent here by Ambrosius to meet you at the crossing. I replaced the prior guard with myself."

He gave a confident nod. "Just in case it was a trap. Obviously it was. Darkmere arrived at the same moment you did."

"But," Thorik began to ask as he tried to make sense of it all, "how did Ambrosius know that we would be here?"

"He's been following your logs."

Thorik pulled the wooden box from his pack. "Did he take the notes from a coffer such as this? Did it have this inscription on the base?"

Santorray worked on his wound and never looked over. "I never actually talked to Ambrosius. His messenger pigeon, Draq, arrived and notified me of Ambrosius' findings. I then rushed over here to meet you."

"Ambrosius must have the twin to this prattle box."

"He's been watching after you for a long time."

"You mean, even before we destroyed the Temple of Surod?" Thorik asked.

"Long before that. He sent Captain Dare down to save you from the Palm Islands, and I followed Ambrosius' instructions to help you find Ericc."

"You knew he was reading my logs all this time and never told me?"

"If you had found out that he was alive, there was a high likelihood of others finding out as well. He needed to heal before Darkmere and his minions started hunting him down again. He couldn't risk letting you know; therefore, I couldn't."

"But now you can? What changed?"

"Apparently you have already been telling others that Ambrosius lives. His secret is out."

Thorik felt slightly guilty for foiling the E'rudite's plan. "How did Darkmere know about us coming here if Ambrosius has the twin coffer?"

Santorray shook his head at the naïve Num. "You've been traveling in Corrockian territory for many days. Do you honestly think that no one would have spotted you and alerted him?"

"But how would he have known to meet us here at this specific bridge?"

"It's the only crossing of the river in these parts, unless you pass at Corrock itself. It's easily determined where you would be forced to cross. I made the same assumption myself. You're a predictable creature, Sec."

"If I'm so predictable, then how is it I was able to stab the mighty Santorray without him being prepared for it?"

"You're right. I should have assumed you would backstab me while I was saving your life." A smirk grew upon the blothrud's face after speaking.

Thorik apologized again for the misunderstanding.

Avanda still wasn't satisfied with their answers. "Why would Darkmere arrive disguised as Ambrosius?"

"Perhaps he was after information," Grewen speculated. "If he had wanted to kill us, he would have just sent a small troop of warriors to wipe us out. But this tactic smells like an attempt to gain our trust to find something out."

Thorik pulled the bandage tight around Santorray's waist. "Well then, he has succeeded."

Santorray sucked his stomach in slightly for the bandage to be tied off. "What do you mean?"

"The only information I have was obtained from Bakalor and Irluk," Thorik answered. "Darkmere will now have plenty of opportunities to ask them both questions once he arrives there."

Avanda looked back toward the bridge, but there was no sign of Brimmelle and Bryus, so she headed back to see where they had gone.

Grewen chuckled at the thought while looking at the recent battlefield. "I would love to see the faces on the Death Witch and Bakalor when they realize their prisoner is actually Darkmere."

Santorray considered the situation at hand. "If it were me, I'd come back to take my revenge. We should stay alert."

"Yes, but we are small ripples in the waves of this pending war," Thorik replied.

Grewen found the comment enlightening and entered his own comment. "You never know what ripples will be the final blow to dislodge a shoreline boulder."

Thorik rolled his eyes at the thought. "Trust me, they have more important issues at hand than to take revenge on a Num trying to travel home."

"Travel home?" Santorray jerked his head with surprise. "I thought you were going to the Govi Glade in order to save your grandmother."

The words took an emotional toll on Thorik. "I… well, I lost the dagger."

Santorray was stunned. "This is not the Sec I remember. You look older, but you are not acting wiser than the last time I traveled with you. You have given up on Gluic, just as you did with Ambrosius' son, Ericc."

"I haven't given up!" Thorik fired back.

"Then why aren't you out searching for it?"

"Because we had to be here in time."

"In time to what? To spring your trap? To see who had been reading your precious logs and notes?" Santorray's voice carried. "This was more important than finding your grandmother?"

"It's not that simple. Brimmelle asked me to leave his mother at peace."

"When did you start listening to him?"

"Hang on. When we traveled with you, you wanted to leave her behind in River's Edge, and then you ended up stabbing her. Why would you care about her?"

"I don't," Santorray barked back sharply. "It's your decision whether you try to save your grandmother. But an actual warrior would fight for what he believes in long before he would be concerned about himself or who was spying on him. A warrior stops at nothing to achieve what he wants. You fought for Gluic then. Why aren't you willing to fight Brimmelle for her now?"

"I don't know. Ever since Bakalor attacked us, it's been different. His curse upon me has softened my courage and made it difficult for me to stand up for myself and fight with confidence."

"That's an excuse!"

"No, it really happened. And I've never been the same since."

"I don't care if it's now harder to fight for what you believe in and what you desire! All that means is that you have to want it that much more. Your curse is an excuse to not have to try harder. It's a crutch that you flaunt in order to justify why you're not willing to do what it takes!"

"No, it's not. It truly has affected me."

"I never said it didn't affect you. It happened! It hurt you! Accept it and stop allowing this excuse from preventing you from getting what you want. Bakalor can't stop you from achieving your goals, only you can! If you want to save her, tell me you are going to turn around and find Gluic! Send Bakalor a message that you are victorious over his attempts to weaken you!"

"Santorray, I wouldn't even know where to start looking for Granna."

"That's Fesh talk!"

"No, it's not. It was somewhere between Lagona Falls and Trewek. That is an amazing amount of desert to search through."

"So, you're going to quit. Yes? Say it, Sec. Say that you are going to quit on your grandmother!"

"I can't just turn around and start marching back the way we came."

"Why not?"

"Because we've come so far."

"Then say it out loud. Say you're quitting on Gluic. At least be proud of your actions, like an actual warrior, regardless if they're right or wrong. Take a stand and make a move," Santorray yelled. "Tell me you're quitting on your grandmother. I want to hear it."

"I could give you a hundred reasons why I should leave her out there."

"There will always be a hundred excuses why not to struggle to accomplish something great. Greatness is only achieved when you follow your beliefs despite your reasons not to. So, tell me right now, are you going to quit on her, or are you going to find her?"

Thorik's voice was now nearly as loud as Santorray's as the two shouted back and forth. "Obviously, I want to find her."

"That's not an option! Either you are going to find her or you aren't."

"I could try for a year and still not find her."

"That's because you haven't decided beyond any doubt that you will find her."

"What?"

"A warrior determines the results they expect first, and only afterward do they determine how to achieve them. You, on the other hand, want to plan your way and hope it results in success. And because of that, every obstacle can potentially throw you off course. A warrior finds a way, regardless of what is thrown at them."

"Failure to plan usually results in failure of a goal," Thorik snapped back.

"But planning only comes after you determine exactly what you want to accomplish. You need a goal so firm and real that nothing will draw you off course. Once you have it burning down in the pit of your stomach, nothing can stop you from achieving it, plan or not. You must become a driven man to be a warrior."

Thorik felt the fire within him growing again. He had lost it ever since they had been in the underworld. His passion for what he wanted had been less than what it once was. But now, with Santorray's words, he was feeling empowered over his own life once again.

"Shout it out, Sec!" Santorray roared. "I am giving up on Gluic!"

"NO!" Thorik shouted back.

"You don't have the desire anymore. Give up!" He taunted the Num.

"I will not give in. I refuse to give up," Thorik screamed at the blothrud. "I will find my grandmother! And I will release her from Varacon!"

"I don't believe you!"

"I don't need you to. I'll find her with or without you!"

Santorray stepped back, as though a wave of energy from Thorik's words had pushed against him. Ambrosius had ordered Santorray to ensure that Thorik make his way to the Govi Glade. The blothrud had not only succeeded in changing the Num's course, but he had strengthened the Num's character. Pleased with his mission, he nodded approval. "And that, Sec, is what a warrior sounds like."

SEARCHING FOR BRIMMELLE AND BRYUS, Avanda arrived back at the tower at the base of the bridge spanning the Squalid Waters. The last time she had seen them was when Grub was spotted and she had chased Thorik into the battle. But now they were nowhere to be seen. "Bryus? Fir Brimmelle?" she called out.

She heard a distant complaining from Brimmelle.

"Brimmelle? Is that you?" she yelled.

"Down here!"

Peering over the edge of the bridge, she found the two missing members within the top of a tree. Bryus' arm had flourished into a robust tree, rooted in the water near the shore. His arm was at the top of the central trunk, locking him into an uncomfortable position as he hung from his shoulder at the peak of the tree.

Laughing at the sight, she struggled to keep a straight face at the scene. "What happened?"

Wedged between two large limbs, Brimmelle didn't find the humor in the situation. "Your friend used his magic. And we all know how that usually turns out."

Bryus glared at Avanda. "Are you sure you cast the spell correctly to attach my new arm?"

Avanda knew exactly what he meant. "You instructed me. You were there."

"True. How about the boiling of my hair? Was there any contamination during the boiling?"

Avanda wanted to avoid that specific step. "Why, what happened to you and Brimmelle?"

Bryus didn't allow her to change the subject. "By now, I should have some flexibility in the new arm, but I don't yet. I should have also started being able to feel sensations with it, but all it does is itch toward the upper end." Bryus was going step by step through every possibility where the error could have occurred. "I'm not sure what went wrong."

"Something always goes wrong," Brimmelle complained. "Avanda, have Grewen get over here and pull me out of this tree!" Brimmelle shouted.

Bryus grumbled to himself, "I've replaced limbs many times with splendid success." The Alchemist gave a nod of reassurance. "Even my daughter has performed this spell with no issues."

"What exactly happened here?" Avanda called down to them.

"Avanda! Go get help." Brimmelle ordered.

"I will." She replied as she waited for Bryus' answer to her question.

"I gave it plenty of time to adjust onto my arm," Bryus said to himself before glancing up at the female Num. "I simply cast a spell to root the wood deeper into my arm. But instead of rooting deeper into me, it pulled me off the bridge, rooted itself in the river, and then grew like crazy."

"And in doing so, he knocked me over with him," Brimmelle said. "Now go get us some help."

28

UNCOVERED

Alone tree stood in the Squalid Waters River near the shore and almost underneath the long bridge which spanned the waterway. Flower blossoms sprang to life on its branches as a giant mognin walked away from the beautiful tree and back toward the shoreline. Grewen carried Brimmelle and Bryus back to the base of the bluffs from this tree after snapping the Alchemist's arm off nearly a yard from his shoulder, giving him the same ugly wooden arm he had had prior to the incident.

With the day nearing its end, the travelers decided to utilize the guard tower as their shelter for the night. After removing the stench left from the krupes' beddings, Thorik lit a fire in the fireplace to cook dinner while Bryus cut off new leaves and branches that had grown on his wooden arm.

Thorik stoked the fire. "So what you're telling me is that, while we were fighting off Darkmere, you were casting a spell on your arm instead of utilizing those great powers of yours to help us?"

Bryus sat on a bench across the room from Thorik. "Yes, that's correct." He appeared to have no issue with his actions.

Thorik was baffled by the candor of his responses. "Did you not see the life or death situation we were in?"

"Oh, without question. I wasn't sure if you were going to survive or not on several occasions."

Thorik was awestruck by the lack of caring for his fellow men. Tossing another log into the fireplace, he continued his discussion with the Alchemist. "If you saw that I was in trouble, then why didn't you at least try to help?"

"Oh, no, I couldn't do that."

"And why is that?"

"Because you specifically told me not to, on the far side of the bridge."

"That was a unique situation." Thorik stepped back from the fire and paced around the room in frustration. "You obviously don't have any interest in helping us, so why are you traveling with us?"

"To take you to the Govi Glade."

Thorik was shocked. "Govi Glade?"

"Yes, you know, where the book of magic is. Vesik awaits." Bryus' smile beamed with intrigue.

"We're not heading to the Govi Glade."

"What? Why not?"

"Because we don't have need for Vesik if we don't have Gluic's dagger."

"Well, no one ever notified me that the plans had changed."

"How could they not change?"

"I don't see what one has to do with the other. Vesik is by far a better relic than the dagger, Varacon."

"But I don't need the book without the dagger."

"That's because you don't know of its powers. It can help us in ways you've never dreamed."

"Can it help us find Gluic?"

"Oh, I have no idea."

Thorik grimaced at the nonchalant attitude. It was driving him crazy. He simply couldn't continue the conversation and found himself sitting back next to the fireplace. Looking down near the burning logs, he noticed a few dozen small rocks placed in a swirling pattern near the fire.

Thorik looked around the room. It was only Bryus and himself. "Has anyone else been in here?"

"More than a few krupes, from the smell of it."

"No, I mean while we were talking?"

Bryus looked at Thorik as though the Num was losing his mind. "If we aren't heading to the Govi Glade, then I will depart tomorrow morning and go my own way."

Thorik leaned down and placed his hand near the small rocks. The air that hung over them was cold, in spite of being near the fire. "We will be going to the Govi Glade."

Bryus now knew the Num was losing his mind. "Collect your senses, Num! You just told me we weren't."

"No, I said we weren't heading there. We will search for Gluic first. Once we find her, then we will head there."

"But what if you don't find her?"

"That's not an option. We will find her." He was firm on this stance. "I'll start by calling out to her like I did once before. I think she is still following us."

Bryus was amused at the idea. "How do you plan to do that?"

Thorik grabbed the Runestones out of his backpack and pulled out the Runestone of Courage. Closing his eyes and opening his mind, he waited for the flow of energy to stream out of the stone, through his body, and then back into the stone.

Amazed by the sight before him, Bryus leaned forward with interest at the new arrival to the room.

By the time Thorik opened his eyes, a semi-translucent figure was forming next to him on the bench. Gluic had returned.

"Granna?" Thorik spoke softly. "Can you hear me?"

"Well, of course, dear. I listen to you every day."

"You do?"

"Yes. I've also had a chance to catch up with so many others that I've lost. It's been a delight."

Thorik smiled. Nothing ever bothered her. "Do you know what happened to you?"

"Surely. As a child, I grew up in Longfield. Then I moved to Farbank when—"

"No, I mean, do you know that the dagger, Varacon, has captured your essence?"

"Yes." She showed little interest. "I told you I would be changing. It's time for me to spread my wings and enjoy an existence with new heights and fewer limitations. I certainly can't do what I needed to do with my old, worn-out body."

"What is it you need to do?"

"Help free those who are forever captive."

"I don't understand."

"I know, dear. Sometimes I don't either." A shallow laugh followed her own comment.

"Granna, I need your help."

"No, you really don't. You've just become dependent upon it. It's an unfortunate fate we give to those we wish to protect."

"I'm not the leader you think I am. I'm constantly second guessing myself, and I don't have all the answers."

"All the answers? Leaders discover the answers. They don't presume to know it all. Leaders show up for the adventure instead of shying away from it or ignoring it all together," she said. "You'll do just fine as a leader. You don't need my help."

Thorik shook his head. "No, this is different. I need to find Varacon so I can free you from it."

"Oh, won't that be pleasant?"

"What? No. I don't know where the dagger is, and without it, I can't free you."

"But I feel free already. What's so wrong with this? We can still chat when you need to."

"It's not the same, Granna. I need to bring you back."

"Why is that, dear?"

The question surprised Thorik. "Because you are my grandmother, and I love you. I miss you terribly."

"Well, I miss you too, but we must let go at some point. Wasn't it nice while it lasted? I did so enjoy our outings."

"But it's not your time yet. Santorray stabbed you by mistake. You shouldn't have been killed."

"Mistakes will happen, dear. Did you know your mother is here? She is very proud of you."

"My mother? Where?" Thorik whipped his head around to spot her.

"Not in this tower. She has better taste than to be hanging around in these types of places."

Disappointed, he turned back to her. "But how do I find her? How do I talk to her?"

"You don't have to find her, but she hears you each time you speak. She waits for you back in Farbank with your father."

"They're both there?"

"I would assume so. They tend to stay in the village."

"So, how is it that you are not attached to the dagger?"

"Oh, I am, dear. I can only stray so far from it."

"But we are a long way from where I lost it in the desert."

"Dear child, I've been lost most of my life," she said with a grin. "You, on the other hand, are but a few feet from the dagger I reside in."

"What? How can that be?" Thorik asked, searching the room with his eyes.

"Go to the Govi Glade and obtain the book of spells. You will need it before your work here is done."

"Therefore, we were correct. There is a spell to release you."

Gluic smiled kindly at her grandson. "You, my dear, will release me, and we shall free those imprisoned." She then stood up from the bench, walked across the room, and stopped near the Alchemist. "Bryus is protecting Varacon for you."

Thorik's eyes grew large, and his jaw drifted down. "What?"

"Enjoy the journey, dear. That's what life is all about." Turning, she walked through the far wall. And with that, Gluic was gone.

The moment of silence afterward was filled with emotions from Thorik as he stared at Bryus.

The Alchemist had little emotion in his glance at Thorik, as though there was no issue at hand.

"Bryus, is this true? Have you had the dagger the entire time?"

"No. You and Brimmelle have both had it from time to time. In fact, Santorray actually had it prior to us, seeing that he activated the spell by stabbing her in the first place."

Thorik stood up and came closer to the sitting man. He struggled with being in shock and becoming outraged at the possibility of this treachery being done by people he had trusted. "Do you have the dagger, Varacon, in your belongings or on your person right now?"

"Now that is a completely different question. If you had asked me that the first time, we wouldn't have had to go through this series of unrelated comments."

"Yes or no!" Thorik shouted.

"Yes."

Thorik bit his lip in anger. "How could you steal her from me and make me think she was lost?"

"Again, that is a completely separate question. I did neither of those."

"You've already informed me you had the dagger."

"True. The rest you assumed."

"Assumed?" Thorik's cheeks flushed with emotion as his anger grew. "If it wasn't you that performed the other actions, then who did?"

Just then, Brimmelle walked into the tower, rubbing his hands together. "Do you have our meals ready?"

"YOU!" Thorik announced.

Brimmelle didn't know what he had walked into. "Me?"

"You stole the dagger from me and told me that I had lost it!" Thorik had fury in his voice that he himself didn't expect.

Brimmelle gazed a nasty stare at Bryus. "You had to tell him, didn't you? Did you also happen to tell him that you threatened to toss me over a cliff if I didn't give it to you?"

Thorik's view changed back to Bryus.

Bryus grinned. He obviously liked this game. "And by doing so, I saved the dagger from being lost forever. If I recall correctly, you were about to throw it over the Lagona Falls ridge."

Brimmelle didn't care any more about the secrecy. In fact, it felt good to get it all out in the open. "Which is why I stole it back from you at the Trewek pyramids. She deserved better than to have her fate in your hands."

"Is that why you tossed her down into the farmlands while entering Trewek? You'd rather have her lost in mounds of mud and manure?"

"Better there than to be with you," Brimmelle protested. "At least now she is at rest."

Bryus reached into his pack and pulled out Varacon. "Apparently not!"

With the horror at the thought, Brimmelle was momentarily speechless. "You found it?"

"What was your first clue?" Bryus asked with an overly theatrical curious expression.

"You lied to me. You told me you couldn't find it."

"You don't know how bad I feel about that." Sarcastic tones filled Bryus' speech.

"Stop it!" Thorik shouted as he reached over and snatched the dagger from Bryus. "I'm furious at both of you!"

Bryus nodded. "Good, it's about time you give us your honest opinion. Let it out, Num."

Thorik's hands shook as he spoke. "And especially you, uncle. I shouldn't have to worry about trusting my family."

"He's right, you know." Bryus pointed at the older Num. "Damn shame he couldn't trust you."

Thorik whipped back around to Bryus, catching the Alchemist off guard. "And you! You have been nothing but a thorn in our side ever since we met you."

"Glad I could keep things lively," he retorted.

"If I didn't need you so much…" Thorik had reached the end of his anger limit and struggled to finish his sentence.

"Ah, but you do." Bryus' smile just added to the issue at hand.

"And you're lucky I do!" Thorik's clenched fist raised toward the man.

"Odd. I don't feel lucky."

Throwing his hands in the air, Thorik knew he couldn't get through to Bryus.

Turning back to Brimmelle, Thorik struggled to know how to convey his anger and distrust. "Why would you do this to your own family?" Thorik asked as his voice trembled with emotion. "Brimmelle, why have you done this terrible act?"

"Because my mother is dead, Thorik. I don't want her memory tarnished any further. Let her rest! She has done her part in this world."

"No, she has one last thing to accomplish, and she can't do it without my help. We must proceed to the Govi Glade and find the spell to release her. And neither of you two can be trusted around this dagger again." Thorik stormed out of the room, furious at his uncle's betrayal.

Bryus raised a single eyebrow and looked at Brimmelle. "I didn't realize they trusted me around it in the first place."

❦ 29 ❧

DEMONS

Thorik's Log: 12th day of the 8th month of the 650th year.

The days are hot and the nights are cold on the dry grasslands. I have attempted to reach out and contact my grandmother several times since we left the guard tower. Regardless, she has chosen not to show herself to me. I am relieved that she is safe and is here with us, but I feel cheated that I can't spend time with her. I suppose she has her reasons. I don't know if I can ever forgive my uncle for his betrayal. We aren't speaking at this time. Perhaps that's best. Our next step is to travel to the Govi Glade so we can collect the book of magic, Vesik, to find the spell to free Granna.

Extreme tension remained between Thorik and his uncle over the following weeks. They had hardly spoken to one another after the incident at the tower near the Squalid Water's bridge, and he could hardly look at Brimmelle without becoming angry. The man had crossed a line, and they both knew it.

Thorik and Santorray had led the group across the grasslands, while Grewen and Brimmelle followed several yards behind. Bryus and Avanda continued to stop and collect various plants and insects as they trailed far behind.

"I don't know if I can ever forgive Brimmelle for his treachery against Granna and me."

Santorray didn't speak as his eyes continued to scan the horizon for danger.

"Have you ever had anyone betray you in such a way?"

Santorray growled at the question. "You have no idea."

"No, I mean someone very close to you, such as a family member."

"Your displeasure in Brimmelle pales in comparison to my past."

"How did you handle it?"

"Like all Del'Undays are trained to do. We take action and then move on."

"Take action?"

"When we are wronged, we take it upon ourselves to take vengeance or allow it to pass. This decision is made and lived out. Once complete, we move on with our lives without the continual emotional ties to it."

"You mean once it's over, you forgive them?"

"We do not forgive, nor do we forget. We move on."

"As though it never happened?"

"Not exactly, but that's close enough for you to understand."

"But how could you look them in the eye again if they had killed a family member, such as your grandmother?"

"My vengeance would cleanse me of my pain. Afterwards, assuming I allowed them to live, we would greet each other as normal."

"I don't know if I could do that."

"As a Num, I wouldn't expect you to live to these standards. These are the demon's teachings that have been embedded into our culture for thousands of years. We are Del'Unday. This is who we are."

"Demons?" Thorik asked with concern.

"You're not familiar with the Del'Unday culture on this?"

"No," Thorik answered. "I know of the demon Bakalor. Is this who you speak of?"

Santorray nodded. "There are actually three demons which the Oracles created for our lands. Rummon, the dragon, ruled the air, the wind, and the storms. He brought rain when he was pleased and drought with lightning when he was angry. Bakalor was created to rule the underworld. He shakes the earth and blows fire from the mountaintops when he is not fed properly. However, he provides us with metals to build weapons and caves to shelter us from Rummon."

"And then there is Ergrauth, ruler of the land and all that rests upon it. Ergrauth's shovel cleared the way for water to flow to our rivers and crops. His axe cut down the forest so the Fesh could graze on the grasslands, and his breath allows life to exist or be taken."

Thorik was amazed at the story. "These three demons took care of all Australis?"

"Offspring helped. Rummon and Ergrauth would often breed with mortals to create trusted henchmen and servants to carry out their needs. It is believed that Bakalor creates his children by cutting off one of his toes, which then takes a decade to fully grow back."

Recalling Bakalor's creation of Grub, Thorik nodded in agreement with Santorray's story. "But if Rummon is a demon, how did he get trapped inside my spear?"

"Ergrauth ordered the making of the most powerful weapon ever, one that could protect the skies above his battlefields. It was decided to send the blind E'rudite, Schullis, in disguise as a peasant to the dragon's lair. As a mighty demon, the dragon underestimated the maliciousness and underhandedness of the meek requester sent by Ergrauth. With his guard down, Rummon's spirit was extricated from his flesh. His body instantly froze in time and forever waits until his soul is returned."

Thinking about the story, Thorik began questioning it. "For all this to be true, the sky and the wind would cease to move until Rummon returned. However, we know this not to be the case. The wind blows, storms come and go, and he has no part in it, so this must be a fable."

Santorray's eyes never left the distant hilltops. "You would be correct if I hadn't already explained that his children took on many duties. Each of the demon's offspring plays a role, and when they argue, like siblings inevitably do, lightning flashes, thunder roars, and the sweat of their battle falls to the land as rain."

❧ 30 ❧

CHUTTLE RANGE

The airy grasslands of the northern Chuttle Range were sporadically marked by large vertical rock formations, that towered over the landscape. Sometimes in clusters, but more often standing alone, the upside down cone-shaped black rocks stood out against the green and gold colors of the tall grass. The thin, rocky points reached hundreds of yards into the sky while the bases bulged out to a meager dozen yards across.

Ignoring the odd scenery, Avanda spent most of her time with Bryus as he taught her the magical properties of weeds, roots, insects, stones, and anything else they could get their hands on. With each passing day, she became more knowledgeable about spellcasting and its few limitations.

As she listened to his explanation of how the legs of some insects can be used as a primer for illusions, she noticed odd stitching in the collar of his shirt. "What's that in your tunic?" she asked, interrupting his lecture as she pointed to the stitching.

Bryus recoiled slightly and covered it up with his hand. "Nothing."

"Well, it's obviously something. What is it?"

Bryus traced the odd thread with his fingers and his facial expression became sad from his thoughts. "It's a memory."

Avanda leaned in closer. "They are hairs sewn into your clothes."

"Yes. My wife's hair." He traced the one on his left side. "And a lock of my daughter's." His hand trembled while touching the one on his right. "This is all I have left of them."

His sadness infected her as well. "I'm sorry to hear that. Is there no way to help save them?"

"I don't know where they are being held." A small tear filled one of Bryus' eyes.

Avanda looked up into the sad man's face. "I'll help you find them. I promise."

He quickly wiped his eye and sat up straight, slightly embarrassed that he had allowed himself to show any emotions. "Thank you, Avanda. I may just take you up on that someday."

Smiling, she reached over and gave him a warm hug before returning to listening to his lecture.

Thorik watched as the girl he had become enchanted with was now drifting away. No longer was she clinging to him and wanting to hold his hand. Instead, she seemed happier around the Alchemist, who had something to teach her.

Unexpectedly, Thorik had missed her soft touch. He found himself spending several hours a day looking back over his shoulder to make sure she was still there. A flicker of panic ran through his chest each time she wasn't in view. These usually only lasted a few minutes, only to find Bryus and Avanda had fallen behind while digging up worms or chasing grasshoppers.

Santorray walked up front with Thorik to scout their path. "She is not in danger."

"Who?" the Num replied in the most innocent way he could muster.

Santorray snorted. "You've been bitten, and the poison will always be in your veins."

"Poison? What are you talking about?"

"Sec, I can see the way you look at Avanda. You have been compromised."

"I don't know what you're talking about."

"Don't lie to me. You're not good at it."

Thorik looked back again, past Brimmelle and Grewen, at Avanda as she laughed after turning a pebble into a frog. "We're good friends who have been through a lot together. Of course we're going to be concerned for one another."

"Now you're lying to yourself."

"Okay, so let's say you're right, which I'm not saying you are." Thorik was absolutely serious. "How does that compromise me?"

"It compromises your mission. Having loved ones always does."

"I disagree. It makes you stronger to fight for them."

"Agreed." Santorray noticed Thorik's surprised reaction. "However, if it came down to choosing between completing your mission or saving someone you care about, which do you select?"

There was no hesitation from Thorik. "If it were between a loved one and a goal to accomplish, it is an easy answer. I would choose the loved one."

"And that is how your mission has been compromised."

"It doesn't have to be that way. We can do both."

"Perhaps. But most great successes require you to give up something equally valuable to you." Santorray scanned the horizon for life. Several Chuttlebeasts roamed in the distance. "If it came down to you saving your grandmother or Avanda, who would it be?"

"I don't like this game," Thorik said flatly.

"Sometimes life places you in circumstances where these situations occur."

"It would be different if you asked me if it was between my own freedom and a loved one."

"Really?" Santorray scuffed. "And you would be so quick to surrender your freedom in order to save another?"

"Of course. Wouldn't you?"

"Thorik, I have had my freedom taken from me. You have no idea what you're committing to."

"Yes, I do. The other option would haunt me for the rest of my life. I could never be happy again knowing that I allowed someone to die when I could have saved them."

Without warning, an explosion erupted a dozen yards behind them. Smoke billowed up from around Bryus, leaving a gray charcoal color over his entire body. His incorrectly attached wooden arm had fouled up yet another spell. His hair smoldered, and one eyebrow was now completely burnt off. Bryus was looking in worse shape than ever.

Laughing at the spectacle, Avanda handed him a cloth to wipe his face clean.

Santorray watched for a response from the local Chuttlebeasts from the blast. As he expected, the explosion caused them to start a stampede. "Pick up the pace. We need to leave these fields before we are trampled and become permanent residents."

31

CUCURRIAN RIVER

Another night had settled in on the land, and the campfires were in a full blaze as Brimmelle made a makeshift fishing rod to catch some of the Cucurrian River's fine selection. The river, as well as the forest they had just entered, was full of life. It had been a long time since Brimmelle had fished, but it kept him busy and helped him avoid Thorik's gaze. The two Nums hadn't spoken in several weeks.

Northeastern Lakewood Forest was much like the southwest part of the forest, but far less spoiled. Few traveled here, and the Fesh'Unday population had grown heavy. Deer, wild boars, wolves, and grazers had not yet learned to fear travelers. In many ways, it felt more at peace to Thorik than his home village of Farbank.

After prepping the camp for the night, Thorik sat near the riverbank, upstream from his uncle, as he watched his unique extended family. Grewen was busy eating an endless supply of plants, while Santorray ensured there was enough firewood for the night before scouting the perimeter for danger and food.

Avanda was busy at Bryus' secondary campfire, rubbing various items together and speaking in odd tongues to evoke spells. Some changed wood into water, while others sent pulsating lights into the air and around the camp. Other spells allowed her to communicate with ground squirrels and other rodents.

Thorik listened as Bryus complained about his wooden arm still not allowing him to do spells correctly, making it difficult to show her the desired results. Avanda, on the other hand, was so mesmerized by the effects she achieved that she didn't really care. Her only issue was the time it took to plan and contrive a spell. She constantly wanted to take shortcuts, to speed up the process. However, when she did, something inevitably went askew.

"Not so fast," Bryus shouted at Avanda. "Instead of this spell allowing us to stay awake without the need for sleep, it could just as easily put us fast asleep if done wrong."

But it was too late, for she had rushed the mixing of components. The spell instantly knocked them both out cold, and they fell softly to the ground.

Thorik's instincts were to rush over, but he had overheard Bryus' comments and thought it was most likely best that they received a good night's sleep. Traveling in the forest would be more difficult than in the grasslands. They would need their strength.

Breathing in the fresh, moist air of the forest, Thorik could almost smell his distant village of Farbank. The sounds of the river lapping along the shores and the wind rustling through the trees were all pleasant and familiar.

The one element that corrupted his cheery memories was the sight of Brimmelle; he sat facing away from camp, fishing by himself. It hurt Thorik to even look at his uncle after his plot to steal Gluic from him. It tore at his heart each time he thought about it.

The two Nums hadn't spoken since that fight, and Thorik didn't know how to repair their relationship, or even if he wanted to. Dropping his head down as he thought about the dilemma, he noticed several dozen small river rocks placed in a spiral pattern near his feet.

The sight inspired Thorik to pull out the Runestone of Courage. Closing his eyes, he concentrated on the Runestone until he felt a presence near him. Opening one eye at a time, he was pleased to see a ghostly spirit sitting next to him.

"Granna?" His voice was gentle.

"Isn't it pleasant here?" she said instead of a greeting.

"Yes, it is. It reminds me of our home."

"And where would that be, dear?"

Taken slightly aback by the question, Thorik answered, "Farbank."

"Oh, I see. You still see that as your home/"

"Well, of course I do. Shouldn't I?"

"If it grounds you, dear. But the entire world is your home." Motioning toward Grewen, who had his feet up against the roaring fire, she continued, "Home is wherever you feel comfortable. Sometimes it may or may not be where you grew up."

"My cottage in Farbank always made me feel comfortable."

"That's nice." She gave an agreeable smile. "Doesn't this place make you feel content as well?"

Thorik glanced around and nodded. "It's very nice, but I think I would get lonely out here."

"I see. So your home is based on being near friends and family."

"I guess you could say that."

Gluic glanced over at her son, Brimmelle. "Do you understand my son is part of your family?"

"No, not anymore." Thorik was clearly being defiant. "He has betrayed us both. You wouldn't be here right now if he had had his way."

Gluic smiled. "True, but he has saved your life more than once."

"And I his. My debt is paid, as well as any debt you had to him."

Gluic laughed. "If mothers began a tally of all the debts their children and the grandchildren owed them, they would run shy of paper to keep track."

"But he tried to prevent me from saving you."

"Thorik, dear." Kindness filled her voice. "This is not always about your journey to grow, but it is also about his as well. Have you not seen the changes in him? He is learning from you every day you're together."

"Learning from me?"

"Is it so odd for someone with more years about them to learn from someone with less? To be honest, you were born an older and wiser soul than he will ever achieve during this lifetime. You are helping him reach what's needed so he can move onto his next life."

Thorik was visibly confused at what she was saying.

Gluic leaned over and moved a few of the small river rocks that Thorik had accidentally kicked. "Be patient with him. He will make you proud in the end."

"But he's so difficult. I can't change him."

"You can't blame a hog for being a hog, and you can't change the hog from being a hog, but you can teach a hog to come when it's time to eat." She followed her statement with a giggle.

"But how can I think to teach him anything when I don't even have my own soul-markings yet? Children half my age have theirs, and Avanda's continue to flourish upon her skin. Fir Brimmelle's markings are so solid and thick; surely his soul is much stronger and more mature than mine."

"Oh, I see. Your lack of soul-markings is holding you back from being the person you want to be?"

"Yes. No. Well, in a way. I just don't feel that others see me as they should."

A soft, warm smile grew on Gluic's face. "It's not your skin or any other physical feature that holds you back. Only your mind can prevent you from achieving greatness."

Reluctantly nodding in agreement, he still felt bad about not having soul-markings like all the other Nums did. "I know, Granna, but when will I get them?"

"When you don't need them anymore, and only after you become the person you want to be by having them." Gluic began fading away.

"Wait, when can I call upon you again?"

"When you are in a room surrounded by death and life as you wait your turn for both."

"Granna?" Thorik looked to see where she went. Asking a few more times, he realized that she had said what she wanted to for now.

Mulling on her words, Thorik eventually stood up, slowly walked over, and sat next to Brimmelle along the shoreline. "Anything biting?"

Brimmelle took a quick glance at his nephew before looking away. "No."

And so they sat for nearly an hour with one and two word questions and answers. Their subjects for discussion were unemotional and unrelated to the events around Gluic or the dagger. No issues were resolved, although the stress and friction between them had begun to clear away.

The camp remained still, aside from the two campfires and Bryus' snoring, until Santorray walked back into camp from his hunt for dinner. He had a dead wild boar over his shoulder, which he had caught with his hands before breaking its neck. He had returned to skin it and feed the travelers.

Walking past the smaller of the two campfires, he kicked Bryus' wooden arm away from the flames. "Wake up. Your arm's on fire," he growled as he continued on toward the main campfire.

Bryus woke from the abrupt kick and quickly noticed the end of his wooden arm was fully ablaze. He had swung it into the campfire during his spell-enhanced slumber. Jumping up from the campfire, he attempted to put it out, but his own spells continued to fail him.

Hearing the commotion, Avanda woke to view the excitement as Bryus ran around in a state of panic. Thinking quickly, she got behind him and began pushing him toward the river to extinguish his flaming arm. The two raced to the shoreline, where Avanda stopped and gave one last shove to the Alchemist.

Thorik and Brimmelle turned in time to watch Bryus fly through the air with a flaming arm and then splash recklessly into the water.

"Done fishing?" Thorik asked in an even tone.

Brimmelle nodded. "I am now."

32

BAKALOR'S NEXT MOVE

Rivers of lava coursed through the cavern like arteries supplying fresh blood to a body. The intense dry heat filled the air as Bakalor slammed his fist on the armrest of his throne. "This is unacceptable!" The demon growled at Irluk. "Where is my son, Grub?"

Floating nearer to the demon, the swirling coal-colored debris of the Death Witch hovered over the demon's hand for a moment before dispensing fragments of rocks which once had been the lesser demon, Grub.

Watching the pieces of his son drop into his open hand, Bakalor was momentarily speechless. "What could have done this?" He pondered the question until the final rocks fell from Irluk. "Was it Ambrosius? Has he returned?"

Moving back from the enormous throne, Irluk landed on the cavern floor in front of him. "We thought it was he, but it was Darkmere in disguise. Our trap was sprung on the wrong E'rudite."

"How could you make such a mistake?" Closing his palm on the remains of Grub, he squeezed his fist so tight that heat and light from the extreme pressure escaped from between his fingers. "I want this to be over! Bring the Nums back to me."

Standing next to the spinning burnt fragments of the Death Witch was the white-cloaked Darkmere. Looking out from his solid white eyes, Darkmere had already healed his own wounds from the attack near the Squalid Waters Bridge. "You have interfered with my plans!" he shouted. "I could have had information out of Thorik about our enemy's war plans and a prisoner to lure Ambrosius into my trap."

The swirling of Irluk's debris increased as she took offense at his comment. "This was not my mistake. Changing your form to look like the one we are all hunting was a foolish idea. My only mistake was believing Grub when he informed me he had found Ambrosius."

"Stop bickering!" Bakalor squeezed tighter on the nearly liquid rocks of Grub and grabbed his mighty mace with his free hand, pointing it at Irluk and Darkmere. "Movement toward war has begun. Someone must ensure that Ambrosius will not interfere."

"Where do we start?" Irluk backed away slightly from the demon and lowered her eyes. "We no longer know where Ambrosius' friends are heading."

The demon slammed the mace into the cavern floor, releasing a massive quake that erupted around them. "Irluk! You promised me you wouldn't let Thorik escape."

She had no response to his accusation. He was correct, and they both knew it.

"I can tell you where he is." Darkmere's statement was clearly a surprise to the others.

With the earthquake fading, Irluk hissed at Darkmere's arrogance. "And do tell, how you know this?"

Darkmere opened a side pouch and pulled out an old, battered wooden box.

Irluk laughed at the absurd item. "A child's toy? You're using a prattle box?" Overjoyed at the stupidity, she waited for Bakalor to lash out at the E'rudite.

Bakalor was not impressed. Opening his palm, he dropped the red glowing magma glob onto the cavern floor. His eyelids narrowed over his diamond eyes, and his teeth began to grind.

"Yes." Darkmere was obviously irritated at Irluk's lack of respect. "It was given to me as a child, to be used as a toy." He confirmed the witch's comment. "However, many years ago, my master, Deleth, instructed me to give it to Thorik."

Irluk watched the steaming ball of magma start to cool and crust over. As it did, she could start making out features of legs and arms. "Then how did you gain its mate?" Irluk snapped back to Darkmere.

"I never did." Darkmere smiled at the confusion. "However, the Dark Oracle, Deleth, also informed me I would need Thorik's prattle box, which will be buried in the future, even though it will show up in the past. Deleth did not explain how, but he provided me with a map of its location near Farbank. The search caused the death of Thorik's parents. I don't know how the Oracle knew my prattle box would end up in a northern canyon, but it did. There are only two boxes. Ambrosius has one, while the other box exists twice; one from my past, and one from the future."

Now fully crusted over, a mouth opened in the center of the round glob, exposing the liquid inside. Grub had returned, and he stood ready for his master's orders.

Irluk avoided staring at the lesser demon and kept to her conversation with Darkmere. "If you knew Thorik and his parents, how come the Num doesn't recall you?" She was more than a little skeptical.

Suddenly, Darkmere used his E'rudite powers and changed his body to look like a typical human traveler. "Because..." He gave a slight bow. "... I was Su'I Sorat at the time."

Irluk scoffed at the name. "A child's toy and a child's game?"

Bakalor looked confused. "Explain!" He struck the cavern floor again with his weapon, causing the ground to vibrate uncontrollably, loosening rocks from the walls and ceiling.

Irluk glanced over at Darkmere before providing the answer to the demon in order to stop the quake from dropping more rocks from the cavern's ceiling. "It's a foolish tradition that the maker of prattle boxes sign their name backwards on the box. Darkmere removed the original name and added his birth name of Tarosius as Su'I Sorat before delivering the box to Thorik."

Bakalor shook his head in anger, causing the ground's shaking to increase again. "I don't care about this! I want to know where they are headed!"

"Their travels lead them to the Govi Glade…" Darkmere changed his form back to his normal white robes, eyes, and hair before smiling at Irluk as he finished his sentence. "… in search of Vesik."

Irluk was shocked. "That's my book! How dare they venture to its hiding place?"

Darkmere didn't allow her complaints to derail his conversation. "They most likely will die in their efforts to find your book, but if they should be so lucky, I need a spell from within it for myself."

"Out of the question," Irluk hissed. "It's mine. It is bound to me. Only I should have access to it."

"The spell I need will allow me to swap locations with my brother, Ambrosius." Darkmere could tell he had their curiosity. "How convenient would this be for the two of you to have him suddenly show up here in Della Estovia?"

Shaking her head, Irluk argued the point further. "You can't perform that spell without possessing a piece of his body."

A thin, evil smile crossed Darkmere's face. "Which you do not have, but I do. Which is why I am now taking control of the hunt for him."

Irluk knew that the Dark Lord had played the game better than she had in front of the demon. The charred debris that made up her body violently swirled as her anger at Darkmere's comments grew.

Bakalor grinned at the idea, and the remaining earth tremors ended. "What do we need to do?"

Darkmere plotted for a moment before glancing down at the lesser demon awaiting his orders. "Send Grub to kill them after they have possession of Vesik. Then Irluk can make haste to bring the book back here."

Bakalor glared back and forth between Irluk, Darkmere, and Grub as he considered the E'rudite's idea. "And what will you do in the meantime?"

"Return to Corrock. I have business to take care of there, just in case Grub fails to perform the simple task of rolling onto a frail Num."

Grub's heat intensified at the backhanded comment.

"Agreed," Bakalor replied.

❦ 33 ❦

GOVI GLADE

———

Thorik's Log: 29th day of the 8th month of the 650th year.

We have reached the edge of the Govi Glade. The open land, surrounded by the thick forest, is far different than I had expected. Then again, this entire journey has not gone as planned, so why would I expect this to be any different? Brimmelle and I are starting to talk again, but I still harbor a lot of anger from his actions. We are so close to freeing Granna and returning to the safety of Farbank that I can't put my excitement into words.

———

The open glade had suffered from the ravages of war between the E'rudites and the Alchemists. Over a thousand years of mystical powers and spells had been unleashed into the mile-wide swath of land coated with grass, clumps of bushes, boulders, and a few trees.

Translucent spheres of energy floated in the glade like room-sized bath bubbles, slowly bouncing off one another as they passed through trees and rock outcroppings, and even into the ground.

The spheres were the remnants of the powerful magic gone astray during the battles. Some provided a view of the glade from another time; others lingered about as a captured spell waiting to be activated. Still others had deeper, darker secrets within thick vapors.

As the travelers reached the glade, they started noticing the signs of the deformities caused by the war and the remaining spheres. The most noticeable was the giant spheres' ability to change the time of the field months and years prior to or after the current date. As each sphere floated along, it erased whatever was there and replaced it with what existed at a different time in history, based on what time that specific sphere was caught in.

Trees were warped, some with branches a decade older than the rest of the tree due to where a sphere had brushed by them. Snow rested upon branches on half of a tree after a sphere engulfed that section before moving on. Twisted and bent by the spheres, few things looked right.

Rock outcroppings were cut away by the spheres, only to be replaced with a layer of tree bark or a frozen snowdrift. Patches of green grass would suddenly turn brown and dead as a sphere raised out of the ground. Dead became alive, the living became warped, and the warped became dead in a never-ending cycle.

"Fascinating." Grewen gazed at the odd formations caused by the spheres. "Past, present, and future all overlapping in our view. What an amazing sight."

Santorray stood next to the giant and sniffed the air. "This smells of a trap that waits for some fool to spring it." Squinting his eyes, he thought of just the right person. "Send in Brimmelle."

Fir Brimmelle shot Santorray a disgusted glance, while the blothrud grinned at the Num's expense.

"Where is Vesik?" Thorik asked Bryus, as the entire group stood just outside of the glade's grasp.

"How would I know?" Bryus stretched his neck and looked about for the book.

Throwing his hands in the air, Brimmelle sighed overly loudly. "I knew he didn't know."

Thorik's face turned two shades of red as he addressed Bryus. "This is the reason we brought you here. You told us you knew where Vesik was."

"Well, of course I do. The book of magic is in the Govi Glade."

"But where within the glade?" Thorik asked.

"That's a wonderful question to ask." Bryus was clearly excited to find out the answer. "The Govi Glade is an ever-changing place. Even if I set Vesik down in one place, the book could be in a different time or place when I looked for it again."

"Different place?"

Bryus' eyes grew like a child who was given a treat. "Yes, a different place or time."

"Then how will we find it?"

"The real question is, do we need to make any efforts to find it?"

"Yes, we do. I need it to save my grandmother."

"Seeing that all things in this ancient battlefield constantly change and move, then it's just a matter of time before Vesik moves right here before us." The Alchemist pointed to a spot just a few yards in front of them as an example.

Brimmelle's patience had worn thin with the entire idea. "Are you suggesting that we just stand here and wait for the book to appear?"

Bryus laughed. "No, no. It's best if we sit down and relax. This will most likely take some time. To be realistic, it would be wise to build some type of shelter for the winter."

Thorik's face tensed up. "We aren't staying here through the winter in hopes that it will appear."

"We aren't?" The Alchemist seemed genuinely surprised by Thorik's comment.

"No, you're going to tell us a faster way to find it."

"Faster? That's easy. Just walk through the glade until you find it."

"It will just be lying there? In the grass?" Thorik was in disbelief.

"Or on a rock, or in a tree."

"How do we know it hasn't already been distorted and shredded apart by the spheres or animals, or weathered away by time itself?"

Bryus laughed. "Vesik is the primary book of magic. It has a spirit of magic all its own that rivals all living things. It's protected from aging and weathering. Even the infamous Wyrlyn couldn't destroy Irluk during the E'rudite and Alchemist War... so the legend goes."

"So, Vesik has been tossed around this field for thousands of years. If it's been just lying in this field, why hasn't anyone else come here to find it?"

A devious smile rolled up Bryus Grum's face, ending at his twitching eye. "Oh, many have tried, and their remains are scattered throughout the glade. The risk has just been too great."

"The risk seems low as long as you watch what you're doing. The spheres are sluggish at best."

Bryus nodded. "True, until you enter the glade. Then the energy of your body affects them, causing the orbs to speed up. The longer you stay, the faster they go. The battlefield stripped this glade of its own natural powers, so it becomes energized once an alternative source enters."

Thorik took a deep breath, wondering what his strategy would be. "I've come this far. I must try."

"Let's get this over with," Santorray announced. "I'll start on the far end and begin working back toward you."

Avanda helped Thorik remove his pack. "I'll go with you as well. We can cover three times as much ground at the same time."

"True," Thorik said, "But the spheres will speed up that much faster with the presence of all three of us in the glade at once." Looking to Bryus for confirmation of his logic, he received it in the form of a nod. "It would be best if I go alone to minimize the effects of the spheres. I'll make a path straight across, move over a bit, and then come straight back. That way, I can eventually cover the entire field."

Growling at the idea of Thorik going in alone, Santorray reluctantly agreed to stay out of the glade. "I'll sweep the perimeter and then follow you from the far side, just in case you need help."

"Avanda and I will monitor you from this side of the field," Grewen noted.

Bryus' cheek twitched. "By your presence being in the glade, the likelihood of Vesik being in one place the entire time is unrealistic. Your scouring of the field will quickly age this land. It could show up directly behind you after your first pass and you would never know it."

Frustrated, Thorik realized that there would not be an easy way to solve this. He would have to do the best he could and rely on some luck to be in his favor.

"Just wait here. I'll keep making passes back and forth until I can't keep up with the spheres. At that point, I'll rest outside the glade so they slow down." Removing all of his gear from his pack, he strapped on the empty backpack, hoping to fill it with the book, Vesik.

Meanwhile, Santorray made his way around the edge to the far side of the glade as he searched. He also kept an eye on Thorik, just in case he fell prey to anything in the open field.

Watching the mostly transparent spheres slowly bounce off of one another, Thorik waited for a clear opening before entering the field.

He had only made it ten yards before he noticed the slight increase in sphere speed. He had underestimated how difficult it would be to look through the tall grass for a book while simultaneously watching out for nearly invisible spheres coming at him from every direction. Running too fast increased the risk of not seeing the book. Going too slow increased the danger and the speed of the giant spheres.

Jogging through the glade, he came upon a tree trunk. The upper half had been cut off, and embedded in the bark was a human arm. The flesh had been infused into the wood, preventing it from deteriorating.

Next was a patch of grass that changed colors as a sphere lifted from the ground directly in Thorik's path. The view inside the sphere was distorted, but it was distinctly the view of a raging battle, perhaps from the very war that caused the spheres in the first place.

Avoiding the giant orb as it rose and lifted over his head, Thorik watched the chaos of the battle continue before running underneath it to finish his first pass of the glade.

He had completed one row. At this pace, it was going to take most of the day to complete enough rows to search the entire field.

Thorik moved over a few yards and waved to Avanda on the far side, and she enthusiastically waved back. The spheres were now at a quicker pace than they had been before leaving on his first trip across.

Jogging a little faster this time, he hoped to reduce his influence on the spheres; however, he was wrong. Nearly halfway across, the ground broke free and opened up below Thorik's feet into a hole created by an underground sphere which had removed the soil. The sphere had passed, but the hole remained, like an air bubble floating just below the water's surface. Rolling to the bottom, he tumbled into the top of a tree, which had been relocated to its new home by the sphere. Thorik couldn't tell if the entire tree was buried below him or if just the top had been misplaced, but he wasn't going to stick around long enough to find out.

Quickly scrambling up the side, he pulled himself up to the grass and rolled to his feet. It was then that he noticed a large leather-bound book sitting in the high grass. A thin leather strap held the overlapping leather covers from opening up and exposing the pages. Symbols had been burned into the leather work, which was old and worn but not damaged. It was not fancy, nor did it glow or emanate any magical lights. But then again, it had survived the Govi Glade, so it must be the book he was after. *Could I be this lucky?*

But before he could run for the book, a sphere lowered itself onto the book and the grass around it.

Thorik jumped back to prevent the sphere from taking one of his arms with it.

The book had been taken underground with the sphere.

He was suddenly torn between disappointment over missing a great opportunity and excitement, knowing that this was achievable. He now knew what they were looking for and he just needed to be prepared.

Returning to his mission, he decided to keep moving forward instead of retracing his steps. It could reappear anywhere, but it seemed demotivating to start all over again each time it was seen.

There was no giving up. Thorik was bound and determined to race this field until he was lucky enough to be in the right place at the right time. He would not fail his grandmother.

The spheres continued to speed up as he spent more time inside the glade. Spheres seemed to come out of nowhere and collide with one another, causing additional small distortions and cracks in the ground. The faster they moved, the harder they crashed, and the more likely these new effects created problems.

Rifts in the ground rose, gale force winds blew out of nowhere, and snow-storms and hail sprang forth from some of the faster collisions. This new uneven glade was now wet and slippery as Thorik fought his way back and forth, working his way across the field.

Time and time again, he had no luck as he raced back and forth across the glade, until fortune fell upon him for a second time. He noticed the book just as it began to slide into one of the new rifts in the ground.

Thorik jumped for it, sliding his upper body into the small crevasse. His hands were wet and cold as he reached out and grabbed onto the spine of the book with one finger and a thumb. But before he could pull it up, a fast-moving sphere rolled itself along the grass toward him.

There was no time to think. Thorik instinctively pulled his arm out of the way. But in doing so, he dropped the book.

Now, with nearly the entire glade done, the sun was starting to set, and many of the spheres were starting to be more difficult to view. A few of them had raging fires or electrical storms within them, and they lit up the glade. Nevertheless, it was the calm ones that Thorik now feared the most, for they were becoming increasingly harder to see in the darkening evening hours.

Racing against the lack of light, Thorik continued with his quest. The grass changed from dry to wet as he ran down the last row for the night with tired but determined eyes. Slipping more than once, he finally fell, slid off his planned path, and crashed into a tree trunk. He had seen this trunk in the glade before. This time, however, the arm was not embedded as far, nor was it protected. Insects were having their way with the fleshy pieces that still clung onto the bones. The remains fell onto the Num upon impact.

Thorik didn't have time to think about the sight before a stray sphere approached and removed it just as he leaped away. By this point, the giant spheres were flying in every direction at a quick pace, and with the sunlight dwindling, they were nearly impossible to see. Suddenly, Thorik was no longer looking for the book. He was trying to stay alive in the minefield of magical distortions.

Jumping to his feet, he bolted for the side of the glade but was blocked. The crashing of the spheres sounded like thunder, and the waves of energy dramatically increased, causing rips in the earth to snap open unexpectedly. Thorik was trapped. His only option was to continue to evade. Each time he focused on an exit, it nearly caused his death.

Diving under a collision caused a wave of energy to flatten him onto the ground. He could feel his body sink into the earth from the force, knocking the wind out of him. Fortunately, it only lasted a second.

Once it passed, Thorik heard Santorray's voice ordering him to run his way. Looking up, he saw the blothrud waving the Num forward as he stood near the edge of the glade. Taking the chance, Thorik sprang to his feet and made a mad dash for safety. Spheres tumbled toward him as though they were consciously trying to block his path, but he slid, rolled, jumped, twisted in the air, and weaved back and forth in this attempt for freedom.

But then it happened. Just a few yards from the edge of the glade, two more spheres rose from the ground and closed in on his path. He reacted without thinking and ran in between the two spheres. Then, just as they prepared to crash and squish him between them, Thorik jumped as high as he could. Unfortunately, the jump was not enough to carry him over the spheres.

As he fell, the spheres clashed, sending out a shock wave which pushed the Num back up into the air, past the edge of the glade, through the trees, and into the arms of Santorray.

He was safe, but he had failed to capture Vesik. They had nothing to show for their efforts.

❧ 34 ❧

CAMP CHORES

Returning to the campsite with Santorray, Thorik held his head down low as he listened to the loud crashes of spheres from the glade. Flashes of light helped him see his way, now that the sun had set, and the cool winds cascaded down from the Cuev'Laru Mountains into camp.

"Congratulations!" Grewen's typical baritone voice bellowed forth once he noticed Thorik walk into camp. The mognin was busy twisting a thick flaming log into the sole of his foot. Sparks flew as he moaned from the enjoyable feeling it gave him.

"Not now, Grewen. I let Granna down and am not ready for an argument."

Turning his foot, the giant began working the fiery end of the log between his toes. "I was being serious."

Thorik sighed and picked his head up to view the camp. There, on the far side of the fire, Bryus and Avanda were reading through the book of magic. "How did you find it? I searched all day and nearly had it twice, but I wasn't able to hold on."

Bryus glanced up at the Num and smiled. "I simply stood on the edge of the glade and waited for it to appear. When it did, I just walked out, picked it up, and brought it back to camp before the next sphere took it away. It was a lot easier than I thought it would be."

Avanda looked at Thorik and winked at him. She was glad to see that he had returned to camp but was at the moment very enthralled with what Bryus was teaching her from the book, Vesik.

Thorik was slightly disheartened by her lack of excitement over his return. Even if she hadn't known how perilous his adventure had been, he still had hoped for her to run over and welcome him back. But she didn't, and for some reason it made his chest feel tight and his stomach churn. He found himself missing her attention.

Santorray patted Thorik on the back. "It doesn't matter how it was achieved. Success of the mission is what's important. The book has been found, and now your grandmother can be freed."

Grewen placed his log back into the fire and straightened his legs so the flames would work their way between all his spread-out toes. "Oh, Bryus makes it sound simple. But if you hadn't stirred up that hornets' nest of spheres, it could have taken months or even years before it would have appeared for him."

"To be honest, I nearly didn't make it." Thorik glanced about to see if anyone was willing to listen.

"But you did," Brimmelle said without any empathy toward his nephew. "Now that you're here, why don't you start cooking supper? We haven't eaten yet."

All of the gear from Thorik's pack had been piled up near the main roaring fire. Bryus had created his own smaller second fire, like usual. No beds had been created, no herbs had been gathered, and no one had even gathered water from the nearby stream. "You waited for me to return to cook for you?"

Brimmelle raised one of his thick eyebrows at the young man's tone. "Don't be ungrateful. We could have eaten hours ago, but I insisted we wait for you."

"I don't know how to thank you enough." Thorik made no attempt to hide his sarcastic tone.

"Well, you can start by making us something to eat," Fir Brimmelle shot back at him.

"I'm not your servant, nor your cook. Everyone needs to share some responsibilities around camp." Thorik stomped the rest of the way into camp and threw his empty backpack down on top of his gear, knocking the pile over. "What would you have done if I hadn't survived? Would you have even noticed until you became hungry? Would you have all ended up starving to death?"

Grewen cleared his throat. "Um, Thorik, not to change the subject, but—"

"No! I don't want to change the subject. I've had enough of this. I'm tired of carrying more than my fair share of weight around here."

Grewen cleared his throat again and pointed toward the fire. "Thorik, your backpack is on fire."

"What?" Thorik yelled and jumped for the pack, dragging it to safety before stomping out the flames. Flushed with adrenaline, he continued to stomp on his pack to take out his frustrations.

Once he had relieved himself of his anger, he looked up from his sorry excuse for a backpack, knowing he would have to apologize for his overreaction. But instead of the glares he expected, he saw Bryus teaching Avanda magic. Several yards away, Grewen was lying on his back, slowly chewing on a shrub and getting ready to fall asleep. Apparently, everyone had ignored his outburst.

Brimmelle sat next to the fire, waiting for dinner. "I'll start reciting our nightly Mountain King readings while you make us something to eat. Perhaps I'll discuss controlling one's temper."

ONCE HE CLEANED up after they ate, Thorik sat next to Grewen, who was also sitting while chewing on local vegetation. Leaning his back up against the giant's side, he watched Avanda, who had been listening intently to what Bryus was saying for nearly two hours. Thorik finally commented to the mognin, "She's really grown up, hasn't she?"

Grewen swallowed a handful of local weeds before answering. "You both have. Your stint in Della Estovia appears to have stolen several years from each of you."

"No, that's not what I mean. Not what we look like, but how much she's matured since we left Farbank."

Grewen had underestimated how much time he had before he would need to talk again, and had tossed half a shrub into his mouth while Thorik was talking. "Yes," was all the mognin managed to say before food tumbled out of his mouth and down his chest.

"We nearly died in Della Estovia."

Grewen gave a quick swallow but wasn't able to get it all down. "If you had, your spirit wouldn't have had to travel far afterward." His little joke slipped past Thorik's ears but caused the mognin to chuckle uncontrollably, spraying leaves and small branches into the fire.

Thorik's focus was not to be swayed away from Avanda. "We became very close in the underworld."

Choking on a limb, Grewen pounded his chest. "I noticed."

"Sharing such trauma can strengthen a relationship, you know." Thorik leaned slightly forward as he watched her.

Pounding his chest again to dislodge the branch, the mognin nodded his head in agreement.

"But I think something existed between us before we went through all that suffering. And I'm concerned that I want to be closer to her." Thorik looked up at his companion. "Would it be wrong to fall in love with her? After all, she was once my student."

A loud snap could be heard in Grewen's throat as the limb finally busted and slid down into his stomach. After a quick sigh of relief, the mognin glanced over at Avanda. "It looks like she is Bryus' student now. She hasn't been your student since I met you."

Thorik's eyebrows raised at the observation. "You're right. She's my equal. But I have another concern."

Pulling another shrub from its roots, Grewen decided to wait until his conversation with Thorik had ended before filling his endless hunger. "And what would that be?"

"Em."

"What about her? Emilen has been gone a long time."

"I know, but I still dream about her."

"Thorik, she led all of us into Darkmere's trap and nearly got us killed. How can you possibly have feelings for her?"

"I'm still not certain if she had control over her own will. Darkmere's amulet controlled his followers. How could she be held responsible for her actions? Instead, we should be concerned that she is still being held under his powers."

"Little man, I know how much you cared for her. But I also know that no matter how strong of an enchantment someone may have over another, you cannot cause anyone to do something that is against their core values."

"You don't know that."

"I do know that. People and events are going to influence you all the time. Some are going to entice you with power or seduce you with lust, while others will enchant you into believing you are doing the right thing. Life is full of temptations. But none of these can force you to do something that you are hard-fast against. They can only play on your existing desires in order to push you further."

"Maybe that's what happened. Darkmere's amulet enticed her."

"To commit murder? To kill her own family? To lead us into a Darkmere's trap? I think not. She had to have accepted these actions in some way to help carry them out."

Thorik's head lowered. "Perhaps you're right. She's just difficult to get out of my head. I still miss her."

"Was she your first love?"

Fending off some embarrassment, Thorik looked at the ground while answering. "Yes."

"Good."

"Good?"

"Yes, now that you have your first out of the way, you are ready to get your head out of the clouds and see what is really available to you."

Thorik peered up from beneath his eyebrows at Avanda. "I think you're right, Grewen." A long pause followed before continuing. "To be honest, she may have been right for me all along."

Grewen waited for the Num to continue and patiently held another shrub ready to eat. He didn't want to talk with a mouth full again.

Thorik stayed silent and watched her from a distance.

The giant finally placed the plant in his mouth and started chewing.

"Should I talk to her and let her know that I'm over Em?"

With a mouthful of limbs and leaves, Grewen sighed. He nodded his answer instead of trying to swallow fast this time.

Thorik stood up and patted his hand against Grewen's thick skin a few times, partially out of nerves and partially out of respect for the giant's wise words.

While walking over to the second campfire, Thorik continued to convince himself that he was finally over Em and it was time to move forward with Avanda. Bryus and Avanda stopped talking as soon as he approached. Both looked up at him and waited for him to speak. Uncomfortable about talking to her in front of Bryus, he rubbed his hands together as his throat felt like it was swelling up. "Avanda, I love..."

Oh no! Why did that come out? Thorik's thoughts raced with emotions. He had panicked and became flustered. Sweat bubbled up from his skin as his audience of two sat in front of him, looking perplexed. His mind raced on how to finish his sentence before it became too awkward. All he wanted to do was tell her he was in love with her and not Em.

"… Em…" Oh no! What am I doing? That's not what I meant. I didn't want to say I'm in love with Em. How can I change this? Can I just run away? Would it be safer to run back into the Govi Glade? "… Embracing new things to learn," he corrected himself.

Rolling her lips up on one side, she squinted her eyes in confusion. "What?"

"Your lessons." Thorik smiled while hiding his panic. "I love to see you have embraced what Bryus is teaching you."

"I thought you didn't like me learning magic."

"Oh no, that's not what I meant. I… um, just don't like you using it. It's very dangerous."

Avanda crossed her arms and scowled. "What's the point of learning it if I can't use it?"

Thorik continued to paint himself into a corner and needed a way out. "So you can recognize magic when others are using it against us," he blurted. "Just thought I'd let you know." He pivoted and walked away before she could ask him another question.

Returning to Grewen, he fell forward onto Grewen's thick arm and placed his hands over his own head in an attempt to bury his face out of the light of the campfire.

Grewen chuckled at the sight. "It could have been worse."

"How? How could it have been any worse?"

"I don't know." The mognin laughed at the situation. "You're probably right. That's about as bad as it gets."

Thorik's face pressed harder into the mognin's arm.

35

GHOSTLY STRUCTURE

The stars slowly moved across the sky as the travelers slept near the fire. Distant howls from wolves and other Fesh'Unday echoed softly in the glade. The glade itself had returned to normal as large clear spheres slowly floated out of the ground and then back below, each time modifying the landscape.

Thorik was the only one awoken by the sound of a wooden door slapping against its frame in a soft wind. Its hinges gave off a soft squeak each time they moved.

Opening his eyes, Thorik saw a wooden shack standing a dozen yards inside the Govi Glade. It hadn't been there before, and he wondered how long it had been sitting there.

The shack was old and worn, its shutters hung askew, and holes could be seen in the roof. The front door and one window faced the campfire.

Thorik wiped his eyes to make sure he was seeing what he thought he was. Watching the shack for a few seconds, he noticed a shadow move behind the window, causing the Num to sit up straight and question himself. "Did I just see someone in there?" he mumbled to himself.

His answer came in the form of the front door slamming shut.

Startled, Thorik jumped slightly from the event before standing up to take a closer look.

As he approached the edge of the glade, he was surprised at the sight of a tall figure leaning against a tree, staring at the shack with his arms folded in front of him. It was Santorray. "There's been movement inside for several minutes now." The blothrud watched the small structure for any threats to the travelers.

Thorik crept his way closer to the shack. "Why would anyone build a home here?"

Leaving his scouting position, Santorray walked over to follow the Num in case he needed protection. The glade was anything but safe, and he knew it would only be a matter of minutes before their presence would affect the spheres of magic that floated within it.

Thorik's pace slowed as he entered the glade and crept up toward the front of the shack. "Hello?" He then made his way closer.

As he approached, the wind picked up, and he could hear movement from inside. Thinking it best to look inside first, he walked up to the window. It was dirty and difficult to see through, so the Num placed his face up against it and blocked out as much campfire light as he could with his hands.

Inside the single-room shack sat a table and chairs, and a fireplace was on the far side. Footsteps could be heard from within, but no one was seen. At least until a hand print slapped against the window, directly across from Thorik's face, from an unseen hand.

Thorik jumped back. His heart raced as he tried to make sense of it. He had seen the shack to be empty, yet the impression of a hand could not have been made by itself. Staring at it, he tried to figure out what he was missing.

Santorray unsheathed his sabers and scanned the area for anything hostile. He found nothing.

But then a single invisible finger pressed against the window from the inside. It moved sideways before it pulled back. A few vertical lines were added as well as a horizontal. Next to that, a circle was drawn, and a backward letter "R", and another two vertical lines, ending with two angled lines stemming from the last vertical one.

Shivers ran up the Num's neck as he looked at the word in the window. His name, Thorik, had been spelled facing inside. Was it a call for him to enter? How did they know his name? Who are they? Questions raced through his head as he stared at his name.

Stepping forward, Thorik peered into the window again, this time without placing his face so near. Again, it appeared empty. "No signs of life," he whispered to Santorray. Regardless, something had written Thorik's name on the inside of the dirty window.

Thorik moved from the window to the door. Taking a deep breath and holding it, he grabbed the handle and pushed it open. The hinges whined as the door opened to unveil the room, with trash piled in the corners. The walls were covered in writings on top of writings, so much so that it was difficult to read any of them. What he could read made little sense, but he still heard scribbling on the walls.

"Hello?" Thorik asked, still standing in the doorway, knowing that there wasn't anyone in the room to answer.

"Hello?" It was a soft faint voice that had replied.

Thorik's body froze. Had he imagined that he had heard the voice, or was it really there? "Watch my back," he said to his blothrud friend.

"As well as the rest of you," he replied.

Stepping cautiously into the shack, the Num asked a different question. "Who are you?"

The pause was long enough to make Thorik feel he had imagined the original greeting, so he stepped farther into the room.

Santorray took one last look around before leaning down to enter the small doorway.

Without warning, the door pulled away from Thorik's hand, slammed shut, and locked, smacking Santorray square on his nose in the process.

Grabbing the door handle, Santorray attempted to thrust it back open. Unsuccessful, he pushed it with his shoulder to dislodge it. Again, it didn't budge the lock. He'd have to break it down. Stepping back, he prepared to use his body as a ram to bust through the door as he howled a warning cry, alerting Thorik to jump clear.

"Stop!" Thorik yelled from inside. The blothrud's attempt to open the door was causing the shack to nearly collapse on top of the Num as beams cracked and ceiling boards fell. "I'm not in danger!" he shouted, just in time to stop his companion from knocking the entire shack down.

Santorray halted his attack and scanned the area before moving to the window, but even with his strong night vision, it was difficult to see through the dirty glass into the dark room. Growling at the situation, he kept his senses on alert for approaching danger. Spheres would soon gain speed and could approach from any angle.

Thorik's eyes adjusted as the falling debris subsided. Only traces of the campfire light now worked into the room through the soiled window. Coughing from the unsettled dust, he stepped toward the table in the center of the room. As he approached, a chair pulled out from the table by itself, as if to invite the Num to sit down.

His options were simple; either he leaves now, or he stays and finds out what is going on. Thorik took in a deep breath before sitting down.

"Get out!" said a low, shallow voice. This one differed from the original voice he had heard. "Leave us alone…" The sound of writing became more intense on the walls, and symbols were added on top of other writings. None were legible to the Num.

Thorik was confused. "You called to me. My name is Thorik. You wrote my name on your window."

The table pushed away from Thorik, and trash in the room began flying about. It suddenly became cold, and when Thorik tried to stand, he found himself held down in the chair by an unseen force.

"…Warning!" the softer voice said near Thorik's ear.

Thorik pushed with his hands in an attempt to get up from the chair as a dark shadow materialized and stood before him, pushing him back down. Papers and trinkets continued to be thrown about the room, and more writings were etched onto the walls. "What warning?" Thorik asked. "What do you want?"

"…Vesik…" The voice faded in and out, often preceded or followed by other words that were too faint to hear.

Thorik didn't like the sound of a warning relating to the book they needed to save Gluic.

"…Avanda…"

"Avanda? What about her?" The idea of her being pulled into this warning struck a nerve of fear down Thorik's neck and back.

A second, larger shadow moved toward the center of the room. It was then that the table next to Thorik exploded into pieces, knocking Thorik onto the floor and freeing him from the grasp of the first shadow.

Thorik rolled to his feet and moved to the back wall, near a small window. Outside of the window, Thorik could see an approaching Govi Glade sphere. His time was up; the sphere would soon take the entire shack away just as fast as it had appeared. "What about Avanda? Is she in danger?"

"…danger…"

The back wall began to disappear as the sphere rolled into its space.

"Thorik," Santorray shouted. "I'm getting you out of there!"

"Not yet!" Thorik shouted back as he jumped from the wall and toward the front door. Halfway across, he was struck with the chair he had been sitting on earlier, and he fell to the floor. "Danger from what?" Thorik asked the shadowy mass after pushing the pieces of the broken chair off him. "What can I do to stop the danger?"

"…Vesik…"

Over half the building was now erased from sight as the sphere filled it in with a boulder. The remaining walls shifted and bent under the pressure of the changes being made.

"What about Vesik?" Thorik yelled as he ran to the door.

"…must prevent…"

The ceiling was now gone, and a thunderstorm raged overhead when looking into the sphere. Thorik unlocked the door and grabbed the handle to pull it open in order to escape the shelter, but the shifting of the walls had jammed the door and prevented it from moving. Thorik pulled again and again, but he was trapped.

The shack was nearly gone. Only the front wall remained as Thorik stood on the few feet of floorboards that still existed. Jumping into the sphere could end his fate inside of the boulder. If it allowed him to live, where would he actually be? Would he ever see his friends again?

Thorik then spotted the handprint on the window and realized his last option. Taking a few quick steps, he launched himself into the air and toward the front window. Unfortunately, the floor buckled from the sphere's pressure, causing him to miss his mark and slide to a stop under the window.

Torrential rain pounded hard from the open roof as the sphere rolled up close to him, making it impossible for him to stand up and jump through the window. He had stayed a few seconds too long and screamed in terror for help.

Crouching down to maximize the time he had before the sphere rolled on him, Thorik heard an explosion as shards of glass and wood sprayed his body. Two large hands reached through the wall and grabbed the Num, pulling him out into the glade, free of the sphere's stormy destruction.

"Are you insane?" Santorray released the Num in the calm night air of the glade only feet away from the nearly destroyed structure. "You could have been killed."

The front of the shack was being replaced with the large boulder as the sphere continued to roll toward Thorik on its way back down toward the ground.

Thorik was far too appreciative of the blothrud's assistance to argue with him.

"Thank you." He was still catching his breath from the ordeal between his words. "Let's get out of this glade while we still can."

"Agreed."

Thorik quickly led the way to safety. "Did you hear the warning? Did you experience the voice?"

"The only thing I heard was a helpless princess voice calling for help. That wasn't you, was it?"

"Yes, that was me. That must make you my prince who came to save me."

Passing the Govi Glade's boundaries, they both had a good laugh as they returned to the camp.

36

ORDERS TO KILL

Heading back out of the Govi Glade before their presence caused the spheres to speed up any more, Thorik and Santorray carefully watched all sides for danger. And danger is what they found, only this was not in the expected form of a rogue sphere.

"Stop!" Santorray ordered. "I sense a new trembling… different from the spheres we have evaded so far."

Lifting out of the ground just outside of the glade, a red glowing mass of liquid rock formed arms, legs, and long teeth. The creature stood between the sleeping travelers back at camp and the two still in the glade. Fire escaped from cracks on the creature's motionless body while its outer surface cooled to a crusty black. Bakalor's son had returned.

"Grub?" Thorik's eyes widened and his mouth opened as he stood speechless for a moment. "But… Rummon killed him."

Santorray stepped in front of Thorik to protect him. However, doing so meant Grub could tell exactly where the blothrud was. Without eyes, the lesser demon used the vibrations in the ground to determine his enemies' locations.

Opening his gaping mouth, which spanned his stomach, intense flames rolled out of Grub as he faced toward Santorray. Then, without hesitation, he charged at the two travelers in the glade.

"Run!" Thorik swiveled around and followed his own advice.

"Split up," Santorray said. "He can't follow us both."

Grub ran halfway before folding up his arms and legs and rolling after them. The massive heat pouring out of the lesser demon scorched a path in the earth as he increased his speed.

Thorik veered off to the left, and Santorray to the right. Spheres increased their speed from the energy of three beings within the glade perimeter. Lightning struck inside some, while others were completely black. Nearly a third of them had sunshiny days within their barrier's grasp.

Looking back to see which one of them Grub was chasing, Thorik had mixed feelings about finding the molten mass rolling behind him.

Banking to the left and then tumbling to the right, Thorik used every trick he knew to lose his chaser. Unfortunately, the small gains he made were quickly lost when he ran straight.

"Get him near a sphere!" Santorray followed from behind, carrying a large branch he had pulled from one of the deformed trees.

The Num turned and dodged a near-fatal attack from Grub. "Why?"

"Get as close as you can and I'll knock him into it."

It may not have been a good plan, but at least it was a plan. Thorik knew he couldn't keep running forever. Seeing a cluster of spheres all rising up near each other, he figured it would increase the odds of Santorray being able to knock Grub into one of them as they ran near them.

Darting off in a new direction, Thorik added a few feet between himself and the lesser demon as they both raced toward the spheres, with the blothrud following behind with his bulky wooden weapon. By the time they reached the cluster of spheres, Grub was on Thorik's heels, and his heat started to burn the Num's back.

Struggling to catch up to them, Santorray leaped forward with all his might and swung at the lesser demon while still flying in the air.

He smacked the fiery mass with the end of the thick branch, causing the wood to immediately ignite into a huge torch as Grub went rolling into one of the winter spheres with an ice storm coating everything in sight.

Crashing to the ground, Santorray nearly impaled himself on the other end of the tree limb.

Thorik skidded to a halt before running back to his friend. "You did it!"

"Not so fast. We're not safe yet." Santorray peered up to witness a few more spheres emerging on their other side. They were now surrounded by them. They were trapped.

A flash from within one of the darker spheres caught Thorik's eyes. He looked inside of it to witness a battle of magic. "The spheres are moving faster. We'll have to make a quick escape once an opening presents itself."

"No time!" Santorray yelled as Grub launched himself back out of the sphere he had rolled into. His crusted-over mass flung through the air, striking and igniting the branch that Santorray quickly pulled up in order to block the attack. The thick wood had prevented Grub from touching the blothrud, but the impact knocked him backward.

Santorray's fall pushed Thorik and himself into the sphere the Num had been looking at. They fell backward in time and into the actual events which had carved the glade into a place of danger. They were now in the middle of the Alchemist and E'rudite War, and the night air was electrified with magic.

Grub followed them through the orb into the glade of the past.

Seeing him arrive, Santorray rolled to his feet and swung his flaming club, knocking the glowing mass out of the glade toward one of the two battling sides.

In doing so, his branch exploded into a thousand splinters. His weapon was destroyed.

"We need to get back out of this sphere before it closes," Thorik yelled over the pounding noise of the battle.

It was a strange statement, seeing that their surroundings had no resemblence to a sphere. The only noticeable sight of their passageway back to their time was a slight hue change to what appeared to be the inside of a piece of concave glass, a section of glass which was getting smaller by the moment. The gateway home was unnoticeable to anyone not specifically looking for it.

As they raced back toward their exit home, a battered old man appeared before them, blocking their way. "Death to all those who refuse to join us!" he yelled before clapping his hands tightly together. Waves of energy sprung forth from his single clap, knocking Santorray high in the air and into the front lines of the battle.

There wasn't time for Thorik to run all the way over to his friend and back as the sphere continued to close.

"Thorik! Run!" Santorray shouted as he became engaged in the battle. "Don't wait for me!"

Thorik tried to determine exactly how far the blothrud had been thrown, but all he could see were the bodies he was tossing up in the air as he attempted to make his way back.

"A Num?" laughed the battered old man. "I'll melt you down where you stand." As the man raise his bracelet-filled arms to perform a spell, Thorik felt his feet become stuck to the ground, preventing him from escaping.

Thorik could see the sphere continuing to close. Attempting to jump, he found that his feet were rooted to the ground, causing him to fall forward. In doing so, he felt a ball of extreme heat roll past his back.

Grub had returned. His flying attack on the Num had missed. When the Num fell, the lesser demon had shot past him and hit the old man by mistake, instantly killing him instead of Thorik.

The spell holding Thorik's feet to the ground was immediately released, because of the spellcaster's death. Freedom to reach the exit was available again. However, Grub now stood in front of the Num, as he breathed a furnace of heat toward the Num.

"Off with you!" came a voice from the side. It was followed by Grub's body being crushed in midair. As he was squeezed tighter and tighter, the lesser demon shrank from the pressure building around him until a bright flash of light blazed outward, leaving nothing but a large diamond floating where he once was.

The E'rudite, who had turned Grub into the gem, grabbed the diamond, blew on it to cool it off, and then handed it to Thorik.

Thorik looked up to see a friend he had missed for a very long time. "Ambrosius?"

"Thorik, get out of here! You don't belong here."

"The sphere is nearly closed." The Num pointed to the small section of floating color distortions hovering in the air. "And Santorray is out in this battle. I can't leave him."

"Get back to where you came before you make things worse. I'll take care of your friend."

Thorik took a step toward the sphere and then turned back to his dearly missed companion. "I have so much to ask you." He hesitated as to his next action. "Come with me!"

"Go!" The E'rudite held out his hand, forcing the Num into the air and back into what remained of the sphere before it closed up.

Thorik rolled out of the sphere just before it went under the ground. Several more continued to float about, and he waited for Santorray to appear from one of them. He knew that the longer he stood in the glade, the more danger he put himself in. But he refused to leave. In fact, he was hoping to increase the frequency and number of spheres in order to increase the chances for Santorray to appear in one of them. It was a risk he was willing to take.

Dodging his way from one sphere to another, he kept on his toes and hoped one wouldn't open up directly below him.

This went on for a while before he heard a loud scream of pain. Looking up, he witnessed a massive creature fall from a sphere above him. The two-headed creature had two arms, four legs, and a tail that had a sharp hook on its end. Long, sharp horns rose from its heads while shorter ones traced down both of its long snake-like necks. Blood from recent cuts and bite marks coated parts of the beast's body and splattered upon the blades of grass. The creature had fallen out of an overhead sphere and into the glade, nearly landing on the Num.

Thorik fell backward from the shock. This was not what Thorik was hoping would appear.

Shaking off the unpleasant landing, the creature stood up and looked down at the Num. Reaching out with both of its arms, it leaned forward to scoop Thorik up as he attempted to crawl away.

But before it reached the helpless Num, Santorray fell from the same sphere and landed on the creature's back. With a bloody saber in each hand, he stabbed the creature deep in its back.

Three times the size of Santorray, the creature arched its back and tried to grab the blothrud.

Bracing his body, with one saber deep into the creature, Santorray used the other one to slice one of the creature's long necks. Blood sprayed from the new gash, glazing the grass and the Num with thick red liquid.

Jerking from the cut, the creature attempted to buck the blothrud off its back. It thrashed back and forth and swung its tail violently to crush its attacker.

Even with his best grip firmly holding onto his saber, the speed and mass of the creature's tail knocked Santorray off its back. Sliding down the beast's side, he dug his arm spikes into the creature's skin, ripping a long, gaping cut down its shoulder and chest.

Flailing about, the creature reached over and finally caught Santorray in its grip.

It was at that moment that Santorray reached up inside the fresh wound with his saber and struck the creature's heart.

A sudden moment of silence followed as the creature realized what had happened. An instant later, it fell forward, while Thorik scrambled to get out from under it before being crushed.

With a thunderous crash, the lifeless body stretched out across the field.

Pulling his arm and weapon out of the creature, the blothrud stepped back from it and wiped his sabers clean.

"Santorray!" Thorik shouted.

"Thorik, what are you still doing here? Did you accomplish your mission?"

"What? We haven't even finished sleeping the night away."

"This is the same night we fell into the sphere?"

Thorik looked baffled. "Of course. Why would you think differently?"

"Because I've been fighting in battles for months. It could be a year for all I recall. Then I saw the inside of this sphere."

"And that creature prevented you access to the sphere, so you had to kill it?"

Santorray shook his head as he sheathed his sabers. "No, he and his two bigger brothers were in my way. He made a run for it once I taught the others a lesson." A hint of a smile crossed his face at the joke as tears pooled within his eyes from a deeper personal meaning that was unknown to Thorik.

During their discussion, a sphere emerged from the ground near the two and covered up the location of the creature's left shoulder and head. As it moved past, those segments of its body vanished and were replaced with grass and shrubs. The parts had been precisely carved away from the rest of the creature's body. It wouldn't be long before the entire body was replaced with the glade at other times in history.

"We need to get out of here." Santorray turned toward the nearest edge of the glade.

Thorik jumped to his feet and followed Santorray, exiting the glade boundary. He didn't understand why the spheres couldn't pass the perimeter, but it was obvious where the boundary was by the row of undistorted trees and brush.

Rounding the perimeter of the glade, the two returned to camp. No one was the wiser that Thorik and Santorray had nearly vanished into the night after speaking to ghostly spirits and falling into a sphere. But what haunted the Num, more than the disembodied voices and not having a chance to speak with Ambrosius, were the words of warning he had received about Avanda and Vesik.

Once they arrived, Santorray began healing his wounds while Thorik woke Grewen and told him of the shack and the adventure that followed. It was important that he didn't forget any details by sleeping on it prior to discussing it.

Grewen sat quietly and listened before responding. "Are you sure you weren't sleeping?"

"Yes, I'm sure. Santorray was with me."

Grewen stretched his long arms out and twisted his head to work out the kinks in it. "You saw Ambrosius? Are you sure it was him?"

"Yes, but he was different somehow. His face... it wasn't burnt. I never met him prior to Darkmere's attack on the Grand Council, when Ambrosius was severely burned across the side of his neck and face. But I know it was him, and he knew me as well. He called me by name."

"Did he tell you how he survived Weirfortus or what his plans are to prevent Darkmere from destroying our lands?"

"No, there was no time to talk. He simply saved me from Grub and then sent me flying back through the sphere. Look, I even have what remains of Bakalor's son." He pulled out a large diamond from his pocket.

Grewen nodded. "We know nothing more about him or what we need to do to help in this pending war."

"No, we will have to carry on as we were. The question I have is whether this is tied to the warning about Vesik."

Grewen's bald forehead bunched forward at the thought. "So, a haunted shack shows up out of nowhere to warn you that Avanda is in danger from Vesik?"

"You make it sound ridiculous."

"I didn't make it sound like anything more than a summary of your story." Straightening out his legs, he hung his toes over the campfire flames. "Would you say it's a fair statement?"

"Yes, mostly. The problem is that I couldn't hear a lot of the words. There was a warning, and Vesik's name was said. And so was Avanda's. So it seems pretty clear."

One of Grewen's large eyebrows raised up. "Perhaps. But could it be a warning that Avanda will destroy the book?"

Thorik hadn't considered that. "Why would she destroy it?"

"I didn't say she would. We're just guessing the meaning of this riddle… we may not even have enough clues to properly perform this task."

"We know enough that Avanda needs to stay away from Vesik. That we know for sure."

"We do?" Grewen wiggled his toes in the lapping flames.

"Yes. I heard it say, 'Warning,' 'Vesik', and then 'Avanda.' What else could it be?"

"I don't know, but that doesn't imply there isn't another option."

"Well, until you think of one, I'm going to make sure Avanda keeps her distance from Vesik."

"That may be a little harder than you think." Grewen pointed toward the second campfire that Bryus had established farther from the glade than the original camp.

Vesik was snuggled up under Avanda's arms as she slept next to Bryus and his campfire. Her face was content and relaxed as she cuddled the large book.

Thorik had no idea if they had fallen asleep naturally or if one of her spells had knocked them both out again. "You know, Grewen, I just get a bad feeling about her having that book."

Grewen yawned and stretched. "You might still be spooked from the shack you saw. See if you feel differently in the morning."

"I doubt it. The book could be dangerous. It might be best if we keep it away from her, perhaps even tonight. At least until we know what the warning is about."

"We may never know. Besides, doesn't this sound like Brimmelle's reasoning for taking Gluic's dagger from you?"

"No, this is completely different. When we first met Ambrosius, he warned us to stay away from magic. Then he suddenly appeared right after I received this warning. Let's face it, Avanda's spells are usually more dangerous than they are helpful. And now we have just given her more power."

Raking his fingers back through his hair, Thorik knew that pulling the book away from her would only end in a fight. "I'll address this with Bryus in the morning. Do you think he would help me with this?"

Looking back to Grewen for approval, he found the mognin already lying back down and falling asleep. Apparently, Grewen didn't feel it was his decision to make.

❧ 37 ❧
OPEN BOOK

Bryus and Avanda woke up early and began searching through the book of magic while everyone else still slept. A leather strap was untied and the overlapping leather cover opened up to reveal pages and pages of handwritten notes, drawings, and symbols. Avanda carefully turned Vesik's large, old pages in order to preserve their delicate appearance and to ensure none of them would be bent or torn. Bryus allowed Avanda to handle the book, seeing that he feared he would damage it with his defective wooden arm.

Within its pages, red and black ink explained the world's most powerful spells in great detail. Most of them were so complicated that the book would need to be present while actually performing the planned enchantment, summoning, or evocation. Divinations and illusions also filled the pages with instructions on hand and body gestures, vocal commands, and physical components such as objects and plants. Some included blood of various species, while others required tears. Vesik was a mixture of the Alchemists' spells used before the E'rudite and Alchemist war.

The vast powers listed between the rich overlapping leather covers caused the book to have a life of its own. The pages they read would glow in the dark of the night, causing the writing to look etched into the pages.

Gazing upon the magical pages, Avanda's fingers gently traced the soft material that held the writings. "We should write these spells down, just in case we lose the book."

Bryus shook his head, but retained a smile. "It won't work. Even with all that this enchanted book has to offer, the book hides one key element from every spell to ensure you don't attempt the spell without Vesik being involved. In fact, Vesik is often one of the components in order to control the use of the spell. Sometimes the book hides writing on entire pages with the most dangerous powers until you can be trusted."

Gently, Avanda turned another page. "Can we try one of the spells?"

Bryus was nearly giddy as he watched the pages of spells unfold. "Absolutely. I'd like to try them all."

"Which one should we do first?"

Bryus closed his eyes and touched a page with the end of his fingertip. "Open it to this one."

Avanda watched the pages fall one after another until she reached the page his finger was holding back.

Bryus smiled. "Very interesting."

"Really? What is it?"

"It's a summon swap spell."

Smiling at the sound of it, Avanda waited for an explanation.

"Who sleeps the most soundly?" the Alchemist quietly asked.

Scanning the group, she quickly responded, "Brimmelle and Grewen."

"Excellent. Let's try Brimmelle. Collect a few hairs from his head and bring them here."

"Hair, again?"

"I'd gladly take a toe or finger, but I have a feeling he'd wake up from such an amputation."

"Good point," she replied as she took a blade. Quietly walking over to him, she gently lifted a few hairs from the back of his head. Pausing, she became concerned about her actions, but a quick glance at Bryus' smile prompted her to complete the mission. After a quick cut, she had half a dozen pieces of hair in her hand, and she quickly maneuvered her way back to Bryus, who had been reading the spell in the book.

"Here they are," she said. "Do I need to boil them?"

"No," he responded, as though it was a foolish question. "Not for a summon spell."

"Sorry. I didn't know."

"You have so much to learn." He took the hair from her. "Now cut some of your own hair off."

"Mine? How about Grewen? He's a sound sleeper."

"He's also bald."

Nodding, she agreed and then reluctantly cut off several hairs from her own head before handing them to Bryus.

"Grab that hourglass I obtained from Trewek."

"Obtained?" she asked, skeptical of how he ended up with a pouch full of items with no way to trade for them.

"Well, I didn't have it prior to arriving in Trewek, and I had it before I left, so yes, I obtained it during that time."

"Did you steal it?"

"Listen, I'm not going to sit here and allow you to call me a thief," he said in a raised voice.

Avanda backed down but still questioned the thought. "Just tell me what I'm supposed to do."

"Reality is, you shouldn't be doing anything with your limited knowledge.

However, seeing that I am currently unable to perform spells correctly, you will do exactly what I tell you to in order to make sure nothing goes wrong."

Avanda nodded and searched for the hourglass in the large pouch. Moving several jars and brass hooks out of the way, she found an hourglass with a metal frame to keep it from breaking.

Bryus watched her pull it out. "Excellent." He then tied Brimmelle's hair onto one end and her hair onto the other. Following the instructions in the book of magic, he had Avanda utilize various verbal and physical commands to prepare the spell. It was at that point that the final verbal commands appeared on Vesik's pages.

"Can you read these?" Bryus asked.

"Yes."

"Good. Now, go cuddle up against Grewen and say those last few words as you flip the hourglass over. Just relax. It will take a while, so you must be patient."

Patience was not one of her strengths, but she would do her best. Reciting the last words to the spell over and over in her mind, she walked across the camp and snuggled up to Grewen, who naturally tossed an arm over her to protect her. She had felt the need for protection before, and he instinctively moved when he felt her body.

Bryus watched with excitement as she spoke the last words and flipped the hourglass over.

She waited for the spell to take effect, but she couldn't see anything happen. Looking over at Bryus, he nodded to her to give it more time, so she did. However, lying still and waiting silently only lasted a few minutes before she fell asleep.

~

"Avanda?" Bryus whispered in order to wake her without alerting everyone else in camp.

Rubbing her eyes, she sat up next to the main campfire. "Bryus?"

"Yes, it's me." He helped her up to her feet as he escorted her to his smaller campfire.

"Why didn't it work?"

"Why do you say that?" he asked as he sat her down on a log, facing the other travelers.

With her eyes finally coming into focus, she could see Brimmelle cuddled up against Grewen, with the mognin's large arm over him to protect him. Avanda and Brimmelle had swapped locations.

Thorik yawned and stretched and stirred as he struggled to sleep. He was so close to releasing his grandmother and ending his journey. Every minute seemed to drag out. Drifting in and out of his slumber, he was nudged awake by the sound of Avanda cheering.

His eyes popped open, and he immediately sat up. Thorik could see the delight on Avanda's face. Bryus was pleased as well.

Tossing off his blanket, Thorik lifted himself to his feet, wiped his eyes clean, and stumbled over to Bryus' campfire. "Did you figure it out?"

"Yes!" Avanda was filled with great happiness. "We did it!"

"That's wonderful." With a grand sigh of relief, Thorik removed the dagger Varacon from his belt and held it carefully in front of him. "Let's get this over with."

Avanda and Bryus looked at each other and laughed. "We didn't figure out that spell," Bryus said.

Thorik was shocked. "You mean to tell me you haven't been working on freeing Gluic? What have you been doing?"

"Are you insane?" Bryus was clearly annoyed. "Asking Vesik for a spell of that magnitude would be improper before we showed her that she could trust us with something less extensive."

"Showed her? It's a book."

"Perhaps, but if not treated properly, she may not provide us with any spells." Using his good hand, Bryus opened the book up to several blank pages. "See, now look what you've done! The spells are gone. You've offended Vesik and possibly lost our opportunity to save Gluic."

Thorik glanced at Avanda and then back at Bryus. "Are you serious? The book has emotions?"

Bryus showed him a few more blank pages. "Every time you open your mouth, the more we lose the chance to see her spells."

"I apologize," Thorik said half-heartedly. It all seemed a bit ridiculous.

Bryus watched the blank pages stay blank as he shook his head. "You will have to do better than that."

"What?"

"You've offended the most powerful and sought-after enchanted item in all the land, and you think a casual apology will suffice?"

"What would you have me do?"

"Indeed, what would I have you do… Ah! First of all, you must lower yourself to one knee and bow to her."

"How would it know if I'm bowing?"

"It? You continue to call Vesik an 'it?' Do you want to save Gluic or not?"

Thorik quickly backed down and lowered himself onto one knee before bowing forward.

Bryus let the Num stay down several moments longer than Thorik would have liked. "Excellent. Now place your hand near Vesik without touching her and apologize for your insensitive comments."

Thorik did as he was told. "I am sorry, Vesik. I was wrong to call you a book. I will treat you with more respect.

Bryus nodded. "Keep going. I think it's starting to work."

"I will never again assume that you or any other enchanted items are without feelings. I meant no harm by it. I have been on the receiving end of such insults and should know better."

Aside from the rustling of the campfire, the camp was quiet. Thorik slowly lifted his head to see Avanda and Bryus holding back their laughter. It had all been a ruse. "Well played." Thorik got back on his feet and dusted himself off.

The other two released their laughs at Thorik's expense.

"Now that you have humiliated me, have you found the spell that we need?"

Bryus had Avanda turn a few pages before he instructed her to stop. "Ah, here it is."

"A spell to release Gluic?"

"Yes," Bryus said sarcastically. "The spell is named 'Releasing Gluic'."

Thorik was not impressed. "Did you find one or not?"

"Understand, Thorik, finding the right spell is difficult. We must combine a spell such as this one, which reverses an enchanted object's spell with one that safely relocates a soul."

"What does that mean?"

Bryus kept his attention on the notes from the spell. "It means, Num, that we will find the spells we need in here."

"Excellent. How long before we can free her?"

Bryus stroked his chin as he continued reading. "How far is it to Ergrauth Valley?"

Thorik thought it was an odd question to ask, but that wouldn't be the first one from the Alchemist. "I have no idea. The Guardians block the entrance, and they are a week or two of travel from here. Why?"

"This spell requires Ergrauthian Spice."

It meant nothing to Thorik. "Can't we purchase some in Woodlen?"

"No, you can't just purchase this spice from your local market. It is special and has natural magical powers. In fact, it's actually two spices that, when mixed together, can negate any spell. We will need this to reverse the flow of the dagger."

"Is this another one of your jokes?"

"I wish it was. We'll need to travel to the Guardians, if not beyond, to obtain the components for this spell."

By this point, the sun had started to rise and Brimmelle had begun to wake while cuddled up to Grewen, under the mognin's protective arm. "What?" He then realized that he was snugging with the giant. "By the powers of the Mountain King himself, what's going on here?"

❧ 38 ❧

CULTURAL DIFFERENCES

*Thorik's Log: 30*th *day of the 8*th *month of the 650*th *year.*

Our journey to save Gluic has changed course. Now that we have the spell required to release my grandmother from the dagger, it has become apparent that we are in need of a critical component to perform it. The only location that holds this component is beyond the Guardian Towers, in Ergrauth's Valley. We will head out this morning, once I have informed everyone of the news. I doubt they will be pleased to hear it.

Morning came, and the discussion of the new destination was not well received. Not only was it one more delay for their return to Farbank and away from any plans to help stop the pending war, but it was also leading them into the most dangerous part of Terra Australis. Only Del'Unday were permitted beyond the Guardians, which stood at the entrance to Ergrauth's Valley.

But Thorik had come too far to give up now and he would travel there by himself if need be. His determination trumped the concerns that any of the others had. Eventually, they all agreed to follow him to the valley to help free Gluic.

"Santorray, I don't understand why you're against this trek. Aren't you originally from the Ergrauthian lands?" Thorik asked as they walked out of the forest that surrounded the Govi Glade.

"It's not a place for you. Outsiders are immediately found guilty of trespassing and are enslaved or taken to the city of Ergrauth."

"But we have you with us."

"I may not be able to save you."

"Why can't we pretend to be your slaves, like we once did in Corrock?"

"The two cannot be compared. Corrock is a far easier place to get away with such deceptions."

"Is that why you left?"

Santorray didn't answer at first, as his eyes squinted at the memories. "I was exiled for crimes against my father."

"Your father? What did you do?"

"I disobeyed him."

Thorik waited for further explanation, but received none, so he coaxed the blothrud for more. "It had to be more than just disobeying him."

"Your culture differs from ours. I'm fortunate to be alive after disobeying my father."

"What? Surely you're exaggerating. He wouldn't have murdered you for such a thing. Your neighbors and local authorities would have never stood for such an atrocity."

"He had full right to kill me where I stood, and no one would have batted an eye. Disrespecting my father in public is one of the worst things I could have done to him. If word had gotten out that he didn't dispense immediate, severe punishment, then he would have lost face, and respect toward him would have been lost by all. He did the right thing by unleashing his fury at me."

"How horrible. What a terrible place to grow up and live."

"No, it was a grand place to live. Everyone knew the rules. Life was very cut-and-dry. You cross the line, you receive punishment. You do what you are told, you are rewarded. Knowing boundaries keeps things in order and reduces unnecessary stress. Many cultures could learn from our structured ways."

"But..." Thorik thought a moment before continuing. "The Ovs in the city of Trewek live just the opposite, and they seem to be happy."

"I'm sure they are, considering they run around without any ramifications to their actions."

"But it seems to work for them."

"That's because the Ov'Unday are pacifists and avoid dealing with real issues. This allows others to take advantage of them very easily."

"I didn't get the sense that any of them were taking advantage of one another."

"And you won't. They will turn the other way and allow the minority of the culture to have their way. Warriors like you and I could never live in such places."

Thorik found it odd that Santorray would place them both in this category. "Why do you say that? I felt very relaxed there."

"You and I could never sit idly by once we started witnessing some individuals get away with murder. They allow their victims to suffer as the city officials try to help the criminals understand that what they did was wrong. Instead of taking swift action to eliminate the bad eggs, they allow them to continue to spread their poison, all the while hoping the offenders will change for the better."

"You don't think individuals can change?"

Santorray growled at the idea. "Few do."

"I hope you're wrong."

"I wish I was. Look at your fellow Nums. Brimmelle hasn't changed much since I have met him. He's still prejudiced against all Altered Creatures and most likely always will be, even though he relies on several to travel with and keep him alive. And then there is Avanda."

"What about her?" Thorik's voice was defensive.

"She will never take the time to get things right. She likes shortcuts and quick results. Her magic is chaotic and risky and always will be. Despite knowing this, you have provided her with a book that provides her with more of these dangerous powers. Your mission to save your grandmother has put our safety in jeopardy by giving her the book, knowing in your heart that she will never change."

"You don't know that she can't change."

"I know that as long as you keep feeding her what she wants, there is no reason for her to change and become more responsible. Pain is a needed part of the Del'Unday culture. People don't change until they feel they are forced into doing things differently in order to survive. As long as you protect Avanda and give her what she wants to learn more magic, she will never grow less dangerous."

Thorik looked back behind them at Bryus attempting to get Avanda to practice a spell, with little luck. As normal, she continued to want to move on to other spells that were more enjoyable to perform.

The Alchemist was sweating from the heat, which was increasing as they traveled southeast toward the Guardians. The sun continued to drain his strength as Avanda tested his nerves with her obsession with studies that were of more interest to her. Worn and tired, he continued to explain the basic elements to her.

"Excuse me," Thorik said to Santorray before he walked back to Bryus. Once he arrived, he asked Avanda to walk up front with Santorray for a while to help him scout for danger while he chatted with Bryus. She was always looking for something different to do, at least until she became bored with it.

"Bryus," Thorik said, once they were alone. "Is Avanda ready to cast the spell we need to free Gluic?"

"Absolutely. I've had more than enough time to explain decades of knowledge to her on how the fundamentals of the components work."

Thorik bit his tongue, knowing that Bryus' condescending tone was just how the man talked to everyone. "Will you be able to perform it?"

"Not with this oak tree growing out of my arm."

"But if we fixed your arm, you could save her?"

"I'm more than capable of purging her from Varacon."

"Okay, so all we need to do is find a new arm for you. Then you can cast the spell once we collect the spice."

"New arm? It will take a year for my body to heal after I remove this one because of the compromised magic used to attach it in the first place. Then, and only then, can I add a new one."

This was not what Thorik was hoping to hear. "I'm not willing to wait that long. You need to find a way to focus Avanda's training just on this spell so she can perform it."

"What do you think I've been trying to do, teach her to plant a garden? I've tried, but she just won't slow down. She has no discipline or fucus. I'm better off teaching her the basics and seeing what she makes of it."

"No, I need her to learn this spell."

"It's a complicated series of movements, words, and components. She doesn't have the patience. And I think I'm just about out of the patience I have. I surrender! I don't need this aggravation."

"Please don't. I need your help on this and am willing to make it worth your while."

The words caught Bryus' attention and caused him to stop walking. "Go on." He quickly exposed a devious smile.

"After she has successfully completed the spell and released my grandmother, I will give you Vesik."

"Avanda thinks the book of magic is hers. She will not be pleased."

"I know, but I will give it to you under one condition."

"Which is?"

"You leave with it, so she no longer has access to it."

"Odd request from someone who is so fond of our little lady Num."

"Not at all. I want her to be safe, and I fear the book will only cause her to harm herself in the end."

Bryus nodded. "That would be a logical conclusion for anyone who has seen her cast spells." He grinned at the idea of not having to steal the book after the spell occurred, which is what he had planned to do anyway. "I accept your offer." He then held out his thin dirty hand.

Thorik unexpectedly paused before reaching out to shake the Alchemist's hand. As he did, it felt wrong, as though he had made a pact with Bakalor himself. Even though he knew what he was doing was best for Avanda, he didn't like the emotions he was starting to feel.

✻ 39 ✻

THE SPELL

Bryus grabbed Avanda's arms in order to stop them from waving around in front of her. "Don't flail your arms about. You must move them in a gentle flowing pattern to the beat of the words. It should feel natural and smooth, not chaotic and sharp."

"I know. I'll do it properly once we retrieve the Ergrauthian Spice. Until then, it doesn't matter." Avanda went back to practicing spells during their midday rest.

Bryus shook his head. "You will only have one chance at this after we gather the spice, so you need to have every movement and word precisely in place and perfected, or else."

"Or else what?"

Bryus lifted his wooden arm that had caused him nothing but trouble since the moment they attached it. "We don't want anything like this to happen again, do we?" Several newly sprouted leaves and limbs had grown since the last time she had looked at it.

"Are you blaming that on me?"

"Avanda, I've performed over a dozen limb attachments, and all of them took. In fact, my head is the only original body part I have left. And in all the spells used to attach these various parts, this is the first time the spell hasn't worked. Care to tell me why?"

"No, I don't," she said honestly.

"And why is that?"

"Because you'll get mad at me."

Bryus actually appreciated her candor. He would much rather have her be honest than to lie or play word games with him. Pointing to his wooden arm, he spoke in clear, crisp words, "This can't happen again."

"It was an accident."

"It was carelessness."

"You rushed me."

"You could have told me you weren't ready." Bryus shook his head with disappointment. "These are the types of mistakes that give Alchemists a bad name."

"What do you mean?"

"Unlike E'rudites, anyone can perform spells if they are taught properly. Therefore, a poorly trained Alchemist can perform a spell and end up doing more harm than good. You know the type, they'll cast spells first and see how they work later."

"I hate those kinds of people." She knew that he was teasing her, so she played along.

"In order to make sure you don't get labeled as one of them, we will continue to practice the mixing of components, the proper pronunciation of verbal commands, and the physical movements required to carry them out."

Taking a deep sigh, she knew he was right. There was just so much to learn, and his desire for her to understand the details seemed to slow her down from learning so much more. "Can we at least practice the explosion spell you taught me? I do so enjoy that one."

Recalling the pain from the last time she had performed it, he declined. "No. We're nearly out of powder, and it takes too long to prepare more. You need to continue learning the spell needed to cleanse Varacon of Thorik's grandmother."

"Cleanse?"

"Yes, Varacon was virgin and pure until Gluic was stabbed. In doing so, she has tainted the dagger."

"Tainted? That's rude to say."

"Perhaps, but the truth is more important to say than worrying about someone's feelings."

"I don't know if that's true."

"Would you rather have the facts or have someone lie to you to make you feel good?"

"Can't you do both by telling me the facts in a way that doesn't make me feel bad?"

"Why waste the energy? The fact is, Gluic must be removed so Varacon can be the priceless enchanted blade about which so many stories have been written."

Avanda ears perked up. "What stories? Do tell."

Bryus had an audience of one, eager to hear him speak of his favorite subject. Excitement gleamed from his face as he prepared to tell his story with all the theatrics that he could muster.

Thorik interrupted their conversation. "Time to go. I want to get past that next ridge by nightfall. We should be at the Guardians within the next few days.

Bryus grabbed his items and stood up, never losing his excitement to tell the tale as they walked. "Long ago, there lived a beautiful princess…"

Avanda smiled as she listened to the story of two lovers, each fighting to free the other. Their day's trek went by quickly as she dreamed about his fable, when they weren't practicing her spells.

❧ 40 ❧

SUMMON SWAP

Night arrived on the grass plains like it did most nights. Wolf howls and the ramming of heads by Chuttlebeasts fighting for dominance carried across the soft hills of the prairie. Lightning from the southwest sparked across the sky in a show, with a backdrop of blue and green ribbons of light adrift in the night sky.

Another long day had been spent walking, and the Nums were exhausted and quickly fell asleep after eating.

Grewen typically was more hungry than tired, but he had dragged his hands in the tall grass during their walk and pulled up handfuls of the plants every few minutes to chew on. With a full stomach, he dozed off halfway through his normal foot cleansing in the campfire.

Santorray never showed signs of being tired. He always ensured that the camp was safe and the surrounding area was secure before retiring for the night. But before doing so, he would often crouch down on his hairy wolf-like legs and stare his dragon-like eyes to the east for several minutes. Periodically, he would sniff in the air before returning his gaze. Eventually, even he would fall prey to the need for sleep.

"Avanda," Bryus whispered as he shook her shoulder to wake her.

Squinting, she looked up and saw Bryus' face, with one eye missing.

Bryus quickly placed a hand over her mouth to prevent her from screaming. "Shhhh. It's me, Bryus. Stay quiet."

The distant lightning added a dreadful look to the man's thin face with his missing eye. Sweat ran down his forehead and down the sides of his face as he apprehensively glanced around. It took her a few moments to fully wake up and realize she wasn't in danger. As his wet and clammy hand released her, she could taste the bitterness of the salt from his wrinkly skin. "What are you doing? Where is your eye? What happened?"

"Keep it down. Everyone is sleeping."

"Bryus, what's going on?"

"Let's perform that spell one more time."

"Spell? Which one?"

"The summon swap spell."

Scrunching up her face, she obviously didn't think that was a good idea. "Listen, it was funny once, but next time we're going to get in trouble."

"Shhh, keep your voice down. Listen, just one more time. I'll never ask you to do it again."

"I don't understand why you want to do this. Everyone is tired. I'm tired. I don't feel like any games right now."

"How would you like to learn a charm spell? Perhaps even a love charm?"

Avanda's eyes gave away her interest.

"Good. We can barter. Cast this spell for me one more time, and I'll teach you a charm spell."

Nodding her approval, she still questioned his motives. "Why now?"

"Trust me, you'll understand later."

Sighing at his lack of forthcoming information, she agreed to perform the spell. "Where is your eye?"

"Never mind. Get started on the spell."

"Whose hair should I cut?"

"No need," he replied, handing her the hourglass with two different types of hair tied onto each end.

"Four people? We're swapping four of us?"

Bryus nodded for her to continue as he pointed at the instructions in the book.

She waved her hands appropriately and said the words needed to prepare the spell before the final words appeared upon the pages.

"Go on, say them," Bryus urged her in a nervous voice.

"Something doesn't seem right about this."

"It soon will. You were nervous about it last time as well, if you recall." Bryus' voice gave signs of anxiousness as he prodded her to complete the spell.

"I suppose. Where do you want me to sit?"

"I don't give a damn where you sit. Just start the spell." His nervous smile had changed to a look of anger.

"Hey, what's gotten into you? Why are you acting this way?"

Grabbing her shoulder with his one hand, he strongly encouraged her to stop asking questions. "Say the last words to activate the spell!" His sharp words were exiting through tight teeth, and sweat poured down his face and his arms.

"No!" She tried to pull away from him, but his grip was too strong.

Raising his hand to slap her, he stopped himself just prior to the act. "You don't understand! You need to finish this spell right now!"

"No, she doesn't!" Thorik announced from behind Bryus. The Alchemist's conversation had obviously been louder than he had hoped.

He quickly turned to face the Num. "Thorik, you don't know what's going on here."

"Get away from her, Bryus."

The Alchemist grabbed her throat and shook his head in defiance of the Num's demand. "Thorik, if you take a step closer to me, I'll kill her. Her blood will be on your hands."

Thorik slowly stepped back, showing his palms to suggest he would obey the old man's wishes.

Wiping the salty sweat out of his eye with his upper arm, Bryus loosened his grip slightly on Avanda's neck.

Seeing this, Thorik decided to take advantage of the opening. "Now!"

Before Bryus could turn around, Santorray rushed forward and knocked Bryus off his feet. Flying eight yards, the man landed and rolled to a stop.

The blothrud wasn't through. He leaped forward, picked the man up, and then slapped him hard to the ground, flat on his back. "You like picking on little girls?"

"It's not like that!" Bryus began spitting up blood from the violent attack.

"Don't kill him," Thorik announced as he walked over to the Alchemist. "I want to know what he's up to."

Shaking his head, his body was held down by one of Santorray's mighty legs. "Nothing. It was just a spell."

"What kind?" Thorik asked.

"Same one Avanda and I did before." He spit up more blood. "Avanda, tell them we were just playing a joke. It was a game."

"Grabbing her throat was no joke!" Santorray growled.

"I was frightened by Thorik's arrival and I panicked."

Santorray looked at Thorik. "He's full of Fesh lies. I should just kill him now and salvage the rest of the night for our sleep."

Thorik raised his hand to prevent the blothrud from killing Bryus. "No. I want to know what he was really up to. Perhaps you can help him recall."

"Gladly." Santorray extended his claws from his paw and began to drive the sharp tips into the man's chest.

"Awww!" Bryus screamed from the new pain.

"Thorik." Grewen had stood up and was walking over to the scene. "I don't like the idea of torture, and I'm surprised that you are condoning this."

"Grewen, you didn't see what he was doing."

"What was he doing when you first approached him?" the mognin asked.

"He nearly hit Avanda for not performing a spell."

"Nearly?"

"Yes, he stopped himself, but he then grabbed her by the throat."

"Should we not give him the right to speak without threatening his life?"

"No!" Santorray was unsatisfied with the suggestion. "His reasons for the crime don't justify doing it, regardless of what they are."

Grewen attempted a different approach. "Even among your Del customs, dear Santorray, it is the victim who selects the response, not an outsider such as yourself. Based on your traditions, Avanda is the one who selects his fate."

Grinding his claws slightly deeper into Bryus' chest, Santorray smiled before looking for Avanda to step forward. "What would you have me do to this Fesh in a human's skin?"

Avanda walked up quietly, tears in her eyes. "Why? Why were you like this to me? I trusted you."

"You don't understand," he coughed out.

"Then explain it to me. Why force me to cast this spell?" She held the hourglass before her and noticed the hair on each end. "Whose hair is this? I recognize Santorray's coarse red leg hair and Brimmelle's black hair, but not the ones on the other side."

Bryus was silent, grimacing at the situation.

"And where is your eye? What does this have to do with it?"

Brimmelle walked up behind her with a cloth wrapped around a small sphere. "I think I found it."

"NO!" Blood shot from Bryus' mouth. "Whatever you do, don't open that cloth!"

"And why not?" Thorik asked.

He received no answer.

Santorray pressed harder onto the man's chest, achieving no results except additional pain for the Alchemist, which Santorray enjoyed watching.

"Open up the cloth," Thorik announced.

"No, please, anything but that," Bryus begged.

Thorik raised his hand to Brimmelle to stop the action. "Tell me why. I shall not ask again."

The Alchemist finally broke down and cried. "Because if you do, my family will die."

"How so?"

"Darkmere has my family in one of his prisons." Bryus struggled to get the words out.

Motioning to Santorray to have him reduce the pressure he was placing on Bryus' body, Thorik was impatient about wanting more information. "What does that have to do with this spell?"

"Darkmere allows my family to live under one circumstance: I must lead him to Ambrosius."

"I knew it!" Brimmelle announced. "I told you he was working for the Dark Lord. Santorray, kill the traitor!"

As much as the blothrud would have enjoyed finishing the battle, he didn't take orders from the likes of Brimmelle.

"I agreed to do this for him in order to save my family," Bryus insisted. "I meant you no harm. If I had refused, he would have killed my family as well as myself. This way, I had time to plan their escape."

It still made little sense to Thorik. "I thought you didn't know where they were being held."

Spitting blood to the side, he took a few needed breaths before answering. "I don't. Which is why I needed the spell."

Avanda held the hourglass up and looked at the hairs on the bottom. She then noticed the unique stitching in Bryus' collar was gone. "These are the hairs of your family?"

Bryus nodded. "Yes, my wife and my daughter."

She squinting as it came together. "You wanted me to cast this spell so your family would appear here with us?"

"Yes, where they would be safe from Darkmere."

"But then Santorray and Brimmelle would have awoken in their place, in some prison."

Santorray scowled and added some weight back on the man's chest.

Brimmelle was outraged at the idea. "You mean to tell me I would have woken up in Darkmere's prison in a distant land?"

"Yes." Bryus squinted at the added pain on his chest. "But you would have had Santorray to bust you out. The two of you would have had a fighting chance to escape. A chance that my family never would have had."

"How could you violate our friendship?" Thorik asked. "We trusted you. I trusted you."

"Why do you think I avoided trying to become friends with you people? I didn't want a relationship. I didn't want there to be any bonds. Every time I found myself getting closer to you, it made it all the harder to complete this task."

Avanda then asked, "How did you choose?"

"Santorray had the best chance of escaping Darkmere's prison, and Brimmelle just annoys me."

Brimmelle stepped forward after hearing the comment and raised the cloth-covered eye as he prepared to uncover it. "I'll show you how I can annoy you."

"No! Wait!" Bryus shouted.

"What does this eye have to do with your family?" Brimmelle asked.

"Darkmere sees through it. He thinks I am asleep right now. If you reveal it, he will see you and know I have been exposed as a traitor. He will murder my wife and daughter."

Avanda considered his point of view. "Have you been plotting against us all this time?"

"I've been trying to save my family all this time. Surely you, of all people, can understand what measures you would take to save family."

Thorik sighed. "And this is why you were persistent in wanting to help us find the book of magic? You needed to find this spell in order to save them."

Glancing over at his wooden arm, Bryus nodded again. "I hadn't expected to lose the power to properly perform spells."

"Which is why you needed Avanda," Thorik added. "Why didn't you come forward so we could help you?"

"There was nothing in it for you. Without a reason for you to get something from it, why would you have helped?"

Thorik motioned to Santorray to free his prisoner and lift him up. He then walked over to the man. "Because we are family. And once you are part of our family pod, we help you out, even when we may disagree with your decision."

Bryus was confused. "You mean you're not vengeful after what I attempted to do?"

"Oh, I'm furious with the danger you put us in, the fear you gave Avanda, and the position you nearly put Santorray and Brimmelle in! I'm disappointed in you as well. So let's make this clear. You are walking a fine line with this family pod, and you have a lot of rebuilding to do."

"And my wife and daughter?"

"I can't guarantee we can help your family out of their situation, but we will try our best once you have proven yourself by helping us save Gluic from Varacon."

Bryus nodded one last time.

"Santorray, escort Bryus back to his bedding. Brimmelle, keep that cloth tight around that eye and give it back to Bryus. The last thing we need is for Darkmere to know we are on to him."

41

GUARDIANS

———

Thorik's Log: 12th day of the 9th month of the 650th year.

Last night we camped just west of the Guardians and the entrance to the Ergrauthian Valley. The Guardians remind me of giant gateposts, as our path sits between the two pointed mountainous peaks. The air is hot and vegetation is sparse in this region. The dry riverbed that leads up to the mountain pass looks like a long tongue extending from two mountainous teeth of the range. I'm feeling less optimistic about our success the closer we get to this eastern valley as we prepare to walk into what appears to be the mouth of an evil beast.

———

Two light gray masses of solid stone pierced the sky on either side of the travelers' path. A thick wall of clouds hung onto the mountain range behind the rock towers as stray wind-gusts forced long streams of clouds down toward the earth, giving the appearance of an upper set of teeth. Thorik and his friends felt as though they were walking into the mouth of the foreign land itself. Adding to this, the sun painted the underside of the clouds with a red glow, as though the valley's mouth was preparing to blow fire toward them. The ominous scene produced a heightened feeling of apprehension for the Nums.

Long cracks raced up the smooth sides of the main two cone-shaped towering rocks as water stains coated the areas beneath them. Beyond these two gigantic teeth, the wide path flowed around the various bends in the desert foothills of the mountains. The dirt road and dry riverbed were filled with bristle bushes, while the foothills were covered with red cacti of various sizes. Most were thin and tall with a few arms at their sides, and nearly a fifth of them had black flowers crowning their highest point, giving the travelers a feeling of being watched by an audience.

"It's like being in the Woodlen coliseum, with thousands of spectators standing in silence." Avanda was in awe of the number of cacti.

She was correct; the initial small valley that lay ahead was bowl-shaped as they walked into the center dirt arena. The assembly of deep red cacti stood eerily silent as they seemed to watch the group walk past them. Silent, at least until a buzzing caught the attention of all three Nums.

"Do you hear that?" Thorik asked. Something was alerting him to danger as the hair on the back of his neck stood on end.

Brimmelle dismissed the noise. "It's the wind." But he himself was too uncomfortable to look up at the hillside audience.

Grewen corrected the Num. "There is no wind."

Scanning back and forth, Avanda watched the foothills for movement. "I heard it as well." The idea of the cacti coming to life was magical, and she looked forward to seeing how they would uproot themselves to walk.

Santorray raised his muzzle and sniffed the air. "Quiet."

The group came to a halt. Brimmelle kept his head low to avoid seeing anything unpleasant, whereas everyone else was on the lookout for movement. As the only one hoping to see something happen, Avanda struggled to stand still.

Breaking off some new small branches from the end of his arm, Bryus was more interested in looking for Ergrauthian spices. "That should do nicely." He then headed for the hills.

"Bryus, wait for me." Avanda immediately followed his lead.

Santorray kept his position as he allowed his senses to determine his surroundings. "The Guardians are coming. We need to move quickly."

Thorik was confused. "The Guardians? I thought the two stone teeth we walked between were the Guardians."

"No, they are the Guardians' gate, where none shall pass."

Thorik chuckled to himself. "We had no trouble entering. It wasn't much of a gate."

"It's not to keep us from entering. It is to keep the Guardians from escaping and destroying everything beyond this point. Long ago, a spell was cast to prevent them from leaving this narrow passage within this mountain range."

"How do the Del'Unday cross into the Lake Valley then?"

"They don't. That is what has held Ergrauth back from attacking and destroying the humans and Ovs for so long. There have only been a few times that he has been willing to risk this journey."

With his body becoming numb, Thorik suddenly realized the danger he had put everyone in. "You mean even the demon, Ergrauth, is afraid to pass by the Guardians?"

"He's not afraid. He just understands the casualties that are likely to come along with doing so. It must be a major play for him to risk the lives of so many of his troops to leave his home valley."

Filling the foothills, the buzzing became loud enough for everyone to hear.

Bryus ran up to the nearest cactus. "Defend yourself, or I shall run you through," he jested as he stabbed his wooden arm into the thick stalk of the red cactus.

Avanda skidded to a halt as she witnessed a thick plume of red dust spray out from the hole in the plant and onto the Alchemist. Avoiding the cloud, she could hear Bryus cough from within it.

"Don't let the spice hit the ground," Bryus choked out as the cloud slowly faded. "Grab the glass jars from my pouch."

Red spice poured out of the cactus as Avanda collected the glass containers and placed the open mouth of one under the stream. A fragrance of fruit accompanied the spice, which poured out over Bryus' wooden arm and into the jar.

Avanda completed her fill, pulled the jar back, and turned to face the Alchemist. In his face, she could see the pain from his ordeal, but she didn't know where it was coming from. "What's wrong?"

His face was turning red as he attempted to pull his arm out of the cactus. It had punctured the plant easily but was now caught inside it. To make matters worse, the hole was reducing in size around his arm. Soon after stopping the bleeding of red spice, the cactus repaired itself and began squeezing his arm.

Even though his vision was nearly useless, due to the spice in his eyes, Bryus quickly cast a spell to open the hole back up. But nothing came of it, for the spice had protective properties. He then performed a spell on his arm. It too was coated by spice, preventing any success. The man was trapped as his arm continued to be squeezed.

Without thinking, Bryus placed a sandal up on the cactus for leverage to force his arm out. But instead of pushing the cactus away, he screamed in pain from the sharp needles that stabbed through his sandal and foot. Unable to pull his leg free, he panicked, for he was now at the mercy of the others in his party.

Avanda had closed the top of the glass jar and set it inside her purse before running behind him. Hugging him from the back, she pulled him as hard as she could as Bryus screamed in pain.

"It's not going to work," Bryus yelled. "We need to mix some of the black spice with the red spice to neutralize it so my spell will work."

"Where do I get the black spice from?"

"The pollen from the flowers on top of the cactus."

Avanda looked up at the desert plants, which had crowns of flowers at their peaks. Bryus' cactus had none, but others nearby did. The shortest ones were easily three times her height. She wouldn't have given it a second thought if it had been a tree, but the thick needles on these cacti provided her with a greater challenge. "Grewen!" she yelled to the mognin.

Meanwhile, Thorik had been standing with Santorray as they watched the other hillside. "The buzzing is getting louder, but I can't tell from where."

Just as the words sprang from his lips, movement could be seen coming over one of the hills. It was a dark tornado growing toward the sky as its base climbed the foothill on the gray, cloudy day. However, this tornado was not connected to the clouds themselves as it moved over the terrain directly toward the travelers.

"The Guardians approach," Santorray growled.

A second tornado appeared behind it, followed by a third from the opposite side of the road.

Not willing to stay long enough to understand exactly what was approaching, Thorik yelled out to his team, "Grewen, pull Bryus free! We're making a run for it!"

As the closest tornado approached, it became clear that the dark flowing mass was actually tens of thousands of fist-sized flying insects, all using the heat from the desert floor to swirl around in a collective group around a larger insect which stayed in the center.

Swarming around their queen, each insect rapidly flapped its wings in order to stay in formation. Red and black external skeletons covered their thin bodies and long, thin legs, and each appendage came to a sharp point.

The queen in the center of each gathering was easily ten times the size of those that protected her. Marked with bright yellow streaks, the red insect had extra pincers in front to help her slay her victims, assuming anything could make it past her army.

A fourth tornado of insects was spotted as the first three closed in on them.

Grewen had already arrived and wrapped his oversized hand around Bryus' wooden arm, tugging it slightly to free it from the cactus. It wouldn't budge.

"Stop playing with it and give it a quick yank," Bryus ordered.

Following his instructions, the mognin made a swift pull. Bryus' body folded up around Grewen's hand from the violent thrust, which freed the cactus from the ground instead of the wooden arm from the cactus.

"You idiot!" Bryus protested, nursing a bloody nose from his face slapping into the side of Grewen's hand. "Can't you do anything right? Put me down." One of his feet dangled in the air, while the other was still pinned to the cactus.

"My apologies." The giant chuckled as he let go of the man's arm. The weight of the uprooted cactus catapulted Bryus forward as the plant tumbled to the ground. "Anything else?"

It was at this point that Thorik and Brimmelle arrived. Anxious to escape the mountain pass before the Guardians arrived, Thorik whipped around to keep a bearing on their advancement. "What's the holdup?" Thorik asked quickly.

Bryus looked up from the painful predicament and noticed the swarms. His face twitched at the sight. "Avanda! Get the black spice. Hurry!"

"No, we have to free you first," she said.

The Alchemist was appalled. "Are you insane? We may only have one chance at cleansing Varacon of Gluic's soul. We must restore him."

Avanda disagreed and moved toward him, but was stopped by his thrashing about with his free arm. "You can't free me without the black spice. Get the spice first," he ordered her.

"Spice?" Brimmelle complained. "We need to make a run for it."

The swarms were closing in; there was no time to argue. "Grewen." Avanda handed the mognin an empty glass jar. "Put some pollen from those flowers into this while we help Bryus."

Delicately taking the small container between two of his massive fingers, he stepped over to a cactus with a full crown of black flowers. Each had long, sharp needles protecting it, and the access to the flower itself was too small for the mognin's thick fingers. Trying anyway, the needles pricked his fingers time and time again. Even with his thick skin, the suffering was tremendous, for each needle gave off a painful poison.

Thorik and Avanda continued to pull at Bryus' wooden arm to free it from the fallen cactus. But without any leverage to hold the cactus in place, they ended up dragging the heavy plant nearly a foot before realizing it was pointless.

The first swarm was now in striking distance as it approached the group.

Brimmelle had been keeping his attention on the Guardians. "They're coming! Drop what you have and run!"

"Avanda," Grewen said, "my fingers are too large. I will have to lift you to do this."

Looking down at the lack of progress with Bryus, she saw the Alchemist's nod of approval to leave. She didn't think twice as she bolted from her position and over to Grewen.

She had climbed up on Grewen so many times in the past that they knew how to get her up high in the least amount of time. Plucking the jar from him, she began scooping out black powder from the center of the flowers.

The Guardians attacked.

Testing their opponents, only a few dozen insects flew from the swirling swarm. The first attack was on Grewen and Avanda as they used the sharp ends of their legs to stab their victims.

Grewen received most of the attacks, as his free hand swatted away any that came close to Avanda.

The insects' abrupt diving at her nearly caused Avanda to drop the jar more than once, but her confidence in Grewen kept her focused on her task.

Thorik and Bryus were also now under attack as they swung their arms out to protect themselves. Thorik rolled away from the attacks and kicked the giant insects off of Bryus, but the Nums simply couldn't keep up. More showed up. One firmly landed on Thorik's back and stabbed the Num deep into his shoulder. Another landed on Bryus and drove a sharp leg into his side.

Brimmelle was not immune from the attack, and he fought off one of the insects by swinging his hands wildly in front of it to shoo it off.

Grewen struggled more and more to fend off their attacks on the little Num, as he held her near the cactus. He had sustained extensive injuries, since he spent no time trying to protect himself. Over a dozen had landed on his body and begun to dig into his thick skin. "I think it's time you get down now. It's getting too dangerous for you."

"Just a little longer." She attempted to scrape off enough black spice from the flowers to fill her jar.

A second wave of Guardians were launched from the swarm.

Brimmelle screamed at the sight. "We're doomed!"

Thorik knew they couldn't possibly defend themselves from this new threat. Bryus was immovable, while Grewen and Brimmelle simply couldn't outrun them. He and Avanda had the only chance of survival, assuming they abandoned their friends, and he couldn't fathom them doing such a thing.

SNAP!

The sound caused Thorik to turn and see Santorray stepping on Bryus' wooden arm. He had snapped it in half and freed the Alchemist from the cactus. "Use Rummon!" he barked at Thorik. Holding the cactus at bay with the broken-off piece of Bryus' arm, he tore Bryus' foot from the needles which held it.

Bryus screamed in pain. Ignoring the Alchemist's agony, Santorray tossed him over his shoulder. "Grewen, take her down this instant!" the blothrud bellowed.

His powerful voice was enough to rattle Avanda and cause her to lean back from the cactus, indicating to Grewen that it was time to take her down. In doing so, he turned and lumbered down the hill back to the road with her in his arms, swatting the attacking insects along the way.

Thorik pulled out the Spear of Rummon and grasped it in both of his hands while pointing it up at the swarm. Feeling the heat radiate from within the spear, he knew the dragon's soul was ready to do his bidding. To his relief, the insects began breaking off their attack.

Brimmelle fell to the ground as his single insect opponent dove toward his face and grabbed onto his head. Its back legs lifted into the air, preparing to thrust down into the Num's throat.

Reaching down with his free hand, Santorray grabbed the insect on Brimmelle's face and squeezed it tight, popping it in an explosion of black pus. The insect's forelegs fell as the Num's mouth, nose, and eyes were coated with the insect's remains.

Brimmelle was horrified. In some way he almost wished the blothrud hadn't helped him.

Picking up Brimmelle and tossing him over his other shoulder, Santorray ran down the hillside, back to the dirt road.

Following his friends, Thorik too made his way to the dirt road, but not to safety. The swarm had followed them down the hillside and blocked their path. In addition, the other three tornado-like swarms had also arrived and blocked any other path to escape.

Thorik lifted the spear up toward the swarm in front of him, causing them to withdraw. But in doing so, the other three swarms moved in from behind. Pulling the spear back, he then pointed it at another swarm. It too, withdrew. But again, the others advanced.

Every second that went by, tens of thousands of Guardians moved closer to their prey. Thorik glanced at Grewen and Santorray for options. They gave him none.

❦ 42 ❦

CAPTURED

Four tornadoes of flying insects surrounded Thorik and his party in the desert mountain pass, blocking them from any escape. Only by Thorik's use of Rummon was he able to keep them at bay, but even that was short-lived as the queens within each tornado swarm worked together to attack from behind Thorik and the direction he held the spear.

The yellow stripes on the back of the queens flashed brightly in order for them to communicate, and the frequency of the light show was intensifying. It was just a matter of seconds before the Guardians would work in complete unison to launch a full attack and destroy them.

Without warning, the flashing lights from the queens stopped. Thorik could hear a moment of silence from the extreme buzzing, as every insect stopped for a moment to change flight paths. The only sound he heard was the thumping of his own heart against his chest as he looked out at the towering endless supply of attackers. His decision to come here had not only failed, but it had cost them all their lives. What had he done?

The quarter-mile high towers of insects dove onto the travelers to carry out the orders of their queens. The sheer weight of all the insects smothered everyone's bodies, and the travelers were quickly covered.

Grewen fell to his hands and knees, sheltering Avanda and Brimmelle from the weight of their attackers, but could not stop the attacks themselves.

Santorray remained standing as his powerful arms and hands continued to destroy the insects. But even he would have to relinquish eventually, and there seemed to be an endless supply of insects.

Thorik turned and faced his friends, launching Rummon's power up in the air and frying dozens of insects every second with the spear's heated breath. But the insects were replaced so quickly that it was barely even noticed by his companions.

A dozen insects landed on Thorik's back, forcing him to the ground with the spear trapped underneath him. The weight quickly loaded on, preventing him from pulling the spear out to use it. He was defenseless.

Continuing with the attacks, the Guardians pounded the travelers until suddenly, there was a second lapse in wing beats. Immediately afterward, all the insects abandoned the attack.

Injured and bloody, the travelers looked up to see the four tornadoes reform above them. In addition, dust was being kicked up from the dirt road as an army approached. A Del'Unday army. Ergrauth's army. As if the Guardians needed help, Thorik thought in dismay.

The army of Del'Unday had come around the bend unnoticed by the Guardians, who had been preoccupied with the travelers. Thousands of Del'Unday warriors filed in around the valley walls, armed with catapults, battering rams, counterweight trebuchets, and wagons filled with weapons and supplies.

It was only moments before the Guardians reacted to the approaching armored troops and quickly launched their attack on the Del'Unday with all four swarms flying toward them.

Fortunately for Thorik, he had assumed wrongly. The Del'Unday army and the Guardians were adversaries, which had provided a reprieve from their attack on the travelers.

"Thorik," Santorray said with haste. "Cover up that spear."

"Why?"

"It once was Ergrauth's spear. If he reclaims it, there will be no stopping him."

Thorik quickly covered it up. "How about Vesik and Varacon?"

"He knows not and cares not about these things. The spear was a special gift given to him, long ago."

The Del'Unday army continued to approach as various Del species came around the bend carrying weapons while some rode Fesh'Unday creatures. Other Fesh pulled wagons and the larger warfare equipment. Flags flapped in the breeze as their masses seemed to grow.

Standing several heads taller than the other blothruds in the ranks was the one that led them. He was a towering blothrud of massive muscles and sharp spikes who had giant red wolf legs, the hairless body of a human, and the head of a red dragon. His red skin dripped with sweat, and his veins pulsed with heated blood. Thick black battle blades and spikes extended from his body across his shoulders, down his back, and on his elbows and knees.

This was the great demon, Ergrauth, and he walked with a confidence of victory, leading his army of Del'Unday warriors toward the Guardians. Each powerful stride slammed onto the ground, causing the earth to shake. Ergrauth was the ultimate Del'Unday. He was the most superior blothrud, or any Del'Unday for that matter. He was the demon of the land and all that rested upon it, and he showed his pride with each massive step.

Seeing the clouds of insects attacking, Ergrauth launched his own forces to intercept them by giving off a deep howl which shook the hillsides. The order had been given, and his army lurched forward.

Smashing with maces and shields, an assault by armed Dels immediately started wiping out the insects near the ground. One after another, they made a path forward past the cloud of bugs.

However, it wasn't long before the rest of the invading insects arrived. By sheer numbers, they changed the tide of the battle as hundreds of thousands hovered over the road, diving and attacking the backs of their victims.

Ergrauth easily swatted them away from his face. He was a master of war and knew when to use the right weapon for the right enemy. Grabbing a horn from his side, he blew into it.

The high-pitched noise was hard for most to hear, especially in the heat of battle. After the long blast into the horn, he placed it back at his side and swatted away the insects near him as though they were nothing more than flies.

The battle raged on as two more tornadoes of insects arrived to help dominate the battle.

Ergrauth watched his army to observe their abilities in this difficult situation. Seeing one of his warriors recoil from an attack by a dozen insects, Ergrauth stomped over and killed the Del'Unday himself. "I will not have cowardice in my army," he announced as he watched his men fight. But his army couldn't possibly hold up against the numbers of its enemies.

He then looked up and saw what he was waiting for. Two dragons were diving toward them.

Covered in blue and white scales, the lead dragon headed in from the back of the battle. Grazing the air just above the soldiers, it opened its mouth and sprayed a fan of deadly frost into the air, killing thousands of the insects that then rained down to the ground.

The second dragon approached at a higher level and sent a series of lightning bolts showering from his mouth as though heat-lightning had occurred without the clouds. Again, thousands of insects were instantly killed and fell to the earth.

The tide of the battle quickly changed to Ergrauth's advantage as the dragons continued to destroy legions of insects with every attack.

Free from defending against the insects, Thorik hobbled himself around to ensure his friends were alive. "He has dragons in his army? I thought they belonged to Rummon."

Santorray shoveled handfuls of dead insects away to free the others as well. "It would appear that he has freed Rummon's children, the Winds of Conquest."

"Those dragons are the Winds of Conquest?"

"Yes." Santorray pulled Bryus up to his feet.

Grewen stood up from his hunched-over position and stretched his back. Standing about the same height as Ergrauth, he was far less threatening. "Trewek's elders must be informed."

"It won't help them. Nothing shy of a demon can stop them," the blothrud said.

Thorik thought about it for a moment. "I have Rummon. Therefore. I am the only one who can stop them."

Santorray scoffed at the idea. "Don't even think about taking that weapon out. Besides, even if Rummon was here in the flesh, he would still have his hands full, taking on both of his children at the same time. His presence inside that spear has no chance, brave Sec."

"Then Grewen is correct. We must at least notify the Trewek elders of the pending invasion."

"We won't have that opportunity," Santorray growled.

Thorik looked down the path at the unguarded rock towers, where they had entered. "And why is that? We can run back to the Chuttle Range before we are spotted."

Heavy footsteps approached the travelers from behind Thorik. Turning, the Num gazed upon the mognin-sized blothrud demon, Ergrauth, only twenty-some yards from him.

The demon stopped and inspected the small band of injured travelers. One of his eyebrows raised at the sight before him. "Santorray? Is it possible?"

Santorray growled at the demon. "More than possible, father."

"Father?" Thorik was louder than he had hoped.

"You are returning to my valley?" Ergrauth asked.

"It would appear so."

"It has taken you many years to finally return and stand at my side. Your timing is of interest, considering I move to destroy the land you have called home for so long."

"You are walking into Bakalor's trap. He is using you to launch this war and sacrifice your troops to do his bidding. He plans to take over the land once you are finished."

Ergrauth grinned on one side of his mouth. "I fully understand what he plans on doing. But I haven't given him all the facts. I will be ready when he comes to the surface. I will be victorious in the end. And with you at my side, I have no doubts about our easy victory."

Blood dripped from the insect cuts across Santorray's body as he stood strong and defiant. "I am not here to stand at your side."

"You have been, and always will be, an Ergrauthian Elite. You have no choice but to fight for me."

"Living for so many years on the terrain you plan to destroy, my destiny is now chosen by myself, not others, and especially not by you."

As the battle raged on behind him, with victory nearly at hand by the Del'Unday, Ergrauth stood motionless for a moment. "You have learned nothing," he growled in disapproval. "You're just as disobedient now as you ever were."

Santorray spit on the ground between them. "I will not blindly follow anyone, including you."

The demon's lips quivered with anger. "I would kill you here and now, but you would not suffer sufficiently for this crime against me. Instead, you shall suffer for all eternity inside of my city."

"You may wish it, but I will not go. You will have to attempt to kill me where I stand."

"Attempt? You are nothing to me. I made you. I can destroy you."

"You can try." Santorray crossed his sabers onto his chest and pierced the sharp ends into his skin before slowly dragging them down, forming a bloody X on his front. He was ready for war.

Ergrauth was not accustomed to being treated in such a way. The disrespect toward him fueled his emotions and heated his body with fresh blood. "You challenge me?" he yelled, staring at the cuts his son had just given himself. "No one challenges Ergrauth!"

Stepping out, the massive demon violently rushed toward the travelers to slay his son. His eyes narrowed, and his teeth seemed to grow larger as his skin tightened and pulled back from his mouth. Using his claws, he ripped into his own biceps to signal his willingness to forgo pain to win his battle.

Santorray also charged forward, as blood dripped from his chest, and spotted the dirt road. With sabers tightly gripped, he howled the war cry of the Elites, which he once led.

His father growled at the sound that he himself had taught his son in his youth, when he had believed that his son would be his finest warrior. Instead, his son turned out to be his greatest disappointment, as he had betrayed him so many years ago.

Ergrauth's thoughts affected his attack by taking his mind off the task at hand for a split second. The two collided, and he had underestimated the skill of his son.

Santorray leaped up and swirled in the air, slicing his sabers deep into the demon's arm and torso before landing firmly on the road, ready for his next attack.

Yelling from the unexpected pain, his father slid to a halt just before stomping upon the Nums. A dust cloud of sand covered the travelers as Grewen pulled Avanda and Bryus to a safer location. Brimmelle and Thorik followed Grewen as the demon turned around toward his son.

Santorray didn't provide his father with any time to realize his son's abilities. He again leaped forward, into the air, thrusting his muscular shoulder and sharp blades into his father's stomach. His weight and speed knocked Ergrauth off of his feet and down into the dirt with a sound that rocked the canyon's walls.

"Not only am I still an Elite, but I am now much more!" Santorray used his fists to hammer a solid blow to his father's chest, cracking a few ribs.

However, Ergrauth's long mighty arm sprang upward, tossing Santorray a dozen yards away from him, giving him some time to recoup. Clutching his chest in pain, the demon revealed to Santorray that he actually was injured.

"You can cut me all you want, boy. But you will never be able to defeat me." Ergrauth kept a keen eye on him as he stood back up. "You know it in your head that you can't win. And as long as I'm in there, you will always lose."

Santorray fought to ignore his father's words. "Go back to your city and give up this war, or I shall be forced to slay you."

Ergrauth coughed out a painful laugh before standing up straight and tall with his shoulders back. "Let me see what my little boy has learned."

Santorray hated his father calling him boy. The degrading tone his father always used had festered into his dreams and nightmares. "More than you think." He then raced back toward his father with his sabers spinning in his palms.

The demon stood like a statue as he watched his son charge at him. Raising his arms straight out to his side, he invited his son to end this once and for all.

Blood sprayed from Santorray's self-inflicted cuts on his chest as he raised his weapons to impale his father. Again, jumping at the last moment, he flew through the air at his target. Ergrauth's chest had no protection. He was vulnerable.

With lightning-fast reflexes, Ergrauth violently swiped one of his enormous arms forward, crushing Santorray's side and sending him straight into the ground. The attack had come out of nowhere, a blow that would have easily killed a Num and most likely disabled the blothrud.

Momentarily clutching his own chest from the pain of the prior attack, Ergrauth quickly grabbed the blades along his son's back and lifted Santorray up in the air before his son could recover. This was an insult more than a tactic, for parents would pick up their children in this manner when they misbehaved.

The demon then ran back toward his army before launching Santorray into the side of one of the military catapults. The wooden weapon shattered upon the impact as splinters and dust shot in every direction.

Before the dust could settle, Ergrauth stepped over, brushed the debris off his arms, and surveyed the damage to his son. Expecting to see a lifeless body, he was astonished to find a large wooden beam from the catapult come flying out at him, striking him in his face.

Ergrauth crumpled backward from the impact, which lacerated his face and broke several of his teeth. He couldn't recall the last time he had tasted blood from his own wound.

Leaping from the catapult, Santorray landed a solid kick to the demon's stomach, followed by a two-handed strike on the back of his neck after Ergrauth bent over from the first attack. The two quick assaults knocked the demon to his knees.

Santorray quickly gathered his strength and lifted the demon up by his back blades. His arms and legs shook from the weight as he attempted to run with him in tow before tossing him head-first into a wagon of supplies.

The wagon burst into pieces as the wheels popped off, and the supplies tumbled out. There was a moment of silence as Santorray waited for his father to leap back out. Instead, Ergrauth slowly stood back up from the far side of the wagon and laughed.

"You still are an Elite. And you have retained everything I have taught you. I'm impressed."

Santorray stood up straight, still waiting for an attack.

The demon smirked. "You are a valuable asset to me. Therefore, I will ask you one last time to join me."

There was no hesitation. "I will not."

"Understood. Nor would I give up what I believe in. But we are at an impasse. And my army will stop at nothing to be victorious."

From his right, Santorray glimpsed several warriors charging him. Pulling out his sabers again, he fought them off. He disabled one, and then another would take their place. He would slay two more, and then three would move in. He simply could not fight the entire Del'Unday Army.

Ergrauth laughed as he watched his son sidestep his way back to his companions as his warriors continued to test his skills. Even with the loss of the demon's men, Santorray was slowly being beaten down with blades and blunt weapons.

By the time Santorray had backed up all the way to the other travelers, he was a bloody mess. It was amazing that he could still stand, let alone fight. It was at this time that the fight stopped and the soldiers backed off, giving way to Ergrauth's approach.

Santorray stood wobbly on his legs as he held out his sabers toward his father. "This is what you call honor?"

The demon laughed. "This is what I call victory. Winning is what matters, not how you do it. Winners write the history to their own favor and tell the tale of victory they want others to know. No one remembers the tales of those who lost."

Santorray spit on his father's foot in defiance. "You are what's wrong with this world. I've known Fesh that I respect more than you."

The phrase struck a nerve, as Santorray knew it would, but the blothrud was too injured to stop the demon's attack as he pounded both of his fists into the side of his son. Santorray crumbled and went tumbling into the pile of insects, which had been killed earlier by the travelers.

Santorray was definitely hurt as he struggled to shake off the powerful blow to his side. Clearing the pain from his brain, he could tell his father was approaching. The thunderous footfalls closed in on him, but he hadn't cleared his vision yet.

Knowing his back was exposed, Santorray rolled to his side and grabbed whatever he could find to use as a shield until he could stand. The first object he grabbed was a large book, which he held up to stop the demon's blow.

"Vesik!" Bryus yelled in horror. His desire to protect the book of magic far outweighed his interest in preserving his own life. Running toward the fight, he screamed for them to stop.

But it was too late; Ergrauth's mighty fist came crashing down onto the book, forcing it into Santorray's chest and knocking the wind out of him.

Thorik frantically called to the Alchemist, "Bryus! It's not worth your life."

But he was wrong. Bryus felt it was worth much more than his or anyone else's life. Ancient magic was history, while each person was only a blink of time. He would do anything to save Vesik. Besides, he believed he needed the book to save his wife and daughter.

The demon stomped a heavy foot onto his son's chest. "You will never defeat me as long as you believe you can't."

Bryus arrived in time to see the book pinned between the demon's foot and the blothrud's chest. Stabbing his broken wooden arm into Ergrauth's other leg, he quickly cast a spell while the demon was taken by surprise.

The spell was intended to liquefy the demon's leg, but because of a failed arm replacement, as well as the red spice still on his wooden arm, it backfired. Instead, moisture from the demon's leg was pulled toward Bryus' wooden appendage, causing it to spring roots into and around the demon's leg. The Alchemist was now attached to Ergrauth.

Removing his foot from Santorray's chest, Ergrauth began kicking his leg in order to knock the Alchemist off, but the roots continued to expand and tighten their hold.

Thorik and Avanda came running to his defense.

"No!" Bryus yelled to Avanda. "Save Vesik!" he pleaded to his young apprentice. "Use it to save my family!"

Watching the Alchemist flail around on the side of the demon's leg, she knew any magic she attempted could easily hurt her teacher. Accepting his request, she stopped at Santorray and Vesik.

Thorik refused to change course. Holding his hunting daggers out in front of him, he charged at the demon to save Bryus.

Santorray tossed the book off of his chest and rolled to his hands and knees, clutching his side in pain. But his father's attacks would not be enough to stop him.

Avanda grabbed Vesik and helped the blothrud to his feet, just in time to see Ergrauth reach down and snap Bryus' arm from his thick demon leg.

"Is this what you fight for now?" the demon asked harshly to his son. Holding the battered Alchemist in his huge hand like a rag-doll, he spiked Bryus back and forth between his hands. "This is what you're fighting for instead of your own people?"

"This is between you and me," Santorray told his father. "Leave him be."

"What interests you about these lesser beings?" Ergrauth looked at Bryus' limp body in his palm. "They are so weak." To display his thoughts, he firmly held Bryus in one hand and used his other hand to pull on the human's arm. Muscles and flesh stretched and ripped as the demon snapped off the man's arm. The bone of the limb was exposed as blood ran down the flesh that had been torn off with it. Holding the arm out toward Santorray to view, he eventually flung it at his son, and it hit him in the chest before it fell to the ground.

Somehow Bryus remained conscious as he screamed in pain, while his left eye jerked from his eye socket due to the demon's abuse. Falling to the ground, it was inadvertently stepped on and crushed.

Looking at the man flailing about in his hands, the demon grabbed him tight again and ripped his right leg from his pelvis, and then followed it with removing his left leg. Each limb hit Santorray after being torn from the human, in an attempt to get the lesser demon to realize how frail his companion was. Tossing the head and torso of Bryus violently at Santorray, he shouted, "They are weak. We are the dominant species!"

The Alchemist was unrecognizable as the mound of body parts splattered on the desert floor. The sight caused Brimmelle to jump and fall back in fear of the demon's strength, while Thorik finished his charge toward the demon with even greater fervor. They had lost a companion who, despite what he had done, was still a part of their extended family.

"No!" Avanda screamed as she attempted to race forward to save her mentor, Bryus. She simply couldn't accept that his journey was over. In addition, her desire to learn new magic had just been crushed by the hands of the demon. Somehow, she had assumed that Bryus' powers could protect them from anything. She turned to charge at Ergrauth and cast whatever spells she could think of.

Before doing so, she heard a soft cough from the mound of flesh and body parts.

To her surprise, Bryus had somehow remained conscious, at least for a short time. She had to assume he retained enough magic to keep himself alive after being ripped apart limb by limb.

"Avanda," he sputtered as he saw her approach. "Perform the summon swap spell. Quickly, I haven't much time left."

"What?"

"Place my hair on one side, the talon from my belt on the other." He struggled not to fade away.

"Why?"

"Let me see my family one last time."

"Then who will appear here? Who will you swap with?" Grabbing the components, she cried as she waited for him to have enough strength to answer her.

"Our family pet. Take care of her."

"We will be long gone by the time the spell is completed."

Coughing and spitting out blood, his words were slurred and difficult to hear. "Keep my rags with you. She will follow my scent to you."

Avanda did as she was told and began the spell, wiping the tears from her face to ensure they didn't fall on the components and corrupt the magic.

"Thank you," he said softly, "… for letting me into your family." Then Bryus fell unconscious.

Meanwhile, Ergrauth had already selected his next victim, which was Thorik. As the Num raced forward to stab him with his hunting daggers, the demon simply leaned down and scooped him up. Thorik never had a chance. He was now being squeezed by the enormous hand of the land demon and would end up as a pile of limbs on top of the late Bryus.

This time Santorray yelled out. "STOP!" The word echoed against the valley walls, causing everyone to pay attention.

Ergrauth was intrigued by his son's stance against the killing of the Num. "You really care about these little creatures, don't you?"

Santorray could see that Thorik was in pain. To continue this fight would only cause the death of all of his companions. "Release him."

With a shallow laugh, he did nothing of the sort. "Why? What purpose could this Num have?"

"I cannot see his fate any more than you." Santorray then gave off a deep growl as he planned his next statement. "But I will succumb to your punishment if you let my fellow travelers live."

"Santorray, save yourself and the rest!" Thorik shouted.

Ergrauth shook his head with disappointment at his son. "You have become weak, boy. Never would I have expected to see the day when an Ergrauthian Elite would forgo his freedom to save a Fesh. You, my son, have been compromised."

Santorray stood firm as the emotional impact played with his mind. "Do you accept my offer?"

By this point, the Del'Unday army had chased the Guardians away and had filed into rank behind their leader. Keeping their eyes forward, they never looked directly at the demon, for fear of swift repercussions.

Tossing Thorik down in front of Santorray, the demon then spit on the dirt near his son's feet. "Santorray, you could have had the world. Instead, you choose eternal pain. You're a fool."

"General!" Ergrauth ordered. "Take these traitors and have them absorbed into my city."

Nearly fifty soldiers stepped forward to surround the travelers. "Drop your weapons," the general ordered Santorray and his friends.

"No," Ergrauth corrected. "Let them keep them. If there is any of my blood left in my son, allow him a chance to die fighting for his life. Just ensure you have enough guards to make his life end quickly should he choose to give up his Fesh ways and be a blothrud once more."

The general nodded. His troops then led the travelers east through the mountain pass.

❦ 43 ❦

DEATH MARCH

Thorik walked between Santorray and Grewen, while the mognin carried Brimmelle and Avanda. Brimmelle's feet bled from the harsh conditions, and both he and Avanda had become overwhelmed by the heat. It was best for them to be carried, and Grewen didn't mind it a bit.

Thorik felt misled by Santorray as he walked alongside him. "I don't understand. How can you be the son of a demon?"

"What's there not to understand?"

"Well, first of all, how is it that you failed to mention this bit of information in our travels?"

"It would have only complicated things."

"Yes, because things weren't complicated prior?" Thorik asked with a bit of sarcasm.

"My relationship with Ergrauth would have prevented you from trusting me, as it has so many others."

"What is your relationship? If he is your father, why the bad blood? What did you do?"

"No one disobeys Ergrauth on anything and lives to tell about it."

"Apparently that's not true, seeing that you did both."

Stopping, Santorray turned to show Thorik his back. "Do you see this scar?"

"I see a lot of scars."

"The largest one. The one that cracked and broke several of my back blades."

The thick deep scar ran from his left shoulder down across his back to his right hip. The blades in its wake were remnants of the powerful weapons that once were.

"Yes, I see it."

"He split me open and left me for dead."

"Just because you disobeyed him? Who would have known?"

"Everyone. I held a position of great power here. I was the general of the Ergrauthian Elite, a force designed to destroy anything and everything in its path. We were not directed to keep order or to ensure citizens were faithful to Ergrauth. Our missions had a single result: death to whomever Ergrauth wished to be removed from the living."

"And you refused to kill someone?"

"Yes."

"Who?"

"A family member."

"He wanted you to kill one of your own kin?"

"Yes."

"That must be the most horrible crime."

"No. Not supporting Ergrauth is the ultimate offense to all Del'Unday. Our punishment will take place in his namesake city."

Thorik realized that something still didn't add up. "But Santorray, you once told me that the Del'Unday don't take prisoners. Will we be executed once we arrive?"

"We will not be that fortunate, Sec. Ergrauth's enemies are utilized to expand the city's size."

Thorik sighed. "If we are to spend the rest of our living days constructing streets and buildings, Brimmelle will not last long in this heat."

"The heat will be the least on his mind, for as soon as we enter the city, they will lead us to the Gateway of Schullis. This passage will strip your flesh from your body and absorb your bones, your muscles, as well as your spirit. By entering the gateway, your willpower will be muted and your obedience will be rectified."

Thorik's eyes had grown large during the blothrud's description, and his face had tightened as though he was going to be sick.

Avanda and Brimmelle had been quietly listening, but now they shot each other looks of concern as they continued to listen to the discussion.

Grewen's stomach groaned from hunger as he grinned at Santorray's comments. "Leave it to the Del'Unday to strip a man of his flesh and bones and then still expect him to follow orders."

Santorray growled. "You disrespect my culture?"

"Far from it," Grewen said in a light-hearted tone. "I find it fascinating that an entire culture is based on fear. Whether it be fear of disobedience or fear of some superstition giving you bad luck."

"You will find out that this is no superstition. The gateway pulls you into the city's walls and streets and roofs. You become part of the fabric of our towers and the building blocks for our statues. The city of Ergrauth is a combination of sand, water, and living tissue. The city is alive with tens of thousands of spirits following a single one who serves Ergrauth himself."

"The city is living?" Avanda asked, trying to understand.

"Yes. The city grows and changes based on the Del'Undays' needs. The crystal structures of the city expand when fed. But unlike anything you've seen crystallized, the spirits can move them slightly, making them appear to be fluid solids. You will understand when you see the lost people press their faces against the walls and scream for mercy. But there will never be any for them."

✿ 44 ✿

ER'QUE DOOMA BADLANDS

Days passed as they marched to the east toward the city named after the demon, Ergrauth. Their trek through the badlands was uncomfortable, at best. Aside from the sparse vegetation, packs of wild Del'Unday roamed these lands. Periodically, these packs were spotted standing motionless on the top of a mesa, watching the travelers pass below.

"They are called kewtalls," Santorray informed his companions. "Mutated and insane Dels. They stand up there on those ridges to mark their territory and intimidate outsiders."

The Ergrauthian guards frequently tried to tempt Santorray to fight his way out, to no avail. They simply couldn't get him irritated enough to attack. The guards also offered the Nums and Grewen the opportunity to escape for freedom if they wished to attempt to travel on their own in these lands.

Santorray shook his head at the Nums, assuring them it was a foolish choice. "The wild kewtalls are like pack animals. They wait for a few individuals to break off from the main group, and then they attack. You'd never survive half a day out here on your own."

"But if we all escaped together, we could make our way back past the Guardians." Thorik looked up at another kewtall on the ledge above them.

"I could, but you Nums wouldn't stand a chance. These aren't Fesh'Unday. They are tribes of Dels who hunt travelers for survival. They are skilled and savage warriors."

Disappointed in his response, Thorik grimaced at the blothrud. "Haven't we proven ourselves to you yet? I think we can support our own." Glancing back up to see the kewtalls, he found they were no longer there. A quick scan back at the other mesa tops showed that all the recent kewtalls had disappeared. "Where did they all…"

Grewen glanced back at the ledges above them and noticed the same thing. "We're just being watched."

"Or hunted," Thorik said.

"They're stalking. Waiting to see a weakness. Looking for a wounded member, or a smaller one they could easily drag off from the rest of the group," Santorray replied.

Thorik swallowed hard and took a quick inventory of his group's whereabouts. "Perhaps you're right. Maybe we don't want to take the guards up on their offer for freedom."

Periodically, the captive party would spot more kewtalls on the upper flats of the desert badlands. They would be under their watchful eye until they had left their lands.

After hours of walking in the blistering sun, Avanda thought her eyes were playing tricks on her. One of the motionless kewtalls swung about, but by the time she pointed it out to Thorik, it was gone.

It was nearly an hour later when she noticed it happening again. This time, she monitored it and watched it thrash about as some type of bird attacked the mutated Del and pecked away at it. This kewtall moved away from the overlooking ledge as well, but the bird remained as it watched the travelers walk past.

Avanda struggled to see the bird high on the ledge. The sun burned her eyes when she looked up, but she could view the bird lift off and fly above them. Circling for several minutes, it slowly lowered itself closer to the marching prisoners.

Nudging Thorik to look up at it, she noticed the bird had disappeared. Thorik wasn't in the mood for games as he attempted to develop a plan of escape.

Frustrated that no one else had seen the bird except her, Avanda scanned the skies to see where it had flown. She watched for kewtalls, as well as the possibility of it resting on a ledge, but found no evidence of it.

"Idiot!"

Avanda heard the voice of Bryus and looked over at Thorik. He had heard it as well.

"Leave me alone," Bryus' voice said again.

Brimmelle heard it and spun around. All three Nums were looking for Bryus after hearing his voice in his typical condescending tone. But he was nowhere to be seen.

"I have to do everything myself." It was clearly Bryus' voice, but this time Avanda saw where it was coming from. The bird she had seen earlier was now waddling along with them as it blurted out comments it had obviously heard Bryus say more than once.

Bright red and orange colors coated its feathers except for its orange and white face. With eyes way too large for its head, it looked like someone had squeezed its neck so hard that its eyes had popped out of their sockets.

Abrupt swipes of the bird's head back and forth nearly caused it to lose balance as it limped along with a talon missing from one claw. "Idiot! Out of my way," it said as it walked past Brimmelle and up to Avanda.

Brimmelle grimaced at the comment. "Great. I was just getting used to the idea of Bryus not being around."

"It's Bryus' pet." Avanda knelt down and showed the bird a piece of rag with Bryus' scent on it.

"How is that possible?" Brimmelle asked.

"I performed the summon swap spell on Bryus and his pet before I left him at the Guardians. He told me that his pet would find us by following his scent." She reached out to pick the bird up. "I wonder what her name is…"

"Idiot!" the bird blurted out.

Brimmelle smiled. "Good enough for me."

Thorik laughed. "What use could this crippled bird be for us? Why would he send her to us?"

Lifting the bird up, Avanda began to pet it. "I don't know if she has a purpose for us. I think the idea was just to get Bryus back to his family. I hope he made it."

"Hi, Idiot." Brimmelle then reached over to pet it.

Idiot snapped at Brimmelle's fingers, nearly taking one of them off. "Leave me alone!" it squawked.

CITY OF ERGRAUTH

Weeks of chilly nights and hot desert days had taken their toll on the travelers. Guards had provided just enough water and food to keep them walking, but not enough to have the strength to escape or fight their way out. Nevertheless, this day would be different, as they grew closer to what appeared to be a distant gathering of enormous red crystals under a thick cloudy sky. But as they traveled closer, it became obvious that it was the namesake city of the demon, Ergrauth.

Dark red monoliths of the city grew out of the pristine white sands of the desert floor at the shore of the Ergrauthian Lake. Dozens of the monolithic towers sprang up from the dune floor as though a growth of natural crystals rose from the convergence of the sand dunes and lake's blue water. Reflecting the sun's sporadic rays off these tremendous towers, the white dunes near the city took on a bloody red hue.

Waves lapped at the ivory dunes surrounding half the city. It had no moat, no drawbridge, and no protection from outside invaders. There had never been an attack on the city, nor could anyone ever imagine one happening. This was the namesake home and the living place of the demon, Ergrauth.

At the entrance was an impressive marble statue of Ergrauth standing victoriously in the center of a fountain, surrounded by a herd of Del'Undays charging along with the demon out toward the desert. Water sprayed out from the feet of the herd as though they were kicking up sand and dust in their rush to fight opposing forces.

The statue depicted the demon with a sword in one hand, showing strength, and a vessel with three spouts in his other. Water poured from one spout, landing on crops carved out leaning against his leg. Red liquid poured from the second spout, which sprayed at the demon's feet, in honor of the blood he had spilled and walked upon to create his empire. The third spout gave a free falling of sand into a vat to symbolize the earth over which he ruled.

Beyond the fountain, the walls and streets of the buildings were made from the flesh and bones of those who died in the city, combined with the desert sands and the lake water. But it was not constructed. It had grown over the years, infused with the physical bodies and the essence of those who were under each step and along every path.

Ergrauth had designed a city that wasted nothing. Those not faithful to him would be absorbed into the city and become part of it. No prisons were needed, for the endless existence as part of a collective that made up the entire city would be the punishment for those who did not obey.

Thorik and his friends were led up to the city. The hard crystal surfaces were glossy and red, and the walls appeared to move slightly as though they were breathing as the travelers entered between two enormous towers. The wall's surface moved and faces and hands appeared to be pressing out from within it, looking at the new captives with whom they would be spending eternity.

The ground had been hardened from the sun's powerful rays, turning it into a sandy and gritty red glass filled with bone fragments. These streets were in use by the locals who went about their business. Various types of Del'Unday pushed carts and moved goods from place to place. Things were orderly, unlike the chaotic streets of Trewek. Residents of this city had clear intentions and rarely stopped to chitchat in the streets.

Pulsing with red fluid, veins clung to streets and towers like vines of ivy. Thin at first near the edge of the city, they grew in girth as the travelers moved toward the center towers.

A low background moaning could be heard from every direction as the dead suffered. It was clear that the locals didn't pay any attention to it. But for the Nums, the entire sight was horrifying.

Even Santorray was uncomfortable, but for different reasons. The traitor, the son of Ergrauth, had returned home. There was a time when all Del'Unday respected his position and his lineage. He was admired and feared, just the way he had meant it to be. But now it was different.

The locals lowered their eyes when they saw Santorray as they went about their daily business. It was a disgrace to see their once mighty hero fall to be a captive.

Few of great strength and stature remained in the city, for the demon had taken most of them to war. What remained were the weak and crippled, as well as the old and the very young.

Ushered into the center of the city, the travelers could see how the city had grown from the center tower, much like a patch of clover expands from its single root. This tower was much larger than the rest and had angled offshoots to all the surrounding towers. Thick veins pulsed fluid from this central location.

Upon this center tower was a great mural of Ergrauth looking over his domain. Words of respect and punishment littered the walls to remind those in the city of how disobedience would not be tolerated. A clear list of rules was carved into front of the tower for all to see, starting with 'Ergrauth's words are law,' and followed by 'Never compromise the mission.' These were just the first two of the many rules for all to obey.

Santorray led his companions in a display of strength, followed by Grewen and the Nums. Even in the face of condemnation and certain death, the blothrud held his head high and was proud of his accomplishments. None of those who looked upon him could say they had stood up to Ergrauth for their own rights.

The city amazed Grewen. He had only heard about it in legends. "It's cleaner than I had expected," he said to his blothrud friend.

Walking behind them, Brimmelle dragged his feet on the streets. Parched and sunburned, the elder Num was struggling to go any further. His eyes glazed over and his breathing became shallow as his legs gave out from under him.

Collapsing onto the street, Brimmelle was kicked by one of the Del guards, who ordered the Num to stand back up. Brimmelle was exhausted and simply couldn't go another step.

A second kick was made by the guard, but it was stopped short. Grewen had reached down to pick the Num up, and his mighty hand had taken the impact of the attack. Grewen flinched slightly from the kick, but it was the guard who felt the pain of several broken toes and claws upon the strike.

"Come on, Brimmelle." Grewen lifted the Num to carry him the rest of the distance. "Stay with us."

Avanda stood defiantly and glared at the guard who had kicked her fellow Num, as though she was going to take him on herself.

"Idiot!" the bird on her shoulder shouted.

As another guard approached, Avanda felt a tug on her sleeve. It was Thorik.

"This won't help us," he informed her.

"What will? We're doomed anyway. Let's at least go out fighting," she replied.

Several guards now approached the two Nums.

"Leave me alone." the bird squawked.

"Avanda, please. I don't want my last memory of you to be during a bloody battle."

"Then fight alongside me."

Thorik softly placed a firm hand on her shoulder. "I've always been fighting at your side, and I always will. But I don't want us to end as dead Nums on the streets of this city. Trust me, we'll find a better way. And when we do, we'll do it together."

"I should turn them into frozen statues." Her voice was intentionally loud enough for the guards to hear.

Bryus' bird flew off from her shoulder and up in the air.

"I'd like to see that, but then the rest of the guards will unleash their rage upon us." Thorik pulled together a half grin for her before being escorted back in line behind Grewen.

"I don't want to die, Thorik." She had finally given in and lost her anger at the guards as her eyes filled with tears. "I miss Bryus, and there is still so much I want to learn and do."

"I know," he said as they walked to the center tower. Wrapping his arm around her, he pulled her in tight. "The opportunity will come, and I'll be there for you."

Avanda leaned her head against him as tears flowed over her cheeks. "Promise?"

Thorik sighed and nodded. He hoped he would be correct.

White droplets splattered on one of the guards from above. Bryus' bird squawked, "I have to do everything myself." Continuing to fly above the prisoners, the bird finally landed back on Avanda's shoulder just prior to them entering one of the structures.

Changing guards at the entrance, four elaborately dressed blothrud guards guided the travelers through two massive doors at the base of the center tower and led them inside, down a few corridors, and then into a large room in the heart of the tower. They were now in the exact center of the city in a room with nothing except a gateway which would absorb them into the structure for all eternity. A dozen massive veins across the ceiling and walls came together at the edges of the gateway.

Two executioners stood near the gateway with long, multi-bladed spears. All four guard escorts remained at the doorway of the room while the executioners managed the events within the room.

Santorray could take out any blothrud, but attacking six at once was a major risk, especially after minimal rations for the past several weeks. He turned his attention to the gateway instead to see if he could destroy it.

Several elder Del'Unday were already standing in line as they waited to be corralled into the gateway. They looked up at Thorik and his friends with desperate eyes. Age had made them unproductive, which was a crime against Ergrauth and his people. Their punishment would be never-ending; the executioners in the room, armed with spears, prodded those on death row to move forward.

Realizing her own mortality, Avanda clung onto Thorik as they entered.

❧ 46 ☙

GATEWAY

The gateway was more of a thick, golden-trimmed doorway with detailed etchings. Inside the doorway was a dark mirror, reflecting the room without the person standing in front of it. To stand in front of it made one realize one's lack of worth.

The travelers stood in line as they waited their turn to walk into the mirror. Thorik and his friends were three from the front, as they watched the process unfold. Santorray continued to stand up front with his chest and snout held high and proud.

Grewen had set Brimmelle back down next to Avanda so he could take the last few steps on his own. Stepping in front of the Nums, the mognin would go before them, hoping his enormous mognin body would break the device before the Nums had to try.

"Idiot!" Bryus' bird yelled out as it stood on Avanda's shoulder and stared at the pulsing veins across the ceiling.

Brimmelle flinched at the bird's yell, since it was so close to his ear.

The executioners gave Brimmelle a scowl, as they assumed the comment came from him.

Brimmelle put his head down to avoid their attention, and Avanda attempted to quiet the bird.

The bird's large, independently moving eyes rolled around and scanned the room. "Fesh face!" the bird squawked.

Brimmelle's eyes opened wide at the remark and then glanced over at the executioners.

Walking over, one of the executioners prodded Brimmelle with his spear to move up in line, right behind Santorray. "Sooner we get rid of your mouth, the better."

"But…" Brimmelle didn't have the opportunity to explain that he hadn't said anything.

The blothrud moved the short Num between Grewen and Santorray. "I don't want to hear it."

It wasn't a position Brimmelle had ever wanted to stand in, for he was half Santorray's height and a third of Grewen's. His view forward and behind was repulsive, so he stared at the floor. But the view was the least of his worries at the moment.

One executioner used his spear to prod the first elder Del'Unday in line to remove his belongings and walk toward the gateway. Reluctantly, the old Del dropped his gear to the floor and walked over to the mirror, stopping a yard in front of it. He gazed at his non-reflection, knowing that he was doomed for all eternity. Stepping away from it to calm his thoughts, he felt the blothruds pressing their spears into his back, forcing him forward.

Once he was within a few feet, his body slid violently against the mirror, as though gravity had changed directions. Tight against the dark reflection of the room behind him, he screamed in pain. Pulling his head back away from the mirror, flesh could be seen dissolving wherever his body touched the flat surface, as though the mirror was comprised of acid.

With the sideways gravity pulling him, he continued to press against the inside of the gateway as he dissolved away inch by inch. Clothes lit on fire and quickly burned away, while flesh melted off. As the skin was removed, the man's muscles and fat broke down into a liquid and boiled away, followed by his bones sinking down into the darkness of the mirror. Fresh blood and flesh pulsed through the veins in the ceiling overhead.

The entire event only lasted a minute, but the horror for those who witnessed it would last forever. The victim, however, would now add to the city's walls and structure, expanding it just that much more.

The scene struck Avanda with overwhelming fear. This was finally hitting her as her end. There was no escape. They would end up as lost souls floating among these halls forever. "The walls are filled with the lives of so many prisoners. Could this be a worse fate than Della Estovia?"

"When we are in a room surrounded by death and life as we wait for our turn for both," Thorik mumbled to himself.

Avanda wiped her tears from her face. "What?"

Thorik let go of Avanda so he could remove his pack and the Runestones within it. He then pulled out his Runestone of Courage. "Granna had warned me of events such as this. I am to call upon her when it should occur." Not seeing anything to lose, he moved between Grewen and the wall to concentrate on the stone as the next old Del'Unday in line was prodded toward the gateway. Now, out of the executioners' and guards' view, he unsheathed the dagger Varacon as he called to her.

Avanda hugged Grewen's giant hand as she waited for someone to save them. Looking up into the giant's face, she could tell he hadn't given up hope yet.

"Every moment is precious," Grewen said to her. "Even if it's your last. Revel in what you have, instead of focusing on what you don't."

Avanda repeated the statement to herself as she tried to determine how to use his words to help. "What do we have?"

In the dim light behind Grewen, Gluic's ghostly appearance flowed from the dagger. "It is time, Thorik."

Glancing back to make sure he wasn't being seen, he questioned her. "Time for what? I've done what you've asked, but we have failed. We are about to be sentenced to a place without life or death. I have fallen short of your request."

"Nonsense. You have succeeded."

Thorik listened to the second man scream in horror and pain as he looked at his friends standing in line. "Only in the deaths of my loved ones."

"This is not your destiny, Thorik."

"I would love for that to be true, but unless you can convince the executioners of this, I'm afraid it is."

"Do you recall what I told you before my death, when I had seen my future?"

Thorik remembered the event. In fact, he had thought of it often, ever since she first touched Santorray with a memory crystal and saw his past and her future. "Your death provides you an opportunity to move into a new body to fulfill a new purpose," he said softly. "But now I can't even give you time to fulfill any purpose."

"But you are wrong. This is what I was meant to do."

Thorik watched the third person in line toss his belongings to the floor and move into position. "You're meant to be heaved into a pile of garments and travel supplies? I think not. I would use you to fight for our freedom, but I fear I would lose you in the process if Varacon were to be scratched."

"No, my grandson. My dear courageous boy. You will not do this. Instead, this is my time to do what has been needed for thousands of years. It is my destiny to free these people."

Thorik held the Runestone in one hand and Varacon in the other as he listened to another brutal death and watched Avanda and Brimmelle cry in each other's arms. "I don't know how to help you save these people."

"Yes, you do."

"Granna, please. No more games. Tell me before there is no time left for us to speak."

"What do you wish to do?"

"Me? I wish to stop these deaths, save ourselves, and release you from this dagger." Thorik thought of what else needed to happen. "And free all those enslaved inside the walls of this city of death."

"Exactly."

"Granna? What does that mean?"

"You must be willing to let go of something you cherish in order to make all of those things happen. Can you do this for me?"

The executioners moved over to the next person in line. It was Santorray.

"Of course, name it! Quickly!"

"Stab Varacon into the vein in this wall."

Santorray unsheathed his sabers and hesitated before dropping them on the pile of gear from the prior victims.

Thorik was sure he misunderstood. "Use the dagger?"

"Yes." Gluic's voice was soft but clear.

"But we have the spell and the components to free you."

"I don't require them. They aren't for me."

"Then why did you have me collect them to free you?"

Gluic smiled. "You must promise me to travel north to the dragon's lair and use them to save Rummon. He will require them for you to be successful in your future journeys."

Santorray walked over in front of the mirror and saw a reflection of the room without him in it. He no longer would exist except in the walls of this city.

Thorik peered back and forth between the blothrud and Gluic. "I can't. I promised to save you."

Santorray bit hard against his lip to draw blood for one last battle.

"You have, and many more. But it is now time." Gluic touched his cheek with her translucent hand.

Santorray stepped up to the gateway, roared with a mighty force, and then attacked, slamming his fists into the mirror as he attempted to pound his way through the gateway to see what was on the other side.

"Granna. No," Thorik stated firmly.

"Courage, my brave little hunter. I will always be there for you."

A howl of pain filled the room as Santorray's fists began to bleed and his flesh started to strip off the muscles on his hands. He hadn't even made a dent in the mirror as it attempted to drag his body toward it. His paws were losing grip and sliding toward the mirror.

"Granna!" Thorik shouted.

Gluic's journey was complete. "Goodbye, my hero."

Santorray continued to pound his fists as pieces of flesh flung off his knuckles as he shouted his last battle cry. Santorray was losing this last battle. He was about to die. His paws slipped, and his body slapped hard against the mirror.

"NO!" Thorik yelled as he plunged the dagger, Varacon, into the wall next to him. The shiny dark red wall immediately turned a dull ivory with a rough texture of sand. This change spread out from the dagger across the room and into the next, like a rapid plague as the veins carried Gluic's essence in every direction. The mirror in the gateway froze solid, its acids neutralized and its ability vanished.

The following powerful thrust of Santorray's fist slammed right through the mirror and the wall it leaned against as shards of glass sprayed the room. The blothrud stepped back to see the sight of the damaged gateway as he raised his arms in the air and roared in victory before smashing both fists one last time, destroying the gateway and the wall behind it.

But his victory was short-lived. The walls were losing their strength, as the city was becoming a giant sandcastle, and it was falling apart under its own weight. Using this to his advantage, he grabbed the spear from a nearby executioner and used it against him before taking out a second executioner as by driving the spear into his gut.

The four guards at the door were confused as to the reaction of the structure around them, but they refused to leave. They had been ordered to stay with the prisoners in the chamber until they had all been through the gateway. To change plans would be to disobey Ergrauth. Ergo, they blocked the exit to stay loyal as parts of the room's ceiling crumbled down on all of them.

Using the chaos to her advantage, Avanda grabbed Bryus' bird and tossed it at the guards near the doorway. "Attack!" she yelled, hoping the bird would respond.

Panicking from the confusion, the bird flew toward the exit and the guards. Instead of trying to attack the blothruds, it was simply attempting to escape the room. In doing so, it recklessly flew toward the face of one of the blothruds.

One guard swung at the bird, knocking it into the face of the other guard, while it flapped and squawked uncontrollably.

It was the distraction that Santorray needed. He quickly grabbed his sabers and headed for the exit. By the time he arrived at the doorway, the guards had knocked the bird to the ground, but they hadn't been ready for Santorray's sabers. With a few swift moves, he cut the blothrud guards down, freeing those in the room.

"Everyone out!" Santorray commanded.

Avanda scooped up Bryus' bird from the floor on her way out of the room. Limp in her hands, she hoped it was only knocked out.

Racing out of the room, just as it fell in on itself, the group ran down one hallway after another. Each one crumbling under its own weight, each one breaking down into its raw elements of sand and bones.

Reaching the exterior, they could see the influence of Gluic, turning the glossy red towers pale. The central region was fully ivory by now as it spread outward.

Santorray led them through the streets crowded with locals screaming from the chaos. They ran for their lives around corners and under archways just prior to their collapse.

A large red section of a tower gave way and fell from its lower ivory sand walls, crashing against one of the streets. The exploding walls sent red blood spraying in every direction.

Dodging around a corner, they avoided the spray as they approached the last row of red towers, which hadn't been affected yet.

The sound of towers crashing and sand raining down on the streets pounded against their backs as they rushed to exit the city limits, passing the fountain statue of Ergrauth. Even with all of that, Thorik thought he heard a familiar voice calling to him.

Thorik stopped and looked around for the owner of the voice, unable to find it until he heard it again.

"Thank you, dear boy," the voice said again. This time Thorik spotted it. It was his grandmother's face, pressing up against the side of the base of the fountain. "I am now free, and so are these victims."

Thorik's eyes swelled with tears. "Granna!"

"You have done the right thing. Now, go become what you were born to be."

"But Granna."

"Become the leader you desire to be and do what you wish others would." Her face faded as the short wall, which surrounded the fountain, was turning ivory. "Goodbye, dear boy."

"I'm not giving up on you, Granna!" Thorik yelled over the roar of the city falling in on itself. But the surface he reached out to was now solid sand. Rough and dry, it no longer showed the face of his grandmother.

"Thorik!" Avanda yelled as she grabbed his arm. She had turned around and come back for him. "We have to leave this place."

A section of wall crumbled into the street, blocking their escape route with over ten feet of rubble made of bones and sand. But it failed to pull Thorik from his state of mind.

"No, not yet." Thorik refused to believe it was over for her. "Granna is right here. It's time for the spell!"

Looking dumbfounded, Avanda jerked her head around at the sights of the city falling in on them from every angle. "There isn't time. We have to leave, Thorik. You have to trust that Gluic knew what she was doing."

"Trust?" Thorik said while the fountain statue of Ergrauth began to crack apart and lean toward the Nums. "The Runestone of Trust!" Thorik quickly tossed off his backpack and dug inside for the Runestone.

Avanda tried to pull him away as she watched the giant statue lose its strength in its base and started falling toward them. There was no time to talk, or even run for that matter; the statue came crashing down upon them.

To her amazement, however, the statue froze in midair. In fact, everything in the city had stopped moving. Everything except Thorik and Avanda.

Thorik concentrated on the Runestone he had once tried in the caves of Della Estovia, after climbing out of the underground river. He had recalled that time stood still when it was activated. "Avanda, quickly! I don't know how long I can hold this." It was taxing to his mental fortitude.

Unnerved by the free-floating statue of Ergrauth hovering above them, Avanda didn't understand what he wanted her to do. "What's happening?"

"I'll explain later. Perform the spell to release Gluic before I can't hold this any longer."

"I can't."

"Yes you can. You have the components and the spell book. Perform it, now!"

Realizing she hadn't practiced as much as she should have, she questioned her ability. "I'll mess it up! I don't know it well enough."

"I trust you. Hurry!" Every second that went by made it more difficult. And as he strained from controlling the Runestone, the objects outside a yard from his position began to slowly move again.

"You shouldn't."

Thorik removed one hand from the Runestone long enough to grab something out of his pocket and hand it to her. The motion outside of his control moved slightly faster until he placed both of his hands back on the Runestone of Trust. The statue hanging over them was nearing their heads.

Avanda looked down in her hand at the object Thorik had given her. It was a blue tinted crystal shard from Bakalor's attack on them. The one she had given to Thorik while on the bridge, while looking over the Lagona Falls. The one that caused her to remember how much they trusted each other and themselves. It was the perfect item, and perhaps the only item, that caused her to straighten up and believe in herself.

Grabbing her components, she prepared her spell as quickly as possible.

"Hurry!" Thorik shouted as he saw the movement increase outside their barrier of safety.

"I'm ready!" She announced. "Wait! We need a body for Gluic to be absorbed into."

Thorik realized he hadn't thought that far ahead. "Have her go into mine."

"No, you could die!" she responded. Looking overhead at the statue just above them, she added, "And if you go, so shall the two of us."

"We have to try!" Thorik yelled, straining to keep time frozen. His muscles trembled from the major toll it was having on his body. Closing his eyes, he used everything he had to keep the Runestone working as he heard Avanda performing the spell.

The statue began to breach the dome of Thorik's time control bubble, causing fragments of the stone to chip away and rain down upon the Nums. With each second that passed, the pieces became larger.

Words were spoken, motions were made, and components were used as Avanda waited for the last steps from Vesik. She sighed with relief as they appeared in the book, as Bryus foretold they would. Performing the final elements, a misty figure pulled out from the base of the fountain and wafted into her new host. The transition was complete, and Avanda finished the spell.

Thorik squinted his eyes from the pressure of controlling the Runestone. "Make haste!"

"It's over, Thorik. Now we need to get out of here."

"Over? But it didn't work," he said through tight teeth. "I don't feel any different."

"That's because I found a different host for her body."

Squeezing one eye open to see who she was talking about, Thorik watched Avanda tossing her items in her pack before collecting Bryus' bird under her arm.

The bird squawked as it tried to clear its throat, and then it winked at Thorik. Wiggling her digits and claws, Gluic rotated its large, bulging eyes in opposite directions. Gluic tested out each part of her new body, including her voice. "Well, this is different."

"Bryus' pet was dead, anyway." Avanda gave a quick half grin before returning to business. "Now we need to get out of here."

Pulling Thorik out from under the falling statue allowed him to maintain his focus on the Runestone. And not a second too soon, for once they were out from under it, Thorik's trembling from the stress caused the Runestone's powers to fade and the statue to crash down behind them.

A loud crack from above caused Thorik and Avanda to look up as the side of the tower near them had broken away and was heading straight for them. The red surface near the top reflected the light from the sun into their eyes as it slowly rotated and plunged downward.

Running back into the city would only put them in more danger as more towers fell and crushed the local Del'Unday. Their only choice was to climb over the pile of bones which blocked their path to safety, but the likelihood of doing so before the tower crushed them was slim to none. Regardless, they would try.

Thorik and Avanda jumped onto the pile and climbed with every ounce of strength they had. Gluic leaped from Avanda's hand and flew up in the air, only to land on top of the pile as she casually waited for them. But the loose bones rolled out from under their feet, causing them to slide back down with every step forward. It was pointless. Every foot forward resulted in a half a foot backward. They knew they would never make it past the crest in time.

Just as they recognized it was over, Gluic flew up in the air and the section of bones they were climbing suddenly fell away, causing them to roll forward, away from the city.

Grewen had used his oversized hands and arms to grab a section of the bones from the far side and pulled it back away, opening a path for them. Gluic had led him to just the right location to dig.

Santorray then leaped forward and grabbed the two Nums from the pile. Placing one under each of his arms, he ran for safety as the tower crushed the location where the Nums had been blocked.

❧ 47 ❧

UNEXPECTED VISITOR

Bones, flesh, and blood shot out from the violent crash of the tower, pelting the backs of Grewen and Santorray. Screams of the trapped souls echoed in the Nums' ears as the blothrud tried to protect them from the flying debris. But they had been too close when the tower had crashed, and the force of the bloody muck knocked Santorray over, causing Thorik and Avanda to tumble out of his arms, far from the blothrud's reach.

A large chunk of another tower twisted and rolled toward the fallen blothrud and Nums with extreme speed. Attempting to stand and run out of the way, the thick, wet debris caused them to slip and fall. They had lost momentum, and only the blothrud was able to grip the ground with his rear wolf-like claws to get started again. Unfortunately, the Nums had slipped too far away for him to save before the tower would crush them. His options were to either save himself or die trying to save Thorik and Avanda. Gripping the blood-saturated ground with his claws and fingers, he leaped toward the Nums.

Red liquid rained down on the white desert sand and bones fell from above as the city continued to destroy itself. But out of the chaos, a tall, blood-covered human ran from the city and scooped up the Nums on his way to safety. Chunks of flesh from the collapsing buildings coated the muscular man's shoulders, back, and head as he continued his escape without skipping a beat. The lifting of the Nums had been a small deviation to his running, as though it was of minor inconvenience.

Santorray was both relieved and angered by the man who had just saved his friends. Not knowing who he was, the blothrud could only assume his motives were not good. He quickly changed his course and followed the man out to safety just as the tower arrived and liquefied into a red mess of body parts.

Once they were at a reasonable distance from any more harm, the man set the Nums down and fell to his knees in order to catch his breath.

Santorray would have done the same if he weren't concerned about displaying any weakness in front of the stranger. "Who are you?" he barked at the man.

The man quickly spun to his feet and pulled out his sword. It was obvious that he was well trained and knew how to handle his weapon. "Stay back, blothrud, or I shall slay you like I have too many of your kin before you on this day." Thick strips of red flesh still coated the man's head and shoulders.

Pulling out his sabers, Santorray grinned at the idea. "I am not like any blothrud you have ever met. I am Santorray, general of the Elite forces, son of Ergrauth, and the only lesser demon of his lineage still alive. A human presents no threat to me."

Standing an impressive height for a man, he was still over a head shorter than Santorray. But he refused to back down. "And I am not your typical human. I am Asentar, the last Dovenar Knight of our great kingdom. How poetic that such great warriors of our two lands finally meet in combat again, for my blade has tasted your blood once before."

"Not poetic. Just unfortunate, for you." Santorray stepped forward to launch his attack.

"Stop!" Thorik shouted as he jumped in between them. "Asentar is our friend. I sent him here to collect the urn for the Winds of Conquest," he told the blothrud.

Scooping a handful of thick, bloody flesh from his head and face, Asentar kept his sword firm in his other hand.

Thorik turned to the man. "And Santorray is our friend, as well as Ambrosius' close ally."

Neither of them looked down at the small Num as they continued to eye each other. Both still expected the other to strike first. But the long delay served to reduce the stress.

Thorik thought it best to keep talking to ease the tension. "We met Asentar in the City of Trewek. He came here to Ergrauth to find the urn in order to prove to the elders of Trewek that the dragons had been released and that war was coming. The urn must be returned to them before Corrock launches its attack."

As Santorray and Asentar squared off with each other, a large multicolored bird with oversized eyes recklessly flew between them before landing on Thorik's shoulder. Glancing over at it, the two warriors noticed the Num smiling.

Panning back to the Dovenar Knight, Thorik cleared his throat. "Asentar, I don't believe you've met my grandmother, Gluic." It was obvious to the Num that everyone assumed his comment was a joke, as they watched the bird fall backward before spreading its wings and flying away.

Still, Santorray and Asentar stood silent, waiting for the other to back down first.

Thorik continued. "Listen, you two are fighting the same battle and need to work together. Ergrauth's army has passed the Guardians and is heading toward Doven's wall. Darkmere, in disguise as the Terra King, has convinced the Dovenar army to move north into Woodlen, away from Doven. This will make an easy path for Ergrauth."

Asentar lowered his weapon, but kept it ready to rise quickly if needed. "Then I must travel to my people and warn them." Glancing down to Thorik, he added,

"You will have to take the urn to Trewek." Reaching into a sack at his side, he pulled out a cracked urn covered in markings and paintings and then carefully handed it to the Num while eyeing the blothrud.

"Thank you." Thorik glanced up to see the bird with Gluic's essence flying overhead in clumsy circles while testing her new abilities. Thorik thought it best not to attempt to convince Brimmelle of his mother's fate, knowing how he reacted the last time she changed form. "But I cannot travel there. I have made a promise to my grandmother to travel north across the lake to Rummon's lair in order to release him."

Brimmelle blurted out his first thoughts about the new plan. "There is no way I am going to climb a volcanic spewing mountain to release a demon that will most likely eat us the first chance he gets."

Asentar's eyebrow's lowered. "Your companion is correct. Nothing but death awaits you in Rummon's lair. In Trewek, however, you can save the lives of many."

"Perhaps, but it is a promise I must live up to nonetheless," Thorik said. "Brimmelle can travel with Santorray and Grewen to the Ov'Unday city. They will have to take this on without Avanda and me."

"No." Santorray's tone was as sharp as his blades.

Thorik turned in surprise at his response. "No? But we need your help."

Santorray began cleaning the remnants and debris from the city off of his blades. "Grewen and Brimmelle will have to perform this task on their own. I must travel to gather Del'Unday who are tired of my father's wrath. We must meet his forces in combat before he rules all of Terra Australis."

"Hold on," Brimmelle said. "I'm not traveling with Grewen. How will we survive?"

Santorray sheathed his clean sabers. "You won't travel to Rummon's lair, and I'm not going to put up with you. Your options are slim if you choose not to travel with Grewen."

Brimmelle looked at Asentar as an option.

"Your little Num legs and wide waist would slow my travels. I cannot risk the delay."

Brimmelle looked at Grewen and wondered how he ever put himself into a position where he would have to travel alone with an Altered Creature.

The mognin grinned. "Looks like you're stuck with me."

"Looks like it," Brimmelle muttered under his breath.

Thorik handed the urn to his uncle. "It is now your responsibility to ensure the elders of Trewek receive this in time to prepare themselves for the upcoming war."

Asentar glanced back at the city as the last few structures fell and countless Del'Unday wandered around in confusion. "We must leave this place without time to heal our wounds. Chaos from this destruction still provides us with a small window of freedom." Taking in a deep breath, he turned back to Thorik. "May your journey be safe and all of our missions be successful. I will see you on the battlefield as we fight for the future of our world."

"Let Ovlan guide our ways," Thorik added.

"Have the courage and desire for freedom to overcome our fears," Santorray added.

Avanda was not to be left out. "And the love of our friends and family give us strength to do what we need to do."

Grewen added his final thoughts to the collection. "As we live within the teaching of Trewek.

All eyes turned to Brimmelle, awaiting his words of wisdom. Everyone else had already spoken. "This is hopeless without the Mountain King's guidance," Fir Brimmelle said flatly.

The group showed obvious signs of disappointment at his comment.

Clearing his throat, Brimmelle added, "Let's be honest here. We have six of us against Ergrauth, Bakalor, Irluk, Darkmere, and all of their armies. We don't even have a crew to carry supplies and a flag for us yet."

Obviously, his words did not stimulate excitement in the group.

Thorik nodded in agreement. "He's right. As much as we don't want to hear it, those are the facts. But in spite of them, I am more confident than ever that we will succeed. For we are an oddity of sorts. When, in history, has a team of this many species come together and put their prejudices aside to fight for the greater good of our land? Never in the minds of evil would they conceive we would work together against them, and that is their greatest weakness. They feed off our intolerance toward one another. But for this moment in history, we shall dismiss these long-taught urges and pull together to take back freedom and our own destiny."

Looking directly at Brimmelle, Thorik straightened up his uncle's shirt. "You are right about our chances of success. But I would rather die in the fight against them than become their slaves."

Brimmelle was struck with a newfound respect for his nephew. He had no idea he had such deep thoughts. Perhaps he had something more than he had given him credit for.

"We all have our missions. We must all do our part." Thorik ended his speech and concluded the discussion.

"I am off to Woodlen!" Asentar shouted as he turned and began running to the west.

"And I am off to stop Ergrauth once and for all." Santorray spit into his hand and shook Thorik's own hand, dripping with saliva. They nodded to each other with respect as a slight grin crossed one side of the blothrud's face. "Goodbye Sec, my little warrior friend. Never forget, it's not the size of the warrior that wins the battle, but the size of their passion and conviction to win." He then turned and ran to the west as well, quickly catching up to Asentar.

Grewen nodded that it was time for him to leave as well. "Every moment I wait here is another moment that could cause the people of Trewek harm. It is time for us to go." Reaching down with his enormous hands, he picked up Thorik and Avanda and lifted them up to his chest and shoulders. They hugged each other tightly. Tears from the Nums ran down the mognin's leathery chest.

"We will see you at the battle," Thorik said.

"I hope no battle is needed." Grewen then set the Nums down, stepped back, and turned to walk southwest.

Brimmelle stood motionless. "You're making a mistake. You should be traveling with us."

"Perhaps, but it is my mistake to make, Uncle."

Avanda gave Brimmelle a hearty hug goodbye.

"Speak the words of the Mountain King. They will help guide you," Fir Brimmelle told her.

Avanda smiled as tears dripped from her cheeks. "I will. You take care of Grewen. Don't let him eat any plants if he doesn't know what they are."

He nodded.

Now it was just Thorik and Fir Brimmelle left to say their farewell. They stood there for several moments, waiting for the other to speak.

Thorik broke the silence. "Take care of yourself."

"I always do."

"I know."

Brimmelle bit his lip slightly as he struggled to say anything worthwhile. "Don't go getting yourself killed. I won't be there to save you."

A light smile crossed Thorik's face. "I'll miss you too." It was followed by a nod and quick slap on the shoulder for luck. His uncle returned the same gesture.

The two parted; Brimmelle followed Grewen, and Thorik returned to Avanda's side as the two Nums watched all of their friends leave them in the middle of the Ergrauthian desert, just outside of the destroyed city.

Misty vapors rose from the fallen city, but instead of fading off, these vapors separated into thousands of individual pieces and roamed the ruins. Moans and screams could be heard from them; they were the freed souls released by Gluic. This continued for several minutes until a dark mass appeared and began tearing through the city, collecting the vapors behind it.

Avanda gasped. "Irluk?"

Thorik nodded as they watched the Death Witch capture a new batch of souls for Bakalor. There was nothing they could do to stop her, and the sight caused them both to feel helpless.

Raising her hands to cover her mouth, Avanda watched as the recently released souls were captured for Bakalor. "Is there no hope for the dead? Are we all destined for this?"

As Irluk collected her bounty, the dark clouds in the sky parted, and intense beams of sunlight pierced down into the city. A sense of calmness filled the air. Vapors quickly moved into the beams of light, immediately disappearing out of Irluk's wrath.

Collecting the last few souls that hadn't reached the beams, Irluk left with her load in tow toward Della Estovia.

Thorik smiled as he noticed how the light appeared to resemble the glowing columns in Della Estovia. But as quickly as the beams of light had appeared, they fell behind the clouds once more.

The trapped souls of the City of Ergrauth had been freed.

Avanda's hand reached over and intertwined with Thorik's fingers. They were now on their own. From this point forward, they had to rely on each other. "Thorik, I know we are fools for doing this on our own, but I believe our trust in one another and our love will allow us to accomplish anything we set our minds on. As long as our hearts are forever together, we are invincible."

Thorik smiled and turned back to look at her lovely face. Somehow he saw past the dirt and debris from their adventure and saw a lovely woman that he had fallen for since they left Farbank. "I can't think of anyone else I'd rather be alone with than you, Avanda."

As they gazed into each other's eyes, it quickly became apparent that they were not alone. There were now thousands of prior residents standing just outside of their destroyed city, many of them spreading out and nearing the Nums. The vast majority of them were Del'Unday, which made sense. But there was also a small band of humans and Nums that had escaped the collapse of the towers as well. They were being led by a Num.

The Num leading the group was a female. Her clothes were ripped and blood-stained, like the rest who followed her. Her long, curly hair was red and golden blonde, and her face looked familiar. "Thorik?" She ran up to him, leaped up into his arms, and knocked him onto the ground. Planting a massive kiss onto his lips, she finally gave him room to breathe.

Thorik was flabbergasted at what he was seeing. "Em? Is it really you?"

"Yes! Darkmere left us in Corrock, and days later, we were all released from his spell." Emilen palmed her necklace, which had held her in a spell under Dark-mere's control. "The Del'Unday that worked for him eventually decided to bring us here to be absorbed into this city. However, just as we showed up, the city started falling apart. I don't know what happened, but I'm so thankful to see you. I've missed you so much."

Thorik laid on the ground in shock. He was sure that his eyes and ears were deceiving him.

Standing but a few feet away, Avanda crossed her arms and glared at Emilen's unexpected return. If looks could kill, the murder of a female Num would have just taken place.

ALSO BY A. G. WEDGEWORTH

www.AlteredCreatures.com

AC's epic adventures continue with the following books:

<u>Nums of Shoreview Series (Pre-Teen, Ages 9 to 12)</u>

Stolen Orb (Book 1)

Unfair Trade (Book 2)

Slave Trade (Book 3)

Baka's Curse (Book 4)

Haunted Secrets (Book 5)

Rodent Buttes (Book 6)

<u>Thorik Dain Series (Young Adult and Adult):</u>

Treasure of Sorat (Prequel)

Fate of Thorik (Book 1)

Sacrifice of Ericc (Book 2)

Essence of Gluic (Book 3)

Rise of Rummon (Book 4)

Prey of Ambrosius (Book 5)

Plea of Avanda (Book 6)

<u>Tilli of Kingsfoot Series (Adult):</u>

Hidden Magic (Book 1)

Final Days (Book 2)

<u>Santorray's Privations Series (Adult)</u>

Betrayed

Hunted

Outraged

Look for other upcoming stories of

Ambrosius

Darkmere

Myth'Unday

Dragon & Del'Unday Wars

and more…

CHARACTERS
PRONUNCIATION GUIDE

Ambrosius: *aeM-brO-zee-ahs*

Asentar: *as-en-Tar*

Avanda: *ah-Van-Dah*

Bakalor: *Bah-Kah-Lor*

Bredgin: *Brehd-gehn*

Brimmelle: *Brim-'ell*

Bryus: *brI-us*

Darkmere: *Dark-Meer*

Deleth: *deL-'eth*

Emilen: *ehM-il-eN*

Ergrauth: *erR-gRahTH*

Ericc: *ehR-iK*

Feshlan: *FehSH-Lahn*

Gluic: *Glu-iK*

Grewen: *Gru-'en*

Irluk: *uhR-luhK*

Ovlan: *ahV-lahN*

Rummon: *Rum-mahN*

Santorray: *sahn-ToR-rAY*

Schulis: *shahL-is*

Thorik: *Thor-iK*

Vesik: *Ves-iK*

Wyrlyn: *Wer-Len*

LOCATIONS PRONUNCIATION GUIDE

Corrock: *koR-RahK*

Cuev'Laru Mountains: *Koo-ehV Lah-Roo*

Cucurrian River: *Koo-kuR-ee-uhn*

Doven: *dO-ven*

Govi: *Gah-Vee*

Kiri: *kE-rE*

Lu'Tythis: *Loo-Tith-is*

Pelonthal: *peL-ahn-THahl*

Trewek: *trU-ek*

SPECIES PRONUNCIATION
GUIDE & DESCRIPTIONS

Blothrud (AKA Ruds): *bloth-ruhd*

7' to 9' tall; Bony hairless dragon-like head; Red muscular human torso and arms; Sharp spikes extend out across shoulder blades, backs of arms, and backs of hands; Red hair covered waist and over two thick strong wolf legs. Blothruds are typically the highest class of the Del'Undays.

Brandercat: *brand-er-kat*

Large lion-sized cats that have scales instead of hair. They can change the color of their scales to turn nearly invisible.

Del'Unday: *del-oon-dey*

The Del'Unday are a collection of Altered Creatures who live in structured communities with rules and strong leadership. These include blothruds, wolvians, brandercats.

E'rudite: *EE-roo-dIt*

The E'rudite aren't actually a species. They are typically humans that have been trained in the basic arts of the Notarian mind control powers which makes them much more powerful than others, but not nearly that of a Notarian.

Fesh'Unday: *fesh-oon-dey*

The Fesh'Unday are all of the Altered Creatures that roam freely without societies. Wolves, boars, raccoons, and most forest creatures are in this clan.

Gathler: *gath-ler*

6' to 8' tall; Giant sloth-like species; gathlers are the leaders of the Ov'Undays.

They are very curious creatures who take their time to investigate the true nature of things.

Human: *hyoo-muhn*
5' to 6' tall; pale to dark complexion; weight varies from anorexic to obese. Most live within the Dovenar Kingdom.

Krupes: *kroop*
6' to 8' tall; Covered from head to toe in black armor, these thick and heavy bipedal creatures move slow but are difficult to defeat. Few have seen what they look like under their armor. Krupes are the soldiers of the Del'Unday.

Mognin (AKA Mogs): *mawg-nin*
10' to 12' tall; Mognins are the tallest of the Ov'Unday. With thick dark hide-like skin, they are can resist most attacks and fire. With opposable thumbs on each side of each hand and a very strong body, they can lift very heavy objects with a great grasp.

Myth'Unday: *mith-oon-dey*
The Myth'Unday are a collection of Creatures brought to life by altering nature's plants and insects.

Notarian: *noh-tawr-ee-in*
These thin human-like creatures have semi-translucent skin and no natural hair anywhere on their bodies. Their motions are smooth and graceful and they have incredible mental powers that appear to be god-like to the other species.

Ov'Unday: *ov-oon-dey*
The Ov'Unday are a collection of Altered Creatures who believe in living as equals in peaceful communities. Typically pacifists. Species such as mognins and gathlers are part of this clan.

Polenum (AKA Nums): *pol-uh-nuhm*
4' to 5' tall; Human-like features; Very pale skin; Soul-markings cover their bodies in thin or thick lines as they mature. Exceptional eyesight.

www.AlteredCreatures.com

Historical Event	Age	Published Novel
2nd Age Begins: Notarians Arrive	2nd Age	
Creation of Unday	2nd Age	
Training of E'rudites	2nd Age	
Creation of Notarian Structures	2nd Age	
Completion of Lu'Tythis Tower	2nd Age	TD5 Prey of Ambrosius
Fall of Notarians	2nd Age	TD6 Plea of Avanda
E'rudite & Alchemist War	2nd Age	SP5 Outraged
Mtn King Temple Established	2nd Age	TK1 Hidden Magic
Nomadic Living & Fighting	2nd Age	
Migration of the Ov'Unday	2nd Age	
Creation of Magical Items	2nd Age	TK2 Final Days
Creation of the Myth'Unday	2nd Age	
3rd Age Begins: Del'Unday Rule	3rd Age	
Del'Unday Expansion	3rd Age	
War of Del'Unday and Myth'Unday	3rd Age	
War of Del'Unday & Dragons	3rd Age	
Del'Unday Civil War	3rd Age	
Rise of the Alchemists	3rd Age	
Victor Dovenar's Revolution	3rd Age	
4th Age Begins: Dovenar 1st Wall	4th Age	
7 Provinces Created in Kingdom	4th Age	SP1 Exiled
Dovenar Kingdom Civil War	4th Age	SP2 Captured
Assassination of Dovenar Knights	4th Age	
Creation of the Grand Council	4th Age	SP3 Betrayed
Matriarch's Cleansing	4th Age	SP4 Hunted
Destruction of the Grand Council	4th Age	TD1 Fate of Thorik
Dovenar Provinces Secede	4th Age	TD2 Sacrifice of Ericc
Reuniting against Del'Undays	4th Age	TD3 Essence of Gluic
The Final Great Battle	4th Age	TD4 Rise of Rummon
5th Age Begins: Frozen Lands	4th Age	SP6 Defeated

Epic Fantasy

Feeling adventurous? Read the stories in a different path from others!

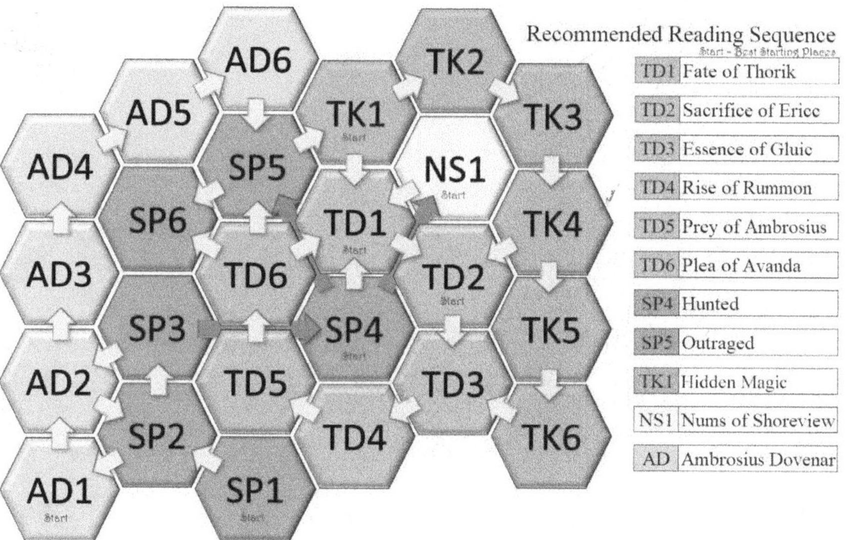